FAMOUS DOGS

OF THE CIVIL WAR

A novel by

Ben Dunlap

Grateful acknowledgement is made to RiskPress Foundation for making The Divers Collection possible.

Cover art by Jack Freeman

Author photo by Mark Olencki

San Francisco, California

For those who knew

HUGH C. THOMPSON, JR.
LAWRENCE COLBURN
GLENN ANDREOTTA

and for ANNE who never doubted

CONTENTS

I

TIME DOES NOT INTERFERE

January 15, 2019

*It is reported commonly that there
is fornication among you. . .*

—Saint Paul

Strange for me to be wondering now about where we actually were back then—in our heads, I mean, and our screwed-up lives while the rest of the world was going to hell with battle, murder, and sudden sex. . . at least one of which had just taken place if it's Caitlin Rosen we're talking about in the story that I've kept telling myself for what's been close to fifty years without my ever getting it straight—at least in terms of who wronged whom and "mitigating circumstances" if that's how the Sixties should be described, like grabbing for beads at Mardi Gras.

Part of the problem's how it's told since it's got to include a loop-de-loop —like, what's it called? an *epicycle*—beginning when summer's just about done in the first year of a new decade, then doubling back twelve months or so and cruising in forward gear from there until everything's back in orbit again. . . except for whatever's lost for good—presidents, protesters, husbands, wars. All but the last were gone by then.

So, we'll focus on Caitlin at the start if only because on that crucial day, when her classes at school are about to resume, she's all too aware of where she is—alone in her bed on South Gregg Street in a heavily-mortgaged one-story house in Cumbria, S.C., but, until only a minute or two ago, in an *in-flagrante-delicto* embrace which, theologically at least, has dumped her into limbo.

That wouldn't have unnerved everyone, so it's also important to note that she's a renegade Catholic or, if you could hear the still small voice that's nagging away unseen, an unregenerate hypocrite like most of the precedents she'd invoke in defending herself if she could. Several will soon be saints, she'd say, and what do still small voices know about how a mixed-up body feels?

She knows her pique is fabricated. It's the Irish in her, she'd contend, a fractiousness laced with knee-jerk defiance and the hint of an alibi too. She's in a quandary, that I'll concede—though, not wanting to seem too biased on her behalf but knowing her as I do, I'll predict what's going to happen. I think she'll resort to prayer.

So, that's how I'd choose to depict her first, sprawling alone in a mussed-up bed while attempting to frame a contrite excuse. I'd mention in an ironic way that—in her own mind, at least—she and the Author of Creation have reached a mutual understanding that she won't impinge on His mercy and time with offenses of a venial sort. But I'd have to note the further detail that the person with whom she's shared her bed is her former husband's former best friend—which, of course, is the heart of the matter.

Next, I'd reconstruct that morning's events—how the mattress had sunk and risen again as that person unnamed (we'll reveal who it was) got up and stealthily left her bed (it could have been anyone, really, she thinks, but rejects at once such a clumsy approach in leveling with the Almighty). She'd opened her eyes and glanced at the clock (5:05 in the digital world), remembered what's scathingly on her mind (an act she'd vowed she'd never commit), and, while idly surveying the dimly-lit room (trousers, socks, and boxer shorts in a trail that leads from the bedroom door past the legs of an overturned wicker chair and album covers strewn on the floor like upturned cards from a tarot deck, the topmost with a wary Bob Dylan decked out in a Triumph Bonneville shirt), she'd more or less started her prayer.

That's definitely where her story begins, and I'll do my best to tell the truth even if it's not edifying—how she's peering about at her surroundings, including the umber Rothko-like smudge of a fully-extended window shade and the hieroglyph of a dangling bra, though her mind's now focused on what she's done and how to present her orison (not sure if that should be sung), knowing it's hardly news to Him that, exactly as the nuns had predicted, she's back in a steaming bed of sin, gaffed and pitched from her choir-girl sleep and into a concupiscent sty with a rabbit-strewn granny gown, tangled and stained, floating like pond scum over her hips (she'd probably like such baroque prose—though, from this point on, she'll be on her own.)

"Lord. . ." she'll start out, still in her mind but testing to see if anyone's there. "You know I'm not one to quibble, Lord, but, really, it's not adultery if, recently widowed as I am," (her husband Danny's four months dead), "I'm weak when it comes to consolation."

She hears an angry growl erupt from somewhere else inside her head and knows that problem looms as well—the sulking golem's crazed reproach, insisting she's somehow done him wrong. Her mouth moves as she shapes his name.

"It's not just that," she'll add to her plea, addressing the Lord of All again. "What hurts so much is knowing he's gone, which makes remorse beside the point. . . and You know I never nitpick, Lord, but, if I'm to

4

blame, as I humbly concede, so is that lying Kenmore machine that made me look so ready to rhumba."

With a rueful expression, she closes her eyes, composing her vaguely pre-Raphaelite face which, depending on someone's point of view, is either bewitching or frankly plain—half-sensual and half-austere, with bluish-white skin and sienna-hued lips framed by a nimbus of reddish hair that curls like the beard of a Ninevite king. . . or as Danny was fond of pointing out, "like the coat of an Irish setter."

She muses on that before she thinks of what she'll include in her appeal. . . for Danny first and then for herself. "I know there're doctrinal issues, Lord, but surely among the Three of You there's room to squeeze him in as well—or, if Purgatory's still in the cards, lodge him for a semester or two on one of those terraces near the top, among the lechers and the wits. My own predicament, as You see, is what to do with Scaramouche, who's gone swaggering off just down the hall to have himself a lordly pee while I dither and have this chat with You before I look him in the eye and say whatever I'm going to say—which depends on what Your answer is if what's at stake is. . ."

Here she pauses to think it through, hacking away with Occam's razor as if it were a palette knife, a skill she's come by only of late as a middle-school teacher of western art who, at 29, is trusted by students half her age who think of her more as an artist herself because she draws so fluently and stutters so badly when she talks that nothing she says seems condescending.

". . . whether it's love or lust," she'll close, framing the issue she confronts. "Or both," she'll add. "It could be both—ask Mary Magdalene, if she's there, or, better yet, ask Dorothy Day, with whom I trust You're on positive terms."

Then, opening her eyes again and fearful she might have overstepped since Dorothy Day can fend for herself, she glances at the magazines fanned over a table by her bed, the ones her cronies also read—the latest issue of *Rolling Stone,* with Jerry Garcia peeking out, a tattered and coffee-stained *Great Speckled Bird,* and two or three *Arts News* in a stack sitting atop a *Catholic Worker,* to which she subscribes for a quarter a year.

That opens a strictly mundane thought overlapping her tentative prayer-line, a plan for what she'll do at school and how that day, in meeting her class—leaving aside the issue at hand and assuming the battered projector works—she'll calm an unruly 8th grade class with a movie she's ordered from A-V on a painter who'd been unruly too, its script as dull as such things are ("Though born in Emilia, north of Rome. . ."), but promising venery for the eye:

A Painter of Flesh:
Correggio

"Listen, Lord. . ." she's about to resume when, hearing a drum-like thump of heels and thinking she'll need a quick maneuver, she puts her matins briefly on hold. The window's brighter, so's the shade—an Albers square in dun and gray—as she mutters aloud so they both can hear, "How in God's name did we get here?"

There's no reply. She's got a little more time to think.

II

AUTUMN WITH TWO ZEROS

August – September 1969

Man ain't really evil, he jest ain't got any sense.

—V.K. Ratliff

Here's how it looks from a God's eye view: there are darkening clouds on the horizon with the city laid out over a number of hills as if hinting at how it got its name—though it wasn't so much from the English moseying upland from the coast as from grizzled Scots-Irish settlers on wagon roads from the north, descending as their kinsmen had done as reivers across the Marches and, declining to christen it after a king, calling it Cumbria.

Had there been a traffic cam aloft on this typical Saturday afternoon, it would have observed the capital city sizzling like spit in a frying pan, for, despite its somewhat misleading name, Cumbria's modest undulations are nothing but sandhills left by the sea at some point during the Paleocene where, in fifty million years or so, Hernando de Soto would traipse through on his way to finding nothing at all and where, in 1786, some equally hopeful entrepreneurs had decided to lay a township out, intending the waste to burst into bloom on streets they'd drawn up on their plan like strings on a giant tennis racket with a ribbon of river its western edge, now spanned by bridges at either end, and, at the sweet spot of the racket, a future "historic" capitol building that would fly the flags atop its dome of both loyalty and rebellion.

Constructed some three of four miles to the south with comparable passions in mind, an empty football stadium squats as if snared in a noose of tangled tracks and fairground lanes alleyways resembling an upturned chamber-pot that's filled and emptied five times a year. And roughly a dozen miles to the east, in a mini-Sahara of scraggly scrub oak and sunbaked sand along with camouflaged barracks and trucks as conspicuous as beach umbrellas, sprawls an enormous Army base with the name of a former President—or, maybe, as Senator Sternbolt crowed when stressing the town's "proud heritage," for the Giant in Gray whose X-crossed flag is one of three on the capitol dome.

Then, were the all-seeing eye of God or that of a traffic cam to veer back towards the center of town, it would look down on a vast arena built for college basketball but on special occasions used for events like Barnum & Bailey's annual show or, at the beginning of each semester, registration for courses to be taught at the third of the city's big enterprises—the

9

amoeba-like blob of CSU, Cumbria State University, with its tentacles spreading in all directions to slowly engulf and finally devour the remnants of a half-dozen mills that used to be the fourth. It's obvious that what's underway must be the enrollment of students.

Adjacent parking lots are jammed, but, aside from traffic across a bridge a couple of miles away and a gold and orange motorcycle threading its way towards the arena, nobody seems in a hurry and even the motorcycle's buzz has dropped to a barely audible hum as it circles the mammoth ziggurat. Tempos in Cumbria rarely speed up, especially during the summer months—though in this particular case, for those who're exiting the building, that's partly because, despite the fact that it's sweltering on the street, it's nearly as cold as Henry Kissinger's heart inside the cavernous Cock-o-Dome, unofficially dubbed "The Rooster Coop," a Babylonian temple of sport named for a mascot chicken but built entirely with pork, thanks to Senator Sternbolt's clout as one of the war's most strident hawks. . . the current war, in Vietnam.

Though Sternbolt's quid for this lavish quo was tactfully kept under wraps, he'd funded the Coop by log-rolling a bill that helped his constituents travel abroad—those who were black, unlucky, or poor. The rest could enroll at CSU which, whatever its lack of Free Speech verve, is as safe as a 2-S refuge can be, and thousands are making the most of it as Registration Day makes clear.

Swooping down from the sky and entering through the doors of the Sno-Cone-shaped arena, we'd see an outer concourse leading us upwards on ramps that lead to widening circles of aisles and seats rising like smoke rings from below. But rimming the edge of each circle today is a series of tables end-to-end with stenciled signs attached to sticks and glum professors slumped in chairs as Weejuned fratboys plod on past like extras from *Metropolis*, their khaki-and-madras uniforms clashing with tie-dyes here and there on Woodstock Nation wannabees and pseudo-aboriginals.

Two of the latter are down below, boldly flouting the White Man's law: THOU SHALT NOT TRESPASS ON THE FLOOR. Paused for effect at the top of the key, near where the scoreboard crashed in June, an Osceola lookalike is explaining to his spellbound squaw how sputnik's nosedive had occurred as Marx and Black Elk had foreseen. Most of the damage has been repaired, though some of the boards are lighter in hue—marking, he tells her, where it fell. He waves his arms as if to warn that the whole arena might collapse when capitalism starts to fail, which could be any minute now, then punches his course-card with disdain.

"Lotta crap!" he snarls and glares at all the conformists overhead.

His wampum shakes. Him plenty hip, that much is clear. But hippies need deferments too, so do as the wise ones have advised—keep peace-pipe stuffed with heap-strong pot.

"OFF THE COURT!" cuts through the air at the moment the stage is finally set, and Michael Dugan now appears from one of the topmost feeder ramps, scanning the tables for English Lit.

He has a knack for arriving on cue—compact and Buster Keaton-like, a hormone-driven innocent out of a novel by Fielding or Sterne, not swaggering as short guys do but bouncing like a terrier. . . your standard Irish bantamweight (light welter, really, needing a week to sweat himself down to make the weight, but feisty, agile, nondescript except for a volatile *je-ne-sais-quoi*, a metabolic overkill that makes cats hiss and babies cry). He's a former Rhodes Scholar who's come back home from Oxford and Harvard after that, searching for something he hasn't found that somehow he thinks he'd left behind—here, in Cumbria, where he's from. It was he who'd been on the motorcycle, a rinky-dink Honda 125.

It's hard to read what's on his mind, but maybe a postcard just received from a coed who must have been in Vienna—of Jupiter, disguised as a cloud, about to plank some pinkish babe who's cocking her leg to tug him in. "Some sauna, huh?" the message says, scrawled just above the painter's name, Antonio da Correggio. So maybe that's what he's musing on, Caitlin Rosen's Painter of Flesh. . . that, or his own licentious mistake that roams the fens as Dunkie Dibble.

"YOU HEAR ME, TONTO? OFF THE COURT!"

A whiff of onions mixed with Brut, a bullhorn pointed like a gun—it's Campus Security on patrol two or three yards from Dugan's ear, addressing the miscreants down below. Sign language from the shoeless chief provokes a clipped indignant beep, launching the cop down towards the floor in a pigeon-toed shuffle, elbows out, weapons a-jiggle on his hip. Osceola, seemingly unperturbed, says something disparaging to his squaw.

I've seen this movie, Dugan thinks, as Osceola ambles off, a blameless nomad on the move. Life imitating Hollywood, the chant breaks loose in Dugan's head:

Hey-yuh hi-yuh ho-yuh huhhhhh!

Who was it sang that on the screen? Bob Many Mules? He can't recall, though movies are part of his métier.

The cop, who's clomped onto the floor, has got his own pursuer now— Ismene von Himmel, in Rooster sweats, the Lady Pullets' lesbo coach. (Horses of many colors, right? Mike Dugan's got no problem with that. Not scaring the horses is the catch.)

"S'cuse us!"

"Thannnnk you!"

Sure thing, you bet. Two recent blondes rake Dugan's bow, squeezing to pass him on the ramp. When he looks back, the chief is gone. The cop's still out there on his own, not far from where the sputnik hit. (Jeff Chandler? Hardly—he was white. Exactly Sonnie? Someone else. The world's a B-grade movie now, and he should know, having worked on some freaked-out student films while camped amid the dreaming spires.)

"Your brogans!" barks Ismene von Himmel.

"Easy, lady," rasps the cop, waving his horn to ward her off, emitting another fart-like beep.

"Listen, you dimwit rent-a-cop! Shit-kickers like yours are not exempt."

His left hand flickers towards his stick as clumps of students pause to gawk. (*What if?* they're thinking. *Even here!* a rumble for The Nightly News—"You shut that sassy mouth a yourn!" "I warned you, bub!" "Well, chew on this!" Say one of them snatches at a gun. A call for back-up, tear gas, dogs. And maybe. . . *maybe!*. . . No, not here—in Sternbolt Country? Not a chance. On campuses like Berkeley, sure—Harvard, Columbia— never here. Nothing ever happens here.)

"Sorrrry!"

"Huh?" The blondes again. All part of the circus, Dugan reflects. He'd called it a movie, but circus is right. The cop has beaten a quick retreat.

"Did you see Doctor Seltzer yet?" one of the blond babes importunes.

"Nope," he answers, playing his part as one of the bozos with a scoop escorting old Jumbo to the Dome whenever the big top comes to town. Not even one of the sad-sack clowns who're chained to their hermeneutical oars high over the squeaky bright shellac and cutesy magic-marker puns— NO HARD SOULS ON THE PLAYING FLOOR. Har-de-har! Back at it again, those stir-nuts assholes in Religion!

Nodding as Coach von Himmel stomps by returning to her lookout post, he checks to see if Dunkie's there. (The scooper scooped, he warns himself—Don't Fuck With Jumbo Or You Die. He'll think of something.

Half past three and she hasn't appeared. Lie low, slink home, and reassess.)

The English section's next to the top—one below Limbo, Dugan thinks, the place where the lustful get their due. She knows where to find him if she looks, but it seems so far the coast is clear along their allotted table space with twenty-odd mere assistant profs strung out along a broken arc and planted in folding metal chairs. It's true, as Tolstoy might have said, that all tenured faculty are alike while, each in his own peculiar way, untenured profs are wholly unlike—from Kravitz who's humming to himself, as frisky as a manatee and Dexter who's like a psych-lab rat to Dugan who's playing it fast and loose, reflecting as he shows up late that, though badgered, defensive, and fighting for air, they'll muster a desperate bonhomie shot through with telltale glimmers of fear that they're trapped in a game of musical chairs that favors conformist sycophants. . . and none of the three fits the bill.

"Second Coming here already, then?" Dexter assumes a Manson-like scowl as if ragging on Dugan for taking his time—and Jesus too for doing the same.

"Still pending, Dexter," Dugan shrugs. "Looks like you've snagged another reprieve. Whatcha got for me, Kravitz?"

Kravitz hunches over his lists. "Well, Beowulf's back on life support, and even my Chaucer's stuck on eight—but let's see here, your three are close to making up." His eyes are rheumy with a cold, a dab of mustard in his beard. "Film course has over forty now, and almost twenty for War Rev Lit, which I assume. . . "

". . . is commie crap!" barks Dexter with a sidelong sneer.

Dugan ignores his nutso crack. Dexter's simply what he is—too paranoid, too many zits, too chummy with the Jacobeans.

"Which rev?" asks Kravitz placidly.

"All of 'em," Dexter says with a fart, inflecting it sardonically and prompting Dugan's witless quip, "Ask Adolf here. He's packing heat."

"You'd be surprised, friend," Dexter snarls.

"Let's act collegial!" Kravitz pleads, thumping the table with both fists.

A couple of students pause to look, and after a silence, Dugan says, "So, okay, guys, here's what it is. I'm sorry I got here late today—I've been trying to straighten a problem out. And, Dex, Krav's right. . . let's both of us cut the crabby gab."

But Dugan knows he's got that wrong as Dexter haughtily lifts his chin. Dexter doesn't gab, he spews, and, after a stubbornly drawn-out stare, renews his semi-manic rant redirected at the scoreboard now which was rumored to cost a million or more—mere chickenfeed for rabid alums equating each losing Rooster team with General Lee's rear echelon ("last chance to offset Appomattox," as Danny had once sarcastically said) suggesting why, in this hapless burg where, according to Chamber of Commerce claims, the "classic" *Birth of a Nation* was set (at least, for a couple of static scenes), "the Sixties" has such an ominous ring.

The town's last rev had not gone well—Sherman had burned it to the ground. Like kudzu, though, it had grown right back, a punch-drunk podunk made-up town plunked down like a shower drain in the sand with CSU at its very heart. "A Cathedral of Learning" its champions proclaim, with Bible-thumpers mustered in-state and Papist "test-score refugees" bussed down from Newark by the herd—though, even without this immigrant crew, CSU can fill a lot of pews. . . so many, in fact, that (zealotry pays!), on the evening the mega-ton scoreboard fell, the Roosters For Christ who normally met at center-court in the out-of-season Cock-o-Dome had switched for a change to the Rooster Pit, where football comes second only to prayer and Coach Ray Don had testified, since Winning-With-Jesus was his theme, that sacking the quarterback was the key to racking up "three score and ten" which, doing the math, he understood as three TDs plus one first down. It wasn't all love-yo'-neighbor, though— "Peaceniks don't go to bowls," he said, "they wallow in Sodom or Atlanta." Some found his metaphors obscure, but, as that was the night of the scoreboard disaster, nobody disputed his basic point that God helps those who get out of His way.

Still, few of the faculty seem to care about what to the Boosters matters most. Except for sporadic dress parades when some fading former Hollywood star or West-Indian drug-lord head of state arrives on a junket designed to prove that CSU is now on the map, most of the tenured profs lie low, letting their juniors "clean the coop," in Dugan's chairman's pithy phrase, at registration twice a year. Today is Dugan's fourth time here, but Dexter, a veteran of many more, is looking to gain a new advantage.

"What sort of problem?" he inquires, returning to Dugan's vague excuse.

"Cut it out, Dexter," Dugan says.

"So, who're you sweating, lover boy?"

Dugan replies in Dexter-Speak: "Right-wing nuts with tiny dicks."

"Don't get your hopes up," Dexter sneers. Then, rubbing his neck, he catches a glimpse of the beaded and barefoot Seminole Chief meandering with his spaced-out squaw. "GERONIMO! Get Custer, quick! Some sort of uprising's underway!"

"Dan George," yawns Dugan. "HEY-yuh HO!" The chant's still rattling through his brain, but now he's managed to dredge it up from a movie he'd been to just last month. It's *Little Big Man*, that's the one!

"You guys, pipe down, huh?" Kravitz complains. There's something green between his teeth—green, like spinach, Dugan notes, though spinach does not, so far as he knows, appear on the Hunt 'n' Peck Snack Bar list. A coed's staring at it too as Kravitz croons, "There's room in Chaucer."

She shakes her head.

"Or Beoooowulf. . . and Sir Gawainnnn?"

Her lips are pursed reflectively as Kravitz, with a winsome smile, leans forward waving his sign-up sheet.

"Shaaaakespeare," he coaxes.

She demurs.

"Lear and Hamlet. . . Much Ado. . . Ro-me-o and Jooo-li-et!"

She seems about to take the bait. "Translated?" she asks.

"What?" Kravitz replies. He's mystified.

"Or is it. . ." Detecting Dexter's growing glee and Dugan's more subdued attention, she hesitates, but then proceeds. ". . . taught in the *original?*"

Dexter howls as Dugan chants

HEY-yuh HO-yuh ho-yuh huhhhhh!

"Shut up there, Dexter! chill out, Mike!"

"Ah. . . maybe. . . something else," she frowns.

"Like War Rev Lit? Sweetheart, come back!" Dexter's guffaw is jubilant.

"Goddamn it, Dexter!" Kravitz fumes. "I hope you're happy. . . and you too, Mike—the two of you scared her off for good. She's heading towards Sociology!"

Like all medievalists, Dugan thinks, Krav takes his job too seriously ("Hey, over here! Look what I got! A blue-light special on *Gorboduc!*"). But she was certainly gone all right—gone with the semi-literate wind, dumped back with belles and KA beaus in that Deep-South Bible-Belt born-again soup, a Jesus and NASCAR-flavored ragout sweetened by just such ripe Cockettes whose Lord & Savior counsels them for Miss Teen

Speedway interviews ("World Peace will be my main concern along with marketing STP. . .") and peppered with dolts like Ray Don Suggs who considers long passes a form of prayer because he knows at Notre Dame they think hail-marys are full of grace, and Strontium Sternbolt ("Stron" for short, but known as "Windsock" on the Hill), guardian of the free (white) world, plus Glubber and Gordo, baleful twins who rule these dark satanic mills (the English/Comp Lit shifts, at least) with Oreen Suber on the side, the draft board's crack redneck valkyrie—an indigestible bouillabaisse on constant simmer at CSU, where gusto, like okra, gets slimy with time.

"Where's Danny?" asks Dugan, looking around.

"Rosen?" says Kravitz. "No idea."

Dexter snorts. "He's pushing his luck."

"We all are, aren't we?" Dugan says. "Reckon that's why they hired us, huh? Shock troops to hold the mob at bay?"

This strikes another nerve in Dex who, still surveying their clientele, abruptly swivels his line of fire. "Gahhhh!" he seethes dementedly, "these hippies make me wanna puke!"

"Easy, Dex, they're why we're here."

"So we're supposed to lick their boots? Faggotty sway-doh beatnik twits!" In Dexter's defiant Hoover-ite view, J. Edgar's flubs are never mistakes. "They wanna get rich without any sweat, same way you pricks are hopin' for tenure." The boils that fester on his neck are like a small volcanic chain. His veins stand out, he flails his hands. "And why? For what? For Marxist chic and group-grope sex? For spouting some half-ass Hindu tune or bullshit Yiddish chutts-pah crap?"

"Fuck off," says Kravitz pleasantly.

"Uh-oh," groans Dugan.

"What's up with him?"

"Cool it," says Dugan from a crouch.

"Our hero's undercover now?"

"Kravitz!" croaks Dugan, tugging his sleeve.

"I'm looking."

"Over there in blue, the walking pup-tent."

"Nope. Not her."

"You sure?"

"Mmmmm. . . yep," Milt Kravitz nods. "This one's more like an Old Norse troll. . . my sort of woman."

Dexter sniffs, "What's going on—your problem again?"

"Bureau recruiter," Dugan replies, resuming his former upright perch. "She's hounding me, Dex."

"Oh, yeah, I'll bet."

"Keeps screaming she just can't get enough."

"Oh, great, you scoffers, laugh away! Trade God and country—John Wayne too—for Beowulf and Bonnie and Clyde. You guys are queer-bait, you know that? You wouldn't know what a hero's like if one of 'em bit you in the ass."

"Blond and Aryan with zits, I'll bet."

"Good one, Krav!"

There's a hint of a smile under Kravitz's beard as a beep goes off in Dexter's jacket—a timing device for cigarettes. He's trying to quit by scaling back.

"I'm taking a break."

"For what?"

"You guess." He aims his voice at his lapel. "Bolero 6 is heading out to rendezvous as prearranged. Any requests from you two chumps?"

"Electroshock might do you good."

"Hah! Later, you losers," Dexter salutes, as genial as he ever gets. Always appearing on high alert, he walks with a backward-leaning tilt as if expecting an attack.

After he's gone, they have a lull before the final rush begins. But by five-fifteen they've drawn red lines at the bottoms of half their sign-up sheets and for virtually everything tailored for jocks, which Dexter, for reasons of his own, has been managing this afternoon but which Dugan will handle while he's gone. Most of those courses are in Linguistics, including the one that closed out first, "Intro to Polysyllabic English," which, according to Krav's report, had been filled in less than a minute from a list of pre-admits submitted by Coach Ray Don, making for big disappointment by those in search of a crip. . . including the owner and sole proprietor of a pair of angora-clad bazooms with a frat pin perched atop the slope as if for a dizzying slalom. When Dugan starts to shake his head, the frat pin shakes in its starting gate as its wearer assumes a winsome pose.

"But I'm planning to major in English!" she says, adding a teasing, "*Pretty* please?"

When Dugan's expression doesn't change, her body language grows intense. It's easy to translate what she means ("I'm daddy's little girl, okay? Sweet as Co-Cola through and through, but daddy's a very rich alum who gets really mean when I'm upset"). The mountains start to quiver and quake.

"Sorry, but no." He knows eye contact is the key. "That course is full. I can't change that. You want to consider something else?"

"Don't hassle us, man. We want it too."

The accent's from the Newark connection, but when Dugan looks, it's the Chief with his squaw—two Seminoles from the Jersey shore edging the alpine boobs aside.

"Look," Dugan says. "All I can do for any of you is put you down on this wait list here, but you can see how long it is."

"Listen," confides the testy Chief, "I gotta stay full-time, understand? How 'bout a creative writing course?"

"They're all full too. You're way too late."

"She-it!"

No doubt about it, Dugan thinks, he's clearly in a draft-board bind as his act grows more chameleon-like. His accent's shifting all over the map and, except for the beads-and-buckskin gear, his manner takes on a rock-star strut. Mick Jagger's who comes first to mind—a rolling stone, that fits the bill! Same matchstick arms and doughboy sulk. Probably smokes a lot of moss.

"Okay," says Dugan, "Tell you what—there's Jacobean, room in that. . . Professor Dexter's seminar."

"Deep Dish?" pouts Mick, the former Chief.

"Say what?"

"You're talkin' that guy Pizza Face. He's. . ."

"What?" snarls Dexter, taking a seat, just back from his feverish Viceroy break, staring Mick down with withering scorn. "Cat got your tongue there, Sittin' Bull?"

"This guy is nuts." Mick puffs his lips, pale freckles across bran-muffin cheeks. He looks at Kravitz peevishly. "So, what you got, Chef Boyardee?"

"Beowulf, Chaucer," Kravitz shrugs.

Dugan attempts to tune it all out. From where he sits, by turning his head, ignoring the shambling zombie horde and peering beyond the concourse doors, he's able to see a patch of grass, a hedge and glinting flotilla of cars above which, like a fishing pier arched over a carp-filled asphalt pond, he spots the concrete overpass leading to weirdly haiku-like signs:

BUY AMERICAN —
DOUBLE WIDE — FREEDOM'S AFFORD-
ABLE — EL CAPRI.

"Oh, gimme a home," runs through his head, "where luxury's crafted out of tin, as mobile as a herpes sore, where the skies are not. . ." But it seems they are. It looks as if it's going to rain.

"Also got *Sir Gawain*," adds Kravitz.

"How 'bout a film course?" Mick inquires.

"Or finger painting!" Dexter hoots as Dugan checks the weather again. The sky's been boiling up all day, but now the clouds are turning black.

Bad news for bikers, Dugan thinks, knowing he'll have to duck and skid with empty beer cans aimed at his head—the price you pay where stock cars roam, especially when, on a one-two-five, he's not exactly king of the road. But then, he's figured out at last he no longer wants to be a king or president or CEO. He's tired of racking prizes up only to learn that, in the end, they weren't real measures of success, just problems for their donors to solve—how to distribute all that shit, maintaining the fiction life is fair and contriving a debt to be repaid by chumps who're grateful to have won. . . while lurking behind those donors' smiles was, "Let's all go home and hoist a brew, these cornball kids give me the creeps!"

"You with us, man? Hey, Rev War Lit!" Mick mugs the way the real Mick mugged with that snotty archbishop on the tube. "You think he's stoned?" he asks his squaw, who answers with a vacant look.

Dugan's framing his own reply when two events occur at once. The first is the chairman looking in for a visit he's certain to describe at the school year's first department meeting, repeating a line he's used before ("dropped in on the troops just to bolster morale, but, as I'm told the dung beetle said, my task proved dauntingly Sisyphean"—yuk-yuk, ole Gordo, what a card! Must get it from William Gilmore Simms).

Dugan salaams without catching his eye, which is fixed at the moment on something else—a new Teaching Assistant he's got in tow who, under her strikingly ample prow is wearing some sort of biker belt that buckles with two big silver hands that seem on the verge of copping a feel, an ensemble triggering reveries that hover above his colleague's heads like an 8-page bibles' comic balloons.

The second event is Dunkie Dee, who's up on the ramp and casting about like a bull on the streets of Pamplona. Hoping he hasn't been spotted yet, Dugan adopts the tai chi pose called Monkey Seeks Needle Under the Wave.

"What's Rev War Lit?" Mick wants to know, addressing the fetal matador as Gordo cordially moves their way.

Dugan attempts to ward Mick off. "Ask him, okay?" He gestures at Kravitz.

Dexter's bemused as Gordo approaches. "Pinko-pacifist crap," he growls, interpreting Rev War Lit for Mick. "Your sort of peace pipe, Medicine Man."

"Gordo! Hi!"

They all snap to, with Dugan in a defensive crouch nervously trying to scan the ramp.

"Gentlemen!" Gordo rubs his hands, gesturing towards the new T.A. "You've met Miss Boozer, I presume?"

The meekly untenured fake faint smiles as Dunkie, some forty yards away, abruptly makes a right-angle turn, spots Dugan, and, wheeling like a tank, starts waving with her pocketbook.

"I haven't," says Dexter.

Dugan, like Kravitz, shakes his head. He sees she's seen him. No way out.

"Ah. . ." Gordo says with lordly delight, his eyes resembling the light in a fridge—while he's talking, a five-watt bulb goes on; when listening, the bulb goes dim again.

"Hey!" Mick complains. "Who's working the counter?"

Dunkie is thudding in their direction. A two-minute sprint is Dugan's guess.

With one hand lightly touching her back, Gordo gestures with the other. "Dexter, Dugan and Kravitz," he says. "Sounds like a law firm, don't you think? Miss Boozer comes to us from Hollins."

Kravitz and Dexter mumble hello while Dugan steps forward with a smile. "That won't be held against you," he says, getting blank or baffled looks all round except for the pair of silver hands that loosen and tighten like a kegel and Gordo's expression of reproof.

"Just joking," Dugan hastens to add. "Old girlfriend of mine once went there too." He knows that's lame, and it's not true.

Gordo turns to his protégé. "Mike's being facetious," he observes. "A modest attempt at British wit to which he's been, ah, over-exposed. Amid a jumble of trendy things, he's planning to teach a course on Joyce, which might be somewhat problematic. Megan. . . Miss Boozer's. . . specialty is antebellum Southern lit."

Oho! *Touché. Le droit du seigneur*—he's practically into her britches now. That biker belt has done its stuff.

"Gordo. . .?"

"Yes, what is it, Mike?"

"Just wondering," (Great & Terrible Oz) "and I really hate to bring this up, but it looks as if it's going to rain . . ."

"You think so, Mike?" He turns his head as if to check, though what he examines is Megan's stack.

"I'm on my motorcycle, you know. . ."

Meg gives him a look—it's just a look, but whattaya know? It's suddenly more like STUD-O-RAMA! Gordo notes this too and frowns.

"You should have thought of this sooner, Mike." (O yes! Correct, Significant One! Wazir of obsequious dabblers in lit!) Meg opens her eyes a little more: you mean he's just a callous putz? No way, not he—not Rufus G. Gordon, corrector of lacunae by Simms. He smiles a tight, magnanimous smile. "That's okay, Mike. You go ahead. We'll manage to keep an even keel." He winks at Miss Boozer-Megan-Meg (and thus, my dear, as you can see, I show favor to those beneath my thumb).

No more than twenty feet away, Dunkie has reached Philosophy.

"Thanks, Gordo."

"Right."

No time to lose, as Dugan knows. He bobs and waves in taking his leave, though Gordo's attention is back where it was (lean forward just a little bit more. . . we're detecting abundant promise here). Megan obliges in a way that's virtually contractual as Dunkie, observing Dugan's wave and thinking his gesture's meant for her, bulldozes obstructions from her path, closing to barely a dozen feet. Not just my booty, Dugan reflects, that insatiable dingbat's after my *pelt!* He hesitates for half a beat, but bad as his cowardly exit might be, Dunkie's reproaches would be worse. She'd bellow a sad, bovine appeal, he'd feel his flesh crawl, show remorse, and there they'll be, back where they've been. . . drunk in the mead-hall, laying pipe.

"Gotta go, guys! I gotta go!"

In motion already, Dugan turns. Now Dexter's pushing back his chair, unwittingly blocking Dunkie's charge. A collision ensues and, looking around, Dugan sees Dexter in a heap with Gordo protecting Megan's boobs and Mick and his squaw applauding the show. Kravitz goes down, but Dunkie's still up, and Dugan perceives his only escape lies down and down and across the court, through no man's land to the Rooster Chute, and maybe, with just a little luck, to a corridor leading out from the Dome. He mimes to Dunkie—"Catch you later!"—then, bouncing down to the bottommost tier and over a railing onto the floor, takes two more steps and hears a roar.

"CAMPUS SECURITY! STOP WHERE YOU ARE!"

No turning back now. He twists half round to check the gap, hoping she's somewhere far above. But she's right behind him, closing fast, her squeaking shoe-sounds matching his as he breaks into an all-out gallop.

"BOTH OF YOU, GET OFF THE FLOOR!"

Glimpsing the cop at the edge of the crowd, he thinks he sees a pistol drawn. The Rooster logo's underfoot as, making a beeline towards the Chute from which he's seen the players emerge, he hopes. . . and yes! Two beet-red doors!

"Mike, honey!" she bawls. She's on his heels.

He strains for an extra burst of speed, praying the doors were left unlocked. He's almost there and. . .

"THIS. . . IS YOUR LAST WARNING! HALT!" That's not the cop, it's someone else.

A sound like gunshots. . . whappity bam! The doors, as he goes crashing through, swing back and forth repeatedly, providing a sort of flip-card view of a slapstick sight-gag in his wake: just a couple of steps in front of the Chute, a woman in sweats explodes from the side—Ismene von Himmel, the Missile of God—chop-blocking Dunkie at the knees. No sound of the impact, silent film. . . except for a bullhorn's muffled beep and a modernist tangle of limbs and heads. The doors swing shut, and the image is gone.

"Nothing to do," he tells himself, possessed of a sudden Zen-like calm while loping along the hallway ahead towards a door with a beckoning EXIT sign. Once through it, he heaves a sigh of relief for what he knows is merely a breather. Then he calmly proceeds for another few steps, a steep ascent, a final door—and there he stands, outside, alone, with nothing to trouble him in this world but a sky that's coiling like Brillo.

• • •

Like a bird-dog hauling itself from a pond, Dugan gives an overall shake, shedding the AC from his pores and surveying the traffic two blocks away that's creeping past a glitzy strip of neon-spangled griddle-and-grease that links the Cock-o-Dome to a bridge over the ankle-deep river. Just past a major intersection, he knows there's a newly built Frank 'n' Stein with Herman Munster looming out front waving a hot dog and a mug. "WHOA!" Herman gestures with his suds, then jerks and smirks and starts again, saluting with his other arm that clutches a wiener in a bun. A blinking sign above his head repeatedly says it's

MONSTROUSLY GOOD!
MONSTROUSLY GOOD!
MONSTROUSLY GOOD!

From his perch outside the auxiliary door, Dugan returns the Munster salute. "Hi, Herman," he says out loud to the sign as *mon semblable, mon frère* he thinks, and, noting the sky is now so dark that security lights have all come on, he makes his way towards the loading dock where his bike is parked illegally. His brain's still locked in overdrive, numbed by the blowtorch sirocco's stench wafting from dumpsters down below reeking of dog days in the sticks, of Crackerjacks, tar, and something else—like piss on a campfire, blocked-up drains, the whiff of a veterinarian's slab. He remembers the beagle he'd had as a kid, braced to endure the needles and probes, then pictures Dunkie down on all fours and, wincing, hustles to beat the storm.

But it's hard to be nimble in cowboy boots, especially a cheap Sears-Roebuck pair. On the next to last step, he snags a heel, loses his balance, twists and spins, and, hurtling awkwardly onto the dock finds a couple of black dudes watching him—one of them tall and whiplash-thin, lounging astride the one-two-five with its helmet, unstrapped, atop his head.

"Out of the frying pan. . ." Dugan thinks, with Grendel instead of Grendel's mother and Grendel Junior off to the side, looking as if they want his bike which—compared to Dylan's T100, much less a mammoth Harley hog—is really just a souped-up scooter. As a gesture of reckless outlaw disdain when parked with tenured Buicks and Saabs, his Honda just barely pulls it off, but muggers might take a different view. The thing to do is play it cool.

"What say there, guys?"

They stare at him.

It's gotten even darker now, and, just as he'd feared when he looked at the sky, he feels a light sprinkle on his arm. The seated brother starts to unfold, looking a bit like Lew Alcindor minus maybe a foot or so in platform shoes and K-Mart jeans—a wardrobe close to Dugan's own. His sidekick wears a tapered shirt, and both sport Eldridge Cleaver shades (how can they see in all this murk?) But sensing how quickly things can go wrong, Dugan adopts a swaggering stance (Hi, bros, hang loose, I know kung fu). "Getting' ready to rain," is what he says, grabbing his helmet back from Lew and snapping the strap across his chin (Goan git this doggie on the road!)

Lew's face is blank as he slides off. The other one's jittery, Dugan thinks, the one to watch (call him Tyrone)—but keep it cool, no hint of fear. He delivers a sort of Bogart nod as, rocking the Honda off its stand, he mounts and, gazing into space, aligns a kick to start it up.

It coughs and dies. He kicks again. It sputters twice. A dumb mistake, he tells himself, not parking in the well-lit lot. He stomps so hard it boomerangs.

"Hot *damn!*" he mutters manfully.

Flipping the key, he tries again as Lew and Tyrone exchange looks, some sort of signal it appears. But suddenly the engine roars (free at last! oh, yes, indeed!) He revs it to a high-pitched howl, watching in case they make a move, then launches his rocket from its pad. So long, there, guys:

I too am untranslatable!

Down to the turn-in, onto the street—it's drizzling, but he's gaining speed, slicing through gossamer curtains of rain, his etch-a-sketch windscreen scribbling up, the dark wet asphalt smooth as slate. Squeezing the handles, he's the man. Night coming on, but that's okay—he's son of Easy Rider now, gliding past Herman's semaphore ("Steady now, Mike, it's slick out there!") as Dennis Hopper comes sidling up, flogging his bike like Wild Bill Cody (what is it with movies on the brain—and Dylan too? "Don't worry about it," Dennis grins. "You've still got wheels, so throttle down!")

He does, and soon they settle back, making the light at the top of the hill and dropping through honey-suckled mist, then up a long tree-shaded slope towards what at the moment he calls home—two barn-like furnished rooms he rents from Dunkie's demented genteel mom, directly descended, as she's said twice, from Duncan, the king in Shakespeare's *Macbeth*. . . on her father's side ("They were Picts, you know, from somewhere east of Inverness"). In Cumbria, family matters a lot—he'd had to pass a pedigree check before Miz Dibble would give him a key ("A widow can't be too careful, you know, especially with a debutante daughter").

When pressed for family anecdotes about their doomed progenitor, the Thane of Cawdor's luckless guest, she claimed the trail had gotten cold ("After the murder, we lost touch"), though she's well informed on her mother's side, the forebears of a squat bald man his competitors dubbed The Sewer King ("*So*-er, not soo-er," she insists), referring to the treadle machines he'd sold from a one-mule wagon seat, amassing the fortune that underwrote his factory on the Congaree, an historic edifice standing still. "Piggie Parlor" is what it says now, but under a dancing neon pig you can manage to make out RATLIFF SEW, a faintly legible palimpsest across a wall of dingy brick, with "R C Cola" clearer still. But clearest of all, stuck over the door like garish lipstick on a sow, is a smaller addendum in gothic bold: SCRIPTURE-BASED BAR-B-QUE, it proclaims,

𝔐𝔞𝔱𝔱𝔥𝔢𝔴 13:31

(mustard, not vinegar, saith the Lord as if ketchup's reserved for basting in hell).

But that's a long way off from here, and Dugan's on autopilot now, leaning as he takes the curves and, hunched close against his plexiglass screen, heading into a tricky stretch where, just after the SCE&G lot, traffic gets funneled to barely two lanes beneath a thirty-foot railroad trestle. He sees the transformers up ahead behind a high fence off to the right while, approaching from somewhere to his left, he hears a freight train's throaty cough. A light emerges through the trees, curving along the high-banked ridge and sweeping towards something Dugan sees—or thinks he sees, he can't be sure—inside the E&G Power lot. The rain has started pelting down.

Rubbing his screen, he looks again at DANGER HIGH VOLTAGE on the fence, a red parked car, an open gate, and a work gang pinning something down that looks at first like a flapping tarp. But his senses go on red alert as the tarp appears to twist and kick like someone in trouble, fighting them off.

Reflexively, he jams on brakes and, feeling a quick centrifugal tug, glimpses his taillight easing past as if it's blithely sailing away. "Slow motion," he thinks, in a Dick-Button spin that's flinging him towards where his rear wheel was while, leaning instinctively into the skid, he hits loose gravel, bucks about, and, lurching and spewing, drags his heels, regaining his balance as he slows.

A light swings towards him and away. He's chilled by the thought that it must be the train but discovers it's just a lamp on a pole that somebody's swinging over his head next to a man who's got some weapon in his hand pointing it at the person pinned down, who looks like a woman—yes, it is! long hair, a blouse, limbs flailing about like a cat with its tail in a mowing machine. Her foot whips out, a thug goes down. She's up for a moment it appears, then snatched back sharply by her hair as the light on the pole obscures his view.

He's seen enough. It's six to one, but a man's gotta do what a man's gotta do. There's a sizzle of sparks, an ozone reek, and hooligans briskly wielding sticks apparently bent on warding him off. Not waving—no, they mean to fight.

"Well, what the hell? Spontaneous me!" he thinks or says, he's not sure which (Jack Nicholson's shouting in his ear, "I'm here if things get ugly, Doo." *Doo* for Dugan?—let's get real!) He tightens his grip and slams into gear, catching the first thug unawares. The thug goes down as Dugan zips by ("Like Dunkie," he thinks. "Ismene and I.")

A blow whacks Dugan's helmet hard sending a shiver to his toes. The light swings back. He pivots one-eighty while revving it up, preparing it for another charge. Then hearing a chatter he can't translate together with a series of flashes ("An uzi!" yells Jack), he gears back down and launches a wheelie—the first of his limited biking career, though he's riding it out like Evel Knieval as if the bike was on its own thumping mere duck-pins through the air. . . first one, then two, then two and a half. The half rears up, gyrates, and falls as bits of gravel tattoo his head.

The woman's redoubled her frenzied fight, shouting to Dugan—so it seems. But in turning to get a better look, he feels a pulverizing blow. . . from what? The lamp, a poleaxe now. He crumples and straightens up again, his arm like a broken baseball bat that's blooped a single into left— it's done its job, now get on base! is all that running through his mind.

Great metaphor, but what's the point? he tries to argue with himself. To save the girl? Good deal, but how? (Yes! keep that question uppermost as, from some pedantic part of his brain, a voice is calmly pointing out that heroics on a one-two-five are roughly equivalent, one might say, to going to battle on a Schwinn. . . which, after all, the Japs had done in chasing the Brits from Singapore.) So, okay, maybe this will work.

Shift down again, he's telling himself. But somewhere else in Dugan's head, he's fairly amazed at what he's done, his own crash-dummy derring-do, so he might as well try to get creative. With Jack and Dennis egging him on, he cuts a high-speed doughnut turn, spoiling the aim of the goon with the lamp who, swinging at him a second time, clobbers another goon's head instead. The clubbee drops as the bike twirls round, knocking the clubber to his knees (oh, yeah! thinks Dugan, piece uh cake!) Goons scuttle like muskrats through the muck as Captain Motocross rides them down.

The girl looks dazed. Her clothes are ripped, and she's splattered with mud. A glance suffices for Dugan to see her hair's as black as her brassiere, a lacy bra with scalloped frills. He thinks she might be Mexican.

"Get on," he yells. She almost falls. "*Hola!* Grab hold!"

Her shrill reply is indistinct.

"C'MON! *VAMOS!*"

Her skirt's too tight. More shots and sparks, the light again, and then he feels her hands take hold. He throttles down, but she slides off.

"Wait!" she calls out, grabbing his belt.

Barely controlling his raging bike, his rear wheel spitting rocks and mud, he drags her, slows, and tugs her on, her skirt hiked halfway up her thighs. His right arm's all but useless now. More thugs erupt across the road, hurrying towards them, waving their arms like umpires in some Aussie sport. "You asshole!" shouts an oaf with a stick. "You think you're fuckin' Steve McQueen?" (Exactly, chum—you saw it too!) He throws the stick as Dugan shoots by, dodging and skidding towards the gate where instantly two lights appear.

What next? A red convertible apparently aiming to run them down, the car he'd seen outside the gate. No time to work that out right now as, using his all but useless arm to steady the bike as best he can, he darts out from the fenced-in lot and, nearly colliding with the car that's trying to block him from the road, he skitters instead on a level path that's part of the railroad's right of way but mostly overgrown with weeds. The lights behind him leap and stab, closer with every bump and swerve, and there's a rumble from someplace else (the trestle? yes!) The train's slowed down to take the curve ("*Where they can't go!*" he hears Jack crow, not grasping what he means at first). The car's within a foot or two when, dropping his

Honda into first and suddenly veering up the slope, he starts a steep climb towards the track, hearing a quickening clickety-clack and Jack's excitement in his ear ("You got it, Doo! We're almost there!") We, my ass! he tells himself, fighting to keep the bike upright.

For a moment it seems he's stalling out—a sputter, but then it catches again, and, suddenly, he's reached the top, fishtailing along beside the freight as shadows flicker on every side. It's all a jumble. What to do? He makes out SEABOARD on a car that's lit like a marquee by his lamp, meaning they must be silhouettes and easy targets from below.

"Sittin' ducks!" he thinks aloud.

"Whaaat?" she asks him in his ear as he decides to douse the light.

"We're sittin'. . ."

"YOW!" he thinks he hears her say as they slam against a railroad tie.

". . . duuuuuuucks!" he finishes upside down, cartwheeling wildly through the air.

But half-accustomed to miracles now, he kicks the Honda as they soar, deflecting it and falling free. She lands atop him. He can't see but rolls and tumbles to his feet, and later he wonders how he did what seems to happen in a blur—hoisting her with him on the run, grabbing a ladder that's suddenly there, swinging and clambering up the side, then sprawling together atop its roof while the shuddering boxcar gathers speed. Not bad, he thinks, with one good arm, though he reckons the train had slowed to a crawl.

Lights bobble behind them, then recede as the thudding that was inside his head has relocated to his arm. He rolls against her.

"Stop," she warns. Her voice is hard.

Not *Thanks* or *Is your head okay?* "I wish I could," he tries to explain.

"Who duh hell are you?" she wants to know.

Prince Valiant is what he's tempted to say, but clever retorts are too much work. She thinks he's just another thug. "Nobody," he says. "Just passing through."

"Working for who den?" she persists. Her accent vaguely rings a bell.

"The Roosters," he tells her. True enough.

She turns her face away from his. He hasn't seen it clearly yet and won't unless she'll look at him instead of at Cumbria down below, searching for something it would seem. Pursuers would be a logical guess, assuming Mack Sennett's been in charge.

28

Slowly the city streets clack by as the tracks descend and rise again. Half-hidden by fitful gusts of rain, it's like a model railroad town—bakery, coal yard, billboard signs ("THE COSMIC CONNECTION," one exults).

"Den why'd you say. . ."

"That car," he blurts, the one that tried to run them down. "Any idea. . .?"

"But you said ducks."

"That's right, I did." Too hard to explain. "I'm shot," he shrugs as best he can, finding his right arm won't respond.

Silence and an appraising stare, which it's really too shadowy to discern.

"My shoulder," he tries to be specific. "It's gone all numb."

"Not shot," she says.

"Oh, I was shot!" He's getting annoyed.

"So why no brud?" Nonsensically, she's ticked off too.

"Dunno," he says. Maybe the bullet passed clean through. Besides, he thinks, how could she tell with both of them soaked and splattered with mud?

He sees her impatiently shake her head. "So, duck or rooster, which is true?"

"Forget it." He feels about for stickiness. (Soup is what he should have said—you know *Duck Soup*? This isn't it.) His arm is numb down to his hand, but the throbbing's returned inside his head. (Lame duck would do—not dead, at least.) He should have ducked, he tells himself.

She's peering back down the track again, clucking as if he's hassling her. What's with such rank ingratitude? Big trouble of some sort on her mind? Or totally stoned—maybe why she's in such a jam now? And, either way, indifferent to any such minor complaints as gunshot wounds or broken bones or how she got into the E&G lot. Something real freaky's going on—part of it doubtless in his head, dealing with pain and probably shock while perched with some hellcat on a train, distracted by thoughts of that lacy black bra and whether she's really Hispanic or not and if she's possibly underage and that toughness of hers a mere façade. He guesses she's just some hippie chick who thinks this decade's outta-sight, a notion that he's too jaded to share.

Her back stays turned, though leaning close as suddenly a bell rings out. They're passing a crossing, and, warily checking the scene for thugs, Dugan knows instantly where they are—headed to Bentsville and beyond, towards new developments gussied up with pools and golf clubs bearing names like Runnymede and Hampton Court. No red convertible at least, but what to his wondering eyes should appear but a baby-blue hardtop, one he knows, stopped at the crossing down below! Same two-tone paint job, chrome grimace, and, lit by the pulsing signal's glow, same goggle-eyed Gordo at the wheel. . . and Meg of the Magic Honkers too! with Gordo the hipster's chatting her up—rapt, absorbed, with a vacuous smile and thumbs like geckos keeping time to some frenzied music he's tuned in. *Professor Mephisto!* Dugan thinks ("How deep and aching are the needs. . .")

"There's the Big Rooster," Dugan observes. "That's who I work for. That guy there."

"Figures," he thinks he hears her say.

In a matter of seconds, the train's moved on, slow as a song by Mel Tormé.

● ● ●

A line of wet rivets under his back—that much continues to seem real while, somewhere in the murk of his brain, he knows there's still a kraken-like pain that threatens pure hell if it's disturbed. But the rest has a crazed Tex Avery feel, including the pile-up in his head ("There's been a wreck, somebody's hurt, you ducks and roosters keep moving, please!") He'll sort things out. Okay, let's see. He's riding a boxcar in the rain with a woman whose face he's barely seen. He studies her back and boyish ass rollicking with the train's vibration, then cautions himself to get a grip. They're bruised and bedraggled, he's lost his bike, his useless arm's gone totally numb, but thinking in Frederick-Henry terms and watching her rhythmic to and fro as they rattle above the street-lighted streets, he's wondering how far they could actually go—to Hamlet, at least, still hours away, the switching yard just over the line ("Mann Act kicks in if she's too young!"), though why, he can't help asking himself, would a rough-hewn bunch of railroad guys decide to call their junction that? Homage sincerely paid to the Bard or lack of any thought at all? A town called Town's a sort of shrug—no people or streets, just shunting trains—like Gordo's blank robotic stare or, crossing some newly-frayed wires in his head, like searchlights prowling a railroad yard patrolled by mindless SS goons.

. . you've met Miss Boozer? Deedy-doo, we jumped a freight once, during the war—the war, you know, in Vietnam. . .)

"If you're planning to. . ."

"Wait!" He cuts her off as he tries to tackle the problem at hand, like tuning a distant station in—some voices and static, then it's gone, but then it might come back again. So, now, let's see, he's spotted a shimmering through the trees, a Bar-B-Que beacon—still unseen, though memory supplies the whole design. . . a dancing pig that jerks and nods on the wall of the Sewer King's former domain where even the heathen can be redeemed through the power of lowly mustard seeds—like Danny, for instance, even him assuming the pork thing's not a hitch. If the tracks lead there as he recalls, it's where they'd better leave the train.

The sign's becoming legible. "See that?" he says as they approach. "That's where we going to bail, okay?"

The twitching flames are bluish white, so it's easy to think the pig's serene, just boogying in its neon pot (like Tom & Jerry's jackboot wit, insinuating pain is fun: Hi, pal, what's up? Here, have a cigar. KA-BAM! Ha, ha, the cat's exploded!) "That rodent's a sadist," he explains, as if his brain's a TV screen that's just as visible to her. Gotta stay focused, though. Yes, we do.

She lets that go until she warns, "I'm not about. . ."

To jump in the dark from a moving train? He tries to flash a calm thumbs-up, forgetting his right arm's out of whack. It sends a telex to his brain: THIS SHIT MUST STOP! So he tries to explain in very few words, "We're gonna slow up on that next curve. Won't happen again for quite a while. Gotta get off there while we can." He's fairly sure the ground is flat.

The pig in a pot goes sliding by as he peers at a stretch of open fields, knowing that's where the city ends and shacks and doublewides begin like wrecks on the shores of a kudzu sea. The maritime simile runs through his mind as, ignoring a darkly nauseous wave that's starting to swell a long way off, he fumbles with one boot over the edge, trying to figure how to dismount while keeping his bum arm by his side. He almost falls, but then his foot encounters a rung, slips off, and slides back on again. The rain appears to be slackening, and smells of dung and damp fodder rush up. There must be livestock down below.

"Ready?" he asks. She's leaning back, her legs drawn up. "You coming?" No, he sees she's not. The clacking and screeching get louder here.

"We're nearing the highway," he explains, losing his balance as they brake, clutching her foot and taking a kick on the kraken he'd hoped would stay asleep. "Ah. . ." he says. "Not necessary."

Still groping, he finds a lower rung, and, dangling by his one good arm, he oscillates like a barroom door. "Sorry I never saw your face." He waits to see if she'll respond, not sure if he's talking to himself. When she doesn't, he gets off one more line: "I guess this is goodbye forever. . ." Worthy of Lubitsch, he reflects, but it doesn't appear to register.

She crouches and peers down past his head as her face, still shadowy in the gloom, assesses what he's just guessing at—a grassy field and long slow curve. Past that, scrub oak, uneven terrain, a deep ravine, and then, he knows from previous trips exploring the countryside on his bike, a sewage stream that after the rain will be flowing with green-brown lumps and curds. That prospect triggers his resolve—Lieutenant Henry bids adieu (Geronimo! as Dexter said, intending what? The point's obscure.)

He jumps, falls clear, takes two quick steps before his right knee buckles back. What follows (he thinks—it's all so quick) is a double half-gainer with a twist. Somehow, he's right-side up again. A forward roll on his functioning side and he's racing across the drizzly field, then slowing and turning to find a blur that's wobbling clumsily in his tracks has come to a halt ten feet away. She'd changed her mind—he doesn't know why. Up to her knees in scraggly weeds, she stares at him as if impressed (Special Olympics. . . what can I say? *Not funny!* a voice in his head objects. I'm handicapped, he tries to shrug, but finds that's not a good idea).

"Okay," he croaks aloud instead, "we'll try to phone from over there," gesturing towards what he takes for a road where a luminous haze is rimming the trees. Piggie Parlor's now nowhere to be seen—he'd waited too late to leave the train. But maybe whatever's making that glow is something besides a liquor store which, according to statewide temperance law, would have to close when the sun goes down. Gas station, he's hoping. . . odds are good—Saturday, and it's early still.

She follows him over the spongy field until they get to a high-top road, skirting a pair of shotgun shacks, one of them with a tin-roofed shed and a lunatic dog that convulses with rage while yanking dementedly on its chain. Because of the dog, they leave the road and blunder into a drainage ditch. Gingerly, he clambers in while she vaults over it in a bound.

"SHUT UP!" yells someone from the house as Dugan sinks past his ankles in muck. With boots like snowshoes, he climbs out, making some noisome-smelling tracks. The barking stops, then starts again. He stamps both feet. A light comes on. She's waded back into the ditch.

"What's wrong?" he asks.

She gestures.

"What?"

"Can't find my shoe."

The dog is frenzied.

"Leave it."

"No."

"Okay," he sighs, indulging her. He wades in too, spots something dark that he plucks free, then watches as, tandoori style, she claps it back onto her foot. He sees she's slender. Supple too. Much more than that he still can't say. . . except for something in her stance, her shoulders, how she holds her head. A dancer or gymnast, maybe both.

A door slams as they move away. The dog subsides, the light goes out, and soon they reach an asphalt road. The rain has now completely stopped but, heading slowly up a hill amid soft sounds of dripping leaves and smells of wet dirt from the fields, they tense at the sound of grinding gears approaching them rapidly from behind. A battered pick-up seems to slow. . . then, honking and swerving, races past to Dugan's undisguised relief. No friends or foes in this neck of the woods, and even the glow he'd glimpsed before has disappeared behind the trees.

But as they top a modest rise, there's a glare like an open fridge up ahead no more than a hundred yards away—a 7-Eleven, Dugan sees—and, in just a few minutes, they're scanning the lot. . . two cars, a pick-up, and a van plus a row of pumps, an ice machine, a trailer sign (DRINK MOUNTAIN DEW!) ignored by the hunkering curb-side crew who're drinking instead from paper bags with bottles of some sort tucked inside (Thunderbird is Dugan's guess, aware that, though they look benign, they could be Huey Newton types).

"Stay close," he tells her quietly, supposing that, in the winos' eyes, the figure they most probably cut is like an ambushed Bonnie & Clyde.

She's fiddling with her mud-caked shoes. He turns to the rehabs hunkering down (Hi, guys! God loves ya. . . So does Allah), trying again to figure things out. Assuming he didn't abet a crime and that her muggers have lost the trail, that they've got a working pay phone inside and Danny hadn't been blowing smoke about staying at home for JLM, the Jesus Loves Me Network of Stars, his chances of making his way back home— if not intact, at least piecemeal—are better than they formerly seemed. . .

though there's still the wildcat woman or girl, and what if she takes a notion to yell, "I'm being abducted against my will"? Or says to him, "I'm Dunkie's friend"?

He holds the door. She hesitates. He looks at her and feels that wave—the one he'd glimpsed far out to sea—is heaving much closer towards him now, but he's still flotsam bobbing about while she's. . . whatever, he's not sure, an Asian of some sort it appears, Viet Cong for all he knows, but Chinese probably in these parts, maybe Korean, who can say? He thinks of the sprinter—what's her name, the one who's always on TV? (Chi Cheng? That's it! *Wide World of Sports!* Same plum-pit eyes and spilled-ink hair. . .) but taller and slimmer, he tells himself (thighs must be like Chi Cheng's too—python-like, could crush a man!) *Aieeeee!* he hears inside his head as he recoils from his own id. Steer clear of that, that's not for him.

She's paused to read his prurient thoughts and apparently reached the same conclusion (though it's not about race, he tries to insist, catching her disdainful look and answering with a wordless reproach—whatever's happening in Canton, he's a regular at the Bamboo House and way too hip to order chop suey). This only takes a millisecond, then she's inside, and so is he.

"You come in here to buy anythang?" a voice behind the counter barks, disrupting his traumatized train of thought that's running through stills from *Shanghai Express* and glamor pics of Anna May Wong. He hears the challenge and knows the type—small face, big hair, a bulldog frame, a surly Pekinese's sneer—a dwarf blown up to monstrous size. "Or you just messin' up my floor?"

"The phone. . ." he mutters, chattering. Wet clothes plus arctic-chill AC further impede what he's trying to do—put his one good hand in the opposite pocket. He fishes up a dollar bill.

She points to a pay phone on the wall. "So, use it."

"Right. I need some change."

"Can't open the cashbox 'less you buy."

"Buy what?"

She shrugs two meaty arms that wobble in a famous way (something to do with Danny, he thinks, from *Rassle Riot* on TV), and then it suddenly dawns on him—it's Awful Oona, former local mega-star, known in the trade as "The Constrictor" (though what in the world's she doing here?) The synchronicity's surreal. *Candid Camera*? Too far-fetched. He thinks he'd better play it straight.

"Some Tic Tacs, then."

"Some whut?"

"You know. . . those little mints in plastic tubes."

Her face is like a wheel of brie—no sign she's grasped a thing he's said. "Excuse me, am I getting through?"

"Whut you see here is whut we got."

"No sweat. Let's see. I'll have. . . a Slurpee."

She studies the cup rack overhead.

"Cola," he adds.

"Uh-huh. Whut size?"

"That little one there. I just want change." He's nauseated anyhow.

"That there's a jumbo."

"Whatever," he says. "The smallest you got."

"This here?" she asks.

"For God's sake, lady! Jumbo or pee-wee, that one there!"

She narrows her eyes, then grunts and turns. "A bantam," he hears her smugly say as if he's made a big mistake. She puts a plastic Rooster cup under a nozzle that, burping twice, evacuates a brownish ooze. She slides it onto the countertop. "We're outta straws."

He takes the cup. "You're what?" he huffs.

"That's thirty-nine cent."

"This stuff's no good without a straw."

"Aisle two, top right, you want 'em so bad." She plucks the dollar from his hand. "There's some down there. They're Dixiebelle."

"Then you're not out."

"You want 'em or not? They're fifty cent."

"Yeah, sure. I want 'em. Gimme my change."

"Forty-four straws in every box. You opened 'em up? Plus two cent tax." She counts it out, then counts again. "That's nine cent change."

"I need a dime!" She shuts the drawer. "Goddamn it, wait!"

"You watch your mouth."

His wallet's gone. He looks around. Chi Cheng's gone too. He understands that he's been stiffed. "You see her leave?" She doesn't reply. "That woman who came in here with me. . . ?"

"The oh-ree-enal?" Oona sniffs. "She left right after you come in. Red Mustang out there blinkin' its lights while you went on about them straws."

The red convertible! Sure, of course. A truck speeds by as he opens the door, an eighteen-wheeler spitting mist, its mud flaps sparkling crimson-eyed. Watching its headlights rake the trees, he feels an operatic pause before the chorus pitches in, the curbside gallery planted there to back his plaintive Where's My Bess?

"She long gone, man!" the first one croons. "Dass aw she wrote."

"Dass right."

"Uh-huh."

So now he gets it, more or less. Putting his Slurpee on a crate, he reaches up to scratch his head and finds he's got a helmet on. Amazing how that's slipped his mind, but then his mind is having to cope with whatever bashed the helmet in. He runs a finger over the dent and knows for sure that he's been had—busting his arm while smashing his bike, saving the girl but losing his dough. It's classic, right? Been down so long, it looks like up, and losing the girl in green knee-socks? Fariña died on the back of a bike. . . though Chi was sockless, he reflects, and, but for his nausea, he concedes, the Slurpee's not half bad.

He looks around, surveying the crowd who're still there squatting on the curb. Where I belong as well, he thinks, with most of the wretched of the earth of any color, every race. . . excluding the schmucks he'd whacked with his bike who, whatever their troubles, had walloped him first. . . or walloped the girl, whoever she was, before they'd gotten around to him. What I oughta do, he tells himself, is get some ripple, sit down, and rap (Say, what's the jive—that Bird's alive?)—and maybe, after a gallon or two, send Oona out to get some ribs (Yo, what it is, it'll kill you too, but there'll be no special hurry. . . dig?)

"HEY, MISTUH!" one of the brothers wails, waving his bag-clad Thunderbird. "You park yo' spaceship down the road?"

Cackles and shrieks. They cough and spit. HEE! HEE! HEE! No brothers to him, then, after all—Lieutenant Henry's on his own. Cocking the thumb of his left hand, he points and squeezes off a round, then goes inside to haggle with Oona: forty-three straws for a penny.

• • •

Back inside the open fridge, he's standing in front of the counter again—helmeted, one-armed, soaking wet, crash-landed in Roswell as it were—while Oona looks on suspiciously. He stares at the pennies in his hand, counting them up a second time and laying them carefully in a line.

"Look, Oona. . ." he says.

"That ain't my name."

"Whatever. . . I'm sure you'll understand. I'm caught in a sort of squeeze, okay?" But how to explain what doesn't make sense? He knows that Caitlin's down at the beach with a couple of junior-faculty wives getting some time off to themselves, and Danny has sworn he'd stay at home watching his favorite TV host on *Jesus Loves Me* ("and my dough")—a televangelist entrepreneur out to reconcile Mammon and God by building an upscale gospel resort next to a glittering dunghill of sin that motorists know as Pancho's Villa (its tacky billboards litter the state). He only hopes Danny told him the truth, the part about staying home tonight.

He only explains the essential details with an emphasis on the TV show. "That's why, you see, I need a dime."

When Oona relents and lends him a penny, he finally gets to make his call. Six rings before he hears a voice telling somebody else to shush. So Danny's got company—no surprise.

"Rosen's the name, Comp Lit's the game—whattaya think of Hermann Broch?" A giggle and then a "Sock-it-to-me!" coming from somewhere else in the room.

"Jesus loves you, Doctor Rosen. . ."

"Hey, turn it down! Real low, okay? Who's this? Hello?"

". . . even if you're not watching his show."

"Duke! Where are you? Drunk or in jail?"

"In deepest doo-doo."

"Anything new? I looked for you this afternoon. They said. . . Leggo! Not now, okay?"

"Danny?"

"Whoa, Mama! Look at that! Not a good time for small talk, Mike. The hamster's loose."

"I need some help."

"Right now?"

"Yeah, now. I'm really sweatin' it, buddy."

A pause. "Where *are* you?"

"Well, let's see. . . a 7-Eleven out Bentsville way."

"You shittin' me, pal?"

"Just down the road from Piggie Parlor. They're holdin' Ramadan on the curb. I'm in trouble for real. . . all busted up."

"What happened?"

"Dan. . .!"

37

"I'll be right there." There's a voice in the background saying
"*Whaaat?*" Some muffled sounds, then Danny's back. "That noise you
hear. . . it's Dharma barkin'. Looks like I'll miss *Pianorama*."

"Hey, Dan. . ."

"Yeah, what?"

"Stay cool, okay?" That wasn't Caitlin's voice he'd heard.

"I'm puttin' the hamster back in his cage."

"You know the place?"

"One seventy-six. The 7-Eleven."

"I'll be inside."

That giggle again.

"I owe you big time, Dannyboy."

A click. What now? he asks himself. Hunt for his wallet in the mud, or
take it for granted it's gone for good? A throbbing pain all down his arm
is starting to make that question moot.

He moves to a freezer down the aisle with speckled ropes of sausage
links coiled like cottonmouths in a box. Nervously searching for
something to do, he slips his left thumb under the lid, lifting and dropping
it while he thinks, letting gray puffs of vapor out. Aware she might take
umbrage at that, he glances at the surveillance disk to forestall Oona
sneaking up and locking him in her Constrictor Grip ("loiterin' fee, that's
seven cent. . . pay up or get your ribcage broke!") But prior to spotting her,
something else goes scuttling rapidly past his feet, reverses and scurries
back again.

"Yeeoww!" he yelps reflexively, knocking some bubblegum off the
shelf. The tentacles stop their thrusting probes, but it's only a black kid
with a mop scrubbing up tracks that Dugan's made. As Dugan steps back,
more tracks appear.

"Thought those sausages musta gotten loose!" he grins apologetically.

But the kid, who's seen bad trips before, just checks him out and looks
away as Dugan scoops bubblegum off the floor and makes new tracks to
the magazine rack—a post from which he can scope the lot for Danny or
goons, whoever's first.

Not much to read, but that's okay. The heavy stuff is over by Oona—
Hustler, *Penthouse*, crap like that. Despite her scowl, he passes the time
by leafing through pulps within his reach. . . a smack-down mag with
pages torn out, a *TV Guide* that's out of date, a months-old Slurpee-stained
Modern Romance.

• • •

Danny shows up in his '51 Merc, a model with gangster-wagon panache—much prized, despite its vintage years, as a sought-after buggy for souping up—and, given its actual mileage-count when Mr. Kappelman passed it on, it drives much newer than it looks. But looks can still convey a lot, and Danny, with his raffish air (Rasputin-like nose and blue-black jaw, gold-braided cap and rock-star shades the color of Milk-of-Magnesia glass) combined with the Mercury's ebony hue plus the missile-rack ornament on its hood and darkly menacing chrome-streaked snout resembling a sand shark washed ashore, commands attention along the curb. But folding his glasses on the dash, Danny stares past them, exits the hatch, and ambles into the 7-Eleven where Dugan is waiting at the door.

"You got a penny?" Dugan croaks as they move back towards the register.

"Jesus, Duke! What happened to you?" Danny's distinctive intonation is like an oboe's piercing mewl in an adenoidal register. "Here. Keep the change. I gotta say your headgear's lookin' the worse for wear."

"I had an accident," Dugan says, putting the quarter in Oona's hand. "In the E&G lot on Sumter Street. . . before finding refuge at this spa."

"The straws," she sulks. "You want 'em back?"

"What straws?" asks Danny. "How ya doin?'"

She squints at Danny suspiciously. He seems much bigger than he is because of the way his shoulders slope, implying raw power in reserve. His gait suggests his legs are bowed, but he rises on tiptoe with each step as if always ready to change direction. His hands hang loosely by his side and his face has a stony, sculpted look until his mouth moves (rubbery)—though, even then, his watery eyes (like those of a corpse dredged up from a pond) stay fixed and unblinking when he talks, his head cocked back, his jaw stuck out, his voice a confidential whine. It's hard to gauge what he might do—like dealing with a rhino, say. . . your first glance warns there's trouble here, a second suggests he'll be okay except in certain states of mind, though it's not at all clear what they might be.

"I get you sumpin'?" Oona grunts.

"You know it," Danny winks at her.

"Whut you see here is whut I got."

"Plenty for me. When you get off?"

She brandishes a length of pipe plucked out from under the countertop.

"Okay," he says. "I can't smoke that, so gimme some Salems. Make it two."

She slaps them down. He opens one up.

"You got a yacht?" she drawls dead-pan but *jiving* with him, acting coy—not just because she's eyed the cap, she's hip to his Danny the Ripper technique. . . where others would neatly tear the stamp, he makes his ciggie pack explode.

"Lady, I got a nicotine habit. I can't afford a boat as well."

"Keep humpin' it, honey."

"Sure, I will." He winks again. "C'mon then, Duke, let's hit the road. And speakin' of sportin' chic chapeaux, 'I *love* the way you wear that hat. . .' *Deliverance*, right? Remember that line? Be seein' ya, hon," he growls at Oona.

She waves the pipe. He's just her type—real men don't need no soda straws.

The curbside crowd, which has dwindled a bit, is ostensibly gazing out to sea, two of them crouched in Danny's way.

"Look out now, guys." He lights a Salem.

"Sho', cap'n."

"Whoa! He launchin' the boat."

The rain's resumed—it's a drizzle again—and Dugan has trouble getting in, tugging the door with his off-side hand. The winos watch this careful maneuver.

"Hey, now. Aw right. Go easy there."

"Stay mellow, guys." The engine cranks as Danny inhales, coughs twice, and asks, "So where to, Duke? The Dibbledome?"

Dugan groans.

"Got it," says Danny, backing around. "Let's find some clean well-lighted place. . . doctors, nurses, x-ray stuff. Durn!" he mutters, shifting gears as he brushes some ashes from his shirt. "You wanna take that helmet off?"

"I can't."

"It's stuck?"

"This arm's defunct."

"I hear ya. Right. So where's your bike?" The windshield's full of shiny specks, but Danny likes to save the juice—anal retentive, Caitlin says. He lets the blades sweep only once.

"On top of the trestle by that lot. . . I had another accident."

"Sure, that's cool." He sees the specks are back again and switches the wipers on and off before giving Dugan a closer look. "But lemme guess where you're comin' from here. It's dark and wet, on top of that trestle, somebody attacking you with a. . . what? A cosh, a sword, a boomerang? Don't answer that. It's all the same—in shadowy, offbeat, black and white. I'd say it's inspired by who. . . Fritz Lang? Some Kraut Expressionist. Early Lang. I'm gettin' close now, am I not?"

If Danny had asked him something else, like how-come they've been such lifelong buds, he might have observed they're just alike—except where he's a terrier type, hell-bent on chasing down every car, Danny's an easy-going hound who only hunts what he can eat. . . and though gab is a pastime Dugan enjoys, to Danny it's slightly better than sex—Caitlin's opinion, but she should know, which maybe explains why he got him a wife with whom he could forge a verbal détente since her stutter's so bad that, in effect, she paints, he jabbers, they get along. . . though she's sly enough to understand her impediment's full of smutty potential, a thought that's skulking in Dugan's mind as he struggles to follow Danny's spiel, something he'd feel more guilty about if she'd ever encouraged him in the least. She hasn't, though. . . so it's Freudian, right? His best friend's wife, forbidden fruit, dark hankerings in his reptile brain? It's lucky they share this Irish thing that draws and respects the line they've drawn—like a neighbor who'll helpfully mind your goat while you're over in Galway having a fling. . . so long as you're not two-timing the goat! Still, neighbor or not, he has to confess that, mired in some dank libidinal swamp, he's sometimes pictured her in the sack like a gasping, spread-eagled Molly Bloom (*Y-Y-Yes! I w-w-will Y-Y-Y-YESSSSSS!*) That snaps him to attention now.

"What?" he asks, as if caught in the act.

"*Public Enemy*'s what I said. . . but, nah, too tough. Or *High Sierra*? Gimme a clue."

"Try brawling in Nighttown," he suggests.

"And your buddy Bloom to bail you out? Oho! My ass!" The wipers stroke and lie back down. "Dunno here, Mike. You S.O.S. from West Be-Jeesus. I pick you up, and, no offense, you're walkin' roadkill, suckin' a Slurpee." He cracks his wing vent for the smoke. "So, now, let's see. . . a sawbones, right? Who won't go blabbin' to the cops. C'mon here, pal! What's goin' on?"

"I jumped a freight."

"Stone sober? Swift! You on your own there, Boxcar Bob—or boogeyin' with the Hobos' Club?"

"A woman," he croaks. "She looked Chinese. I was doing my best to save her tail."

"Uh-huh, except. . .?"

"Except I guess she wasn't so thrilled."

"Sure," says Danny, "makes perfect sense. . . so that's why Bruce Lee beat you up." He pauses for his ritual—the wipers are on, and then they're off. "I guess we gotta face it, chum, bum scripts are damagin' your career." He yanks the dashboard ashtray out. "Well, hell! I thought she'd emptied that." He sniffs a butt, then holds it up. "Tareyton Light. . . who smokes this shit? It's not old Adlai, that's for sure."

"Condolences, Dan."

"Sure, that's okay, we all get old. Just wish she hadn't nailed his ass. Talk about saving somebody's tail! She set him up."

"Aw, come on, Dan. The dog got hit. . ."

". . . by a Budweiser truck—that ring a bell? Know what her uncle Archie does?"

"Distributes beer?"

"Co-in-ci-dence!" He taps his cigarette in the tray. "So anyhow. . . what's there to do? I took him to a funeral home. I wanted cremation, simple and quick. They said they'd pick the body up. I told 'em I had it in the car. The bastards freaked—they don't do dogs. 'A kosher dog,' I told the jerks. Try Dunkin' Donuts, they advised. . . comedians, right?"

Dugan coughs. "What happened then?"

"Eleven at night? I drove him down to Longstreet Park and torched him on a cook-out grill. A neighbor complains, the cops show up—'Crematin' widout a license,' they howl. Twelve months' probation, whattaya think?"

"I hope you'd do the same for me."

"Yeah, well, they told me one more pyre, I go to the clink. Do me a favor and wait a year." He flicks his cigarette again. "Ole Adlai. . . he was quite a dog. He went out like a Viking, buddy."

They drive in silence for a while. Then Danny asks, "You droppin' a tab?" Twin jets of smoke shoot from his nose.

"I swear."

"No sweat. You jumped this freight. . ."

"I told you, Dan."

". . . with Princess Aura—it slipped my mind. And where'd the two of you park the bike?"

"We wrecked it."

"Yeah? And where's she now?"

Another awkward semi-shrug. The traffic's sparse, but every jolt sends urgent instructions towards his brain. That nauseous wave is hitting the beaches. Surf's up, he thinks, surf's up for real.

"Stop, Dan!" he blurts.

"We're stopped, shithead. The stoplight. See?"

Danny exhales a cloud of smoke while Dugan throws open the door and pukes, just missing a white and gold Corvette pulled over because the light's "too short."

"What?" Danny asks the occupants, who're staring at Dugan as he heaves.

"As soon as we're ready to go, it's red. . . it must be broken," the driver complains, gunning it while her tape-deck blares that Whitey has landed on the moon. Her dual-tones match the hues of her car, like those of her equally spaced-out friend. "Can't get more points on my license," she adds, watching as Dugan heaves again. "Bummer," she says.

Her friend looks on attentively, engrossed by how he clears his nose. "Far out!" she comments.

Dugan nods. "I'm just. . . a freaked-out cynic," he says.

"Green!" the friend squeals. "Give it some gas!"

"No, wait. . . it's red. See what I mean? We'll never get home."

"We must have been here over an hour!"

"You've got it in park."

"What?"

Danny adds, "How long have you two girls been blondes? Just put it in drive next time it's green."

"I told you! See?"

"It's working! Wheeeeeee!"

They whiz away.

"Nice girls," sighs Danny with a shrug, waving a V at their exhaust. "A cynic, huh? Accordin' to who?"

"Hold on," chokes Dugan. One more heave. "Dexter," he bubbles, leaning back.

"Well, Dexter's wrong. Believe me, pal, you're one fucked up romantic."

• • •

To Dugan, the ER waiting room looks disturbingly like the 7-Eleven—same lighting, same floor, same clientele, with the careless and indigent waiting their turn and the sullen and wrathful looking subdued. One with an ice pick in his head sits upright with his mouth agape, looking bewildered but serene. The woman beside him's on the phone, stretching its cord as far as it goes while complaining that Nathan's ruined her blouse and owes her a new one P.D.Q. Nathan appears okay with that.

Closer to Danny and Dugan's seats, a kid whose T-shirt says "TUNE IN!" is walking his fingers over the chairs, murmuring rhymes beneath his breath. His mother, whose purse is on her lap, sits stolidly in another row.

"Jason, you git on ovah heah!" Her eyes are all she sets in motion, but wrapped in a flowery gingham print, she looks like Oona's negative image.

"Why he wearin' a helmet?" Tune-In asks.

"Dugan?" barks Big Nurse icily, plucking him from his reverie and steering him through some swinging doors. His name sounds like an accusation. "Wait there," she points. He says okay, taking another plastic seat.

When she returns, she grabs his arm, the one that's hanging like a leash attached in an oddly precarious way. Her fingers don't apologize. (Green shower caps in fashion here. . . like Russians on a Black Sea beach, ex-Soviet doctor refugees? He ponders that—the squirrels are back in his attic now along with the newly awakened pain. But that's okay. No need to rush. If ice picks in the brain can wait, what damage to him could prompt such haste—unless Big Nurse is Russki too? Big Nurse is speaking English, though. *Disjecta membra*? Used to that. . . assuming his arm gets numb again. He likes the numbness, it's his friend.) Some x-rays? Sure, and then we'll see. Who'll see? he asks.

Big Nurse replies, "The man with the stethoscope over there."

Beside them in the little room, a doctor dwarf's perched on a stool, smiling at Dugan as he says, "So how'd we do this?"

"We?" Dugan asks.

"Uh, Mister Dun-what?"

"Du-gan."

"What? Nurse, help me out."

"My name. . ."

"Not now. We'll get to that. I asked you how we managed this. Let's see the file. Aha, of course! A murder-cycle accident. That's what I call 'em. . . what they are." He looks at the clipboard in his lap, reading some sentences Danny wrote. "Well, Mister. . ."

"Dugan."

"Please hold on! Just wait a minute till I'm through. Your shoulder's crushed. Not much to do, but we'll strap it up in an elbow sling. The weight of the arm will help it set." (Like speckled sausage links in the fridge—keep it on ice a day or two.) "Does he speak English? Nurse, look here. Has anyone gotten through to him?"

"He said okay."

"That doesn't mean much. He's still in shock. Would you try to get that helmet off?" He shines a light in Dugan's eyes, moving a thumb from side to side. "Feel dizzy?"

"No."

"Just watch the thumb. I think we're starting to come around."

"I've *been* around."

"I'll say you have. This looks like a piece of your former machine."

"Where'd you get that?"

"I'll ask the questions," carps the dwarf. "Allergic to any medication? Read over this list. Okay, that's good. I see you're working at CSU—grounds crew or what?"

"I teach."

"Hello! The joke's on me. Whatta you teach? That's good, right there. No, hand me that. The water. Right. Okay, let's see. Take two of these to lessen the pain—you'll be feeling it soon. Take two right now. Just swallow. Good. I'd say you're lucky, Mister Doyle."

"Doctor."

"What?"

"All sorts of things."

"Here, give me a hand. Just ease him up. That's it. Okay. I'd like to keep you here awhile. For observation overnight."

He shakes his head to tell him no. (Can't do that, Doc. Got things to do. . . like bury my Honda, watch Chi Cheng run, recover my wallet, save the world. . . by teaching, you know, one class at a time.) "How long. . ." he gestures, short on words—it's hard to get them out he finds since swallowing those little pills

". . . before you can use it?" nods the dwarf. "Impatient, aren't we? That's okay. Six weeks for sure, it could be ten. You're feeling woozy? Sure beats pain." (Doc's gliding away, like everything else. . . the wrong end of a telescope.) "Good night, sweet ponce," the doctor says—or does

45

he? This is very weird. "Here, nurse. . . hello?" (This doesn't make sense—
it's out of Grimm. The dwarf appears to be amused.) "Whoa. Steady there.
So you're a professor? I don't suppose," he nods and beams, "you're
teaching any football players?"

"Lots," he lies.

The dwarf is hopping up and down. "Go easy on 'em."

"Right," he says or thinks he says. Then someone's guiding him
through the doors. The crowd looks up. He tries to smile. The woman's on
Jason's case again ("You touch that ice pick one more time. . .!") He's not
just woozy, he feels blitzed. A blip and they're back in Danny's Merc
("Your grandpa, Dan, he doin' okay?") A final traverse and he's lying in
bed, his shoulder holstered in its sling (a pistol? Oops! before he can draw,
it's something else—he's not sure what, but then, before he closes his eyes,
he sees it for what it really is. . . a gauze-wrapped sugar-cured ham).

● ● ●

Bright morning sunlight streaks the floor past islets of scattered
clothing and shoes to a penny, some fuzz, and the plastic cap of a ballpoint
pen kicked under the shoulder-high "chifferobe" (plantation talk, Miz
Dibble has said) along with a rented tux-shirt stud that Dugan had dropped
and never retrieved after squiring the ardent Miss Dunkie Dee to the
previous season's Cotton Boll Ball.

In its coverage of that event, *The Cumbria Impeder* had truly outdone
itself, declaring on the following day that "amid the elegant revelry, the
evening's thunderous climax came with a ne plus ultra rigadoon"—
circumlocutions that Dugan recognized as a reference to Dunkie's lead-
footed jig fueled by four or five flutes of champagne, though it baffled the
paper's readership and led to a newsroom contretemps for the maverick
reporter Billie Swick, whose wise-ass polysyllabic wit would get her
summarily reassigned from Society Notes to movie reviews submitted by
her as FLIX FOR HIX but appearing bi-weekly as "Movie Talk." She'd
probably written the caption too for a photo of Dunkie and her date:
"Stunning in Cotton Boll Ball gown and gloves, Miss Duncan Ratliff
Dibble," it began, proceeding to a bigger fib, "granddaughter of late
philanthropist Vernon K. Ratliff, Esq.. . ."

The Sewer King? Philanthropy?

In response to Dugan's tactful inquiry, Miz Dibble had offered a few details. Ratliff, it seems, had concocted a scheme to rehabilitate errant Cumbrian youth. With hooded eyes and trim moustache, he too had posed for a photograph—in rumpled white linen and Panama hat, a Colt revolver on his hip, overseeing some black men glumly clad in black-and-white horizontal stripes.

"But these are convicts! Look, Miz Dee, this bald one's chained to his sewing machine!"

She'd sniffed at his effrontery, invoking a Gospel parallel on the subject of visiting folks in prison and reminding him acerbically that, "Even our Lord & Savior did time" (and what if He'd asked for guidance too—say, seventy hours of guidance a week with Sundays off to offer up thanks for His servant Pilate's helping hand? he'd wanted to ask but thought better of it). Miz Dee had confided even more. "That nigra there, with his foot on the treadle, his niece was J.C. Kingdom's aunt." The All-American running back? Whom Dugan advises—did Miz Dibble know that? She'd nodded as if they both held stock in J.C.'s future pro career. "She raised that boy to run from whites," she added as if revealing all. "Right there in Gadsden down the road." She shook her head as if to say God truly works in mysterious ways when it comes to broken-field runners.

But J.C.'s riddle was bigger than that. He'd never divulged the Christian names for which his two initials stood—maybe because a cousin of his, the fatherless corner-back Regis Jones, had been callously razzed by rival fans who'd learned that his birth-certificate name was Regis U.S. Pat Off Jones, prompting an even uglier claim that his namesake was a patent citation on one of the frequently idle machines in a laundromat of ill-repute attracting a late-night clientele. Though the evidence was non-existent, the insult had been clear, resulting in a nickname "Tumble Dry" that followed him to the NFL where, like the wrestler Gorgeous George, he wore it as a *nom de guerre*, making detractors rue the day they'd ridiculed him for his hot air. Still, J.C. thought himself forewarned, and, when pressed by reporters about his name, he'd only shrug and smilingly say, "Ah runs 'em lak ah sees 'em, boys, 'cause talkin' don't put no points on the board"—the sports-page leader on the day when the rest of the caption that Billie Swick wrote said, "Next to Miss Dibble (face a blur) is MITCHELL DUGNA, PhD."

There wasn't much point in setting them straight, but Dugan had tried to anyhow. "Dear Miss Swick," he'd written to Billie, "Ole Mitch don't care if you screw with his name, but he happens to be J.C.'s advisor, a matter of moment to your peers ('Applied Dynamics, bagged a C? Keep up the good work now, you hear?') He knows the secret of those initials but ain't goan tell proofreaders like you."

"Who's askin'?" Billie Swick replied. "You're lucky they didn't call you Dung."

Dugan was lying anyhow—J.C. was keeping his secret close. But the press-box guys were in search of relief from weekly accounts of Rooster defeat, especially on the day of the Ball when J.C. ran eight kick-offs back, one for the home team's lone TD. So, ignoring the score, they'd tried to promote what they trumpeted as "A GRIDIRON ENIGMA" with a challenge they'd posed for their readers: "Can You Decipher Those Two Initials?"

> Loyal Rooster fans have still had a lot to crow about this season in the dazzling footwork of its All-American running back J.C. Kingdom. But both he and team spokesmen have remained so stubbornly mum about what those initials stand for that negative rumors have once again been reported in the Upstate. Now, thanks to an authoritative source, we've got a big announcement to make—and this is where you readers come in: send your best guesses to The Impeder along with why you think you're right, and, if your answer proves correct. . .

Well, whattaya know? was Dugan's response—a contest Lester Mattox could love ("Le'ss christen that boy in plenty of time for next year's festive Ku Klux Bowl!") But the reward had boggled his mind:

> . . . you'll get VIP seats for all remaining home games plus tailgate catering by Piggie Parlor Bar-B-Que in amounts that equal J.C.'s playing weight—nearly 250 lbs. at last report!

He had no interest in the meat (roughly ten Adlais, he supposed), but assuming J.C. had cut a deal for something other than barbecue, he'd submitted an entry anyhow. "Jesus Christ is my best guess" (nailed at the 12 but back on his feet and into the endzone from the 3). He never received an acknowledgement, maybe because he'd signed his card as "Morton C.

Glover, Ph.D." (an inside joke for Danny and friends since Glubber wasn't known for wit any more than for basic decency) and no winner was ever announced (presumably because, like the S in Harry S Truman and like J.C. himself, they simply were what they were).

All this conflates in Dugan's mind on the morning after his accident with flashbacks to the Boll Weevil Ball as it's known to resentful outsiders—which is to say, to Catholics, Jews, and anyone even slightly darker than a moderate Pawley's Island tan or, as Miz Dee had tactfully put it, those who wouldn't feel comfortable among the community's "old elite" of high-born Cumbrian businessmen, bankers, and prosperous realtors-slash-slumlords along with smatterings from the professional class of doctors, judges, and architects, including the town's first periodontist whose darkly ominous hectoring had earned him the sort of wary respect accorded to preachers and undertakers, plus dozens of lawyers shrewdly adept at fleecing Yankee litigants. Though they were the ones who'd furnished the dough, their wives had the leverage to assure that former member's widows and sons got invited to the annual ball, which is why Miz Dibble and Dunkie were there and Dugan too for that matter. . . his father had once been a member—though, long before he'd moved away, he'd neglected to pay his dues.

The event was tribal to say the least, confirming the club's priorities of status, booze, and strutting about with affluence a rolling bass and pedigree the official theme. The officers in beribboned shirts, smug with lecherous bullfrog pomp, stood, hands in their pockets, chests puffed out, ogling the debutantes skimming the floor like mayflies over a moonlit pond—blithe, bare-shouldered, off the beat.

The orchestra stuck to the tried and true (tried by hacks like Lawrence Welk and true to a Muzak-like ideal), but getting requests, they'd tackled a shag, inspiring a gassed-up Oldsmobile dealer to try some moves from Myrtle Beach that caused two members to intervene, whereupon the drummer, trying to help, began to shake a pair of maracas—at which a bachelor haberdasher skipped out while warbling "Cha! Cha! Cha!" until an officer took things in hand by instructing the band to play a waltz, and Miz Dee, grabbing Dugan's arm, coyly said if he insisted.

He'd steered her like a Zamboni driver, easing her out onto the floor, self-conscious at first but then surprised to find how nimbly mobile she was, as fluid as something mounted on wheels—a vacuum cleaner sprang first to mind, or, better yet, an ambulance, her sequins flashing as she spun.

"You're such a good dancer, Doctor Doogan!"

"Like blocking for J.C. Kingdom," he bowed.

But his compliment sounded too obscure, partly because, for all his fame, J.C. would not be welcome here except to help pour cheap champagne from diapered bottles at the bar. Dispatching Dugan to fetch them some as soon as the "Tennessee Waltz" was done, Miz Dee remained with three of her chums comparing notes on the Dee Ell See, the gossipy club to which they belonged, while Dunkie watched placidly, head hung low like a buffalo on a nickel.

It took him a while to wend through the crowd.

"Mike Junior!" gushed a matronly blonde, blocking the doorway with her hip just as he'd almost reached the bar. "I swannee you're the *spittin'* image!"

"Ma'am?" he'd parried, edging away.

"Don't you ma'am *me*!" She came on strong, her push-'em-up bra displaying its wares like a couple of wilted canapés. "I knew your father. . ." she confided, dropping her voice to a harpy-like growl. "He was a handsome dawg," she purred, putting her hands on his lapels. "Weesa Spratt—I was a Heyward. . . from over near Ellenton, you know where? The old one, not the new one, now."

One of the wuzzas—sure, he knew.

"They built that bomb plant," (she said bum) "where I went courtin' with my beaus." She poked him with her fingernail. "I reckon that makes me radioactive! How long since you got back to town?"

"A couple of months now."

"Doin' what?"

"Teaching at CSU," he said.

"Well, I declare. It sho' beats working, as Moon would say. My husband, Moon—you know him, don't you? Your momma did. . . and how's old Edna getting' on?"

"Who?" he asked.

She rolled her eyes. "Your pretty momma!"

"Ella, you mean."

"Honey, slow down. Don't talk so fast."

"Her name was Ella."

"Elll-laaaa! One of the Urquhart girls, all of 'em cute as possums too! You look like you're right cute yourself. She stayed with your dad?"

"That's right," he said.

"And moved. . ."

"HEY, WEESA!" someone roared, a sweaty man without a chin. "Listen, son!" he chortled to Dugan. "You know what a woman. . .?"

"Russ, GO ON!"

"A woman of fifty. . ." (squeezing his arm) "Dooby! How's it goin' there, bud?" (tightening his grip and looking around) "Know whut she's got atween her jugs that her teenage daughter dudn't?"

Dugan shrugged.

"Her *navel!*"

"RUSS!" She smacked his chest.

"*Navel!*" he whinnied, turning away.

She reached for Dugan, yanking him back and bringing her face up close to his. "Hold on, Mike Junior. . . what's the rush? Your precious momma moved to *where*?"

"To Sarasota."

"Well, listen here. . ." (her hand inside his cummerbund) "I've been in the circus too, you hear? I guess we both got stuck with a clown."

"No, ma'am."

"No, whaaat?" (an intimate tug) "You mean your daddy wudn't a clown? You hear that, Russ? He wudn't a clown."

Russ took that in and said with disdain, "He was with a lampshade on his head!"

Dugan said quietly under his breath, "He ended up on a trapeze."

"So little El-la married a *swinger*! Who'd a thought it?" Weesa clucked. She looked for Russ, who'd gone again. "I knew he had a drinkin' problem."

"He never dropped her, though," he said.

"Then what?" she asked. "They both still there?"

"He died," he told her. "So did she."

Her face hardened a bit and then relaxed. "You should've looked after her better," she said.

He took that as calmly as he could. "Yes, ma'am, I should have," he replied before adding sarcastically under his breath, ". . . and I wonder who's looking after *you*?"

She narrowed her eyes and poked his chest. "Sweetie, don't try to mess with me. Your little tuxedo ain't all that cute."

"WEESA! HEY!" A paunchy man had shoved through the crowd, arriving in sections like a train. "S'cuse me, son. Hey, Wees, look here! You gotta come see whut we got goin'."

"Mike Dugan. . . you remember him?"

"Come on now, Wees."

"Stop talking and listen." She pointed to Dugan. "Ella and Mike. You hear me, Moon? You see that knock-off standin' there? His daddy's lack of manners too."

Moon looked him over and shook his head. "What happened to Mike? He moved again?"

"In a manner of speaking," Dugan said.

Moon's expression remained a blank. "Well, hell. Too bad. Here's what we did—we found this mijjit down in the lobby, and gave him a twinny to break on Red. . ."

"'Bye, Mike," she winked. "You better look out. Smart alecks are six to a dollar here."

"Mike who?" Moon asked, spilling his drink while leading the wuzza to watch their prank.

By himself in the doorway, Dugan could see both where he was headed and where he'd been. Out on the dance floor in his wake, the band was revving up again with Chubby Checker's whitest hits. Ahead, at the bar, there was room to maneuver, though a man with a leathery pockmarked face sniggered as Dugan bellied up. Dugan replied with a neighborly nod, ignoring the man's belligerent look.

. . . let's do-oo the twist!

The stranger sipped and glanced away.

"Champagne," said Dugan. "Make it three. Hey, keep the faith," he told the man who, munching an ice cube, told the wall, "I'm no Ephesian, Sunny Jim." Or don't, said Dugan to himself, returning to find Miz Dee cranked up amid some zealots from her club discussing what she was wont to call "an aristocratic heritage."

"A never-failing resource," she trilled, "upon which people like us can draw. . ." She looked around as he walked up.

"Miz Dee. . ." He held three glasses out.

like we did. . . last suh-huh-mer!

Dunkie took one and chug-a-lugged as her mother concluded her cliché, ". . . in times of difficulty."

"True, so true,' piped Opal Tubbs. "And collard greens too I always say."

52

"What started that?" he said to Dunkie.

She shrugged and gulped another glass down, putting it back and eyeing the third as "OPAL!" Miz Dee sternly said, "IF YOU WON'T WEAR YOUR HEARING AID, YOU'RE GOING TO MISS OUT ON A LOT."

"I heard the same thing," Opal said.

A hand was clapped on Dugan's neck, jostling some champagne from his glass.

"Mike! It's Gordo! How's it going?"

Dugan turned. "Oh, Gordo, hi."

"You get here on your motor-sickle?"

Good one, Gordo. Har de har. You with that student you're tryin' to screw? "My bike?" he answered. "Not tonight."

C'mon! c'mon! Let's do-oo the twist!

As Dunkie polished the last glass off, Miz Dee spied Dugan's empty hands. "I thought you went to get champagne."

"All gone," he said. "You know each other? Professor Gordon. . ." Gordo bowed. "Miz Dibble and Dunkie. . . Opal Tubbs. And Miz DuBose."

"Rufus G. Gordon," Gordo smiled, pleased with himself for being there along with the General from the Fort and one or two other invited guests. "I'm Mike's Dutch uncle, you might say."

"On which side?" Miz DuBose inquired.

"WHAAAT?" asked Opal with alarm.

"The ENGLISH Department!"

"And the Dutch? Weren't they on our side in the war?"

"OPAL! Really, never mind."

"I don't see why that band's so loud. Like opening up a box of Pandoras."

"Well. . ." Gordo answered, looking bemused.

"If music be the fool of love. . ." Miz Dee observed.

"True. . . so true!" Miz DuBose agreed, leaving Opal with nothing to say.

"That's 'food,' Miz Dee."

They studied the shrimp dip's empty bowl.

"Food's always been the fuel of love," quipped Gordo, now in papal mode. "Oysters, chocolate. . ."

"And *champagne!*"

"OPAL!"

"What? I *love* champagne!" Opal defiantly stood her ground, wistfully following Dunkie's hands waving the flutes like smoking guns. Then turning to Gordo, Opal exclaimed, "And I miss *The Saturday Evening Post!* I hate that awful Mister Butts."

"Ah. . . Mike," said Gordo, looking around. "Why don't you make another run?"

"No, no. We're fine," Miz Dee broke in. "It's time you youngsters had some fun."

"Right," Gordo chortled, catching on. "Go on, there, Mike, let's see the two of you get down and dance the light fantastic. . . dance." He smiled at Dunkie, wagging his head, as cordial and basically insincere as Nixon's plan to end the war.

Slyly, Dunkie had raised her hands, her fingertips stained a curried pink from munching the shrimp dip wearing gloves. Drunk as a skunk, she shot him a glance that in its shy, slow, sullen way was disconcertingly lecherous. Gordo stood looking benignly on while, fired up by its bland success, the band reverted to R&B.

"Give us the glasses," Miz Dee said, as Dunkie took a half step back, steadied herself and seemed to shiver.

As the mirror-ball flashed, the band cut loose with fortissimos of "ShaBoom! ShaBoom!" Dunkie was swaying with every boom, her eyes on Dugan, measuring him. Time for the rodeo to begin.

"Okay, hot mama," Dugan winked, tugging her gently from her stall.

"YATTATA YATTATA!" yelled the band.

● ● ●

But Dugan's bravado has taken a hit. Back then he'd had two workable arms plus a wallet and a one-two-five, though minus that missing-in-action stud that daily, if unbeknownst to him, gets touched by a probing finger of dawn. On the morning that follows his accident, it seems some sort of conjunction occurs—for the instant the stud begins to shine, a rapping intrudes on his sedation.

His hypothalamus hears it first, reminding him of his duplicitous role since Dunkie decided, after the Ball, that Cinderella was taking charge—

along with her scheming mother, of course, who's made it perfectly clear to him it's irrelevant whether the slipper fits. He doubts if Dunkie's confided the worst, but no matter how affably he demurs, Miz Dee's not letting him off the hook. He's Dunkie's prize and hers alone, let jezebel poachers be advised.

If some alley-cat huntress on the prowl visits him past the sermonette, there's no hot water until she's gone—literally, his pipe's cut off, though how it's done is unexplained. . . something to do with Harlan Tull, a crackpot neighbor living next door with whom Miz Dee has an iffy détente. Her solicitude is even worse: if he's hung-over after a spree, a clucking Miz Dee is sure to appear to dole out vile "plantation receipts"— restorative potions she's devised while Dunkie, his would-be bartered bride, morosely waits outside the door, ready to grapple yet again.

They'd dragged him off to the Dibble Hunt—half-wits with shotguns blasting birds while mutts like Dinkie gum the scraps (Dinkie's the Dibbles' cutesy name for a scruffy malodorous rat-like pooch that, other than hating Dugan's guts, prompts thoughts of the devil's own S.A.T. with a question that fills his heart with dread: "*In this progression, what comes next: Dunkie, Dinkie, Dibble. . . what?*" The answer that troubles his sleep is "*me!*")

Then there's the matter of Mister Tull, an alcoholic sociopath who, leaving the nuclear Navy behind, had settled in with ole Jim Beam, promoting free enterprise in his head by shooting the squirrels in Miz Dee's yard as they raided the feeders meant for birds. "Free-loading bastards!" he would rail, firing off .22 rifle shots that, whizzing across her patio, would thud into her potting-shed. The body count was piling up— just squirrels, no people as of yet—but as Harland was armed and dangerously nuts, dissuading him was a tricky task for which Dugan was hand-picked by Miz Dee. Met with gruff suspicion at first, Dugan had made a twisted case that shooting the bastards was much too slow and risks of collateral damage high. So Harlan, who'd managed torpedo tubes, had rigged high-voltage power lines converging on Miz Dee's feeder tray, intending to fry each furry marauder flicking its tail at Adam Smith.

"They're gonna *feel* that invisible hand!" he cackled dementedly to Miz Dee, proceeding to blow the transformers out that served the eastern half of town—which prompted a visit from two stern men who told him his one-man war was done (in fact, they carted him off to a place where Harlan himself was likely to get high-voltage adjustments to his plans), after which he'd been more subdued, reverting it seemed to submarine mode.

Dugan got credit—for nothing, in fact—though he could detect in Miz Dee's mind the thought that his leash had gotten slack and Dunkie too passive to rein him in. His handicap here, as he perceives, lies in an aversion to being rude, while her great strength is playing dumb—for which, of course, she's superbly endowed. That and gradually wearing him down as, antennae aquiver at break of day, she raps and repeatedly calls his name along with a frenzied snuffling from Dinkie, the scrofulous numb-numb devil-dog.

"Doctor Doooogan!" she coos through his patio door that's also riddled with Harlan's slugs.

"Ye gods!" he groans despairingly as last night's debacle bubbles up like Drano in his sleep-clogged brain. He opens an eye to look around, hears a key turning, glimpses her head, then catches an unmistakable whiff of gardenias mixed with Listerine. Thank heavens he'd put the chain-latch on, but what and how could she possibly know?

"Girl in the dorm! Whooeee! Look here!" She's banging the door against the chain.

He won't respond. His shoulder aches. His head's a pummeled cantaloupe. Her cheery voice assaults his ears, echoing a sappy radio show that just went off the air last year.

Good morning, Breakfast Clubbers!
Good morning to ya!

To make matters worse, the idiot dog's been whining and scratching at the door, frantically trying to wriggle through.

"Syllabub time!"

For breakfast? Gag. The woman's insane.

"No use playing possum with me," she purrs, inserting her nose as far as she can.

"Go 'way, Miz Dibble."

"Certainly not. I added some bourbon to help things heal."

The scratches and clicks abruptly stop as Dinkie, who's wormed his way inside, stalls out beside a laundry pile. Then something connects. He goes berserk, attacking a pair of jockey shorts.

"HUSH UP, NOW, DINKIE! You come back here!" She peers in past the still latched door. "Oh, Doctor Doogan, just look at you! I knew that contraption. . . Never mind. . . Dunkie can chauffeur you around."

He stumbles numbly to the door, unlocks it, and then returns to bed.

"Motor-sickles!" she chides with disgust, putting a tray down on the bed. "That damn fool Harlan Tull is right, anyone rides one gets a plate." She taps a finger to her head. "Or pins, or maybe something worse. He said you're hiding a loco streak, living a wild vicarious life. And I told Dunkie just last week while driving home from the Ratliff reunion, that precious little professor of yours is going to smush his sweet brains out."

"Miz Dee, excuse me. . . *The Impeder*?" He sees she's brought one with the tray.

She shakes her head. "I've got a bone to pick with you first. DINKIE, STOP! Put those back down!" She yanks the shorts from Dinkie's mouth, twisting his head a full three-forty.

"Good thing I wudn't still in 'em, huh? That dog's got leprosy, Miz Dee. Can I just look at the front page?"

"No, you can't. Now, open wide. I'm not asking what you did last night." She jabs a spoonful at his mouth. "From the look of things, you were up to no good. Carousing and roostering, I suppose."

"Did you mean roistering, Miz Dee? I wasn't, no—I'd been at work and had an accident coming home. They've put me on powerful sedatives, so mix it with some of that stuff you've got and I could croak right here and now."

"I doubt it," she says. A glob of syllabub hits his arm. She uses his shorts to wipe it off. "Dunkie. . ." she says, as Dinkie growls, snapping at one of Dugan's boots. She swats him with the folded *Impeder*, after which Dinkie wanders off. "She thinks you've gotten in some kind of trouble. I only hope it's not illegal."

"I wrecked my bike."

"Was Dunkie with you?" she demands.

Dugan's surprised. "Of course, not. Why?"

"Well, something's happened to her as well—she won't say what, some sort of fall, she called to tell me from her dorm. Very peculiar, if you ask me, and she says you've been avoiding her. I told her you're just like any man who's scared of what he really wants, especially if he's lived in England. The men over there are all so shy. . . because of their teeth is what I hear. At least, that's what my dentist claims. . . he's Doctor Clinkscales, you know him? You saw him at the Cotton Boll Ball. He says if we get socialized, we're going to learn just how they feel, they're practically communists over there, which accounts for what's happening to their teeth. But yours look fine. Except for the one that's chipped up front—I said to Dunkie, 'His teeth look fine.' Did you know Kris Kristofferson?"

"At Oxford?"

"Yes." She nods her head.

"A little before my time," he says. "My friends were from places like Arkansas. Or Liverpool—same sort of place."

"He's sweethearts with that Indian girl—oh, what's-her-name? They sing together. And both of them have beautiful teeth." She gives him a coyly suggestive look. "Dunkie's part Indian too, you know."

"Any particular part, Miz Dee?" Her teeth, for instance, for a start?

"A very small part, if you must know. But that's not what you and I need to discuss. She's very banged up this morning too according to what she said on the phone. I'd hate to suppose. . . if. . . oh, you know." She slows and sputters to a halt.

"If what, Miz Dee?"

"These motorsickles. . . boots and things. . . What Harlan Tull as good as said. . ."

He's puzzled now—since Harlan's too bats for a confidant, he wonders what's on her devious mind.

"People are trying all sorts of things," Miz Dee continues breezily. "Experimenting, acting wild. . ." A wad of syllabub falls with a splat, followed by Dinkie's menacing snarl—he's cornered a sock and teeters up with half of it dangling from his mouth. Miz Dee grabs hold and whaps his head. He drops in a heap, then lurches up and staggers out of the room again. "He's always liked her friends before." She drops the sock atop a boot that's shedding shards of reddish clay. "Long hair and beards, they're not so bad. Hippies and protests, alcohol—maybe even a little pot. . . I'm not completely out of touch. But if you and Dunkie. . . well, you know. . . we just don't come from people like that."

Like Adolf and Eva? Who's she mean? "Like what?" he asks.

"Like. . . playing too rough." She looks away, then back again. "I've heard of a book called *Savage Love*."

"I thought you said she's Indian?"

"Just Pocahontas. No one else." She puts the *Impeder* down at last on a bedside table next to him.

"Miz Dee," he says. "I better confess. Dating a redskin turns me on, but kinky coupling's not my thing—no matter what Harlan Tull might say. Dunkie and I are friends, that's all. I'm sorry if you. . ."

She cuts him off. "A worried mother has to ask. This syllabub's medicinal."

"For what?" he asks. "Delirium tremens?"

She slaps his arm. He yelps with pain. "I'm sorry, but it serves you right! There're things that we don't joke about."

"Like syllabub?"

"Like family tradition."

"I'm gonna throw up."

"You've got such promise, Doctor Doogan. I hope you don't just flub it up."

He opens his mouth. She shoves some in.

"It tastes like Sterno," he complains, using his elbow like a prod to nudge *The Impeder* onto the bed.

Dinkie, who's fetched the other sock, stands watching them warily out of range as Dugan flattens the front page out, hoisting it just an inch or two, and Miz Dee lets her words sink in. After an interval, she resumes. "It's tragic, you know, what happened to her." He's not sure who she's talking about. "She died so young." She sighs and frowns, referring, it seems, to Pocahontas. "I'll leave this syllabub here," she says. "You can finish it later on your own. I don't know why I waste my time trying to help such headstrong men—they just don't know. . . YOU PUT THAT DOWN!"

"Huh?" He lets the paper fall.

Caught munching again on Dugan's sock, Dinkie breaks wind and stares at the floor as he, like Dugan, comes to heel.

"Give it to Mama!"

Dinkie complies, eyeing the syllabub on the floor. Miz Dee, who's also noted the splotch, bundles the sock into a lump and places it on the bedside table. "All Dibble Retrievers love to hunt. They're born that way, like Dunkie and me. Those doctors should have their heads examined, releasing you after a thing like that."

A thing like what? And how did she hear?

"Hand me that paper, Doctor Doogan." She crumples a back page into a ball, using it first to wipe the floor—then Dinkie's muzzle after that, leaving a sort of creamy goatee. "Dunkie called five minutes ago." The dog goes nuts at Dunkie's name. "She says she's heard you had a wreck."

"How. . .?" he asks inaudibly above the snarls that Dinkie emits whenever Dugan starts to speak (the little bastard knows! he thinks).

Miz Dee yanks Dinkie by the tail. "HUSH UP NOW, DINKIE! Dunkie says. . . YOU BETTER BEHAVE!. . . I don't know how she got the news. She's very intuitive, you know that. And she worries too much—she's on her way over to see for herself what parts of you are still intact." She glares at Dinkie. "I'M WARNING YOU! I tried to tell her how stubborn you'd be."

"The paper, Miz Dee, you're messing it up."

"Oh, take it," she says. "ALL RIGHT, THAT'S IT! GET. . . OUT OF HERE!" The dog retreats to the still opened door, his toenails clacking on the floor. "You get some rest till she gets here."

The door thumps shut and opens again. "You eat that syllabub now, you hear?"

● ● ●

He thinks about resetting the latch, but tendons twanging on jagged bone make him decide to put that off. He props the *Impeder* on his knees, scanning it quickly to see what's there: syllabub stains and overseas news along with Westmoreland's declaration regarding his briefing from Vietnam: "Without censorship," he'd told the press, "things can get terribly confused. . . in the public's mind," he'd hastened to add in his weirdly deliberate nonsense-speak. Other than that, just routine stuff— body counts, moon rocks, Willie McCovey. Nothing about last night's melee, not even among the local-news squibs. No ruckus or shoot-out. No Chi Cheng.

He glances up at *The Peaceable Kingdom*, the last of the posters left behind by girlfriends eager to mark their spoor—like leaving eye-liner on his sink or pantyhose draped above the tub, layers of claimants taped to the door: WAR IS NOT HEALTHY under the Hicks and Van Gogh's bedroom under that, a Tibetan mandala, and, wholly unseen, a woman by Goya that Dugan acquired as wishful thinking on his own—Señora Sabasa Garcia by name, but he'd covered her up when Danny complained that, except for the color of her hair, that was his wife on Dugan's door. The mandala had come from The Cosmic Collection.

He studies *The Peaceable Kingdom* again: the simpering lamb (or maybe a goat?), the leopard quivering for a fix ("Holy be-jeesus! all this

MEAT!") But the meaning's changed for him of late, with Dugan the Carefree Predator feeling more like a would-be prey.

He catches a whiff of the tangerine peel he'd dumped in the trash just yesterday, which makes him think of his big mistake in the back of the Merc eight months ago. Danny had lent him his gangster wheels to serve as a dogcart to the ball, forgetting three citrus sacks in back that Caitlin had bought to use as props (she'd entered her abstract green-fuzz phase, letting fruit rot to putrid blobs while seeking what Danny dismissively called "the m-m-multi-hued p-pathos of decay"—like Rembrandt's cellulited nudes, a long, gross way from Peter Max).

So. . . looped in the aftermath of the ball, Dunkie and Dugan had clambered in back, laughing and having some grisly fun. They'd rolled across a couple of sacks, enveloped in clouds of tangerine smells (still fairly fresh, no problem there)—this after they'd swiped some extra champagne, a couple of bottles for the road, and dawdled to tipple in Sternbolt Park, riding the plastic piggies-on-springs that threatened to crumple as Dunkie swayed, serenely shit-faced, back and forth. Then, soon as the last of the bubbly was gone, they'd skipped to the Merc where Dunkie, aggressively Rubenesque, had put her hand in Dugan's crotch as if in a friendly game of jacks, snatching whatever she could grab. It was one of those moments, he recalls: the tangerines like a beanbag futon, the princess oblivious to the peas, the radio playing Jingle Bells. . . and, what the hell? He'd seen them smirk when the man on the bandstand called her name, mustering svelte debs on parade. He'd help old Dunkie stuff her stocking.

A clamor disrupts his reverie—the devil-dog barking through the wall at footsteps on the patio. He watches the knob, on full alert. Too stealthy for Dunkie, not Miz Dee. Who else, then? Could it possibly be. . .?

"How's it goin' there, Flipper?"

Faithful Dan.

"Partyin' on," is Dugan's reply, delivered with a wry grimace.

"Pharmaceuticals, pal—they'll do that for you."

This prefaces Danny's entry routine: take two steps (yo!) into a room, snatch something up, inspect it (huh?), and launch into a manic spiel. "You done with your Evel Knievel stunts? Don't bother to answer—I know what you'll say. But you're looking much better than I'd have thought." He discovers a book that he greets like a friend, yanking it down off Dugan's shelf and waving it like a tomahawk. "Yee-haw! Damn *right*!" Their superstar colleague's famous work, a novel and now a big-bucks flick.

"Looks lak we got ourse'ves a SOW!" Jamming two fingers into his nose, he louvers it up into a snout. "C'mon now, boy! Less heah you squeal!" His head flies back. "Sooooo-iii?" he calls. "*Squeal lak a pig!*"

But Dugan's reverted to where he was—in the backseat of the Merc again incited by those inquisitive paws, still stuffing those britches with Christmas cheer. It makes him wince. At least she's off now in a dorm. Otherwise. . . he shudders to think.

"What's eatin' you, boy? Your motor-sickle?" He puts the book back with a cluck.

"I made a mistake."

"Head-on, I'd say."

". . . with Dunkie."

"Yeah? At the Rooster Coop? I heard she got her cockles von Himmeled."

"Not that."

"Then what?" He looks at Dugan, who's shaking his head. "You buffed the brillo with Godzilla? Not really! *Why*? Don't answer that—there're some illusions I want to keep." Spotting the food tray Miz Dee left, he lifts the cup and gives it a sniff. "What have we here—some syllabub? Don't mind if I do. . . okay with you?" He uses three fingers to scoop it up. "Musta spiced this up with lighter fluid. Not bad, though. Ummm. So Dunkie got planked." He puts the empty cup on the floor as Dugan, in fractions, leaves the bed.

"I'm gonna shave." He's never tried with his left hand.

"Don't s'pose you've heard yet from that girl? Forbidden topic? Suit yourself. You should ventilate this place, you know—it smells like gerbils."

"Listen, Dan. . ." He's by the sink foam-lathered up, but the razor keeps slipping in his hand.

"Ugly, man. You want some help?"

"I need some help retrieving my bike."

"You're bleedin', buddy. Seen the news? Yours wudn't the only game in town. A meltdown at the Rooster Pit—first game of the season, no defense. Coach Ray Don says it's negative thinkin', and Ray Don's right. . . we gotta get it outta our heads. I'll help you on one condition, Duke— ease off this Rider Haggard crap."

"You got it."

"Right. You saw the game? Nah, 'course you didn't. . . but here's the scene. As soon as the Roosters get the ball, this guy with a bullhorn starts to chant, 'JAY! SEE!' then waits for the fans. 'KINGDOM!' half of 'em shout back. Then 'JAY! SEE!' 'KINGDOM COME!' Now everybody's joining in. 'JAY! SEE!' 'KINGDOM COME!' 'JAY! SEE!' 'KINGDOM COME!' And frat boys in the end-zone seats are waving this giant prick on a stick. . . like Number One, you understand? Except this ain't a finger they're wavin'. 'GO COCKS!' the drunkest of them yell while jabbin' their sticks up in the air and others are screamin' KINGDOM COME!" He checks the syllabub cup again. "Empty! Damn! Now, listen up. My question for you—since you weren't there, but prone to gettin' so stoked on race—is regarding the color those frat boys chose for each of those humongous pricks. What do you think it was, old chum? You take your time. That stuff was delicious. The answer, my friend. . . the answer is RED! Can you fuckin' believe it? A mestizo!"

A trickle of blood seeps through the foam.

"I hate watchin' you cut your throat like this. Just grow a beard."

"Dunkie's part Indian."

"Sure she is. I dig that too! But Rooster fans. . . you see their dilemma. They'd sell their sisters for a win but can't go wavin' this big black dick above those little blond coeds' heads! So whatta they do? Treat him like Tonto, ain't it great?"

"What's in your hair?" He wipes his face and steps aside so Danny can peer at his reflection.

"Ashes. . . what else? It's Caitlin again." He dusts his forelock. Flecks sift down. "She knows I'll go back to Longstreet Park. . . to fetch what I can of old Adlai, see? Just ashes and fur and bits of bone, which I put in a Piggly Wiggly bag and leave on the kitchen countertop while I step away for a minute or two. But when I get back there're two bags there—one's from ashtrays in the Merc and probably all around the house, the other one's Adlai. Hey, which one? 'It's all the same,' is what she says. 'My ass,' says I, 'did Adlai smoke?' 'J-Just once,' she shrugs. 'THAT'S IT!' I yell. I take the one that smells like him, and that's the one I throw away."

"Throw where?"

"Well, see. . . I'm on probation. I gotta be prudent. So I take this bag out for a walk and, wherever he used to drop a log, I sprinkle a bit—like holy water, know what I mean? But soon as I see the filter tips, I know she's out-maneuvered me—let me scatter a bag of half-smoked butts while she, perfidious shiksa minx, tossed Adlai in the trash compactor. I pull him out, but what can I say? How do you scatter a bouillon cube?"

"That's shitty."

"Yeah. But more like peat, mixed up with coffee grounds and stuff."

They brood for a moment.

Then Dugan says, "Life's full of unexpected turns," referring to either one of them. "What I just learned from Miz Dibble is that Dunkie's part Powhatan."

"No kiddin'? That's cool. I've often said that some of my best friends. . . No, wait, that's wrong—from Indiana's what I meant. They're hoosiers, right? Some of my best friends come from there. Here, gimme that!"

Dugan's been locked in one-armed strife with a shirt in a box from Nice-'n'-White. Now Danny helps him put it on.

"Just slip your arm through—there you go! Regarding the Dunkster," Danny adds, "that's what they mean by 'feedin' the bear.' It follows you home, and, after that, you gotta keep feedin' it or you die. Your option is to change your home. As a matter of fact. . ." He checks his watch. "We better get started towards your bike. What's that? A pill? A purple one, huh? That's. . . Yowwww! LOOK OUT! Hostile incoming on the way. . . from the perimeter to your right!"

It's Dinkie, like a rabid mop, skittering over the rugless floor to stop stock still in a quivering pose, sniffing the sole of Danny's shoe. Miz Dee arrives in Dinkie's tracks.

"Knock, knock again! It's only me!. . . Oh, Doctor Rosen, how are *you*?"

"Fine, Miz Dee."

She gestures at Dugan. "Please tell him he's got to stay in bed. Dinkie, you stop that right away!"

He's humping Danny's Cordovan.

"That dog's possessed. What's wrong with his skin?"

"DINKIE! You ate the syllabub!"

"Must be an aphrodisiac!"

"Don't be so silly. DINKIE, YOU STOP! I'll put him out on the patio."

"Don't bother, Miz Dee. We gotta go."

"But Dunkie. . ."

"No, ma'am, we really can't wait. We gotta go find my motorcycle."

"You don't *got* to do anything of the sort!" She turns to Danny, tapping her jaw and pointing to Dugan's bleeding chin. "What in the world has he done to his *face*?"

"Him let him scalping knife get dull. . . But, joking aside, I want you to know your secret's safe with me, Miz Dee. I can honestly say—and this is the truth—you don't look Indian to me."

64

"I think somebody's been pulling your leg." She looks at Dugan. "And I know who."

"Ow, cut it out, Mike!"

"Really, Miz Dee, we're goin' now."

She follows them out. "I think you're making a big mistake."

"The story of his life, Miz Dee. But you gotta admire his get up and go—we got him up, and here he goes."

A breeze kicks in as they move towards the Merc, wafting a tropical post-rain smell. Danny pulls out his Nemo cap. "C'mon, now, boy, le'ss hear you squeal. . ."

The rest is lost in the deafening wail of a chainsaw starting up next door. It's Harlan Tull, who's gone A.A. since his return and taken to logging the neighborhood. He says it helps to calm his nerves—especially during Rheingold ads on *NFL Today*.

• • •

From under the water oaks lining the street, the fine white sand looks ochre and blue—a tableau Caitlin might describe as like a Sisley or Monet. . . Arles in Summertime, Deauville Dawn, Cumbrian Sunday Comin' Down. There's darker mud with herringbone tracks inside the SCE&G lot, but on a weekend, no one's there. The gates are chained and padlocked shut. Inside, the big transformers loom like monoliths flanking a windowless red-brick box that hums with energy like a hive buzzing with innumerable bees. Danny and Dugan peer through the fence.

"Right over there."

"Where?" Danny asks. No sign of a scuffle anywhere other than spots of scuffed up mud.

"Beside that grid. I came out here and went up there." He gestures towards a narrow path that drops like a plumb line from the track.

"They locked up when you left, I see."

Dugan takes note but doesn't reply. They follow the fence to its corner post, past DANGER HIGH VOLTAGE and PRIVATE KEEP OUT. Then, picking their way past lumber and rocks, they reach the slope and struggle up. No definite tread marks to be seen, though the angle's as steep as Dugan supposed, making him clamber in a crouch and causing his shoulder to throb with pain. When they get to the top, they both look down.

The lot's some thirty feet below, the trestle a few yards up the track, its near end shaded by a tree.

"Up here?"

"Uh-huh. Along this stretch." He tries to guess how far he'd gone before he crashed into a tie at about the same speed as the train.

"That was after the little men beamed you up. . . before they snatched your bike away?"

"Funny one, Dan. And my wallet too—I'm looking for that."

"I'd say you're lucky you kept your pants." He shakes his head. "She hustled you, pal. I don't know how. . . drugging your Slurpee, I assume."

"Nah, nothing like that. . . that couldn't be it."

"Oh, sure. That's it. Nobody could get a bike up here."

They peer back down the precipitous slope, then up and down the curving track. The air's grown hot with occasional gusts wafting quick whiffs of creosote over the litter on the tracks—a sock, some cardboard, pieces of glass, an empty half-pint of rot-gut gin, the wrapper from a Sugar Daddy with hardened globules of caramel. . . but nothing that Dugan's hoping to find. Some shade on the tracks looks splashed from a bucket, the tracks like filaments in a bulb. On reaching the shade, they stop and sit, each perched at the end of one of the ties.

"You got a Salem?" Dugan asks, his boot heels wedged in the gravel bed.

"You bummin'?"

"Yeah."

"Well, whattaya know? Hold on, I'll see." He's got his usual mangled pack. Just two are left, and one of them's split. He throws the unsmokable one away, dividing the last one deftly in two. "Half for you and half for me. You get the filter end, okay?"

The sound of the Zippo's tinny clink has a frog-in-the-Zen-pond sort of ring. Perfect serenity while they smoke with no traffic on Sundays during church. Exhaling audibly. Never mind. The rest of the fucking world's insane.

"'Salem Country,'" Danny reflects, citing the slogan from the ads. "You know what, Duke? It's always the same. Fresh and green, with birds in the trees, never some cowshit-ridden terrain designed to humor the Marlboro man. We're talkin' tobacco in *paradise*! I want you to trust me on this one, pal—I've spent a lot of time out here. For you it's just a page in *Life*, stumblin' over a trunk-sized pack like maybe some giant's schlepped around and put it right there for you to find, tellin' yourself, what luck, oh boy, I been lookin' for someplace just like this, some trestle with gravel and weeds and tar where I can puff on those magical sticks." He sucks on the butt and flicks it away, pushing his cap back on his head.

"But then, before you know it, Mike, you're making excuses. Just one more time, you promise yourself—a last long ride on one of those logs! But it's never enough, you get my drift? You're hooked on trips to Salem Country, like hanging out nights in an opium den. No pressure, right? Just taking a break. But that's when the accidents all begin, meshugana wrecks with murderous chinks. . ." He pitches the package over the edge.

"So that's it, Duke. Before you bummed, I thought, 'Okay—no heavy karma for a smoke.' But now I'm kissing it all good-bye. It's sayonara. . . all gone. . . kaput." He stretches and yawns, then gets to his feet. "I'm glad we had this talk, ole buddy." He gazes down at the E&G lot. "You know what I mean? I really am."

What Danny means, as Dugan *knows, is whatever you're smoking's cool with me, just don't get weird, we'll see this through*. That's friendship for you, Dugan thinks, even when it's irrelevant. He's turning to stub his own butt out when he suddenly spies an amber glint lodged in the gravel off to his right and leans to get a better look. "Wait, Danny, right there at your feet! Bits and pieces all over the place!"

Danny shrugs. "Just plastic, Duke."

"It's my fuckin' reflector!"

"Sure, it is—and chunks of Moses' tablets too, and, if we keep pokin' around up here, we'll find Amelia Earhart's plane. That candy wrapper over there, could that be maybe her last meal? No, *listen* to me. . . just listen, okay? What if you hit your head down there? You skidded your bike into a tree or hit the fence—I saw that dent in the helmet that probably saved your life. And, listen, you better. . . I'm serious, guy." Dugan is gazing down the track. "Forget your wild hares for a while. Look after your ass at CSU."

"My ass? Oh, yeah." He cranes his neck. "The part of me that's not in a sling."

"This isn't the time, I realize. What they're sayin' is Glubber. . ."

"Bloody hell!" He'd tried to spit like *A Fistful of Dollars*, but it clotted and dribbled down his chin. "Mort Glubber, huh?" He wipes his jaw and whips his hand, but most of the slobber won't shake loose. "There's one like him in every department."

"Don't be so naïve, Billy Budd. The guy's a thug."

"If you say so. He's still third-rate."

"You're missing the point, Duke. Listen to me!"

But Dugan's opinion of Morton C. Glover is widely shared at CSU where, known as "Glubber" to all but his friends (a klavern consisting of Gordo alone and maybe Ed Doggett when he's sloshed), he covers the chairman's dubious bet that, out of the Babel of critical claques (a blather of esoteric cant that Gordo's frankly baffled by) there's one that might serve as a refuge for him. The trick is to follow Hamlet's lead, reducing it all to words, words, words—mere grist for the bibliographic mill, purged of reliance on taste or wit in a way that Glubber has made his own, enlisting Gordo in his schemes, siphoning funds and wangling a chair while abusing the students Gordo bribes to work with "CSU's scholar squirrel"—the nickname coined by Billie Swick before she left for *The Impeder.* "The rudest man I ever met, and maybe the dumbest," Billie swears, "because at bottom he hates ideas—and, most of all, the people who have 'em." Dugan supposes he's one of those.

"So what'd you do to piss him off?"

"The guy's a jerk. He picks on people."

"He wants your ass is what I hear. I heard it from Doggett the other day."

"Yeah, well. . ."

"For what?"

"For nothing. For trash. At that party last spring, at Gordo's house, when Glubber was holding forth on the war—something about a light in the tunnel—I said it's more like Plato's cave, and he said blah-blah fuckin' Rhodes Scholar, he'd never known one who's worth a shit. So I said coming from Karshish. . ."

"Who?"

"Karshish. You know. . . from Browning's poem. 'The Picker Up of Crumbs of Learning.'"

"Jesus, Duke! You called him that?"

"He gets to say whatever he wants? I thought he had a sense of humor."

"Humor? Come on! Try Heinrich Himmler."

"Yeah, well, okay. I made a mistake."

They muse on that, then Dugan says, "Is he gunning for *you?*"

"Who? Glubber? Nah, I'm not a threat." He looks around beneath their feet. "Hey, where's that ciggie I threw away? Looks like I must have stepped on it. Oh, well, that's it. I really quit." Nevertheless, he picks it up, examines it closely and, heaving a sigh, tosses it into the gravel again. "It's all about priorities, Duke, keeping our eyes on the glitterin' prize. . . by which I mean the mighty T, a lifetime of feedin' at the trough. Tenure's the thing, as Chairman Mao said—not castin' about for beauty and truth and all the stuff you're tryin' to teach. Speakin' of which, you goin' tonight?"

"To that reading by Blunt? My shoulder's hurt. Who schedules things on a Sunday night?"

"C'mon and go. We'll pick you up. Caitlin'll let you check out her gourds, maybe some squash. . . you'd like that, Duke. Her style's evolvin' pretty fast. Soup to nuts. I'm dreadin' cheese." Looking beyond the E&G lot, he gazes out over Hampton Park as if trying to guess if the darkening clouds are auguring more rain later today. "She's always thinkin' though, you know? Truth in decay's her bag these days. Stashin' her produce under the bed, tackin' putrescent pictures up—I can't even take an honest dump without some pockmarked Rembrandt face watchin' me like an oatmeal cookie. Believe me, pal, Tim Leary is wrong. Life with Hieronymus Bosch is hell." He pauses to grind a foot in the gravel. "But all of a sudden it hits me—wham! I think she's really onto something. What's missin' for you and me is a *schtick*! No, wait a minute, hear me out! Given the guys who're keepin' score, profundity won't get us squat. . . and that movie course you started up, in their minds that's just fun and games."

"Enrolling half the students we teach!"

"I know, but they dismiss it as glitz. So, listen, Duke, to what's come to me here. If it's rotten to start with. . ."

"I thought we'd come to find my bike. . ."

"Hang on. . . I'm gonna save your ass. First of all, quit messin' with Joyce. Avoid those big guys like the clap—or if you can't, don't try to think. All that's doin' is wearin' you out. . . like subtlety, right? Take Glubber and Gordo, whatta they do? Count and collate whole mountains of crap. . ."

"Like laundry lists."

"Correct. But *whose*?"

"Writers nobody's about to read—like, I dunno, like Timrod or Simms."

"Spot on again! But say it with confidence, say it proud! You gotta go *sell* it to make it work. 'For guys like William. . . Gilmore. . . Simms!' C'mon now, boy! You getting' on board?"

"You're sayin' we oughta play their game? But there's sellin', Dan, and sellin' out! Who wants to spend his time on Simms?"

"Ah, that's the beauty of it, Duke! It makes no difference who it is. Choose anybody you want to read, and you're free to count whatever you can! Commas or crosses, fucks or farts. Anything you can quantify. . ."

"Phallic symbols or fisher kings?"

"Not bad! But take it from a guy whose dissertation was fables recurring in modern lit, we can do a lot better here if we zero in on the animals. Like famous author's household pets—Fanny and Flush and even the lobster that what's-his-name, that lunatic Frenchman, took for a walk. Add the lobster quadrille and you've got a lot more plus Dali's lobster telephone, so there's a subject you can *count*! No thought required. . . maybe conclusions at the end, but you gotta remember the mantra, Duke, 'Enumerate, don't analyze.' Short bios at times, but mostly lists. It's foolproof, see? No way to lose. The road to tenure's paved with shit."

"Like man's best friends who went to war. . ."

"Or famous dogs. . ."

". . . of the Civil War!"

"He's *healed!* Oh, Lord, my boy is saved! It's famous dogs of the Civil War!"

But Danny stops in mid-benediction. A breeze has started to stir the air, tossing the trees that litter the park, and, peering down through scrims of leaves, he spots a cortege under way.

"My bike!" yelps Dugan, seeing it too and starting back down while Danny squints. "Those guys are trying to roll it off!"

"Get back to the Merc! We'll head 'em off."

"Looks like they'd headed towards Carver Field!"

But Danny's slowed by his slew-footed gait as the scavengers near a line of posts dividing the separate but equal parks, both of them mostly overgrown except for a well-worn sandy path that leads from some shanties along the tracks some three or four hundred yards away to a bus stop near the E&G lot. As Danny and Dugan are scrambling down, they catch more glimpses of the bike being led like a heifer to a fair. Once back in the Merc, they see it again, much closer to being lost from view.

"Hang on!" yells Danny, slamming into a lower gear and grinding across the rough terrain. The pilferers turn with a look of alarm as, bouncing and weaving over the field, the Merc roars up and skids to a halt. The doors fly open and Dugan sails out, flapping his sling like a signalman's wand, followed by Danny in his cap.

"That's stolen property!" Danny barks, grabbing the handlebars. "Turn it loose!"

"Shee-it!" the kid in goggles says.

"The key was in it!" the other one howls.

"We thought it was junk," the tall one adds.

Dugan is trying to figure this out. These same two kids had been eyeing his wheels before he left the Cock-o-Dome—but how did they know he'd have a wreck, and who could have told them where to look? These questions are rattling through his mind as he studies the damage to his bike. Not nearly as bad as he'd supposed. Not totaled, really—just conked out.

"How 'bout the wallet?" Dugan says, looking at Lew and then Tyrone.

They glance accusingly at each other.

"You found a wallet?" Danny demands.

They shake their heads.

"No way."

"Huh-uh. We ain't no thiefs."

Dugan stares with a gimlet-eyed look, then turns to Danny nodding his head.

"Thanks, guys," says Danny, flashing a five.

They hesitate until, sullenly, Tyrone says to Lew, "Aw, let the dude have his scooter back."

"Ain't nothin' but a piece o' junk." Lew takes the bill and turns away. "Dumb-ass place to dump a bike."

They amble off, not looking back. Then Danny rolls the bike to the Merc, and Dugan helps lift it into the trunk. The trunk-lid flaps. They tie it down, chipping some paint off as they cruise, sedately now, to the Dibbledome. Unloaded and propped against a tree, his Honda appears for the most part intact. But Dugan knows it isn't so—whatever he'd felt for it is gone. It's like saying good-bye to a statue.

● ● ●

It's a stellar event for CSU, though like numberless Brits washed up in L.A., Augustus Blunt has the soul of a surfer, still skimming the college lecture scene despite the loss of his board, as it were, with celebrity based on authors he "knew" when Bloomsbury still could get it up—a quip he frequently uses himself—and on sundry privations that he's endured (contemptuous critics, bad reviews, Beluga-less gigs in dumps like this) as well as on his once-modish verse which continues to be, for reasons obscure, inescapably anthologized. A garden-party Trotskyite, he maintains Stalin had silenced his muse (strangled it during the purges, he says) while his "dewy-eyed innocence," such as it was, got done in by Cousin Tony's guile (though the problem was Cambridge, Blunt will explain, a loyal Oxonian to the core). No dummy but clearly out of trumps, at bottom he's now a pragmatist, a genial twice-wed sodomite determined to stay atop the wave as, lean and patrician, boyish still, he adds to his memoirs year by year, riding the remnants of his fame on through the pipeline of the Sixties. . . abetted, it's whispered back at home, by funding from the CIA—a charge he's been at pains to deny by calling himself a left-wing nut ("or testicle," as one wag said).

The venue itself is semi-surreal, with décor Caitlin Rosen compares to Meret Oppenheim's fur-lined cup because, despite being part of the lavishly humdrum Business School, its Strontium Sternbolt Auditorium had been given a weirdly surreal flair by lining its ceiling, floor, and walls with a uniform carpet-like fabric that creates an odd acoustical sheath in which sounds merge and disappear like ingredients in a blender, an effect that's even more disconcerting because of the Pepto-Bismol hues inducing a mood of fetal regression—as Kravitz had incautiously pointed out during a Faculty Senate debate, prompting the B-School dean to reply that, not having a venue of their own in which to hold such large-scale events, humanities profs should hold their tongues before trying to book his space again. . . though, after Gordo had added a course on "Business Audits as Literature" to smooth the way towards a bachelor's degree for semi-literate business majors, the B-School dean agreed to relent. . . hence, the present occasion.

Like everything else in these volatile times, it draws a hodgepodge crowd of dissidents and devotees. Not counting Dexter's nuke-'em group who're festering sulkily in the rear, attendees include some forty professors with dowdy demoralized wives in tow scattered across the middle rows, a dozen or so grad students down front (half of them sporting perky wives and one, Meg Boozer, seated alone but closely monitored by the rest), four "extra-credit" undergrads (from Tony Schifoso's modern-lit course, shifting uneasily in their seats while checking their watches obsessively), a number of curious culture freaks plus scattered groupies and wing-nut strays (including a ferret-faced anti-bomb geek with HELL NO - I WON'T GLOW stickered across her string-net bag) and Billie Swick, the movie reviewer, who'd once, as a student assistant for Glubber, informed on the kickbacks he'd skimmed off as chairman of the Library Committee—an action that led to Glubber's report that Billie lacked "scholarly acumen," effectively altering her career.

Though few have come to be edified, many have hopes for scurrilous dirt on Isherwood at Max Schmeling's gym or Auden's encounter with "Miss" Babette whom he'd spotted in Cocteau's *Blood of a Poet*. But Blunt won't squander his stockpile here—he's saving the good stuff up for Cavett, the talk show host who went to Yale and interviewed Katherine Hepburn twice. Instead, Blunt says in an offhand way, he'll read some bits of early verse, an announcement that's met with tepid applause and querulous grumbling here and there.

One of Schifoso's guys gets up as if at some urgent mute command, though everyone hears his seat snap back. With a patient if vaguely quizzical grin, Blunt watches him amble from the room. He presses his book flat, pauses, and says, "I wrote this little bagatelle, 'The Skipper of the Kipper Smack,' when I was barely seventeen. . . after John Grierson took me aboard for a sail in a North Sea squall."

He lets "took me aboard" sink in a bit before proceeding with a couple lines about brawny fishermen seen from behind while hauling in their heavy nets. But midway through, he glances down and, with a suddenly furious glare, wrenches the microphone aside and huffs, "I want this thing cut off!"

"WHAT? CAN'T HEAR!" shouts Billie Swick.

But Blunt's incensed, ignoring her cry. He's pointing to something below his waist. "I want this thing removed right now!"

"A little late for a bris, I'd say," growls Danny to Dugan Groucho-style, leaning past Caitlin who's in between. He's wearing the Guatemalan shirt she'd given him when she still assumed he'd be a blank canvas she could fill with tints of flamingos and refried beans. It's embellished tonight by a shoestring tie that dangles in front of her as he leans, prompting attempts to brush it away as meanwhile, on the womb-like stage, Gordo has summoned an A-V guy who, peering inside the podium, reaches and yanks a cable free to disconnect some sort of recorder, holding the cord up like a snake.

"So now. . ." Blunt wanly smiles at the crowd, "can you HEAR me NOW?" He clears his throat. "Can everyone HEAR. . .?"

"NO!" hoots Billie.

Blunt drones on inaudibly nonetheless. "SurVEILlance" pops out and then "beTRAY." The rest is soaked up by the rugs.

"You need a mike," says the A-V guy.

". . . if I'm talking like THIS?" Blunt's lips keep moving. ". . . Foster DULLes. . . HOOver's THUGS." And then, to Gordo, "LASKY and I. . ."

"WHAT?" yells Billie.

Blunt's very perturbed. He says this place is sinister. He's right, thinks Dugan. Seated in back, two suit-clad strangers have the look of Sternbolt's Citizens' Watchdog Group, and he'd heard as they were coming in that Dexter's right-wing student troop, convinced that Blunt's a Comm-Symp stooge, are planning to protest mid-way through by silently brandishing *Atlas Shrugged.*

"ALL RIGHT," says Blunt. The mike's back on. "So. . . you can hear me?"

"YES!" bawls Billie as Blunt resumes—audible now, but still soporific:

Roistering home with a boatload of seamen!

A nervous cough across the aisle as Kravitz, idly scanning the crowd, fishes a fuzz-caked Luden's up. He nods at Dugan, rolling his eyes, and Dugan, who's thinking of popping an extra pill, let free association reign, recalling the mayhem with Chi Cheng—whoever she was, whatever she'd done (dealing is what comes first to mind, some sort of courier up a creek for hustling somebody else's score, but why this particular backwater creek?) Not many like her in this black-and-white burg (no soccer balls either or artichokes, and, given the choice of either or both, how many would know which one to kick?) Something to think about, he concedes. but at least she's not his problem now—though Dunkie. . . he'll be seeing *her.* (His shoulder hurts. He shouldn't have come.)

He looks around and swallows a pill, hearing the activist rattle her bag, and, midway through "The Ethiope's Ear," a libidinous paean to Haile Selassie, sees Dexter's group get up to leave waving their copies of Ayn Rand's book—though one of them's got a Gideon Bible, and Dexter himself remains in place, as if detached from their commotion.

Augustus Blunt is unfazed too. He feeds off this, though his listeners can't. For them, as they hear the doors boom shut, the EXIT signs that bracket the stage exhort like Dr. Pavlov's bell. They tighten their seatbelts, hanging on as Blunt's stale tropes drift overhead (exhaust fumes, Dugan tells himself, from a decade that nearly wrecked the world). Blunt's into

74

his overworked "Málaga" next, a eulogy for the Popular Front with Franco-in-a-tanko rhymes that float through the room like mustard gas.

Now even Gordo's chin sinks low, drooping until it touches his chest. He furrows his brow and jerks his head but almost at once succumbs again despite being seated next to Meg, whose blank expression doesn't change—like the bowsprit of some motionless ship. The two of them make a poignant tableau that causes Dugan to ruminate ("Alice and Dodo," runs through his head. "Oh, yes, my dear, come sit on my lap and, whoops! my word! I'm growing bigger!")

Some mild applause yanks Dugan back. He starts to clap, which ought to hurt. It doesn't. . . odd. Catch Gordo's eye. Clap harder. Good. There's Kravitz with cough drop, Danny bored, Caitlin between them turning to smile. She tilts her head and widens her eyes, a trick she has like a spreading of thighs, a. . . (WHOA! he groans, let's censor that! slamming the trapdoor shut again). She nods and claps, but not so hard.

Blunt's manner implies indifference to praise, but pursing his lips as if weighing requests, he says he'll only read one more. The ferret-faced woman shakes her bag. Blunt squints his eyes to read her sign—intrigued, it seems, by I WON'T GLOW. The rattle fades. He strikes a rapt telegrapher pose. . . receiving some signals, just for him, transmitted from a far-off place. When he resumes, his voice is low.

Suave minotaur with your swollen rivet. . .

"Queen of the Night!" somebody exclaims—the world as a hijacked produce train, a piece they recognize at last.

Unzipping the night to nuzzle and swive it. . .

"Good Middle English verb," adds Blunt, arching an eyebrow, looking amused. "Swive it!" he repeats the phrase, seeming to savor the sound.

The crowd's attentive, listening now. Not Dugan, though—for a moment he's back on another slow train, riding the rails with what's-her-name (he needs a name, Chi Cheng won't do, to go with the sling his arm is in). But something more urgent intervenes or, more specifically, enters his nose, informing him that he's going to sneeze. He tries to stifle it, knows he can't, and, just as Blunt says his engine "beseeches" while "thundering through lush Yorkshire's beeches," Dugan emits a booming "KAAA-CHOO!"

"Please stifle that soundtrack!" Blunt requests, completing his triplet with "whimpers and screeches." But Kravitz, as if conspiring with Dugan, unleashes his own explosive "Ahhhh-SHOO!"

A titter and looks of consternation, as—clearly miffed, but still rhapsodic—Blunt slows his fruit-train to a crawl. "Two shuddering. . . hillocks. . ." he declaims.

A pause.

"KAAAA-CHOO!"

Blunt patiently waits for the reply. Like mating loons they call to each other.

"Ahhhh-ka-SHOO!"

Dugan attempts to shake his head. "Sorry," he gasps as, cannily into working the crowd, Blunt waits a beat and then resumes:

Two shuddering hillocks that invite. . .

Cupping his hand up to his ear, Blunt now adopts a comic pose, eliciting laughter plus applause as Meg indignantly looks around. But stoked by the treacherous feel-good pill, Dugan's libido is taking charge (a scene from *The Conqueror*'s in his head—she's Susan Hayward, he's John Wayne, head honcho of the Golden Horde: "Y'er byootiful in yer wraath," he drawls, his warriors perched on Harley hogs). He winks at her salaciously, but she ignores him. Blunt does not.

Supposing the wink is meant for him, Blunt lifts his eyebrows quizzically and says in husky tremolo, "Ah, well, you know, as Spender once put it in Madrid. . . good sex involves an awful din!" That's too outré for most of those there, though a couple of cackles accompany him as he starts to warble his final line.

Like the smirk. . .

He pauses, searching the crowd, then locks in on Dugan, winking back as if chiding his heckler with a leer, revising a key phrase just for him:

Like the *sneeze* of some cheeky catamite!

• • •

"Zuh diagnosis, Herr Professor?"

Danny adjusts his rearview mirror, clenching a cigarette in his teeth. He hadn't intended to light it he said, but the reading tonight has driven him to it.

All Dugan can see reflected back is Danny's dark glasses bobbing about. He always drives at night in shades—*hommage* to Thelonius Monk, he claims, whether the real Monk drives or not, the illogic of which prompts Dugan to say as Danny launches his Freudian riff, "Turn counter-clockwise, know what I mean?" He's still half-tripping on his pills.

"*Jawohl!*" nods Danny who knows, of course, though Caitlin won't, which she'll resent for being excluded causing Danny to double down on his schtick while Dugan attempts to hold him in check which she'll regard as two against one until she blows her Irish stack, and, from that point on, amid the debris, they'll count on Dugan to clear it away. God knows what they do when he's not there, though it's easy enough for him to guess without getting too graphic in his thoughts.

"But zuh diagnosis?" Danny repeats.

"Micro. . . phobia," Dugan chokes, finding it hard to breathe in back.

In shotgun, Caitlin fans the air while Danny puffs on maniacally. "*Sehr gut*, Herr Duke, but heff you seen vhut Schpielberg says?"

"About what?"

"You know. . . *vagina dentata*?"

"Open th-the d-damned w-w-window! PLEASE!"

The knob's gone missing on Caitlin's side. Danny and Dugan both comply. The rain whips in.

"I'm gettin' wet!"

"Haff you seen *Jawss* yet?" Danny is pumped. He wipes the windshield with his hand as Caitlin's getting a Kleenex out to help him clear a porthole view. "In zuh poster he showss his hand. . . so to schpeak."

Dugan laughs. He's got a point.

"Y-Y-You're b-both disgusting."

"*Nacht und Nebel!* All fogged up! Roll 'em back up! Yeah, back where they were. . . we'll equalize the pressure, see?"

Adjusting his glasses, he rubs again, streaking the windshield even worse with smoke-swirls bouncing off the glass (like sixth-grade science, Dugan reflects—milk bottle, match, and hard-boiled egg—a gulp, and they're inside the jug). "Hey, you remember. . .?"

"W-W-Wait! Look out!"

A skid, a thunk, a shrill whoopee as a white-and-gold Corvette guns on past, running a stop sign, honking in time as a couple of blondes yell "GO, COCKS, GO!" (blitzed valkyries, Dugan thinks—friends of the Rooster backfield, sure, but those two chicks they've seen before).

"You guys okay there?" Danny drawls.

"Th-they s-s-scraped us!" Caitlin's voice is accusatory.

"Two nights running," Dugan shrugs, which once again is a mistake— he keeps forgetting there're moves that hurt no matter how many pills he takes.

"We c-c-could have b-been *killed!*"

"Yeah. . . swived," he says.

A jogger's been marking time on the curb. He now jogs past them looking back, reflective strips across his heels like tracer bullets, zip zip zip.

"Ass I vass sayink," Danny resumes, unwilling to stop in mid-routine. "Ein obvious case uff phallic dread. . . engendered by fears uff man-eating twat."

They're passing the jogger once again.

"But, Doctor, I feel I have to ask. . ."

"Vutt?" Danny pounces, taking a drag. "Zuh fact that zis cigarette's in mein hand? Don't jump to conclushuns, Brother Duke. The reason I know that I can quit is (puff) like Alex Portnoy (puff) and not like Herr Augustus Blunt, I (puff) am not renouncing twat and am not now nor ever have been an anal retentive (puff puff cough). Jeez, you know, I hate these things!" With thumb and finger pinching the butt, he cracks his vent and flicks it out, scattering sparks as it flies by. "You know his mother was Jewish, right?"

"B-B-Borrr-ing!" Caitlin interjects. "C-Can't we t-t-talk about. . ."

"Fruits, Miss Emily? I declare, you're enigmatic, tha'ss a fact. Up in your bedroom all the time, just paintin' away at squash and gourds! Whattaya say we split a lark? You workin' on a comeback there or all-of-a-sudden tongue-tied now?" A pause for Danny to reload. "Your Bloomsbury boy's a lark for sure—a bit of a fruitcake too I'd say, but, hey, you know that artsy type. So split the lark, and whattaya get?" He looks at Dugan, sniggers and says, "B-B-Bloody fingers, for a start."

That's meant for Caitlin, spousal talk.

"F-F-Fuck you, Danny!" she fires back.

"Witty reply there, Miss Recluse. Le'ss write that on some little scrap."

Dugan knows when it's time to break in. "Hey guys, it's me! Remember me? Little Mikie with the broken wing?"

"Screw little Mike!"

"God bless us every one, okay?" Still riding his pills, both hands are numb. "Just want you to know that other than blondes there's slaughter and death out there on the road."

"Outlined against a blue gray sky. . ."

It's bardic, thinks Dugan. We know the lines. "*October* sky— hexameter, huh? Crowley, Miller, Layden. . . and who?"

"Conquest, slaughter, death. . ."

"And plague."

"Nope, plague and conquest are the same."

"What's he smokin' on Patmos?" Danny demurs.

"They're on the same horse is all I know—which goes for war and slaughter too. So it's. . ."

"Conquest, slaughter, death. . . and what?"

"M-M-Misogyny."

"Oh, Jesus Aitch! How 'bout drownin' in shit?"

"Aw, come on, guys!"

"We leave that out? Or won't you tell Dear Abby here she can't go shuttin' the Sunset Lodge just 'cause some fag humps Haile Selassie? We're talkin' stallions, are we not? And minotaurs with swollen rivets." His snicker builds into a wheeze. "Shi-*it*!" he cackles.

Dugan coughs.

"Th-The thing is," Caitlin finally says with her temper barely under control. "He kn-kn-knew them all. S-S-Sickert. H-Hulme. . ." she rubs her knuckle on the glass. "Wy-Wy-Wyndham Lewis."

"Excuse my raising a touchy subject. He didn't just *know* 'em—he buggered 'em, right?"

"POSSUM!" Dugan interjects, pointing at a rat-like wad that's scurrying past a parked Peugeot. "Close call, huh, guys? Well, yessirree. Ole Pogo there 'most bought the farm. Not saying that possums light my fire—just cats gone wrong, if you ask me—and cats don't like me as a rule, though fat girls do, and most neurotics. Babies, no, but faggots, si. . . which may be why I got that look, at the end there, from the Fairy Queen."

"N-N-Not. . ." says Caitlin, chin tucked in, her voice a baleful octave lower. "N-Not you too."

"Don't lump us together. Danny's a schmuck."

"I am?"

"Pipe down. I'm talking now. Let's work along the food chain here—to chickens which, though you might not have guessed, don't like me either—an' you know why?" He's asking her.

"I know."

"Back off there, Dan! You wanna know why?"

She utters a sigh and shakes her head, knowing his solo's mainly for her.

"Come on, now, Caitlin, listen up. We're twelve years old, State Fair, okay? This booth for—what's-it? R.E.A. Rural Electric's big back then. HATCHING THE FUTURE is what it says with slowly revolving racks of eggs laid out inside this incubator with lots of light bulbs keepin' warm. Fill out a card an' you might win! Win what? Who cares? Whatever they got. There's a woman in calico lookin' on like an extra left over from *Grapes of Wrath* who says, 'no use'n you boys signin' up, my son's goan win them baby chicks.' So Danny says, 'Well, madam, we'll just have to see—this guy I'm with wins everything.'"

A bell is ringing. Danny stops, and Dugan's surprised to see where they are—same crossing as the other night, where Gordo had waited behind the wheel (he wonders what Chi Cheng's up to now. . . nothing good, he's sure of that). Tonight he sees what Gordo saw, sees SEABOARD rumbling by again and listens to the ding-ding-ding as if it's the intro to a song that somehow he's obliged to sing.

"So as I was sayin'. . ." he's into it now, "some six or seven days go by, and I'm by myself at home, okay? when two menacing guys in overalls start pounding on the closed front door. I open it up and one of 'em says, 'You Michael B. Dugan?' What if I am? I want to say, but maybe these guys are undercover. Danny and me, we'd had a fight. . ."

"You started it, asshole!"

"Yeah, like hell. But maybe I'd really made him mad. Maybe he's out to get revenge, and this is his idea of a joke. I'd said some things. . . well, anyhow, there're these two guys, and one of them clearly knows my name. 'So, what if I am?' I actually say, and the big one, who's not takin' no guff, growls 'Reddy Kilowatt says hello.'"

The train's caboose goes clattering by.

"'Oh, yeah?' I say, 'he's just a cartoon.' So the other one waits a beat and says, 'We got your chicks out in the truck.' My what? I ask. 'Four hunnert fifty to be exact. You want us to leave 'em on the stoop?' You're kiddin', I tell him. He says they're not."

The Merc, like a tin can full of smoke, goes bumping over the Seaboard tracks.

"C-C-Cut on the g-g-goddamn windshield wiper!"

"It's only a drizzle," Danny says.

"C-C-Cut. . ."

"Okay!" A single swipe. "Sorry, Mike."

"No problem, guys."

"Nah, go ahead! So how do they package all those chicks?" Danny knows the story by heart.

"In cardboard trays."

"Like Nehi Colas. . ."

"J-J-JESUS, D-Danny! L-L-Let him talk!"

"I thought you said. . ."

"Hey, guys, okay! I'm only twelve—I told you that—but that particular afternoon my schedule was actually pretty tight. . . I've got this birthday party, see? So I get 'em to lay the boxes out wherever there's room on the living room floor, and, just when I'm about to split, I hear these desperate peeps cut loose. 'We're suffocating!' is what they say, but the guys are gone, so whatta I do? 'Lift the lids, or we're gonna die!' You won't run off? 'Just let us breathe!' I take a peek and Danny's right, they look like Nehis in a crate. 'Okay, you promised.' And then I leave, thinking I'll get back in a jiff."

"You don't, though."

"No, but when I do, I find my mom's already there, and she's got the vacuum cleaner out, using the nozzle that sucks up lint to get to the ones she couldn't reach. . . under the sofa, places like that."

The wipers make a single sweep as the windshield speckles up again.

"And wh-wh-what?" asks Caitlin, knowing full well and knowing what lies behind his spiel. She knows that for Danny it's the same and that endless insouciance takes its toll. Sometimes he pays the piper too.

Dugan coughs before he resumes—it's once again getting hard to breathe. "Well, she puts 'em back in the cardboard trays, and, except for some guano here and there, all she needs then is an explanation. I tell her I won 'em at the fair and can use 'em to get a merit badge that none of the other Scouts have earned, which is when my dad gets home half-crocked and says he'd raised chicks too when he was a kid, something I'd never heard before—fed chicks, milked cows, and walked to school. My mom's for sending 'em back to Reddy, but eventually, to my total surprise, they say I can have my poultry farm. . ."

No rush to finish—they're almost there, passing the subdivision gates.

"T-T-Turn left," points Caitlin.

They go right. Caitlin sighs and folds her arms. The road slopes up.

"You raised 'em on your screened porch, right?"

"Made a waterer from a five-gallon can and roosts from a folding laundry rack. You took a wrong turn back there, you know."

"No, this is the way."

"Okay," he shrugs—he'll finish for sure. "In three weeks comes the first hard freeze. I'm up at six to check on my brood, and it looks like photos of Wounded Knee. . . bottom of the Inferno, right? Chick-sickles keeled over everywhere."

"Huh-unh!" squawks Caitlin, playing along.

"My dad's asleep, but my mom looks in and tells me to help her gather them up. It's like picking lead soldiers off the floor and layin' them out on cookie sheets while she thaws 'em out at Pre-Heat Bake."

"L-L-Love it!" chirps Caitlin.

"'Ohhh, where am I?'" Dugan moans, adopting a sluggish baritone. "'Whoaaaa. . . peep. . . peep!'"

A dead end looms. They stop and start to turn around, and Dugan recalls the other night when (whoa, peep, peep) he got himself thawed on an ER sheet. What goes around. . . he muses on that. It strikes him as profoundly true.

"Okay back there?" It's been a while since Dugan spoke.

Where was he? Right. "So. . . four out of five get back on their feet, stumping around like wind-up toys, but after a couple of freezes and thaws, I've lost a lot more and the ones that survive lose all ambition. . ."

"Speakin' of which, you know this year. . .?"

"L-L-Let him finish."

"Sure, okay."

"We sold 'em, and I got a dog."

She looks annoyed. "So wh-what's the p-p-point?"

"That's a good question," Dugan shrugs, ignoring the pain. "It happens, you know—you take what comes. Go right at this corner and straight ahead. After a few more freezes and thaws, really about ten years or so, both of my parents were dead as well. . . there was no point, that's what I learned."

Another pause. Then Danny jumps in. "But sure, there was—there're lots of points. First, that you lacked a four-footed friend. The two-legged types will let you down. . . including most humans, that's a fact. And so will cats—steer clear of them, no matter what the leg-count is. Famous or not, you need a dog. My second point is whatever you do, don't get a job in some chickenshit place. . . like, well, let's see, like where we are. Too late, I know," he puts on brakes, "but here's some gravel for your craw. It's the Year of the Rooster this year, Duke."

"Is that a fact? Coach Ray Don know? I think that's it up there on the hill. . . the one with all the lights," he says.

They bump up next to Dexter's Rambler. SUPPORT OUR FIG his bumper says—the rest of the sticker's torn away. A house is shining through the trees, circled by glistening parapets.

"Hey, looks like Doggett's doing all right."

"Married a shoppin' mall," Danny sneers. "Love ya, babe. Got your umbrella?" He pecks her neck. She turns away. Then, looking at Dugan, he cocks his head. "No dumb-ass moves tonight, you hear?"

"I'm mellow, Dan." He really is, stroking his Not-With-Sternbolt tie with peace signs strewn on crimson silk—hand-crafted for Saks and ordered last month from a *New Republic* back-page ad.

"You know who else raised chickens, Duke?"

Oh, sure, he knows. They've reached this point in the script before with Danny citing his Q.E.D. of a murderous, hate-crazed Goyaesque fowl that only purported to be a man. . . but Himmler had actually looked the part, allowing an opening to reply, "I don't believe I resemble a chicken."

Danny steps out, then ducks back in. "Tell that to Colonel Sanders, pal."

Caitlin's baffled by that exchange.

● ● ●

The whole gang's there—Gordo and Glubber with Doggett their host plus Millie their hostess somewhere in back having a migraine, still in her wrap but, after another drink or two, likely to buck up and appear. Some senior professors are scattered about in various stages of decay, their rumpled impunity signaled by tweeds, a jocular ease, and Hush-Puppies shoes while their juniors, dressed in khakis and jeans, affect a hip placidity that's undercut by a glance at their wives who vary in looks from drabness to panic. It's the graduate students, unattached, who're lit up like convenience stores, thrilled to have made the A-team list—most notably

Gordo's biker-belt babe whose peasanty blouse addresses the room with greetings from somewhere east of the Don, evoking arch *dobry-vecher* salutes from a trio of hirsute, jittery men whose open-necked shirts say I'M CREATIVE, their tight smiles adding "kamikaze"—hinting at egos, Dugan knows, as fragile as what he's got in a sling. . . the writing instructors, he reflects, first to go when a pogrom occurs.

The house exudes a moneyed air, resembling a *Southern Living* spread except for its incongruities—its chic and costly sofas and chairs contrasting with a low-budget bar and high-priced gadgety objets d'art displayed on shelves with book-club sets, their jackets still in mint condition. For the tenured it's like a country club—they've paid their dues and they belong. For the rest it prompts both envy and scorn, though most have read enough Wharton or James to adapt with a gluttonous nonchalance. . . which helps explain the cut-rate bar.

Dugan's first move is to locate the booze—unwise, he knows, but there it is. The kings of the dungheap have dispersed with Gordo expounding on Timrod and Simms while Blunt the poet looks gravely on and Glubber skulks about on a prowl that Caitlin insists she'd like to paint ("Komodo Dragon in Search of a Goat"). Doggett has briefly disappeared, but tending the bar is a grad-student vet who's studied with Dugan once or twice—the second time without signing up.

"Hey, Doctor Dee, what's going down?" He gestures at Dugan's bandaged arm.

"Some wise-ass black belt in a bar said Whitman's just a talentless fag. I took issue with the talentless part. . . straightened him out, but he bent me up." He gestures in a knowing way. "Got something special under there?" He figures Blunt for high-priced Scotch

"Why, Michael, hi! What happened to *you*?" It's Tony Schifoso quaffing some dreck. Gunning all out for tenure too.

Dugan attempts a one-armed shrug, ignoring the twinges that provokes.

"But what'd you *do*?"

"Just kissin' ass, I slipped 'n fell."

Schifoso looks before he laughs, exposing the rack of bull-moose teeth below his drooping handlebar. "Ah, ah, ah!"

"Glenlivet? I thought so!" Dugan nods.

The grad student pours him half a glass.

"Better hope you don't get caught at that."

"Fuck off, Schifoso," Dugan says.

"Bad luck," he whines. "Your arm, I mean."

"But I can still dictate."

"Sure," he grins.

"I'm finishing up my Joyce piece now."

"JOYCE?" he sputters—his specialty too.

"That monograph. I thought you knew. The one the *Quarterly* wants to see."

"I thought you were into movies now. I hadn't heard you'd gotten that far!"

He hasn't, of course, but maybe he will. "Sanskrit puns in *Finnegan's Wake*. Ramifications, lots of 'em. Here, wipe that off before it stains. How can you drink cheap shit like that?"

He turns to confront a cylindrical head with pulpy lips and pig-like eyes that together create a total effect like that of a kicked-in trashcan.

"Hi, Mort," he says in a faux-friendly way.

Mort Glover glares and edges away.

"Ignore th-th-that shit."

"Whoa, cut it out! I think I'm in love." It's Caitlin, apparently bumped from behind, whose tit is burrowing under his arm.

"G-G-Good whisky, M-Mike. It d-d-does that to you."

Whatever the purpose of her tease, he knows it's not an invitation, so they stand for a moment surveying the scene as the action shows signs of ratcheting up—literally from Bach to rock on Doggett's room-to-room Hi Fi. "Oh, yeah! Get down!" the tenure-less crow while, noncommittally, Blunt looks on like Her Majesty at a Hottentot bash. Danny's now moseyed back to the bar, and Gordo's chatting his *pupsik* up. Caitlin's proximity's as it was.

"Hey, Babe. . . I can't stand it."

Her mouth's in his ear. "W-We'll have to g-get rid of D-D-Danny, Mike."

". . . ALLOW ME," booms a British voice,

. . . to introduce myself!

Dugan's played Caitlin's game before. "Can't we just leave him here?" he asks. "He's married to his music, right?" (Cornel Wilde in *A Song to Remember*, but he doubts if Caitlin knows the flick.) She lowers her voice and shakes her head.

"N-N-No survivors, M-Mike," she says. (Merle Oberon! She's got it right.)

I'm a man of wealth and taste!

preens Mick, boasting it seems on Doggett's behalf. There's an audio-rip and Mick is gone.

"Come ON!" yells someone angrily.

Dugan begins to disengage, muttering into Caitlin's hair. "Okay, I'll take the sucker out."

She grabs his belt and tugs him back. "You kn-know. . . wh-why he hates you. . ."

"He knows I love your ass, that's why."

"N-n-not him! *Him*." She gestures towards Glubber who's back on the prowl, browsing through Doggett's 33's ("Horst Wessel Song"? It's gotta be there!) She pauses and widens her eyes again. He keeps himself from falling in. "Th-That le-le-let-let-let. . ."

"Letter," he tries to help her out. "The one I sent to the *Observer*?"

"Uh-huh," she nods. "Y-You know th-that's why."

"Nah, Glubber's no hawk," he disagrees. "Hawks fly. He crawls. He's too unprincipled to care."

"R-R-Right. . ." she says, but then shuts down. Whenever she's stalled, she works her eyes—closing the lids and, after a pause, lifting them slowly, yielding a glimpse of a place where words can't ever go. "B-B-Billy. . . Budd," she finally says (agreeing with Danny—whattaya know?)

Still mesmerized by Caitlin's trick, he's plummeting in a slow free fall when Millie Doggett grabs her arm and Gordo's goose-girl bustles by (Whoa, Megan, hi! Remember me—the guy with the Honda? Hey, wait up!). Meg moves like a catapult towards a wall.

"Uh, Mike. . ." Ed Doggett blocks his view. Loose-jointed, tall, and angular with a candy-apple sort of head creased by an ever-sarcastic smirk and topped by a bit of thinning scuzz (like Pumpkinhead is Dugan's thought—from where? He tries to dredge it up. An Oz book, right? Or Ichabod Crane. But what's the use. . . compared to the likes of Gordo and Glubber? Restrict yourself to countin' 'em up.) Ed's nodding confidentially.

"Hi, Ed. Nice party. Sure beats the reading."

Doggett nods without a smile, then looks around as if they're conspiring and gestures towards a swinging door. "Can I have a word or two with you, Mike?"

They enter a kitchen that's all aglow with the hue of its stove and matching hood plus freezer, dishwasher, Frigidaire—all in a shade called Harvest Gold, deftly accented throughout the room by a multi-legged two-toned butcher's block and racks of copper-bottomed pans. The taint of gentility, Dugan thinks. Caitlin's taught him to notice that.

Gordo's standing by the sink. "Hi, Mike," he says.

Then Doggett dives in. "We're worried, Mike."

They lean together as Doggett confides while Dugan examines the canapés laid out on the waist-high butcher's block. Something about them seems unreal, like plaster tidbits on the tray in Beatrix Potter's *Two Bad Mice* (he's getting regressive in his citations—must be the fallout of those pills).

"People. . ." says Gordo, rubbing his eyes and sliding his glasses back in place. "Some people feel. . . ah," (snicker-snack) ". . . you're not. . . ah. . ."

Doggett takes his cue. ". . . fulfilling your full potential here."

Gordo's expression conveys concern. His gaze has wandered to Dugan's tie. "That shoulder of yours looks pretty bad. I've been hoping to get a full report."

Oh, yeah? thinks Dugan, not from me. Something inside him bubbles up, as if Glenlivet's reaching the pills.

"It's broken?" asks Doggett.

"Crushed," he says—he doesn't know why.

"That's incapacitating, Mike. I know you'll do the best you can, but. . ."

". . . you're going to be half-speed for weeks."

". . . with months of therapy after that."

Both of them use a lowered tone he hasn't heard since fraternity rush. Doggett lights up a Tareyton.

"The point is. . ." Gordo taps his arm. "You need a leave of absence, Mike."

"A medical leave. It's temporary."

"A chance to get things back on track."

Dugan blinks.

"We can cover your classes. I've found somebody at Chantry Mount. . . a young post-doc who's in your field. Well, more or less. Non-tenure track, but he can help out. . ."

Something is very fishy here. "Gordo, gee. That's nice of you. But I can still. . ."

There's a glance exchanged. "I don't know how to tell you, Mike. . .
you're very. . ."

"What?"

They hesitate.

". . . vulnerable," Gordo frowns.

"We've heard how good your teaching is. . ."

"But," nodding at Doggett, Gordo adds, "you need more arrows in your
quiver."

Right, thinks Dugan, that much is clear. A Glubberectomy's just the
thing. "I've got a monograph on Joyce. I'm well along."

"That's good!" beams Gordo.

"On. . ." (*Finnegan's Wake*? Well, limit the lie.) ". . . on *Dubliners!*"
he improvises.

"Good," nods Gordo once again.

"You'll get a chance to work on it."

So everyone's lying, Dugan thinks, as Gordo's spelling out details.
He'll need to meet his classes once and sign some forms that Gordo's got.
Then good, good, good. We all feel good.

"Stop by tomorrow," Gordo smiles. "And Mike. . ."

"Uh-huh."

He takes his hand. "Let's keep this entre nous, okay?"

"Thanks, Mike. Good luck," nods Pumpkinhead.

"As you can see. . ." he starts to say, but, cutting him off, the two depart,
their haste confirming what's unsaid: you're outta here, so long, good-bye.
The swinging door goes thwop thwop thwop.

Alone amid the Harvest Gold, surveying the Hi-Ho canapés, Dugan
revisits Famous Dogs, Danny's astute but futile scheme. Cracker, cheese,
and olive slice. . . so quantifiably banal. The olives, he notes, are what give
it away. No slap-'em-together and damn-the-cost—somebody's counted
those slivers out, one to a cracker topping the cheese. He picks the olive
off of each, recalculating as he chews, then pops another little pill. No
special reason. It feels good.

Back in the living room, nothing has changed except he's feeling
slightly fried. Dexter's pinned some guy to the wall, apparently in a manic
spiel. Kravitz is standing by the bar, keeping an eye on Billie Swick who's
talking to Doggett's mother-in-law. He elbows Kravitz in the ribs.

"Luden's 'n' gin'll kill you, pal."

"And screw you too, my battered friend." Kravitz is cloaked in Vapor Rub fumes. His voice sounds hoarse. "Where's superstar colleague gone these days?"

Dugan is getting his glass refilled. "Like who? Big Jimbo?"

"Who do you think? Out hunting pygmies with a spear? Who's that with Dexter?"

"No idea. Hi, Billie. . . seen *Midnight Cowboy* yet?"

"Can't hear," she mouths. She points at his sling.

He gives a mono-shouldered shrug, then catches a signal from the scrum that's surging back and forth near Blunt. It's Danny, who rolls his eyes and grins as Dugan strolls over, feeling loose, a pleasant buzzing in his ears. The circle of acolytes looks enthralled.

"He was a naughty boy back then. . ." Blunt's making room for Dugan's approach without appearing to notice him.

"*Ish*-erwood," Schifoso chirps, calling attention to himself.

"With Wystan, he. . . *experimented*." Blunt licks his lip licentiously. Then, after a millisecond's pause, he turns to Dugan with a smile. "Ah, Mister Oover, I presume—fellow Oxonian, are you not?"

Anticipating Dugan's response, Jim Morrison answers with a snarl,

NO TIME TO WALLOW IN THE MIRE!

The other Doors commiserate.

"What are you drinking?" Blunt inquires, putting his hand on Dugan's glass, wrinkling his brow and taking a sip. Half a head taller, he's very patrician. "We seem to be. . ." He lowers his voice. ". . . the only ones here not drinking swill. Come talk to me."

The huddle begins to dwindle discretely. Danny backs off so Blunt can't see and, hooking two fingers in his nose, starts hoisting it upwards towards his scalp. Schifoso tries to block their way. "Did you know Agee?" he persists, not wanting to take a powder yet.

"A marvelous boy," the poet says, sliding his hand up Dugan's sling. "What happened to you?"

"Believe it or not, I jumped a freight?"

"And let me guess." He leans so close that Dugan can see white nostril-hairs protruding and twitching as he speaks. "You ran into. . . a railroad dick?" He delivers the line like Lenny Bruce.

"Look. . . Mister Blunt. . ."

"It's Augie."

"What?"

"That's Chester's idea of a joke. I lived in Chicago for a bit."

"Like Augie March?"

"Exactly. Indeed. Big-shouldered Chicago. Ummm-*umfff!*" he mewls, so frankly salacious in his tone that Dugan takes a half-step back. "Another sip?" He reaches again for Dugan's drink.

"Well, Augie, look. . . I think that, ah. . . you're barking up the wrong quiver. . . Augie."

The squint of an eye. "Why, so I am." With a smile that hardens into a sneer, he moves his hand to the top of the sling and gives it a squeeze and sudden half twist—like starting a blender, Dugan thinks. Quick and sharp, the pain whirs up.

"Better take care of that," Blunt declares. "Oh, hello there!" He lifts his glass to Tony Schifoso. "Freshen me, won't you? There's a chap!"

Schifoso leaps to get Blunt's drink while Dugan unsteadily reels through a door, suddenly drunker than he'd thought—the pills, the pain, the slugs of Glenlivet have guided him to a precarious place, out on the porch now, gazing down at reddish-brown tiles a long way off, apparently many feet below. The tiles are wet. . . he notices that and knows what every high diver must feel, that sooner or later the drumroll starts and after that it's up to you. Beneath him, through a circle of fire (or lights in a puddle, it's not clear which), the pool is beckoning (jump! it calls), the size of a thimble far below. In just a moment, maybe he will from the platform he's been clinging to.

The drizzle's become a steady tattoo, music and crowd noise from inside as the Comp Lit guys are on a tear, inspired by the girl from Sholokov ("*Vy ochen' krasivy!* Whattaya say?") But having apparently sought him out on the brink of his death-defying act, she's there beside him on the porch with twin balloons inside her blouse that are floating her just beyond his reach—she's hovering inexplicably as he speaks from the height of his unease. "I keep forgetting—what's your name?" Her boobs are inexpungible.

"Excuse me?"

"Hi." He's sitting it seems—he wonders how. The boobies have drifted farther away. "Would you please tell me. . .?"

"Megan," she says.

He struggles to get back to his feet. "I've got a question for you, Meg. . . I don't suppose, from Hollins and all. . . considering what I've been through, Meg, I don't suppose. . . you'd like to fuck?"

She's gone. He's on the porch alone as run-off shimmers in the sand, a curtain of beads that shake and shine splashing across the russet tiles. Something's in motion, he perceives—he's not sure what, it's probably him. He's in mid-air, it's him all right. . . from which he infers he must have jumped.

Then, just as his cheek is kissing the tiles, he mumbles a *dosvidanya* for Meg. "I didn't think you would," he says.

• • •

No syllabub at the Dibbledome on the morning after his debacle. He tries to fry a Krispy Kreme he finds left over in the fridge, but spills his Coke while yanking its tab, attempting to grip it with his knees. He stoops to wipe the foam away, which makes his head and shoulder ache. He'd like to pop a purple pill, but knowing he'll need to use his wits, he thinks he'll put that off awhile. When part of the doughnut sticks to the pan, he tosses it out and guzzles the coke, the inch or two that's still in the can. That leaves two problems unresolved—a recalcitrant zipper on his fly and the memory of last evening's finale. He tries to come to terms with both, beginning with what he'd rather forget.

"WHO'S SEEN THE ONE-ARMED WIOLINIST?"

It runs like a horror show through his head—Caitlin urging him towards the door and Meg the Buxom's prim rebuff when asked if she'd like to hear him play. He sees himself with a silly expression, like Archduke Ferdinand out for a ride, busking absurdly for the crowd.

"YOU ALL MUST SEE THE WIOLINIST!"

He'd looked at Meg. She'd turned away and Gordo frowned, but Tony Schifoso shushed them up. He must have had a premonition.

"Hold on!" said Dugan, turning his back, so ripped he couldn't stand up straight. Somehow he'd managed to loosen his sling with the help of his pill and a gulp of Glenlivet. Then, after he'd fixed his arm in place— the broken one—inside his belt, he'd draped his coat Italian-style and swiveled to face a silent room, a pencil held in his good hand. He'd seen this stunt at an Oxford bump-supper, but some part of his brain suspected the truth: he wasn't the Archduke after all, but Gavrilo Princip, master musician, aiming his instrument at himself.

"LADIES UND CHEN-TEL-MEN!" Gavrilo sobbed, echoing Danny's Freudian schtick and waving the pencil like a bow. "Vhut can I say? Since loosink my arm, I only play. . . on special even-inks like ziss."

His former student, leaving the bar with jugs of sherry in either hand, had paused to gawk. Schifoso grinned.

"We haff in our midst a man from Parnassus. . ." A bow to Blunt and a patter of claps, dampened by Blunt's aloof expression. ". . . a radical bard. . . who knowss his *roots*. . ."

Gordo coughed. "Let's all. . ."

"VUN MOMENT, Gordo! *S'il vous plaît!*" He'd brandished a handkerchief ("Now I begin!"), closed his eyes and, with a sigh, folded the cloth beneath his chin as if tucking away a violin. He seemed to count. Then, dipping and swaying, with eyebrows raised, he'd coaxed his music from the air, sliding the pencil back and forth. "Waa-waa-waa wa-wa-waaaaaaaah!" he hummed in a high-pitched nasal whine.

Some laughed, some didn't. Blunt did not. Schifoso was squirming with elation. "Beethoven!" he told the edgy crowd as Dugan fiddled dementedly, a self-destructing artist-assassin driven by something he couldn't name—rebellion, impulsiveness, even (who knows?) some talent it was death to hide. . . though what that might be remained obscure, aside from his gift for acing exams while playing the ageing *wunderkind*, a role he appeared to disavow with every stroke of his makeshift bow.

"Wa-wa-wa wa-wa-waaaah!" His forehead, perspiring, grew beady and damp, but what could he do to remedy that? He blinked and blew at a sweat-stung eye, still sawing the pencil as he hummed: "Waa-waa-waa wa-wa-waaaaaaah!" He glanced at the handkerchief under his chin. Up at his forehead, down at his chin. The crowd was growing restless now, but no one moved to lend a hand or help him wipe his dripping brow.

"Waa-waa-waa. . ."

The music stopped. He took a breath. . . and, after a ghastly doom-ridden pause, completed his misbegotten stunt—though, even with booze and two of his pills, a hot wire seemed to be probing his brain along with a crazed futility that he ignored or maybe enjoyed. He bent his legs so everyone saw his trouser fly had been left unzipped.

"Good God!"

He heard a lone guffaw as something fleshy-pink emerged, apparently with a life of its own—stretching and curling, peering about, until, as Dugan lowered his hand, it gripped the Eagle No. 2. Only then, as he mopped his brow, was it clearly a finger attached to the arm the wiolinist had done without.

Everyone looked on, stupefied. Gordo stood speechless next to Meg while Blunt, as if released from a spell, began a disdainful anecdote concerning The Cuban Superman, whose act involved what Wystan had called "the artistry of a well-wrought stern." Danny emerged from the edge of the crowd, reaching for Dugan's one good arm.

"I thought we said no dumb-ass moves."

"Yeah, well. . ." crooned Dugan, looking at Blunt. "Callipygian is the word you want."

"And where were *you*?" hissed Caitlin to Danny. "Just get him the hell away from here."

"How 'bout some Janis?" somebody yelled as Dugan moved leper-like towards the door, feeling things sag in weird slow motion while peering into a round gilt mirror (a newsreel of the Hindenburg—the crowd like bb's dropped on a floor, the fireball blossoming like a rose, a face that looms before the lens. . . his own? Uh-oh, the movie's real!) He slid from the mirror, moving on.

"Gordo. . ." he said from a long way off, still clutching the pencil through his fly. ". . . very vul'rubble. . . I know that."

"Tomorrow, Mike. We'll talk it over."

"Jus' wanted t' show. . . wha's in my quiva." He'd brandished his pencil like a wand, and, as if it were scripted, Janis had screamed, repeating his fellow Rhodes Scholar's plea:

I'D TRADE ALL MY TOMORROWS. . . FOR ONE
SINGLE YESTERDAY!

Noticing Kravitz in the crowd, he'd earnestly offered good advice. "Stay 'way f'um th' oll-lives, Krav," he warned as Caitlin gave her umbrella a shake and Danny stood waiting on the walk, his face impassive behind his shades. Caitlin moved stiffly, Dugan thought. He scoped her bony Irish ass, her low-slung tits and reddish-blond hair (like Lizzie Siddal's, he tells himself). Her face so stern when she looked back. "N' hide your nuts! You hear me, Krav?"

He saw the kitchen door swing shut, but not before he'd caught a glimpse of Gordo and Glubber tête-à-tête, outlined against the Harvest Gold.

• • •

Recollected from his Oxford years, "*Þæs ofereode, þisses swa mæg*" keeps rumbling back and forth in his head—some scop who'd knocked back too much mead consoling himself for getting canned with the sentiment that "this too shall pass" (Deor, thinks Dugan, that's his name. . . wonder if Gordo's heard of him?)

The Cock-o-Dome's a mile away in the other direction from "Pecker Place"—a puerile nickname students use for what's officially called The Roost, where athletes with their special needs are lolling together in sumo pomp except for excursions during the week when they (or their proxies) go legit with courses in which they're obliged to enroll ("foolin' around with fairy farts," as Coach Ray Don so scathingly put it). Mere profs, as a rule, don't count for much, though boosters do and politicians who come and go with clockwork dispatch despite a conspicuous shortage of clocks in places such visitors rarely see—like Humanities classrooms for a start, where above each blackboard is a hole from which two naked wires protrude, awaiting some future allocation.

Sports budgets, of course, are sacrosanct—though, according to faculty scuttlebutt, two years before when funding was tight, the deans had begged Ray Don for alms, knowing his "Rooster Recruitment" stash outstripped the pittance they'd been consigned but oblivious to how incensed he was by their cutting his pre-game prayerthons. To put things bluntly—and Ray Don's blunt—those no-show profs had flunked a test. So, prior to any donation from him, he wanted some sign of real contrition, and Gordo had scrambled once again, making amends by staffing a course for which Danny insisted the only text was a box of magnetized plastic letters. Highly unlikely, Dugan thinks, but just as improbably, that was back when he himself had risen to fame by advising the Rooster's superstar, a distinction he'd earned in a curious way.

As Miz Dibble herself had cattily sniffed, the blonde in the duplex across the street apparently had a very green thumb for more than just a few potted ferns. Thick loops of vines festooned her porch entangled with yuccas, orchids, and palms, their overripe fruit and bruise-dark buds pervading the neighborhood with their fumes. What Miz Dee decided to keep to herself was that secretly, at the heart of this fen, more than thumbs had been at work mulching a bed for the Roosters' coach who, finding his post-game solace here, had parked his less luxuriant wife in a villa on Alabaster Lane.

Dugan's complicity was a fluke. Late one Saturday out on the town, he'd engaged in some prurient badinage at a Shoney's Big Boy's closing time with a hostess whose moves were as slyly lubricious as a girl he remembered from junior high, but only to cross the eponymous Boy who emerged from the kitchen with a scowl and matching Hells Angels skull-faced tattoo. So, canceling his trip down memory lane, he'd headed back home alone on his bike, and, as he was rolling it up the drive, noticed a muddle across the street involving a mobile rubber tree that was gliding away from the duplex's porch. A man in black was directing its course.

"Hey!" Dugan had yelled, alarming another black-clad pair who dropped a huge ceramic urn, concussing the neighborhood with its thud, then scattered like roaches towards a van. An engine revved. Porch lights came on. The van squealed off in a cloud of exhaust with two lame ninjas in pursuit—the smaller one female, Dugan thought.

Dugan had rung the duplex bell. The door cracked open less than an inch through which he'd spied his neighbor's head, her hair pinned flat as if for a wig.

"Robbers!" he'd yelped, his mouth to the crack. "Swiping your plants, and one was. . ."

"Thanks," she'd calmly replied as if accepting a Mormon tract. But he'd gotten a better look inside, and, lurking behind her in the room, was a gentleman-caller Dugan knew, wearing an apprehensive look along with some bright red boxer shorts.

"Hi, Coach!" he'd chirped.

"Okay," she'd almost whispered back. "No problem. Thanks."

"You want the cops?"

She shook her head.

"But look at this mess! Your porch! Your car!" He turned and saw it wasn't her car. It was Ray Don's white 150SL, adorned with honeymoon-type graffiti: FORNICATOR! FUCK RAY DON! And, scribbled in scarlet across the hood, FLAGGED FOR ANOTHER ILLEGAL PASS! "Sorry," he said. "I. . ."

"That's okay."

It didn't seem civil to leave it at that. "'night, Coach," he'd waved.

The great man bowed. The door squeezed shut, and, when Dugan set out for work next day, all signs of the night before were gone. He'd confided in Danny but no one else, leaving Ray Don some room to maneuver. . . which is when he was made J.C.'s advisor—the fruits of discretion he supposed, along with some box seats now and then and soaring status around the town with crackpot fans like Rolly Dehon, proprietor of Wild Rooster Gulf where players got lubes and retreads free while others were lucky if they got gas after waiting for Rolly to amble over, bestowing his toothy benediction. He'd never attended college himself, but Rolly had fought on Okinawa and definitely had some grit in his craw.

"How's J.C. doin'?" Rolly would crow as soon as Dugan rode up to a pump.

"Doin' okay."

"I'm glad to hear it. Now, what you need?"

"Couple of gallons. He's worried, though."

"About the dawgs?"

"Yep," Dugan would nod.

"Their tailback's good."

"He's got V.D. They're skittish 'bout hittin' him from the rear."

Shorty and T. J. listened in. "I hear you."

"Whoo!"

"You keep 'em straight."

Thumbs up. You bet. Gotta pass courses in order to play. ("Come on, J.C.," he'd repeated for Danny, "look out for those gerunds now, you hear?" Aw, man, dis verb-agreement shit is startin' t' make me aspirate!" Really? No—but more to the point, J.C.'s a bright guy underneath if only they'd let him do the work instead of saying, "Just tote that ball!" And lift that cotton, Danny had gibed.)

All that's where Dugan is coming from on the morning after his fall from grace, plodding on foot towards Gordo's lair while brooding on whether the Ray Don link might be of use as a bargaining chip. Probably not, he tells himself, since Gordo's a sometime fan at best and his own ignominy's so complete. . . though Gordo had once believed in him, or trusted he'd churn out meaningless crap to match what he and Glubber produced. He hadn't, and now they figure he won't.

He trudges along on Secession Hill, past what was formerly "colored-town" with its scattered array of tin-roofed shacks where cooks and yardmen used to live, though white-flight schools and grants from HUD have primed it for Caucasianization. Already some houses are being razed, exposing the privies and washing pots guarded by rat-faced curled-tail dogs that yap at whites and scurry away.

"Not things you notice from a car," is Dugan's thought on reaching the tracks a few hundred yards from the site of his crash. No purple pills so far today—he's keeping his head as clear as he can despite a throbbing that won't relent and the incline that he's still got to climb to the prison-like fortress up ahead (described by Danny as "cellblock modern," their workplace if he still has work). But just as he's starting the ascent, a deafening clarion makes him jump:

R - E - S - P - E - C - T!

He flinches reflexively from the din as a second metallic trill is launched, a shotgun blast of R & B:

FIND-OUT-WHAT-IT-MEANS-TO-ME!

The fanfare's followed by a squeal and a red-and-black Firebird's silky hum. "Hey, Doc, that you?" the driver calls, a Smokin' Joe Frazier look-alike whose T-shirt seems spray-painted on. "You gonna walk, or you wanna *fly*?" He lifts his Ray-Bans with a thumb, grinning at Dugan as he speaks. "You bitches go on 'n' git 'n back!"

Two sulky black girls open the door, and, languidly doing as they've been told, earn J.C.'s patented end-zone smile. Dugan is barely in the car when it fishtails off with another cadenza.

WHAT-YOU-WANT-BABY. . . I-GOT-IT!

"Who's been messin' with you, Doctor Dee?" Sliding his glasses back in place, J.C. is nodding at Dugan's sling.

"Crack-back block. A guy named Glubber. Chairman just looked the other way."

"Sheee-it!" He waves at a couple of blondes whose Corvette's headed the other way, then growls to his leopard-like minions in back. "You lookin' at one real crazy honkie!"

The girls in back absorb this news. It's an early September morning still, the sunlight barely touching their skin, but both exude a coppery glow with a scent that Dugan can't define but thinks is probably sandalwood.

"Work goin' okay?" he asks his charge.

"Whatta you *think*?" the superstar grins. "Made Dean's List, Doc! You didn't know that? You fixed me up in science good."

97

A joke, thinks Dugan, since science is J.C.'s nemesis, mainly because they all have labs—Botany, Psych, and "Rocks for Jocks," they've tried them all with no success. But he also knows he's dumb like a fox and as canny with words as Mohammed Ali ("Ah'm gonna make more than Frankenstein," he'd told the *Impeder*'s sports reporter, "just doin' what I natcherly do." Did you mean *Einstein*, J.C.? "Ah mean ah'm a monster runnin' back—you ever see Einstein with the ball?") But his eligibility was at stake, and, knowing they needed some science credits and hearing Fred Kurtz had gotten so vague he was handing out random B's and C's, he'd dispatched J.C. to a long-shot choice, an "Intro to Cosmology" course, hoping he might somehow sneak through.

"You did okay?" he asks his charge.

"Got talent, man! Here, gimme that pad." He's looking at one of the girls in back. "Yeah, that one there. Now open it up."

Dugan's astonished by what he sees. J.C. has made his first B-plus by taking a new extension course in the School of Domestic Sciences. "In *Cosmetology*?" he asks.

"Woulda made uh A," J.C. allows, "if I hadn't fucked up mah cawn-row lab. . . at which I'm a master since back then." He nods towards one of the girls in back. "Show 'im, Latonia!"

Slowly, she turns. Her hair is in an intricate braid with beads and seashells woven all through it. Dugan inhales that musky smell, the scent of a hay-bale after rain. It makes him think of blue-black chiefs in places like Juba and Khartoum—of women sent up from Zanzibar, perfumed and oiled and jangling with brass. It stirs his loins just thinking about it.

When they get to the edge of the faculty lot, there's nobody there to see him descend.

"Stay cool," advises his advisee, slamming the Firebird into gear while blasting out another salute to football and learning at CSU.

WHAT-YOU-NEED. . . YOU-KNOW-I-GOT-IT!

The girl with the hair-do smirks and waves, as if she's read the tarnished mind of Cumbria's former golden boy.

• • •

In its vacuous functionality, Rufus G. Gordon's office resembles a dentist's waiting room with narrow beige-colored matchstick blinds in dark-brown metal frames along its outside wall and floor-to-ceiling bookshelves lining the other three. The shelves are densely packed with blue back-issues of PMLA, not-for-resale anthologies, and multiple sets of works by Simms—all part of a minor commissar's stolid style that's all too familiar to Dugan who closes the door as Gordo requests and follows his gesture to a chair that seems much lower than Gordo's throne. Ensconced behind his massive desk, the chairman appears to be immersed in some paperwork he's got in hand. Eventually, he clears his throat and stares at Dugan myopically.

"Ah. . ." Dugan begins, "about last night. . ."

But Gordo signals for him to wait. He signs a note and looks back up, like a specialist with some dismal news. "Yes, Mike?"

"I want to say how sorry I am. . ."

"A little late for that, I fear." Gordo squeezes his hands together. "Augustus Blunt was not impressed."

Dugan nods reflectively (he would have been, Great & Terrible One, if he'd managed to get into my quiver). "Maybe if I apologize. . ."

"He's gone to The Citadel," Gordo intones, removing his glasses and rubbing his eyes, then carefully putting the glasses back on. "No doubt, he'll make you famous there. It's Meg—Miss Boozer—to whom I think you owe a sincere apology. She's reported what happened on the porch."

Dugan imagines her lurid prose (he said he wanted to ravish my body, strip me buck necked then and there, and touch me all over, here and here and even here!) "I was. . . a little out of control."

"Mike, I want to level with you—as a friend and colleague, I owe you that." He grips his desk and stares at Dugan. "Your fiddling around's been pretty sophomoric. That incident at registration, the wreck that's so. . . improbable, then last night's. . . shall we say, bad taste? But what I'm really disturbed about. . . is what I only heard this morning." He pauses a beat. "I hear you're on drugs."

"Drugs?" gapes Dugan. "It's medication. I shouldn't have mixed those pills with booze."

"I really don't want the squalid details. I want you to know there are some things here. . . that CSU just can't tolerate. We can't and won't. No! Let me speak." He looks at the vista outside his window, like something conjured by Albert Speer—stark, rectilinear upright slabs with streaked facades and windows sealed as airlessly as mason jars, bordered by prickly barricades where passersby might otherwise sit beside its sole embellishment, a House-of-Usher-like cement tarn, its brackish water littered with trash beneath two giant dunking birds that hunker immobilized in the drink. . . an artsy concept run aground at the feet of the humanities.

Gordo's still in a reverie, gazing so long that Dugan has time to scan the office's bleak décor, including what Gordo's hung on the wall—a Leonardo notebook page with heads and limbs all jumbled together. He tries to analyze Gordo's choice (a sort of a spare parts catalog for people with interchangeable parts?)

Finally, clearing his throat again, Gordo begins to ruminate. "I'm from another generation, Mike. I grew up in the Great Depression and went to college during the war. . . the big war, Mike, the one that saved what we've got here." He gestures outside, and, clearly moved, resumes in a slightly lower voice. "I couldn't wait to fight for my country." He checks to confirm that Dugan's listening, then runs his eyes back up the wall. "We didn't have any protest marches, no signs to 'Get Out of Guadalcanal.'" He swivels his chair but loses his balance, then rights himself with an aimless glare. "Those kids out there who're roaming the streets, half-crocked on dope and rock-and-roll. . . hypnotized by some disk-jockey's guff whose malarkey goes out by radio. . ." (You got it, Gordo! Wolfman Jack! It's people like him who've caused this mess!) "They're lost, perplexed, don't know who they are, where they should go, or what to believe. That's why, when they come to us for help, we've got to set a good example."

He pauses as if for a reply (though all that enters Dugan's mind is a tremulous God-bless-Captain-Vere!), then leans towards Dugan cocking his head.

"I hope you hear what I'm saying, Mike, because. . . well, let's just say I care." He holds out a memo that he's signed, the document he was working on. "Medical leave. You'll get half pay. Just sign in triplicate where I've marked."

"Gordo. . ."

"No. What's done is done. I've extended an offer to your replacement."

Already? That figures, Dugan thinks. Like ridding the rest home of a corpse—the sooner removed, the better for all. He signs on the line where Gordo has x'ed. "That it?"

"That's it. But listen, Mike. . ." Gordo rises, extending his hand. "Good luck," he says with an earnest sad smile. He puts his other hand on top, so

Dugan adds his other hand and, stick-stack, it's no-take-back until Gordo leans the other way. "Professor Glover showed me your letter, the one you sent to the *Observer*." He cogitates, still holding hands. "You've become. . . a bit of an agitator. Not an ideologue, I recognize that. A trouble-maker—a show-off, Mike, and I'm sorry to add, despite the exceptional promise you showed, you've been, shall we say, 'a flash in the pan'? Popularity's not the name of this game, and credentials don't really amount to much. . . unless you produce. You know what I mean. Mort Glover was skeptical from the start. 'not a scholar, but an entertainer'— that's what he said when you first came, and I'm sorry to say you've been proving him right." He blinks and stares as if surprised at the sight of his spare-parts sketchbook page. "You'll think that's a harsh assessment, I know, but Mort means well, and hear this, Mike, I'm telling you this for your own good. There's a snatch of verse that comes to mind. . ." (Dugan assumes he knows what's next—breathes there a man with soul so dead?) "It might have been written with you in mind. I think it's Byron, or maybe Hood, or even Browning, but anyhow. . ." He frees his hand and starts to quote: "But, oh, beamish nephew, beware of the day,

If your snark be a boojum. . .

Te-dum te-dum te-dum te-dee." He looks at the ceiling and wrinkles his brow as if to retrieve some fleeting thought. "Just think about it. By the way. . ." he adds with a nod, delivering the coup de grâce, "did you happen to meet your replacement last night?"

"At the reading by Blunt? He's in town now?"

"At the Doggetts' reception, just passing through, on his way back to Chantry Mount."

"I didn't," says Dugan.

"I wish you had. I know he'd like to make a trade, your place for his. . ."

"In Chantry Mount?" Another state?

"Well, it's late to be looking around down here, and, after last night it crossed my mind you might just welcome a change of scene where there's none of this baggage over your head and you can rehab, so to speak. I hear they've got a housing's shortage, so trading leases makes lots of sense. Good libraries there. . . that sort of thing."

What sort of thing? is Dugan's thought. Penitence, exile, savorless bread? (He gets the point. It's Meg's revenge. Don't nobody mess with

101

Black Bart's girl.) "Well, sure, why not?" he says instead. "He got a name?"

"It's on this offprint," Gordo says, holding a pamphlet upside down so Dugan can read the words out loud:

THE ANGUISH OF COMMAS GONE AWRY:
ANOMALIES IN TIMROD'S TEXTS
by
John M. Dough

"Some sort of alias?"

Gordo frowns. "He pronounces it Duff."

"You gotta be kidding."

"He's working on Simms. . . with more on Timrod in the works."

The message is clear. His quiver is packed. (Well, boffo, chaps! He'll fit in here.) No point in dawdling, Dugan thinks, this evisceration feels complete. "I better go meet my class," he says, "to tell them about my change of plans."

Gordo nods. "Take care now, Mike." He's headed back towards his cluttered desk, when, quizzically, he turns half-round—but changes his mind, and Dugan's dismissed.

On his way out, he runs into Meg, who's waiting in Gordo's anteroom pretending to read a magazine. When he enters, she primly turns away. . . prompting in him a sort of regret. Now that there's something they could share, he wishes they'd had the tête-à-tête that Gordo said they needed to have. He might have confided that he too knows what it's like to get screwed by Gordo.

• • •

Architecturally speaking, the two adjacent buildings are like fraternal twins—one tall and thin for offices, the other for classrooms short and squat, but both with dark brown metal frames for windows shaped like parapet slits and narrow beige-colored matchstick blinds, though most of the blinds in 202 are bent or stuck and hanging askew. The students are like and unlike too, with early-arrivals in fixed-seat desks dressed mostly in jeans and polo shirts while a late-comer spillover lounges about resembling a roadshow cast for *Hair*.

The course is wildly over-subscribed. It should have been closed at thirty-five, but Dexter has signed up every freak who showed up late for registration—Abby and Eldridge lookalikes, Paul and Ringo, Aitch Rapp Jones—while Kravitz has duped sorority types, the ones who'd turned *Piers Plowman* down, by promising movies and romance ("Like *War and Peace*, you've heard of that? With Audrey Hepburn, Mel Ferrer?") There're thirty or so without a seat and a general commotion in the room. Too bad, thinks Dugan—could have been fun.

With a valedictory look around, he notes a coincidence new to him: the bleakness of the room's décor is Gordo's office on the skids, and both are that of a 7-Eleven, fluorescently lit and sporadically mopped. As usual, there's no chalk in the tray, but scrounging a half-inch nub from the desk, he prints the course's name on the board.

L-I-T-E-R-A-T-U-R. . .

Pinching the fast-diminishing nub, he labors to write with his left hand.

O-F W-A-R & Я-E-V. . .

He sees the last R got reversed, erases it, and draws it back. But O-L-U is as far as he gets before the chalk is all used up. "That's 'Revolution,'" he explains.

"Yeah! Right on!" yells Aitch Rapp Jones.

"We've got a problem," Dugan says.

"Whole friggin' country!"

"Say that again!"

"Okay, stay cool—here's what I'll do. I'll call the roll and make an announcement. Answer me when you hear your name."

When he gets to the end, he asks for omissions.

"Me." Alias Mick, the Seminole chief. . . Dexter must have let him in.

"Name?"

"Lonnie Brazell."

"Your number?"

"What?"

"I need an I.D."

"That's fascist crap. You got my name."

"That's why they left you off the roll."

"Who you working for, then? You with the Man?"

"We'll leave it off. Anyone else I didn't call?"

"Hey, wait!" yells Mick. "Let's air this out! Internal passports, you want that? You sellin' this class out to the feds?" The accent's more like a local's now.

"Hold on, okay?" He gives his voice a patient edge. "You're not on the roll—I'm not sure why, but I'll bet that missing number's to blame. That means no credit, no degree. But what's all that to Chairman Mao? You with me, Mick?"

"It's Lonnie!"

"Fine. You want the prize, you play the game. Nobody rides the merry-go-round unless he tells us his I.D. No tickee, no washee—get the point?" Power to the people, Mick.

Now somebody else is raising her hand.

"Should we be taking notes today?"

The frat-pin girl. She's signed up too? And next to her—he should have known! His kidneys ache in a furious way as the rancor he'd felt he feels again, a sense that he'd been suckered in. Whatever she wants, it can't bode well.

"Name?" he asks her, business-like.

But Rapp sees something's going down. The Asian kids take engineering.

"Lowes Lee," she says. "I've got duh ticket you're looking for."

"Whoa!" mutters Rapp.

There's a snicker or two. In slacks and a scarlet-colored blouse she looks as young as most of them, but not like a student. . . something else, and they're gawking at Dugan for a clue. That ticket must be his wallet, he thinks.

"Your first name, please. Would you spell that?"

"Like duh frower," she says. "Urr. . . oh. . . ess. . . ee."

Their eyes are locked. She's going to make this mano-a-mano.

"Dig it!" says Mick.

The girl with the frat pin looks confused.

"Anyone else?" Dugan stays cool, wagging his sling like Frank 'n' Stein's mug. "All right, then. . . here's the bottom line. Because of matters beyond my control, this course is canceled as of now. Somebody else might teach it instead, but as of now that's up in the air."

Gasps and groans. "Aw, shit!" says Mick.

"What *sort* of matters?" Aitch Rapp demands.

Most students stand, but no one leaves. They're waiting for an explanation.

"So how'd you get so busted up?" one of the frat boys tries to pry.

"I got what you get for interfering."

"Oh, yeah? In what?"

He tries to shrug. "That's not germane."

"COME ON!" yells Mick.

The room is fraught with tension now, of a sort on campuses everywhere—the ones in the news—but arriving this morning in Cumbria too, if only in a mild-mannered way.

"Check with the registrar's office," he says, raising his voice to make himself heard. "They'll tell you what options you've got left."

"ANSWER THE QUESTION!" Aitch Rapp yells, taking a step in Dugan's direction.

"In what?" a shrill voice backs Aitch up. The sorority girl—yes, even her, shaking her clenched fist in a snit. "You interfered in what?" she yaps, the frat pin bobbing with every shake.

"Yeah, what?" two voices say at once.

Dugan relents. "An unfair fight."

They think he means a demonstration. Since Grant Park—really, since *Medium Cool* and "Look out, Haskell, it's for real!"—beatings by pigs are radical chic. He's raised the ante and won the pot. They wait for him to tell them more, and somehow it seems they've all deduced whatever he means pertains to her, the woman who's got his ticket she says. . . or number is what her manner conveys.

"That's all," he says. "Somebody's been hired to take my load. I haven't been told what he's planning to teach. . . but nothing like this, I'm pretty sure. My other courses are canceled too."

"Aw, man!" whines Mick. "I needed this course."

"I'd like to see Miss Lee for a moment." He looks around and she's not there. He's not surprised. "Try drop-add, Mick. That's it, okay?"

More grumbles and curses, one or two *fucks*, some envious glances at his sling as the room is quickly emptied out. He puts the class-roll back in his bag as if he's going to need it still (he won't, of course, that's sinking in) and reflexively turns to wipe the board. It's all connected, he tells himself, knowing he's got to figure it out before she tries to make a deal—his wallet for something. . . but what's her game? If he wasn't a target, he must be now (he supposes that somewhere in its head a praying mantis must wonder the same shortly before it gets devoured).

"You wanted to see me?" She's reappeared, exactly as he'd guessed she would, ready for clever repartee.

"Yes, I did." He runs through lines he doesn't use ("There were easier ways to cancel my class!") Instead, he tries the silent look that Bogie gives Bergman in *Casablanca*. It doesn't appear to register, despite her fondness for movie clichés.

"Your warret," she says to him, holding it out. "I found it where I lost my shoe."

He takes it, and they hold it together. Again he feels what he'd felt before, as if he's known this had to occur.

"You need a lift?" he wryly asks. The fact that he's got no lift to give is less to the point now, he concludes, than where the red convertible is.

"No," she says. "We need to talk."

● ● ●

He's wary of walking into a trap. His office isn't an option, of course (he's not ready for any goodbyes just yet, though he'll have to clean some stuff out there to leave with Danny if he can), and (assuming his name is still on their list) the Faculty Club requires a tie—a rule the Rooster Boosters made when, taking their business clients there, they'd found a bunch of scruffy profs made closing deals more difficult, a problem the dress code helps to resolve, along with having upped prices enough to keep the egg-head riff-raff out. The service is lousy anyhow, and Dugan's not up for a backdrop like that. So where can the two of them go to talk—his turf this time, not a 7-Eleven?

He runs through the options in his mind. Seoul Food's out for an obvious reason—"no tickee, no washee" was bad enough. Piggie Parlor's too far and hardly the place, and Frank 'n' Stein's just weenies and suds. That leaves the anti-war coffee house that's fairly nearby on Lower Main.

BETTER READ it used to be called, implying its patrons were all well-read while punning on "better red than dead," though the latter is what most Legionnaires urged, partly because their Legion Hut's bar had catered for years to teenage drunks who now prefer a caffeine high. . . or, rather, according to Legion complaints, the spritzers of commie

106

subversion-and-sin their leftist competitors use for bait. When a doctor named Milstein from the Fort said no to training Green Berets but yes to Acapulco Gold, the Legion decided to make its move, alleging that Milstein used the café for recruiting some GI saboteurs—and, given the beads-and-tambourine dread infesting the dreams of righteous folk, such hooey got treated as gospel truth. In a matter of days, Doctor Milstein was gone, spirited off to Leavenworth on charges the Army ordered sealed, which, according to scuzz-buzz, also claimed he'd admitted to being a fag as well. That was when vandals defaced the sign, changing the name to BETTER HEAD and prompting the owner's irked response of calling it simply "COFFEE POT."

After all that, its trade went slack until a local councilman, accused of siphoning funds from trusts, huffed he, for one, would not stand by while pinkos and queers polluted the state. "COFFEE POT?" he'd bawled out its name. "You think *caffeine* is sucking our kids into that godless left-wing sewer? It's not the cawfee, but the POT! Drugs, sedition, and *nekkit* wimmen!" That, plus a rumor Jane Fonda was coming to help keep COFFEE POT afloat, drew hordes of hippie-like hangers-on who, added to undercover observers, kept things in the black for a couple of months—at the end of which the owner ran off with a short-order cook well known about town for adventurous sex, including once balling Mama Cass or so he claimed with no real proof. Then the owner's ex-wife changed signs again. UP YOURS the new one brazenly said, and, under that, WE SERVE NO MEAT.

Up Yours it is then, Dugan decides. Though it couldn't be called a commercial success, it draws a sullenly picturesque crowd opposed to the war and anything else that doesn't rely on chlorophyll. But none of that clientele is there when he leads the purported Rose Lee in, past Lomotil muffins under a dome and jars of tarry Muesli crud to a table with festive roots and twigs, a shaker of wheat germ, and a card with a calligraphic design declaring there'll be NO SMOKING HERE—provoking some anarchist wag to add "But You Can Fart" with a ballpoint pen.

"Hi," Dugan says to the pony-tailed guy behind the counter shelling peas. Ponytail nods, not lifting his eyes, as if he's busy sorting the peas.

The place has an oddly vacant feel, like a barely-in-business country store with a lot more space than items to sell. Anti-war posters share the wall with Dylan in profile, rainbow-hued, and letters that dangle from a string: W-O-O-D-S-T-O-C-K-N-A-T-I-O-N by the door and B-E-H-E-R-E-N-O-W above a shrine that quotes two lines from William Blake—"all truly wholesome food is caught/without a net or a trap"—with a silhouette of the poet's head in what looks to be a beaver hat.

"Coffee okay?" he says to Rose, a name as Irish as Dugan to him.

"Black," she answers, impervious but taking things in.

He relays the order to Ponytail who shrugs as he goes on shelling peas.

"Excuse me a moment," Dugan says, walking over towards the counter. "You got that, right? Two regular coffees," he repeats, then heads towards the men's room's paint-stripped door with the pain in his shoulder so severe that, despite hopes of keeping his brain alert, he's decided he's got to pop a pill. As he's choking it down, he looks in the mirror trying to guess why they'd need to talk and why she's suddenly reappeared except, of course, to give him his wallet. . . though, if that's the case, why wait until now?

He pauses to study his haggard face, aware of what's flashing through his mind like a rapidly shuffled deck of cards. She's extremely good looking, he's noticed that, wearing her hair with a part in the middle— something his mother had also done, like Vivien Leigh and Hedy Lamarr. Maybe she's really in trouble, he thinks, but what's he prepared to do about that, exiled as it seems he's become? But before that question's been addressed, it's succeeded by how annoyed he feels at Ponytail's smugly superior air, so passive-aggressive to the core—as if Up Yours is the peaceable kingdom and Dugan a two-faced carnivore. And yet, he thinks, even given all that, there are touches to which he feels himself drawn, like dark-stained sawdust-sprinkled floors that are nothing but whimsy to cynics like Dexter. But Dexter was born in Minnesota and takes it for granted that people down south are prone to Faulknerian complications— and how can you tell a twit like that that the dimmest of fans at the Rebel 500 knows Thunder Road from hard-scrabble fact and the saddest of losers in Agee and Coles say, "So, maybe the meek ain't inheritin' squat, we'd rather get even than get ahead. . ." which, aside from how self-defeating that is, doesn't make rednecks better or smarter, just not what dopes like Dexter assume.

All that goes tumbling through Dugan's mind, not as a logical train of thought, but like an avalanche gathering speed, compounded by anything in its path and running its course in the blink of an eye. Some basic things he knows he knows—that, if lions are lying down with the lambs, it's only because it's in between meals; that peaceniks like Ponytail yelling at troops who're herding scared villagers into a ditch are not about to get in the way if risking their own hides comes into play; that Gudgers and Ricketts are carnivores too, Scots-Irish like him and appetite-driven.

And what can he say for such violent kin? As any recruiter might attest, in kilts or camouflage they're the ones you'll want beside you covering your ass when their murderous counterparts open fire—though they're just as obstreperous minding their turf, so when Dennis and Peter roll up like punks, oozing their *Easy-Rider* scorn, their bikes are sure to get blown away. Such people don't take to being demeaned or even to getting criticized. Some call them trash swept out of the mills, their politics (i.e., bigotries) from Tillman to Sternbolt making it plain they're gonna get screwed on their own terms (but they're grounded—at least, he wants to believe—in something other than avarice. . . stubbornness, maybe, kith and kin).

Still, what does *he* know about life in the mills? Essentially nothing. Caitlin does, for what that's worth—which is little to Danny and less to him—given her family's moving about from Swansea to Roebuck and back again plus migrating to the artsy class (though stuck with a stringy hard-bitten look that's wrenchingly forthright in its way, like some of those photos by Evans and Lange). As for peaceable kingdoms dixie-style, where would he and Danny fit in? He summons the painting back to mind, looking for signs of Danny's tribe with ole Ezra the Peddler out of sight on a barge down past the river's bend—part-Solomon, part-Lenny Bruce—while Dugan's rep is Willie Penn, fellow Oxonian on a roll naively assuming goodness will win, trusting that probity will prevail (one's parlaying upstage left and the other off somewhere in the wings, but both are peripheral to the charade of eaters and eaten front and center). So Danny schlepps out of a bar-mitzvah class and ends up teaching goyishe lit, while Dugan, the sometime altar-boy, comes home, as Danny himself insists, more Jewish than Danny will ever be. But (next card, please) for Dugan those aren't what's troubling him most.

What does it mean, he's asking himself, to share a Confederate soldier's name, repudiate his Great Lost Cause, then wander into a drab café, nostalgic for those wide-plank floors and childhood years in his grandfather's house (when Monroe—wasn't that his name, who showed up every few months or so?—was down on his knees with a brick in a rag, buffing that aristocratic sheen for a snot-nosed white kid to enjoy?) Black losers, they're the other sort—and he could report how his nominal friends, whose fathers had preened at the Cotton Boll Ball, would ride through "colored-town" at night shooting out porch lights from their cars, how four of them pissed in a milkshake cup on the night of the Booker-T senior prom and cruised until they found a kid out struttin' in a rented tux. . . but that's all over and they've grown up, hoping the guy in the tux forgot, or moved away, or decided that M.L.K. was right. They're expecting to be the ruling elite (like rednecks, though, they feel no guilt—he does, they don't, and he can't figure why. . . except, he has to ask himself, was it always a shill, that chivalrous pose which he'd so earnestly tried to adopt? He hopes not, but it seems it was, which leaves him nowhere in this town that he'd once thought of as his own). So what if he likes the losers more? It doesn't imply they're going to win or shrug things off or that anyone should. . . which means, he concludes, the issue's moot and he can savor what's basic here—the smell of the sawdust on the floor, the sham of its nouveau poor-white pose, the memory of Quentin Compson's lie (the last card falls, the shuffle's done. . . I don't hate it either, he tells himself).

Maybe two minutes at most have passed as he heads back to his waiting chair—and whattaya know? Rose Lee's still there along with two coffees Ponytail brought before returning to his post. He sees she's slipped dark glasses on and is muttering comments up her sleeve as if recording evidence, ignoring Ponytail's goggle-eyed stare. Together, they've thrown him into a snit as, stopping his squirrelishly busy hands, he lets a pea roll onto the floor, watching it bounce like a grenade to less than an inch from Rose's shoe, then freezing with his lips pursed tight as if waiting for it to detonate. But the moment Rose lifts her blank-faced gaze, Ponytail jerks back in alarm—though looking at Dugan, not at her, prompting an irrational hunch that Rose and Ponytail know each other. Ponytail's voice is querulous.

"You lookin' for something?" Speaking to Dugan.

"Right. We are."

"Like what?" He's back to shelling peas.

"Like, leaving aside those mummified muffins, what've you got in the way of food?"

"No meat."

"That's fine."

"We don't serve pigs." He wipes his mouth with the back of his hand.

"You what?"

"You heard me," Ponytail glares. "Think you and Madame Nhu fool *me*?"

He's pointing at Rose. She's Madame Nhu? Unless he's really in on the game, he urgently needs a B-12 fix. He's angry, though, or seems to be, like one of those mugs the other night. The whole world's bent on violence, even this rat-faced vegan on speed.

"Back off there, pal," is Dugan's retort, bending to sweep the errant pea up. "We came for some coffee. Hold the peas." He places it on the tabletop and adds a couple of dollar bills.

"Oh, sure, Mister G-Man. I'm naïve. Think I don't know what you're up to here? What'cha been hidin' in that sling? Had to activate it in the head?"

Rose watches as if she needs translation, looking about while poised for flight—same as she'd done two night ago before they entered the 7-Eleven.

"A box full of roaches, you silly twit! I took its lid off in your head."

Rose shifts uneasily, scraping her chair, while Ponytail reaches towards a shelf to flip the knob of an amplifier, unleashing a crazed metallic shriek. She's ready to scram as Ponytail, leaving the peas behind, comes out from the counter headed towards them while Jimi Hendrix rages and fumes and Dugan fires back as he gets to his feet, "I'm callin' the health inspector next!"

Ponytail wipes his hands on a rag. Up close he reeks of cauliflower. "Oh, yeah? I bet! You leaving already?" He's nodding like a bobbing doll, first at Dugan and then towards Rose. "I thought you'd like the national anthem!"

Rose is now headed for the door, and Dugan remembers how it went—he'll look around and discover she's gone. She'd vanished in the classroom too.

"You want Pat Boone, I got Pat Boone!" The veins in Ponytail's neck knot up. "Think I don't know what you guys like? Oh, wait up, Miss! See what I got. How 'bout some Captain & Tennille?"

"Hey, fella, look!"

"Or Mantovani. Better than Jimi Hendrix, right?"

"There's something I think you oughta know."

"I'm short on protein? Sure, you wish! And how're you're fixed for colon cancer?"

"Your man up there. . ." He points at Dylan. "He wudn't at Woodstock, you know why?" They're eyeball to eyeball, and Dugan can see the bastard's out of his meatless mind. "He wanted more jack—the fascist hyena."

"Your type all smell like what you eat."

"Which type?"

"Uh-huh. Think I don't know? Tell Wonder Woman I'm onto her. And you too, Steve. Bang bang woo woo!"

Ponytail stops inside the door as Rose half-turns three steps beyond, waiting for Dugan who takes his time, still hoping he'll pick up some detail as a clue to what's really going down. A puff of wind lifts Rose's hair. He notices how she leans away, like Nike atop her flight of stairs, and he leans too, like a relay runner, speaking so Ponytail can hear.

"The guys at the Bureau got it right. This mess is worse than the Legionnaires said."

Great leapin' lizards! Whattaya know? His paranoia now confirmed, Ponytail shows a wild elation, shouting with Jimi, whirling about, wiping a table off with his rag. Then he's back in the doorway, waving his arms. His outraged howl sounds high and thin. "Kissinger sucks!"

They keep on walking.

"Nixon's a dickhead! Hear that, Steve?"

A furious pounding, oinks and snorts. "YOUR DIRTBAG BOSS. . . WEARS ARGYLE SOCKS!"

Dugan turns with a mild-mannered smile. "Thanks for the coffee. Keep the change."

• • •

So they're walking again, as few others are on a day like that, while buses and trucks are cruising past and one or two cars keep circling the block as if in search of a place to park, though nothing's clearer to Dugan now than it was in the dark two nights before. He's doing his best to play it cool, which for her is seemingly effortless, as if there's no hurry to straighten things out. Maybe she'd said, "We need to *walk*"?

They pass a place called Dixie Fish exuding an offal and fish-gut smell and a specialty shop called Flushed With Pride dealing in toilets and urinals, its whimsical fly-specked window display presenting a PCV mandala, and then, on the corner, Nice 'n' White, a place to drop dry cleaning off where draft-age boys are peering out past rapidly pulsing neon signs—1 HOUR! 1 HOUR!—as if the time is running out before they'll hear from Oreen Suber ("Greetings! Take a Trip on us!") Dugan can feel their eyes on Rose and, aware of how exotic they look— like walking a borzoi through the town (unless, of course, she's walking him)—he guesses it's probably crossing their minds that Saigon might not be so bad (dream on, you twerps, it won't come cheap, that's why his shoulder's in a sling). As if to emphasize that thought, he takes her arm with his functioning one, leading her back the way they'd come but crossing before they reach Up Yours, defying an asshole driver in shades who gawks at Rose with a "hey-baby!" grin as he idles his two-door yellow Camaro.

They skirt the campus perimeter, veer left, and, heading west again, are passing a row of parking meters when, just as they're drawing abreast of one, it suddenly flicks its time's-up tongue—at which Dugan, as he usually does, pauses to fish about for a coin while tucking his satchel under his arm, then pushes a quarter into the slot.

"Power to the people, huh?"

He sees she thinks he's showing off—which he is, in a way, but not just for her, though she seizes the moment to say to him, "I tink I owe you. . ." Then she stops, letting her hesitation sink in, watching to gauge how he reacts.

He's ready to counter this opening move, but finds he's disarmed by something else—the husky tremolo of her voice, enticing but oddly matter of fact. Also, before she'd donned her shades, he'd noticed a vague unfocused gaze—eyes black as seeds inside a pear. . . innocent-seeming to him at first, though it's probably just astigmatism.

"I *think* I owe you. . ." she repeats, struggling to get the fricative right.

"Nothing," he says, implying it's more than she's likely to pay.

". . . an expranation," she plows on, pausing and gesturing at the sling.

"My shoulder?" he drawls, attempting a shrug and putting a weird hitch in his gait (he'd like it to look like Steve McQueen but reckons it's more like Long John Silver). "It's broken," he adds, "as I tried to tell you the other night. . . by one of those goons, whoever they were."

She compresses her lips with the faintest of frowns, her shades obscuring what's unsaid, and they amble in silence for a bit.

They've entered the oldest part of town, the part the Yankees didn't burn, where sidewalks cracked by live-oak roots have carpets of acorns underfoot crunching and rolling as they walk. He'd grown up here, in his grandfather's house. No need to tell her that, of course, or how the house he'd known as a boy, built years before his mother was born, had porches appended to three of its sides, a sundial on a cement urn denoting how slowly time went by, evinced as well in other ways—like droning fans on hardwood floors, or lawn-mowers' lingering thrust and return, or lazy larghetto street-sellers' cries for okra, peas, and butterbeans—or how, the

113

minute his grandfather died, while Dugan was stuck in Harvard Square, the house had been sold by uncles and aunts, and he, in Quentin Compson mode, had decided he'd never go home again. Still, here he is, despite himself, immersed in the feeling he always has whenever he's in that neighborhood that eternity's eddied up to the doors but never quite managed to seep inside and that, only a block or two away, his family's still holed up where it was like characters in an O'Neil play with ceiling-high mirrors in the hall, table and hunt board, harp-backed chairs, "Wild Turkeys" by Audubon on one wall and Lee & Jackson on the other (at Chancellorsville, in their moment of glory, just minutes before a jittery picket would murder his country by mistake). A heritage of mistakes, he thinks, beginning with what the war was about—though, no matter how much of it he rejects, there's a cavil he can't eradicate. . . we are, alas, what we have been.

But why's she prompting these thoughts in him?

They reach Gervais and start uphill, glimpsing the flags on the capitol dome—for country, state, and something else. . . for ludicrous, headstrong valor and pain—unjust, deluded, all those things, but reckless as a scalded dog, the product of a self-righteous snit whose relics lie stacked in a lusterless room he dimly remembers under the dome, where birdlike widows rocked and talked in plaintive high-pitched twittering, keeping the swords and sashes bright. But nothing's immutable, even the past—re-edit, rewind, and release it again on those underlit screens inside their minds as Griffith and others managed to do ("I say, there, Gen'l Longstreet, suh, I'd like you to meet my fiancée. Name's Chi Cheng—a little shy, but faster'n blueboys at Manassas!" "Har-de-har! I reckon tha'ss what we need now, boy—some slanty-eyed rebs to he'p us out. Order us up a coupla million!") No matter what, he wants to believe, we're only what we're willing to be. The cause was wrong, and that was that.

She jerks her head impatiently as if she'd tapped into his thoughts. "I'm trying to explain," she says, getting every consonant right.

"Oh. . . explanations. . ." he evades. Like what? Like smack? Like Fu Manchu? (Duh drop-off get a lidder confused, better for you keep owdda duh way!) Chinoiserie in Dugan's mind is mostly a matter of wonton soup plus Ezra Pound and a dash of Pearl Buck, but it's all clichés and stereotypes—endurance, guile, and clannishness. . . like Scots without predestination, same stinginess but better sex. Footholds along the Yangtze, yes, but also, on the porno screen, dark-nippled boobs and pubic smudge more like a goatee than a beard, savored once in a double bill, in

Ann Arbor on a scholarly jaunt when he and Danny had cut a talk on glottal stops in Syr Gawayne (its proper spelling says it all), preferring the marquee's coded text to the drivel dished up at MLA: GEORGINA SPELV IN DEV MS. JONES/JOY BANG IN ORIENTAL KITT. Through each debasement, Joy had smiled. "Exemplary," expounded Danny.

"Are you still wid me?" Rose intrudes.

"Sorry," he says. "My id and the pills can't seem to agree." (But weren't they discussing what's happened to him?)

He watches her process what he's said. "Okay," she answers, marking time. It's clear an apology's not in store. (So solly, Joy Bang kept telling Long John, who'd prematurely lost his load—that's okay too, her smile implied.)

They pause at the edge of the capitol grounds, where an outfield of statues has been deployed too late to shag the cannonballs that Sherman lobbed from over the river, their improbable hits awarded plaques— bronze stars affixed to the building's façade, beneath which lurks a peanut man in overalls and Rooster cap who, standing in shade at the base of the steps, signals with fake Masonic signs.

"Cap'n, Missis, how-dee-doo?" Nightmarishly, he sucks in his teeth and folds his face into a blank, then grins and resurrects his nose. "Parched or boiled, how many you need?"

Dugan declines with a wag of his sling ("us one-armed men can't shell no goobers"). Rose nods and smiles. The man persists, "Maybe the lady wants some, though?"

"I'll let you know."

"You change yo' mind, I'll be right here."

"Good deal," says Dugan, brushing him off while noting that Fold-Face winks at Rose as if he too is in on the game (are those pills now making him paranoid?)

"Gimme a bag of boiled," he nods.

"Thanks, Cap'n. Fine." He swallows his nose, restoring it like a Murphy bed. "That quarter's good. You want some change?"

"No." Dugan sees her look around.

"Dis way?" she asks while leading him on.

"You ever tasted these?" he asks, following her towards the statuary.

Not since she was a kid, she says, declining the chance to try them again. *Boiled* peanuts? He's incredulous—he'd thought they were a Southern thing. "Chinese," she says. Like baseball, huh, and peanut butter?

She shakes her head. "Like fye-yuh drills and egg foo yung." So she's Chinese? From where? he asks.

They're standing where two paths converge as she turns her shaded gaze on him as if he's somehow crossed a line.

"All over duh place. From San Francisco. . . Chinatown."

"Your accent. . ."

"Yeah, I know. . . in whatever language," she concedes. "My mudder was French, my farder Chinese. Sometimes it seems to come and go."

"I grew up here," he volunteers. "I went away and came back home— from England and Boston, places like that. My accent's kind of mixed up too."

Has he ever been to San Francisco? Once, he says, to visit a friend. . . on a Greyhound out and back again. She asks if he knows Union Square.

Awkwardly, with just one hand, he opens the bag and shucks a nut, sucking the salty contents out and dropping the hull at his feet. A pigeon scoots over to check it out, pecks once or twice, and waddles away. A lot more trouble than that was worth—he thinks the bird would probably agree. What was the question? Union Square? Yeah, more or less. He knows where it is.

"Dere's a sign in one corner," she starts to explain, "or used to be, in Chinese wid English underneath. Red and gold—big letters, okay?" Young Lee, it said, her father's name—"den Wash & Press by Hand - One Day."

He didn't remember. No surprise. What she remembers best, she says, is the laundry bins where she took naps when she was maybe three or four. . . one customer for every bin, so all the bins had different smells. He tries to guess—like sweat, cigars, perfume, or sex? Like jars in a Chinese pharmacy? She lets him conjure what he can.

He nods to let her know he's there. "Go on," he says, and she resumes, taking him through it step by step. When customers pick their laundry up, she learns their names and correlates. He knows that word?

"What? Correlates?"

He does. Okay. She correlates their names and smells. Also, she learns how fabrics feel. Rich ladies' underwear is best, silk camisole and frilly bra. McGonagall bin was best of all—her husband owned a lot of stores. "Close wid a cedar-closet smell," she says, "like incense sticks, but not so sweet." She'd smuggled a bra once to her room, planning to put it back again after her own clothes had that scent. But her father had caught her. "'Litter Lowes,'" he'd frowned and said, "'you got no need for one uh dese.'" She pauses to let the point sink in—he couldn't pronounce his daughter's name. "So, when were you in San Francisco?"

He jerks himself from a reverie concerning the bra he'd glimpsed on her. Maybe all his suspicions were wrong. "Six years ago. . . were you there then?"

They're walking and pausing. She shakes her head, then shows a perfunctory interest in him by asking if his family's here.

"In a manner of speaking," Dugan says. "My father was a lawyer," he adds. "He died a couple of years ago." These peanuts aren't much good, he thinks, tossing the bag into a can. At thirty, his father had fought in the war and never really got over it. His nerves were shot, things went to hell. . ." No need to tell her any of that. "My mother too, not long ago."

"The same," she says with lowered head.

They've come to a place where they can sit, where benches encircle a sort of shrine constructed out of granite and bronze. Wade Hampton's staring out over their heads, resolute, dead, equestrianized with the sites of his battles carved underneath on the sides of his seven-foot pedestal, names familiar to Dugan from birth. A lot of men had died in those places—for what? he wonders. Making us free? Not hardly. What? To help preserve a way of life premised on some not being free. The general looks reconciled to the cost. His horse's balls are painted red.

Rose takes this in, surveying the scene, then, brushing her hair back, takes a seat, patting the bench to beckon him down. A Southern girl would have wiped it first, especially wearing light-colored slacks.

"Fraternity boys," he says to Rose, gesturing towards the crimson balls. "They want you to know he's riding a stallion."

He drops his satchel on the grass. Half-hidden by the pedestal's base, a bum clears phlegm three benches away as if vexed by getting roused from sleep. No signal, just a spit and cough that Dugan regards attentively. A naturalist would be amazed by how life teems on these capitol grounds.

"Red's good for luck," Rose Lee observes, gesturing at the blouse she's wearing. "I want to tell you what I do. . ."

"I'd like to know. Unless, of course. . ."

"I need to tell you."

"Okay," he says.

She hesitates, appraises the bum, then turns back towards him. "Here's duh ting. Soon as I started to talk, you see, I worked duh counter for my dad and learned duh way things are, how it's not duh same if you're yerrow

117

or black. We couldn't own land out dere, you know, or marry a white. . . dough my farder did."

He hadn't known there were laws like that, but he's puzzled by how her accent's grown. No discernible pattern, slightly weird.

"My mudder was what we cawr a ghost. When she got sick, two brudders showed up to take her back to Cincinnati. Take me and farder too, I said. Dey wouldn't, dough."

"She named you Rose?"

She shakes her head. A little too vehement, like a child—a motion he wants to see again. "My farder chose it, you know why? My ticket out of Chinatown. My mudder got out anudder way, against her will, but. . . anyway. . . After she left, he cried so hard I thought he'd ruin all the clothes."

She gives a caustic little laugh, maybe because her accent's gone, then takes her shades off, meeting his gaze as if to assess what impact she's had. He notes a mole beside her ear, and a pinpoint like a blue tattoo between her eyelid and her cheek. He thinks about those laundry bins, but despite the heat, he catches no scent, just newness like a glossy book— Rizzoli, Abrams, one of those. Another pause. He looks at her. . . and finds he's lost his train of thought.

What language did she speak at home? What language? Yes, when her mother had left, what language did her father speak? Mostly Chinese is her reply. A little English now and then.

"You also had a Chinese name?"

She puts the shades back on again. "Lowes Lee, okay? But funny, huh? My farder could never get duh joke. When customers laughed, 'Hey, Gypsy Lowes! A nickel if you take it off!' he had no idea what dey meant. You listening. . .?"

"Mike. My name is Mike."

"You listening, Mike?"

"I'm listening, sure." He looks at her and she looks back, as fixedly as he at her. He thought he'd heard they never stare, unless. . . that's wishful thinking, though. (Be careful, Duke, he warns himself, but "somewhere, surely," Whitman trills, "I ate with you, and slept with you" when your hair was still cut straight across, Prince Valiant bangs and crimson silk and skin the hue of ripe persimmon—like *Broken Blossoms*. . . funny, huh?)

"When he found out, it made him cry."

"Again?"

"So maybe he liked to cry."

Or maybe she exaggerates? He's an English professor, doesn't she know? For a moment they tune each other in. He waits for her. She catches up, as if she's down to business now.

"Movies?" she says. He waits. She adds, "You like dem, right?"

Of course, he does. He likes them a lot. Bergman, Fellini, Truffaut. . . sure. And Hitchcock too. "They're truth," he adds, "as Godard says, 'twenty-four times a second.'" Truth of a sort, he's committed to that.

He's heard of a critic, Pauline Kael? Who hasn't? he says. *Kiss Kiss Bang Bang*, he knows that book? Surprised again, he says he does (Kael really despises what's genteel, and it crosses his mind she wouldn't like him, which strikes him as odd. . . he's not genteel—at least, he doesn't think he is). Rose knows he's wandered off again. That's true all over, doesn't he think? Think what? "Duh kissing and banging. . . you agree?"

"Well. . ." he hedges.

"In Hollywood and Taiwan too."

"Really?" he says. He's not surprised.

Well, sort of, she shrugs. "No kisses dere, but lots uh bangs." She asks what Chinese films he's seen.

Coincidence—there's just Joy Bang. Whatever he says, he won't cite that.

So, none at all? Does he know they make a lot of them here? Here in the States? He didn't, no. He thought they made them in Hong Kong. They do—kung fu, that sort of thing. "But udder stuff. . ." Her voice trails off, and Joy Bang's frolicking in his head.

Rose takes a breath and looks away, then turns her shades on him full bore. "When my farder died, nobody cared if litter Lowes Lee was taking it off or leaving it on, and, after I finally needed a bra, I got a chance to be in a film. . . or I could marry duh ginseng dealer who had dis. . . what? You call it 'wen'?" She touches her cheek. "So you can guess." She lets him guess, which brings Joy Bang to life again.

"It wasn't so bad." her face looks blank. "Just jerk-off stuff, know what I mean?" She sees him wince. The shades go on, her lips compress. "If Ming vase break, you sorry, huh?"

"Maybe it only bounces," he says. It's the best he can do, but making a quick adjustment or two, he's thinking that meeting a soft-porn star is better than some of the things he'd feared. . . and not nearly as bad as what's occurred to his shoulder, bike, and teaching job. "So, then. . ." he asks while mulling that over, "you made a lot of movies like that?"

"Dat matter to you?"

119

He tries to shrug. There's nothing to say. He sees a man in a cotton-cord suit who's laboring up the capitol steps, so out of breath he has to stop to wipe his forehead with his hand before slowly climbing the last few feet.

"I made a lot. . . just T & A." Her voice is flat and—unmistakably, he thinks—vaguely accusatory. "But maybe dis comes as news to you, a lot of you white guys really get off just tinking about us Asian chicks. A litter skin is all it takes. . . it's what you'd call a kirrer deal." Then, "Killer," she corrects herself.

"I wouldn't know."

She's staring at him once again, brushing her hair back with her thumb as if about to let him have it. The point is now she's syndicated. . . twenty-four rich old Chinese men subscribe to see that bit of skin. Not white guys, no (they're digging Joy Bang), but Taiwanese bachelors late in the game hung up on dreams of what they've missed. Sex of a sort, but good-girl sex. "Dese old guys want a Ming vase too." So the dutiful daughter talks a lot, she takes a bath, gets dressed, undressed, and goes to bed. But gradually they've asked for more. She'd said okay—"More bang bang den, but not more sex." (Sinking in quicksand, tied to the tracks, a Perils-of-Paw-Ling sort of thing except the danger's not the point. . . it wasn't for Pauline either, he thinks.) "Pay for tickee, see washee's not enough," she says as if to snap him to.

The bum gets up to tighten his belt, then shuffles away, not looking back. Dugan should probably do the same, but it seems she thinks she's got him hooked and it's only a matter of reeling him in, at which point she'll reveal her hand. That's what he supposes. He's curious too as, all matter-of-fact, she's starting to share some business details about sending out episodes once a month in Super-8 first and then 16. He nods. . . he's worked in 16 too.

"Good deal for me, and business is good." (Would peep-show proprietors say the same?) "But soon duh subscribers want even more—like white guys, huh? more bang for duh buck." (Did she say fuck? He's not quite sure.) "So now. . ." She pauses, looking around, seeming to time how long she waits as if knowing he knows it's for effect.

"Now. . .?" Dugan repeats, accepting his cue while pondering Joy Bang's repertoire.

She says the bang bang matters more, which means including more thrills and chills. She's switched to tape instead of film. . . to video, he understands? In the studio maybe, he replies, but not in the field—video's not that portable and mikes at a distance wouldn't work. It's tough, she allows, but there's new stuff out and they're using RF for better sound. . . "radio frequency," she explains as something starts bubbling up in his brain, some sixth sense sounding an alarm (the traffic, he wonders—what has he missed? The statues, the bushes, a plane in the sky?) "The other night. . ." he starts to say.

Two kids in Ray Bans wander by—Lew and Tyrone, he's pretty sure, another odd coincidence. They nudge each other as they sit. Beyond them, by a naval gun from the *casus belli* battleship Maine, a man all in black is up to something, fiddling around with a shoulder bag. (Hold on! squawks Jack, who's reappeared with Dennis and Peter by his side, waving their arms at what's going on.)

"Dat's what I'm trying to tell you, Mike."

He sees it coming like a shell. The man with the bag. . . (He's loading the gun!)

"We'd gotten behind." She's talking fast. "Duh power lot scene we grabbed on duh fly. . ." His left brain's piecing it all together, his right brain's howling to get through. "A couple of minutes was all we needed, but you showed up and after that. . ."

He shakes his head at Lew and Tyrone as she plows on, trying to keep his attention on her while the man by the gun is aiming at them. Dugan instinctively starts to duck, then straightens up and points at him. "Aw, Christ!" he bawls. He feels incensed.

"I was gettin' to dat."

"To Allen Funt?"

Dugan's now gotten to his feet, but she stays put on the bench. "Hector," she says. "He's working for me. But he's. . ." She searches for a word, using whatever she thinks might work. "How do you say? *Irrerevant.*" She struggles but gets it mostly right. "A bodyguard-cameraman who can drive."

"And where've you got his RF mike? Wedged in somewhere between your knees?"

Lew and Tyrone look someplace else.

"I'm tryin' to give. . ."

"You giving, my ass! You're taking, babe! And not just me—these guys, that bum. . . all of us *what*? Just camera fodder?" He glowers at Lew and then Tyrone. "You part of this too? You guys in this filmflam like those two?" They gape at him, but neither moves. He's savoring his wasted puns. "I'd figured drugs. . ."

"Hey," Tyrone says.

Rose takes her shades off, eye to eye. "Just one more scene, that's all I ask. We need it. . . for continuity."

"You must be outta your mind!" he barks, turning his good arm towards the gun and letting his middle finger talk. The granite soldier off-screen left, perched on a column gazing north—in the general direction Sherman took—appears to think he's in on the scene as he nonchalantly cradles his gun. Across the street, in the shade of the trees, a grave bears Henry Timrod's name.

I need not tell the brave survivors

He's not about to fall for her line, watching her as she bolts to her feet while Hector's screwing his eyepiece tighter. Shades now in hand, she's looking pissed—but is it for real? Has he got her in frame? How's it going to look when you see it on-screen?

"Oh, sure," she says. "You bang up my extras, mess wid my shoot, and nearry get me kirred as well. . . an' I'm the one who's outta my mind?" She's in his face, furious now, invoking his stupid gaffe again. "No tickee, no washee! Big fuckin' deal. An' dat phony crap you fed your crass! An unfair fight. . . you innerfered! What bullshit, huh?" She points to Hampton on his horse. "You tink you're like dis big shot here. . . you got the brass, just missin' de balls!"

"Easy, mama," Lew chips in.

"Be quiet, you!"

"Le'ss boogie, man."

"His ass is grass."

They rise and exit from the set. She points to the general on his horse. "Dis fathead here, so what he do?"

Is that a joke? Confucius say? "Birth of a nation," he replies as Rose continues her tirade.

"At. . . Seven Pines? And Manna Sass?" She reads the place names on the plaque.

"Manassas."

"So? Who gives a fuck? It's nuttin to you since you weren't dere, but you know why? You're chickenshit! My farder wasn't chickenshit. Somebody messed around wid me got glound-up lowes hips. . . you know dat? it's itchin' powder. . . dumped into aw his underwear!"

"YOU GET THAT, HECTOR?" Dugan yells.

The sun streams out from under a cloud, and, right on cue, some men appear, suffused in light, on the topmost of the capitol steps—the governor with his wing-tipped aides, including the man in cotton cord who laughs at what the great man says. They stand like goths in double knit beneath the Roman portico.

"CUT!" Dugan yells.

He frames the shot. One of the aides looks down and frowns, but from his chair John Huston grins (Nice work there, Mike, let's all take five). Joy Bang deserves an Oscar.

• • •

Dugan stalks off as if on stilts, but after he's walked a block or so, he remembers how far he's got to go. He's thinking of popping another pill at the moment a red Mustang appears—the one that had tried to run them down, the one that Oona reported she saw blinking its lights for Rose to leave—with Hector the Cameraman at the wheel.

The puzzle's looking nearly complete, except it's still nonsensical. Insatiable Chinese movie buffs browbeating their star into crazy stuff for which she needs a volunteer? He'd wrecked her shoot, which she's trying to save by using him in another scene—that much is plausible in a way but not bloody likely he's telling himself as the Mustang pulls abreast and slows to give her time to placidly say, "You need a rift?" She's stealing his line—though, yes, as a matter of fact he does. Those pills must work like tranquilizers.

After letting her wheedle him into the car, he listens as she elaborates on how she and Hector had studied the rough and, whatever it lacks as *cinéma*, it's got more than enough of *verité* and is simply too good to throw away, so all they need is enough for a bridge, an exit to match his sudden intrusion. He says that sounds too ominous unless he ends up getting the girl (a pretty good line, he tells himself as she smiles and reaches to pat his arm as if to confirm they've made a deal). "I mean it," he says, "no broken bones." She smiles again and nods her head, noting they'd need to start at three. "Or handstands either," he tacks on.

Hector's stayed silent throughout the ride but seems to know where Dugan lives, and, though his irrelevance still seems vague, Dugan thinks he can deal with that—he's poached on other preserves before, and this one seems to be worth the risk. . . which is where things stand when he gets home with plenty of time to sort things out before he resumes his acting career.

Nevertheless, "Are you utterly nuts?" one part of his brain keeps bringing up as he watches the Mustang drive away. She told him she'd panicked the other night because, a couple of months ago, a triad gang had gotten involved—he knew about those Chinese mobs? Not really, he said. "Dey're very bad." They'd moved in like a protection racket and wouldn't put up with any delays. She's desperately sorry he'd gotten hurt, but she's hoping he'll "interfere" again in what's really for her an unfair fight, et cetera, et cetera. What pops unbidden now to mind are the lyrics to a new song out about trucking on when it seems there's "nothin' left to lose,"

feelin' near as faded as my jeans. . .

which is pretty much where he is now.

But even losers need wheels, he thinks, and for riding a bike you need two hands, so he'll have to finagle something else, and, given how few resources he's got, the only place for that sort of fix would have to be The Cosmic Connection—they'd glimpsed its billboard from the train, a head shop/pawn shop/hippie-boutique that's close enough for him to walk.

It's almost noon as he sets out, three hours before he sees her again in her blouse the color of luck, she says. . . except, of course, that's not what she'll wear since continuity's her concern (or so she says, he supposes it is, which means it'll be the ripped-up one from the previous shoot along with the lacy scallop-edged bra, the memory of which has, somehow or other, lodged itself in his libido as if for the purpose of luring him on to what he knows is lunacy (the sex of no-sex—it's insane, like opening up the Sunday Times and spotting amid the grisly news a model in panties regally posed, presiding like Artemis over the fuss) though, blathering on about getting the girl, he'd ill-advisedly agreed and, in any case, the blouse was tan.

But faced with a milelong walk ahead, he lets his pill-soaked brain digress in ways that ignore how her accent improves as soon as she gets whatever she wants or why, being asked, he's agreed to her scheme which might be ascribed entirely to lust if he hadn't surmised from what she'd said that his chances of scoring are virtually nil (a lot of white guys really get off. . .) So his mind wanders off onto other things like back to the color red again, auspicious for her but not for him since he favors a shade of deep blue-green—magnolia leaves, a summer wave, his well-thumbed copy of Wuthering Heights with its cover the hue of Roquefort mold, a tipoff, he's been candidly told, to the sordid condition of his soul, an insight sternly confided to him by a stacked ex-gymnast Theosophist who'd detected his aura one afternoon while making out to "Feelin' Groovy."

"Uh-oh," she'd sighed, "too far from satori."

When, in search of an ectoplasmic boost, he'd changed the record to "Ball and Chain," she—Sunbeam, formerly Cindy Bohm—whose wigwam-friendly hippie name ("an enlightened appliance," he'd agreed) had caused him to say he'd call her that if she'd agree to call him "Whopper," had objected that he was missing the point.

"It's not that easy," she'd explained. "You can't switch karma like. . ."

"Yeah, like what?"

"Like. . . you know." Then her eyes went blank. She was strenuous, supple, even shrewd, though Sunbeam's schooling, such as it was, had mostly been confined to a gym, leaving her in her adult years articulate only in her joints. Which meant when stumped, she acted spaced.

But Dugan had pressed her anyhow. "Like what?" he'd repeated.

She'd frowned as if they were on the brink of something deeper than R.D. Laing. "Like. . . you know. . ."

"What?" he'd said again.

". . . condoms," she'd blurted out at last—her most original observation, that and her inadvertent pun, "I wandered lonely as a crowd," misquoted when Sunbeam reminisced about her road trips with the Dead.

But for all her stunning vacuity, she'd had an Olympic-caliber bod for the sake of which he'd swotted up lines, including a couple from Jerry Garcia, to prove he could tune her frequency in. He'd crib things like "the songs on this record are not so much songs but exercises in tonal control." She'd look at him and answer, "What?" To which he'd replied on one occasion, "There are two kinds of people, normal and simple." Not knowing he'd quoted sacred texts, she'd told him he over-analyzed—unfair considering where they were: locked in a Tila-Tandulaka embrace from the *Kama Sutra*, Chapter 2, keeping time to the humpback-whales' refrain from *Songs of the Amniotic Sea* (in Sunbeam's Yaqui Indian view, sex was an ecological act, but over-analysis wasn't cool). "How can you say that?" he'd demurred, grunting in unison with the whales. "You're into denial," Sunbeam had said, halting her acrobatic thrusts.

"I'm not."

"You *see*?"

Then her kegels resumed, prompting a guttural drawn-out groan and spasms of high-pitched whistles and clicks.

"Stay in me!"

"What?"

"You're losing momentum."

"You hear those humpbacks? Losing their loads."

She said she'd help him work on that. He needed to find his proper place in what she called the "ecoverse," a realm where style-points matter a lot.

"I'm coming anyhow."

"No, not yet." A double tuck.

"Aieeee!" and a throaty chuckle from her.

Though demonstrative in other ways, she'd kept her orgasms to herself, clutching him in a wrestler's hold that sometimes made it hard to breathe but arching her back and sticking her dismount as if Kinsey himself was keeping score—"maintaining her Tantric focus," she said. "I'm not a screamer," she'd explained. "Us Scorpios never are, you know." He'd lamely confessed that was news to him, but Sunbeam admitted she wasn't surprised—for somebody with a PhD, he had some pretty scary gaps which wouldn't be all that easy to fill.

She was full of eclectic twists and turns, though in most respects an open book—as deep as Pat the Bunny, say, though ingenuous in her self-centered way. She braided her hair like a Navajo maiden and dreamed of living in a yurt with birds in Froot-Loop color schemes and musical dwarfs (Hi-Ho! Hi-Ho!). At twelve she'd loved a balance beam and at fourteen a licentious coach whose Humbert Humbert hankerings would get him deported to Bucharest. By twenty she'd mastered all sorts of moves that Dugan had never seen before, and, after they'd gone their separate ways, he'd come to miss that squat strong body.

In retrospect, he'd done his best, but in the end it hadn't worked out. He'd tried to close his psychic gaps, but even a gauzy Indian shirt (with round red beads that buttoned in front) couldn't offset the crucial flaw she'd diagnosed along the way: he wasn't what she called "polymorphous."

"That's *so* unfair," he'd counterattacked. "I'm as poly as morphoi generally get."

"You're not receptive."

"Yes, I am."

"To what?"

"Let's see. . . to Baba Ram Dass. I was very receptive to him, I thought."

"You weren't at all. You called him a butthead."

"That's right, I did. But I was receptive. True faith's accepting what's untrue."

"That's Castaneda."

"Sure. Him too—all refugees from inner space. Like whattya call it? Eckankar."

He used a term he'd learned from her, but saw at once he'd made a mistake, reminding her of a recent fiasco. She'd been told by a Rosicrucian friend that all felines are "psychotropic," a fact well known to most adepts engaged in frequent spirit travel.

"Cats store up energy in their fur and use it whenever their chi gets low. Like the ancient Egyptians, see what I mean?" No, he'd said, but she'd just shrugged, "You can see what this means for Eckankar." He couldn't, though. She'd have to explain. "Well, duh! They've learned that smoking the fur. . ." *Cat* fur? he'd asked. They're *shaving* their cats? "Don't get so clinical," he'd been told. "Most get so high they coast back home. It's really effective is what I hear."

She'd invited him to try some out, and, when he refused, had produced such a stench that Miz Dee had pounded on his door, and Sunbeam, as "a token of love," had presented her with a ankh-shaped pull made by a friend in pottery class. Mistaking it for a crucifix, Miz Dee had hung it on her wall next to the "high church" Sacred Heart that Dunkie had cross-stitched by mistake ten years ago at summer camp, producing what Danny had aptly described as "Sonny Bono with a tumor." Eventually, Sunbeam had to concede "the cat fur thing" had been a hoax, fooling a lot of "receptive adepts."

But having met Danny, she thought he was cool because, she said, "He goes with the flow. You're too attached. Things seem to matter a lot to you." Things? Dugan had scoffed indignantly, pointing to all her occult gear, which triggered a snit in which she blanked. "But I'm tuned in," was all she'd say, and the following week she'd learned his sign—his driver's license gave it away, and Sunbeam couldn't wait to pounce. "You Sadges are fire and very intense. Not subtle," she said, "but entertaining." (What, Sunbeam too? First Glubber, now her!) Bad luck that she's a Scorpio— she hoped his sub-sign was ascending. What's that? he'd asked. But she got cagey. Astrology is a complex art. He needed a reading right away.

She had an acquaintance, Moondog II, who was doing accounts for Merrill Lynch, casting their clients' horoscopes. She thought he'd probably do her a freebie.

"You know," she told him late one night, "this reading could mean a lot to you." Naked except for amber beads, she'd flattened her jugs across his chest so he could feel the tom-toms beating. "Right on," he'd grooved. He'd caught her drift. If Wooloo the Thunder God was pissed, they'd have to do what Wooloo said. The day and minute that he was born? December seventh—write that down. One-twenty-three in the afternoon. Nineteen forty-one, okay?

"Oh, WOW!" She'd flipped when she got back. "This is extremely heavy shit!" He'd feigned indifference, but Sunbeam freaked. "Moondog checked it over and over. He's never cast a chart like this!" Did he think he was ready? Ready for what? "To learn that you're. . . a TRIPLE SADGE!"

It wasn't safe. He might combust. But at least their future together was clear since "Sadges and Scorpios just can't mix." By the end of the week, she'd changed her name to Cindy Moonbeam Bird-in-Hand and packed her Vedic incense burner. Miz Dibble was glad to see her go. He got his hot water running again, and Moondog got what he was after—assuming that's who she'd showed up with at Baba Ram Dass's squat 'n' chant on his second attempt to enlighten the town, the pockmarked guy with matted hair escorting a client whose mid-calf socks, exposed while assuming a cross-legged pose, resembled long tubes of PCV out of the window of Flushed With Pride. Ram Dass kept nodding at them and smiling as if his investments were doing well—but still a butthead, Dugan thought.

Since Sunbeam left, his wardrobe has changed. His Indian shirt's not worn much now, its berry-like buttons dangling untouched. He'd bought it at The Cosmic Connection—"The Cosmic Rip-Off!" Sunbeam had sneered after buying a poster by Peter Max and finding a sales tax added on. "Wouldn't you know?" she'd complained in a huff. "Establishment lackeys, Moondog says!" an indictment with somber overtones for a hireling employed by CSU, especially if his radical chops were as shaky as Dugan's appeared to be. For Sunbeam, soon to be Bird-in-Hand, the Sixties were such a mind-blowing trip that she couldn't osmose why his bags weren't packed. Metaphorically speaking, she'd said in a fret, "It's like you don't mind missing the boat." He'd pondered a bit before his riposte, "Most of the boats I might have caught are now at the bottom of the sea."

That had stopped her in her Birkenstocks, though Dugan was merely quoting Man Ray—or maybe Max Ernst (he wasn't sure which). She'd looked so deflated he'd hurried to add, attempting to make some verbal amends, "But maybe I'm manic depressive, okay?"

"Most Sadges are," was her reply, adopting a contemplative look. "Bad acid does that too," she'd said, suggesting a couple of useful rules that nearly every deadhead knew: trip with your friends, don't sleep with the drummer, and never buy tie-dyes at a place where tourists in Weejun moccasins go—which brought her back to The Cosmic Connection. She'd approached the Weather Underground to get it onto their target list, but she'd written again to take it off after she'd gotten some incense free on Jonathan Livingston Seagull Day—though, as she said, that was just a reprieve that didn't apply to everyone. "Stay away from that place," was her advice, and except for the shirt and a couple of books imbued with a scent of sandalwood, he pretty much had until making a couple of impulse buys like a Hare Krishna starter kit he'd bought as a birthday joke for Danny and a single off-beat 33 whose album cover had caught his eye, not only because of the name of the group,

7he Sufi Choir

printed in pseudo-*Rubáiyát* script, but because of a curious photograph that showed, in a caftan by the sea, surrounded by airheads perched on rocks, a guy he'd known in graduate school—Brad Tittlewhit, reborn out west as "Aga Jamshyd Abdullah Khan." He looked like Jesus wearing a lei with slippers made out of banana peels. "Carmel is blessed," the liner notes said, "by this sign of a spiritual revolution." The album bespoke a *vita nuova*, and Dugan had studied it for a clue. Whatever it meant, he told himself, the Sixties parade had passed him by.

But all that's history too by now for Dugan himself has been remade. Like Jamshyd formerly-known-as-Brad, he's shedding his former job and self while Cindy Moonbeam Bird-in-Hand shacks up with Bernie Levinson (alias Moondog, brokers' friend), all of them reinventing themselves like actors trying out new roles. So give it a shot, he tells himself. It's Dugan the Psychically Dispossessed who's arriving on foot at The Cosmic Connection.

● ● ●

The sign up top shows a sun and moon reeling through ribbons of clouds and stars. A pungent potpourri seeps outside, which, past the threshold, grows intense, layers of drug-dog-baffling smells like cardamom spiked with Ty-D-Bol, garlic, anise, and curry powder. Dugan steps into a barn-like room full of flower-power bric-a-brac.

"Peace!" hails a voice from inside the gloom.

"Hallelujah, brother! Wave the snails."

"Hey, man! Don' gimme no right-wing jive!" The accent's black, the voice is Mick's—the sometime rock-star hippie chief.

"You work here too?"

"I own it, doc." He peers past Dugan towards the door. "S'cuse me a minute. . . WAIT UP, DUDE!" He collars a guy in baggy fatigues. "Empty 'em out." The freak complies with a zombie-like move, coughing up several one-point-fives. Mick pulls the packets over the counter, then picks out one and pushes it back. "Have a good trip," he tells the guy, who nods and slouches out the door.

"My old man's notion of revolution," he says to Dugan, shaking his head. "They wanna drop out, we're gonna cash in." He sighs and leans on the big glass case, referring apparently to himself. "Merchant hippie still going to school. . . a hassle, man. What happened to you? Oh, yeah, you said you interfered. You dropping out or turning on?"

"Look, Lonnie," he asks, "you want a bike?"

"What sorta bike?"

"A Honda."

"Yeah?"

"A one twenty-five."

"That's a motorized skateboard, not a bike."

"I'm sellin' cheap."

Alias Mick squints down at some bongs above a row of plastic nargilas. "It's busted up?"

"Not really," he says. "A broken reflector. Runs okay." That's mostly true. He hopes it is.

"Hmmm," Mick considers. "How 'bout a trade?"

He's got an old Pontiac parked out back—purple and derelict, built like a tank, with visor and portholes like a Brinks, left by a guy whose number came up—expense-paid trip to Vietnam. Still ran last time he cranked it up.

"Sounds promising," Dugan says with what starts out to be a shrug. "So take a look." He'll do the same, wherever it is.

The Pontiac's moored like an ironclad. After kicking its tires and lifting the hood, they drive it over to see the bike and, finding less to kick or lift, agree right off to trade straight up. Dugan negotiates one detail, peeling his parking permit off and sticking it onto the car's rear bumper. At that point, noting it looks like rain, he warns Mick that the bike might skid, especially since its front wheel's bent. Also, the headlight needs replacing. No sweat, says Mick, but Dugan should know that one of the Pontiac's wipers is shot. The driver's side. What else? That's it, aside from taking up too much space. Okay, they're cool. Load up the Honda, drop it off, and Dugan can haul his wagon away.

That's what they do. Now Dugan's got wheels. But in less than a mile the downpour begins, and, steering from shotgun where he can see, he peers out through a streaming cascade—better than from the driver's side which looks like a post-sign-off TV. For nearly a block, he's driving half-blind, but then decides he'd better pull over. . . letting a Corvette slide on by, honking and swerving (Barbie rules!)

Those blondes again—but never mind, it can't be part of Rose's game. What matters is that his shoulder aches. . . bilateral stress, or maybe the rain. No sweat. He stops to gobble a pill, then pushes the seat-recliner knob. The lever he's pushed snaps off in his hand. That's okay too, he tells himself. He stows it in the glove compartment, surveying things from the starboard side. Let's see, he thinks. There's Danny's apartment, not far off, but he reckons he ought to wait this out. A little zazen will be good for the nerves. BE HERE NOW. He's here, it's now. Look out again—what's there of note? Two dumpsters plus a pile of brush, a plastic Big Wheel missing a wheel. He tries the radio, gets the news, hears "thunderstorms, with occasional floods," gets country, rock, and R & B, then, after some static, turns it off.

In twenty minutes it hasn't eased up and satori's no closer than before. *So improvise*, his right brain exhorts. With what? His feet. Still sitting in shotgun where he can see, he probes for the pedal with his foot, and, finding he's able to start it up, eases the Pontiac out from the curb— steering it deftly with one arm and letting it coast whenever he can. Everything's easy but the brake, but without any other traffic in sight, that's not a problem at the start. The problem arises picking up speed in a long downhill that ends up. . . where? In a steadily spreading muddy brown sheet, sprung out of nowhere in the dip. Just hubcap depth, he tells himself as, deciding to take the flood head-on, he hits it like a log off a flume. The Pontiac plunges, ramps, and stalls. He drifts for a while before subsiding.

The main point now's to keep his cool. Thunder and lightning, torrents of rain. Inside the car, it's almost snug. Outside, the water obstructs his view. No radio, right? Electrocution. Merton was murdered in his tub. Same with the horn but give it a try. . . we're only talking a few volts here. He hammers the chief's head on the wheel—a couple of clicks, and, after a pause, some belches bubbling up from the hood. So whatta we do? Try blinking the lights. But they're submerged. No problem. Damn! They've shorted out too. Cigarette lighter, ashtray. . . check! Hood latch, hand brake, blinkers, vents. . . no, not the vents, a big mistake!—that's major seepage on his shoes. Ignition's gone. The window? Stuck, but shotgun's still above the flood. Signal to dry land? No one there. Think Aga Jamshyd Abdullah Khan. Om, om. Okay, it's rising fast. He'll force the door and equalize. . . just wait for water to fill the car, then swim for shore. Good thinking. Right. It's almost touching the steering wheel.

He exits from the passenger side and flails in a sort of one-armed crawl until he feels his feet touch ground, wading/half-swimming to a yard where he's met and sniffed by a curious dog who follows him as he trudges off to notify Wild Rooster Gulf.

"Go home!" he yells. The dog turns back. When he's half-way there, the rain slacks off.

Rolly Dehon dispatches a truck without much comment or surmise, sending Dugan with Shorty in the cab. When they get to the Pontiac, there's a crowd—women conferring with folded arms, kids in shorts, and several dogs, including the one he'd met before who barks at Shorty's clacking boots.

A man in waders has taken charge. "Damnedest thing. Juss plowed right in. The guy in shotgun cut 'n run." He lowers his voice behind his hand, shooting a glance at the women and kids. "Driver's still down there."

"No, he ain't."

They stare at Shorty. How's *he* know? If the driver's not down there, where'd he go?

"Ask *him*," says Shorty, leaning down, not indicating who he means.

They have a hunch, though—jutting their chins at the guy resembling a squeegee mop. One witness swears she saw two men, or maybe a woman. . . she breaks off. A mother sends her kids inside, and somebody mutters "Chappaquiddick." It's about to turn ugly, Dugan notes, as Shorty hurries the tow in place and radios that he's on his way, tugging the Pontiac out of the drink. The man in waders shakes his head as he cranes to look in the soggy back seat.

"Nope," he says with a nasal twang.

The car keeps draining as they go. Back at the station, Rolly shrugs. He'll do his best to vacuum it out. "A'course," he drawls, "I guess you know, this model ain't sub-mersible." They ask him if he needs a ride, but Dugan says a friend's nearby.

The rain's long gone when Dugan arrives, his wet boots thudding on Danny's porch. Hearing some scurrying sounds inside—a muffled voice, an expletive—he wonders what he's caught them at. . . a sudden storm, the power out, the two of them making bee-lines home (Hi, Hon! Bip-bam, some one-thirty woo.) He waits for Danny's sheepish face, but it's Caitlin instead who opens the door.

"M-M-Mike!" she says, in a flustered way.

"I wanted you guys to see my car."

"Y-Your car?"

"But it sank." He notes her collar's buttoned up wrong with the topmost button out on its own. "I really came by to share the news. I'm blowin' this joint. I'm outta here."

"W-W-What? W-When?"

She glances behind her, just a glimpse, but then he looks for what she's seen and, over her shoulder, through the pane, he catches a snatch of yellow and blue—an anorak he's seen before, furtively gliding towards the street. Ed Doggett, he thinks, not taking it in (the implication's on her face, the sinkhole into which they've slid. . . sofa, sideboard, table, chair, with Dugan and Caitlin in their wake). She doesn't try to look away.

"S-S-Sorry, M-Mike." She lifts her hand as if to help.

Clearing his voice, at last he says, "For Chrissake—*him*?" But neither moves. "Tell Danny. . ." he adds. "I wanted to see him. I need somebody to check my mail."

She nods okay. He turns his head. Branches and debris litter their porch as if they didn't own a broom.

"M-M-Mike."

He stops but doesn't look.

"I luh-luh-luh. . ." Still working her mouth, unable to speak, she waits for Dugan to relent. He's pulling her towards him with one hand when, sucking a sharp intake of breath, she's able to finish without a stammer. ". . . loved your letter, you know that."

That's just another complication. He'd have held her longer if he could, but she utters a hiss and slides away.

• • •

At 3:13, they're underway with Rose still looking lucky in red and Hector squared off behind the wheel with his features, like the Mustang's grill, set in a vaguely disgruntled grimace produced in part by a keloidal scar zigzagging through his weedy moustache and changing color according to mood like a pinkish chameleon in the bush. In other respects, he's like Desi Arnez, a perception that Dugan keeps to himself as he offers a box of Cheez-Its around.

"For luck, hey, Hector? Give us a smile." He gets a Sonny Liston stare. "C'mon, then, Rose!" He gives her a nudge and shakes the box. She briefly trains her shades on him as if to look him back into line, then shakes her head and turns away. "Old Hollywood custom," Dugan persists, annoyed by her pretentiousness (whatever they're up to, Shakespeare it's not), "like break-a-leg. . . or whatever expendable body part. I guess you've noticed that these pants are. . ."

"Do me a favor!"

"Favor? Sure."

"I'm trying to think."

Well. . . that makes sense. He'll do the same." (You get on somebody's boat, he thinks, and all of a sudden she's Missus Queeg.) He cranks his window halfway down and chucks the Cheez-Its into the air.

"*Chinga tu madre!*" Hector freaks.

"Do us a favor," Dugan begins, then looks and sees the speed-trap cops with Cheez-Its bouncing off their hood, pulling out now into the road. Hector's scar's a livid zed (the mark of Zorro comes alive!) No siren, but the cops catch up until they're riding the Mustang's bumper. More verbiage from Hector, clearly obscene, as Rose and Hector altercate and Hector adopts a Driver's Ed air, adjusting his mirror to watch the cops in their teasingly cat-and-mouse pursuit.

Their game continues for more than a mile before the cruiser pulls abreast, then drops back only a yard or two as Dugan discovers the cop he can see resembles the Campus Security guy who'd run afoul of Ismene von Himmel (another hired extra? surely not, but nothing's impossible anymore). Musing on this coincidence, he imagines what the cops must see—three multi-ethnic litterbugs on a Miami-New York run with Florida tags the giveaway (Dugan had noticed them getting in) while putting down all authority with various acts of provocation, like tossing Cheez-Its at the law. The cop keeps scowling, then yells out, addressing him like a pig to a truffle.

"Hey, freedom rider! You in back!"

Dugan politely cocks his head.

"Y'know what that guy Harpo got?"

With his squinty-eyed made-in-Bombingham look, the cop seems primed to have some fun. He and his partner argue a point before he cups his hands again. "Arlo," he bawls, correcting himself. "Fuh lidderin'. . . you know whut he got?"

Dugan gingerly lifts his sling as if explaining the Cheez-Its box. "Slipped out of my hand," he tries to mime.

The cop ignores his explanation. "So what you think he *oughta* get?" He flashes a quick cold-blooded smile, inviting the perp to dig his grave.

But Dugan's now gotten up to speed. Guffawing as if he's in on the joke, he whoops with a nasal redneck twang, "That longhaired Yankee S.O.B.? Shore hope they whup his hippie ass! Don' git 'im no Cheez-Its, that's fer shore."

The cop in shotgun, looking surprised, turns away, then back again. "You goddamn right" is all he says. He thinks for a minute before he adds as if to a kinsman skirting the law, "So where you from then?"

"From rite cheer. . . from Cumbria High."

"Oh, yeah? Whut year you graduate?"

"Fifty-eight it woulda been. . . except fo' going overseas."

"That right?" says Shotgun. "Sixty-one, an' bin with the force here evah since. Listen here, hoss, I tell yew whut, yew keep those tostada chips to yo'seff. . . an' tell that bandito ahind the wheel I'm juss itchin' to dee-port spics like him."

"He don't speak English," cousin Mike yells. "Yew can't tell folks whut they don' know." His accent's suddenly gotten so thick the cop has trouble comprehending. "He's drivin' this lady from Veet Nhai-um."

"I hear you, friend." He pauses, then adds, "Damm wetbacks think they own this place."

A nod.

"Damn rite."

"You betcha, Clyde!"

After the cops confer with each other, the cruiser abruptly shoots ahead with Hector reminding them where to go. He mutters until they're out of sight, ignoring Dugan's "Sorry, folks." Rose looks at him, expressionless.

No conversation for a while until they're ten miles out of town, reaching an unpaved country road and bumping along as far as it goes before turning onto a high-crowned track that leads to a ROAD ENDS barrier, half-hidden behind some waste high weeds. Hector stops to move it aside, then gets back in and idles the engine. Rose tells him something terse and low, following which he puts it in gear and eases around a bulldozed mound, continuing at a snail's-pace speed. Somebody's scouted this location, but Dugan's not asking for the plan—he doesn't even try to guess as he shifts his thoughts to flash-back mode, going back over the last two hours. . . the awful look on Caitlin's face.

Leaving her standing on the porch, he'd hustled back to get his car and found it perched on Rolly's rack, still dripping ignominiously. They'd promised to have it ready to go as soon as the Mets and Braves were done. No sweat, he'd said, and walked on home. But things were tense at the Dibbledome, where the Dee Ell See had run into snags that kept diverting it from its theme of "Living the Dixiecratic Dream."

He's asked Miz Dee about those initials. We're Daughters of the Lost Cause," she'd said—though Opal Tubbs, deaf as a turnip, spoke up at every meeting, it seems, claiming "Lost Chord" was part of its name when it had been founded decades ago (an assertion she'd try to corroborate by trilling in an off-key voice, "Seated one day at the organ, I was weary and ill at ease. . ."), then proceeding to disrupt members' remarks with Tourette-like non-sequiturs ("Somebody in Gaffney found it, I hear!") Otherwise, so far as he knew, at meetings they mostly chatted and sipped, but because, theirs was the Vernon K. Ratliff Chapter and this would have been his centennial year, today would be a special occasion with a Bircherite dentist scheduled to speak on Senator Sternbolt's storied career and why, in general, the time had come to reconsider the Eighth Amendment.

Dugan had waited in the hall until he could catch Miz Dibble's attention. As soon as committee reports were done, he'd tried to confide his painful decision to relocate in Chantry Mount. It hadn't been easy, he'd maintained—she'd always treated him like. . . a friend. Gordo was almost certain to call about fulfilling the rest of his lease.

"I've talked to Doctor Gordon," she sniffed, apparently taking his news in stride.

She'd been fully apprised of Young Doctor Dough ("a vociferous reader, I've been told") who'd be needing a quiet place to stay while editing William Gilmore Simms. "One of our favorite authors," she'd smiled before getting back to the matter at hand, which was Dugan's departure P.D.Q. Pursuant to that, since learning the news, she'd called to get the meter read, and a man from Southern Bell had come. Dugan had wanted to know for what, but to check the line was all she knew, and it wasn't for Dugan to worry about. Though he'd told her he wasn't posthumous yet, she'd quickly moved on to something else—the pepper jelly in the fridge ("Bottom shelf right!" she'd suddenly barked). He hoped that Dunkie. . . ("Fritos too! They're there in back—behind a package of stone-ground grits. No, in the closet—not the fridge!") Dunkie would always. . . ("Never mind!") She'd turned to look him in the eye. Her daughter's dance card, Miz Dee said, had filled up in the past few days. He got the message. That was that. He hoped the lecture went off well ("the cruel and unusual part").

She'd shrugged and left, and he was through except for swiping the Cheez-Its box. Then, just before he reached the door, Rikki-Tikki-Dinkie struck, a leprous missile aimed at his leg, skimming dementedly over the floor. Revenge is mine! the animal snarled as, through both layers of khakis and socks, Dugan could feel its teeth sink in. He kicked, and the dog went airborne again in a slow limp arc towards the twittering dames.

"HAPPY LANDING, YOU MANGEY MUTTFUCKER!" he yelled, pleased to have found the perfect *mot juste*.

"He certainly is," chirped Opal Tubbs, supposing he meant Earl Warren.

• • •

They slalom through scraggly stands of pines, schussing across thick carpets of straw to a tangle of kudzu-festooned scrub that's clearly where the Mustang stops. Rose lifts her shades to study the scene while Hector, with the engine off, taps cha-cha-cha on the steering wheel and gives a little shake of his head. Dugan deduces it's not the place, or, if it is, it's not what she wants. Hector says something with a shrug, eliciting a cluck from Rose, another shrug and an irate retort. Then Hector gets out to study the scrub and, yanking a rope of kudzu loose while giving a barely perceptible nod, returns like a wind-up doll to the car. Though seemingly pissed by what she sees, Rose indicates that they've arrived.

As Dugan gets out, she leans back in and, deftly removing the top she'd worn, discloses that magical bra again—twin smudges and light Mazola skin pent up within its lacy nets—before she dons the ripped-up blouse and turns towards Dugan, buttoning still (continuity after all, he sees, when he'd supposed it was only a con). He points with his left hand at the sling.

"But what about. . .?"

"What? Voice-over," she says, unzipping her jeans and sliding them down (wearing white panties, Dugan observes—no match there either, careless details). "Don't worry about it," she declares, shaking a skirt and twisting it on as if wholly on top of his concerns.

Hector smirks. Rose shuts the door, bumping it deftly with her hip. Hector, who'll set up somewhere else—as Dugan surmises, no one says— cranks the car and is driving away before she's tossed her shades back in. She purses her lips but lets it go, looking at Dugan appraisingly. He hears a gnat whine near his ear.

"Your pants are ripped."

He glances down. "Four-legged assassin. Fought him off."

He feels no need to elaborate, patting the pills he knows he'll need as Rose pulls out her pad again—as diligent, he tells himself, as that child in bangs he thinks he knew collating her lists of undies and socks. This is what's running through his mind, not questions about what happens next. Think zazen, right? No reason to stress. A ping-pong ball on the ocean of life.

Peering about, he catches a glint buried amid the tangles of kudzu. A closer look, and they're tracks, of course. He should have guessed, but what does it matter?—he's past all prudence anyhow and has got the pills to see him through, the first of which he swallows now. The sun is white in a cloudless sky. A one-note bird keeps repeating itself with urgent insistence overhead. Da da da da da da da.

Rose bows her head, consulting her watch as if checking the gaskets prior to launch. Then, hearing the tracks begin to hum and grabbing his arm with a quizzical smile, she leads him waist-deep through the vines. They're bumping together, nudging thighs as he wrenches his foot from a kudzu snare. Glancing up, she drops his arm, and, brushing her hair back with a thumb, gestures down with the flat of her hand. They crouch and wait.

In seconds, there's a swelling din—a rasping like a grinding-wheel and a clatter like barbells hitting the floor, a change of key as it slows for a curve, and suddenly looming, bearing down, like a ravenous dragon the train appears, glaring before it grumbles past in search of a pathway through the scrub. Dugan discovers he's short of breath, but no sooner has he breathed in deep than Rose is giving him a shove. As he bends, she nods and rises up like a mermaid from a kudzu wave—a movement he tries to duplicate, though he's more like a drowning sailor at sea clutching whatever he can grab.

To his surprise he gets there first as, nabbing a ladder with his hand and swinging as if on monkey bars, he struggles for footholds, hanging on. Then, steadied by Rose two rungs below, her breasts a clamp behind his knees, he finds his balance and starts to climb, feeling the sort of manic elation he's heard ascribed to adrenalin highs. It doesn't last long. Once he's up top, he discovers the metal's hot as a stove, so hot he's trying to squat on his heels when the whole train gives a headlong lurch, sending him skittering like a puck flung slap-shot towards the boxcar's edge. When he brakes in mid-skitter by snagging his sling, his brain lights up at the bloodcurdling howl that he understands is coming from him.

Rose clutches his foot and reels him in as the train starts gathering speed again. Pain prompts a stark lucidity when a second pill pops out of his shirt and rolls to within an inch of his head. He snuffles it up and settles in, his forehead pressed against her knee. As soon as a pleasant numbness sets in, he lifts his head to look around—and, whattaya know, the dancing pig, a multi-limbed Shiva during the day devoid of his nightly neon twitch. They're slowing gradually to a stop, then backing, reversing, backing again as if there's an argument in the cab ("So, okay, smartass! Know so much! Let's see if Savannah's back that way!") He's trolling for landmarks when he spies a 7-Eleven slipping by. Same one? Not sure. It's strange terrain. They change direction several times more. Each time, he tries to stay down low, until—surreal coincidence—they've stopped somewhere in the middle of town, and (doo-dee-DOO-dah) TWILIGHT ZONE! There's Gordo's Buick where it had been, with Gordo back behind the wheel and Meg of the Magical Honkers too. And what he sees, or thinks he sees—maybe they're not in the town anymore—is Meg in the midst of an artful ploy, pumping old Gordo for all he's worth on something other than Southern lit. Not really. No. Must be the pill. But Gordo appears to be singing now, rolling his head from side to side as Meg instinctively glances up, spots Dugan and points as Dugan stares back, defiant as a treed iguana.

The signal winks. The train starts up, and Gordo and Meg grow smaller and smaller until they vanish from his brain along with a number of other things.

• • •

How much coincidence can you take? This question's troubling Dugan's mind, though, given the spirit of the times, synchronicity almost seems routine. What's typical of such mental tricks (he's getting receptive, as Sunbeam would say) is meeting the same thing coming and going. . . and sometimes both can happen at once. Jung said as much, as he recalls— he's not sure where. The collective unconscious gets so roiled that personal flukes seem commonplace, so you're hardly surprised to discover you're cast in somebody else's melodrama ("The strawberry birthmark! Mother McCree! My long lost. . ." Ahhh, we've been through that!), and, just when you think you're playing the prince, you learn you're the footman after all as Eliot himself had pointed out ("because I do not hope to turn. . .") though he's off the staircase Dugan's now on, admittedly loopy from his pill and thinking he's glimpsed his destiny, which looks a lot like Barnum's sign (THIS WAY TO THE EGRESS, ladies and gents!), and, as always, it lies straight ahead.

They've rumbled on while he ruminates, but the moment the kudzu reappears, he loses his bearings as before. A sterile landscape's scrolling past, a couple of shacks on cement blocks, and then, beyond a baronial gate, three golfers on an emerald green, some faux chateaus, designer trees, and, parked in a driveway. . . there's the Jag! The bastard's homestead, can it be? Oh, yes, for all things flow together just as the cabbala claims: a sports car, palm tree, phony facade ("Crimson Slug by Dead Palmetto"). It's Glubberama in The Dunes, and on a golf course (nature embalmed!—the perfect setting, Dugan perceives, for the Digger O'Dell of literature).

But palm trees yield to sand once more, and Dugan's attention turns to Rose. He studies the prospect she presents, the slender neck and upswept hair, pinned loosely up with a cheap barrette (wasn't it down the other night?) The curve of her lissome back and ass (taut as a teaspoon, he observes), her lean long-stretched-out sprinter's calf—no wonder they pay to watch her bathe (and, if her twaddle's to be believed, they'll be paying to watch *him* on a train?)

His pill-addled mind is thinking this through when, like a slowly ascending balloon, a head drifts up between two cars. ("Glubber," he mutters, "has boarded the train!") The head looks back. Not Glubber, no— a Warren Oates lookalike glaring at them. A brakeman, maybe (or railroad dick dispatched by Blunt from who knows where?), waving a stick and starting to crawl towards where the two of them are sprawled.

"OFF!" Rose snaps as if it's for real, pushing him towards the boxcar's rim where, finding the ladder, he starts to descend. She's right behind him, hovering, and so's the brakeman with his club, raising it with a menacing scowl. The club comes down. It misses her head, but Dugan sees it coming again, apparently aiming at his hand. He frantically gropes with his toe for a rung, finds it, and, as the brakeman swings, snatches his hand and body away, plummeting backwards from the train. He hears a yell and, in mid-air, looks back to watch her nose-dive too (instructions for Hector from her pad: a TILT and PAN to tight shot of a woman, arms outflung like one of the divers in Riefenstahl, SLOW MOTION of brakeman gazing down, a russet boxcar, swatch of sky, train rocketing quickly out of frame, then CUT to fall-guy hitting the ground after twisting adroitly in mid-air—one step, two, then three-four-five in rapid succession, racing to leave the pain behind).

He stumbles and falls, the pain shoots past. Then, turning, it's headed back his way, picking up speed alarmingly. He desperately fumbles for a pill, forgetting he's already swallowed two.

"What are you up to?" She's annoyed.

"Acting," he says as the pain thunders past, leaving him for the moment unscathed. He remembers what happened to the pill, reflecting it wasn't that long ago and maybe. . . relief! it's all in his mind, lapping his ankles, rising fast (soon, some soothing voice declares, he'll close his eyes and go to sleep).

"*No! Get up quick!*" Rose Lee's now urgently tugging his hand.

(But what's the hurry? Simmer down.) He's drifting into a pastel zone.

"Come ON!" she yells. They've made a mistake.

(It's okay. Look, he'll do the crawl. . . the backstroke. . . whoa!)

They're off again. He sees the pain—it's like a crazed bull looming ahead, just waiting for him to try to run (that napalmed girl in Vietnam, sprinting a step ahead of her scream. . . she ran flatfooted—not Chi Cheng, who's loping beside him, turning her head, but what's she saying and why's he here?) A fence of some sort. (What's she got? A prop from nowhere cutting the wire.)

"Now you!" she barks as she's squeezing through.

He gives it a try but catches his sling (one pill too many's a problem here). She turns back towards him, ripping it loose. Wherever they've landed's not in the script—or maybe the plan's to feign alarm. He sees a familiar hedge ahead, and "steeplechase" leaps into his brain. They've blundered onto the Springdale track! There ought to be stables over there, and jumps and rails, and over that hill. . .

A sudden whinnying makes him turn, expecting to hear a thudding of hooves. Instead, its concussion knocks him flat. A rain of dirt, a walloping boom. (The horses are blowing up! he groans—and highly regrettable, he reflects.) But there's only a crater and swirling smoke. No body parts? He examines the hole. (What sort of delirium is he in?) Another roar. It's overhead. A helicopter wheeling around, looking for something. . . maybe for them.

Rose seems completely unnerved now. Another whine and a second big burst that's farther off, but just as loud. He's baffled by this turn of events—and yet, he's weirdly focused too, with one thought uppermost in his mind:

Run, run, as fast as you can. . .!

But Rose now seems more resolute. She's dragging him with her towards a shack that stands alone atop the hill. His instincts buzz. "No, no! Not there!" She slips and falls. The shack is blown to smithereens (Hector is staging Armageddon!) A thunderous growl erupts to the side, behind a stand of bushes and pines. "*This way!*" he pants as a long-barreled snout slides menacingly into view, beginning to turn in their direction. "BAAAACK!" he bawls, reversing field as it swivels its turret towards his voice, apparently bent on sniffing them out. A second snout, with obstreperous pique, is starting to rip the hedges apart.

Hearing a lunatic grinding of gears, he stumbles backwards, grabs her hand and starts a galloping zigzag race. One of the panzers is gaining fast as they approach a head-high ditch that, like an incision, gashes the field. They leap down into it, land in a creek, and splash along its sandy track. A third tank's battering through the trees, unable to trace them from above as they stumble along to the shallower end and exit the gully spattered with mud.

While staggering up another hill, they turn for a moment, catching their breath, and see their pursuers stalled below like thwarted rhinos shaking their heads, staring with one eye, then the other. Higher and higher. Pebbles and shale with streaks of erosion, clumps of grass, scrub oak and pine. For a moment it seems they're in the clear (you can't catch me. . .

I'm the gingerbread man!)

But Rose, ahead of him, comes to a stop as Dugan half-turns to follow her gaze. The tree line seems to be moving piecemeal like extras cast as Birnam Wood, shouting odd slogans as they go.

"Vee See! Vee See!" some smilax yells.

"Lai day! Dung lai!" a creeper adds, raising itself on camouflaged legs.

A shrub that duck-walks towards them says, *"Ong manh joy kong. Chow ong! Chow ong!"*

A crackle of static intervenes before the smilax calmly adds, "Roger, Lobo. . . that's affirm—my men have captured two Vee See."

The shrub's edged closer, bristling with twigs. "DISARM!" it snarls. More bushes rush up. "Interrogate!" His sling comes in for special attention.

"Talk, motherfucker! Understand? Or I'm tyin' your nuts to one of our choppers and shovin' yo' yaller ass out the door."

"Ain't nearly so yaller as I'da thought."

"All 'causa Calley," grouses the shrub. "I say we scrub this gimpy putz and body-search the mamasan."

"SHUT UP, YOU TWO!" the smilax says. "Rawhide calling Alpha Coyote!"

Static, and then, "Wuz wawk bzzz on?"

"I'm askin' *you.*"

"Bzzz wawk bzzz wawk bzzz personnel repeat unauthorized personnel."

"You tellin' me. . .?"

"That's what bzzzz wawk there're no Vee see in these maneuvers."

Holy chamoly! Dugan blinks, trying to pull himself together. They're at the Fort, a firing range—some sort of war game's underway! Did Rose plan *this*? He doesn't think so. The guys in botanical drag are pissed. "Big trouble, Bub!" the nearest one says. His helmet's swathed in poison oak.

"You war protesters?" the shrub-man coughs, checking his testicles with a smirk. "This part of what they're testin' us on, pacifying this civvi shit?"

"Incredibly life-like."

"Even the tits!"

"Yee-har! Whoo, boy! I'll take that test!"

Rose closes her blouse in no special hurry. She finds her shades. The lens are cracked, but sliding them on, she stares at Shrub-man steadily until, with a salacious leer, he hoists his belt and looks away.

"Mean fuckin' mama-san," he jeers.

After a while, a jeep appears off in the distance, trailing dust. It passes the tanks and bounces up, stopping about ten feet away. A soldier with captain's bars gets out, escorting a man whose steel-rimmed specs define his role like a swagger stick. Psych Op is what they clearly say.

"Mind telling us who you are?" he says, acting as if Rose isn't there.

It's hard to stay focused, but Dugan replies, "According to the Geneva Convention. . ."

"CAN IT, BUB!" A vigorous prod.

"And answer the question! Who the fuck. . ."

"Sergeant," snaps Steel-rims. "By the book. You heard me?" addressing himself to Dugan again.

"Dugan, M.B." Essaying a crisp left-handed salute. "I'd like a word with General Blatz." His brain is starting to function now.

"You what?"

"With Blatz. With General Blatz. It's classified, but he'll confirm."

Derisive looks from all but Rose, who trains her broken shades on him.

"Of course," drawls Steel-Rims caustically.

"Don't make a mistake here," Dugan says.

The captain blurts, "You're pushing your luck."

Dugan nods. "Sir, that's affirm. Tell General Blatz Mike Dugan says. . . that Maxie's knickers are in the cabana."

Steel Rims loses some panache. "You actually think. . .?"

"You tell him that. And remind him that Dugan took the rap."

The Captain leads Steel-Rims off to the side. They hesitate, but it seems clear they won't need blindfolds after all. Dugan adopts a jaunty pose, then turns to the poison oak with a shrug.

"Don't s'pose you got a Salem. . . Bub?"

• • •

Too bad his sex drive's in remission. Aches and exhaustion, too many pills—all Dugan wants is to soak in a tub, assuming Miz Dee left his hot water on after Dinkie went airborne thanks to him (no Dinkie, no washee, she might have decreed, a turn of phrase that makes him wince as they're riding home in the general's car). But disgraced and dismembered though he is, he's had a few triumphs during the day—dropkicking that hellhound for a start, and, even after his pain's returned, savoring Rose's puzzlement. Despite her Dragon Lady pose, she's been both startled and intrigued.

They'd each been questioned separately about their fouling maneuvers up, trespassing in a security zone, and damaging government property (one of the tanks got stuck in the ditch). He'd given a lengthy deposition, explaining their part in a scavenger hunt that was organized by the Legionnaires—they'd thought that tract was private land until the fireworks started up. Nobody had fallen for Dugan's b.s., but that's okay—he was Blatz's boy, and Blatz looked after his off-beat friends (including Maxie, Steel-rims winked). It wasn't so clear what Rose had divulged, but Dugan is certain whatever she'd said was less improbable than the truth. Still, Blatz had taken him aside and said in a brusque avuncular way he hoped his weapon was fully loaded.

"I've got it on automatic, sir," an answer that made the General wheeze with nostalgia for his aide-de-*con* days, tomcatting it in the Philippines.

Steel-rims himself then drove them home, Rose wearing some outsized WAC fatigues dug up by one of the general's guys. "This caper," says Steel-rims when they stop, "I wouldn't repeat it."

"There won't be a sequel," Dugan agrees.

Rose snorts but doesn't elaborate, hugging her bundle of muddy clothes. Dugan can see Steel-rims conclude she's just as inscrutable as he'd thought, a message she'd probably meant to send. . . though maybe she'd meant it for Dugan too ("you round-eye twits are all the same"). But then, of course, he'd saved her hide and has an advantage for the nonce.

The sky's still streaming red and black as Blatz's staff car pulls away and they're starting up his private walk. A Rooster sunset, Dugan reflects, assessing the grotesque price he's paid and how much steeper it could have been ("Ex-CSU Prof in Custody/Part of Subversive Porno Ring"). What portion was scripted? What comes next? And where was Hector all that time? Such questions are churning in his head when Rose impatiently blocks his view, turning her cracked shades full on him just as she had on that oaf at the Fort and asks if he's planning to go inside. His mind had been wandering as they walked, but now they're standing in front of his door.

"Assuming my key still works," he shrugs, knowing that's hardly guaranteed, but playing it cooler than before, thanks to his ego-numbing fatigue and mystifying clout with Blatz—though while he's still fumbling for the key, a sixth sense warns him something's up. . . like Dunkie in the bushes, say, or Dinkie with some rabid pal, or Harlan Tull, the patriot, who'd shared his chauvinistic creed in a letter to yesterday's *Impeder*: "We stole this land from the redskins," he'd raged, "and, no matter what Stokely Carmichael says, we're not giving it up to the [SNCC]!" (though leaving the first of Tull's slurs intact, they'd clearly omitted a second, supplanting it with what they had as if it were a euphemism). With crazies like that on the loose nearby, it was prudent to look about.

"Lose something?" she asks half-mockingly, as if to regain the upper hand.

"My reputation. No great loss. Been whittling it down for three days now." Briefly buoyed by his own wit, he glances into the farther room, then back at her as she stands by the door. "What can I get you—a drink, a phone, or something else? A second-edition *Leaves of Grass*? All three can easily be arranged."

She stops in front of *The Peaceable Kingdom*, rubbing the mud-streaks on her neck. Seizing the moment, he steps in.

"Like the guy in the coffee house," he explains. "Bean sprouts and tofu save the world!" He makes a professorial sound, an ummmm preceding his homily. "Hicks from the sticks imagined that scene—a pacifist Quaker layabout. . . also, it seems, a hopeless sot. It's all about resisting temptation, though Quakers would say it's something else." His spirits are reviving now.

"Isaiah," she says emphatically.

He looks surprised.

"I went to a Cattolick school," she shrugs.

"Real psychodrama," Dugan allows, referring to Hicks and possibly Rose, though her movies don't seem so peaceable.

She turns her head and sniffs the air as he, with an awkward nonchalance, is slyly sidling up to her, recalling the wisecrack Danny had made about a need for ventilation—though all he can smell is his own spoor, a sort of this-is-my-hamper reek mixed in with whiffs of tangerine.

146

He takes a chance and nuzzles her neck, not hoping for much but taking a shot. She leans away as if mildly annoyed in the midst of trying to concentrate.

"They're signing a treaty," he resumes. "One of just two we actually kept with the people we'd planned to civilize. That guy on the left is William Penn, who's advocating peace and love. . . pacification, you might say."

"Dese animals here. . ."

She turns her head, and they're face to face until it's clear he's made his move and she'll endure his pedantry. Just that, no more.

"They look too trusting, I agree. The sheep's a ninny, so's the goat. The leopard now, his brains are fried—he's verging on a breakdown, see? Those eyes. . . dose eyes. . ." He tries again.

She slips her mouth away from his. "A bad idea," is all she says.

"Yeah, yeah." he nods. "They all say that." The boys in the picture both have slings—he's never noticed that before. And the girl at the bottom is tugging on one as if she's using it for a leash. He puts his finger on the girl. "Whatta you s'pose she's doing here—keeping that kid from wandering off?"

"Looks like his sister."

"Are you sure?"

She breaks off with a sidelong look. "Look, Mike," she says, with a hand on his arm. "Dis afternoon you helped me out. You made up for duh udder night, and, I promise you, I'm grateful for dat. But I'm telling you dis for your own good, I'm one of duh cats, Mike, not duh lamb." A sucker-punch, but he's not down. She sees he's coming back for more—so much for keeping it in remission. "But maybe you're after less den I think. Maybe it's only sex you want?"

"I'm willing to do whatever it takes. . ." Shot and counter-shot, up for more. ". . . so I can be a movie star too."

She shifts her angle, changing tone. "So what's duh part you wanna play? You wanna be dis guy kneeling here, duh one taking blankets outta duh box? Big give-away swap, is dat duh deal?" Her accent's rocketing off the rails, but not her targeting, as she knows. "Whatta dey after? All dis land plus slaves plus. . . whatta you call it. . . *nookie* too? How much you tink you oughta get? One tumble or two, a daily double?"

Stung, he takes a half-step back. She follows, reaches for his sling, and asks in a different register, "Treaties are easy, aren't dey, Mike? It's gettin' screwed dat gets so hard. Just ask dese ten litter Indians here." She points and laughs or doesn't laugh. "What udder requests you got for me?"

He's silenced for once. She sizes him up. Then, after a pause, she seems to relent as if it's merely been an act required by the back-and-forth of their scene. "Hard to fly wid a broken wing," she says as if commiserating but still in an acerbic tone. "So now we got dat straightened out. . . anyting else you need help wit?" Fight's over, she thinks, she's won the bout (a mistake they always make with him—no matter how big a palooka he's been, he'll get up off the floor again). He fumbles about for a retort, though aware of how stilted his umbrage sounds.

"You want an accounting, do you, Rose? Of course, you do, you've made that clear. So what has it cost you getting those scenes, anything more than a ripped-up blouse? For me, the price has been pretty steep— an arm, a job, a reputation. What else? Oh, yeah, what sort of requests? Shampooing my hair and tying my shoes. . . both are much harder than you'd think, but those I can handle on my own. What's tricky as hell is wiping my ass. Other than that, it's not so bad." He shrugs and sighs and drops his guard. "Forget it, Rose, I'll tell you what. . . I'm really and truly out of gas." That much is truer than he knows.

She nods as if they've averted a wreck. "So, okay den. You got a tub?"

"A shower too."

"Nope. Want a tub." Retrieving her bundle from the Fort, she tosses it onto his chifferobe. "And maybe a shirt. My skirt's okay, duh browse is shot."

He opens his closet. "Take your pick." A going-out-of-business sale.

She flicks through stuff appraisingly, amused to find the gauzy shirt. "Dis doesn't look like you," she says.

"You'd be surprised."

"One of your gurrfriends," she opines, picking a blue work shirt instead, as, facing the closet, raising her arms, she lets the WAC fatigues slip down. She turns back towards him, donning the shirt while leaving it mostly open in front (a signal that she'll be trusting him now?), exposing her mismatched underpants and something looped around her neck—a palm-sized box with wires attached to a small black disk on a lavaliere. "RF mike," she points and says. Then tugging it up and over her head, she adds it to her stack of clothes. "Starting duh water," she declares, as peremptory as a home-room teacher but coy in a comically menacing way that says they're back on peaceable terms.

"Help yourself." He'll wait his turn.

148

Disconcertingly quick at switching roles, she brushes on past him towards the tub, then turns to catch him glancing down—not at her fundament, at her calves (always what he looked at first when watching a woman walk away—like Bitsie Spann in junior high, first glimpse of her through the snack-bar door, selling some kid a Nutty Buddy. . . her saddle oxfords, bobbie sox, the way the tendon joined her heel, one look and the pursuit was on).

"What are you staring at?" she demands.

"Your legs."

"Well, don't. No Gypsy Lowes. Mudder Teresa, unnerstand?"

Like Chinese checkers, he reflects, you gotta be quick to stay in the game. "I'm lookin' at what you show me, luv." He's trying to play it as it lays, the title of a book just out.

"Remember dat." She pads away, then reappears with hair tucked up. "You duck," she says.

"Me eagle, maybe. Never a duck."

"Don't be a dork, Mike. Lower your head." He stoops, she lifts, the sling comes off. "Now sit." She takes off both his boots and socks, unbuttons his shirt and loosens his belt, then tugs him back onto his feet, leading him to the bathroom door. He'd thought the bath would be for her.

"You sure you know what you're doing here?"

"Oh, sure," she says. "What you can't do." She slides his trousers to his feet, revealing a swagger-stick in his shorts. "Tell you what. . ." She pats his arm. "Soon as you think your ass is clean, you let me know. I'll help wid duh mud in your hair."

"My ass is always clean," he says. He follows instructions anyhow, slipping his shorts off, nudging the door, and stepping carefully into the tub, finding it hotter than he'd thought. "Oh, help!" he warbles, sloshing down, as beyond reproach as William Penn.

"Problems?" she answers, farther away, as if she's rummaging through his room. She's welcome to what she finds, he thinks, but maybe she's reading a magazine. "Way too hot," he hollers back.

He hears the phone ring. Rose picks up, but Dugan can't make out what she says.

"Who's that?" he yells.

She looms in the doorway, looking down. "Phone company says dey'll call you back. You set?"

For what? For Cho-Cho-San? Mixed signals coming from all directions, but that's okay—the bout's a draw. Besides, he thinks. . . or doesn't think (the warlord from the Gobi groans with messengers galloping from his crotch to the farthest-flung outposts of his brain. LUST! the fearful envoys leer, and PAIN! the high-cheeked children cry). He spreads a washrag over his groin. It rises like a circus tent, autonomous, beside the point.

"Lie back," she says indifferently.

He tries to grab the side of the tub, which lets the washrag float away. "Damn Southern Bell!" he says instead, trying his best to redirect. "They bother to say what they're calling about?"

The work shirt's closed, but when she kneels, her thighs jut out enticingly. "I didn't ask. Come on, lie back."

He feels the washrag float away. She brushes her hair back with a thumb, leans over the tub and squeezes some Prell. With both eyes closed, he feels her hands, massaging his head and the back of his neck, her fingers like some musical thrum on. . . what's it called, the Chinese lute? Maybe there's something better than sex, maybe it's this, what Hicks foresaw—the loins shall lie down with the lamb. (Okay, he thinks, the warlord's spent, it's time to let the sensei speak.) "My future's here and now," he slurs. (The pipa, he recalls its name.)

His voice sounds hoarse. She doesn't reply, but putting one hand beneath his neck, she rinses his hair off with the other.

"Okay, aw finished."

"That's it?" he asks.

"For you," she says. The tub's now full of muddy water. She pops the plug, rocks back and stands, snatching one of his towels down. "Your back is cut. Hold on, let's see."

"The wire," he says. "This afternoon."

"It's just a scratch."

Plus his shoulder, of course, and Dinkie's chunk (he's running low on body parts—he's mentioned that, he thinks he has). He's slightly dizzy getting up and puts his good hand on her hip, doing his best to steady himself. She lifts it off but leads him out, then goes back in and shuts the door.

He hears the tub fill up again. But, totally zonked, he tells himself it's really just sleep he's craving now. The ache in his shoulder's tamped down low, a pilot light that flutters and purls. Another half pill. . . oh, swallow it all! He does, and, creeping into bed, lies lapped by the sounds of Rose's bath, thinking about her blue-black hair. . . as black as what? as carbon paper. Small breasts, of course—no problem with that—and one tooth slightly out of line (just as it should be, he observes, though love of the other is what it is. . . beautiful in a special way, but definitely not domesticated. . . selkie, asrai, grindylow, figments that haunt his Celtic blood).

Then, drifting deeper into sleep, he's nearly submerged when she slips in puts on his gauzy hippie shirt, and, wading out to where he lies suspended in that deep slow stream, sidestrokes beside him, hip to knee. He tries to catch her scent again (expecting some distinctive smell like ripe fruit on a pantry sill or clotheslines in a winter sun) but comes up empty as before. There's nothing there. He guesses his body's wafting towards her the rancid stench of a carnivore, a big-eyed cat who'd hump the lamb—except she claims that she's the cat, and he's. . . well, he must be the dog.

"Mike!" she whispers, nudging his thigh.

"Huh?" he groans. He's barely awake.

"Terr me what you said to him."

"Said. . . to who?"

"Your friend, duh general. General Bratz."

"Nothing. I made a story up. He didn't believe me."

There's a pause.

"So why'd he let us get away?"

He doesn't reply. She nudges again.

"I'll tell you later. Gotta rest. . ."

"Tell me now."

"Huh-unh," he says.

He's scudding off. She slides her leg up over his knee, moving a hand across his chest. "But how'd you get us out of dat mess? Explain it to me—wake up, Mike!"

(It was during the war—I can't discuss it.) "So tired. . ." he yawns. (I spent too long in the sewers, okay?) "I did him a favor."

"The General? How?" Her skin feels cool.

"I've always had dumb luck," he says. "It's just. . ." She puts her hand on his. "Somehow I never seem to get. . . whatever it is I really want."

Her fingers hint this time he might. "What sort of favor?" she persists.

His mind's more focused now, awake. "The six-months option saved my butt. . . you've heard of that? Okay, just wait, I'll get to Blatz. They draft you and you serve two years, but for a while they offered a deal—six months and then you did reserve. You got off light. No Vietnam. . . unless they called you up again."

"De're udder ways uh ducking out."

151

"Well, yeah, that's true—a guy I knew shot off his toe. Six months seemed easier to me." He tries explaining to himself the trajectory of his brief career, the acrid barracks in the pines, the sand and heat, the dumbing down. "First thing they do is cut your hair, then weigh you, spray you, check IQ. They like things in the middle, see? Extremes don't regiment so well. What happened to me, I took the test and knew exactly what it was— the Wechsler Adult Intelligence Scale! I'd studied that sucker word for word, a whole semester in this course. . . Human Cognition 305, why this was asked instead of that, why that was right and this was wrong. . . You followin' this?"

She nods her head. It bumps his chest.

"I missed a few on purpose, right? I wanted to make things look legit. They freaked, of course, but whatta they do? Here's Einstein, their new recruit, and whattaya think they make him do?" She's pressed against him. Boobs are sweet, but not so tempting now as sleep—he tries to wind his story up. "Whattaya think they make him do? He gets to drive the general's car."

"Don't unnerstand."

"The guy's chauffeur. I drove his car. It kept me out of trouble, see? But Blatz kept laying pipe all day—some macho thing, don't ask me why. His wife caught on. . ." He vaguely wishes he'd lied to Rose, inventing a more heroic story. At least he's through, he'll get to sleep. "And that's when Dugan took the rap."

"Dat's it?"

"That's it. He owed me one." He hasn't told her everything—he's left out stiffing the Reserve and Oreen Suber hunting him down because, when he got home again, he'd failed to write and didn't drill. No point in bringing up the Rhodes, the years at Harvard he'd cashed in, the hot-shot future he'd outgrown.

She rolls away. He thinks she yawns—a stifled sound, he can't be sure. She could be chuckling. Then she's still, and, lying stretched out side by side, like knight and lady on a tomb—or the two of them on a boxcar's roof—he grooves to the tune of the Frigidaire. The tide he'd drifted through returns, tugging him under, dragging him down. He opens his eyes and sees the clock, watching the seconds pulse away with a low faint buzzing new to him—why hasn't he heard that noise before? He listens harder while, just outside, the surges of crickets rise and fall. He must have slept. The room is dark, light from a window ribbing the wall. He touches her neck—no blood-beat there. He moves his fingers further down and, where the flesh begins to yield, discovers a rhythm in his hand that flows from her and into him, striking a chord so resonant it goes on droning through the night. "Whatever. . ." he thinks, or almost thinks, before he's fallen asleep again.

• • •

His first thought is that he's waking alone, but then he squints and makes her out, tiptoeing through the shadowy room. He tries but can't locate the clock, supposing it's sometime after five.

"Whattaya want?" he quietly asks.

"A shoe. . . a shoe."

She straightens up. Her legs are like a carving fork beneath his ruby-buttoned shirt, so sheer it's hardly more than a veil for what's half-visible underneath—including the plain white underpants (from J.C. Penny is his surmise) without the lacy scalloped bra. He'd fallen asleep too soon he thinks as he struggles to get his wits engaged.

"I'm talking existentially." Not a good line. He edits it down. "Pragmatically speaking, whattaya need. . . besides a shoe?"

"Here's one," she says. "You see duh udder?"

"I see them both. That shirt looks good. I think it's you."

"I'm taking duh blue shirt," she replies, ignoring his sophomoric crack. Good thing she does. He's trying too hard. She shakes the shoe she's got in her hand.

"It's in front of the hamper over there." He's on one elbow, pointing it out.

She turns. "Okay." She picks it up, then sits beside him on the bed, looking a lot like Kuan Yin—locally sold with benches and urns as whimsical backyard statuary. The Goddess of Mercy, Dugan knows. Danny's grandfather Kappelman had sold them for years to garden clubs instead of black-jockey hitching posts.

"So, then. . ." he asks her pointedly, noting her disquieting stare. "In terms of where you're off to next, what's your plan?"

She pats his leg. "No plan," she says. "It's how I survive. Hector chooses where we shoot."

"But what you shoot might matter more." He twists into a sitting position. "What I've seen of your scripts is sorry-ass stuff. You need a writer—hang on, don't laugh! Without a story, the rest gets dull, no matter what crazy risks you take."

"You know somebody?"

"Well, it happens I do."

"Can't do it all on pills," she says. "No good wid one arm in a sling." Leaning above him, mocking him now. Her tits smirk too beneath the gauze.

"You've no idea what I can do."

"It's true, I don't." She's closer still. "So, tell me, Mike. What could you do?" She's propped one foot up on the bed, leaning down towards him over her knee.

"Whatever you want."

"Whatever?"

"Sure. Say what you want—snuff Spiro Agnew? Shoot my dog?"

"You got a dog?"

"Not at the moment, no." That's lame.

"But you'll snuff Agnew, won't you, Mike? You wouldn't say what you don't mean?"

"I didn't."

"No?"

A power play, and whatever he does he's going to lose. . . unless that liquored-up Quaker was right—he plays the goat, the ninnies win. He's not a goat, though, that's the thing. That's not a game he wants to play.

"Listen," he says. "I've interfered twice and saved you once. If you need me to do it, I'll save you again—though, to tell you the truth. . ." putting his hand down on her foot, which is chubby and child-like—big surprise, he'd expected a slimmer, more elegant shape, "if the breakage continues, that'll get tough. But meanwhile, sure, whatever you say."

With that he lifts her foot to his mouth, which tips her over onto her side. He kisses the foot and on up her leg, feeling her fingers in his hair.

"Stop," she chokes, conceding the point.

Feeling elated, he raises his head, watching her as she rolls to her feet and unhurriedly tugs her skivvies down. Then, stepping out of them, letting them drop, she remounts, laying hold of him (put this too on his can't-do list), and, bracketing his thighs with hers, inserts him slowly, leaning back (*you're out deep now!* he hears Walt say), bracing herself by grabbing his shins. He winces as she rubs the bite. Already in motion, she hears him yelp. "What?" she asks him, turning to look, repeating herself with every thrust.

He shakes his head. "Highly. . . advanced technique," he groans, as, like a hovercraft gathering speed, she skims above what he's just said, her "What?" repeated, driving hard: what? what? what? what?

"Kama. . . Sutra," he explains, hoping to make this witty sex. Heroic it's not, but that's okay. "Undoubtedly. . . the move. . . called *phut*."

She's closed her eyes, compelling him now, forcing him out beyond the surf to where the swells are slow and deep. He waves to Walt who grins and says,

I will you to be a bold swimmer.

(It'll have to be the backstroke, Walt!) He looks and sees her head thrown back, her nipples lisping through his shirt—an image that's mixed up in his mind with memories of the Dibble Hunt (the dove he'd shot, limp-necked and warm, as if it still could fly away), the widows rocking, dressed in black (a girl in bangs who watches them rock. . . and rock, and rock). He's falling now, plummeting through a ring of fire but hugging her to him as he falls a long way off from where he's been.

They bob like seals (the tide is strong). She waits for maybe half an hour, until she's sure he's really asleep. The bedsprings creak as she gets up, but he's still drifting far from shore. She frowns in the midst of changing shirts and pauses for another look. He's stranded like a drowned Phoenician.

She nods to Hector. "Dat's a wrap."

III

WHILE THE UNIVERSE IS ERUPTING

September 1969 – May 1970

*I should have made my way straight to you long ago,
I should have blabb'd nothing but you, I should have
chanted nothing but you.*

—Walt Whitman

"Dear Sirs," he'd written *The Charlotte Observer* shortly before he wrecked his bike, "Our country's the conscience of the world—that's how we've always thought of ourselves. But given what's happening in Vietnam, it's getting increasingly hard to assume. So I have a suggestion I'd like to share.

> Our leaders keep telling us war is hell, and commies
> who mess with Uncle Sam will wish they'd never left
> Hanoi. But what's hellish is innocent people who die by
> tens of thousands every year, the ones we call "collateral"
> who keep blundering into lines of fire or dawdle in
> leaving our "free-fire zones."
> Our forces have been under great duress and didn't set
> out to cause those deaths. We Americans don't smear
> stakes with dung or booby-trap babies with grenades. We
> defoliate and pacify and try to help villagers understand
> that sometimes we'll have to destroy their homes in order
> to save them in the end.
> But if that was the plan at My Lai 4, our critics are
> asking what was saved and why, on finding no Viet Cong,
> we mowed down women and children instead. Protestors
> are claiming photos don't lie, and, frankly, speaking for
> myself, I'm very disturbed by that *Life* magazine
> spread—not just the corpses, they've gotten routine, but
> injured villagers still alive, waving their hands and
> begging for help. . . making me think of Wounded Knee
> or someplace else I'd rather forget if we're the conscience
> of the world. Even down here in Sternbolt country, my
> neighbors are starting to get confused about how to tell an
> atrocity from what's become an atrocious war.
> The issue for me is trying to keep things in perspective
> and seeing these things for what they are, which is where

159

my modest proposal comes in. If we're dealing with an obscenity, let's be more forthright than we've been. Forget apologies or excuses. Instead, in every toilet stall where words like "fuck" or "shit" are scrawled—or "cock" or "cunt" or "eat my dick"—let's add "MY LAI".
. .

The last few lines had asterisks in place of some language Dugan had used. "An ex-Rhodes Scholar," the editors noted, "currently teaching at Cumbria State."

Some fan mail reached him in a week. "Dear Asshole," one of the cards began, "how 'bout Old Glory up your butt?" That query had come from Fayetteville, just a whoop and a holler from his new home.

● ● ●

Regarding the Seaboard railway line—which Dugan has ridden twice of late—he learns, as he's gassing the Pontiac up for the final leg of his five-hour drive, that the gang who'd laid its circuitous track after a festive Fourth of July had been too soused while heading north to manage a simple straightaway. That's what he's told at Boffo Gas while confirming the route to John Dough's place which isn't exactly in Chantry Mount. "Near Lugton" is what his directions had said, but Lugton's not near anything. Twenty-five miles from the campus itself, it's where some freight trains used to pause to take on water from a tank set up on stilts beside a spur. . . pretty much all that happened there, except for some slanderous imputations.

"Track's like a corkscrew down the line," drawls an attendant in overalls, leaning against an Orange Crush crate and working a plug from cheek to cheek. "Trains had to slow up long enough for Lugton girls to ply their trade." He squints and spits for emphasis. "Hope yo' frenn's down near the river there. Rest o' that town ain't worth a shit."

"Truth is," nods Dugan, "neither am I." He figures his battered set of wheels helps cover such backwoods repartee.

"Yep?" says the attendant, spitting again.

"Yep," Dugan confirms as he drives off.

After another half-hour or so, he stops in Historic Lugton's heart, parking beneath a dying oak with one of its arms a lopped-off stump. Behind him whirrs a plywood plant, in front is Beasley's Feed & Seed/Post Office/& Lugton Savings & Loan with the Fire Department parked out back. Past that, some scattered tin-roofed sheds, two sycamores, and a gravel lot containing a truck with one of its tires propped up against a vine-draped pump.

"Agee and Evans," Dugan thinks as he studies the picturesque country store, with maybe a Gudger there by the door to greet whoever might mosey by—like a couple of strays from the northbound freight that Dugan and Rose had been aboard ("What say there, boys?" Well, howdy, Mike! Y'all durned sure had yo'se'ves a ride!) That reverie flutters through his mind, but then it's gone. His focus shifts. The bug-gummed windshield is his past, his new life here's about to start—a *vita nuova*, he tells himself (like Jamshyd formerly-known-as-Brad, maybe he'll change his name to Lug to give it a neo-Snopesian ring), but first he's got to settle in.

Vamoosing from Cumbria wasn't that hard—a week at the Rosens' culling his stuff, leaving great heaps except for his books for them to keep or give away plus refilling a tube of those magical pills that have helped him coast to where he is now, about to enter the Beasley's store. The Pontiac makes a choking sound long after he's cut the engine off and climbed the steps to its double screen-doors while still appraising what he sees—the moss-scabbed brick and paint-peeled wood, the plate-glass windows speckled with flies, the cardboard cut-out of a girl hugging a big loaf of Merita (with lipstick and an upswept perm, she's sporting a knowing jailbait smile), all proclaiming that he's come to a place where Judy Canova could feel at home (Judy Canova? when was *that*?) It's not just neo, it's congealed.

Sputtering in a final appeal, the Pontiac heaves a tubercular sigh as he moseys inside the all-in-one store, finding a dark-stained wide-planked floor that's sprinkled with sawdust down each aisle (what Up Yours tried to imitate) and inhaling its musty dry-goods smell. He notes the crisscrossed croker sacks and jumbles of orphaned odds and ends stacked up in barrels by the wall (though not quite sure what dry goods are, he pictures large bins of crowder peas with big tin scoops to measure them out and aromatic kernels and beans that vary from ochre to chocolate brown, to be cooked with fatback, served with greens). He sees the bedpans stacked on shelves aimed like howitzers at the door, the washtub wringers on the wall, the boots and straps and pickle jars—standard

Southern Gothic, sure, but more than mere nostalgic ooze. You understand it or you don't. He tells himself it's in his blood.

Nobody's in sight, but behind a partition, he hears Bob Barker calling 'em down, an audience clapping, then a cough that's rasping behind him like his car. He turns to meet Ma Beasley's stare, her eyes two raisins pressed into dough with a torso apparently made of the same ensconced behind a counter-top and bracketed by a pair of scales with a trickle of string from overhead (for packaging dry goods, he assumes), waiting for him to state what he needs. He's glad he has the common touch.

"Ah'm Mah-kel Doogun. . ." he explains, his accent soaked in honest sweat. "John Duff wuz s'posed tuh leeve thuh key."

She studies him distrustfully.

"It's fuh mah house."

The scratchy cough behind a partition hocks up a stubborn wad of phlegm.

"Thuh ole Duff place." He wags his sling. "I'm s'posed tuh git thuh key rat cheer."

"PUR-VIS!" she bellows. "Come out heah!"

The laugh-track fades.

"Whut?" someone whines.

"Turn that thang off and git out heah!"

A man in highboys shuffles in—parched and creased with wispy hair and a buzzard-like neck supporting his bean. "Most time fer Hollywood Squares," he croaks.

Folding her arms, she jerks her chin to signal for Dugan to speak again. "Would you tell him what you just said?"

"Ah'm Michael Dugan. . ."

"Hole on rat thar," Pa Beasley rasps, grasping a wrinkled window sash that hangs from a nearby metal hook and carving a wedge out with his knife. "Yew tell me whut yew thinka that." He drops the wedge in Dugan's hand. Heavy and dark with a leathery skin, it's like a semi-petrified turd. "Cured rite out back. Go on," he winks and rubs his teeth. "You ever taste any jerky like that?"

"Nope," Dugan replies. He tries to chew, then shifts it over to his cheek. "Ah'm gonna live in John Duff's house. He said he'd leave. . ."

"Hit ain't no house. More lak uh hut."

"Built you know where," Ma Beasley sniffs.

"Ah *don't* know," Dugan tries to shrug. "Ah'll need directions too, ah guess."

"Uh-huh," she mutters.

"Whuut?" he asks.

"Thuh colored section," Pa explains. He turns and limps behind the partition. Ma juts her jaw at Dugan's sling.

"You. . . drive like that?"

"Yep," he agrees. "It ain't so hard."

She acts as if she thinks he's dim or hasn't mastered English yet. "You. . . aim. . . to stay. . . in Lugton long?"

"Ah guess ah will."

"Your friend. . . got on heah pretty well. Lived like a hermit some folks said."

"Ah wooden know."

"A right good customer, though," she adds, pausing with a meaningful look.

He takes the hint and peers about. Some basic provisions should do the trick—coffee, sugar, bread, and milk. Vienna sausages, pork-and-beans. Ma watches him as he stacks them up. And Kellogg's Bran Flakes, he decides. He finds all that, then turns again.

"Hep you with sump'en?" Pa's come back.

"Y'all got enny raisins?" Dugan asks.

"Yew lookin' right at 'em." Pa says with a hoot, flapping his arms and stretching his neck. "Nexx to thuh Dutch Boy Cleanser rack."

Ma scrutinizes Dugan's pile. "That it?" she asks.

"Hold on," chokes Pa. His Adam's apple works up and down. "Yew puttin' thuh raisins on that bran?"

"Shore," Dugan says.

Pa slaps his leg and turns away like a spectator glued to *The Price Is Right* with all the answers in his head. "They're both rite chere in this one box!"

Dugan can't think of a retort.

"See! *Raisin* Bran!" Pa Beasley crows, putting the box in Dugan's hands.

"Mah lawd!" says Dugan, feigning surprise.

"Don' git so soggy," Pa allows. "An' saves uh little do-re-mi."

That observation sets Ma off. She squints at the jar of Taster's Choice. "This coffee has went up ten cent more. I told you, Purvis."

Pa looks vague.

"I said to mark it up last week."

"Yep," Pa admits. He chews his beard as she scribbles the new price on the lid. "She did," he adds with a vigorous nod.

"No problem," says Dugan, on his way to being a right-good customer too. "An' gimme two Slim Jims while you at it."

Ma stares at him. "You eat those things?"

"Bess eatin' I know."

"Cause cancer's what Ralph Nader says. That rebate offer's over, though. How 'bout that jerky in your mouth?"

The window sash. He shrugs. "Okay."

"Eleven cent." She writes it down. "A dollar eighty-six," she frowns. She gestures at a plastic box—a kid in orthopedic gear. "You want the pennies?"

"Nah."

"Uh-huh. You suit yourself." She counts out change. "And heah's the key." She takes it from Pa and slaps it down.

"Ah still need. . ."

"What?"

". . . directions."

Bing! She shuts the drawer with her hip and starts to wipe the counter down.

"Purvis! Will you hep this man? Mistuh. . . what?"

"Mike Dugan," he says.

"I'm Loraleen Beasley," she replies. "You come to me for 'most anything—groceries, loans, and postage stamps. You go to *him* if you're on fie-yuh." She squints and scowls, nodding at Pa. "Just jokin', a-course. He's chief of the Lugton Ladder-and-Hose, which is why he kin handle die-rections too. Come back to see us soon, you hear?"

Pa clears his throat and starts to recount how he would get to John Dough's place with all the road signs shot away. "Durn tarket practiss," Pa explains, escorting Dugan down the aisle. They pause when they get to the puppy chow. "Yew got uh dog?"

"No," Dugan says. "Not yet, at least."

"Hit's huntin' season," Pa observes. "Ah'd ware brite colors, I wuz yew."

Thanks, Pa, he thinks. Right neighborly. I'll put up sandbags when I can. Hugging his groceries, he can't wave. "See y'all," he nods as he bumps out the door.

Pa's face conveys what he won't say. He's too polite to argue the point, but in these parts at this time of year, the odds are pretty much against most one-armed men in the woods.

● ● ●

"Folla thuh blacktop haff uh mile (ain't got no city blocks out heah), turn leff at In Ho's beauty spot (thuh trailer sportin' pink winder trim, uh sign says In-Ho's Hair Apparent—Roscoe Moseby done brung her home affer haff his toes had 'most froze off while fightin' fuh freedom in Koh-rea). Back rite again jess pass uh scraper been thar since Sharleen Phelps run off with hits negligent wetback operator—jess dumped hit rite thar in thuh ditch an' leff in Sonny's new Camaro ('don' never truss uh man,' he says, 'with hearts 'n' roses on his arm and writin' in thuh Mexican tongue'). Go ovah thuh bridge 'cross Highway One an' enta twinny squar miles uh scrub tha'ss mostly thar fuh colored people. Yew'll see uh row uh nigra shacks set back ahind some chinaberries. Turn leff furse chance— thar ain't no sign (them coloreds ain't learnt t' read nohow, jess wastin' paint an' taxpayer munny). Red clay been scraped uh good long stretch till affer you git pass Trueblood's place. Yew'll see his collards, big as hawgs (collards, not coloreds—thuh ones tha'ss green!) Road's mostly yourn from that point on, woods taller an' thicker—good huntin' land. Look fo' uh mailbox on th' groun' (some durn fool aimed his truck at uh deer an' flattened the U.S. Mail instead), thass whar yew live, turn in rite thar (too steep fuh when hit freezes, though)."

Dugan can't spot the chinaberries, but seeing three cabins at a place where asphalt stops and red clay starts, he takes what looks like a landing strip, scraped out of the dirt and cleared of stumps but undulating straight ahead. As he's passing more houses on either side, he's vaguely aware of being watched from next to wash pots in the yards and screenless windows edged in blue ("mos' whytes don't travel down that-air road without they got some business thar. . . or pack a gun, yew got uh gun?") The rat-tailed dogs race out to bark, then slink beneath the shacks again, their low-slung tits between their feet.

But just before the road slopes down, on a plateau hedged by locust trees, is a cabin with a wide front porch and flourishing fields of collards and corn in the midst of which, knee-deep in the vines of a melon-patch, is a giant off of a Niblets can, his arms akimbo, watching the car. . . not jolly and green, but big and aloof, hardly acknowledging Dugan's wave. "Trueblood" was what Pa Beasley said.

Another half-mile and, on its side next to a brush-clogged drainage ditch, is an uprooted mailbox marking the start of a driveway with a ski-jump pitch. Having geared his car down to make the turn, Dugan chugs up the steep ascent and comes at last to a shuddering stop. With a sputter and sigh, the engine dies.

Dense woods crowd in on every side. According to Gordo, John Dough had affirmed that rentals were scarce in Chantry Mount, that even Arthur Godfrey's son had pieced together tobacco barns to fashion himself a make-shift pad which had prompted his own idea in turn—a former mule-shed gentrified to form a rustic scholar's retreat on leased land Dough had characterized as semi-romantically out of the way. "Bucolic" was Gordo's colorful term, describing how Dough had found a site "atop a majestic river-view bluff" with an eye to "decreeing his Xanadu" (like Kamo no Chomei, heard of him? Gordo had not—he merely blinked as if Dugan had coughed to cover a fart).

Now Dugan discovers how far Dough got in building his pleasure-dome in the sticks. . . a single board-and-batten hut—some twenty by twenty, he would guess, and possibly just a few feet more—with a roof, three windows, and a door that's shut by a hasp and a Master lock for which Ma Beasley had coughed up the key. A lone frayed power line sags through the woods, attached to the hut in a dirt dauber's nest that's underneath the nearest eave. It wouldn't take much for an overload.

"Furnished," it turns out, means a cot, a table, two chairs (one missing a back), a sofa that's covered in Naugahyde (its innards oozing onto the floor), a lamp, and a bureau missing some knobs squeezed in between a cold-water sink and a two-eyed hotplate on a shelf. A kerosene heater squats on the floor (Aladdin it's named enticingly, not needed as yet but ready to serve). The rest of the plumbing's rigged outside—an outdoor shower spray nailed to the wall (its water source obscure at first until, behind a waist-high bush in back, he spots a gasoline-powered pump bolted atop a cement slab, evidence of some sort of well) and, fifteen or twenty feet away, a phone-booth privy-in-the-pines, its glass walls painted baby blue with suns and flowers on the door above a scratched out quarter-moon (a hole's been cut in the metal floor beneath a squared-off outhouse seat, no phone but a phonebook ready at hand with most of its yellow pages intact—in case of emergencies, Dugan assumes). That whimsy recurs inside the hut: brown floor, green walls, and scarlet beams, low-vaulted ceiling painted dark blue with paste-on moons and shooting stars. The front door's plain, but its jamb's cerise and its three wooden steps unfurled below resembling King Crimson's tongue.

He'd figured Dough as an asinine twit getting his rocks off reading Simms, but the twit, it seems, is something else—an Aleister Crowley in the bush whose pen pal might be Squeaky Fromme. He'll have to work that out somehow.

But first things first. He walks across to check the tap and feels the shed begin to tilt, moves back and feels it rise again (Chaplin's *Gold Rush* comes to mind, though it seemed much funnier on the screen). Outside is a crumbling cinder block under one corner of the hut. He jams a log into the gap and fetches some ballast from the car, a couple of boxes of records and books, a suitcase and his groceries—including Pa Beasley's Raisin Bran, which he eats while perched on the topmost step, his back against the plywood door. He tries some jerky, spits it out, and, unscrewing the lid of his Taster's Choice, finds roofer's compound in the jar or something too similar to ingest. No coffee, then. But he's still okay, listening to whippoorwills through the trees, feeling the soft air on his skin, watching it turn crepuscular ("an' gettin' dark," he says to himself, a grad school joke that rises unbidden).

Nostalgia overtakes him now, reflecting on other moments like this, thinking of Keats (he's not sure why but "Give me women, wine, and snuff" goes flashing absurdly through his mind), then textual anomalies, Timrod, Simms, Augustus Blunt, and, reaching the weary end of the road, his present improbable situation. "Lugton," he mutters, "or Life in the Woods," determined to live deliberately, to front the essential facts of life and see if he can't et cetera. "My future is here and now," he adds, brooding on that thought for a while before noting his formerly snow-white sling now looks like an auto mechanic's rag, which brings him back to more practical matters and, pursuant to them, returning inside where he finds a message he'd missed before.

"HOUSE RULES," it says on an index card,

MAXIMUM VOLTAGE AT ANY ONE TIME:
TWO LAMPS & A HOTPLATE—ANYTHING
MORE, THE POWER GOES OFF. TWO-MINUTE
SHOWERS ARE THE MAX—ANYTHING
LONGER, THE WELL RUNS DRY. WHEN

YELLOW PAGES ARE ALL USED UP, SUGGEST YOUR MONOGRAPH ON JOYCE.

He squints to read the final word, which looks like "TOUGH" but could be "DOUGH." (Who told him about the monograph?)

The green wall has a rosy tint. He checks and, through a gap in the trees, sees the sun's top rim sink under a cloud—sedately, though, he tells himself, like an old man settling into his bath. The wall turns colorless bit by bit. The sill goes next and then the sky. The lamp works, though he likes the dark and, by raising the windows, lowers the heat enough to think he'll get some sleep. But his shoulder's begun to pulsate again and, wearing only his undershorts while sprawled atop the twanging cot, he hears a mosquito summoning friends to join him through the patchwork screen. He's propped a book to block a hole when the ceiling above him starts to blink. The stick-on stars, he thinks at first, then discovers it's roaches making their way across the galaxy overhead. After a sketchy half-hour or so, he surprises himself by dozing off.

At ten p.m., when shots erupt down where he thinks the river must be, he reassures his citified brain that somebody's got a possum treed. At one o'clock, there're two more shots, apparently now from up the road. At four, they boom from somewhere else, across the road but farther off. Either that possum's like a fox or possums in these parts must be doomed. Dugan's awake for more than an hour, and, just as the birds are beginning to stir, is back on the verge of sleeping again when, suddenly, he hears a blast, a crack, a swish, and then a thud. Whatever it is is closing in.

"YOU MOVE YO' ASS!"

Alarmed, he jerks himself awake.

"Goddammit! You HEAR me? I said MOVE!"

Another roar and a splattering sound like water from a garden hose tracing a path across his roof. "Birdshot" Dugan wonders aloud, as, prodding his wits, he tries to think. One of Dough's cronies come to call? Some neighbor out to even a score ("Bugger y'er Simms! Ted Dreiser's the man! No diddling with his anomalies!")? He looks again and sees in the woods what looks like an ad for *Field & Stream*—Mister Potato Head with a gun, a dog, red vest and camouflage hat, reloading his weapon thirty yards off.

"Jasper... shit!" Potato Head yells. "Git off yo' sorry ass 'n' FETCH!"

Though Jasper moans, he doesn't budge.

"Don' lookit ME! Go git thuh BIRD! Rite ovah THERE by that run-down shack!"

The shotgun swings in Dugan's direction. He hits the floor as it goes off and hears the log support pop loose. The shed is sinking.

"Judas PRIEST! Now lookit whut yew made me dew!"

Dugan remembers Pa's advice—huntin' season and what that means, armed numbskulls prowling loose in the woods. He's crawling backwards towards the door, his brain now ratcheting into gear (James Bond, he thinks, his piecemeal gun). He spots a stack of 33s, his KLH still packed away, and, grabbing components one by one, assembling the units as he goes, he sets up speakers on the sill (tough work to manage with one arm).

"Fergit thuh shack, dew whut I SAID!" Potato Head's poking with his gun. "If yew don' git that goddamn BIRD an' fetch it rite this fuckin' minute, ah'm gonna BLOW yo' ass away!"

Jasper whines.

"Ah'm countin' to THREE. . ."

Dugan is working as fast as he can. Reach for the outlet, plug it in, switch PLAY, and turn the volume up as high as he can make it go.

"When ah git through, hit's aw-she-row. . . okay, thass TWO!"

The needle drops into a groove.

"Juss wag away! It ain't goan hep."

"𝕺 𝔉𝔯𝔢𝔲𝔫𝔡𝔢!" booms the baritone, so loud it shakes the pine-straw down. The hut shakes too, reverberating.

"Shee-it!"

A pause, then "𝔑𝔦𝔠𝔥𝔱 𝔡𝔦𝔢𝔰𝔢 𝔗ö𝔫𝔢!"

Dugan, who's listening from the floor, hears Jasper's howl and then a shout, "Goddammit, dawg, yew GIT back heah!"

But "𝔖𝔬𝔫𝔡𝔢𝔯𝔫 𝔩𝔞𝔰𝔰𝔱 𝔘𝔫𝔰. . ." drowns him out, followed amid diminishing barks by an orchestra and an *Ode to Joy*. Mister Potato Head's final cry is uttered as an indignant reproach, "Come back, you dumb mutt! Ah said STAY!"

By record's end, the coast is clear, leaving aside a parting shot presumably aimed at Tito Gobbi. Dugan then cuts the music off. As soon as he's dressed, he cracks the door, waving his peace-tie on a stick. Drawing no fire, he ventures out, feeling the hut tip forward and back.

Instead of shots, he hears a sound like somebody dropping croquet balls repeatedly on a cement floor, a hollow muffled sort of thrum that resonates throughout the woods as full of foreboding and regret as the music for a

Hitchcock film. He tries to track it for a while, but, flitting ahead, it disappears, leaving him standing on a path that seems to lead to the edge of the bluff. With another few steps he's past its crest and on a precipitous downward course before he's noticed how steep it is.

His forward lean picks up momentum, accelerating step by step until he finds he can't slow down. Twisting and sliding in his descent, his sling like a half-furled sail in a storm, he's barely controlling his breakneck rush when, nearing the bottom, kicking up clods, he starts to stumble, spins, *chassés*, and, pivoting sideways, hits a dip that snaps his knees back, pitches him up, and stops him cold by some white-barked trees spindlier than the ones up top. He's aware of a steady loom-like hum and, twenty or thirty feet ahead, the glint of a flattened watery slab like sheet-metal coursing through a mill.

In a very short stroll, he's on the bank with a spillway lying straight ahead and to his right that shifting expanse as smooth and bare as a tabletop. It's maybe a hundred yards across but, starting below him to his left after the spillway's twenty-foot drop, floodwaters have cut a second sluice that branches through the rocks and trees. The path is harder to trace from there but, once he's got it fixed in his head, he strides along past towering trees—cypress, tulip, and sycamore—until he sees far overhead what looks like a Roman viaduct, its concrete pylons lifting a span over the tallest trees in the gorge.

He guesses it must be Highway 1, a conjecture confirmed when he stumbles across an historical marker on its back, dropped or fallen from up above, repeating its litany to itself—that, a hundred eighty-nine years ago, Cornwallis had forded here with his men, not only assured things were going well but indifferent to winning hearts and minds since in Camden only shortly before they'd whipped the ragtag rebel troops and followed them north to mop things up. There was plenty of time, they must have assumed, to pillage, wreak havoc, and win the war, so they'd torched a mill on the river's edge and dawdled awhile to watch it burn before searching, destroying, and cantering on.

No traces remain. It feels serene with a few leaves already sifting down and clumps of flotsam clogging the stream—plastic bags and six-pack rings snagged in the limbs of fallen trees with bottles, cans, and Clorox jugs—conveying a sense of things used up, of future history zeroed out so that nothing of note could occur there again (the nymphs are departed and their friends, the doxies and their baggage-trains. . .) He sees a station house up ahead, its steel doors locked and windows barred, and, on past that, a railway bridge. No reason to go that far today.

His ruminations mellow him out but getting back up is such an ordeal that he wonders if maybe, whenever there's time, he ought to install some sort of winch. The catch is who would crank him up—like who can help him fix his hut? His boots keep slipping on the path, slowing his climb, and, near the top, he watches a rock his toe's nudged loose go bouncing downwards towards the stream, leaping and tumbling through the trees, thudding invisibly far below, followed by the continuous hum.

He listens and, without knowing why, feels better than he thinks he should. He sniffs the air—a scent of pine and cool damp earth benignly warmed by an early fall sun. He's winded and his shoulder aches, but when he's atop the bluff again, his mind reverts to the see-sawing shack and, rather than drive for help in his car, he keeps on walking through the trees, along the driveway, down the road until he gets to Trueblood's house.

It's more of a hike than he'd supposed. The road, scraped raw, is desolate, but topping a slope after nearly a mile, he pauses to take a leak in the woods, which gives him a doglike satisfaction, marking his bailiwick with his spoor. In another few yards, surmounting the hill, he enters the Jolly Green Giant's realm—collards and melons, a dry-stalk field, a rusty roof beneath a tree, a porch with a car-seat raised on chocks and, mounted upon it like a throne, the cacique holding a corncob pipe, his hand so big it cradles the bowl as if it were a chinaberry.

Two girls peek out through the closed screen-door. "Hey!" Dugan smiles. They duck away. "Your daughters?" he asks the seated man, who smokes as if he hasn't heard.

"M' grands," he says eventually. His gaze is steady in a way that signals what his words leave out. His voice is mild. He puffs the pipe, then checks the bowl and murmurs to Dugan, puffing again, 'They pa's a railroad man lak me."

"You're Mister Trueblood?" Dugan says.

He hears a giggle from the door.

"That's right." A puff.

"I'm Michael. . . Dugan."

Trueblood nods.

"That was me going by. . . uh, yesterday. . . last evening in the Pontiac." Another puff. "The purple car. I've moved in down the road from here. John Dough's old place. . . just down the road." He isn't sure he's understood. "You know?"

A nod.

"Well. . ." Dugan explains. "The problem is. . . it looks like one foundation's gone."

That seems to register. After a pause, "I'll come to-reckly," Trueblood says in a way that ends the conversation.

As Dugan is heading back towards the road, he thinks he sees a woman's head, with paper curlers, watching him go. But when he turns, there's no one there. He waves to Trueblood on the porch and continues on back the way he'd come, across a ditch and down the road. Before he's halfway up his drive, he hears the gasket-rattling thump of Trueblood's pickup gearing down. He waves again as Trueblood brakes and eases past the Pontiac.

'That was quick! Can I help?" Dugan asks as, exiting carefully from the cab, Trueblood smiles with his eyebrows raised as if he mightn't have understood. "Can I give you a hand?" says Dugan again, not needing to add it's a limited offer.

Trueblood turns and shakes his head. He's brought a railroad jack along and cement blocks that he unloads like sugar cubes in either hand. Feeling he's useless, Dugan talks while Trueblood deftly does the job, answering softly now and then but mostly mute as he raises the house, replaces the blocks, and dislodges the jack. He moves in the slow, deliberate way a barefoot man would walk at night crossing a barnyard in the dark. When Dugan confesses there's one thing more, he counters blandly, "What you need?"

"A ceasefire." Dugan shakes his head. "Had a lunatic blasting away at dawn. . ."

"Uh-uhhh," says Trueblood, hoisting his jack as if it weighs no more than a twig.

". . . fired birdshot up against the house. Treated it like a free-fire zone."

"You got no gun?"

"For firing back?"

"So you don' hunt? You got no dog?"

"No gun, no dog."

"If I was you," Trueblood allows in the same slow gentle baritone, "I wouldn't make no sudden moves." He shoves the jack back in his truck and slams the tailgate into place.

"How much I owe you?" Dugan asks as Trueblood's getting into the cab.

"Heppin' each other," Trueblood declares, "don't nobody have to pay for that." He turns his head to back the truck, prompting some sputters and a knock that sets the whole machine aquiver. He's in reverse but rides the brake to give him long enough to add, "Go on 'n' let'um know you heah. Do lak this mornin'. That was fine. Yuh made mah collards droop," he adds with just a hint of a smile.

● ● ●

Since Trueblood hadn't let him pay, Dugan returns to the Feed & Seed looking for something to "hepp" the grands. He finds a plastic teacup set— labeled, he learns, with an obsolete price. He wants it anyhow? Yes, he does. Ma rings it up as Pa observes, "Them little cups don' hole so much. Rite dainty, ain't they?"

Dugan nods.

"Tea pot too."

"Yep," Dugan says.

"Yep." Pa thinks hard before he adds, "Made in Taiwan. . . I reckon tha'ss why."

"Could be," says Dugan, nodding again.

Pa chews his beard. "They's mosely mijjits is whut I hear."

A big-hipped woman waits in line with king-sized Cokes and Oreos, watching as Dugan stirs the bin that holds fluorescent plastic toys.

"Sepp those bigguns that wrassle," Pa says to her. "You seen those fellas on TV?" She shakes her head. "Same show as that lumberjack competition."

"Add these two Barbies," Dugan says, laying them by the teacup set.

Ma looks askance. Her face is set. The big-hipped woman shifts her load as Ma asks Dugan with a squint, "Mine tellin' me why you want them things?"

"Whut thangs?" he hedges. (F' private rites—I'm gonna need lottsa hatpins too.)

"Are they fer coloreds?"

"Trueblood's grands."

"Purvis!"

"Whut?" He hasn't moved.

"Get him two o' them other dolls."

173

"Barbies?"

"No. Them other ones."

He fetches two cocoa-colored dolls. Smaller than Barbies, poorly made. Ma holds them up.

"That all?" she asks.

He says it is.

"Four ninety-one."

She slides the Barbie dolls aside and starts on the big-hipped woman's batch, reaching out for the Oreos. Dugan considers, but lets it go, grabbing the teacups and the dolls and laying a five on the countertop.

"You want them pennies?"

"*Lincoln* pennies? Yessiree!"

Pa merely looks puzzled as Dugan salutes, pockets his pennies and leaves the store, driving the toys to Trueblood's house and getting a collard in return. He's never encountered one in the wild and wonders if it's unusually large—more like a body-snatcher's pod than something he's apt to cook and eat. Taking it deep into the woods, he leaves it where it might get shot. Then, crouching to check beneath his hut, he finds scrap lumber as he'd hoped, including a couple of two by tens. It's not that easy with a sling, but when he's through he's made a bench, nailed onto the trunks of two big pines in the clearing outside his hovel's door.

Feeling he's making headway now, he finds the bottom half of a rake, and, combing the pine-straw mat away, discovers an ancient wheel-shaped stone about a manhole-cover in width, dragged up, he reckons, from below—from that mill the marauding Brits had torched. . . or, maybe, if hauled from somewhere else, as part of something never built. Either way, a weird *trouvée*, like shark's teeth on a mountain peak.

He's interrupted by a snap (C'mon now, boy!) He spins around (SQUEAL LAK A PIG!) and catches a glimpse of a man with a gun attempting to duck behind a pine. (Potato Head or somebody else?) He looks again. The man is gone. He knows he's got to keep his cool, so, directing his comment to the tree, he nonchalantly wields his rake, tapping the top of the half-buried stone. "Can't figger out how they got this heah." No answer, but he carries on as if he's back at the Feed & Seed, dealing with half-wit bigots and cheats. "Guess it mussta took a mule."

A voice comes floating from the woods. "Th' weed o' croime bears bitter fruit!" The accent's weird. "Y'er bluffin', mite. Yuh can't see shit. . . an' don't know th' password either," he adds.

An Aussie assassin? What comes next—a gang of drug-crazed kangaroos? "*The Shadow*, right? I see your hat."

"Oh, Oi doubt that." But, after a pause, "Wot sorta 'at?"

"A Hopalong Cassidy sort of hat. Mind comin' out so we can talk?"

Another pause, then, "Roight! Don't move. Juss 'old 'em hoigh." A hat emerges atop a man—a knobby, hawk-faced, bandy-legged man—holding his gun at shoulder arms. "An' oo the 'ell are you?" he asks.

"Who do yuh think? The occupant."

The Aussie irregular waves his gun. "Black fella 'ere?"

"Whut?"

"Where'd 'ee go?"

"He went back home. After fixin' my house. I'm gonna put my hand down now. You're from Australia?"

"So Oi'm toll. An 'oo are you?" the Aussie repeats, blinking and sniffing, jerking his gun.

"The guy who got this house from Dough. I'm living heah. Ah told you that." Dugan can match him, brogue for brogue. "An', judgin' from whut Ah've seen so far, Ah've moved into a bloody zoo."

"Moinus th' kai-jes," the Aussie says (translated as "cages" Dugan concludes). "Less 'ope it's not *too* bloody, mite." Rubbing his eyes with the back of his hand, he suddenly plops down on the bench. "Fagged out, all roight, Oi'll tell yuh what. . ." His barrel sags as he doffs his hat. "Been under siege 'ere for a month. Black fellas in th' woods with guns. Razors, machetes, God knows wot." He looks around. "Gotta sty vigilant, am Oi roight?"

Dugan is speechless.

"Ian Bob!"

"Whut?"

"Ian Bob." Extending his hand.

"Dugan, Mike." He offers his left hand in return.

"Yuh're at a disadvantage there. Yuh juss move in?" He squeezes hard.

"Yesterday." He can't squeeze back with a back-handed shake, but he's able to study the gunman's face—skin taut and tanned like an animal's hide, its nose resembling a bird of prey, a jutting chin, and feral teeth that get exposed with every "mite."

"Yuh tike this mornin'," Aussie Bob fumes. "They 'ad some sorta ceremony. Screamin', shootin'. . . shockin' row. M' dog's still underneath th' 'ouse."

"My hand." It's locked in a claw-like grip.

"Wot?"

Dugan's slipping his fingers free as Bob examines the half-buried stone. "Black fellas musta put it there. Some sorta altar, seems t' me. Don't touch it 'til you know f' sure." A wind blows and the pine trees creak. "Mumbo-jumbo voodoo shit. Creepy, innit?"

"Looks lak a millstone," Dugan shrugs.

"T' you 'n' me. . . but not t' them." He shuts his eyes and rolls his head. "Oi'm really beat. Patrol 'til six, then slap m' wife 'n' kip a nap, write, correct, 'n' send crap off, then come up 'ere t' check you out. . . loife under siege, mite, can't relent."

"Mike."

"Sigh *wot*?"

"My name is Mike."

"Ian Bob," he says again, distracted by some distant noise. They listen together and hear it again, a hollow reverberant series of thuds. Whatever it is, it's far away. Bob takes his hat off, rubs his scalp and leans his gun against a tree. His blondish hair is thin on top. "Oi woulda styed in bed," he says. "But then that racket started up. Hullo, Oi've 'eard that sound before—or somethin' bloody like it, roight?" He works his fingers on his neck, massaging it as he turns his head. "Oi whited 'til it simmer'd down. Then, working m' why up from th' road, Oi spied th' blackie through th' trees and tried t' circle back downwind. . ." His fingers stop. "So wot's with Dough?"

Hacked by his bearers, whatta think? "Moved away. We traded bunks."

"Frenn o' yours?"

"Not really, no," an answer that seems to reassure Bob.

"Frankly. . . that Dough's a wee bit strynge. . . a perfessah, y' know, no good with guns. Yuh been in th' service?"

Dugan nods. "Special duties."

"Roight," says Bob. He pulls a Lucky Strike from his shirt and holds the pack out. "Want a smoke? Don't blime yuh—nothin' but cancer sticks. Kenya. . . Katanga. . . Oi was there. Rhodesia. Merely rehearsals, mite." He strikes a light. "The comin' storm could start roight 'ere." He sucks smoke down and starts to cough. "We're nighbors, eh? I'm down th' road."

"I thought. . ."

". . . that y're the lass on a dead enn road? Lass but one, mite. Oi'm at the enn." He picks tobacco flakes from his tongue. "Me an' m' woife. . . she's preggers."

"What?"

"M' woife," he says. He looks around suspiciously, black fellas seemingly on his mind. "Can't trust 'em, Dolan, remember that. Yuh foolin' yerself yuh think yuh can."

"Dugan."

"Roight. Think I don't know? Get used t' 'avin' 'em around—all Mister this and Mister that—and, then, one noight. . ." He draws his hand across his throat. "Do as y' loike, chum. My advoice is keep y' distance." Bob gets up. "Could use a 'and, though, when it's toime. If yuh're fit by then. Two 'ands, I mean."

"You do Lamaze?" He's thinking hands and delivery-room teams, how Kravitz's wife, as D day neared, had said she'd pitch if he'd play catch—resulting in what, in scoring terms, was reckoned a passed ball by the nurse who'd snagged the pop-out as it fell. Both hands are needed now and then, though sometimes two are not enough.

"Wot?" Bob objects.

"You an' your wife—you do Lamaze?"

Bob squares his shoulders. "Sod you, mite! I got her preggers—that's all you need t' know from me without discussin' 'ow I do it."

"You said. . ."

"You Yanks don't listen, do yuh? Live an' let live, dog eat dog—it doesn't matter which t' me. Black fellas know I'm onto them. They 'ear me out thair ev'ry noight."

"So that was *you*?"

"Ten, one, and four—'ight 'undred yards between each styge—from different quadrants, soundin' all clear. Woife doesn't 'ear me, what's she t' do? Get out th' shotgun, call for 'elp. . . though, course," he glumly rubs his chin, "those buggers will 'ave cut th' loine."

Neither speaks. Bob lifts his gun. "So, what yuh runnin' from?" he asks. "Th' 'ousing shortage or th' law?"

"Huh?"

"Why'd yuh move 'ere?"

"R&R." He wags his sling. "I write," he shrugs.

"Sime sorta crap as yer frenn Dough, or somethin' a bloke moight wanna read?"

"Don't know for sure. I'm findin' out. An' you're a bounty hunter, right?"

"Don't push me—wotzit?"

"Dugan."

"Roight. *Th' Tarheel Planter*—'eard o' that? *Progressive Farmer* redneck style, but oughta be called th' Roight-Wing Cracker. Got readers in ev'ry one-'orse town—my sorta nighbors, Fyodor, armed t' th' teeth 'n' mean as snikes 'n' out to castrite Doctor Spock. I edit that. . . roight down the road."

"No shit?"

"Oh, yeah, there's plenty o' shit." Bob's smile is like drought-stricken corn. "But Oi didn't sigh that, did Oi now? Manure's a big thing where they live." He does a three-sixty, scanning the trees as, weapon at ready, he's on his feet. "Y' got no dog? Oi'll bring moine by t' get yer scent. . . don't want 'im rippin' out yer throat." Bob tips his hat brim with his gun and steps into the underbrush.

"You let him roam?"

There's no reply. Bob's melting back into the woods. A twig cracks and a blue jay squawks, then crickets make the silence seethe.

• • •

One thing comes clear in less than a week: Thoreau was lying when he proclaimed that life in the woods gets simplified. What Dugan gets done "deliberately" is prime the pump, compost the trash, wash out some socks, and look around, by which time half the day is gone. If he also opts to check the dam, buy Raisin Bran, and get his mail, or—after he's bailed a half-sunk boat found caught in an eddy after a storm and both his arms are back in use—go rowing to get some exercise, there's no time left. . . it's after dark.

And then there're trips to Chantry Mount that are harrowing in a special way. The shortcut route he generally takes leads past a plant called Lickety Split, where chickens get "processed" into lumps (i.e., dismembered) for KFC. He learns to speed up through that stretch, its stench so bad he holds his breath as soon as feathery tufts appear winking in trees or on the ground as if the birds had been detonated. Sometimes he spots a runaway, zigzagging through the charnel waste, and "If only for decency's sake," he thinks, "you know you oughta stop this car and give that multi-piece dinner a lift" (though he doesn't, of course—he motors on, like any good German Bayreuth-bound, thinking what matters are culture and brains except, as he learns in a couple of trips, what matters most in Chantry Mount is not just brains, but basketball. . . or brains applied to basketball, intricate feats of speed and height creating a sort of Watusi mystique combined with narcissistic aplomb that, allowing for all the standard clichés of beards and jeans and working-man's boots, derives from a single repressed chagrin that, whatever it is, it's not Ivy League. It's an academic Provincetown attempting to be both quaint and hip with a smugly bohemian backwoods air, a Holly Hobbie village façade, and beatniks and rednecks smoking grass like denizens of the Peaceable Kingdom (funny how back in vogue that is). Dugan's not comfy with the scene and ends up spending most of his time, despite his Famous Dogs resolve, holed up inside the library's stacks thinking about his book on Joyce.

He's conscientious at the start, working on some of the early stuff at a dimly lit carrel off to himself. DUBLINERS is what he writes at the top of a blue-lined index card followed by an abbreviation, LC-1, referring to his initial thoughts on Joyce's story "A Little Cloud" and numbered because it's meant to imply that, though they're about a small detail that happens to have caught his eye, they're only the first of many. "The title refers to something quite small that proves of great significance (cf. Elijah's forecast of rain from a cloud no bigger than someone's hand), and, given Little Chandler's name (n.b. same initials as "Little Cloud"), we might think that allusion applies to him. . .

> But as we learn in the course of the story, he's even
> less than meets the eye, and the tiny but crucial
> neglected detail points, all but unnoticed, to somebody
> else. L.C.'s a shallow self-pitying dabbler who thinks
> of himself as being Byronic (e.g., an Irish everyman)
> and considers his wife a hopeless drudge who's
> squelching his true romantic self. Three times [cite
> each] he's been on the verge of taking a volume of
> Byron down. (note: Joyce is very specific here—"the
> volumes remained [there] on their shelves.") BUT. . .

Dugan resumes triumphantly,

> when L.C. slouches morosely home, convinced his
> brood is dragging him down, Joyce almost in passing
> lets us know that "A volume of Byron's poems lay
> before him on the table" [THIS is the little Irish cloud

foretelling the ending of a drought—for who's been
reading the book and why? It can only be his misprized
wife! Like Gretta Conroy/Molly Bloom, she knows
much more than L.C. thinks and the dabbler himself
does not know shit!]

For a moment after jotting this down, Dugan feels he's been inspired—
an original insight, how about that? He finds Caitlin Rosen springing to
mind with Little Chandler's prurient dream of "darkly oriental eyes"
("how full they are of passion," he croons). But almost at once, the
euphoria fades. This sort of thing is pointless, he thinks, what Danny
would call pedantic drool. The light around him inspissates (i.e., grows
thicker) as he leaves off, slouching morosely to the loo—an oubliette in
the library stacks with graffiti on every inch of its wall from a neo-
Mansonite school of wit: gigantic dorks and 8-shaped bods with holes
gouged out strategically, psychotic ravings, numbers, dates, and, over the
urinal scrawled in red, a line in caps from William Blake,

O, ROSE, THOU ART SICK

notated below with "She's got the clap." Joyce might have savored that,
he thinks, though he shudders to guess who'd authored the rest—grad
students gnawing on their fists, professors giggling as they scrawl,
Raskolnikov the Janitor deciding what will go or stay. Dugan examines
this wall of shame, takes out his BIC, and prints two words between "Rock
Hudson Is A Stud" and "Stop Me Before I Swill Again."

MY LAI

Okay. He sheathes his pen.
    Returning to the parking lot, he spots an imitation Che at a table in front
of the student center—a coed flaunting a red beret with olive fatigues and
working-class boots recruiting for some radical group. She's a dialectical
piece of work, a hip Brunhilde hackling the crowd with tangles of
uncombed curly blond hair exploding from under her Maoist cap while
she, in a boldly assertive stance (hands on hips, feet planted apart, a braless prow that's bursting free though pinioned in crisscrossed bandoliers
and a freckle-faced, pink-cheeked, snub-nosed face that's set in a Debs-

for-Castro sneer) is distributing flyers to passers-by, daring the frat-boy business-school types to bad-mouth what she's handing out.

He detours for a closer look and gets a poster in return. COMO EN VIETNAM, it says, depicting a girl in a rice-field hat who's cuddling an unfired cannon shell more or less like that girl on the Feed & Seed door holding a loaf of Merita. It's crudely drawn but looks like Rose. There's another that says just VENCEREMOS.

"Whut th' hail. . .?" he says to Che, who greets him with a provocative smirk.

By now he's gotten his act together—his accent and his wardrobe match, he's found a used-dog for his hut (a collie-shepherd advertised as Moving/Forced to Liquidate/Non-spayed Female/One Year Old). He's calling her Credo on a whim. "It goes with the hut," is how he'll reply to cracks from Danny or anyone else maintaining such whimsy's out of sync with his nouveau poor-white masquerade. It's quixotic but hopeful, he'll admit, an assertion of faith against all odds to name your best friend I-Believe. "So, okay, cool. . . belief in what?" a flake like Sunbeam might demand. "In possible virtue," he'd reply. Besides, he'd want to point out to her if, in her own Pavlovian way, she'd counted on him to get it up whenever she hummed "Sh-boom, Sh-boom," why shouldn't his sidekick salivate to something more stirring than a bell? Like Ludwig, say, whenever she eats? It's the *Missa Solemnis* he has in mind. He'll sing it as he serves up scraps, (the "Credo, Credo"—all he recalls), but, no, it's not just shi-shi crap like dotting your i's with little hearts. . . which, according to Sunbeam's new-age disdain, is a symptom of nymphomania (as she should know if anyone does). That's nympholepsy, Dugan says. "But whut thuh hail' (as he'll tell Che), "belief in sumthin's not so bad"—especially when, as somebody's said, you can't always get what you want.

So, beginning a month ago at his hut, he'd sung to Credo every night when putting her supper into a bowl, and, after he'd sung, he'd start to talk—at first to try his accent out, but then, because she'd seemed engrossed, to share his thoughts on Joyce as well. Uh-oh, he thought, like blessing snakes. . . the hermit syndrome, lost at sea. Which is why, for a while, he'd cut back somewhat on their chats, and, when he resumed, stuck mostly to stuff like weather reports and local news picked up from Pa at the Feed & Seed. Still, that did wonders for his brogue.

The upshot is it's gotten so good that even some locals can't be sure unless he gives himself away with leftie-speak like "hawks" or "pigs" when talking about the power elite. Poultry and plywood always work—

and with chickens, of course, he's on firmer ground, though that can get him in trouble too, as when Ma Beasley reported her niece had picked up work at Lickety Split, and he'd replied, "What scalds mah grits is all thuh road kill 'round that place." He'd seen Pa glance at their frozen food locker, and Ma asked Dugan to say up front if he had anything stuck in his craw. Hastily patching up his gaffe, Dugan allowed that what he'd meant was how shockingly coddled our chain gangs are—instead of keeping the highways clean, they keep demanding luxuries. . . like toilet paper and color TV. Pa had nodded his assent, and Dugan said, "Hit's 'at arrogant dadburn'd Suth'un Bell," invoking a universal gripe. "Them operators gall my soul." Using their pay phone off and on, he'd been having some trouble getting through when calling long distance to talk to Dan. "Becuzza how yuh talk," said Pa, and Dugan was flattered, supposing he meant that's how they treat us good ole boys. But, after reflecting, Pa declared, "Hit used t' happen t' Roscoe's whyff. . . 'Course she was speakin' some kinda Koh-rean."

It was talking to Credo that did the trick. Now even the Beasleys have overlooked how peculiar his accent seemed at first. Add unkempt hair, sweat-stiffened jeans, and hands hard-callused from rowing his boat, and this is the package Dugan presents on that afternoon in Chantry Mount when, approaching the Cuba-Si! table and babe—one Bonnie Gewertz, as he'll soon learn—he studies those posters, the one he's got with the bomb-cradling girl and the other that spells out *venceremos*.

"Whut th' hail. . . ?" was how he'd begun, and "duz this thang say?" he finishes up, pointing his finger at "Vin-ser. . . vin-ker. . . Ah don' know!"

Bonnie adjusts her bullet-belts. "We shall overcome," she says, then comes closer to finger the one he's got. "Como means 'like,'" she adds with a frown, unsure of where Dugan's coming from but clearly intrigued by what she sees. "'Like in Vietnam.' We're going to win." She tosses her curls assertively. "In Cuba they're just like Viet Cong." Though she's aware that her words are trite, her eyes are saying something else—I'm privileged, sure, but hip to this: the wretched of the earth still fuck, and it's possible we might work things out so long as you don't call my bluff. He understands her well enough to push his accent to the hilt.

"Caumeau?"

"It's Spanish," Bonnie says.

"In Vee-et *Nam*?" pronouncing it so it rhymes with ham. "How come they're dinks instead uh spics?"

The bigotry of the oppressed. She's sized him up and likes what she sees, a bottom-dog victim she can help. She wants to go somewhere and talk, and, though that's all she specifies, the implications are intense. They gab for a while beneath a tree. He tells her how his family fared on their Alabama tenant farm, describing every plank and chink in a cabin lit by kerosene. Though life was hard, they'd had each other. She listens as raptly as Robert Coles. When he adds that struggling through Thomas Wolfe had made him hitch-hike to this school, her eyes get misty. He has soul. He's older than most students here, and not officially enrolled, but he's found his way into the stacks to study works by guys like Joyce. . .

"JOYCE?" she snorts indignantly. He should be reading Franz Fanon. What about Marx? Marcuse? Mao?

He's read so little, he admits. His family used to call him Duke, but they've all been wiped out by pellagra. He hadn't planned to tell her that, but it feels so good to get it out. What else? she asks. His run-down shack, he'd take her there if it weren't so far—and, anyhow, she might get scared. He lives alone there in the woods, the only white amongst poor blacks. Her eyes are shining. Can't she go? She'd really like to see his shack. She also grooves on his Pontiac, exactly what she thought he'd drive. He says it was salvaged from a flood. She waves to a friend, they go for a ride, and, in less than an hour, turn down the road past Trueblood's place—where two little black girls smile and wave.

Impressed with that, she *loves* his hut. The privy, though, is disappointing. "It's not authentic," she complains.

"It's junk," he argues.

"True," she nods, reversing her stand. The people's art is often junk, and vice versa Hegel said. . . or was it Marx? She's not quite sure—one stood the other on his head. His hut's decor is "primitive," which means it's got integrity despite its air of the occult. Not junk, but kitsch. It's all the same. She's studying sociology. "I like this place. It's totally cool. Straight out of *The Whole Earth Catalog!*"

"Th' whut?" he asks. He says he's never heard of that.

"You're really amazing," she declares. She steps up close and kisses him, then moves away like a bull in a ring, head-down before it makes its charge.

"Ah'll lite th' heater," Dugan says.

"I love the smell of kerosene."

"Oh, yeah?"

"What's this?" *The Peaceable Kingdom.*

"Uh zoo," he says.

"Oh, no, it's not. We studied that. You know what's going on down here?"

"Looks lak a party. Wait," he says, unrolling the poster he'd gotten from her. "Ah'm gonna stick this one up thar too."

He fumbles with the row of nails he uses for coat hooks by the door, impaling COMO EN VIETNAM. When he turns back, she's done a trick—like yanking out a tablecloth while leaving the plates and glasses set. Though the bandoliers are still in place, her top is gone. Her hair so blond, her nipples pink, she's like a busty kewpie doll tricked out in boots and cartridge belt. "Put on some music," she suggests.

He switches on his KLH, which he claims some students had thrown away. She thinks it's stolen. Stepping back, he gestures towards the nasal voice. "Th' people's Shakespeare."

"Elvis?"

"HANK!" He'd bought it with just such use in mind. "Now try th' sofa," he invites. "That leather's genyu-ine Naugahyde."

He's got her on the psychic run. When she sits down, he joins her there and gets his hand in her fatigues. She listens for a couple of bars, then says she's glad it wasn't him. Who? *Elvis*, he's (her cheeks are flushed, his hand gripped tightly by her thighs). . . the tool (she gasps) of the. . . exploiters! Sorry to hear that, he declares. "No. . . move your. . . there! That's it!" she says. She drowns Hank out when she arrives like Lenin to the Finland Station.

Afterwards, she's magnanimous. In her red beret and cartridge belts luxuriating on the couch, she says she'd like to meet his dog—even if, as he's already warned, it's tuckered out from chasing coons. He makes a Hello-Doggie noise as Credo haughtily stalks in. "Hey, Plato, how's it going, girl?" (Has he no shame?) He pats her head, making the pathos extra plain—though dropped-out from a one-room school, he's named his dog for an ancient Greek whose work he'd never encountered in class. . . and class is whut it's all about.

"I'm going to help you," Bonnie vows.

She tells him her minor's in Modern Dance, which helps explain what happens next—a strenuous choreographic feat ("Nimble Monkey Tames the Snake") that breaks a lamp, knocks over a chair, and nearly puts him in a truss.

That's only the beginning, though. Radical sex is Bonnie's bag. Orgasms equal agitprop. She likes rough names—"rich bitch" is one, and "cap'talist cunt," and others that she instructs him to use pertaining to either hygiene or money. She never shaves her body hair, endowing her cavities with a scent that lingers on his hands for days (he'll later tell Danny it gets so bad he puts on gloves to brush his teeth). At teach-ins, when the program's dull, she likes to rummage through his crotch and grunt obscene ten-letter words. Her favorite site is in the stacks, the men's room Dugan had found on his own, and she likes to do it from behind, her hands propped up against the wall like an S.D.S. militant getting frisked. She reads graffiti as he humps and screams "Que! Que!"—or maybe "Che!"—not familiar with Spanish, he's unsure. . . though he notices on one such trip that his own graffito's been removed, inked over by a silhouette that looks like Richard Nixon's nose.

She brings him books and magazines: *Ramparts*, Roszak, *Mother Jones*, *The Anvil*, and *The Protean Radish*. Wilhelm Reich has a lot to say, but Norman O. Brown's a waste of time—"sophomoric crap" is what she says. At first he thinks she's read all that, but once he learns she's blowing smoke, merely repeating what she's heard, he ends disputes by asking her if that's what Lukács really said. "It's what he meant to say," she smiles, and tells him not to think too much—it's balls you'll need when it hits the fan. "The people are always getting fucked. . . remember *that*," is her schoolmarmish line, confusing herself with the masses.

Her friends consider him insincere. When asked to go cut sugar cane, he says he'd love to help Fidel, but Kropotkin's taking up all his time. "Try hacking your way through that," he laughs, but they glower at him with consternation. Kropotkin, huh? Kropotkin's a shill, and so is Dugan they suspect. They're not sure why, but they think he's a phony, a "prole on the make" as one of them sneers, "probably spying for the Man." As for Bonnie herself, she too begs off from joining the junket to Havana—and, since salvaging Dugan is her excuse and sleeping with Bonnie is everyone's goal, they're miffed with Dugan and let him know it. Bonnie dismisses them with a shrug.

"They're premature ejaculators."

"Whut?" Dugan blinks.

"Like McNamara—heard of him? The Secretary of Defense? Just look at his eyes when he's on TV. You learn to size 'em up," she says.

You do? Oh, sure, she's worked it out. "Think of the Puritans," Bonnie exhorts, "harping on God but crazed by sex, clutching a blunderbuss in the woods while dreaming of fucking Hester Prynne." But what if, he asks, when we talk about sex, what's really in our heads is God? (Perry Miller had said that first—he'd heard it at Harvard while he was there—but she cackles as if his thought's absurd.) "Look, don't you read the stuff I bring? It's very important," she maintains as if she thinks it really is. He's caught off guard when, in order to prove her point it seems, she yanks a library book from her bag, locates a page, and starts to read that, "Sexually awakened women" (clearly a reference to herself) "affirmed and recognized as such, would mean. . ." she pauses for effect, "the complete collapse of. . ." what does he think? ". . . authoritarian. . .?"

He can't guess.

". . . ideology!"

"That's a big mouthful," he concedes.

"Huge," she agrees, stroking the jacket of her book—a vaginal landscape by O'Keefe with letters like daggers adrift in the sky. *The Mass Psychology of* he sees with the rest of the title blocked by her hand. *Fascism*, he finally makes it out. For a course? he asks. She shakes her head. He can't believe she's found it herself, but maybe so. . . and, after all, there's Little Chandler's wife to consider.

Bonnie insists he take the book—he needs to read it right away, before he has another orgasm. How long does she think that's likely to be? It all depends. Depends on what? She has him read Chapter 1 aloud while she's translating into fellatio. He stops at a climactic passage.

"How far did you get?" she asks with a smile.

"Page three," he answers. "Paragraph two."

She tells him to mark it. When he does, he notes the book has similar marks, mostly on pages one through two. He wonders if one was by McNamara.

But, for all her hedonistic flair, Bonnie can be surprisingly staid. One day at his hut, while warming up with a medley of martial arts and sex, she says as if she's quoting Marx that she just can't do it *in front of her*. She means the dog.

"Like doggie style?"

"Not any style. I don't like how she's watching us."

"That's paranoid." He means bourgeois.

"Also," she says, "please give her a bath. I leave here smelling like a vet."

"A whiff of dharma's good for you."

"You're talking funny," she objects. "Like what's-his-name, with L.B.J.? Bill Moyers. . ." she says—he's starting to sound a lot like him."

"Ah been watchin' TV," is his excuse.

He'd gotten careless. Bonnie's right. He promises that he'll clean things up. The dog goes out and she goes down. They hammer out a little more Che, and, by the time he goes for beer, he's gotten his accent back on track. No "dharma" again he silently vows as he fetches a six-pack from the store, but just as he's nearly reached the hut, he hears two voices, then a slap, followed by laughter and a howl that sounds like Ian Bob in heat. He turns the corner and there they are—Bonnie in high-boy overalls posed like a barefoot odalisque with her on the bench and him on the steps, his hat strategically on his lap. Bob greets him with, "'ey, Gilligan, look! It's th' *perfesser!*"

She laughs as if that showed some wit. They talk awhile and drink a beer. Then, letting Bob know the party is over, Dugan tells Bonnie he'll drive her back. They're halfway there before she asks why his neighbor had called him what he did.

"He's such an asshole," Dugan says.

"He's funny."

"Trust me."

"Trust you how?"

"He's an Aussie, okay? Two words will do. . . genetic pool."

"But he's aware. Politically, he's very aware."

"For chrissake, Bonnie! He's deranged. A wacko racist *sturmbahnfuhrer.* . ."

"A what?"

He knows he's slipped again. "He don't want flow-ride in th' wawtah."

"Uh-huh," she says sarcastically. "Like all your neighbors here are black, and suddenly you know so much." She hooks her thumbs and yanks her bib, displaying her braless line of thought—something that Bob had surely observed. "Your neighbor's a very thoughtful man. And not as right-wing as you think."

"They come from convicts," Dugan shrugs. "That must affect their politics."

"He's organizing farmers here. Know what he thinks this country needs? Some *national* socialists! So, you see?"

He sees but keeps it to himself.

"You know what else?" She's sporting a smirk he's seen before, the day she wore her red beret. "He thinks I've got nice boobs," she says.

• • •

If Bonnie's not exactly swift, she's good at getting what she wants—as, for instance, at Sigmund's Kosher Dogs ("A Lingam in a Yoni Bun") while spouting instructive Maoist quips, she asks how well he knows McLuhan, clearly with some ulterior motive. They're seated beside a long glass wall that serves as a sort of window display for the latest in counterculture chic set off by an orange and green décor that, according to something Bonnie's just read, can work to suppress the appetite. It's here she likes to rendezvous where Dugan alone eats Sigmund's wares while she's seen feeding the destitute.

Unsure of what she's getting at, he slyly considers what she's asked. "Old Mighty Mouth!" he finally says.

"Whut?" Bonnie frets. Increasingly, she talks like him—an affectation he resents.

"They call 'im Denny."

"Ah don't know. . ."

"Won thirty-one games lass yeah f' Dee-troit."

"Yew got 'im mixed up," she explains. She smooths her hair and takes his hand while he eats French fries with the other. She means the global village guy. Technology and who we are. Awareness, wholeness, Gutenberg.

"Whutever."

"Look." She strokes his hand. "Th' car, th' watch. . . not jess TV. They're tools we use t' mediate. See how hit works? Through ritual. That's whut we need t' understand becuz that's how hits message gits through."

"Hit is?"

"Of course."

"That don't make sense."

She sighs and leans back in her chair, tugging him forward over the table and gazing into his eyes with such an intense and proletarian abandon that the ketchup is knocked onto its side, she drops her voice and earnestly asks, "Yew evah been to a football game?"

"Well. . ."

"Level with me. Tell th' truth. Ah mean a big-time college game."

"Uh, lemme see. . ." He stalls for time, uncertain of where she's taking this. "On TV count?"

"Thass jess mah point! Hit's lak yew've never been t' church. Yew've heard 'em hollerin', am I right? but can't relate to why they holler."

"Ah guess so."

"See. McLuhan's right. Th' medium is th' people's massage. Hit's also blatant exploitation."

"You mean hit's fixed?"

She smiles and points a schedule out, taped to the wall behind his head. Why does he think they advertise to watch the underclass at play? What sort of underclass? he asks. "What Cleaver calls 'em. . . menials." That sounds degrading, he concedes, and where did Eldridge Cleaver play? She says he ought to ask instead how much we waste on circuses when some are going without bread. "But not those menial running backs who drive those fancy foreign cars?" This makes her frown. He's missed the point. He needs to find out for himself. "This weekend's when yew oughta start."

"Start whut?"

"Yew know. Th' CSU game. Yew said your friend. . ."

"Ah know ah did." "

He'd mentioned Danny once or twice, implying that Danny pushed a mop among the jocks at Pecker Place. That's how he'd met that running back contending for some big award. The Heisman Trophy? That's the one. She says she'd been exploited once, cheerleading for a high school team, but got free passes now and then. She bets his friend does. Maybe, yeah, since they're playin' down there.

"So, call 'im up."

"Okay. Ah will. . . assumin' I kin fine his numbah."

Their dueling accents make it hard for either to communicate, but back in Lugton later that day, he tries the Beasley's phone again and finds this time he's getting through.

"Mike!" Danny shouts. "What's wrong with your voice?"

"Whut'n the hail you tawkin' 'bout, bo?" Hoping he can't be overheard, he strains to get his old voice back while murmuring in an undertone. That makes his accent weirder still, but Danny treats it like a joke.

"Them mountain men abusin' you?"

"Hail, yes. Look, Dan, I know it's late. . ."

"Hang on a minute, Mike, okay?" Commotion at the other end while Dugan stretches the phone cord out to check on Bonnie in his car, nodding her head to "Purple Haze" or something that makes her jerk around as if she's on a carnival ride. He looks at the Red Man on a shelf, Brown Mule, and stuff for roll-your-own. Ma Beasley starts to wipe the scale as if her mind's on something else. "Hey, Mike," says Danny, "Caitlin and me. . .

we're havin' a little trouble here. Nothin' that JLM can't fix. . . but what you need? You back in jail?"

"Some tickets for this weekend's game."

"With Chantry Mount?" He hesitates. "I wouldn't know where to start on that. The paper says they're all sold out."

"No problem. Just give J.C. a call. I'll never be able to reach him from here. Ask him to leave whatever he can for Dugan to pick up at the gate."

"How many you want?"

"How many you think?"

"Just checking, pal. Another flake?"

"Sort of. . . you know. . . I can't discuss it."

"Wire taps, right? I'll do my best. You tell Aleksei four oh ten, a range of fourteen hundred miles."

"I read you, Strangelove. Keep the faith and sodomize Henry K as well. I owe you, Dan."

"Stay cool."

"You too."

To Bonnie, he merely says, "Okay." He never learns what's up her sleeve. It may be someone's tipped her off and this is her way of checking it out. Or maybe it's his rival prole—a jerk blown in from Malibu, allegedly a migrant worker, who's claiming that Dugan's not for real and getting some traction with Bonnie's friends. To counter that, he's agreed to go. . . exactly what he shouldn't do.

At least he's got a set of wheels that lend him credibility, and three days later they're on their way, rattling along in the Pontiac. Halfway there, Bonnie observes sententiously that—in its present state, at least—they're in an authentic "people's car."

"A whole lot roomier," Dugan says.

"Than whut?" she asks.

They've stopped for gas and are stretching their legs—in Hamlet, near the railroad yard. The trains are lined up ten tracks deep. "Vee dub-yous."

"Whut?"

"Folks waggins, rite? You said jess now. . ."

"This heah's a Pontiac," she frowns.

"This heah?" he mocks. "They talk like that in the suburbs now?"

"*Whut*?" Bonnie's incensed. "An' who are *yew*, Mistuh Spiro-Agnew-from-the-Sticks? If yew're gonna improve th' way yew talk, choose somebody better tuh imitate."

"Like who?"

"Yew name it. Say-zar Chavez!"

The guy from Malibu, all right—Dugan discerns his sabotage. But back in the car, as they resume, passing the boxcars' dots and dashes, Dugan decides to hold his tongue, watching the town as it slips by—railroaders' houses, chain-link fence, a scoreboard over a football field (HOME OF THE FIGHTIN' RAMS, it brags). The field is empty. Bonnie sulks.

"You put down everything," she complains.

"Ain't that whut revolutions do?"

"You see?" she huffs. "That's whut I mean. You used to be so. . ."

"Whut?"

"You know. So. . . mentally undernourished," she says.

"Those wuh th' days!" He touches her shoulder cajolingly. "Come on, now, whutta we squabbling ovah? We're gonna go see a *football* game!" She slips both hands beneath her bib as if she's warming them in a muff. After a minute, Dugan adds, "Listen, ah'll tell yew somethin' cool. Yew know how this heah car got named? Th' Pontiac?"

"A town in Michigan," she growls.

"Huh-unnh," he says. "Yew see that thar?" He points to the logo on the dash. "That thar's a chief named Pontiac. . . who went t' see th' Master of Life, an' th' Master give 'im some advice. He said t' drive th' white man out."

"Drive him how? Like a chauffeur?"

He looks at her and gets in return a clearly ironic *who-me?* stare, first time she's ever let him see she knows he knows she's playing dumb. She's shrewder than he'd thought she was. Everyone is, he tells himself. They're speeding towards a cross-shaped sign—GET READY HE'S COMING! it forewarns.

"See that?" he leers.

With a satisfied smirk, she rubs her hands like guinea pigs humping under her bib—as if to say, "An' so am Ah, Ah'm comin' too, no matter who Ah'm doin' it with." He has a sudden revelation, that, leaving aside her working-class pose, Bonnie's a queen-bee through and through, serviced by all and bound to none. Whatever his prospects as a drone, she, in another five years or so, will be shaking her pompoms, like as not, for an NFL expansion team—the L.A. Studs or Malibu Dinks—without a thought for Franz Fanon. He lets another minute go by before returning to Pontiac.

"So, ennyhow, he enns up thar. . . as an orna-mint that's stuck on a hood."

"I still don't get it. What's your point?"

"There's not any point," he shrugs—something he thinks he's said before.

• • •

By half-time when they reach the lot, the guards have left the VIP gate, so Dugan brazenly drives on in, trying to squeeze the Pontiac into what's clearly less than a space between a post and a Mercedes.

"Yew scraped hit," Bonnie yawns and says.

"Th' coach's car? Oh, shit!" he yelps, then tries to blow his comment off. "Looks lak a coach's car t' me. C'mon! We're gonna miss th' game."

A deafening roar erupts inside, so sudden and loud they feel like mice in the path of a mega-sized mowing machine. It rumbles past them, then subsides. The ticket window's still not shut. Nearing it, Dugan tells her to wait. They need to be discreet he says.

"You're Doctor Dee?" the ticket guy asks. In Cumbria, folks still dress for a game—the Lugton look is not in vogue, and Dugan looks too alien.

"That's right," says Dugan, doing his best to keep from being overheard.

"You got an I.D.?"

"The Dee's just my initial, see? I'm a sorta professor. . . on leave," he adds, showing the guy his faculty card.

"This stuff is for a guy named Dee."

"What's wrong?" asks Bonnie.

"Nothin', sugar. You wait right there. I'm talkin' with. . . Mister Wilcox here. Okay, then, Wilcox, here's the scoop. You see who left that? Take a look. He's gonna have 'em nail your ass if we don't get to see this game. In fact, I'm gonna tell the press you wouldn't let his cousin in."

"His cousin?"

"Right, you racist twit! You wanna discuss those famous initials? Jobless Chump—you got that down? Guys lose their thumbs for less than this."

"But you're not. . ."

"Now I'm getting' pissed! His dad's my uncle, understand? And that's a problem you don't need. We're well-connected, get my drift?"

"I'm still supposed. . ."

"Does Grandpa Sternbolt ring a bell? Just fork 'em up, an' you're home free. You don't, I tell the Senator, you move someplace outside this state."

"I shouldn't do this."

"Yeah, you should."

He takes the package to the gate where Bonnie says, "I'm sugar, huh? How come yew treat me lak I'm shit?" She doesn't like to be upstaged. "What's all that stuff?"

Press passes, camera and two caps—the camera's made by Fisher-Price. "My friend's a joker. Put these on."

"What organization?" asks the guard who's standing by the elevator, bemused by Bonnie's dreadlocked hair, a new addition to her look.

"P.W.I." At least, that's what the passes say.

He lets them through, a first for Poor White something or other (International's Dugan's guess). From there it's easy—off the lift and down the ramp, past one more guard, another gate, and then they're strolling onto the field. His camera draws some curious looks, but once their Rooster hats are on, they blend in with the sideline crowd who're busily snapping the halftime show. The scale of things is dizzying.

Out on the field a giant egg, towed on a cart and swathed in smoke, has people prancing all about, rushing up to touch its sides, flailing their arms and leading cheers. Surrounding them is the Rooster Pit—a bowl whose steep sides tower up, a rack with seventy thousand heads that at some signal start to shout, "DEATH! DEATH! DEATH! DEATH!" Bonnie is baffled. Huge black flags are suddenly raised and raced in lines around the track, dipping and rippling in the breeze. The Roosters' colors are red and black.

"The dee-fense," Dugan yells to her. "It's called Black Death."

A drum starts throbbing on the field. Behind it, marching through the smoke, two hundred instruments appear along with sequined majorettes chop-chopping with fiery-knobbed batons. They stop and launch into a tune that Bonnie hums for several bars, then turns to Dugan.

"Know whut that is?"

"*Also Sprach*. . ." he starts to say.

"Two Thousand One! You didn't see *that*?"

How could he? He was in the fields with beri beri, out pickin' cotton, totin' bales. The egg is rocking, so's the crowd. "DEATH! DEATH!"

they're chanting again, applauding a giant head with legs that represents their masterful coach. The drums are buttressed now by brass, a theme that rises like the bone tossed in the air by Ray Don's head (a *heel*-bone! laughs a local reporter). The bone descends and drums pound on like a count-down for apocalypse. BOOM-boom BOOM-boom, BOOM-boom BOOM-boom.

Dahhh Dahhhhh DAH-DAHHHHHHHHH!

The egg cracks open, smoke swirls up, and out steps what appears to be a Loony-Tunes cartoon sprung to life—a man-sized rooster in a suit, nodding and waving to a crowd that answers at first with delirious joy. Sparklers converge, and trumpets soar. Big yellow feet and smiley beak, he boogies as the crowd looks on and, only gradually, one by one, noting a problem that leaves them stunned. Although the music thunders on, a hush falls over them like a tarp. They've seen what, locked inside his egg and wearing a huge and cumbersome head, their Rooster-man presumably hasn't—a new appendage like a tail that's flopping and swinging between his legs. . . except it's red and sewn in front and looks distinctly circumcised.

A gasp goes up as he cavorts—some titters, and then outright guffaws. The band's pursuing its diagrams, but a couple of tubas get unnerved, back up and take out half the drums. A pile-up follows, cockettes sprawl, the woodwinds fizzle like Alka-Seltzer. With his vision impeded by his beak, the Rooster deduces something's wrong but thinks he'll somehow save the day by flapping his arms and boogying on despite the band's atonal turn.

Dispatched to get things back in hand, two troopers are racing onto the field when Rooster-man, by chance it seems, discovers what's causing all the fuss and desperately tries to rip it off. But his yanking and tugging spin him around, sending him spiraling to the turf where, jerking spasmodically, kicking his heels, he flops in an onanistic heap. A trooper has seized him by the claw when, leaving that part of his costume behind, the rooster lurches back to his feet, running for daylight as the crowd, aghast but more and more amused, begins to cheer the flasher on,

FORTY... THIRTY! ... FIFTEEN! ... TEN!

Rooster-man is in full-stride, the goal line just a step away, when his drooping upholstery gets in the way and tangles beneath his one good claw. Like somebody poleaxed, he goes down, lying inert as troopers with mace subdue the non-tumescent garb. A stretcher's brought out from the stands to take him to a holding tank where, news reports will later say, they find him stoned but not to blame for what *The Impeder*'s reporter will term "a regrettably tasteless Chantry-Mount prank" while others will privately share a belief the mascot himself had hatched the stunt after munching peyote mailed by a friend from an orchid shop in Laredo.

The teams begin the second half, though Rooster-man's fate has cast a pall. Action is sluggish for a while, then CSU starts to move the ball—a couple of J.C.'s patented runs slashing off-tackle and cutting back, a pitch-out to him going wide. He jukes and fakes the halfback out, reverses direction and heads upfield. He's at the forty when he's nailed, knocked out of bounds at precisely the spot where Dugan and Bonnie have set up shop. Dugan leaps clear, but Bonnie goes down like foam laid under a DC-9 with J.C. atop her as they slide. He rides her with her legs spread wide until they reach the Rooster bench and lie there grappling for a bit while the ball veers towards the Gatorade. Her dreadlocks are what catch his eye.

"Girl. . . do sump'en wit' 'at hair!"

It's lust at first sight, as they say. Officials are trying to whistle him back, but J.C. takes the time to grin, "Meet you in the end zone, bitch. . . In three mo' plays. Hey, Doctor Dee! You made it, huh? So, how's my old professor doin'?"

"Pretty good." His cover is blown.

"I gotta go," J.C. observes like Romeo saying he hears a lark. The crowd is yelling out his name. He winks at Bonnie, looks at the stands, and holds three fingers in the air.

His fans let out a rooster cry, and three plays later roar again as J.C. darts across the line, busts the ball, and piles on Bonnie. She answers with a pelvic thrust that announces what level she's playing on. Dugan, who's back at the thirty-five, can't read what J.C.'s telling her, but it seems to involve a rendezvous because she lingers by the fence, not far from several pricks-on-sticks waved by frat boys in the stands. The kick-off teams are on the field as Dugan encounters a resolute face in shades and headphone by his side. "Hi, Coach," he says.

He gets a curt, suspicious glance before the great man turns aside to shout instructions to an aide. "Who're all these bozos?" he demands, nodding his head in Dugan's direction.

There's not much point in hanging around. A last long look and Dugan leaves, not pestering Bonnie with goodbye.

• • •

His Pontiac's been towed away.

"I had a sticker," Dugan protests.

"For motor-sickles, sure," he's told by Wilcox at the ticket booth—who's been waiting, it seems, for Dugan's return. "Guess J.C. stands for Junkyard Car."

"How long d'you take to think that up?"

"You call the Senator. . . okay?" He slams the ticket window shut.

Dugan has turned to leave on foot when he sees a Corvette backing up, swerving erratically through the maze of Caddies and sports cars left in the lot. It slams on brakes when Dugan waves, a tail-light brushing past his thigh.

"Stuck in reverse," the driver yowls.

"It only goes backwards," bawls her friend.

They giggle. Both are bonged way out. He says his car's been towed away.

"Bummer!"

Then they laugh again. He asks for a lift to look for his car. "Wherever it's gone," he adds with a shrug.

"Wherever? Sure!" the passenger clucks. She finds his plight hilarious.

"If you can get us outta here," the driver says with a serious look.

"Okay, move over," Dugan says.

He slides the gearshift into first. The car bucks forward.

"Whoops!" shouts one.

The other blonde cheers. They're almost out when they get stopped. A hulking figure lifts his hand.

"Uh-oh," says one.

"Shhhhh," says the other.

They both sit stiffly as the hulk stalks over to the driver's side, tapping against the window trim and leaning his head officiously in. He's got two watches on his arm and wears a jaunty safari hat encircled by a leopard-skin band. He nods to each of them and smiles. "Don't ever do nothin' like this again." His air of cordial menace hangs like beer breath in the autumn air. "I'd kinda like. . ." He looks around, rubbing his mouth with the back of his hand and breathing heavily after each phrase. ". . . to see this town

196

die peaceful." He waves and smiles his famous smile, acknowledging Dugan's sly salute, then straightens up and pushes off.

"Oh, wow!" says a blonde as they drive on.

"Strangioso," says the other.

"Sheriff Bullard," Dugan notes, but neither of them has seen the movie.

• • •

Now solitude poses problems of its own. A light rain's pattering on the roof, the wind keeps lisping at the door, and Dugan, back in anchorite mode, is lounging on the Naugahyde with a *Charlotte Observer* in his hands while Credo snoozes on the rug. Though the heater turns out some short-range warmth, the walls give off a radiant chill as he peruses recent news and ponders a question of profit and loss. Think McNamara, he tells himself. "The waste, the waste," he mutters aloud, remembering a person he'd never met who'd preceded him as a fellow Rhodes, top graduate in his class at the Point, among the first to die in Nam. What do we get that's worth the price. . . to us, to them, to anyone else other than Rusk and Kissinger? The cost-accounting seems surreal.

"An isolated incident," is Nixon's reassuring phrase in a speech he'd made two days before. My Lai, he says, was "deviant," but our people will get to the bottom of it. They'll seek out those responsible—if somebody was, if it happened at all. Meanwhile let's not prevaricate by ignoring the excellent progress we've made. A million two hundred thousand men are how many we've sent to Vietnam, and "virtually all of them," Nixon declaims, "have helped the people of Vietnam. . . in one way or another." They've built roads and schools, he wants us to know. They've built churches and pagodas too, and, in point of fact, he declares, "The Marines alone this year have built over 50,000 churches, pagodas and temples for the people of Vietnam."

But that's appalling, Dugan thinks—in less than a year? A thousand a week? A hundred thirty-six a day? No wonder we're at a standstill there— we're wasted from all that temple-building! At this rate, in another ten years, we'll be looking at. . . what? a half million more? At a thousand or so square feet apiece, that's nearly a billion square feet in all. Some 20,000 football fields! Built by our Marines alone on a manic-obsessive-compulsive jag in a country that's not as big as Missouri! It boggles the mind, but the remedy's clear: WE'VE GOT TO STOP THE BUILDING NOW! while there's still room for rice fields left. Or, maybe, just maybe, that's why we should bomb. . . to roll back the pagoda glut. There's only one question he'd like to ask: when everything's totally out of whack, how do we know what's *deviant*?

My Lai, you say? Not all agree. Some argue that it's not unique, that both sides murder all the time. General Westmoreland espouses this view on the very same day as Nixon's speech—and neither one mentions a massacre. "But is it okay," a reporter asks, "to kill civilians?" Well. . . let's see. The General hears the question posed and tilts his Easter Island head. "Not unless they're armed," he earnestly says. But there've been cases, he points out, where women have killed our fighting men, and children have planted booby traps and thrown grenades and served as combatants in such ways. Can he say how often such things occur? Well, "these are not unusual." But then, he adds, reflectively,

I wouldn't say they are commonplace.

Credo lifts her head to stare as Dugan emits a sort of yelp. Atrocities and an atrocious war—the difference is what? he asks himself as he'd tried to ask in that letter of his. He crumples the *Observer* up and tosses it on the hut's cold floor, unable to say which he loathes more—their hokum or his own sanctimony. He's growing truly sick of himself as, living his arcane Robinsonade, he's learned how digressions can roam unchecked like roaches over the ceiling at night, and the babble is driving him up the wall (his thoughts, that is—the roaches stay mum, the advantage of feelers he reflects). He'd like to shut the hubbub out, but what can he do here by himself? He's in his hut, they're in his head, like Russian dolls inside each other.

He hears a growl beside his ear. "I never knew, and never shall a worse man that myself" (that's only because you haven't looked—keep at it, chum, he tells the voice that must have sprung from something he's read). Who is it then? He's not quite sure—it's vaulting like a ventriloquist's trick from floor to ceiling, wall to door.) "Then, too," it adds from near some socks abandoned by Bonnie when she left, "I've never dreamed of any. . ." (what? Some super-illicit act of sex?) "enormity. . ." (the magic word, you've got that right—excess is what defines our time!) He corners the growler in a book face down beneath the Grateful Dead. It's *Walden*-boy, he might have known. He hears a twang from Jimi too, but the

198

growler's not giving his rostrum up. ". . . greater than I've committed," he adds. (Well, get a grip there, buddy roe—we've got enormities to spare). Two men in huts, he tells himself, more than a hundred years apart—and Chomei, back eight hundred or so (all crazy as bedbugs after a while, and Jimi might be losing it too).

It's cold and dim outside the hut. An icy run-off trickles down. He closes the book to silence Thoreau, though silence bugs him even worse. "You nattering nabobs," taunts a drawl as he's tugging some vinyl from its sleeve, but Spiro's out of his element here. "There must be," Jimi starts to wail, "some kinda way. . ." and Dugan's joining in with a howl as "outta here" they both entreat.

It's been a month since Bonnie moved on. His shoulder's almost healed by now, but the rest of him's in lousy shape. He strums along, his fingers numb even when playing air guitar. He needs to get more kerosene.

"Too much confusion," Jimi snarls.

Uh-huh, he nods. That's it, all right—*Como en Vietnam*, okay? So what's the Pentagon got to say about what happened at My Lai 4? "Assault with murderous intent" is how they're now describing it. Mitchell and Calley will take the stand, and, at the Department of Defense, its bullet-domed spokesman, Melvin Laird, says dozens of others will soon be charged.

Maybe. But Jimi's skeptical. "Can't get no relief," is his complaint, and Dugan's unable to shut it out—the reverb of what he'd had to see, and shouldn't see, and can't forget. There's a furnace-voiced clanking in his mind behind the rasp of Jimi's guitar. The thing that haunts him's in the room. He sees its cover sticking out and yanks its title into view. LIFE, it says ironically. Too late to stop, he opens it up and there's the ditch in its double-page spread, the photo that's seared into his brain. Amid the jumble, right in front, the girl who sculls across the pile with knees raised high and head thrown back, her fingers clutching at her groin. A shriek cuts loose like an alarm—it's in the ditch and in his head. Useless to shut it up again, nothing he does will turn it off. It blends with Jimi's ripsaw whine and, even when buried out of sight, the killing, he knows, goes on inside.

I have no right, he tells himself. I cannot know, I have no right. Ah-womp-ah-womp! is Jimi's reply. Life is a bitch, his music sneers.

Credo's scratching to get out. There's something outside she wants to chase—she must have smelled it through a crack. He opens the door and she explodes across the clearing, through the trees. He watches her stop and sniff the ground. Then, after a minute, she trots back.

"Big deal," he says. "Don't bother to wag. . . and look at the mess you're tracking in!" shutting the door, he bangs his thumb, muttering testily under his breath.

She answers with a cool-it grin, and, knowing whatever she needs to know—only that and nothing more—circles about and settles down, eyeing him briefly with a look that says, if he's got nothing in mind, she thinks she'll take a little nap. (I know what's in the ditch, he thinks, but don't know if what put it there might also end up loose in me.) That rends my soul, he tells himself as Jimi hoots sarcastically, "Let us not talk falsely now!"

"You're driving me crazy," Dugan complains, and, in the silence that fills the hut, neither says anything more.

● ● ●

Wet pine straw under dripping trees, a 40-watt sun, an ice-rink sky. His trouser legs are soaked to the knees as Dugan and Credo cut through the woods, impelled by the fever in his brain. Hunting season's over at last. The winter day is fairly warm. They jump a red-clay drainage ditch and follow the roadway to its end where, stating the obvious, there's a sign attached to a saw-horse barrier—NO THRU ROAD it says to itself. To its left is a driveway snaking its way past a trio of stumps, a Road Runner with a CB antenna, two camouflaged fifty-gallon drums, and, stolidly perched on rock supports, a two-story newly-roofed clapboard house built about ninety years ago, refurbished enough to give it the look of Pa Beasley with a metal toupée.

A ladder's been propped against one wall with a woman atop it scraping boards in raincoat, scarf and fuchsia socks—it's Marianne, Bob's preggers wife, who looks back down as B'wana Bob in chukka boots strolls onto the porch to check things out. She's missed a patch. He points that out, then hears the clink of Credo's tags.

Their mongrel mastiff, black-and-tan with over-sized head and steel-trap jaws, sails out to meet the interlopers, its fur ruffed up and head down low. But Credo deftly alters course, leading him off into the woods. "Shy!" Bob barks and disappears into the shadows or somewhere else.

200

As Dugan had learned from Marianne, the dog had just appeared one day, half-starved and ravenous as a wolf. She'd put some food out, wheedled, and coaxed until he'd dug himself a lair amid the debris under their porch from which he emerges now and then with the breakneck stealth of a crocodile—a crafty one-eyed desperado who must have discerned in the mismatched pair the same gaunt look they saw in him. Marianne calls him "Mister Shy," though Bob, preferring one-syllable names, addresses their squatter simply as "Shy."

Distrusting humans (much like Bob), Shy won't set foot inside the house, preferring his snuggery under the porch and one of the blankets from their bed (Marianne's way of sharing Bob). Also he's mute. "Black fellas 'ate that," Bob's declared. "'E slips up on 'em loike a shark!" Man and dog have reached a détente based on their mutual lone-wolf traits, though Marianne's much harder to read and far too taciturn to reveal if she's as ill-used as it seems. From her ladder she watches Dugan's approach as, presumably, Bob's still doing too—though if he is, it's from out of sight.

Coughing discretely, Dugan says the renovation's looking good. She nods and pauses, scraper in hand. Bundled in overcoat, sweaters, and scarf, she's like a carelessly tethered balloon that could drift away in a gust of wind.

"Bob back inside?"

"Can't tell from here." She scrapes some more.

He clomps across the empty porch. No sign of Bob as he ventures inside the shotgun hallway's barren space, hearing an orotund anchor-man say he'll "check in a moment on Conrad and Bean." Then music and singing, homage to Zest.

The hallway opens along one side to newly sanded hardwood floors, two filing cabinets, shelves, and desk with a green Selectric under its shroud, and, parked by itself against one wall, a heater exactly resembling his except the Bobs have turned theirs up despite the relative warmth of the day. The air's so dry it's hard to breathe.

"It's a beautiful sight!" the announcer resumes from a small TV on an orange crate. The set's not working properly—its vertical hold keeps going awry, flipping the picture off its screen—but Dugan examines it anyhow, recognizing Cronkite's voice and deducing there must be astronauts picking up samples on the moon. A NASA spokesman describes the terrain, saying it looks defoliated, a sort of lunar DMZ. "It is," that resonant voice declaims. "It always was and always will be. . . from time immemorial."

Dugan's still peering at the screen when something is pressed against his neck—the cold thin edge of a razor-sharp blade an inch below his Adam's apple.

"Jesus, Bob!"

"Oi'd been a Mau Mau, yuh'd be dead."

"There's Richard Gordon still inside," Cronkite's observing on the tube.

"'Old on," croaks Bob.

". . . and on the ground at Houston Control, where everything is A Okay. . ."

Bob sheaths his knife and cuts the sound. The picture flickers silently. "Sty careless, mite, and y'er gonna regret it. Caught two of y'r fr'ens down by th' dam this Froiday mornin'."

"Doin' what?"

"Said they were fishin'. 'Ave a seat."

"And?"

"One of 'em briefly 'ad a pole." He joins his hands behind his head. "Dropped it, though." He starts to laugh but coughs instead, retrieving some scattered paperclips which he pensively drops into a jar. "Shy 'elped 'im with that last decision." He puts the jar in front of him, then moves it slightly to the side. "So whatta yuh up tuh down there, mite?"

Fomenting uhuru, you dumb fuck. "Nothin' momentous. . . tryin' to think." Already woozy from the heat, he's not sure what he's doing here— except for an urgent need to talk to somebody other than himself. The weird thing is that, even here, it feels like he's still inside his head. Bob's wry expression prompts him to add, "A witness to our time, I guess."

"This country's full of witnesses." Bob gestures towards a lay-out page with photos of bearded hippie types protesting at some army base. "Not activists, juss auditioners. . . f' wot?" he crows. "Reality, mite! These yoyos can't be sure it's real until they've seen it in th' news." He's talking about a photograph but, reflexively, they both glance up at the sizzle of dancing video dots, now stabilized enough to show two figures hopping up and down.

"Is that a golf club?" Dugan asks, watching a spaceman stroke a putt.

Bob nods and shrugs with a mirthless grin. "Clobber uh golf ball, kill a gook—th' medium's not th' message, mite. It's 'ow yuh interpret wot yuh see. 'Ere's a suggestion from my boss." He hands across some galley sheets to go with the protest photo-shoot—a rabidly paranoid diatribe about how godless mongrel tribes, conspiring with Marxist-Leninist queers, are undermining all we love with protests, drugs, and subliminal ads brainwashing gullible Christian kids—the usual ultra-rightwing crap, updated to note such pending events as the so-called Moratorium which pinkos have dubbed a "March Against Death," though according to Bob's mad-dog boss, it's actually a sinister plot to sap our fighting men's resolve. "How many soldiers AWOL now, incited by just such leftist crap? A million and a half," he writes, "plus 50,000 known deserters and 60,000 'emigrants' who've made their way to Canada. It's time to stop this hemorrhage," he says, and do it by going straight to the source. "If every reader will target a traitor—long hair and beads, the hippie type—and make it zappatista time. . ."

"Incitement to murder? Who'd listen to this?"

Bob hums the Howdy-Doody theme (how's he know that? McLuhan's right. . . moon walks, soap, and vapid TV mixmastered into a witch's brew). "Th' woods are full uh cry-zies, mite."

"You can't print this."

Bob smiles again. "Yuh bleedin' 'earts are all th' sime, 'opin' that 'uman nigh-ture will chainge. No stomach fuh th' why things are."

The air's so parched that Dugan reels, but Bob appears impervious, a lizard grinning from a rock. Scraping is audible through the wall, insistent and methodical.

"Not stomach. . . conscience!" Dugan bleats, a phrase that Sunbeam might have used. "What's real is that people get hurt in wars. Non-combatants. . . like Marianne. . . and kids who can't get out of the way. Zappatista time in Vietnam for a quarter-million civilians so far—how can we possibly justify that by saying we're gonna make them free?" He's on a roll, so he keeps going. "They've got their own bad guys, I know, but what's bogus is claiming they want us there. We know we'd lose an open election."

Bob's eyelids drop as Dugan rails. "Yuh come down 'ere t' tell me this?" He rubs his forehead with his hand. "Nah, 'at's okay. Keep talkin', chum. Don't get much chance t' chat like this. Dough used t' show up 'ere now 'n' then, but didn't have much t' sigh on th' war. . . So war 'n' peace, that's wot we're about? Like salt 'n' pepper, am Oi roight?" His tongue flicks out and in again. "Oi wanna tell yuh somethin', mite. . ."

Dugan is feeling slightly sick. The heat, he thinks, he needs more air. But Bob's begun to tell his tale.

"We 'ad this stretch of 'ighwhy once, me and m' fellow soldiers o' fortune. Luanda was a long why off—just fifty klicks of road it was, 'at's wot th' map said, enn t' enn, but th' capital was a world a-why. Oi was th' driver of a truck our commander 'ad filled with fifty men. Villagers, roight? from near our camp. 'Ad trouble roundin' fifty up, so they'd mixed in some o' th' older boys. Th' man that Oi reported to told me t' drive. Oi drove a klick, he said t' stop and pulled a man down by th' road. Myde 'im kneel an' shot 'im. Bang. Bullet went in 'is skull, just 'ere. . ."

Dugan now feels he's suffocating. But Bob continues, sleepy-eyed.

"Another klick, 'e picks another. Th' sime procedure. Fifty klicks. A man a klick is th' idea, as a warnin', y' see? Keep out o' this war. But this is where th' humor comes in. . ." His smile is crooked with contempt, exposing his sharply pointed teeth. "We reach th' village at th' enn. . . and 'ave two buggers still in th' truck. Leff over, roight? Th' maps were wrong. Not fifty, it was forty-ight! Oi'll never f'git th' looks on their fyces." He lets his story register.

"This room's an oven," Dugan says, seized by a sudden nostalgic pang for the stamp-album world of his innocent years with pink for Churchill, Kipling, and Rhodes, blue for Babar and de Gaulle—Nyasaland and *Indochine*, engraved in fastidious miniature. . . zebras grazing with giraffes, round thatched huts with canopied trees and bare-legged natives harvesting jute, imperial fictions hinged and glued before the advent of TV (regarding the latter, Dugan notes the picture tube, now stabilized, is cutting from astronauts bouncing about to shots of near-deranged elation as a woman with lavishly lathered hair is showering with orgasmic zeal. To calypso tunes, she gasps and smiles, indifferent to assholes on the moon or piteous truckloads in Angola. SHORT & SASSY trumpets the screen. That's all it takes, a good shampoo). "I better be getting' back," he says.

"Come on, yuh 'aven't asked me yet. . ."

"Asked you what?"

"Th' two leff over, y' sensitive sod! Yuh want t' know wot 'appened t' them?"

It's just a story. It's not real.

"We turned 'em loose," Bob says with a snort. "We weren't barbarians, y' know."

"All th' same. . ." As Dugan gets up, he has a thought. "I know somebody you oughta meet." He totters slowly towards the door, afraid he's going to find it locked but pleased with the image in his mind—

Glubber and Ian Bob on the moon, making it safe for goofy golf. A flickering picture on the tube.

As he opens the door, he hears Bob shout, "I met 'er already, you f'get?"

"Who. . . Bonnie?"

"Roight. Wot 'appened to 'er?"

"She's screwin' a friend."

"Oh, yeah? Too bad. She 'ad nice boobs."

The air outside has a soothing taste as Dugan attempts to gulp it down. He hears the sound of scraping pause, but takes a while to move his tongue, glancing up at Marianne. "How much you charge to work on mine?"

She turns and smiles, then looks away. *Rosemary's Baby* crosses his mind. The boards she's scraped look scrofulous. The roof has the sheen of Congolese tin.

• • •

Credo rejoins him in the woods, cajoling him when they reach the hut to keep on going towards the dam. She's right, he thinks, just keep things in motion long enough to scrape my grungy psyche clean. Once at the spillway, he squats down, plunging his fingers into the flow—cold as slate, opaque as stone, the way he wants his mind to be. How did he get so over his head while wading in such a shallow puddle? (The horror, the horror, and what way out when Marlow's off on medical leave and Kurtz is hawking fertilizer?) The more we think, the more we lie. (And memory, then, does that lie too? Do lies torment us like the truth? Is any nostalgia half so strong as what we're trying to forget?) Ignore the words, take images—the pictures his brain has filed away, randomly stuck like bogus stamps on unmarked pages from the past. Two ants he saw on a wooden step, a raindrop making two trickles converge and running together in a stream on the oval back-window of a Dodge (the image expands sea-monkey style—he's four years old and hiding out while his mother's calling him in for a nap, he smells the car's upholstery). What makes such images sacrosanct? (Eventually, they're lies as well.) *That girl. . .* he shuts his thinking down before he even sees the ditch, but knows whatever he claims is true will have to coexist with that—at least, as long as he remembers (he will, he swears, but to what end? how long before it's warped and bent like stamps steamed off forgotten mail?)

Come on! says Credo with a nudge.

"I'm on the edge," he tells his dog. He knows he needs to talk with Danny, but while phoning him from the Feed & Seed with Credo waiting in the car, he doesn't let on what shape he's in. It's Danny who's manic, probably stoned.

"Get down here, Duke! Right now. Tonight."

"I can't."

"You better! You know what's on? It's Tricky Dick—a major speech. Our President, pal. We gotta confer.'"

"I'll try. . ."

"Don't get evasive, now. I need ya." There's a background thump, another voice—it's Caitlin's this time, answered by Danny's, "Sure, he will! He's coming down. . . Hey, listen, Mike, I can't talk now. You heard about what Dexter did?"

"Buggered a choir boy?"

"Holy shit! You haven't heard? Gaudy details, man. Caitlin says. . . say what? By six? She says you gotta be here by six. For supper, okay? A double bill—Nixon and Dexter. COME ON DOWN!"

• • •

An unspoken subtext marks the scene: Dugan the racehorse thinks he knows what most of his counterparts fail to learn—that running in circles, fast or slow, will get you nowhere in the end—while Danny, who sees himself as a mule, thinks stubbornness always beats out speed. . . and Caitlin, cast as the put-upon mare, can only kick the door of her stall.

For Dugan it's close to coming home with some of his own stuff on display. The furniture's mostly thrift-shop eclectic with unframed canvases on the walls, painted in Caitlin's current style—mega-scale views of rotting fruit like pocked and moss-grown panoramas. He looks around and announces his mood.

"Escaping from Elba does me good!"

Danny chuckles and Caitlin nods. There's tension between them, Dugan sees, but Caitlin's typically circumspect and Danny's upbeat with his news. Meg Boozer's flunked her comps for starts and Gordo's maintaining there's a vendetta. Directed at whom? Directed at him—he's set Meg up with a second committee. Ed Doggett's getting a divorce. And then there's Dexter's dénouement. "A last act, pal. True Grand Guignol. I can't believe you haven't heard. Hey, Caitlin!"

"Whaaat?"

"WE NEED A BEER!"

He's in a crewneck riddled with holes revealing a yellow shirt beneath. She's clomping about in skirt and boots like Esmeralda, Gypsy bride, somewhat allaying Dugan's sense of a mean-hearted specter haunting the room, something akin to that feeling of dread skulking about at Ian Bob's. He knows enough to hope he's wrong, but whatever it is keeps sneaking back in, lurking beneath the ostensible fun of slouching their way towards Bethlehem.

"Believe me, Duke, it's revvin' up! You wouldn't have noticed it in the sticks, but check the RPM down here. This place. . . hey, where you goin', babe?"

"To g-g-get y-your beers." She pauses long enough to add, "C-C-Cook or m-maid, I c-can't b-be both. And *maybe*. . . "

"What?"

She gives him a look.

"Well, hurry on back. I'm tellin' you, buddy—when you're movin' this fast, you look for the brakes. For avoidin' collisions, know what I mean? Ya gotta know when enough's enough." He waits until the door swings shut, then grabbing the phone and turning it over, he prises its bottom lid off with a pen.

"Paranoid, Dan?"

"Nah, she's a fink. I've known it for years." Fumbling around, he plucks out a joint and snaps the phone parts back in place. It utters a ding when he sets it down.

"Okay," he puffs while lighting up. "The story you drove down here to hear. . . it's Tenure and Pro-MOTION time!" (more Howdy-Doody—Danny too?) He chortles with glee, exhaling smoke. "Remember our plan for Famous Dogs? Well, Dexter hasn't got a plan—most kamikazes don't, you know, and not enough gas to get back home. When Doggett's committee turns him down, suggesting he'd better look someplace else, he calls 'em a bunch of commie fags. Puts it in writing, which they reject. So what comes next? Submit a formal appeal, you think?" He squints at Dugan through the smoke. "Here, take a toke. Whoa! Easy, big fella!

Leave me a little! So, Dexter. . . he goes to Gordo's office—and while he's there, pulls out a gun. Locked and loaded. A forty-five."

So some of those rumors had been true, at least as far as packing heat. "No shit?" says Dugan as Danny resumes, hunched forward with elbows on his knees, nodding his head for emphasis.

"Ole Gordo's pretty cool at first, claiming the whole thing's out of his hands—nobody but God can change things now.'In that case. . .' Dexter cocks his gun, and Gordo edits what he'd said to 'God or Sternbolt, nobody else!' Whereupon Dexter points to the phone. 'Get him,' he says. . . Hey, gimme the joint!" Dugan sucks twice and hands it back. "But Gordo's left his intercom on, an oversight that gets word out. His secretary calls for help. The campus cops just stand around, but after a while they send for SLED. . ."

"The swat-squad guys?"

"The F Troop. Yeah. . . This shit's no good. Been savin' it for a special occasion, but nothing's what you want it to be. . . So, anyhow, they call him up. . ."

"Who? Dexter?"

"Nah, the Senator's guys return the call, tellin' him Sternbolt's out to lunch, under the weather, in the john. . . while Gordo's office is under siege. SLED's got it surrounded, so come on out! But Dexter announces he's all wired up—he'll blow the place if they storm in—then makes a call to Channel 10 and asks if Mister Knozit's there, the weather-man dude slash kiddie-show host, the only reporter he says he trusts. To this point, Dexter's makin' sense. But now he says he's got some demands, the first of which they better get straight. . . a deep-dish pizza, extra cheese, sausage, no mushrooms, make it quick. By now the whole town's tuning in and Mister Knozit's very hip, playing deliveryman on his own. 'I'm glad you felt that we could talk.' You got the pizza? Dexter asks. He looks and it's got mushrooms, right? He threatens to shoot the person who brought it—that's Mister Knozit—still with me, pal?—who's crowded in with his camera crew. . . and Dexter looks like he means it too. But then he laughs. It's just a joke. He won't kill anybody, see? so long as Sternbolt gives him tenure."

"They've gotten a camera crew in there?"

"He lets 'em in and they go live as Dexter reverts to where he was, claiming that he's been cheated again. He'd said no mushrooms—look at this! The camera tries to get in close as Dexter yells 'WHOSE PIZZA IS IT?' He's suddenly pissed at everyone there, pointing his gun and waving the box. 'EAT, YOU PIGS! IT'S ALL ON ME!' And one or two crewmen start to eat, but right in the midst of this moveable feast, Meg Boozer strolls in from the wings. Nobody knows how, but there she is—Miss Famous Dugs incarnate, right?—telling the camera what's happened to her. It's not poor Gordo who's to blame—she looks at Gordo, still in his chair smilin' back wanly at her words—but she's been victimized as well because she's a woman. . . *with balls*, she adds, the first sign she's been on the sauce. It looks like maybe they're turning a corner with so many actors in the scene, but then the man from SLED arrives, wearing a ski-mask (God knows why), rappelling like Spiderman from the roof and planning to toss some tear gas in as soon as he's able to break the glass. Meg Boozer spots him, points, and screams. He's bouncing against the outside wall when utter pluperfect hell breaks loose. The pizza falls into Gordo's lap as Dexter, reflexively reaching out, flips it over in mid-air. They wrestle and Dexter's gun goes off. . . apparently aimed at Gordo's crotch."

Danny pauses, takes a toke, and squeezes the roach into a clip. "Between his legs as things turn out. But there it is, on live TV—the gun, the pants, the deep-dish mess looking like mangled private parts. Meg takes one look and starts to shriek as Gordo struggles for the gun. It's all on camera as Gordo succeeds and waves the pistol over his head while Meg keeps sobbing, 'O my God!'"

"Unbelievable, Dugan says.

"It gets much weirder," Danny exults. "The man from SLED now makes his move, aiming to crash into the room. Maybe the gunshot's spoiled his aim. He swings and there's a muffled thump, and then he's gone. Just disappears. There's all this smoke where he'd just been and then a shot of him in a hedge—there must have been a back-up crew—spread-eagled and choking on the gas. Jump cut to back inside the room and pan to Gordo from the rear, his arm round Dexter's shoulders now, the loaded pistol in his hand. There's Meg, who's babbling, on her knees, still wiping the crud from Gordo's fly, and Mister Knozit with a mike and both men weeping with relief as Gordo looks at us and says that rather than lose the woman he loves, he'll abdicate, he'll quit his job. He tells Mister Knozit, 'I RESIGN!'"

"You're kidding! *Gordo*?"

"Just like that. Then Mister Knozit starts his wrap and, seeing that Gordo's still intact, Meg starts to cry and Gordo smiles and Dexter's looking pretty beat. It's damn near operatic, Duke, but suddenly, without a break, we've segued to *The Brady Bunch*. The rest is rumor. What I hear is Dexter's gonna beat the rap—it seems he's got some powerful friends who think his work's of consequence. They're talking about a grievance committee."

"Well, I'll be damned. What sort of work?"

"Been keepin' tabs on us, I'd guess, something to do with Sternbolt for sure. . . Here, take it!" he hisses urgently, passing the clip as Caitlin comes in. "Big Nurse!" he warns as if it's a joke.

She stops with a reproachful look. "Th-Th-Thought y-you'd quit."

"Hey, babe, I did! But that menthol shit screws up your brain."

"Y-Your b-b-beers," she glowers, and leaves the room.

He hesitates a beat and shrugs, "Fucked up again. Oh, well," he says, "at least we'll both have appetites. So how's life on the sidelines, pal? Sounds like you pimped us to a win."

He means your turn to talk awhile, so Dugan tries to catch him up, from Lugton to the parking lot where Famous Colleague smiled and said, "Don't ever do nothin' like this again," and BUSTED's what those girls were thinking.

"Yee-haw!" yells Danny. "Hear that, babe?" He's looking at Caitlin by the door, munching on Fritos from a bowl. She's come back in as Dugan talks, her off hand in an oven mitt.

Dugan continues, "Anyhow. . . he waves us on. The chicks were totally zonked, of course—like, 'What a trip!' and 'Whoa, that's cool!' that Sergeant Sunshine let 'em off. 'He's kinda cute,' the tall one said. The short one bawled, 'You'd bang a NARC?'"

"Wild!" Danny snickers, unamused. "I ran into him too last month. He's got this hat. . ."

"With a leopard-skin band?"

"It's ocelot. I tell him Hi. He's got that way of swellin' up. You know," he glances back at her, "like layin' claim to half the room. He points at me and. . ."

Dugan finishes the line. "'You must. . . change your life,' he says."

"How'd you know that?"

"Claims it's from Rilke. Prob'ly is. Been doin' translations is whut Ah heah."

"You better control that accent, Duke."

They pause as Caitlin munches on. The specter's back, whatever it is, crouched in the corner of the room. Danny and Caitlin know it's there.

"So where's he now?"

"I hear he's off to Yucatan."

"Oh, yeah?" says Dugan, wondering why—to muse a while in a mummy cave? To hunker down with knees hunched up and choke on Fritos—like, let's see. . . well, whattaya know, that sounds like us! After a ponderous moment or two, he finally asks, "What's going on?" trusting that no one's going to say.

Caitlin sighs.

"I mean it, guys. You're draggin' about like somebody died. Jeez, here we are! Let's rock 'n' roll!"

"Right," Caitlin smiles. "So where's my mitt?" Finding it's still on her left hand, she leaves to fetch the casserole.

"Hey, Mike," says Danny, watching the door. "It's gotten a little complicated. Caitlin's had. . ." He drops his voice. "Yeah, well, you know. . . she's had an abortion. I know what you're thinking—we'd wanted a kid, but. . . see, right now the timing's bad. She needs to paint." They hear the oven door bang shut. "It's brought us together in a way. For one thing— and I mean it too—no more screwin' around for Danny boy. And for another. . . here she comes!"

The door swings open, and Dugan sees what he's been hoping to avoid—her clam lasagna, more than enough, it seems at a glance, to pave the streets of Palermo.

"C'mon in the dining room," Danny says.

Big Nurse, no kidding, Caitlin awaits as if to administer tetanus shots. She gestures for Dugan to pass her his plate.

"I'm not really hungry," Dugan says, prompting a baleful stare in reply. "Ah. . . just a little. At the start."

She points her mitt for Danny's plate.

"Oh, yeah," says Danny. "Lousy news. Remember Leon. . . Leon Stoops?"

The black kid who could hardly read? In Dugan's first summer back on the farm, he and Danny had done a stint instructing kids in need of a break. "Sure," he says. "From Upward Bound."

"He just got killed. In Vietnam. The paper said. . ."

"Aw, damn! Not him."

"Outrageous, huh? They're shipping him home."

"That's. . . fuck! That's. . ."

"Yeah."

They sit without talking—nothing to say—forks poised above the clam lasagna.

"W-Well!" says Caitlin. "R-R-Rock 'n' r-roll."

211

"I'll get the vino," Danny proposes, leaving the room and coming back unscrewing the cap of a Gallo jug.

"To us," says Dugan as Danny pours.

They swallow and take a dutiful bite.

"Hey, this is good, babe."

"Really delicious!"

They chew in unison, chase it with wine, and look at the big clock on the wall.

"Uh-oh!" whoops Danny with frenzied glee. "We almost missed it. Know what's next?"

Caitlin's mum, so Dugan replies, "Tricky Dick?"

"You got it, my friend! Oh, yeah, you bet!" He sashays towards the TV set, spreading his arms and starting to sing. "It's. . . Tricky DICK-y time! It's. . . Tricky DICK-y time!" Howdy-Doody rides again. He hits the button and Nixon blooms in color and close-up, totally mute.

Dugan's still crouched above his plate, hearing that puppet-show tune again, disquieted by the parallels. Caitlin distracts him by touching his arm, turning her soulful eyes on his and asking him in a quiet voice, "T-T-Tell m-me the truth. . ."

He says he will, wondering if he'll have to lie.

"Y-Y-You d-don't. . ." She pauses to study his face. ". . . l-l-like my lasagna. . . d-d-do you, Mike?"

"I like it fine."

"N-N-No, y-y-you don't!"

"Come on, you two! I'm turning it up."

"Y-You're lying, M-M-Mike."

"No, I'm not."

"LADIES AND GENTLEMEN. . ." Danny brays, turning the TV's audio up.

"Then, have s-s-some m-more!"

She lifts a wedge on a spatula and is moving it towards his still-loaded plate. Somehow, as Danny starts to expound, lasagna's dumped in Dugan's lap.

"Jeeze Louise!" It weighs a lot.

". . . THE PRESIDENT OF THE UNITED STATES!"

Caitlin wheels in Danny's direction. "B-B-Bastard!" she snarls, her purpose clear.

"Right on!" says Danny heedlessly, thinking it's Nixon Caitlin means.

Zapruder-like, the whole scene stalls, jerking towards Danny frame by frame. . . and then it's over, the deed is done—tomatoey sauce from head to toe, the emptied casserole in his lap as Caitlin flaps like a bat from the room. A door is slammed. The whole house shakes.

"My fellow Americans," Nixon says. Dugan is frozen in his chair.

"It's shitty lasagna," Danny shrugs. "Sooner or later, she had to know."

Nixon declares he won't be moved by anything war protesters do. We'll stay the course in Vietnam. Our loyal allies are counting on us.

"Ah, well, of course," is Danny's response. "Those who refuse to learn from the past are condemned to do what Dexter did. Which is why this crapola's in my lap." He strokes his head to locate a clump, peels it off and holds it out dangling like seaweed from his hand. "Clearly, I gave her this dumb idea."

"Me too, I reckon."

"Maybe so. It's Dexter's revenge."

". . . silent majority," Nixon drones.

"What's he saying?"

"God only knows. The guy's so furtive. Just look at him!"

"He looks unhealthy."

"Much too pale."

But the President's message rambles on. We'll fight until democracy's come to all the people of Vietnam. No sacrifice will be too great.

"BULLSHIT!" yells Danny, winding up and flinging lasagna at the tube. It wobbles obscenely through the air, then clings like viscera to the screen. "Load up, old buddy. Take a shot." Grabbing a clump, he fires again. "Aw, shit, I missed! But see how it works? Ya hit the nose, ya get deferred."

They fire together and then at will.

"Homing in!"

"He's hard to hit,"

"Look out there, Dick!"

"WHOMP!"

"This is great! Got any more?"

"Jeez, look what we did."

"What?"

"Over there." An early abstraction, beige and blue, resembling three band-aids on a bruise. "Caitlin's painting. We overshot."

"So what?" he shrugs. "It needed some color."

"Easy, Dan. You better back off."

"Can't live in fear, pal. Look at that!" He gestures at Nixon's pasta-decked face. "Good therapy, huh?" He wipes his fingers on his shirt. "Hey, where you're going? Sit back down!"

"Out of ammo. Gotta run." He knows they've reached the end of the scene.

"To Chantry Mount? That's crazy, man."

"To Lugton, yeah. I gotta get back."

"For what?"

"My dog. I got a dog. And I owe you, Dan. This trip was good."

"Owe me for what? Two-thirds of a joint? A load of lasagna in your lap?"

"For some sanity, man. A little perspective. But you and Caitlin. . ."

"Naahh, we're cool. We're through the worst. A week ago it was pretty rough. Tonight. . . just lettin' off some steam." He scrapes at a blob of tomato paste. "What sort of dog?"

"A female dog with a mind of her own. Good company, though. The best of some lousy decisions I've made."

"They're talkin' about your babe from the game. I hear she wore ole J.C. out. As a matter of fact. . . now, where'd it go? Caitlin said she'd put it aside. More news of Miss Dee's post-deb moves." He lumbers into the little front hall, yanks at a drawer, hunts around, and finds what he's been looking for—a newspaper clipping tucked in a vase. "Read it and weep."

There's a picture of Dunkie looking serene. Engaged to be married. Cool. Read on. Her fiancé's an English professor. . .

Dr. John Mack Dough, B.A., M.A., Ph.D.

"Well, whattaya know?" So Birnam Wood's back on the move. Dugan's amused and slightly miffed. He looks at Danny, thumping his chest. "It kinda gets you here," he says.

They walk together to his car. No sign of Caitlin. Never mind, she'll come around in a decade or two. Regarding the nuptials, Dugan concedes there's a euphony in that blending of names that would mortify even E.A. Poe. "Dunkie. . . Dibble. . . Dough," he chants, "in her most immemorial year." Miz Dee must be in high gear now, she and those blue-rinsed varicose-brains who're part of her precious DLC—they'll do ole V.K. Ratliff proud. Ducking to slide beneath the wheel, he cranks the engine. There's a bang, and the Pontiac starts to cough up phlegm.

214

Danny leans in on the passenger side. "Ugh," Danny sniffs. "Like hermit crabs."

"It got submerged."

"Outstanding. But. . . just hear what I say. I gotta make sure you get the point. That clipping is more than social news. If you're plannin' on comin' back next year. . ."

"I'll let you know," is Dugan's reply, surprised to discover he already knows his fling with old CSU is done. "Tell Caitlin the food fight. . ."

". . . was your idea. Already thought of that," Danny nods. "We're gonna be okay, you know."

Dugan looks up and waggles a V. "All of us, hey?"

"Damn right. You bet."

"Hang loose."

"Okay."

He puts it in drive. The Pontiac wheezes out from the curb as Danny delivers a jaunty salute. But watching him in the rear-view mirror, Dugan can see he's lingering there, looking both up and down the street as if he's uncertain where to go.

● ● ●

Halfway home, it starts to rain, just as he's leaving a Dairy Queen—a drizzle that turns into a squall with a loud tattoo on the Pontiac's roof. Both wipers are back in working order which, like events at CSU, is minor progress of a sort. If the bullies and psychos are freaking out, that's reason enough to celebrate. But what's happened to Caitlin and Leon is grim, and, listening to his wiper blades clack, he dwells on Danny's other remarks to help dispel those darker thoughts. (Whap and whap.) Like hermit crabs, huh? (Wet Airedales maybe. . . or balled-up socks, which look a lot like hermit crabs). So, yeah, okay, he'd had a point. Speaking of which, a clammy stench wafts upwards from his wine-dark crotch—a cause for alarm at Dairy Queen (Oh, that? I've just been circumcised)—which, given their mutual mishaps with food, prompts a return in Dugan's mind to Gordo's weird non-sequitur while trading him in for John Mack Dough. What was it he'd said as if musing out loud? "But, oh, beamish nephew. . ." Surely not Simms. An allusion to something—yeah, but what? "Beware," he'd said, "beware of the day. . ." The highway glistens in his brights, short white dashes unspooling in spurts like arrows fired at the chief on his hood. "If your snark be a boojum. . ." Dugan recalls. It's nonsense verse, he'll look it up.

Next day, he drives to Chantry Mount, determined to track the doggerel down if only as a purposeful act. There's nothing in Bartlett's, but that's okay—in Oxford's index there's a clue: "S. be a Boojum. . ." Closing in. "CARR" and a number. One more step.

He pauses to case the reference room—grad students mostly, he concludes, passing some time in purgatory while avoiding the hell of Vietnam. Two Peck & Peck sorority types are trolling the scene for possible catches. They check him out when he arrives and, a split-second later, pull in their lines—no bottom-feeders in their creels. One whispers and the other laughs.

CARR's for Carroll. "I'll be damned!" His guffaw causes heads to turn, looks of annoyance here and there. "Out-thunk," he adds in his Lugton brogue, further provoking *habituées* who act as if they think he's on drugs. He smooths the book, leans forward and reads. "But oh, beamish nephew, beware of the day / If your Snark be a Boojum! For then

> You will softly and suddenly vanish away,
> And never be met with again!

That afternoon when he gets to his hut, he tells himself he'll get in shape. He jogs sedately towards the Bobs', then sprints uphill to the collard patch. His shoulder's got a rusted hinge, his legs are like extension cords. But the following day he's at it again with Credo next to him— dawdling along until they're near the top of the hill, then scooting ahead with a bark and a grin. In a couple of weeks, he's closing the gap, and she's panting much harder towards the end. More than once, when they finish their run, Trueblood presents him with a collard. "You lucky t' have 'at dog," he says, puffing benignly on his pipe.

When Ma Beasley confides that Marianne is craving lard and collard greens, he deposits the collards in her yard while Credo placates Mister Shy. Bob must have deduced the ultimate source, but, getting more covert every day, he chooses to ignore the bestowal. For his part, Dugan's fairly amazed by his prowess as a running machine—no thinking involved, it's all in his feet.

But three weeks into this new regime, Ma Beasley says he's gotten some mail forwarded from his old address. He gets so little this seems odd.

Though Purvis is down with a touch of the flu, Ma says he'd noticed a home-made card arriving for Dugan without a stamp. "Don't know how it got here," she observes, handing it over reproachfully. "I ought to be charging postage due."

The card has grease stains at the top and FREE scrawled out in ballpoint pen. He knows in an instant what it is. "Dear Doctor D," the message begins,

> youll never guess where I got this card –
> C ration box can you beat that? in 12
> more days Im outta this place a hellhole
> firebase in the hills – our president says
> were fighting for peace – better believe
> its what I say – like fucking for virginity
> - youre former student Leon Stoops.

God damn this misbegotten war.

• • •

Next day's the Moratorium. Overcast skies and not so cold. Great numbers of people will take to the streets in Washington, Boston, cities like that, and even in places closer to home—like Fort Bragg, outside Fayette Nam, where Leon Stoops had earned a stripe *en route* to his trip in a body bag. That thought's recurring in Dugan's mind as he sets out for the Feed & Seed, but then impulsively hangs a right, not thinking about what he might do, just chugging along past dry-stalk fields, through Colon and Sanford and, south-southeast, past porches with sofas and doublewides in Swann, Olivia, West Spout Springs, arriving before he's decided to go.

It's past endurance, he tells himself, as he reaches the U.S. army base inexplicably named for Braxton Bragg, a general Jefferson Davis sacked. Just after a day-glo fast-food strip are berms on either side of the road and fences topped by razor-wire, then a visitors' gate that's open wide, apparently suckering marchers in as choppers buzz watchfully overhead.

Nervous about his first demonstration, Dugan parks well away from the gate, perceiving that many have done the same—locking their cars in a casual way, but ready to make a getaway. Maybe they do this every week, but what if they've just showed up like him on the spur of the moment, without a plan? He tries to guess what might come next with stills from *Potemkin* in his mind and civil rights marchers in Birmingham. Tear gas is standard, he assumes, with dogs and hoses in the mix, horses and grapeshot optional—especially if the press attends. . . as they probably will since, enticing a crowd, two mega-celebs have been announced. But so has Jesus. Whoop-dee-doo.

More confident with every step, he mingles with the downhome types who're streaming past him towards the gate. He's glad he's got the Lugton look. If people who look like him are there, that's part of the message they'll convey—everyday folks who've had enough. The freaks are there to say that too. With so many fed up, this war's kaput. A helicopter hovers and gawks, then moves on off and disappears.

MPs assigned as traffic cops direct them past a barricade onto a field that's scallop-shaped, some eighty or ninety yards across with grassy ramparts on each side enclosing the long slope to a stage. Armed men are stationed on the rim while others in mufti here and there seem to be signaling back and forth. Thinking again of Eisenstein, he looks more closely at the crowd—bigger and younger than he'd thought, with not so many K-Mart types and more subscribers to *Mother Jones*, hippies and freaks who forage like goats or gambol smugly with their kids, some calmly recumbent, looking spaced, others in aromatic clumps—plus super-freaks who're CIA, the ones to watch if trouble begins, and counter-protesters who'll stir up fights. . . no sign of them yet but biding their time. The kids won't have a chance, he thinks, their Deadhead parents out to lunch in ways that are hard to comprehend. Judging from all he's read and heard, protests are rarely a parlor game. Theater, yes, but not a game.

He calmly sits in the midst of the crowd, but feeling the pressure of a stare, he scans the crowd around him again, not letting on that he's aware a couple of Dostoevskian monks are nodding their heads in his direction. They seem annoyed—he can't think why. Among their hollow-eyed entourage, two women are staking out their turf, unfurling a banner between two sticks: a helmeted pig with a circle and slash and words proclaiming "A MEATING OF MINDS" plus "OVO-LACTOS AGAINST THE WAR" (the first two O's are shaped like eggs, each with a dot resembling an eye—they could be tits, it's hard to tell). He's glancing reflexively back at the monks as whines burst forth from a speaker box, four thunderous thumps and "1-2-3" directing attention to a scrum that's moving slowly towards the stage. Voices around him speculate.

"You see her?"

"Who?"

"Is Joanie there?" asks a Dunkie-sized girl to Dugan's right in sandals and a rainbow serape.

"Can't tell," her freckled friend replies, craning her neck from a kneeling position. "I think I see a bass guitar."

"I heard she's going to Hanoi."

"Bob Dylan says she broke his heart. She's. . ."

"Sad-eyed lady—God, I know!"

"Who's that?"

"Who's where?" Serape pleads.

"The tie-dye, see? Oh, God, it's her!"

"It's Joanie? Where?"

"In that red mini-mumu! There, by the stairs."

"That's just a groupie," Serape sighs. "You're such a spazz!"

"I hope she shows."

"She probably won't."

The rest of the crowd is restive too, awaiting the rumored visitation.

"Oh, well."

"I *told* you!"

Both sit back. The plump one has a bag of snacks that she's just begun to rummage through when a pair of black Levi's grabs the mike, announcing the Reverend Nobody's name who's going to pray for something or other. Not much applause but just enough, as the prayer begins, to mask click-clicking from the hill. Dugan turns round to look at the troops, supposing they're taking their safeties off. It's photographers, though, compiling their files. . . to be used for what? Some credit checks is Dugan's guess and auditing of your income tax followed by wire taps. But who cares? Put all of us on your suspect list and fight your damned war by yourself! There're news photographers up there too.

An "AMEN!" resonates from the stage as a guy with a hoarse professional voice grabs the mike and shouts to the crowd, "So give the reverend cat a hand!"—guiding the clergyman towards the stairs.

"Yeah!" someone yells as the man scampers down. Hoots of derision and scattered applause as the guy with the hoarse voice babbles on. "Tell 'em," he rasps at the top of his lungs like a cheerleader through a megaphone. "C'mon now, let 'em hear you say. . . are we gonna go to their

219

fucking war? Whattaya know. . . are we gonna go?" Anemic denials. "No, no, no."

"How's that? Can't hear! Are we gonna go?"

"HELL. . . NO!" A few dozen more.

"Tell Henry K if WE'RE GONNA GO!" His voice is frenzied, pleading, wild, and answered now a hundred fold.

"HELL, NO! WE WON'T GO! HELL, NO! WE WON'T GO!"

"Tell Nixon too." He's waving his hand like a choral conductor, strolling across the forty-foot stage, prompting an angry, maddened reply.

"HELL, NO! WE WON'T GO!"

"No what?"

"NO WAR!"

"Are we gonna go?"

"NO! NO! WE'RE NOT GONNA GO!" they chant in unison, belting it out. "HELL, NO! WE'RE NOT GONNA GO!"

It's just a sort of Simon Says, but Dugan's uneasy joining in with a rant as mindless as the war, and, when they're starting another round with HO! HO! HO CHI MINH! he ducks his head and waits it out. It isn't, he thinks, that there're not any rules—it's that merely obeying them isn't the point. . . but neither is joining a lemming drive. If he's a lone wolf, what of that? When lone wolves die, they die unmourned. But Leon, he thinks—he's mourning for him, for the moment forgetting Bob and Shy. When he looks up, he sees the monk staring with bulging, red-rimmed eyes as if recalling some affront.

"RENNIE WIENER!" the hoarse guy shouts, announcing it like a bingo card. A minor celeb but better than nothing, one of the brash Chicago Seven acquitted for lack of evidence. A wiry poodle of a man— in jeans and work shirt, cuffs rolled up—he bounces over to the mike, waving and sneering, "Kay Gee Bee!"

That momentarily puzzles the crowd until they see what he's pointing out, surveillance teams up on the bank pointing their cameras down at them. "Let's all of us do our Sixty-nine while they do Nineteen Eighty-four!" Some catch his allusions, most do not. But that's okay, he's rambling on in a rhythmic style—denouncing the Pentagon's "Merchants of Death," suggesting Mick Jagger might cast a spell to exorcise McNamara's brain, then switching his theme to private parts. "Whose *prick* is bigger?" he demands.

They cheer at that, but Dugan gets lost in the rigamarole, remembering the Roosters' pricks on sticks and wondering if there's some sort of connection. Something to do with Puritanism—at least, so it seems, in Rennie's mind where, when that breaks down, right-wingers snap and wallow in a sick nostalgia, killing for God and raping for peace (as Leon Stoops had pointed out, anticipating Rennie's spiel. . . or maybe repeating it, who can say?) "Sex and drugs for the President's thugs!" The point's obscure, but never mind, the crowd's now frantically lapping it up. "Right on! Whoo-hoo!" and they're shaking their fists, with "Ho, Ho! Hey, Hey! How many kids did you kill today?" Tell it to Hank. To Henry K. . . Kissinger ought to hang by dang, be shot bang-bang, and shipped to Danang! Rennie's now into Dr. Seuss, his rapid-fire patter trailing off into a scornful nasal drawl: "SHOW THE WAY! FUCK HENRY K!" Then "ARGGGH!" he shrieks against the beat. "Where'd it come from. . . all this BLOOD?" He grabs the mike and strangles it. "I gotta know! It's like a flood!" Maybe he's seen them getting bored, or, possibly, planned this all along. "You see it? Man, it's everywhere! Saigon! My Lai! Hanoi!" he screams. "And who's behind it? TELL ME WHO?"

The crowd's apparently missed its cue, so Rennie exhorts by providing a clue, throwing his hands out towards the bank, "THEY DID! THIEU DID? WHO'D YOU SAY?"

"THEY DID!"

"WHO?" He points to the troops and gestures beyond.

"THEY DID! THIEU DID! NIXON TOO!" Some of the crowd don't get the Thieu, but Rennie's frenzy's unrestrained responding to their improvisation.

"YEAHHHH!" he bellows, spurring Serape onto her feet. Her friend's up with her dancing about and waving their snack bag overhead.

The crowd's on the brink of going berserk, though the men on the bank keep snapping pics as if it's just a wedding reception. This is when Dugan, glancing up, feels something flash on in his brain. At first he's baffled. Nothing there. But then he sweeps the bank again and feels the same subconscious alarm. More slowly then. Back up. Pan left. The man up there dressed all in black is. . . Hector! Yes! *And if Hector's there. . .*

"LET'S SHUT THE FUCKERS DOWN!" yells Rennie.

Now Dugan's thoughts accelerate. Follow his lens—he'll be aiming at her. . . apparently over there, he thinks, where the monks and Ovo-Lactos are.

". . . END OF THE TUNNEL. . . MARSHAL KY. . ."

But don't stand up. Just stay down low, move in a crouch on through the crowd. Hoots and jeers, they're shifting mood.

"YA-HOO!"

"Siddown."

"FUCK SPIRO TOO!"

Groping and fumbling, losing his way, he checks his bearings. Hector's there, his camera's pointing. . . over here? At her? Can't tell. She's turned her head, giving him time to reconsider whether he's up for mayhem or not.

"FUCK MARTHA MITCHELL!"

Closer now—he's not sure why. Freak families bunched up all around, snotty-nosed kids and strung-out moms. Reconnoitering. . . almost there, keeping his back to Hector's position. Then, close enough to touch her hair, he sees it's not her after all. What he's feeling at first might be relief, but somebody's lips are by his ear.

"Herro, peergrim, lost your way?"

She'd seen him first, that much is clear. . . and that's the best that she can do? Whatever she is, she's no John Wayne. He's on the verge of telling her so when a sudden elation whips the crowd. People around him strain to see while Rennie shields the onstage mike to let the emcee fill him in. Then Rennie nods. He's got big news. "Listen," he says. "IT'S JOAN BAEZ!"

Wild whistles and cheers. What's there to say? If Joanie's with *us*, the Pentagon's through! Where is she, though? They've come for this. They're sure she's here. It's Dugan alone who's stunned to perceive how the funnel of time has led him on, each turn in the road, each asinine whim, propelling him towards this *mise en scène*, this next-installment rendezvous that Hector's up there getting on film. . . on tape or whatever, cuneiform. Who's scripting this? It doesn't make sense. Beamed down from nowhere, Rose, in shades, is kneeling beside him on the grass, the rest of her face expressionless as she launches another sarcastic crack, "I guess you drove duh general here?"

Aware she's merely stalling for time, assessing what risks he might present, he poses a question of his own. "You still touring with the USO?"

"Free country," she says. "You got nuttin' on me."

It's all he can do to keep a straight face. Her accent's seemingly gone to hell, and her dialogue needs a lot of work—like watching old movies from eons ago. For old time's sake, he'll play the game. "How 'bout leaving the scene of a wrecked career?"

"Yeah, whose?" she answers bitterly.

So maybe he hadn't thought of that amidst their screwball repartee. The crowd's becoming more restive now. Is Joanie really here or not?

"I tried to warn you," Dugan shrugs. "Your plots are too predictable."

Except for briefly compressing her lips, Rose's expression doesn't change as people start a synchronized clap, forcing her closer to his ear.

"I knew you were lying all duh time. Dat guy who called you out was right."

What guy? he wonders—does she mean Mick grousing about his canceled class?

"So why'd you forrow me here today?"

"Sheer accident. I came on my own."

She studies his face. He sees she's trying to make up her mind.

"Same as before." He holds her gaze.

The hubbub's like a gathering wave. She looks away, then back again.

"Nobody to *truss*." She hisses the word.

The crowd chants and a drum joins in, drowning their conversation out. "Joa. . . NIE!" Boom-boom-a-boom! "Joa. . . NIE!" Boom-boom-a-boom! They've spotted the singer near the stage.

"She's here!"

"Down there!"

Boom-boom-a-boom!

"So, where's the MIKE?" he shouts at Rose, making his skepticism clear. He leans in closer in order to hear.

She rolls her sweater bottom up, revealing the small black box with wires attached to the belt-loop of her jeans. There's no green light, which means it's off. She glances quickly at the hill. "I'm in a herr of a bind," she says, as if struggling to pronounce the l's.

BOOM! BA-BOOM! BA-BOOM! BA-BOOM! while Joanie begins to mount the stage.

"And what about your sidekick there?" He doesn't turn, and neither does she.

"Part of duh bind." Her face is blank behind the shades. "I said I'd give dere money back. Dey say no way. It's gotten a litter scary. . . Mike."

BOOM-A-BOOM!

At least, he thinks, she remembers his name. The frenzied crowd noise seems to swell as her lips are brushing against his ear. "You heard uh snuff films?"

He recoils, resisting a knee-jerk urge to laugh. Sure, he's heard. There's a wave of applause before he asks, "You doing the snuffing, I assume?"

"Eedda way. Dey're out for blood."

Dose kinky Taiwanese again. "Then cut 'n' run," is his advice. "You're good at that."

She lowers her shades just far enough to fix him with a glacial stare, then nods at the uniformed men on the bank. "So who're duh big-time snuffers here? And fuck you too. . . I forgot dey'd made you a chauffeur. . . so you get to cut widout havin' to run."

He doesn't flinch, mainly because he sees it now—why she's so pissed, bookended by Hector and the feds. The feds are what he couldn't get straight, but it wouldn't take many scenes like this to get her name down on some lists while maybe, in between the two, she's crossed that triad gang somehow and snuffing's simply what they do. . . more thrills and chills for her subscribers. But what sort of script would bring her here?

"Tell me what's going. . ." he starts to say.

"HEY! GIVE HER A HAND!"

"It's gonna get messy," Rose confides. "I wanna get out. . . I'm rearry scared."

They've handed Joanie the microphone. She says hello, the crowd's ecstatic, and, affixing the microphone to a stand, she starts to sing a song they know, prompting a rapt attentiveness while, furtively, Rose, to prove her point, reveals the small black box again. She flicks a switch, a light goes green—then switches it so it's off again while Joanie trills to credulous ears "this land was made for you and me. . ."

"Wait," he says, "just one more thing." He doesn't know why he's asking this, but as she's sliding her shades back up restoring that blank impassive mask, he puts his fingers over hers, assuring the box's light stays off. "If you're asking me to interfere. . ." He waits until she seems to nod. "Okay, a deal," he's nodding back. "Don't leave me holding the bag again." It's sheer bravado. There's no plan, and why's he being a chump again?

"Would you please SHUSH?" a woman snaps while nursing a porcine babe-in-arms who looks more like a small adult. The singing's stopped and Joanie speaks out, complaining that she's been misconstrued. Like all her friends against the war, she's really *for* our fighting men—that's why she works so hard for peace. That's why she'd like for everyone here to join her in what she's singing next. "I've sung it in fields and coffee houses. . ."

For two of the brains that hear that phrase, the man from Lugton's and the monk's, that sparks an instant epiphany. Dugan remembers Ponytail who, as if with a sudden protein surge, recalls encountering Dugan and Rose. "I KNOW YOU ASSHOLES!" Ponytail rails. "Don't act like you can't hear me! HEY!"

"SHUSH!" barks the indignant Leche-League mom, an irate nipple popping out. The nursing dwarf's infuriated.

"I'll sing it on the White House lawn. . . New York, Saigon and Timbuktu. But first I'll sing it here with you."

"Burma Shave!" a cynic yells—a counter-protestor, Dugan suspects—but Joanie's bell-like voice rings clear with a throng of admirers joining in.

Oh, beauuu-tiful. . . for spa-cious skies. . .

"J. Edgar's boy!" snarls Ponytail, explaining his righteous whacked-out rage to sproutheads around him singing along

. . . for am-ber waves ovvvv grain. . .

"STILL UNDERCOVER?" Ponytail yells. "OINK! OINK! Hey, lady! Madame Nhu!"

More heads are turning. Rose shrinks back, checking the action up on the bank where Hector, focused on what he needs, has locked his shot too tightly on her to notice this unexpected threat.

"Hey, MUSSOLINI! I'm talking to you!"

. . . above the fruuuu-ted plain. . .

Ponytail's got the vegans stoked, fixated on Dugan and ready to pounce like fruit flies on a rotten peach. Dugan is thinking as fast as he can. Assuming that Rose is telling the truth and that, even if Hector fathoms what's up, he can't get down from the bank in time, a diversion's the obvious tactic here—maybe involving Ponytail, whose ovo-lacto suicide team has started to crawl in Dugan's direction.

Amerrr-rica! Amerrr-rica!

Think! he urges his churning mind. What worked before might work again. Some other scenario he can filch (like *Bonnie and Clyde*? No, don't think so. . . or Mister Memory, *39 Steps*? Not quite it but getting there).

Ponytail's crew look semi-deranged ("Meat! Meat!")—they're closing in (afternoon of the living dead). "Here, Piggie, Piggie!" one of them growls.

. . . and crowwwnnn thy good. . .

Rose pulls her feet up under her rump, ready to bolt in any direction. There's a flickering now in Dugan's mind—the set of her jaw, the tilt of her head. Add freckles, dyed hair plus Albert Hall—and who's he's straining to recall? Bouncy and vapid, tough as nails (who, according to Danny's scandal file, during all-nighters on their bus would hoover Les Brown and his Band of Renown while belting out "Que Sera Sera")—her name? Come on! And what's the flick?

. . . with bruuu-therhood. . .

The vegans are clawing at Dugan's boots, but the answer's on the tip of his tongue—a Hitchcock remake. . . *Doris Day*! The girl, the target, and the gun—*The Man Who Knew Too Much*, he grins. The cymbals clash. But who's the assassin and where's the gun? Dugan's frantically stalling out.

. . . from seeea too shininggggg. . .

Yes! He knows! He's on his feet and pointing at Hector on the bank. "JOANIE! LOOK OUT! THAT MAN IN BLACK IS POINTING A GUN!"

Heads snap around. A piercing shriek from the Dunkie-sized girl, and the end of the song will never be sung as even the vegans back away (though, if anyone actually paused to reflect, they're surrounded by soldiers armed to the teeth—they've *all* got guns—but Hitchcock's right, nobody reflects, or, if they do, they think "Grant Park! We're gonna get hammered, gassed, and jailed!") Panic erupts as groupies down front nonsensically try to rush the stage, rebounding and then, in disarray, clashing head-on with a second crazed wave who've followed them blindly down the slope.

In seconds, mad havoc rules the field, though up on the bank there're cooler heads converging on Hector who, still unsure if they're targeting him, hesitates just a moment too long. He drops his camera, takes two steps and finds he's struggling with a man who knows some specialized wrestling holds. Apparently, Hector draws a gun. A shot rings out and chaos reigns with screams and yells and bodies colliding. The mike-stand falls with an amplified thump as Joanie is hustled off the stage and MPs converge from either side, hoisting their shields and waving batons, the sight of which prompts a general stampede. The troops suppose they're being attacked. Tear gas is fired, and Serape spins and staggers about, flailing her arms in a silent-film way—it's Eisenstein, but it's for real. Her friend bends down to help her up, then sprawls headlong when she's whacked too.

People are weeping, rubbing their eyes. The burning in Dugan's eyes is bad, but it's evident Rose can't see at all. Groping and stumbling, her face in her sleeve, she lets him lead her out of the fray. He moves against the prevailing flow but finds, as they're approaching the gate, it's not where he'd thought it ought to be. Some new recruits are streaming in, strapping on gas masks as they run. By keying on them, he finds his way, waiting to let them hurry past and heading back towards where they'd been. He notes that two with tangled masks are frantically trying to get them on, and one of them rings a vague sort of bell as a smaller (and buzz-cut) Lew Alcindor. They jog on past at double time as Dugan leads Paw Ling through the smoke, past mass confusion and out the gate. Like Orpheus, he tells himself, tugging naively on her hand.

● ● ●

Police cars speeding towards the fort ignore the old-model Pontiac. The radio report is terse. Fort Bragg has had an incident: a plot to murder Joan Baez has prompted a quick, decisive response. Details are sketchy, though sources say a suspect's now in custody. Rose rubs her eyes as the voice drones on, "Protestors were asked to leave the base. A Fort Bragg spokesman praised the troops for handling the crowd with such restraint. And back in our nation's capitol. . ."

"Rich!" says Dugan, cutting it off. "Restrain 'em back to the stone age, huh?"

Rose reaches to cut the news back on, prompting a wry expression from him. "Whoa! Be my guest," is all he says, not bringing up the Cheez-Its box and how she'd "needed to think" that day or pointing out that, once again, he'd found a way to save her ass. "I'm only the driver," he observes.

227

But so was Hector—think of that. *Part of the bind* is what she'd said, so if Hector sets out to track her down, will it be for the money or something else? But that's. . . irrelevant, he hopes, unwilling to think where that might lead.

The news has moved on to Washington now. Some estimates of the D.C. march are claiming half-a-million or more, though police are reporting a smaller crowd that eventually made it to the Mall. Most marchers protested peacefully despite reports of sporadic assaults by splinter groups with Viet Cong flags, prompting arrests at various sites.

"In other news, the Pentagon. . ."

"Okay," she says, but neither moves. Both are too stubborn to cut it off.

"Heard enough?"

". . . brought murder charges. . ."

"Tell you what. Let's do it together."

"Do what?"

"No points for playing dumb."

"Okay," she says a second time, though not agreeing to anything.

He cuts it off, and neither speaks as Pineview township straggles by and Rose continues rubbing her eyes. After another five minutes or so, he asks her in an off-hand way, "So. . . what had you and Hector planned?"

She turns her watery eyes on him. "No plans," she says, enunciating carefully. "Whatever it was, I didn't know." Her voice is flat as if suspicious of him as well.

"You said it was going to be a mess."

"It aw-ways is."

"For you?"

"For me." She pauses a beat. "It gets much worse when you show up."

"Oh, yeah?" That's just partly true, she's clearly having second thoughts. "I could say the same about you, you know, but no messiness in my life now. Ever heard of Kamo no Chomei?"

"Sounds Japanese," is all she says.

Neither had Gordo, he recalls. "Well, I'm living like him in a hut in the woods. . . in the middle of nowhere, off the map. My shoulder's more or less working again, but, as you can see, I myself am not. . . and, whatever you think, I'm not undercover. You know who that guy was in the crowd, the one who kept calling you Madame Nhu?" He sees this seem to register. "Same screwball we met down in Cumbria."

She studies his face. "So, if meeting me was an accident, what'd you go dere looking for?" Once more she'd carefully nailed the l.

"Other than opposing the war? Nothing until I'd spotted Hector standing up there with the troops. Then I started looking for you."

"Dey'll try to find me too, you know. And Hector. . ."

". . . if he gets the chance, will have to look for somebody else. To snuff, I mean. In Mexico would be my guess, after he's done a little time." He hopes that's true. Besides, who cares? He understands she's good at this game, but he's much better than he was. Better than what? he asks himself—some quasi-Oxonian post-Harvard mug with Douglas Fairbanks on the brain? He brakes and pulls off to the side, letting a pick-up sputter past. A bristling silence stretches out.

"Are we going someplace?" she finally asks.

"I'm headed back to where I live—a place in the sticks an hour from here. Not even a place, it's what I said. A hut in the woods that's off by itself."

"You're taking me dere?"

"I'm. . ."

". . . taking me dere." Her accent makes it hard to gauge if she's being sarcastic when she adds, "I mean it, you know, dey'll look for me."

Oh, yeah? Who's dey? Dose rich subscribers? (You see our girlie run dissa way, escape quick-quick from movie-man?) That's not what Dugan says, of course. Instead, he asks, "So whatta they want, your lunatic fans? Just tell me if it's drugs, okay?"

She shakes her head.

"Next question then, who knows my name? Does Hector, for instance?"

"Probably so. He might have forgot. He doesn't keep notes when we finish a shoot."

"So, he might. Okay. But he probably won't be out on the loose—and why would he try to implicate you? They'll get him on a weapons charge. . . and maybe a whole lot worse than that if they think there're two of you in cahoots disrupting their bases more than once, even if that's a coincidence. With all this craziness going down, habeas corpus is a joke—no charges pressed, but they'll shut you away if they figure you're any sort of threat. But say they decide to let him go, how would he know what's happened to you? You just vamoosed, he'll have no clue."

She's thinking hard. He's thinking too—has he really offered her what he thinks? Then he might as well push it if he can.

"My life has changed a lot," he says. "I'm like a hermit with a dog. My nearest neighbor's a good way off. No job, no phone, no indoor plumbing.

If you're looking to hide, it's a pretty good place. But I come with the hut, so that's the catch."

"Duh probrum. . ." she says, and he perceives she's willing to negotiate. "I'm in a mess I can't explain, but. . ."

"What?" He waits to hear her terms. She knows what he's asking better than he.

"No concubine."

"You think that's what I'm asking for?"

"Aren't you?"

Is he? He's not sure, and in any case she's telling him no. "I'm improvising. Suit yourself."

"Roommates den. . . for just a why-uh?"

He knows she's trying to nail it down as maybe she'd done with Hector too.

"Also the dog." Ménage à trois, he'd told her that.

She hesitates. From Hitchcock to *It Happened One Night*—it's not an easy transition to make. "Some tings. . ." she says as if thinking aloud, "I gotta go buy."

Of course, he thinks, like bullet-proof vests and stun grenades—or Tampax, dental floss, underwear. Another long silence seals the deal, and he eases the Pontiac back on the road.

The drizzle has started up again as the land slides by on either side as raw as acne under a beard. He flips the wiper switch with his thumb while Rose is pulling her shades back down and waiting a bit before she says, "Bad things could happen to you. . . Mike."

Probably will, but good things too. And, after all, how bad is bad? The wipers answer whappity whap (but O beamish nephew, beware of the day. . .) "And you?" he asks.

"Dey awready have."

They drive in silence a few miles. More fields, more trees, Rock City signs, IMPEECH EARL WARREN on a barn—as if they don't know he's retired (impeach his commie ass anyhow!) He turns the radio on again and gets some Dylan, just in time, singing about a mail train ride and how I wanna be your lover (well, don't we all? is Dugan's thought—he wants to say can't buy a thrill, been leanin' on the windowsill, cold showers and wind sprints every day and here I am, pal, back on track, headed towards where I've never been). But Dylan the Switchman's skeptical: "Don't say I never warned you," he drawls, when your train gets lost. . .

Dugan hears, but he's unmoved. The Sixties are almost over he shrugs.

• • •

Alone in a Sanford parking lot while Rose is foraging through the mall, Dugan's rethinking Dylan's song and recalling Blunt's hijacked produce train. "Lighten up, Duke," he tells himself, swabbing his eyes while taking stock of this weird and dizzying turn of events. He's come through yet another debacle with faculties on the whole intact, no broken bones, and the damsel in tow—so why does he have this ominous dread (metaphorically speaking, he insists) of being in over his head again like those hugely tumescent manikins in those underground comix by R. Crumb who're attempting to mount humongous babes? Okay, he muses, get this straight—the mismatch isn't just one of size, but of wit, maturity, savoir faire, and, if that's what this episode's headed towards, Oxford and Harvard ain't enough to saddle this amplitudinous nag? Apparently not if he's uptight. He needs to chill out, take it slow—though she was the one caught up in a snit at having him bail her out again, persuaded at first he'd tracked her down to screw around with her porno show. . . or bust her drug ring, who knows what? In addition to being no John Wayne, she's no Fellini either for sure—though she's made a circus performer of him, conning him into her Sennett-like stunts, putting him off, then coming through. . . but only on her terms, hers alone. More "bad tings" really might be in store if he's as gullible as before (did she say *things*? he thinks she did—like everything else that comes and goes).

Drill down, he tries to tell himself, confront yourself and get to the truth. Caprice and deceit are part of her game, but, knowing that, he's playing along. Why? he wonders, trying to probe what's loose at the moment in his id. Not just some naïve love-of-the-other—that's part of it, sure, but only part, though racial complexity's in his blood as much as movies are on his brain and everyone else's that he knows. What's real may be what they see on a screen, but what asses like Bob have failed to perceive is that often it's unintended things, developments unforeseen in scripts, that become the true reality for those who watch with a practiced eye—like the flush-faced actress truly in heat because of some errant

231

pheromone or the actor who's suddenly horny for real after the tenth or twentieth take. You can read it so clearly on the screen, that helpless spiral. . . into what? What Cary and Ingrid really feel down in the cellar faking lust, or Ingrid again with Bogie at Rick's. No clumsiness there on Bogie's part—Bogie had always played it cool, but those letters of transit were a shill. It's Bogie's banana she's panting for. . . apparently not the case with Rose, or maybe only by fits and starts. And Bogie looks tall—well, taller, at least (in fact, they both stand five foot eight). Here's looking at you, kid. . . from below if the kiddo in question's wearing heels. He guesses that Rose is maybe five six.

Then there's Patti, of course. . . was that her name, the diva who diddled General Mite? He wasn't as big as Bogie's dick, so hose-length wasn't her concern—though, being half-Sicilian herself, she must have dug the blue-black jaw that he and Bogie shared with Mite, nearly from childhood he recalls. Not that it helped much early on since he'd played Mordred year after year, the darkly malevolent sneak-about in Holy-Grail shows in middle school, while Danny was Merlin, and everyone else could saunter and preen as Round-Table twits while Dugan had been instructed to skulk.

Is it really that buried in his past, why he's so willing to put up with Rose? He's still got time, so he might as well probe why so many such memories are coming to mind, so oddly related to middle-school years before his big winning streak had begun and he was dismissed as a "smart-alecky kid" because he'd refused both bridle and bit and breaking such broncos was the rule no matter how quick or clever they seemed. If that was most prevalent in his school, it was much pretty much true across the board, even at Christmas pageants in church without his displaying any dissent. Tall beardless kids got the glamorous parts with crowns and coffers filled with myrrh while he was assigned a union-suit with mittens and footsies the color of snot—a "Wild man of the Woods," they said, who'd come to worship the new-born babe, frog-marching with the shepherds' flocks. He'd begged to try out for the ox, manure-boy, half-wit, anything. But Miss Roberta (e.g., De Mille) had told him to hush and work on his hop, which left the teenybop angels atwitter (excited to be like Maidenform ads decked out so skimpily in their slips—a cause for further bitterness. . . they'd sing for the shepherds, he surmised, but not for long-johned missing links).

What had brought about a change of tune was Dugan's decision to camp it up—he'd played that yeti like Harpo Marx, bugging his eyes at Balthazar, looking for cooties in Melchior's hair, ogling the angels until they shrieked, wagging their pert tits in a row. It went down hard, upstaging God, and Miss Roberta had cut his part, re-casting him in her next year's show as Saint Luke speaking through a mike from offstage in the vestry room. But she'd relented his final year, entrusting him with a starring role normally played by the senior-class male most likely to go to seminary—or it might have been her wry revenge, since he was Joseph in a year that Mary could easily have lugged her spouse along with the donkey and Son of God to Bethlehem and back again.

Mattie Jo Lumpkin wasn't just tall—she threw the shot-put like a pea—but she was winsome in her way, a jungle gym he'd wanted to climb since long before he learned in class that she was at least as smart as he. And now his role was comforting her as, impelled by a Caesar Augustus decree, he'd cuddled her up and down the nave Actor's Studio to the hilt, using both hands beneath her cloak while wooing his shy colossal bride in ways defying common sense though fraught with doctrinal appeal—our Lord's paternity re-confirmed by sheer proportions, Q.E.D.

But Mattie, like Patti, had liked 'em petit—or "every which way," as Dugan inferred from some of the leering older boys. Despite a few sectarian qualms, he'd come close to laying her in a manger when Miss Roberta intervened. After catching him feeling Mattie up, she'd had King Herod dog their tracks whenever they tried to slip away, frustrating Dugan, and, in the end, provoking a close call on the set.

En route to Egypt, as it were, he'd learned that Mattie was stuffing her bra with halves of Wilson tennis balls, the homemade falsies she'd devised to make herself less angular. When shortly after he'd copped a feel, one of them turned up in the hay, a couple of shepherds had threatened to blab—which meant, of course, embarrassing Mattie, effectively making Dugan a cad. . . and, even then, that wasn't his style. So, Dugan had taken the blabbers aside and said it worked like Benadryl—you chewed enough and you got high. Mattie was hooked. "But give her a break, she's knocking back twenty balls a day." The guys were hip, they'd both clammed up. The truth of the Virgin's falsies was safe, but that's as close as Dugan would get to knowing her in a Biblical way.

Still, he's made headway since back then in learning to tailor his appeal. Long before Dunkie's gruesome pursuit, he'd learned that big girls found him cute, scatterbrains liked his intellect, and smart ones left his hands alone if he recited the Rubáiyát. With other sorts, you never could tell. Though Bonnie and Sunbeam fell for his act, Rose's not the bimbo type. . . he'd have to think of something new. Like what? concluding his meditation more or less where he'd started out. By being who you really are, his inner Bogart says with a snarl, and, if that doesn't suit her, fuck her (sure, but that's what he won't get to do). Don't be so crass, he tells himself, there's more to life than chasing tail. At the moment, though, he can't think what, given the moves he's already made.

He sees her heading back towards the car with a hardened expression on her face—like Maria Casares in *Orphée*.

● ● ●

Rain's drumming lightly on the hood when, turning from asphalt onto dirt, they splash past Trueblood's collard patch towards Dugan's hideaway in the bush. Their previous stop at the Feed & Seed was Rose's turn to wait in the car while Dugan got groceries for that night. He was its only customer.

"Somebody with yew?" Pa inquired.

"Uh frenn," said Dugan, knowing the rain was making it harder for Pa to pry.

"Startin' t' slack off," Pa observed, straining to get a glimpse through the door. "We've had aplenny, but yew know whut? Uh spell uh winner rain lak that. . ."

"Yep?" Dugan replied, not paying attention.

". . . hit kinda stitches thangs back together."

He's quoting that as they drive away, but Rose's mind is someplace else. After they get past Trueblood's house, there's nothing but woods and red clay road descending for roughly half a mile, his mailbox still beside the ditch (what mail he gets is *poste restante*, mostly handouts from CSU and occasional notes like Leon's card together with letters from Ed McMahon implying some sweepstake might be his as randomly as Leon's death), and then the driveway, soaring up for which he drops down into first, jerking Rose forward in her seat. They slide but, as his wheels take hold, vault upwards to a shuddering stop some fifteen yards from Dugan's hut. The phone booth's visible through the trees with a ribbon of pathway to its door.

With her shades now off, she takes this in while tugging a poncho from a bag. Red vinyl, he notes, her color all right. She yanks it free and, as she does, a tag on its hem flicks Dugan's cheek. She glances at him when he ducks, their eyes meet and he sees in her something he hasn't noticed before—same smooth-as-silk impassive mask but subtly older, slightly worn, more like a distance runner now. . . even (admittedly, splitting hairs), while less alluring than he'd recalled, more of a stranger than he'd thought. He gestures and they both get out, sheltered by surrounding trees.

"Down there's the river, under the bluff. The rest is pretty much what you see—the hut, the driveway, lots of woods with one old farmhouse down the road. It dead-ends there in half a mile with a drop off and more stands of trees, a drainage ditch, then Highway 1 that'll take you to Raleigh an hour away. . . except you can't get there from here unless you go back the way we came to that store you saw and on from there—twenty minutes or so in all, I'd say."

He's rattling on like a Lugtonite while she listens the way he'd listened to Pa when asking directions to his house, except it's like she's scouting locations. . . or maybe escape routes, who can say?

"Also, the dog I told you about." He calls her name, and, right on cue, as if she'd gotten a wrangler's nod, Credo sashays around the house, her tail a tightly wound propeller. Rose hesitates, but then leans down, rubbing her hands in Credo's ruff and uttering bits of doggie-talk—an effort of will, he duly notes. That's how they're going to play it, then, at least until things settle down. Stay on the surface, make it work. . . though her surface is a kaleidoscope, and he sees she's gearing up again for what will be a mano-a-mano.

"Credo," he says with no explanation, remembering Rose's Cattolick school, while Credo submits to Rose's attention, looking at Dugan with a grin as if she's got the drill down too. "So. . . any more questions?" he inquires.

"Duh hut. . .?" she nods in its direction.

He hears her dubious change of tone, so he adjusts to counter her feint. "Twenty by twenty, just one room. Not much to look at," he admits. "Not much to live in, come to that."

Her look says, "Why'd you ask me then?"

"I manage," he shrugs. "I don't need much" (a loaf of bread, a jug of wine, some books of verse. . . and thou, it seems—though that's the catch he mustn't admit). "Don't s'pose you've read *The Rubáiyát*?" He guesses she hasn't. "Useful advice for life in the sticks." He trusts she's letting his blather go because it's all beside the point. For the moment, at least, she's got no choice, and he's doing his best to hide his cards.

He leads the way to his plywood door, sliding the bent nail from its hasp. "I've got a lock inside the hut. The key's outside on a shower knob, but seeing as how I never lock up. . . and that's the privy over there. Outdoor plumbing," he concedes, "but Redneck Rustic's right in style. No phone, of course, so no wrong calls. . . But come on in, you're getting wet."

He notes she's cautiously holding back, peering inside as he opens the door. "It's. . ." using her querulous tone again.

"Yeah, you're right, I see what you mean—reminds you of a tacky pagoda, but browse around, you can't get lost." He'd forgotten how cramped it'll have to be. Still, slightly irked that she won't go in—she's the one in a raincoat after all—he says, "Okay, I'm getting' soaked," and, squeezing past her into the hut, turns back to add, "It's all I can offer. . . think it can work?"

She studies his face, not budging an inch. "How long you tink I'm gonna stay?"

"A day, a week, whatever," he shrugs. "Same goes for me. . . I've no idea."

"So you're worried I'm trouble and. . ."

"Trouble?" he says, exasperated. "What else is new?"

"Dere's just one bed."

"For God's sake, Rose! We've been through that. . . there's a sofa there too." She seems to know he's improvising.

"And where's duh river?"

"I told you, behind you, it's right down there. But I'll show you tomorrow—it's way too steep and slippery too. If you're thinking about a getaway, you've gotten away. . . at least, for now."

But she stays put, nodding impatiently towards the Bobs'. "You said duh road dead-ends down dere?" He sees she's checking the gaskets again.

"There's an Aussie and his pregnant wife who keep to themselves down where it ends. He's paranoid, but we get on."

"So one way in, duh same way out. . ." She looks at the surrounding woods. "How else would you get out of here. . .?"

"If the posse showed up?"

"Duh what?" she asks.

"The people who're chasing you. Well, let's see. . . unless they're parachuting in. . ."

She stays impassive, a face like glass.

236

"You can see there're woods in every direction. But, yeah, I'd take the steep way out. . . so steep you gotta know the path."

"Show me," she says.

"Tomorrow, okay?"

"Prease," she says, a change of tone that catches him totally by surprise.

"That's crazy. Why?"

"For fun," she says sarcastically.

"For fun?" He knows it's push and pull, but, given an inch, she'll take a mile. "With you, that turns out orthopedic."

She nods and smiles, then notices Credo in the rain, seemingly waiting to go inside, though it's slackening to a drizzle now. "I'll bet it's fun for *her*," she says.

Credo appears to understand, hearing Rose cluck and point towards the bluff.

He feels betrayed but decides give in. "Hang on," he says, "I'm grabbing a coat. You'll both regret it before we're through," as, donning his slicker, he closes the door while dog and woman are starting off.

Rose slips before they've reached the bluff. So what? her expression seems to say. With red clay smeared all down one leg, she runs one hand through her wet hair before tugging her hood back up with the other. Her skin's the hue of Credo's coat, which he notes while supposing he knows what's in her mind: "I do my homework," she'd explain. "When I don't. . ." Oh, sure, disaster strikes—like socks mixed up on laundry lists or jumping off freights in free-fire zones, persnickety but error-prone ("Dese not your socks? What socks you mean? Maybe look diff'rent now dey're crean"). And homework's what you do at home, not cops-and-robbers folderol. She'll break her neck, he tells himself, taking the lead as they start down, bracing to catch her when she slides and sprawling beside her in the mud when they get to the most precipitous stretch, high over the spillway's silky buzz.

"Jesus Aitch!" He helps her up and slides again, collapsing in a tangle of limbs.   Halfway down, they stop for breath with both of them wet and splattered with mud. She studies Credo's sidelong descent.

"How much fardder?" she asks.

He kicks a rock. It ricochets and hits some trees.

"Hey!" Credo signals from below.

He guides Rose down the last steep bit, on past the spillway, up the path until they're under Highway 1. How far does the path go? He can't say, he's never gone any farther than that. How wide's the river? He's not sure.

.. maybe a hundred yards, he'd guess. He's got a rowboat above the dam but has never met anyone on this path or heard any hunters this far down. He leaves out Ian Bob's report of meeting some anglers somewhere nearby.

"I remember a place like dis," she says.

"Probably not in Chinatown." He doesn't ask her where it was.

"No," she says reflectively as he points to rivulets through the rocks, too fast and deep to wade across and too slippery to try to hop across.

"It's easy at first, when the boulders are big." He steps from one that's on the bank to one with a crest that's shoulder high, expounding from his lecturer's perch. "I've made it halfway once or twice, but the smaller the rocks, the wetter they get. . . it's not a route you'd want to take." He makes his point by propping a boot against the nearest mossy rock—it slips, of course, and his leg slides in, soaking his pant-leg past the knee. "Let that be a warning. . . yow!" he bawls as he's forced to plunge his other boot in. "Actually. . . I need a hand."

His mummery leaves her unamused—though, in some indefinable way, her mood has changed (or started to change, he's not sure why) as she's sizing up the task at hand and Credo's racing back and forth, barking out her mock reproofs.

"Be careful," he warns.

One step, then two, and she's where he'd stood, bracing herself to give him a tug.

"Whoa! Pretty good! How'd you do that? Must be those rubber soles of yours."

They squeeze together on the rock as, grabbing his pockets and holding him steady, pursing her lips in concentration, Rose does a sort of high-wire act, her wet hair brushing Dugan's cheek. For the briefest of moments, they're balancing there like tango dancers on the beat with water like music rushing by. Then stepping away, her foot slips too. She reaches back to grab his arm and poises like Mercury on one toe. He pulls her towards him in a hug, and, stepping together onto the bank, they part as soon their feet touch shore. But something has been decided now. He can't exactly spell it out, but it seems to include some sort of agreement—she'll stay until she's in the clear, though clear of what he's still not sure, and, after that, who knows? They'll see.

"It's trickier in boots," he says.

• • •

When they've made their way back up to the hut, it's Credo's turn get in a snit because, by forgetting to fasten the door, he'd let her rug get soaking wet. She seethes as they unload the car, then watches while Dugan lights a match and stoops to start the Aladdin up. She waits for him to notice her.

"Go sit," he says.

She drops her head resentfully. But Rose comes over, squatting down and purring her words, almost getting her consonants right, commiserates in a female way. "You're wetter den we are. Let's dry off."

"My towels?" he squawks. He's only got two.

"Cool it," she says while kneeling down and starting to rub, reverting again to doggie-talk as Credo's sybaritic stare confirms their sisterhood is strong. They both glance up. He's losing this battle, but he's amused.

"A laundryman's daughter. . ." he starts to chide, catching the drift of Rose's maneuver and seeing it works a lot like jazz—a constant shifting of rhythm and tone, making him hustle just to keep up. But he's on to her now. He thinks he is.

"Yes?" Rose responds half-mockingly, mud-woman to the smug mud-man.

". . . should be setting a better example here. Her name. . ." he starts his own new riff.

". . . means 'I believe.' I went to a Cattolick school, okay?" Exactly what he'd known she'd say.

But he knows nothing, really, does he? Watching her peel her wet socks off, hanging her damp jeans on a chair, he thinks how fatuous it would be to gamble on the here-and-now assuming that what she lets him glimpse will outweigh what he doesn't know. He likes the way she turns and smirks, the way she cocks her head askew when, glancing up, she meets his look. But what's for real? And why does it matter?

"I'd better go dump the trash," he says, "while I'm wet from our kamikaze tour."

In mid-November, night falls fast. Returning from the garbage pit, he looks and sees his windows aglow with Rose inside, preoccupied, apparently whipping up a meal—another unpredictable turn. The rain has slacked off once again. Nothing but soft drops in the leaves from boughs that shake against the cold. He stops and eavesdrops, mesmerized, like a fisherman with a mermaid-wife who, caught in a net he'd cast in the surf, is sitting amid the opened cans that gape like clam-beds in his hut. She's got his Rooster sweatshirt on.

"Whattaya doin'?" he inquires, as if he's just come home from work.

"Where's duh salt?" is her reply. She's jauntier now. The tempo's changed. This syncopation suits him fine.

"Behind you—there, it's on that shelf. Both shakers say pepper, but that's the salt."

"What's dis?"

"Slim Jim. A carcinogen."

"Omit duh Jim. I'll add more salt."

"So what's my job?" They're playing house, though what that means is unclear too. Both towels are dirty. Never mind.

"Sit down and wait—I'm awmost trew."

"You do this often?"

"Never."

"Great."

He'll watch her play this new theme out, as fetching as it is banal. His sweatshirt reaches past her hips. . . white socks, bare legs, and hair pulled back in a comically stubby ponytail, barely a tassel behind her head. He studies her lean, well-muscled calf, aware that, barring a meteorite or other improbable act of God—like angry subscribers burning his hut—they're going to have this night together. . . and maybe a lot more time than that. But it's only a movie, don't forget. Remember Bogie. Keep it cool. She'd counseled that too as he recalls.

"So any more questions for me?" he asks.

"Questions?" She pauses, knife in hand. She's chopping up everything in sight. "*Como en Vietnam*," she reads while pointing to it with the knife. "You been dere?"

"No. . . a gift from a friend."

"Uh-huh," she nods. "Duh lamb's now loading duh lion's gun. . ." Each of her ells is almost an are. "But maybe it eats her anyhow."

That's good, he thinks, compared to her "herro, peergrim" line—it's her cleverness as much as her looks that's got him increasingly captivated. "You found the kitchen on your own. . . anything else about this place? Neighbors, escape routes, flora and fauna?"

She thinks for a minute. "Duh privy?"

"What?"

"I'm asking you."

"It's outdoor plumbing like I said. A privy's an outhouse."

"Right," she nods. "And duh big stone wheel you got outside?"

"Mayan calendar. Very rare."

"Uh-huh! It's blank."

"Dull year so far. I'm aiming to make a coffee table as soon as I get it up on legs."

She shrugs and starts to chop again. This is how birds talk, Dugan thinks—here, I'm here. . . you're over there. . . you're there, I'm here, we're in the clear! The moment he thinks that, Rose observes, "You act like you got someting to hide. . . all wisecracks wid no expranation, nothing from you but euphemism which, as I remember, just means a lie."

"Polite evasion." But he's impressed. Her accent's still a sometime thing—which could be meaningful, maybe not. "Like supper, huh?"

"I guess we'll see." She's dumping some edibles in a pan. "I just don't get why you're up here."

"If I told you the story, you wouldn't believe it."

"Den you probably need a better writer."

"Touché!" he says. "But here we are."

"Here we are," she repeats like a bird.

He thought they'd been here once before, if here implies some sort of rapport—though with modest results, as he recalls. But nothing's forever, this is now, and, if posturing's what it's all about, he's got a repertoire of his own. He'll have to play it as it lays.

"So what can I do to help?" he asks.

"Too late," she says.

"Put on a record? Read from a book?"

"Read what?" she asks as if, with *The Peaceable Kingdom* in mind, she knows he's launching one of his lines.

"Let's see," he persists. "You might like this." He finds his paperback *Leaves of Grass*, something he almost knows by heart. All he can do, he thinks, is try.

She's started to stir-fry what she's chopped—onions, tomatoes, garlic, and meat (she's used the Slim Jim after all). Sizzling and popping fills the room along with clouds of pungent smoke through which she glances at the book.

"Ahhh. . . 'White Man' doesn't sound so good."

"Where'd you say you went to school?" He sneezes once and sneezes again. "And what'd you Cattolicks have to read?"

"Whatever the nuns provided," she says.

"Well, this is heretical. . . check it out." He opens a window and cracks the door. "It's how I always thought it would be. . . and I swear to you it's not just a line."

"I guess we'll see."

"Well, at least I haven't used it before—I just thought that maybe someday I would. I'd open this book and read it out loud, and the woman in question—in this case, you—cohabiting in a snug little hut, would listen and say, 'that's just how it is!' So here's the part I thought I'd use. 'I have somewhere lived. . .' Well, shoot! Hold on. I've lost the place." He riffles the pages with no success. "I can probably quote it anyhow. 'I have somewhere surely lived. . . a life of joy with you.' You see, it's about what has to be, of knowing that they belong together."

"Uh-huh. You wish."

"But here we are as we both just said."

"Berieve me, you weren't in Chinatown."

"He means it metaphorically—you know what. . .?"

"Sure. . . a euphemism."

Birds do this better, Dugan thinks. She puts some rice into a pot, pours water atop it, and gives it a shake.

"Okay, I've found the place again. 'All is recall'd as we flit by each other. . .'"

"Frit!" she hoots. "Let's try *corride*!"

"'. . . fluid, affectionate, chaste, matured'. . . I think you meant to say 'collide.'"

"Who *is* dis guy? He talks like you." At least, she's willing to play along.

"Walt Whitman—it's what I used to teach. 'Fluid' sounds slightly loopy, I know, but that's what he does that's really so great. Words are like something he's just invented. Like Adam in paradise, know what I mean?"

"Duh muddy professor's showing off!" She's speaking to Credo but really to him in a way that says this game's okay.

"Maybe so, but listen to this, 'You grew up with me, were a boy with me or girl with me. I ate with you and slept with you. . .' That's romantic stuff if you ask me."

"Who's he talking about?"

He closes the book and gets to his feet. "It was probably another guy."

"A guy? You mean he's. . .?"

Dugan nods, glad he's winding up home-free.

"Well, dat's okay."

"Sure, that's okay." He waits a beat, then takes a step, circling both arms about her waist and pressing against her from behind, though he knows as he does it he's gone too far. She'd suckered him in, he took the feint. No, that's not true—it's his mistake. He watches her turn the hotplate off, and, putting her fork and spatula down, wheel like a dancer slowly around, elbows in, hands under her chin, shoving him gently in the chest as if they're in a pas de deux, but not the one they'd danced on the rock. He takes a step back, she stands firm. Their supper's not what's simmering here.

"Look. . . Mike." She stops to rub her nose, then pauses to let her words sink in. "Maybe we didn't get dis straight. Dose films of mine. . ." She looks away. "I did some tings I didn't like, some tings I didn't want to do."

"Who cares?" he says. He's thought of that.

She stops him with a withering look that makes him rephrase what he meant.

"Whatever you did's okay with me. We'll pick back up wherever you say."

"Oh, you tink so? Now you're duh big subscriber, huh? You tink what happened means anytime, whenever you want it. . . dat's why you wanted to bring me here. . ."

"That's not what. . ."

"Bullshit! Yes, it is! 'Just one more ting' you said at Fort Bragg, if you could get me out of dere. What udder ting you got in mind? Fucking, of course. It always is."

He gestures palms up, peaceably, as she's trying to yank the sweatshirt off only to get it stuck halfway. The rooster rhumbas about a bit, but then she's twisted it over her head and stands there in her underwear, the bra and panties still mismatched. He hopes the striptease ends right there, but she's not letting him off just yet.

"You get what you pay for, dat's duh rule." She reaches back to unhook the bra, tossing both it and the sweatshirt aside. "No touchee, no feelee, but look-see fine. So take a look, you want it so bad. Dat turn you on, you peep-show creep?"

Her backbone's like a knotted string—he notes that when she turns away. When she turns back, she's icy calm. "Tomorrow morning I'm outta here. Nobody gets to fuck wid me. Not anybody anymore."

"I'm going for a walk," he says. He tries to look her in the eye. "You wanna stay, that's fine with me. You wanna go, just tell me where.

Nobody's beatin' up on you." She's way too shrill for this to work. He'd thought it was music, it's just noise.

He clucks to Credo, holds the door and leads her with him from the hut. They follow the driveway to the road, but find it's started to rain again and huddle under a sycamore that hardly shelters them at all. They squat awhile, then trudge on back.

Barelegged in socks, in his sweatshirt again, she's reading a magazine on the bed like a Hollywood starlet in between takes. A smell of garlic fills the hut, much stronger than it had been before. The room is hot. He lifts the latch.

"I'm gonna let some air in here. You might wanna put your britches back on."

She turns a page, ignoring him. It's clear she's played this scene before—or so he tries to tell himself. She gets off yanking him around, but he's at his limit, fed up now. He's been a seducer, not a cad, and feels entitled to set her straight.

"I wasn't presuming anything. I helped you out—not once, but twice—and what it cost was pretty steep. That's why I'm here. No place to go." It's not exactly true, of course, but neither was what she'd hammered him for. He waits for her to look at him. "But unless you're planning to leave on foot, you're stuck with me for the rest of the night. You want to sleep, we'll go to sleep. Or we can eat if it's edible."

"Close the door," is all she says, leaning down closer to the page as if absorbed by her magazine, then looking up at him again—less angry now than wary, it seems, out of some centuries-old mistrust about which he can only guess.

He goes to the hotplate, turning it on and shaking the contents of the pan, gobbets and chunks of this and that which, after twenty seconds or so, he dumps onto two mounds of rice that shake as if they'd grown in clumps. She watches him sulkily from the bed as, grabbing some Gallo from a shelf, he lifts a plate with his free hand, holding it towards her—yes or no? She's non-committal. Getting up, she tugs the hem of her sweatshirt down and, reading a final word or two, tosses her *Mother Jones* aside. She makes eye contact as she sits while Dugan's pouring two glasses out, ignoring the irrepressible thought that he's hosting another lasagna bust. The only time he's in control is when he doesn't give a rip.

He lifts his glass. "Chin chin," he says.

She stares at him.

"That's not Chinese."

"Who said it was?" He's staring back.

She cracks the faintest hint of a smile. It looks contrived—take one for a scene they'll shoot again. Or not—who cares? Who gives a shit? He'll wait to see what she says next. She takes her time before she asks, "Why'd dey send you to Siberia?"

"I asked somebody else to fuck."

"You're totally hope-ress," she declares.

She knows he's telling her the truth, not all of it, but it's enough. He understands she's backing off, and, furthermore, she'd faked that r. "Whatever it takes," he wryly replies. "That tear gas whets the appetite."

He clinks her glass. She picks it up and takes a sip, glancing at Credo. "What's wid her?"

"Pay no attention. Miffed, I guess. She thinks she ought to eat with us."

"So feed her den."

"I'll get her bowl."

He fills it with some dry Purina, then adds two spoonfuls from his plate. Putting it down, he drops his head and mumbles out a chord or two.

"What's dat?"

"Her name."

"You're singing it."

"Yeah. Doctor Pavlov is our vet."

When Credo's through, he lets her out. He pours more Gallo, then he asks, "You recognize that music?"

"What?" It's his move now, she's tossing it back.

"What I was singing."

"Should I?"

"No. Not really, except. . ." He feels a slight buzz when he stands. Maybe it's worth another try, but not for what's clearly not to be—the fisherman with his oddball catch, scaly and beautiful, cold as ice. The fisherman's drunk. She's still a fish.

"My theory is. . ." He's telling the truth. ". . . if we're the last best part of creation, God must have been hoping for something more. More than us—than Spiro and me." He fumbles through the record shelf. "Otherwise, it makes no sense—why go to all that trouble, right? inventing the world and everything else as backdrops for the human race?"

She sees he's hauling his best stuff out. He knows, of course, though he means every word, that, even when it's improvised, life as we live it's still a script. The bard was right, the world's a stage, but, going back to his thoughts about birds, there's something that means much more than words.

"So here's my great discovery," he says. "It was all for this." He holds it up, Otto Klemperer's thunderous take on the *Missa Solemnis* on one disc. "You see," he adds pontifically, "it's all a huge Rube Goldberg machine, the living and dying, space and time, designed to produce this single work by a half-mad genius who was deaf. The rest is just an afterthought."

"Beethoven?" she asks as if reading a script, surmising it from the record cover.

"The credo's what I sing to her. I'd play it but she gets upset. A feeding frenzy, know what I mean?" Then, attempting a long shot after all, "If you're still here in a couple of weeks. . ."

Nice try, she nods. "No promises," is her reply, meaning she's where he'd hoped she'd go—though with her, he thinks, he's never quite sure.

"A little more Gallo, then," he says. "To Ludwig and to White Man too."

"To Ludwig maybe," she relents, draining her glass in one long gulp and saying she needs to use the phone.

"There's a candle and matches on a ledge."

She bumps the table leg getting up, then bends to locate both her shoes. He joins her at the open door.

"A little chilly dressed like that. You see it from here?"

She says she can't.

"Here, take a flashlight. . .right over there."

He watches her as she splashes off in sweatshirt, shoes and underpants, and he then, while taking a piss in the woods, looks over his shoulder to see the booth lit up like a tiny boat adrift. He shakes himself, the light goes out. When he gets back, the hut feels snug, its walls as warm as somebody's skin.

Yanking the tub from under the sink, he starts to stack the pots and pans, then leaves them outside on the bench in case it rains a little harder. If it doesn't, he'll wash them sometime tomorrow. Tomorrow's another day, he thinks.

When he goes back in, she's brushing her teeth in panties and sleeveless undershirt—flaunting her rule of gawk-all-you-like but do-not-touch-the-merchandise. He thinks he knows how her viewers feel as he strips down to his boxer shorts and tells her he'll flip her for the bed. He's kidding, of course. The sofa's for him. Héloïse sleeps in Abelard's bed.

"Good night."

"Good night."

246

No hanky-pank. The lights are off and heat turned down when he hears from Credo, still outside, scratching indignantly on the door. He gets back up to let her in. She gives him another sarcastic look, lit by the glow of the kerosene heater. He shrugs and returns to the Naugahyde, which is pliant and yielding except for the lump that prods him in the small of his back. The bedsprings twang across the room. Long day, he thinks as he hears two shots, resounding maybe a half-mile off.

"Our crazy neighbor," he says aloud. No answer from Rose, so Dugan adds, "Crazy but harmless," waiting a bit and feeling his watchfulness start to ebb as layers of somnolence settle in.

He's almost asleep when she speaks up, so quietly she says it twice. "Just roommates, den?"

"Whatever," he mutters, meaning okay.

So life's surprised him yet again. But nothing's surprising really, he thinks. New lines, same script, but different results—at least, for the moment. . . maybe they'll change. But no more sequels, this is it. He mulls that over. This is it. There's an endless array of couplings on-screen, but no matter how much they doctor the roles, the chemistry always stays the same. You try to vary it as you can, hoping to get a different result. You don't, though—that's a cruel fact. That's Hollywood, he tells himself. It's life as well, but what of that? The window glass is damp and cold. The heater faintly ruminates. He hears its flutter, sniffs its smell, detects a rhythm in its hum.

● ● ●

Awake before her that first day of what he'll call his "Jake Barnes phase," he pauses at the head of the bed to study her face while she's asleep—as if, by meticulous scrutiny, he'll make the poet's whim seem true, turn what he's conjured into fact, invent a past from sheer desire. He ponders her features one by one—a mouth the hue of apricots, a bridgeless nose and lampblack brows and, smeared a bit and beginning to fade, eyeliner in a blunt blue stroke from the corner of each almond-shaped eye. He memorizes what he sees. But then her breastbone prompts the response he'd implicitly promised to suppress (at least for now, he edits the thought).

"No good." She catches him unawares.

"What's wrong?"

"No good. Not gonna work." Peremptory but not annoyed, she says by way of explanation. "Can't deal wid dat turtle head pokin' about."

"It's. . . been hibernating," he's started to say when Credo alerts them with a growl, and, knowing it's not an idle alert, he gestures to warn that something's up other than what's inside his shorts.

They watch the windows, listening hard. A footstep's crunch, another growl, and then an unshaved jaw appears, two gimlet eyes beneath a hat, a rifle barrel's muted glint. Rose tumbles sideways through the air, yanking her blanket after her as Ian Bob, still trying to see, holds up an arm to block the glare.

"G'dye!" he grins half-drunkenly, tapping his fist against the glass.

A saucer falls. Rose crouches low. Her eyes are darting, wall to wall.

"It's okay!" Dugan semaphores, the blood departing from his groin. He'd followed her to the cabin's floor.

Bob raps again. "Just checkin', mite."

"Goddammit, Bob!"

"Jungle telegraph, y' know." Bob waves his rifle towards the road. "'Urd y' moight be ennertyning." He tips his hat. "Oi see yuh are."

"It's okay," Dugan says again. "That Aussie fool from down the road. I don't know what he's doing here." He stands and pulls his britches on. "Stay put. I'll find out what he wants."

"He's got a gun."

"I know he has. He always does."

Credo, as Dugan's lifting the latch, having discerned it's only Bob, slips out for a sunrise look-about. Bob pushes inward on the door, trying to gawk past Dugan's chest. "Wot's this? A secret 'air salon?" He winks at Rose. "Is cawfee on?"

"No," Dugan says. "The kitchen's closed."

"C'mon, then, mite. Give why a bit." He shoves his way into the hut. "'Ello," he says. "Oi'm Ian Bob, servin' as yer 'ouseboy 'ere. No, don't get up, Oi know m' why."

Wrapping the blanket like a shawl, she watches as he grabs a pan and switches on the hotplate's eye.

"Look, Bob," says Dugan, "we're not dressed."

"Easy, chum. Oi'll lend uh 'and. M' dog was nervous. 'E's out there." He gestures vaguely towards the woods. "'E knows when there's a strynger 'ere." He sets the saucepan on the eye. "Oi'll fetch th' mess y' left outside while y' two set y'selves to roights. Looks loike y' 'ad a banquet 'ere." He turns back halfway through the door. "Y'er not a Jap by enny chance?"

"Go on, get out!"

"Yanks might've forgot. Us Aussies ha'n't. . . Back in a jiff!"

Rose gathers herself and gets to her feet. No acting—she was truly scared.

"A nut. . . I told you," Dugan says. "The guy's a clueless sociopath."

"Oi 'erd that!" Bob's outside the hut, fumbling with the shower knob. "'Ow's this cut on? OWWW! 'oly be-JEESUS!"

Hearing him soak the dish-filled tub, they snatch some clothes up, starting to dress. After a while, Bob knocks on the door and, sticking his head in, chummily says, "Good thinkin', mite. Y' caught me there. Oi see y' got it booby-trapped." He turns his questioning back to Rose. "So what's y'er name, then?"

"Back off, Bob. Her name is Rose. And yours is mud if you don't blow."

"At ease, there, chum! Just tryin' t' 'elp."

"No thanks," barks Dugan, shutting the door. "Might as well humor him," he tells Rose. "The son of a bitch can't take a hint. He's probably hopped on Dexedrine." And in any case, whatever he's on, a long way from the Angolan assassin.

"Comin' back in!" advises Bob.

"Wait up there, Bob." He turns to Rose. "You dressed?" he asks her.

More or less—she signals yes. But reaching back to bunch her hair, she tugs the rubber band too far. It snaps as Bob comes through the door without the tub he'd gone to fetch.

"So 'ow you loike it? Black or whoite?" He looks at Rose, whose back is turned. "Or sorta muddy colored. Which? Tell me 'ow y' loike it, Rose."

"Brack, no sugar. Mike. . .?" she asks, as if they've got this routine down. "You got anudder rubber band?"

Crouched shoeless while fishing for a sock, he says, "That box of paperclips right there, on the floor beside the stack of books."

"One black. No sugar," Bob repeats, reaching for mugs above the sink. "Y'er Chinese, then?"

"Last time I looked." She hits the l's right on the head.

"Well, I dunno. . . it's 'ot, watch out." He sets a mug in front of her. "G'd Earth an' all that sorta thing, but gotta keep th' roadwhy clear. Can't 'ave yuh marching 'ight abress—no en' tuh it then is wot I 'ear."

"Piss off, there, Bob. You're being a schmuck."

"S'long as y'er not 'avin' kids. . . *Yum sing*," he adds as he blows and sips. "We're 'avin' a kid, th' woife 'n' me. Guess you muss study at Chantry Mount?"

"Right," Dugan says. "She's in drama and film."

"No kiddin'?" He rubs his face with his hand. "Is *yum sing* roight?"

"*Yum sing. Wen lie*." She tightens up a second braid, then lifts the mug and takes a sip.

Bob looks around. He's out of steam. "'ere comes m' dog." Shy's reappeared with Credo trotting by his side. "I gotta go crash. I'm woiped out, mite."

"Good idea, Bob."

Bob tugs his hat brim. "See ya, Rose. Y' need more caffeine, lemme know."

Dugan escorts him towards the road, but Bob veers off—Shy's right, he says, it's too exposed. Much safer these days in the woods.

"Look," Dugan requests before Bob's gone. "Two things that you can help me with—the first one's privacy, okay? She's sorta old fashioned and really shy. The second's a problem with my bed. . . you got a mattress you can spare?"

Bob's way past empty. "Oi'll ask th' woife. Or foller me back 'n' ask 'er y'self."

In twenty minutes, Dugan returns, a rolled-up pallet on his head. He dumps it on the Naugahyde as Credo sniffs to check it out and Rose picks bits of saucer up.

"Movin' roight along!" he says.

● ● ●

Rolled up like a futon during the day and stored in a corner behind the bed, the mattress looks like uncooked dough, a pig-in-a-blanket minus the pig. They both know who's to play the pig, but that's not uppermost in his mind—what, confoundingly, matters much more to him is whether she'll choose to stay at all with him in his somewhat neutered role and Aussie Bob, though clearly deranged, providing protection of a sort along the perimeter every night while steering clear of them during the day. That scheme appears to meet her demands, and he ventures to say as much to her on the afternoon of an overcast day as they're strolling downriver past the bridge, where the path gets lost in overgrown weeds.

She's changed a little—not so uptight, but chafing at her predicament and puzzled, she says, by his purposeless life. He doesn't see why. He's got plenty to do, and merely to raise an issue like that confirms an Asian stereotype. He spins not, neither does he weave while making the most of what he yet may spend, et cetera, et cetera, plus something or other by Lao Tzu. . .

"No good," she tells him once again.

No good as a hippie, he concedes. He's on medical leave for now, he says, but not going back to CSU because he's done with jumping through hoops other than ones he'll choose for himself. . . as he'll definitely do, he always has. Still, during this awkward interim (he's improvising), he aims to get to the bottom of something—which might as well have to do with her, or whatever it is she represents. . . he's not sure what, he's working on that. Surviving on just one's wits, he thinks.

"Eloquent bullshit," she observes, dismissing him with his own sort of phrase. He's affronted because he was telling the truth or coming as close as he can get. They walk for a minute, then she returns to what sounds like a Taoist notion to him—wherever he's headed, he's on a path. . . she's just in limbo, twiddling her thumbs. (Had he edited what she'd just said or had she gotten that tongue-twister right? It's reaching a point where he's not sure.) But really in limbo in less than a week? She needs to unwind, he tries to suggest. The way to do is to be, he says. Besides, she's *safe*, that's no small thing. It is and it isn't, she demurs—she might be better off on her own. She might, he admits, but she's very conspicuous in these parts, and shouldn't she let the trail grow cold. . . for a couple of weeks, a month or two? (He can't believe he's saying this.) She thinks about what he's just said, then stops to let her words sink in.

"You're generous, Mike. You're not asking for much. . ."

"I'm not offering much. . ." he interrupts.

She pauses, then tells him, "Here's duh ting. . ." (is that for effect?) "you drive to the store to get what we need, you be duh rooster, dat's okay." She's wearing his CSU sweatshirt again and plucks at the mascot's upraised beak. "But when you get back, I can't be duh hen. . . anudder rooster, someting else. Maybe somehow we work it out. . . until. . . until I don't know when."

He doesn't know why she's so hung up, but it's clear to him now she'd meant herself when talking about his purposeless life (probably Eve's objection too, incensed at never getting to town). It's okay if she sets the terms—it's all provisional (life is too).

"If I could share a capon's perspective. . ."

They turn upriver, back towards the bluff.

"A what?" she asks impatiently.

"A chicken who's looking to live in peace, which is what I hope we can manage to do. . . for as long as it works for both of us."

"Dat's fair enough" She takes his arm as if relieved by updating part of some tentative plan.

"Birds of a fedder," he replies.

What follows is totally new for him so far as dealing with females goes, though he manages most things fairly well except at night when, hormones all on red alert, he struggles to think of something else (like banging his head against a tree) while ignoring divestments prior to bed—a back half-turned, a flash of skin, then panties, socks and undershirt like Wonder Woman's uniform (who was it who'd alluded to that? Ponytail raving at Up Yours, presaging Dugan's future role as Steve the celibate aviator?) But what else could she possibly do, cohabiting in a one-room hut? It's not as if she's rubbing it in, though often she chooses to wear no bra, and, once, before he rigs something up for privacy in the outdoor shower, he impulsively sneaks a furtive look. It's a sunny but chilly afternoon with bright backlighting from the sky. She's stamping as she rubs some soap across her shoulders and over her chest, shimmering when she reaches back (her nipples like rubber plugs of the sort they used to use for soda bottles). He doesn't know if she sees him or not, but he hangs a curtain the following day.

When it freezes, he wraps the pipes with rags, and, moving the washtub into the hut and warming some water up in pots, he goes for a walk before she strips (imagining what he doesn't see), and, finally, it gets so bad that he's ready to flog it in the woods (what am I doing? he asks himself). He ponders Roscoe Moseby's toes while trying more wind sprints down the road and inventing more off-site needs to pursue—like scouring the nearest towns for a wok. In Sanford, at the hardware store, they listen to his awkward description and sell him a galvanized stove-vent cap ("in commonist China, hit's a wok"). He takes it home and hands it to Rose, saying at last they'll "wok and woll." She's not amused but tries it out and figures a way to make it work.

Otherwise, what's there to do? He watches her attentively—the way she sighs when she gets bored or lifts her eyebrows at a joke or closes a drawer by leaning back and straightening her arms to push it shut. Some things seem gross (the way she chews) and some grow more beguiling with time (like how her thighs don't taper down but join her hips like tinker toys). He sees her strolling on the path with head half-bowed and shoulders low, her hips shoved forward in an S and fingers laced as if in prayer (*Les Très Riches Heures*, he tells himself, but maybe more like a Tang dynasty scroll), adding that to a growing list of enticements that he's identified together with a reddish mole behind a shoulder to one side. What mole? she asks him, dubious. He shows it to her in a mirror. Reproachfully, she studies it. Where she comes from that's very rude—such blemishes are a private matter.

"In California?" Dugan scoffs. She shouldn't be hyper-sensitive.

"You mean inscrutable?" she retorts.

They're not the same. It's just a mole. Not worth a hassle."

"Who's hassling?"

"You." It's limbo fever, he explains. He's seen it coming—classic signs. . . moody, irascible, slightly bored.

"Speak for yourself!"

"I am," he says, and she backs off. They're companions now and almost friends, as one-time lovers sometimes are. But has the professor got a cure? she asks him half-facetiously—something to keep the mind engaged, other than present company. Of course, of course. He's sure of that? Right here on the premises, he replies, though nothing is sure but Shakespeare and Keats. Are any great books a certain cure? Only two, my child, he says—*Wuthering Heights* and *War and Peace*, either of them should do the trick unless she finds them too verbose. . . too wordy, he says. She rolls her eyes and says she'll try a double dose, reading from both books every day. After a week he gets a report. It's clear Émile has no knowledge of women, but Lea's perceptive. . . very aware.

"You've got it backwards," he protests. The woman is Emily, not Émile, and Leo Tolstoy was a man. But Rose persists, she won't back down. One's a woman who thinks like a man, the other's a man. . . Is she putting him on? She catches his smile. He knows they're only playing a game but finds it's like lines in that Whitman poem he'd read aloud from once before. "You grew up with me," old Walt had said,

> . . . were a boy with me, or a girl with me,
> I ate with you, and slept with you. . .

It's almost as if they're acting them out, but, again, she seems to be reading his mind. So why'd he'd singled those two books out? They've got nothing in common that she can see. Both authors were mystics of a sort. "Nope, only one," according to Rose. "This one," she says (it's *Wuthering Heights*), that's why the other is so much better. Dugan points out how reckless it is to draw conclusions before she's done—she's hardly started on either one. "I start in duh middle," Rose explains, "beginnings and endings always lie."

She's caught him unawares again, snookering him at his own best game, which also means she's figured him out far better than he can figure himself. She's right, he thinks, in her whimsical way, as effortless as she makes it seem (a Chinese Natasha, a neutered Pierre, a rural backwoods southern steppe). But whimsy is volatile—as is she. As soon as he starts to take it for granted, her cold, peremptory side appears. Off balance repeatedly, he's surprised by the pleasure he gets from letting her win. When she stumbles across the notes he's made, half-heartedly, for his essay on Joyce, she asks in a dubious monotone, "But why'd you do this?"

"I really don't know," is his honest reply, except he's learned what L.C. learned, and that's too difficult to explain.

He discovers she cheats at five-card stud with Loser-Washes-the-Dishes at stake. She slaps her cards down. He objects. She smirks and tries to rub it in.

"You lose!"

"I don't."

"Oh, yes, you do." Untethered, her tits are vehement.

"There's something funny going on."

"Oh, yeah? So what? Unlucky in cards, dat means someday you lucky in love."

"Not lately," he shrugs as he shuffles the deck. She probably knows what he does in the woods.

"You keep on hoping," she shuffles and says. "Maybe tomorrow things improve."

Maybe, he thinks with a cynical nod. Celibacy can mess with your mind.

● ● ●

Next day he visits the laundromat where what was Delbert's Muffler Shop is now Marvita's Wash 'n' Slosh, the end of an agrobusiness dream that Delbert had up and left behind when federal agents, nosing about, discovered the pot fields underground. Even with washers and dryers installed, his ex-wife halved her energy bills and saved whatever Delbert had paid to have his assistants "cut the grass."

Dugan has been there several times but not with panties in his load, so he's relieved it's empty now. He puts such things on DELICATE and runs the rest in one big heap. But just as the undies cycle out, a busybody he's overheard hobnobbing at the Feed & Seed, loads two machines and settles down for his intimate folding-table show. No folding, then—lump stuff together. He's stuffing the dryer load in his bag when something catches on the door. The panties.

"Damn!"

He yanks. They tear. The woman stares as if she thinks there's something kinky going on—which she'll report at the Beasley's store. . . and maybe Ma, who's not so dumb, will figure out he's got a guest who, if Pa had seen her in the car, he might remember looks Chinese. Dugan's aware he mustn't get lax. Next time he'll drive on down the road to where he feels anonymous, to a rival in Corinth called WHITER THAN SNOW ("Wash Me and I Shall Be Whiter than Snow"), the Pentecostal laundromat beside a Philip's 66 that sells French ticklers in the head.

WHITER THAN SNOW was on his mind when, unloading his pillowcase at the start, he'd sniffed the panties on the sly. No special smell. He'd sniffed again. The gossipy woman, though missing that, looks primly aloof when he checks out. Transvestites running wild in the woods—he'll make an epic tale of it when he recounts the encounter to Rose.

But just as he turns and is gearing down for his driveway's short steep uphill climb, he glances instinctively to the side and meets the milky one-eyed stare of Mister Shy slinking off furtively into the brush. He spots more movement in the woods and, past the driveway, near his bench, a collard like a monstrous zit erupting from the ruddy clay. Not far away is Trueblood's truck.

Jerking the Pontiac into park, he hustles towards the front of the hut where, like a low-budget production still, he stumbles on a mute tableau of Trueblood with a two-by-four and Credo several feet away, both gazing upwards at the door where Rose is standing, looking down—not at them, but at a gun. His footsteps seem to break a spell. All three jerk quickly, then relax. He instantly puts the pieces together.

"That Nazi bastard," Dugan says. "He. . ."

Trueblood calmly shakes his head. "I caught him by surprise is all." He plucks the rifle from the ground. "You better see he gits this back. The two by fo' belongs to you."

"He's crazy."

"Sho'. We all knows that." He looks at Rose, who turns around to check on something in the hut. "I don' s'pose he be comin' back. I sho' do like 'at dog," he adds, as Credo peers into the woods.

"I saw the collard."

Trueblood nods. "I chunked it towards 'at other dog when this one bark to say look out. It comin' at me like a snake, but once I snatch this board heah up, it think of somethin' else to do. Then Mister Bob come round th' side. . ."

"Pointing his gun?"

"S'cuse me," says Trueblood quietly as Rose emerges with a plate on which two water glasses sit. She holds it out. They both take one. "Well, now," he says. "That does taste good." He drinks it slowly, wipes his mouth and sets it back onto the plate. "I better get back on up the road. You short uh collards, lemme know."

Dugan's enraged but mystified. He walks with Trueblood to his truck and watches as he backs around and rattles on up the red-clay road. Trying to reconstruct events, he guesses that Trueblood reached the hut as Bob and Shy on some crackpot patrol were prowling in the woods nearby. How Rose fits in, he isn't sure but, when he gets back, he sees a bruise that's darkening along her jaw.

"What happened?"

"Nothing."

He persists. "He threatened Trueblood with his gun?"

"Ask him," she shrugs.

"He tried to. . .?"

"No."

He reaches out to touch the bruise. She parries his hand and turns away.

"He hates duh Viet Minh," she says.

That's all he gets from her that day, and, later, when he asks for more, she says she's through discussing it.

• • •

Next day he takes the rifle back, leaving it on the Bobs' porch. A week goes by, then several more, marked by Rose's darkening mood. It's still unclear what she's going to do but, in her non-committal way, she settles into their joint routine. He does his chores, she mopes about, Bob does his skulking somewhere else. Though not what Dugan was hoping for, just living together would seem enough except for his role as eunuch-in-chief, wondering how much her subscribers had paid and what they'd managed to do with themselves in between getting installments from Rose.

One day, returning from the store, he finds that she and Credo are out, presumably on their favorite walk along the path below the dam, and can't suppress the paranoid thought that Ian Bob's showed up again. A few minutes later when both are back, he keeps his anxieties to himself. But then one day on the way to the store, he stumbles upon some vital news—the man arrested in a plot to murder folk-singer Joan Baez has been deported from the States. Hector ("Protector") Manuelo Lopez is on his way back to Panama City. Illegal entry. No details.

"Good news for Rose," is Dugan's first thought—though, driving home as he's mulling it over, he thinks it might be bad for him, making it safer for her to leave. But if Hector can't hope to follow her now, he still could share whatever he knows—which is little enough. . . except, of course, for Dugan's name which Rose has conceded he might recall. Could somebody track her down with that? It would take a while, but who would bother? Dose dwatted subscweibers? That's far-fetched. Nobody hires sleuths to trace Joy Bang. So back to the question he's raised before: with Hector effectively out of the way, why should Rose linger there with him? Why shouldn't he keep this news to himself? That would be lying—he wouldn't do that. . . or would he? No.

As soon as he sees her, he blurts it out, provoking a curious frozen smile. As if in a game of crack-the-whip, she's still as a statue until she says in a low flat voice, "I need duh car." For what? he asks as he hands her the keys. She shakes her head. No problem, he says. She takes a step, stops, turns, and sits. "Forget it."

"What?" he asks.

"Dere's nuttin' to do."

"For him?" he asks.

She doesn't reply. He waits a while before he asks if Hector was really from Panama. "Probably. . . more or less," she says—the truth is that she doesn't know. And how and where'd she connect with him? "Connect?"

she asks distractedly. He waits again. "With Hector?" she shrugs. "No card, work hard." She'd hired him cheap. "Dere's lots of Hectors in L.A." Ruthless, macho, out for themselves, deported and bouncing back again. "Dey gave him bonuses on duh side." The subscribers, she means. She folds the car keys in her fist.

"Is there anything I. . ."

She shakes her head, preoccupied by something else.

"Then try," he says, "whatever it is." What if she's an illegal too?

She looks him searchingly in the eye, then rises and leaves without a word. Whatever it was, when she returns in a couple of hours—quelling a fear she'd abscond with the car—he tries to furnish a positive spin by saying with Hector out of the way, they've both got cause to celebrate. She asks him why. Well, lots of reasons, he explains. Her freedom, his birthday. . . yeah, it's true, he's twenty-nine that very day. It's no big deal but, anyhow, he's been planning a cook's night off for her, though he'd turned around to share the news and needs to run to the Feed & Seed. She nods to acknowledge what he's said but says she'll need another trip too.

She sees the expression on his face. "It'll be okay," is all she says, "after a little mopping up."

He's used to that—it's standard with her, but he wants to ask before she goes how old she's been supposing he was? She hasn't wondered? That's okay. But, also, he's a hell of a cook, so be forewarned. Yeah, that's a joke, but he's going to try—whatever's happened someplace else, they might as well make the most of things.

"As best we can," is all he adds. The bets are down now, he reflects— today's the day we'll be showing our cards. He fixes the moment in his mind as sunlight slides like faded silk across the sill and up the wall.

● ● ●

Dugan gets stuck at the Feed & Seed. He'd promised to hurry, and he tries but has to bandy words with Ma.

"That Chinese woman still out thare?"

He hesitates. "Out whare?" he asks.

"Out thare with you."

"She's studying at Chantry Mount."

"Uh-huh," she sniffs. "What's all this for?"

"Ah'm makin' chili."

"Well," Pa chirps up, holding a tiny pepper up. "This heah's thuh fella you should git. You usin' beef?"

"Instedda whut?"

Pa's heard they like to mix in dogs. Who told him that? Well, who you think? Roscoe with the froze-off toes!

"You tell old Roscoe that's a myth, raw monkey brains is what they eat."

"Tasted pig brains," Pa allows. "Dadblasted good with scrambled eggs. But pigs is smart."

"Yep," Dugan says. "Yew wouldn't catch them eatin' dawgs."

When he gets back, Rose looks upset, still undecided what to do. She grabs the keys and drives away.

● ● ●

So, it's three o'clock. For a couple of hours, he's got nothing to do but lose himself in four-alarm chili. "We'll see," is what he tells himself, referring to Rose as well as the chili. Re-checking the clock—it's 3:02-- and morphing into a master chef, he readies his basic array of tools: the cutting board, the serrated knife, the stove-vent cap (a.k.a. wok). He hunts for Rose's wooden spoon and finds it soaking in a pot she's left unwashed inside the sink (an ominous sign, but maybe not—does somebody checking out for good clean up before she leaves or not? Most women would, he tells himself). He picks a yellow onion up and peels its flaky outer skin. He peels another, then he carves. It's down to barely half its size before he minces what he's got and cuts the beef up into cubes. His concentration's soothing him. Two garlic cloves, some olive oil, and, adding heat, he reaches a point where every motion has a voice, producing an orchestral fugue. The mixture's bubbling golden brown. He adds the meat, its basso thud provoking a sizzle that's blending in. He stirs and hears the onions sing. He adds hot peppers, four in all, and suddenly a cloud of smells spreads everywhere like violins—the peppers' acrid high-pitched whine, the garlic's sweet but husky drone. He hums along, and, in his mind, the sound is comparable to Bach (the beef, he thinks, the rolling bass). He puts tomatoes in a pot with water, basil, celery seed. Green peppers, bay leaves, cumin, salt. . . transfer the rest, it's nearly done—

reduced to mere continuo. The room's fogged up, the windows wet, his clothes a Mexican sachet, but only one decision's left—to use the kidney beans or not. He lets that simmer while he walks for longer than he thought he would, then rushes back with a sudden fear he'll find his hut's burned to the ground.

It hasn't, but it's getting dark. He takes a leak, as Credo squats and wanders off. From where he stands outside the hut, it's got a sad-sack *Gold Rush* air. . . the party-favors by the plates, the chili ticking like a bomb. Oh well, he sighs and grabs a beer, one of the Heinekens on the sill. Maybe she's gone, and maybe not. At eight o'clock, he adds the beans. At nine, at last, he hears a car and thinks at first it's someone else, but then she's coming through the door and he's affecting nonchalance.

"You get things fixed?"

She seems to nod, throwing her sweater on a chair.

"Wrong question, huh? Sure took your time."

Still no response. At least she's back. She shuts a bag up in a drawer and plops down with a frazzled stare.

"How 'bout a Heineken?" he asks, raising the window. Frigid air. He slams the window shut again. "Okay, *tovarich*, whattaya say? *Za vashe z'dorovye*, eh?" That had gone over big with Bonnie's friends but not with Rose, who lets him jubilate alone. No effort from her, which he resents along with her drama-queen woe-is-me and whatever it was that took so long. It's clear he'll get no explanation.

"To us," he proposes, faking esprit while popping her tab, then chugging his own. "Wamme to get you started there?" He sips from hers. "Okay. . . to me! I'll drink to that." Another chug and then a sip. He's depositing loops of moisture rings—one more and he'll have an Olympic seal. "Hey, this is festive. What's the deal?"

"Tired is all."

He wants her to know she's pissing him off despite the fact that she's returned. "To you, to me, to Texas Pete! Hang on, I'm gettin' us both a bowl."

He ladles big globs of chili out.

"Pipin' hot." He takes a bite and sweat breaks out. Another bite—his tongue is scorched. Too many hot peppers. "Shoot," he says. "I messed it up. I'll get us some Spaghetti-O's." He swishes the beer inside his mouth. "Don't even try it. Okay. . . what?"

She shakes her head, remaining mute.

"This chili was a bad idea. Would you believe. . .?"

Her eyes are closed.

"You sick or what?"

"I'm tired."

"For sure. You take a rest."

"Uh-huh." She sprawls across the bed.

"Things really got fixed."

"Fuck off," she groans.

"That's better," he says. "Don't let my clambake interfere."

Too bad, he thinks. Misfired again. Or maybe—who knows?—she's into drugs, which is why she's been so secretive. . . Hector had formerly kept her supplied, and, now in a panic, she's managed to score with something that's thrown her for a loop. He scrapes the bowls and feeds the dog and takes the beers in off the ledge—no point in tempting nuts with guns. After a while, he prods her leg. There's no response, but she's breathing fine. He slips her Nikes off each heel.

"Hey," Credo whines. After letting her out, he smears some bread with peanut butter. Happy goddamn birthday, me. He chases the sandwich with a beer.

With one boot off, he's up again when Credo's scratching on the door. "My toes are Roscoe-cold," he thinks but lingers there outside the door, standing with Credo on the steps. The dirt, the bench, the straw, the trees, the darkness lapping at them all—a tide is turning, he perceives, whether it's headed out or in.

When both go in, he shuts the door and wrestles the other boot off his foot. Then, keeping the chili's stench at bay, he lays his folded mattress flat, turns out the light and gets undressed. Almost at once two distant shots, like muffled pops, erupt far off. His stomach growls. He shuts his eyes.

When he wakes up, the room is warm and there's a low-pitched coughing sound coming from over by the tub. He thinks it's Credo, but it's not. It sounds like a penitent's mumbled plea—but it's Rose by the washtub, throwing up.

"You sick?" he asks her stupidly.

Her hair swings forward as she heaves, so primly that it seems at first she's only fighting back a sneeze. The heater's light is just a glow. He reaches out. She shakes him off and heaves again. He puts his hand along her spine, which bows and shudders as she rocks. She seems to mew.

"Say that again."

He thinks she says she'll be okay—"No doctor," if he hears aright. He helps her fumble back to bed. Her skin is hot. He cuts the light on by the shelf and grabs a dishrag from the sink.

"Huh-unn!"

"What's wrong?"

Her face knots up. She pukes but doesn't reach the tub. He drags it to her, takes the rag and uses it to wipe the floor.

"Lie down," he says. "Get back in bed."

He carries the rag and tub outside, rinses them out, and then returns. When he gets back, she's leaning up, her T-shirt plastered to her chest. The heater. What? She wants it off. He nods and, opening up her purse, finds a note pad, coins, a comb, and, under all, some Tylenol. He melts two tablets in a glass. She spits it out. He tries again. He gets a Kleenex from the box and wipes the corners of her mouth.

"Huh-unnh!"

"It's clean."

She starts to scowl but then relaxes into sleep. Too bad he'd quit old Troop 14 (the "Sternbolt Youth," according to Danny, "Christian brownshirts on the prowl")—he might have learned some useful stuff like what to do in case of shock, lower the head and raise the feet, then tie a sheepshank. . . what's a bight?) Am I asleep? he asks himself. Her face looks stony in repose but tranced and dreaming like a mask.

He wakes at some point in the night, still propped against a table leg. Sky's dark but turning gray he thinks. Her fever's raging—what to do? He tries to get more Tylenol down and, when she chokes, supports her head, holding it cradled in his lap.

"You hear me, Rose?"

She murmurs back.

"Where'd you go? I need to know."

She digs her fingers into his arm. "No. . . doctor."

"Right, I got that part. But tell me what. . ."

Her hand slips loose. She turns her face into his lap and makes the sort of choking noise the Pontiac makes when shutting down. As if in consort, Credo whines. They alternate, then harmonize—a choke, a whine, a cough and wheeze, a drawn-out sputter and a howl.

"Too much, you guys! C'mon, pipe down."

They stop abruptly. Rose lies back. Her breathing eases up a bit, then modulates into a purr. Credo affects an instant doze while Dugan, intending vigilance, succumbs as if they'd flipped a switch. When he wakes up, it's broad daylight and Credo's pacing by the door. He has to take a leak himself but checks on Rose, whose hums and clicks sound regular, like snores instead of anguished sobs. He steps outside. It's sunny and cold (the sort of morning on the moors when Olivier picked Merle's body up and carried it towards the closing credits).

He makes some coffee for himself—then, noticing Credo's empty bowl, opens the 12-ounce Liver & Bits he'd bought for her as party food and leaves it on the lowest step. She's trotted off. He goes inside, drifting into a fitful snooze, then waking to check on Rose again.

She's scorching hot—sweat-matted hair and splattered shirt, her vomit like the Liver & Bits. He peels her T-shirt over her head while hugging her close to prop her up, the two of them in an exhausted embrace like partners in a marathon dance. Surprised to find how frail she seems—stark collarbones with teacup tits, dark nipples sagging to the side—he bathes her with the loofah sponge she'd told him they would have to have, then tugs a clean shirt over her chest—a debonair Mickey Mouse in spats decked out to look like Fred Astaire (a whim of Sunbeam's un-reclaimed). With her socks pulled off, he hesitates, but noting a sort of mucous stain, he rolls her knickers down as well, lifting her up to slide them free. Her legs are splayed. He takes a look and sees some sort of menstrual pad. There's not a lot of pubic hair, a fact he notes with a clinical stare while scrubbing the inside of her thigh, unable to think what else to do. With a shock, he sees she's watching him.

"*Jo mei-a?*" she asks, retracting her knees and grabbing his hand indignantly. "You give me. . ."

"What?"

She takes the sponge, still hunched as if for a bobsled run. "A towel."

"Here." He looks away. "Are you. . .?"

"You don't. . . know anything."

It's true, he thinks—way out of his depth, he's doing his best to muddle through. She yanks the sheet up, lying back. He smooths it out. "Some water?"

"No." She turns her face, her chin now planted on her chest. In twenty seconds, she's asleep.

He stirs two Tylenol, lifts her head and helps her swallow them while she sleeps. He feels a twinge, a nervous jolt, like waking up behind the wheel (did I doze off? he wonders again. . . is what's been happening for real?) He ought to rinse the tub again and clean the hut and go for help before he conks out from fatigue (a paralytic in the tub, the water rising, he's alone—oh, help! he warbles, sloshing down, but that was very long ago).

It's midday when he wakes back up. Though blurry-eyed from his long snooze, he senses something's gotten worse. He looks at Rose, and there it is: the sheets are crimson, soaked with blood. She's bled to death? A suicide? His heart is throbbing in his throat, and, once again, she's watching him.

"A box in dere."

He doesn't know where.

"That drawer dere." Her voice is strong. "Just hand it to me."

He complies while averting his gaze as answers start forming in his mind followed by questions he can't resolve. Not drugs, he thinks, biology—but he gets flummoxed either way (was life with mermaids half this hard? No fishy vapors once a month but eggs ten thousand at a time—all females are others, he perceives). When she's sleeping again, he steps outside, still reeling from the night's events though muffled in layers of fatigue, still trying to think through what she's done. He wonders if maybe it was his.

• • •

To his relief, Rose quickly mends. He buys new sheets and burns the old in his cement-block incinerator, which is really just a garbage pit. In less than a week she's back at the wok, and Dugan, though rattled by recent events, detects a change in their status quo. She's lower-keyed, more matter of fact, and almost wistful in her moods. They seem to talk a little less and bump into each other more—like people who're stumbling from a wreck, intimate in a somnambulant way.

Now, on occasion, raising his head, he thinks he catches her watching him, and once, when she's reading as he comes in, appraising him quickly and looking back down, then checking to see if he'd caught her out. He notes her brief discomfiture before a curt dismissive smile that's meant to say it's no big deal—though maybe it is, as he concludes, when they're walking together below the dam on one of the coldest days they've had.

She bumps into him on the path.

"Sorry," he says.

She bumps him again. He takes her hand, and they walk for a dozen steps or so before he stops and, facing her, says, "It's freezing down here, don't you think?"

"Should we go back up?" She's talking to Credo, not to him, puffing out clouds with every word, then lifts her head and holds his gaze, making no effort to free her hand.

"Well, it's New Year's Eve—remember that?—and I've thought of something we can do."

"What sort of thing?" Her face is blank. "Don' wanna be trustin' you weary-nearry."

He understands she's flirting now. "Don't worry," he says. "No hanky-pank."

"No what?" She doesn't know the word, or, if she does, she's playing dumb.

"Nobody tries to break the rules."

"In udder words, no sex," she says.

"No sex by devious means," he shrugs.

That's devious in itself, she says. Not necessarily, he explains, for, as it happens, a previous guest has left an illegal game-box behind. What sort of game's irregal? she asks. Nothing dangerous, he replies, but he offers to show her and she'll decide. What's her name, that previous guest? Bonnie, he tells her. Bonnie? she says, as if tasting the word. The name sounds promising, she declares. They should rummage together through Bonnie's box—though, frankly, she hopes they'll find some game he's better at than five-card stud. Or one at which she doesn't cheat? She'd said if he keeps trying. . . True, but lately he's been winning at cards. Sometimes maybe she likes to lose—though losing can be a relative thing. That's true as well, she says with a smile. So they hurry back up and, once in the hut, Dugan retrieves the sandalwood box where Bonnie had stowed her smokable fun. He feels his luck's about to turn.

● ● ●

"Someting I've noticed. . ." Rose confides.

They're facing the windows, leaning back, partaking of Bonnie's elegant stash after stacking their pillows on the floor and plucking King Crimson down from the shelf.

"Head music," he says officiously, upping the sound while puffing a joint prior to passing it on to her. Like Danny, he's claimed he doesn't smoke, but, what the hell, it's a special occasion, a holiday high can't hurt a thing—and, serendipitous though it seems, they've reverted to roles they've played before, like Warren & Faye in *Bonnie and Clyde* who've just decided to rob a bank, disrupt maneuvers, or ruin a film by launching dumb stunts and wrecking the set. . . or not, he thinks, no need for that. Everything's comedy in the end.

The hut's grown hazy with pungent smoke and Greg Lake's solo's underway ("innocents raped with napalm fire. . .") when Rose observes with a wave of her hand, "Someting I've noticed. . ." She takes a hit, repeating the words that she'd just said. "And I mean dis in duh nicest way. . . in some ways—did I say dis before?—sometimes you act just like a dog."

"And you can be catty."

"No, not me. . . we're talking you."

"In some ways, yeah, you're probably right. When I piss in the woods, I look for a tree."

"No, but listen. . ."

"Okay." He listens. "To what?"

"What I'm saying is dis. . ."

"You have a particular dog in mind?"

"Like any dog, you're aw-ways smelling tings," she says. "Whatever's in front of you. Like a book. . . whenever you read, you smell duh book." She picks some reefer from her lip.

"I do?"

"I've seen you. Every time."

"Gimme!" he gestures, takes a drag, and, pinching it, offers it back to her. "Okay," he says. "I'll tell you what. You've heard of Samuel Johnson, right?"

"Lyndon's brudder?"

He rolls his eyes. "A famous eighteenth-century Brit."

"Take it," she says, returning the nub.

With lids half-closed, he tilts his head, switching to professorial mode. "Okay. So now I'm gonna explain. . . why smells are so neglected here."

"Neg-rected where? Not here in dis hut!" Her accent's thicker than it was. Lately, it's hardly been there at all because, as he'd thought a few days ago, he'd simply stopped hearing it any more—just as he couldn't hear his own. He hears hers when she wants him to, or when he's irked. . . or, as it turns out, when they're both stoned.

"Don't be a wise-ass," he replies. "Here in the States and England too. In England and America both."

"I'm really hungry," she declares as, kneeling and reaching up to a shelf, she grabs a bag of tostada chips and, tearing it open, holds it out. "Want some?" she asks, her own mouth full.

He shakes his head. He'd rather talk. "So anyhow. . . this Johnson guy was such a wit that this other guy just dogged his tracks writin' down whatever he said."

"No kidding?" she munches. "Really great!"

"Not everything, though a lot of it was. Some was like 'Hey, it's lookin' like rain—gimme a beer, and charge it to him.' The guy was human after all."

"Too bad." She takes another toke in between more tortilla chips.

"Nah, that was good. Especially since this other guy, who seemed obsessed with gettin' stuff down, was there, like, with a tape recorder. Not really, you know. . ."

Crossing her ankles and folding her arms, she squints like an Utamaro print. "Not rearry, of course."

"His name was Boswell," Dugan adds. "At first, he shows up everywhere. . ."

"Like Hector."

"Well, if you say so. Same sort of thing. A dipstick with an eye for detail."

"Dime a dozen."

"I wouldn't know. But here's the sort of thing he sees. Oranges then were hard to find, and whenever old Johnson got hold of one, he ate it, right? like anyone else. . . but then he pocketed all the peels."

"Kirr it," she tells him, passing the roach.

"Huh? That's okay. There's plenty more." Watching her stub the first one out, he clumsily lights another one up, puffs, and holds it out to her.

"So where's it come from?"

He's confused. "From Bonnie. I told you."

"Duh orange? Duh!"

"That's not the point."

"Oh, I doubt dat."

"From Spain—who knows? Seville, okay?" He snatches the joint back, takes a toke, and waves it like a magic wand. "But all this time what

Johnson's missed is that Boswell was watching him tuck stuff away. And, finally, he. . ."

"Who?"

"The Scottish guy. I told you that. Here, take it."

"Tanks. What Scottish guy?"

He watches her exhale through her nose. "The one who's writing everything down. So Boswell goes up to Johnson and says I've noticed you hide those orange peels. . ."

"He writes it down?"

"It's what he says."

"Don' unnerstann. I taught you said. . ."

"The Boswell guy, he's talking to Johnson. . . asking about the orange peels. Then later he gets it written down. But Johnson takes on this injured look and answers with something really neat. 'Sir,' he tells him with chagrin, '*I have. . . a great fondness for them.*'"

She nods her head.

"You get it?"

"No."

"You got it," he says.

"Then what's a chagrin?"

"A sense of injured dignity." Reclining so their shoulders touch, he takes the joint back, sucks some smoke, and sets the roach down on a plate. "I know the feeling."

"So do I."

"Not in my company."

"Yes, I do."

"Well, that's where I'm headed. What Johnson does is he sniffs them, see? When he gets back home, he takes them out. . ."

"And sniffs dem! Sure." She looks at him with a loopy grin. "Well, Mike. . ." she croons.

"Yes, Rose?" he asks.

"Dat's a wundafah story! Makes no sense. . . but dat's okay."

He squeezes her knee. "It makes a lot of sense," he says.

"Huh-uh!" She shoves his hand away, and, leaning sideways, reaches back to stack the pillows up again. The reefer rolls onto the floor. She swats it and it falls apart. "Sorrrry!"

"No sweat. . . I've had enough." His knee is pressed against her thigh, a fact that registers on them both prompting her to move her leg in a slow and very deliberate way as if it takes gymnastic finesse. But they're shoulder to shoulder, and, where they touch, there's still a synapse both can feel.

He sighs and says, "I guess you're right. What that story's really about is. . . *smell*." Ignoring him, she's closing her eyes, rolling her head from side to side (zonked, he thinks, but so is he). He touches her arm to get her attention for what he considers authoritative. "Okay, listen to this. . ." He clears his throat. "Out of all the memories we store up, the ones that have to do with smell are our most intense and persistent—did you know that?" he asks. "And taste is basically the same. . . which is why, in Proust. . ."

"You know," she yawns, "it's been a rong time. . ." Her voice trails off.

"Me too," he says, his hand on her knee.

She shakes it off a second time. ". . . a long time since I rearry relaxed. Confuse me wid Bunnie's a big mistake."

"Bonnie."

"Whoever."

He agrees. King Crimson wraps with cymbals and drums ("I fear tomorrow I'll be crying"), so Dugan asks for any requests. Some Dylan you say? He grabs Grace Slick and flips the switch to automatic ("Every day I try," they start to sing). Dat's not Bob Dylan. Sure, it is. ("So hard to know your mind," they add.") That's him on fuzz bass. Hey! that hurts. ("And find out what's. . .") She socks his arm. Or maybe not—it's what I heard. (". . . inside you!") Ow! He thinks he's cool. "You're not," she says.

"Don't change the subject." Which is smell, and it matters a lot because, even before those two were gone. . ."

"Johnson an' dat udder guy."

"Right. Johnson and Boswell. . ." He tries to remember where he was. "The thing here's smell. . . which had vanished completely until after Napoleon had come and gone and an Englishmen showed up saying in verse that his 'whole soul grieves at the moist rich smell of the rotting leaves,' and they told him that sounded too indecent, so he too started omitting smells. . . and you know why there was all that fuss?"

He's on a tear, unable to stop, but so's Grace Slick who's getting up steam, making it hard for either to hear.

"Dey made it ir-regal?" Rose replies, dropping her head and hugging her knees.

"Just improper," Dugan says, moving his face a bit closer to hers and brushing his mouth across her ear.

"Wait!" she reaches behind his head to pilfer a pillow from his stack. He's got too many. Yeah, like fun! He lunges as she's leaning back and bangs her head on the table leg. "Oh, no," she wails. "You clobbered it."

He rubs it. Yep, it's clobbered all right. But as he was saying—or hadn't yet said—there's a guy in a book he's been working on who grooves on a sautéed-kidney smell.

"What's wrong wid dat?"

Her hair's like corn silk to the touch, looking much thicker than it is—and maybe a couple of strands are gray. That's something he hasn't noticed before, but, really, it's hard to see in such light. . . though, now that he mentions it, it's too bright. He'd like to get up and turn it off, but that's more trouble than it's worth and he's on a roll now anyhow, explaining that for the guy in the book, that smells reveals his zest for life (the soap commercial comes back to mind invested with a kidney aroma slathered across the shining skin of a woman ecstatically in the shower—could it be Rose? decidedly not, but the image prompts him to admit that he'd tried and failed the olfactory test). "What's wrong with that is wrong with me."

She mumbles as if from far away. "Failed duh what?"

He tries to explain that he's like Johnson, hip to smells, but he'd sautéed some kidneys in a pan and found the stench completely revolting—which meant he might be one of them. One of who? she'll probably ask.

In fact, she's long since closed her eyes.

"The puritans," he rambles on, "and the hidden connection of sex and smell. . . like taste and smell, what old Johnson was really into, see?" He asks her if she gets his drift. Though she doesn't reply, he's undeterred, repeating himself with, "Two hundred years, smells disappear. . . oh, maybe you'd turn up one or two, like Keats or. . . hey, are you asleep?"

"Um-hnnn," she smiles, "but not in France. *Je reviens sur le troisième jour. . .*"

How'd she know that? "*Ne te laves pas.*" So she speaks French? She reads the perfume ads in *Vogue*. With hardly an accent, he observes. "*Mon père l'a voulu, tu comprends?*" He understands what she's just said—which is not to suppose he's figured her out, but, other than that, she's. . . what was he saying? He seems to have lost his train of thought.

"Smells," she helps him.

Yeah, okay, right. The Airplane's asking them how they feel—he wants to answer pretty good if slightly fuzzy about the edge. But the edges are where this game is played, and, even pleasantly ripped as he is, he thinks he augurs promising signs. Instinctively, he spies his goal.

"So I lived in England," he admits. She says his accent's very good. Despite her irony, he persists. "You know about Baudelaire?" he asks. The poet from France—she's heard of him? She has? That's good. "Well, when he describes this woman's hair, he says it smells like cheap perfume and sweat and stale tobacco smoke. No Englishman could have written like that until somebody crossed the Channel and learned. . ."

She sits up straight impatiently. "You puttin' dis on the final exam?"

He pauses momentarily.

"I'm bored, professor," she complains.

"Don't make me stop! It's gettin' good. Those Englishmen I'm talking about, the ones who settled New England, see? They were puritans too, which is why we've got such lousy cuisine—taste and smell. Remember that? The French eat stuff that rots in caves. We've got McDonalds. . . see what I mean? Now, here's the question I've got for you—as far as culture is concerned, what's America's biggest gift to the world? Take your time. You think it's Whitman, Satchmo, Bird?"

He nudges her shoulder. She shakes her head.

"You're right, Miss Lee! We wish they were! Know what it really and truly is?" He notices Rose looks comatose and rubs her arm to get her attention. "Hey, where'd you go? C'mon, wake up!"

She opens her eyes as ear-splitting shrieks zip out of the high-fi speakers like bats, soaring with Grace as she ascends up towards some musical empyrean. "What?" asks Rose reflexively.

"*Deodorants,*" he says to her, putting his face up close to hers. She leans away as he persists. "Erasing smell. . . repressing sex. You see where I'm going, Odorless One?"

She sees, all right. "But it's not gonna work."

He gapes at her with consternation. She gives him a shove, and he recoils. "You mean. . ." he blusters, "you really think. . . that I'm just tryin'. . .?" He straightens up. "Despite your fragrant-sounding name, I've got some interesting news for you. . . in the nicest possible way, of course. You're the only woman I've ever known completely devoid of pheromones!"

"What are you saying"

"You've got no scent! Nada, zero, not a whiff. An utterly odorless olfactory void. To put it discreetly, you're firing blanks."

She glares at him as if incensed. "I've got plenty of scent."

"It's probably just some Chinese thing. . . or maybe you lost it along the way, like Peter Pan without any shadow."

"He wudn't Chinese."

"That's not the point. Good thing you didn't try Smell-o-Vision—your subscribers would want their money back."

She holds her arm out, sniffing her wrist. "So what about you who failed duh sautéed kidney test? I guess you tink you smell so good."

"Not saying that. But see for yourself." He lifts his arm. "An abundance of scent!"

She proffers hers. He hesitates fastidiously, then runs his nose along the vein from hand to elbow. "Sorry, but. . . nope."

"Ridick-alous!" She lifts her arm up over her head, exposing an armpit.

"Cheating again. That doesn't count." He's seen her rubbing the Mum stuff on. Of course, there *is* one way to tell, but, no, she wouldn't be up for that. They'd have to examine a patch of hair without deodorants or shampoo.

"Out of duh question," she declares.

"Sure, I knew that."

"Den why'd you ask?" She sighs as if exasperated. "So all dis time, you've been settin' me up?"

He shrugs. It's no big deal for him. He wasn't going to bring it up. She said she'd noticed he's like a dog, so he's explained what she'd observed. Pheromones mean a lot to him. She's like a. . . what? Like something carved from ivory. Or maybe. . ."

She snorts impatiently. At first he thinks she's going to stand as, leaning forward, reaching down, she turns a strange expressionless face up at the ceiling, then at him. "You promised," she says. "No hanky-pank?"

He nods. Agreed. Whatever each of them thinks that means (at least, until she changes her mind, the odds of which have just improved).

She rubs her hands down the seams of her jeans. One sniff's enough?

There's no set rule—but probably, yes, one ought to do. She starts to comment, holds her tongue, unsnaps her jeans, and slides them down.

"Okay."

"Hold on." He's breathing in. "I'm clearing my Eustachian tube."

She lays her hands atop his head. "Dis doesn't seem so scientific."

"Hang on. I'm upside down, you know. It's not a science, it's an art." He sniffs again. "It's hard to tell." She starts to pull the jeans back up. He stops her hand. "Elusive, but. . . I think it smells. . ."

"Like what?" she asks.

". . . a lacquered box. The inside of a wooden box in which some precious jade is kept." He slides his face up to her mouth. "Or maybe cheese." She starts to laugh. "No. . . jade was right." He's pulling her to him, kissing her mouth. "So I was wrong about no smell."

She kisses him back, as if she's known they'd end up here since long before it crossed his mind. The music stops and starts again, and the whole equation seems to shift—expecting less, he might get more. She slips a hand behind his head, her other hand down between his legs, exhorting him like a conductor's baton. If their pact has been that she'll say when, the message she clearly sends is now.

They roll together and apart, like beansprouts whisked about a wok, twisting and grappling, shucking things off. She moves her heels up under her rump and starts to rock as he slides in. The tempo shifts to a steeplechase run—galloping, soaring, prompting a shout that arpeggios to a whinnying gasp. And suddenly it's cinematic—from Griffith to Brakhage, a dizzying rush. . . two timber wolves (the montage starts) rutting ferociously in the snow, savage and fierce, and, O my soul, it's Lillian Gish and the cataract! They're headed towards the precipice now as a jumble of images harkens back to every great movie ever made. Grace Slick is reaching the iron bridge. He spies her with her crimson flag (not crimson—no, it's Chinese red!), the Cossacks bunched to ride her down, their pent-up walls of hide and fur (slow, fast, and faster, here they come). Her mouth yawns wide. . . he hears her scream. Feed your head! she's wildly beseeching,

Feeeeeed your heh-eaaaad!

Then, clutching at Rose, he's somewhere else, out of the maelstrom, floating free. The movie's spooling on the floor as they both waft upwards towards a light, like mermaids through a kudzu sea towards beaches of dry tostada crumbs. Yep, Brakhage, he thinks—he should have known. A lap dissolve and he's closer to home beside some sort of moonlit stream with lightning bugs that flock like stars and musky aromatic scents reminiscent of a laundry bin. When he pulls back, she holds him in.

"You lied," she says.

He lets that go. Like Herman Munster, he just gloats, waving his weenie at the world.

● ● ●

Both mattresses now go on the bed and Dugan can feel their lives contract, whole subplots slipping off the screen. No mind-games now—here, on this terrace, penitents dance, and the syncopated double-backed beast is frolicking nightly in their shack (like Fred and Ginger in the park when music from nowhere catches them up and Ginger's reluctance melts away in a wisdom-of-the-body gavotte). "Like teacup to saucer," Danny would say, defining an ideal liaison as objects without needs or guile in passionate proximity. "Just think entelechy, Brother Mike." Not Stanislavsky, Meyerhold. Not Freud or Jung, but Wilhelm Reich. The hut's become an orgone box.

One day, returning from the store, he catches her reading an old *Observer*—the one with his letter about My Lai, which he'd left beneath a pile of books. She looks at him but doesn't speak, letting it drop back on the stack. He buries it wordlessly in some files he's stuffed into a cardboard box, and neither would bring it up again just as they never mention Joyce. She doesn't ask, "Why'd you do this?"

He buys a newspaper once a week, from Charlotte if he wants it thick or Raleigh to get some local news—either will serve to stoke the fire that sends their garbage up in smoke. With no TV the war gets lost along with bulletins from Fort Bragg concerning a brutal incident: a captain's wife and kids are killed and ACID IS GROOVY scrawled in blood or chanted by the perpetrators, the work it's thought of hippie thugs like those at a protest months before, the last to be permitted there at the military base. An all-out search is underway. Weeks pass, and one day driving home with laundry washed at Whiter Than Snow, he learns that the Fort Bragg murder case has taken an unexpected turn—the captain himself is under suspicion. The station fades on Trueblood's hill and Dugan's still fiddling with the knobs as, gearing back down to take the drive, he glances ahead and spots a car—it's Danny's Merc among the trees. A weird convergence is underway.

No sign of Credo as Dugan gets out and, rounding the corner of his hut, sees Danny poking a querulous toe at the ancient-Mayan-millstone dig. Danny looks up at Dugan's approach.

"How's it goin' there, Duke?" He hoists a beer, while Rose smiles wanly from the bench. She shades her eyes as Danny says, "Just lookit whut I got us, boy! Some real antiques—Atlantic Ale! 'It's *Schweitzerized*'—remember that? whutever the hell tha'ss s'posed t' mean. I found it at your crossroads store." Adopting a pseudo-Lugton brogue, he lifts the carton to reveal that five are left for them to share. "Couldn't get Rose to give it a try, which means, I guess, she's got good sense. But you're still apeshit, ain't you, Duke?"

"I'm mellowing." It's warm today. He frees a beer and twists its cap, then, seeing she's antsy, says to both, "So. . . Rose meets Rosen."

Neither smiles. "Head-on," is Danny's wry report. "I think we both surprised each other."

Dugan's arrived too late it seems. He takes a swig as he's sizing things up. "Wayne Poucher. . . Jeez!" he says to one. "On the radio," he adds to the other, including her in their memory trip. "He reported the local bush-league games. . ."

"Even when they were on the road and he was holed up in some studio readin' live from a tickertape while addin' a soundtrack of his own."

"Same noises and voices over and over. . . he might as well been makin' it up."

"'C'mon, Daley, get a hit!' every time he comes to the plate."

"But really hypnotic in a way. I'd be lyin' in bed and listenin' at night, waiting to see how things turned out and wake up to that sizzle of static with no idea who'd won the game. . ."

"Still, all you'd remember anyhow was what he'd tell you every half-inning, 'Atlantic Ale. . .'" and Dugan joins in, "it's *Schweitzerized*!"

They're laughing together.

"It's not so bad," Dugan concedes, not commenting on the marketing ploy of its Gone-with-the Wind plantation cans. "Must be about as old as the Merc."

"Nah, maybe fifteen no kiddin', though. You're in a real time-warp in these parts." Then Danny goes through the motions again, offering a can which Rose declines. "Well, suit yourself," he says with a grin, tipping his own up in a toast. "Good luck if you're waiting on Chardonnay. To war and peace! You know the rest."

"Aw, grow up, Dan."

"Too late for that. There's never been a good war, chum." He winks and chugs, wiping his mouth with the back of his hand and launching an obnoxious, "Ahhhh!"

Dugan attempts to break the spell. "Let's back up here, and start all over—and stay for supper," he says to Danny. "I want you two. . . to know each other."

But Danny insists he's gotta get back. He's only here to deliver some mail.

"Break bread with us, man. We're talkin' what—a couple of hours?"

Looking impatient, Rose gets up. "I'll have to run some errands den—you got duh keys?"

"They're by the door. Where's Credo gone?" He peers about.

"Shy came to call. Nice meeting you," she says with a nod.

He figures she's planning to drive around as long as it takes for Danny to leave. But hoping he still can make it work, he says to both, "Hey, mellow out, guys—let's drink to friendship and move on. One swallow," he appeals to Rose.

Shaking her head, she steps inside, looking around to find the keys.

Danny shrugs. "She's right, you know. It tastes like shit—they probably meant it's scheiserized."

"Stifle it, Dan! Stay with us, babe."

But Rose is clearly nobody's babe, flipping the finger as she goes.

"Hard!" nods Danny, waving his ale.

"You're making it harder," Dugan says. The cast has changed, but the play's the same—he's back to the thankless peacekeeping role he'd played at the Rosens' months ago. "What happened here?" he wants to know.

"What can I say? I fucked it up. I've got a gift for fucking things up."

"Well, now you've really got to stay—she's headed towards a grocery store that's more than a dozen miles away." He knows she's not but raises his voice to let her hear—she's just within earshot, starting the car. "He'll stay!" he shouts in the Pontiac's wake as it chugs and grumbles down the drive.

Danny agrees but only because, he says with a squint, the risk of lasagna here looks nil—the sort of semi-offensive crack that ends a bad B-movie scene. Then Danny gets down to why he's come, fetching a shoebox-full of mail, mostly junk with a couple of bills and four or five letters stacked on top he'd found in a CSU mail-room pile. "That first one's really what brought me here. From Oreen Suber—she's trackin' you down."

"Dear Reservist," the letter reads, "Your file has been referred to us." How's his recovery? Still employed? They'd like to have his claims confirmed. From Gordo too, there's a genial note. "Dear Colleague (stricken through in ink with Dugan's first name scribbled in), the status of your continued leave. . ." PENDING REVIEW is Gordo's phrase, with what's described as "complications." Two things are clear from what he's read: he's entering into no man's land without the encumbrance of a job.

"Refill?" asks Danny, back from his car with another six-pack of redneck brew, enough to last all afternoon.

"Don't mind if I do."

They guzzle and sigh, then Danny reports with a serious air, "Look, buddy, here's the thing, okay? That Dough boy's really kissin' ass. He's stakin' out claims all over the place."

"Yeah, well. . ." burps Dugan with a shrug. He puts his can down on the bench, scanning his comforting stockade of trees beyond which lurks a sinister world.

Danny appears exasperated. "So. . ." he says, and waits a beat. "You plannin' on headin' back our way?"

"Dunno. Depends." A hollow drumming sound erupts, then pauses before it starts again. "Woodpecker," says Dugan, burping again. It seems the woods are full of them.

Danny attempts to follow his gaze, sees nothing, and studies the hut instead. "This mondo bizarro—yours or Dough's?"

"Whatta you think?"

Danny affects a Groucho look, working his eyebrows up and down. "You're into some weird shit, kemosabbee. Maybe it's part of this kooky new you, this Sergeant-Pepper-lost-in-the-bush, or maybe you swiped the basic idea and are screwing around like that Tittlewhit creep—except, instead of the Sufi crap, you're into some half-ass Chinese cult. You've lost it, Duke! You've really freaked. I hardly know you anymore. And, say, remember 'Famous Dogs,' our patented fail-safe tenure tool? I happened across the liner notes to Dylan's 'Highway 61.'"

"'Revisited.'"

"Oh, yeah, and how! I can't believe you ripped him off."

"*Hommage.*"

"My ass. You plagiarized! And I used it, man, repeatedly. . . until Meg Boozer came up to me at one of Doggett's lame soirées. 'So you're a fan of Dylan's too!' Like whattaya mean, my buddy and I. . .?"

"Lighten up, Dan. It's no big deal."

"What's bigger?"

"C'mon. I'll show you around."

"Answer my question."

"Jesus, Dan! It's you who've changed."

"And you're business-as-usual with Anna May Wong, shacked up in this Yellow Submarine?"

Dugan considers Danny's dig—not the part about Rose, but at Dough's décor (drab on the outside, vivid within, like. . . uh, let's see, not the obvious thing. . . though, Danny's dyspeptic view aside, it's his and Rose's refuge now, so its meaning has changed to something else, something he knows he'll never convey. . . like the colors of Trueblood's granddaughters' dreams).

"Hey!" snaps Danny. "You trippin', man?"

"Hang on there, Dan," he tries to explain. "There's plenty to count, but not many plots. . ." (he's thinking of Joseph Campbell now) ". . . and no matter how freakin' inventive we get, we're always living out one of those—like dancing a tango by yourself, following those footprints on the floor." (That's pretty good, he tells himself—he hasn't completely lost his touch.) "Find it, fulfill it, whatever it is. . . For you it might be *Moby Dick*—get out your harpoon, chase the whale. For me, it's this whacked-out Joycean thing, living out 'Highway 61'. . ."

"*Re*-revisited?" Danny scoffs. "Gibberish, Duke. . . and Joyce, my ass! A Portrait of what? An ex-Rhodes Scholar down on his luck? You livin' out *L'Avventura* here or 'Debbie Does Dallas' Hong Kong style?"

But Dugan doesn't rise to the bait. He's on the verge of telling the truth—that he might have found the very thing he didn't know he was looking for, but it sounds so schmaltzy he says instead, "I'm grabbin' for all the gusto I can get." Then, pausing to reflect on how much they both hate Schlitz, he adds in a calmly pragmatic way, "She's worth it, Dan."

"Oh, sure. You hope. But pussy's never worth the price. Trust me, pal, I'm readin' your mind. You think it's like those liner notes—like, what's he call them. . . Savage Rose and doodly-squat who've shacked up somewhere in the woods? Oh, yeah, that's cool—you got the shack part down all right." He thumps the side of Dugan's hut. "A Chinatown whorehouse, you ask me! This dog of yours a figment too?"

"She must have gone to the store with Rose." He's surprised to discover how unruffled he feels in the face of Danny's wild assault.

"How long's she been here?" Danny demands. "How long you think she's gonna stay?"

It's Rose he means, but Dugan replies he'd bought her in Raleigh second hand, adding he knows how pissed she'll be to learn she's missed out on a walk. But why don't they mosey on down the bluff while there's still light enough to see? He's got a boat, they can row on the river.

"Who is she, Duke? Don't fuck around." An actress? Yeah, so's Lady Macbeth. So why's she here? She's on the run. From who? "The beer!" What? "Bring the beer!" They'll talk about it as they go.

"Ignoring shit won't flush it, you know! Speaking of which. . ." he points to the privy. Dugan nods. "That's what I thought." But he sets out with his slew-footed gait, following Dugan towards the bluff.

Halfway down, they lose a beer. It bounces once and disappears soundlessly into the trees until they hear it ricochet. They get in his boat and row upriver, exploring the farther shore on foot—across a meadow, through some trees, downing more beers and ambling back to find a crowd of sullen cows waiting as if they're planning to board. Danny's afraid they might attack. Stay calm, he urges, they smell fear. The dirt's been churned into a muck that sucks his penny loafer off. Leave it! he shouts but picks it up and backs aboard with snarls and barks. The cows recoil.

"Quick!" Danny insists. "Shove off before they see it's a trick!"

The cows look on attentively, watching the barking man recede as he's ferried across to the opposite bank. But mid-stream, Danny's alarmed to find the current flows over a cataract. *Way Down East!* He should have known. What happens if the boat stalls out? Taking a last despairing swig, he tosses his empty ale can in, watching it bob towards the lip of the dam and snag on the limb of a half-sunken tree. "That could be us, you know," he warns.

He tries to dislodge it with a stick retrieved from underneath his feet, but after nearly capsizing the boat, he settles morosely into a crouch as if they're headed across the Styx. The instant they're back, he leaps ashore, waving his arms and slapping his sides. "Jesus, I'm a nervous wreck! This Natty Bumppo shit wears thin."

They walk along the lower path, trying to find the old rapport.

"How's Caitlin doin'?" Dugan asks.

"Better. Though sometimes. . . it's been rough." Things rub her wrong. A couple of doozies, one with Dough—at that party of Doggett's he'd mentioned before, she and Dough got into a fight. Seeing the two were having it out, Doggett had stupidly butted in, and she'd called Dough a sock of shit. Silk sock, said Dough, let's quote it correctly. What matters, said Caitlin, is the shit.

They laugh and Dugan identifies what seems so different in Danny's looks—his teeth look unbelievably good. Danny intuits what's on his mind, baring his mouth in a bull-moose grimace. "I thought you'd never

279

notice," he says. The problem's basically periodontal. Say what? His gums.

"Damned dentist claimed there's no hope left. A thousand bucks! 'Or what?' I asked." He uses a finger to wiggle a tooth. "See that?" See what? That's what he means. "'Extract the choppers, then, McTeague'—I was callin' his bluff, this Blue-Cross schmuck." So which costs less? he'd asked the bum, keepin' 'em in or pulling 'em out? By far the latter is what he's told. "Oh, yeah? Okay, so pull 'em all out! Right now! Let's go! I'm sick of your candy-ass hectoring." And what'd he do? "Just what I said. The front ones are plastic—garish, huh? For the molars in back, I got a reprieve. I'm using this special little brush."

"You floss?"

"You bet."

"We're gettin' old."

They walk to where the path runs out, then back to just below the dam.

"You worried Oreen might screw you, Duke?"

Another shrug. "Who knows?" he says, but he thinks he'll probably be okay. He reckons his shoulder's like that brush, a stopgap that should get him through, though he's sick of her candy-ass bullying too. And, at bottom, you know, ole Ernie was right—he's stronger in the broken places. Plastic's a miracle, Danny says. *The Graduate*, Dugan says with a smile. "And push-ups, man, like you wouldn't believe! I'm gettin' it all together now." Sounds like a cult is Danny's reply. "Beats kissin' ass." He guesses it does. "It's all a matter of where you aim." They laugh together, and Dugan says, "But there's something I oughta tell you, Dan." Oh, yeah? What's that? "In a cook-off, Caitlin wins hands-down."

"No shit. Okay—no egg rolls, huh? Hey, look at my can there! Still hung up. I'm glad you leveled with me, Duke. You order for me when we get back. Well, I'll be damned, the fucker just sank! So much for being Schweitzerized. That barking I hear? Must be your dog."

"Yeah," Dugan nods. "They must be back."

"Your neighbors come bargin' in up there?"

"Not very often." Why'd he ask?

He'd stopped for directions at the Bobs' who didn't take to his pokin' around. "Besides," says Danny, shaking his head, displaying his Teddy Roosevelt teeth, "For a guy who's got it all worked out, you're lookin' snuck-up on, Hiawatha."

• • •

It's half-light when they get to the hut, and Danny and Rose both seem prepared to try a bit harder to get along. Danny collapses on the steps, recounting how he'd fought off the cows and the tragedy of his fucked-up knees—he could've made the NBA. "Tell her, Duke." Climbing that bluff had taken its toll.

"It's all a lie."

She wants to move the table out. The weather's so warm. She'll get the chairs. They turn the table on its side, scraping the wall with two of its legs and tearing a poster that falls to the floor. COMO EN VIETNAM scrolls up as the table is angled out through the door—following which, Last-Supper-wise, with Danny and Dugan at either end while Rose in the center serves them both, they all look out at the purplish woods. Most of the sky's the hue of her skin but bright as a furnace down below, while thousands of feet straight overhead, a jet stream moves out from the trees like a scalpel's incision bleeding light and leaving a keloid scar behind.

Dugan unscrews a Gallo jug to match the various gobbets and bits of stir-fried, spiced-up this and that. But Danny decides to pass on the wine. He'll have another beer instead from another six-pack retrieved from his car. "Good thing I came prepared," he says. He chugs and listens for a while as Dugan describes the Lugton scene.

Nobody's had more than a mouthful or two when Danny attempts to seize on a pause. "So where're you acting, Rose?" he growls.

"Same place I'm teaching," Dugan says.

"Hey, who asked you? But, since you mention it, let me point out regarding this many-splendored thing, your half-pay only runs through June. Then what, Pinocchio? Thought of that? You're fiddlin' while your tenure burns. . . that's meta-talk," he says to Rose, drawling his words and steeling his voice like a diplomat declaring war. "Okay," he adds, "the moment of truth. . . a term I picked up in Pamplona. I'm gonna tell Rose just what I think, and she can tell me to go to hell—so can you. . . but listen, Rose, my friend here more or less had it knocked until a couple of months ago when suddenly he lost his job. . . his shoulder, his bike, and now his mind. Maybe you're worth it—I wouldn't know—but, whatever you're up to, I really hope you're not just messing with his head. This guy is fucking up his life. . . So there, that's it. I gotta go."

"For chrissake, Dan! Rose, sit back down. You're treatin' me like a bartered bride."

But like any deft actor given the chance, Rose seizes on this overwrought cue as if Hector was taping them from the woods. She delivers a look of withering scorn, then says to Dugan ferociously, "Stay here and talk about Uncle Walt or whatever you call your White-man shit. You round-eyes make me wanna puke." Stacking her plate on top of his, she reaches for Danny's. He yanks it back.

"I'm not a round-eye. I'm a Jew." The stand-off lasts until he adds, "Okay, I'm sorry. I'm a jerk. Don't take my plate—c'mon, siddown. I'm harried, nothin's goin' right. . . for me, for Duke, the whole damned world. Tact's not my strong suit, as you can see, but, hey, if you think you know what you're doin'. . . ." He samples a bite of Rose's grub—then, sticking two fingers in his mouth, pulls out a microscopic dot. "Whattaya know? You wouldn't think this late in the year. . . poor bastard's dead." He lays it out. "Good protein, though. And tasty too." Rose hasn't yet moved from where she was. Standing with two plates in her hand, she reaches out once more for the third and this time Danny lets it go. She takes the stack inside the hut, exiting left. The scene goes on.

After a long pause, Danny says, "Well. . . looks like I've been here long enough." Nodding to Dugan, he gets to his feet, sways a bit, and points to the sky. "You know. . . we don't know, that's the truth. It might rain popcorn. Keep the faith."

The table between them, Dugan stands. "You gonna be okay?" he asks.

"For what?"

"For driving."

"Tha'ss a laugh! It's not my ass that's in a sling. Z'okay I ask a question, though? I gotta ask. You do it. . . ?"

"What"

"You know, like this." A sideways gesture with his hand.

"Go fuck yourself."

"I do that every day, ole chum." He slouches around the side of the hut, stops, and says with a baleful stare, "You wanna keep playin' Dimitri, Duke, you better read that book again." After a pause, he turns to say as if it's just an afterthought, "Remember that time we had that fight?"

"No," Dugan lies. "That wudn't a fight."

"What was it, then?"

"A wrestlin' match."

"Sure," Danny says. He waves and stumbles as he leaves, much drunker than he'd seemed before.

"Be careful, dumb-ass!" Dugan yells.

Rose reappears as the Merc backs up, its headlights raking the tops of the trees.

"I don't know what he meant," she says.

"You don't?" he asks incredulously.

"What's meta-talk?"

"Elaborate circumlocution," he says.

"A lie?"

"Yeah, sorta. He meant we always lie to ourselves whenever we try to tell the truth."

She thinks about that, then she says, "Was he expecting someting else?"

"We all do, don't we?" he replies, putting his arm around her waist and noting again how slim it is.

• • •

He wakes up in an oddly shadowless world reminiscent of paintings that Caitlin loves—by Piero della Francesca, say, whose stately paper dolls pose and preen, too evenly lit for any real depth, or Simone Martini's gilded realm, his circumspect Virgin so Chinese despite pink cheeks and flaxen hair, the angel's tidings frozen in air, his mantel coiled like hammered bronze. . . "subtraction and replenishment," the sort of jargon art teachers use, though that's what's running through Dugan's mind as he reaches out in bed for Rose and sees (as Martini might have seen) his languid model, nonchalant, as focused on nothing as a cat but seeing it all, bare-legged in socks (with one sagging down) and leaning both elbows on the sill, his sweatshirt's sleeves pushed up her arms as, shoulders hunched, she looks around.

"Snowing," she says, voice matter of fact.

"How deep?"

"Don't know."

She answers in a monotone. The heater emits a fluttering sound. *Verweile doch!* he tells himself, unable to hold his pedantry back and moved enough to hesitate before he breaks the spell again.

"Where's Credo?"

"Out."

He shuts his eyes so he can drift in the luminous silence swaddling him, "Come on! Get up!"

"What for?" he groans.

"Auspicious day!" as if she's excited by the snow.

She shakes his shoulder, and he responds by sweeping his arm behind her knees, catching the smooth cool backs of her thighs, then pulling her towards him. She grabs back. They grapple, part, and, jujitsu-like, he's out of bed and onto his feet, stepping into his trouser legs and finding their chilliness gratifying as if, in connecting cool to cold, he's able to build a sort of rhyme, discover a structure, ferret out links. . . a notion he's vaguely pursuing still when, quickly dressed and out the door, he stabs his boots into the snow—a fresh soufflé without a dent, so pristine that he feels a pang making new tracks behind the hut. But then he crunches past his car and starts to piss into a drift (not Proust, he grins, but Hemingway, like butter in a mashed potato). A soft thud makes him look around.

His shovel still juts atop a mound beside his postponed millstone dig. Beyond it is a swatch of tan that shakes and, bursting from the woods, comes kangarooing towards the hut. Credo's buoyant. Understood. He follows and they clamber inside.

"Sky's dark," Rose says, again at the window gazing out. "A lot more snow."

"You still not dressed?" He stamps his feet. "What happened to your auspicious day?"

"Duh way to do, round-eye, is be."

He stamps again, knocking the loose snow from his boots and making the jelly glasses clink. He'd quoted that line to her, of course. "It's just as true in reverse, you know. Now that I'm up, I'm ready to go!"

"After some coffee," she declares, "it's possible that I might agree." Her voice is grave, but with a lilt he's heard on several occasions before— when they both got stoned on New Year's Eve and once or twice while playing gin. Her knees look chubby from behind. "What're you doing?" she demands.

"Getting my yin and yang aligned."

"Well, stop, and put duh pot on, please."

She makes some toast and, wordlessly, they breakfast together looking out and watching the snow wafting erratically fast and slow. Bored with inaction, Credo yawns, gets up, and scratches on the door. "Make up your mind!" is Dugan's reproach as she looks around and minces out. He shuts the door and sits with Rose, beside her on the Naugahyde.

"Like drifting in a houseboat, huh?" He bumps her shoulder with his own and, after getting no response, launches another banality. "You know what I can't get out of my head? That old radio ad for Ivory Snow—"ninety-nine and forty-four one-hundredths per cent pure!'" She shakes her head impatiently, preferring the silence. So does he—but sometimes he can't help himself. "Remember that?"

"Pure what?" she asks reluctantly, squinting at him and looking away as if she's thinking only snow—which is swirling about in gusts outside like specks inside a paperweight. He says as much, and, with a sigh, she turns back towards him to reply. "As if it's mufflered," she agrees, her voice so mild he's caught off guard.

"A muffler's a tailpipe," he objects, draining his cup while squeezing her knee. "You meant. . ."

"It's mufflered," she affirms. "What do you wear around your neck. . . when it's cold outside and snowing too?"

He thinks they're back in game-playing mode. "You wear a muffler, am I right?"

Her smirk invites what follows next. "Sure. You're right."

"Of course, I am!"

He slides his hand into her lap, but only to have her grab it and say while lacing her fingers into his, "No, way too cold—juss look at dat!" as gusts of snow are swirling about so densely the phone booth can't be seen. He manages to kiss her neck, her nose, the corner of her mouth.

"You ever see snow like this as a kid?" he huskily murmurs in her ear.

"Not ever," she answers distantly but nestling closer, clutching his arm.

Obligingly, he stumbles on. "Me either, really," he confides, inhaling the scent of her new shampoo (she's fussy about her pheromones now) and is instantly back in his grandfather's house with its butler's pantry's musky smell of peaches, cantaloupe's, ripening pears lined up along the window sills, the light diffused in a similar way within that calm and orderly nook where everything had its proper place like well-tied flies in a tackle box (the old man had been a punctilious angler, and yet he'd been a dreamer too as evidenced by the stories he'd told which Dugan remembers even now). He'd like to share those memories with Rose but finds they're hard to put into words, so he settles on a non-sequitur, "I'm Gaelic, you know, I'm not Teutonic."

"Uh-huh," she says as if his remark had made good sense, "but you've somewhere surely lived a life of joy wid me. . ." almost getting the consonants right.

"You've been reading my books!"

Laying her head on his shoulder, she adds, ". . . all is recawed as we frit by each udder. . ."

He knows she's letting it come and go, but how long had it taken to dig that up? and why'd she bothered? he asks himself. The fritting's over, he concludes as they gaze together as if entranced, watching the wavering curtains of snow. Then Dugan resumes his amorous patter—the treble to his hand's low bass, inquiring and insinuating. "My grandpa was a story-teller."

"Ah-aw," she yawns.

She's bored already? "Not yet," she says while closing her eyes. She's never heard of Cormac, right? "No," she purrs, she doesn't know that. Know what? he asks. Whatever he'd said, "The car-mat thing."

"Cor-*mack*! He's Irish. That's his name." His grandpa's? "No, it belonged to a guy there long ago." Like Hamret? "Except in Ireland." So it's a play? "It's a story, okay? But this one's true, the way some made-up things are true. You wanna hear it, yes or no?" He gestures with both hands in the air. Sure, sure, she nods and opens her eyes—what's it about? she wants to know. "A prince." Of course, it always is. "A princess too—that's better, right?—and an evil magician."

"Nope, nope," she scowls, "too many uh dose."

Yeah, well, that's how this story goes—the magician's just abducted her. "Is she uh virgin?" Probably. . . why? "Just making sure she's pure as soap." So far, he says, but not for long if the evil magician gets his way, and he's carried her to his castle, okay? It's perched on a cliff high over a beach so, if Cormac tries to rescue her, the magician can spot him a long way off. "What's his name?" The magician? he asks. Nobody's ever said his name—which is totally sinister, I agree, but this is crucial, so listen up. Cormac has got some mojo too, some magic jewels in a pouch. "How many?" Good question, he's got three—an emerald, a ruby, and a pearl. "Where from?" Where from? "Sure, where're dey from?" She sits, palms flat along her thighs like the effigy of Queen Hatshepsut. That thought distracts him. Hatshepsut, the one in the Met (where'd *that* come from? he's asking himself). "Duh jewels?" she says, reminding him.

"Nobody knows. From far away. His father left them in his will. What's funny?"

She shrugs. "Duh usual number, I think, is two." Her fricative's on the money again.

"Well, look," he says, exasperated. "These interruptions. . ."

"Sorry," she says with a grimace, her head lolled back, her fingers tugging her T-shirt's hem. "It's like duh story of my life."

"More than you know, but different too." No Hector Protector—just a prince. "You ready to listen?"

"Sure," she says for the third or fourth time.

"So, then, okay." Her eyes are closed, her fingers dancing under her hem as if she's playing an andante. He concentrates and then resumes. "Prince Cormac to the rescue, right? as, just in time and out of the blue, he shows up on his faithful horse. The color of the horse is white—I know that's what you're gonna ask—the horse, the prince, and the castle are white."

"But duh princess?"

". . . is like a golden pear." He tries again to nuzzle her ear, but she squirms again just out of reach. "Or maybe a bar of Octagon soap."

"Like he's the coror of Ivory Snow? I guess duh magician must be brack."

"Dunno," he says. He's taken aback. "They come in all colors I suppose." He pauses a moment before he adds, "That's what I think a prince would say. . . which maybe makes it harder for him than trying to act like a magician." He thinks that's true. He hopes it is. He's not sure about being a princess though, which was probably part of what she meant. "Where was I?" he asks.

"Duh prince's jewels," she replies.

"Oh, yeah, okay. So, this mojo of Cormac's comes with a catch—he's got to shout some special words whenever he uses one of those jewels, tossing it towards what he's fighting against with a '*Rippla-rippla-rippla-ree!*'" (He hears his grandfather's baritone.) "You got that down?" he's asking her. "Three ripplas followed by a ree."

She's hitching the sweatshirt up her thigh. "So where's dis princess when he shows up?"

"Where do you think? On a balcony at the top of some stairs in a tower that's up above everything else. . . from which she can spy a princely speck that growin' bigger while she looks. Mum's the word since the evil magician's standin' there too, but she can't help smiling to herself. 'So wot's th' dale 'ere?' asks the magician who'd left his glasses down below but can see the expression on her face. 'Oh, nothing special,' she insists—

she's just enjoying all his stuff, expensive gadgets, silks and furs. She looks so innocent. . . yeah, but wait! There's somebody down there on the beach! 'Yuh little bitch. . .'"

"Dis guy is *bad*!"

"Just gettin' started—even worse." He glances at her ochre thighs. "He whippin' up this super-dark spell and clouds of angry bees appear. They swarm towards Cormac, stinging his horse, making the princess whimper with fear—which really chafes the bad guy's ass. 'Shut up, you. . .'"

"'. . . rittle bar of soap!'"

A double take. She nods her head.

"So Cormac tosses out the pearl. . ."

"'Rippla-rippla-rippla-lee!'" She gets everything right but the last r.

"That seems to work. And in a flash, the bees are gone! So Cormac spurs his white horse on, and, looking up from way below, he can see the princess gazing down. . . and whattaya know? She looks *Chinese*."

"Told you!"

"Right. But now the magician's really pissed. He mutters and makes the sky grow dark. A thousand monkeys crowd onto the stairs, rush over the drawbridge, down to the beach, jabbering as they scratch and pinch. But Cormac gets the ruby out, and. . ."

"'Rippla-rippla-rippla-lee!'"

"They're gone like that—in a puff of smoke! Now Cormac's close enough to wave. She tries to smile, but. . ." Rose smiles too. She's fiddled with the hem enough to let him see what he's left out—the princess wears no underpants. He moves his hand. She drops the hem. "The bad guy weaves his scariest spell. . . mobs of drunk Irishmen waving clubs, howling like banshees, grabbing the horse."

He snatches, but she twists away, sliding across the Naugahyde. He grabs, she yanks the sweatshirt down with both hands squeezed between her legs. "No! No!" She tries to slide away.

"Don't be an ingrate! Cormac's here!" He clasps her waist while yanking his fly.

"Hold on!" she pants. "What happens next?" She twists enough to spoil his aim. "Duh story."

"What?" His head's on her shoulder from behind.

"What happens next?"

"He rides his horse right over the bridge, and. . ." pausing behind her, dipping his knees, "enters into the castle hall."

He demonstrates. She helps him out.

"He didn't. . ." she gasps.

"He didn't. . . what?"

"The emmera. . ."

"Right. . ." He slips one hand beneath her shirt, the other in between her legs. "He's savin' it. You never know." She covers both his hands with hers.

"And. . . duh. . . *magician?*"

"Jumped," he groans, "from that topmost turret. . . headfirst," he adds. For a moment the snow seems floating up, then settles and sifts back towards the ground. "But there was still magic. . . in the air. As soon as the prince was safely inside. . . snow. . . started to fall all over the place, like Ivory flakes—or heavenly dandruff. . . hominy grits. . . the first snow that she'd ever seen, and it got very. . . very cold. . ."

She makes a noise, but neither moves. Her head sinks back against his neck.

"And they. . . both froze."

She murmurs a protest into his ear. "I taught you said dis story was true."

"It's true, all right."

"How. . . long?" she whispers, "were dey like dat?"

"Well. . ." he blabs, ". . . until they came."

There's a pulsing he's sure they both can feel though nothing's in motion but the snow—and, after a while, it seems to him he's entered inside her mind as well. He feels her thaw. Her breathing slows. He's followed her to the utmost verge when a shadow emerges, then a shape, just past the tree line watching them, a spectral ice-encrusted form—of Sergeant Bob with his sled dog Shy—surveilling them from the netherworld. He doesn't suppose she's noticed Bob who tips his hat brim with his gun and disappears into the woods.

"Did you. . .?" she asks.

He hadn't, of course. The evil guy had reappeared.

"Car-mat fell off his horse," she sighs.

Winter was still icummen in.

· · ·

The bluff looms over their slow-moving skiff. The snowfall's stopped, but the cold persists with the midmorning sun a sallow smear and the river resembling scuffed-up slate. They're facing each other in the boat with Dugan rowing in the stern.

"Fweezunggg!" she attempts to say.

Watching the puffs float up as she speaks, he tries to tell her never mind, his own lips mismatched blocks of wood.

"Say whaaat?" she shivers as she asks somewhat more successfully.

"Just thinking about. . . a book," he says, working his lips to warm them up as he misses his stroke and slaps some spray.

"Yow!" she yelps, sounding like him.

"Sorry," he croaks. "That's not in the book."

The oars rise up like heavy wings, bright dribbles sliding off the blades.

"Which book?" she asks, not interested.

"By Hemingway," he answers her, dipping the oars back down again, "escaping together in a boat."

"Nope, nope, nope. . . too cold for dat." Then, beating both fists against her knees, "Dis wasn't a good idea," she adds.

He pulls again, the oar-locks squeak. "The world is fucking crazy," he says.

"So?"

"So we need some sort of plan."

"What's that?" she asks, peering upriver behind his back.

He turns to see another boat with men in yellow anoraks about to glide behind some trees, too far away to hear their motor. The one in the stern throws out his arm, seeming to point in their direction. Were they signaling? she wants to know. "To us? Guess not," is all he says, returning to where his thoughts broke off. But how can he know that? she persists. She's agitated. He understands. Has he seen any boats down here before? He hasn't, no, but it's no big deal. "Relax," he urges, prompting a scowl. And then, intending to put things right, he launches into some anodyne patter about the things that get us upset—"must go back eons," he observes, "spotting a predator in the grass, seeing some tracks that don't bode well. . ." What scared her most when she was a kid?

"What's scaring me now—don't patronize."

He tugs one oar and feathers the other, letting them swing into a turn. He's heard some kids get petrified that pulling the plug when they're in the tub will send them spinning down the drain. Fred Rogers says that, he's been told. "But really it never crossed my mind. . ." What? He sees that something's wrong.

"I'm like an ice-cube," she complains.

He assures her that they're heading in. "What haunted me when I was a kid. . ." He pauses until their eyes lock up. "We still in conversation here?"

"And what if we're not?" she glowers back. It's like a switchblade— just that quick. One flash before she folds it up. She gives him an ironic smile.

"I might get professorial."

"What else is new?" Then she relents. "Keep rowing while you talk, okay? Let's hear what used to frighten you?"

"It's no big deal," he says again.

"Come onnnn!"

He shrugs.

She leans her elbows on her knees. "You're actin' like an asshole, Mike."

"I am?"

"You are. I've gotta be carefuh, you know that. What haunted you? I wanna know."

He starts to alternate the oars. Some fancy rowing. Lah-di-dah. "Three things," he says, "when I was a kid, scared the be-Jesus outta me. . ."

Barking erupts from the top of the slope. It's Credo demanding where they've been—she'd been off in the woods when they set out. He pulls on both oars once again, yanking so hard the bow leaps up. Thirty or forty yards from land, he matches his phrases with his strokes.

"To be tortured by Nazis was the first. Second was the electric chair, and third," he says, "was the loony bin. . . lobotomized by some arrogant shrink." He rests on his oars as they coast to the bank. "They're all the same—you get my point? Authority gone loco, see?"

He hears the spillway to his left and, yanking an oar, corrects their drift. When he looks back, she's shaking her head, both elbows cradled in her hands.

"What?" he asks her.

"Nuttin."

"What?"

Expressionless, she hugs herself. "It's aw-ways uh mistake, Mike. . . not to come."

"Uh-huh," he grunts. "Confucius say." (Joy Bang too, but what of that?)

She pounds her knees. "My buns are freezing off, okay?"

"'bout time!" barks Credo, dead ahead, a burst of russet on the shore—looking overweight, he notes, hoping it's just her winter coat.

• • •

As soon as they get to the top of the bluff, he says he'd better go back down—he'd meant to tie up extra well but can't remember if he did. He sends Rose on while he descends, not sharing what's really troubling him but seeing at once the coast is clear. The boat's okay. Nobody's there. Only a rapidly darkening sky, looking as if more snow's to come. He fumbles with the stiffened rope, then takes it easy as he climbs to keep from gulping frigid air. Up top, he notes this extra trip has taken nearly half an hour.

Blanketed in the snowy woods, his hut looks made of gingerbread with icing on the roof and sills. The windows, though, have turned opaque as if the place is full of smoke. Alarmed, he hurries up the steps and enters to find she's in the tub, head back and arms along the rim. She waves for him to shut the door.

"All clear?" she asks offhandedly, more serious than she's letting on.

"Of course," he says. He stands on one foot, balancing, while tugging his boot off from the other. "Like frozen cod! Just look at that!" He peels a sock off one white foot.

She's not impressed. Her hair is up—she reaches to adjust a pin as he removes his other boot.

"Hard-hearted woman, what's it take?" Doffing his jacket and trousers too, he tugs his manhood into view. "Oh, no! This too?"

"*Tant pis*," she says dismissively.

"*Miséricorde!*" he answers in kind, displaying *le pauvre petit soldat*. It's shriveled and dark, a blunt blue bolt.

"*Assez*," she says. "I got here first." She plays it like Claudette Colbert bobbing about in asses' milk. "*Un peu plus d'eau, s'il vous plait, mon chéri*—and do make sure it's *très très chaud*."

"What if I say 'my hut, my tub'?"

"*Ma chatte*, okay? And put dat broken toy away. Duh way for me to do. . ." she says.

"You're getting repetitive," he objects.

". . . is to float like a bar of Octagon soap."

He fetches the pots she's pointed to.

"It doesn't," he says as he starts to pour. "Octagon soap is like a brick."

"More. . . more," she croons, her shoulder dipping to the side, hands floating up across her chest. "Stop staring."

"At what? Don't flatter yourself." Staring, he empties two full pots and goes to the sink to fill them again. The washrag spread beneath her chin, she slides her rump against her heels, then shuts her eyes and pats the rag while he, deciding to mull some wine, starts rummaging through their storage shelf. "You seen the cloves?"

Tuning him out, she lifts the rag, glancing at her dark-knobbed breasts, then drops it and adjusts a pin. "Maybe I ought to wash my hair."

"I know we had some, where'd they go?"

"But maybe not. Dis feels so good."

"And lemons too—what happened to them?"

Credo lifts her head to yawn, lazily watching what they do.

"Lemons and cloves, they've disappeared."

"In dere," she points.

The bureau drawer. "You're stashing them with your *underwear*?"

"I got a great fondness. . ."

"No, you don't."

Credo settles back down again.

"Dey're like sachet."

He studies the spices with a shrug. "I'd planned to mull us up some wine. . . but now it's gonna taste like socks."

It doesn't, though. It tastes much worse, which somehow makes it drinkable. She soaks and sips for half an hour, spitting out cloves and rising at last, apparently now half-mulled herself—enticingly so, it seems to him. She dons his ratty terry-cloth robe and plops down on the Naugahyde, clipping her toenails while he stands in water the color of vichyssoise, the soapy remnants of her bath. He calls for her to get the pots. She's busy lining slivers up.

"You better!"

"Nope."

But then she sighs and says okay, dumping more water in the tub. It sloshes over as he squats, prompting her tipsy "Never mind." The heat spreads towards him. "Yessss," he groans, relaxing in the sudsy soup. He's got an idea for a film. He tells her so.

"Don't bodder me." She gets more wine.

"Move Credo's rug," he interrupts. "The hero's gonna be a frog—you listening to this?"

Sure she is. She listens to him all the time. He gulps a mug of what he calls a beaker of the frozen north while she's examining her toes.

"This idea's yours for free," he says. He might talk drivel now and then, but the *tao* of a ping-pong ball, you know, is not confined to a single bounce.

That garners another ironic look. "Depends how many times it's hit."

He lifts his mug, which she ignores. "The hero meets a dragonfly." Meets it where? "That's not the point. It's sort of tragic in a way. He feels this stirring deep inside, this pang he's never felt before." She gathers her bits and slivers up. "The problem for the frog, you see. . ." She lifts the latch. "Whoa! Jeezaree! Hey, close it quick!" She dusts her hands unsteadily, then leans until the latch clicks shut. "The problem's that she's much too big." Too big for what? "To swallow." Oh. "So all that crazy wild desire, if it's not hunger. . . must be love." She looks at him and starts to titter (just make 'em laugh, it never fails!) So, then, what happens in the end? "Not sure," he says. "Really," he adds, "I need more wine." There's not much left. "Maybe it's time for White-man, huh?. . . unless of course. . ."

She rolls her eyes. He thinks it works like Spanish fly? "So read it," she says craftily.

He's in the tub, her turn to read. She'll mispronounce it, she objects. "Who cares?" he replies as, reaching up and plucking it down, he tosses it to her on the bed to which she's moved and is sitting with her chin on a knee. "Come onnnnn!" he coaxes, echoing her. "Assume you're talking to a frog. Pick any page, an' let 'er rip!" She bends it double, clears her throat, unbends it, scowls, flips back and forth. "Just read it."

"But it doesn't make sense—'Come nigg. . .'"

"Come what?"

"Enn-Eye-Gee-Ahch."

"That's 'nigh'—like 'high.' It means up close."

"'Come nigh. . .'" she reads.

"Come nigh to who?"

"Stop interrupting! '. . . nigh to *me*.'" Propping her back against the wall, she holds the book up to the light. "'Come nigh to me. . . you rumber-hipped man.'"

"*Lumber*-hipped? That can't be right."

She looks more closely, getting it right. "*Lim-ber*-hipped man." She knows that word? She runs her left hand down her flank. Oh, that! he says. "Pipe down, you Phirristine!" she replies. "'Stand at my side until I lean. . . as high as I can. Fill me wid. . .'" What's wrong? he asks. She studies the book. "'Fill me wid all-bee. . . aw-bess. . .'" So spell it. No, she's read enough.

"Just spell it, Rose!"

She flashes a mock glare, then resumes. "Ah-Ell-Bay-Aa-Ess. . ." There's no such word he sternly says. "You wanna bet?" She bends to show him, leaning down, disclosing what's under her sagging robe.

"*Albescent*!" What? "A word for white."

"Not again! Duh man's obsessed!" Her robe's unbelted, open now, her body like a new-peeled stick.

Fill me with albescent honey

She makes a face, but he's got news of an urgently rampant ascent—GODZILLA LIVES! Up from the deep, the monstrous *soldat* has revived.

"Stop! I mean it! Put dat up."

Too late for expostulation now. White-man's taken a sudsy dive, but naked and slippery though he is, Dugan takes two steps from the tub, hooking one arm around her waist as Credo scoots out from the fray. Rose slips a foot behind his leg and then they tussle, chest to chest, like dancers in a voodoo cult. She's got more leverage than he'd thought and uses it. They hit the bed. The mattress creaks as she squirms free but, vaulting up to grab a sleeve, he flattens her with a flying burrito, a move he'd once seen Oona use or close enough to call it that, slamming them both onto the bed. Houdini-like, she's out of the robe and wrenches him into a hammerlock.

"Kung fu!" he snorts. "I should have known."

She answers with a triumphant squeal as he's wedging a knee between her thighs. She tries to twist in a quick reverse, but he counters her move by holding her tight while she thrashes and wriggles, ducking her head. She barks a phrase—it's in Chinese—and tries to brush away her hair. "*Gwailo!*" she cries. They're eye to eye and side by side, laughing, panting, gasping for air. She pulls him towards her, lying back, tilting her hips to meet his thrust, and he's riding up the steps again into the warm wet castle hall, hell for leather, galloping home. He hears her groan—she's urging him on—and answers with an urgent sound that rises to a rhythmic howl as, both arms planted and head thrown back, he irretrievably detonates, unleashing what, as *soldats* know, nobody's likely to survive. He topples slowly on her chest, his elbows on the terrycloth.

"*Ngo.* . ." she moans into his ear, digging her fingers into his skin.

Sex is sex, he tells himself, and nothing's untranslatable.

". . . *ngo ngoi lei.*"

In English, he figures, it's the same.

● ● ●

Another shift in how they relate—they're intimate now in little ways, habits and crotchets that they share, though subject to cabin fever at times. An ice storm hits in February, then snow again, and still more ice. Some trees go down, the power's out and, depending on how much traffic they get, back roads stay blocked until whenever. Trueblood and Bob do what they can, but checking for tire tracks every day, Dugan surmises after a week that something's awry at the end of the road other than what he's long since known. Despite his personal loathing of Bob, he goes to check, evading a string of booby-traps to wind up standing on their porch while Shy lurks mutely in the woods—to waylay Credo, Dugan assumes, though Credo, who's clearly pregnant now, has chosen to stay at home with Rose. Whatever'd occurred with Trueblood that day, Bob's kept his distance ever since. Still, Marianne's surely almost due, and who else is there who might care?

He knocks and waits. Then, hearing a thump, he thinks he sees a shadow flit and hears, from a pocket radio that seems to be somewhere off to the side, reports of a calamity. "In outer space. . ." a calm voice says, but no matter what's up with Houston Control, he knows it's one of Bob's maneuvers. In two or three seconds, that's confirmed.

"Y' blink an oilash 'n' y'er dead!"

"A what?"

"An oilash. Rise y'er 'ands." Bob prods his shoulder from behind.

"Just cool it, Bob. You both okay? I came to see if Marianne. . ."

"Y' with yer niggers ur yer chinks?" Bob swings his shotgun towards the floor. "GALLIPOLI," he barks at the door. The radio adds it's looking bad, then Marianne peeps out through a crack.

"NO SURRENDER," she replies in her typically flat affectless tone. "They've got a problem," she confides.

Dugan waits as latches are flipped. He hears a deadbolt sliding back, then Marianne herself appears.

"The countdown's stopped."

"Go back inside."

She's walking like an astronaut, wearing a knit maternity smock with saggy long-johns, day-glo socks, and a look that says she's had enough. She nods to Dugan. She's okay.

"Guess it won't be long," he says, meaning before the baby comes, but Bob, adjusting a bowie knife tucked handily in a shoulder sheath, supposes he's talking helter-skelter.

"Got that roight. Th' power goes out, yer Hottentots grab their bleedin' spears, an' it's Rorke's Drift all over agin." His head darts forward like a snake's. "But they're pushin' their luck round 'ere, ol' chum. Goes double f' you and yer concubine."

"Oh, yeah?" snorts Dugan under his breath, surprised at how his kidneys ache. Bob's lunatic bigotry drives him nuts. "You know where you can shove it. . . mate."

Bob squints but hears him well enough. "Come prancin' down this why agin, y' get a log behind yer ear. Same for y' soddin' Mau Mau friends." Clint Eastwood-like, he sets his jaw, leans in and bites off a "G'dye."

"Fuck you," says Dugan pleasantly.

Bob lets him get ten steps away. "Y' truss a dink, y'er crazy, mite. Worse than th' niggers, come t' that."

Yeah, maybe so, you son of a bitch—but I'm through abetting a psychopath. Rorke's Drift was Zulus anyhow. He looks for presumptive stud-dog Shy, who's lying low but watching no doubt as Dugan slogs back to an empty hut. It seems to happen every day—he turns his back, they disappear, both Rose and Credo, down to the dam or up the road to visit with Trueblood and his grands.

He tries the dam first and they're there, perched watching beside it. . . looking at what? A flat and shimmering scroll of silk? A cauldron of unending change? It's both and neither he decides. Time's ever-rolling stream runs smooth but has its grim hydraulics too—they're in one now, he tells himself, though neither's panicking just yet. Suppressing that amorphous dread, he sits beside them on a rock. They gaze awhile and go back up.

In a couple of days, the sun comes out. He cuts out letters for a note, using some headlines from the *Times*. "Dear Doctor Gordon," it begins. "One John M. Dough in your employ, formerly of Chatham County,

is **SUSPECTED**
OF
unnatural **ACTS**
with
TEENAGED GIRLS
and
LIVESTOCK

He signs it with a felt-tipped pen—"A Friend of Higher Education"—and mails it from the Feed & Seed.

In March, when Credo's litter arrives—accepted with a rueful shrug as what dogs do without TV—she drops them underneath the hut and then, when he can coax her out, watches him move them to a box decked out with blankets in the yard. Nine pups, he counts, but looks again and finds there're ten, including of pair of newt-like Shys. He wants to move the box inside, but Rose says no, and, while they talk, the brood's returned to where it was, beneath the floorboards which, for weeks, are seething with plaintive squeaks and mews until, while chopping some celery up as he recounts the latest news—more action in the Parrot's Beak is threatening to widen the fighting again—Rose snarls, "Dat's it! It's dem or me!" She points her knife. "It's just too much. Dey're making me sick!"

Code-Name Medea's his response, a plan to distribute Credo's pups among black neighbors up the road, upgrading their curly-tailed mini-mutts with hounds that might give Bob a pause. It takes a while to dole them out, but once it's done, he feels relieved—and so does Credo, he concludes, though her *mater dolorosa* air requires some therapeutic walks and a couple of deep-massage shampoos.

On one of those walks down by the dam he discovers his boat's no longer there. Not swept away—he checks that out—but probably towed upriver, he thinks, by one of the men in anoraks who'd spotted it on the river that day. . . the original owner, like as not, though it's news he doesn't share with Rose for fear she'll think her getaway's gone and her pursuers closing in.

He's ticked off, though, when he happens to find she's used his Short & Sassy up. "So get some more," is her retort. That's not the point, he says in a huff as they're getting undressed that night for bed—she should let him know when things run out and she knew it was there for Credo's coat who. . .

"Get off it, Mike! We've been trew dis. Could I. . . *please* get a litter sleep?"

Oh, sure. He marvels that she can. All the same, they're still at odds in that trivial way when she shakes him awake at four a.m. because, she says, she's heard a gun somewhere nearby in the woods. He mutters that it's just Bob's patrol. She'd wanted sleep, now so does he. "Trust me," he tells her.

But she won't, and five minutes later it erupts. Two shots. A third. A burst of four, then somebody yelling not far off, maybe a quarter mile away. (Uhuru! Christ! Fort Bragg again—except somebody's firing back. He trusts it wasn't Marianne letting Bob have what he deserves. . . or Helter-Skelter from Fort Bragg.) "Nobody's coming here," he shrugs.

Nobody does. The shooting stops, but, lying awake in the panic-scorched dark without much chance of dozing off, he gets hung up on that matter of trust, brooding on things she's never divulged that might be keys to her gonzo world of crazed subscribers and murderous gangs, even such piddling personal things as whether she's got a Chinese name. . . he's asked repeatedly, knowing she must, but on every occasion, she's blown him off. Now all he wants is a token of trust as, quietly, he asks again, but she pretends she doesn't hear.

The heater's off and a window's cracked through which he smells the seasonal change, a nighttime whiff of things unsheathed.

• • •

Next morning a battered truck drives up. Credo alerts them with a bark, then, having advised that it's a friend as Dugan arrives to check things out, she follows him like an aide-de-camp while switching her haunches from side to side.

"Trueblood!" Dugan calls out to Rose.

She greets him with their protocol, glasses of water on a plate. Trueblood nods and takes a sip, noting the weather's doin' fine, he plans to get to plantin' soon. "Sho' do," he smiles. "This weather's good." He sweeps the bushes with his eyes. "You mighty lucky wit 'at dog."

"We offered you pick of her litter, you know. . ."

"Now, tha'ss a fack." He wipes his mouth and drinks the rest, the glass a thimble in his mitt. "Jus' can't commence no pup," he says. "Too bad about them astronauts."

"What happened?"

"Well. . . they turned around."

"They did?"

"Sho' did." The crickets drone, or something does. "That shootin' you musta heard last night. . ."

They pause to check an alien sound, a helicopter in the sky. The DEA out looking for pot?

"Was anybody. . .?" Rose breaks off.

"Hurt?" asks Trueblood. "Reckon so. But Mistah Ian, he okay. His wife is too—they jus' druve by. Lease-ways," he adds, "she *looked* okay. Those other men got messed up, though."

"What men?"

"See here, now, tha'ss th' thing." He hesitates. "Two cars uh white men, not from heah. They ast for you. F' both uh you."

Dugan thinks quickly. Hector? No. Her film buffs? No. Not even Dough, resenting his note, would want to start a shooting war. Who then? And why? "Were they foreigners?"

"Well, yes 'n no. They talk like yankees at th' start, but affer they ast, some cracker say that I ain't gone tell 'em what I know. So I tell 'em th' folks they lookin' fuh was in the lass house down th' road." He gestures past them towards the Bobs'. "I know they ain't goan see yo' light, and Mistah Ian. . . he's a-quipped." With a knowing look, he nods his head, placing his glass back on the plate. "Juss thought you two would want to know. . . they been discouraged, tha'ss a fack."

"Thanks," Dugan says as Trueblood declares it's time for him to be getting on back. They walk together to the truck, discussing what the ice storm did and how his grands had liked the snow. The littlest one ("tha'ss Azalee") has had the sniffles off and on (but "'cepp for that, they both doin' fine. . . sproutin' like collards," Trueblood says). Starting his truck, he leans back out, "Whatever y'all need, I'm down th' road." Dugan attempts to thank him again as Trueblood adds with a wave of his hand, "I reckon you know how the ole hymn goes. . . row f'uh th' shore affo' it's dark."

• • •

It's happening. They both know that—whatever it is, he thinks again.

"We've got a litter why-ah," she says as if it's just a weather report, moving the tub into the yard and kneeling to scrub some skivvies out.

"Maybe," he says, but maybe not.

He stands there. She looks up and squints, then leans back down to dump things in, kneading the sudsy clumps like dough.

"Whoever they are," he says to her, "Bob bought us some time while they regroup. . . thanks to Trueblood," he reflects.

She shrugs and goes on scrubbing clothes.

"What are they after?"

"Me," she says. "Dey'll wait to see what I do next."

"Which is?"

She gestures, then resumes, meaning she wants a chance to think. Fine with him. . . he'll ponder too, going back over signs he's missed, listening for noises he's ignored, the sliding and rustling sighs and creaks, and, under them, the things that wait, the silences that take up space. A blue jay's answered by a horn, far off but saying something back. . . a rumbling freight, a barking dog, and, on the river's farther shore, a chainsaw's predatory whine. Too much out there to rein it in.

"Looks like they want you bad," he says, ending his moment of zazen.

"Dey won't try comin' in again," she says as if she's thinking aloud. "Dey'll be waitin' for me when I go out. . . but de're udder ways to get out of here. . ."

"I'm goin' with you," he declares.

She looks at him as she's wringing things out and stacking them on the bench he'd made. Then, stepping aside as she's tipping the tub, he trips on his still unfinished dig, the millstone lying in its hole like part of a Mayan chieftain's grave—he's thinking he ought to bury it back along with everything from the past. As usual, she seems to intuit his thought.

"You'll have to be reavin' a lot behind—whatever can't get into duh boat."

301

"The boat is gone." She stares at him, expressionless, obliging him to try to explain he'd found it drifting after a storm, and one of those men they'd seen that day was probably its original owner who must have towed it back upriver.

"You didn't tere me," she objects.

He hadn't wanted to worry her. He'd thought it wasn't that big a deal. "We can climb out by the highway bridge."

"And do what from dere?"

She's got a point. "You go alone, I'll pick you up."

She shakes her head, "Dey know duh car, dey'll forrow it."

Trueblood, then? He's done enough—if there's shooting again, he'll be. . . (she pauses to recollect) a sittin' duck, was that the phrase? They can't ask him to take the risk. She's standing now in front of him.

"What?" he asks.

She shakes her head. "Sad movie, Mike." Her arms akimbo, sleeves rolled up, she's disconcertingly matter of fact. "Whatever happens. . ." she starts to say.

"Prince Cormac's got an emerald left."

She hesitates, but he's locked in, certain of what he's telling her. For a moment he feels things slowing up as she looks far off, out towards the river. He's with her looking that way too, here and now and maybe forever if they can somehow nail it down. He doesn't want to hear it said, whatever it is she's poised to say.

"Mike?" she asks him.

"Sorry," he tells her, snapping to.

She touches his shoulder.

"Right," he says. He's studying her—her hair tied back with rubber bands and sweaty wisps at either ear, refuting the blindly gnawing thought that he and she and whatever they share could be as fleetingly insecure as light on the pine trees, clouds in the sky, sound of the chainsaw whining again—except, no way, the thought's absurd. Ridick-alous. His heart would break. . . or not, he argues with himself, rejecting such hyperbole. There's plenty of time to pack the car, get out of Dodge, go down the pike. . . whatever the hell that might involve. What sort of film-buffs travel with guns? "Who are they, Rose?" he asks again. "And what are they after other than you?"

"No use. Won't work," is all she says.

"It would if you'd tell me. . ."

"What?"

"Enough so I can help," he pleads, exasperation showing through.

"You can't," she says emphatically.

He thinks she might be mocking him. He knows she's not, but angered by his own despair, he lets his fury loose on her. "For once," he leans in close to her. "Just once in your lying fucked-up life, tell me the bloody fucking truth!" He grabs her wrist and squeezes it hard until he's sure he's hurting her.

She makes a throaty chuckling noise and yanks her arm free, shaking her head.

"Trust me with something," he implores. He feels the funnel narrowing, a spiraling downwards towards the drain—he might get sucked down after all.

"Like what?" she asks with pitying scorn.

He thinks it's scorn. He can't be sure—Blake's ravenous worm's at work again. "The truth about that night you puked, why Hector was packing a loaded gun, or what your subscribers. . ." he sputters, stalls, and then blurts out, "Just let me know your fucking name!"

"My what?" she chokes.

"Whoever you really are," he adds.

A startled look, so he repeats, "Your bloody fucking Chinese name!"

She hesitates, then starts to laugh.

"That's funny?"

"No, dat's really pathetic. None of duh guys I've ever fucked. . ."

He slaps her, sees her head recoil, feels shocks of pain course up his arm. She turns, her face still half concealed, a hand thrown up and then held flat to catch the blood that's crimson red. "Goddamn it, Rose!"

Like throwing a switch, her eyes go cold. She's going to hurt him back, he knows. "Fuck you and your White-man shit!" she seethes. "Think words and sex solve everyting? So what you want? The same ting now? *Yún Yǔ?*" she shrills. "Dat what you want? *Yún Yǔ! Yún Yǔ!*" Then seemingly checking what she's said, she snarls in a voice that's full of pain, "Get out uh my way, you hope-ress ass!" hissing as she brushes past.

Hearing the water in the sink, he follows her back into the hut. "I didn't mean. . . If you'd just listen. . ."

"*Yún Yǔ!*" she savagely repeats, holding a washrag to her nose.

"Is it broken?" he asks her stupidly.

"Satisfied now?" is her reply, checking the rag and peering outside, seemingly back to business again. She wipes her nose and looks at him as if it's pointless to contend. "What dey want from me is idiotic."

"Don't do it then. Just disappear. There're lots of places we can go. Forgive me, Rose!"

She looks for a towel to dry her face and, finding it on the back of a chair, reaches up to her swelling nose, examines the washrag, folds it up, and starts to dab with the towel instead. He waits until the process ends.

"What have they got on you?"

She lifts her chin and looks away, watching a bird that's lit in a tree. He sees it too, and it sees them. "Dey're after me, not who I'm wid, but dey didn't expect I'd have a gun."

"I'll do anything," he tells her again, knowing he's said it once before.

The bird they're watching flies away. She turns and, looking him in the eye, places her palm against his cheek, a gesture that catches him by surprise.

"I know," she says, then tilts her head, smiling what might not be a smile.

Slowly she turns to leave the hut. Through the window he sees her nearing the car but loses track of her after that. He doesn't hear the engine start and discovers the keys are on the sill. For a moment he stands there, clearing his mind, knowing the worst is about to begin. He follows her out and browses about, wandering Bob-like through the woods within a whisper of the hut, considering where to position himself if and when her pursuers return. An ambush would be easy here, assuming that they'd come strolling in (he's in the bushes with a gun—if Trueblood, say, would lend him one—they're in his sights, he picks one off. . . or, no, he lets them see he could, yells "Fuck off, guys—I mean it, blow!") They wouldn't, though. They'd waltz on in, and. . . say they nail him, what's she do? She talks. She says they've got the whole thing wrong, it's Hector who ruined their video game—unless it's Hector who's showing up (or Glubber, Dough, and Kissinger too with Calley leading their sick platoon. . . but jump-cut then, they're on the path, just Rose and him down past the dam with Credo trotting on ahead the way it's been so many times. . . it's simple, really. . .) There's a car. He hears it pausing on the road and sees Rose closer to the hut, cocking her head towards where he stands as if there's something he can't hear, behind him maybe. Turning too, he looks around, then back to find she's disappeared. He checks the driveway. Nothing there, but glints of metal through the trees, the sound of an engine on the road headed, it seems, down towards the Bobs. He shouts out, "Rose!"

She answers "What?" inside the hut, obscured behind a window screen.

Relieved, he tries to reassure. "Must be the Bobs," is all he says.

"Must be," she answers through the screen as the car goes rattling past again, a dust cloud pluming up behind.

The Bobs retrieving what they need? Or someone reconnoitering? He'll have to take his cue from her. He scratches Credo, kneeling down to run his fingers through her coat. Here and now, he thinks again. Flaky pine-bark oozing sap, a smell of new leaves, russet clay. Just keep it together, he tells himself—she needs you now, and you need her.

She acts as if they've still got time. They eat with careful courtesy. Her face is swollen, he's contrite. He tries to think of Hemingway, the fourth dimension—this is it: she's sitting there beside him now. It lasts forever. That's not true. He searches her face. She gives no clue.

"Shouldn't we. . .?" he says at last.

"No," she answers. "It's okay."

"You're sure?"

"I'm sure."

She's somewhere else—he doesn't know where. He's in the vestibule of hell.

• • •

With nothing more to say or do, he does whatever he'd need to do if they were planning to move on soon—culling the things he'd want to take, disposing of what he'd throw away. At the moment he's burning bags of trash, poking them idly with a stick while enveloped in clouds of acrid smoke and musing on Brits two centuries before who'd torched a mill not far from there and sauntered on off to what came next, winning some battles but losing the war. The burned-out miller must have stood more or less where he's standing now, looking for light at the end of the tunnel. Things don't really change that much, he thinks.

In scenes like his, the wait's not long. There's barking, then the sound of a car, and he guesses at once what's taking place. He'd left the car keys in the hut (why? he asks as he sprints inside. . . because she might be needing them?) A note's beneath a two-pint jug of Short & Sassy amber goo, casting its shadow like a stain across the "Rippla-rippla-rippla-ree." Not bad, he thinks, but gimme a break! Her message could mean a couple of things—that she's got some mojo of her own to deal with whatever's been tracking her or she's counting on him to save her again, though where and how he hasn't a clue. But if he's to follow her, where'd she go? Towards where she thinks they want her to go—but that means what? he tries to surmise. That it's not just Rose herself they want but something only she can do. Of course, that's it. But where she goes depends on them, on who they are and what they're after. Soft-porn videos? Not a chance. . . though what if she's just protecting *him*—from them or from screwing the whole thing up before she pulls off what she's planned or they've got planned for something big? The readiness is all, he thinks. He'll get there in the nick of time to save her from the evil magician— and there's only one person that can be.

It's clear to Credo something's up. She'd tried to warn him with her bark. Big deal he's telling her now to "stay" (what for, big guy? *you* let her go!) She tries to follow him down the road, but he turns back to tie her up—something he's never done before—then hustles on down to Trueblood's house. When Trueblood's daughter says he's out, he says if they don't mind he'll wait.

The grands peer shyly through the screen until the daughter ambles out to offer some water, assuring him, "He soon be back."

"How long?"

"Toreckly."

So he stays, sitting morosely on the steps, his boot-tips white with garbage-pit ash, a glass and saucer on his knee. He hears a radio inside— gospel, commercials, R&B, all sounding much the same to him. A fly investigates his head, zooms off and buzzes back again with a sense that here's where something ends. A station break, and then some news. "Incursion" the announcer says as if it wards off halitosis. Hard to decipher what he means. "Safe havens" and "Cambodia," more clashes with the Viet Cong. When Trueblood's daughter checks on him, he asks about what's going on.

"Gone to th' stow," she reaffirms. "He be back heah affoe too long."

"Sorry," he says. "I meant the news."

She looks around at the radio as if unaware that it was on. He listens and hears a new voice say our troops are in the Parrot's Beak with an enemy base within their grasp, and President Nixon's telling the world we won't be stopped by a line on a map—he won't stand by and watch us behave like "a pitiful helpless giant" he says. When one of the grands peers through the screen, he asks her if she saw the Bobs.

"Nawsuh, I'se sleepin'," she reports.

He asks about the night before. Did those strangers say where they were from?

She shakes her head. "But wunna dem was. . ."

"You! Azalee!"

She turns around, her hands pressed flat, still pushing outwards on the screen.

"You git in here!"

Trueblood's daughter reappears. "What you gone haffa do," she sulks, "is ast my daddy. . . we don' know." She steps back as a gospel tune describes how Jesus turns the tide.

"The reason I ask," he says to the screen as if addressing an oracle, "we had some trouble down the road. My girlfriend and my car are gone. I'm worried, so I came down here." A shadowy outline through the screen. "I'm sorry to bother you," he adds, and, hearing his own apology, he feels the enormity of it all.

The woman steps out onto the porch. "There be those days," is her reply.

He nods and, handing back the glass, says, "Tell your father. . . let him know I'm rowin' hard to get to the shore." There's really nothing more to say.

She promises she'll tell him that, and, rather than wait, he thinks he'll walk. He knows she's watching as he leaves.

●　●　●

Reaching the store by half past ten, he finds the keys in the Pontiac and understands he's there too late—unless, of course, he follows her guided by nothing but a hunch that, rather than simply getting waylaid, she'd driven this far to make a deal and is now on the lam with somebody else. . . another of her irrelevant thugs.

Ma Beasley's been expecting him. She stops part-way through ringing up snacks for a woman who looks tubercular. The woman's son keeps picking his nose and wiping it on the T-shirt stack beneath a school-supplies display above which, next to the register, is a sign in Crayola that proclaims, "THE BOBS HAVE HAD A LITTLE GIRL."

"They have, huh?" Dugan takes his time.

Ma Beasley nods officiously. They're doing fine, she sniffs and adds, except for Bob, who's gotten shot—he'll be on his stomach for a while. "Purvis! Turn that tee-vee down!" The baby's over seven pounds. Who shot him? Well, he shot hisself. Some sort of booby-trap they think, but who can say in times like these? The coloreds down that way are bad as most folks round here ought to know. She lifts her chin and sniffs again. He asks if Rose had used the phone. "Purvis!" she yells, and Pa appears, holding a grease-stained towel up.

"Plugged four pro-testas in Ohio. Juss uh minute. . ."

"Turn it down!"

A burst of music, then it stops. Pa reappears with empty hands. Ma speaks to him impatiently. "Will you tell him whut you toll me?" She glances at the customer, who whacks her son atop the head, knocking some T-shirts to the floor. He picks them up and stuffs them back, now speckled with sawdust. Ma looks irked, but Pa's oblivious, clearing his throat.

"She come in heah 'bout one-fifteen. Rite affer *Jeopardy* was through. Uh re-run whut I'd seed before."

"The oh-ree-enal," Ma explains to the woman with the snot-nosed kid.

"Ast me could she use thuh phone. Long distant call. When I allowed she'd need more change, 'I'm callin' colleck' was whut she said."

"Dee See," adds Ma, her lips compressed, not seeing the sneaky brat reach up to swipe some Milk Duds from the rack.

"'Dee See' is whut she said," Pa nods. "But then I couldn't heah that good—*Hollywood Squahrs* was comin' on. An' whut she's talkin', hit seemed to me. . . lak what hit wuz wuz Red Chinese."

"Hit wurn't, though." Ma takes over now. "In-Ho come in to get some gum and, soon as that woman sees her face, she switches so In-Ho couldn't tell whutever it wuz that she wuz sayin'." She folds her arms and says to the woman, "When Roscoe brung his war bride home, I said Koh-ree-ans fit in fine so long as they 'spect our way of life. . . which, settin' some hahr-style issues aside, In-Ho has always done real good, an' how she acts and whut she eats is pretty much like most white folks do." She turns to Dugan, squinty-eyed. "But when the FBI come by to ast us wuz your girlfriend here. . ."

"Did you see proof they're FBI?"

But Ma, in full stride, thunders on. "They ast us wuz that fureigner here. . . 'cohabitin' with an ox-i-dental.'"

"'n' Ah said. . ."

308

"Pa said. . ." Ma's in charge, though pleased to repeat Pa's clever reply. "'He ain't no Baptist, tha'ss a fack.'"

"I did," nods Pa. "An' when I ast could she repeat whut th' woman had said in normal speech, In-Ho said no, hit wurn't Chinese but somethin' else, she don't know whut."

They look at Dugan, who, thinking this through, assumes the "agents" were a shill. The language bit is puzzling, though. Ma sees his frown and hammers home the point she's itching to deliver. "Mister Dugan, I'm goin' to tell you the truth. You've been a right decent customer, but there's things that money just can't buy. An' no matter what brought her to these parts, if that fren a-yourn's a Vee-et Cong. . . we won't be needin' her business here."

"I 'preciate that," he says to Ma as well as the other two standing there—Pa and the woman ignoring her brat who's over by the corn-meal bin preparing to relieve himself. "Y'all got it wrong, though, 'bout my frenn. You ever heard uh Marshal Ky—you mussta seen him on tee-vee?" He's deep in his Lugton brogue again.

"He got a *muss*-tache?"

"Tha'ss th' one! Big annie-commonist of ourn. He wears this scarf. . ." Pa's now built up a head of steam. "I seen him. . . shore. . . like Snoopy in the funny papers!"

"Well, he's my girlfrenn's uncle, see? An' he's thinkin' about investin' heah, rite c'heer in Lugton if, yew know, thang's don't work out in Vee-et Nam. He sent her here t' scout around." He nods at both of them and shrugs. "Discount stores is whut he does. . . that K in K-Mart stanns fuh Ky. But his plan fuh here's to build uh dam an' start in on vacation homes to he'p resettle some uh his frens, an' then, yew know. . ." They get his drift, but he pauses a beat before his kicker. "When he shows up, most folks go broke—he undersells 'em pretty bad. But ennyhow. . . whut's there to say? Free ennerprise is whut it is."

"He's comin' heah?" Pa asks, aghast.

"I reckon so." He waves his hand. "If I wuz yew," he says to Ma, meeting her malice eye to eye, "I'd start layin' lots uh noodles in. . . and git me some yaller Barbie dolls."

• • •

He doesn't know if he's coming back, so Credo's what he deals with next. There's not much point in saying good-bye (arf arf, so long, it's a dog's life, pal!) She circles and sits on Trueblood's porch, ignoring him as he drives away.

She'd watched him as he packed the car, weighing the trunk down with his books, his records, and his KLH. He was lugging his Smith-Corona out when he noticed the tell-tale bootlegger's sag that would probably get him stopped on the road. So he'd changed his mind and carried stuff back, everything but a heap of clothes that filled the trunk like a laundry bin. He'd taken the Short & Sassy too but, as he was making a final pass, tripped over the millstone stumping his toe, and, in a blindly irrational snit, dug both hands underneath its edge, prised it loose, and lifted it up, fairly astonished that he could. Then, holding it braced against his knees, he'd slipped his grip along the top, thinking he'd lean it against the bench and find some chocks to set it up—just one damn thing that he'd complete. But taking two halting, crablike steps, he'd felt a pffft inside his chest and eased the stone back on its rim, waiting to see what damage he'd done. None, he'd concluded—lucky for him, unlucky for the goddamned stone. He'd rolled it awkwardly like a wheel, poising it at the edge of the bluff and letting it lurch and leap away, crashing like Big Foot through the trees. He'd heard a final crunch and thud before the spillway's hum resumed. Ashes to ashes, dust to dust, the millstone back to where it had been.

● ● ●

Kent State, the hoarse announcer says, appears to have been the proverbial match lit carelessly in a gas-filled room with protests exploding all over the map, vigils and teach-ins, marches and mobs, dissent erupting in every big city. He thinks he's picked the likeliest one, continuing northwards through the rain, regressing at first through barren fields as if in some seasonal retrogression, then into Virginia where spring resumes from Richmond up to Petersburg—the landscape of a failed Rebellion, a thought that dovetails with more news he hears about on the radio. . . there's a meltdown in Cambodia. Lon Nol is in and Sihanouk out ("succeeded by a palindrome" is Kissinger's callous epigram as if it all comes down to this, that backwards or forwards it's the same, another coup, more people dead). He tries to grapple with what he's heard, imagining chaos in Phnom Penh with a short squat man at a big teak desk, newly in charge (for the moment, at least) and, pondering what might unfold next, scribbling down "Noxin?" on a pad, "Wenga? Smarba? Regnissik?" Then sighing and trying it in reverse. Meaningless still. There's no way out. Esor, Nagud, Caitnop. . . pleh!

● ● ●

Washington's like Alaric's Rome with hordes of barbarians at the gates (*Sign of the Pagan*, Mister Jones), jittery workers under siege, and a tambourine army in the streets (tomorrow they'll sack the Pentagon!) Odd, he thinks, how we suppose we've quarantined nightmares overseas only to find them loose at home, not guessing the cause is in ourselves (we're threatened by what we've always been), though it's festive in a surreal way.

He finagles directions to a church *The Catholic Worker* recommends— in Georgetown, on a steep side-street beside a take-out ("Doctor Wok") and in back of a storefront sign on wheels that features a line he recognizes,

WE ARE SINGING TODAY
OF THE WIPE-OUT GANG
Holy Mass & a Blessing of Joints
Kropotkin Dancers 8 pm.

Inside the darkened parish-house gym, he finds a makeshift gypsy camp—bundles and bedrolls, buckskins-and-beads with fuck-you beards and sad mustaches. He bumps into a Seminole chief who's smoking a reefer near the door.

"What's happenin', man?" inquires the chief.

"Wish I knew," is Dugan's reply, giving the chief a double take—he looks so much like Lonnie/Mick that maybe. . . who knows? (Zhivago's law—that we and the people who matter to us are running somehow on parallel tracks, drawing abreast and moving apart.) But then, all hippies look alike. Instinctively, he searches for Rose the way somebody who's lost a ring believes he'll find it in the grass, but doesn't—although, with every step, knowing it only takes a glance, he keeps on hoping until at last, not giving up but wearied out, he goes to sleep as a last resort, thinking

311

he'll dream and find it's so like Adam waking up to Eve (Keats' answer, more or less).

So, after a quick pass through the streets, he works the rat-pack in the gym ("A Chinese woman. . . say, yay tall, late twenties maybe, thirty at most, probably wearing something red?") Then, heading back out along the street, he tries to question Comrade Wok ("*Yún Yǔ*? Hey you! You know *Yún Yǔ*? Wait up! Come back! Hey, open the door!") Finally, close to two a.m. with a sliver of cold moon in the sky, he crashes on the parish floor to wake up, stepped on, just past six, by marchers getting underway (but Keats was wrong, she isn't there).

Still sure a convergence is underway, he stumbles out onto the street where Nursing-Mothers-Won't-Feed-War are serving up cans of apple juice to drowsy marchers on the move. Buses have lined up down the block and geeks are waving people on. He's watching a group in caftans board when someone sings out, "Grab a seat!" He does, and, asking who they are, discovers that they're the Sufi Choir. From Carmel, right? Well, whattaya know? You heard of Jamshyd Tittlewhit? Glum faces: he's apostate now, a hypocrite, a carnivore. Oh, yeah? Too bad. Well, lemme see. There's always Omar—he's okay? Omar *Khayyám*? Oh, he's our guy! "And this first summer month. . ." he quotes as Sufis on either side of him cheer. ". . . that brings the Rose. . ." They cheer again. The lines just popped into his head. Is he a Sufi, one of them? "A fellow traveler," Dugan shrugs, a lot like Omar in a way. Let's hear it for Omar! WHATTAYA SAY? THE TIMOTHY LEARY OF HIS DAY! He's into it now and up on his feet, ready to chant the rest of the verse. "Shall take Jamshyd and Kaikobád. . ."

aWAYYYYY! they shout in unison.

Then into the traffic, waving at cars, flashing a fist, thumbs up, a V ("Scissors cut paper! Yay, yay, yay!") A man up front is playing the spoons. "This land is our land!" someone sings while somebody else is lighting a jay. The air brakes wheeze, they stop and go, wait twenty minutes while they're stuck behind a beer truck with a flat, get out and see above the trees the Washington Monument's phallic spire— "Strangelove's Hard-on," Dugan hears from one of the caftan-clad elect.

"Hey, saddle up! We're near the Mall!"

"Eowwwwww!"

"Let's go!"

"Who's got the drum?"

"Damned apple juice! I gotta go pee!"

The hundreds turn into thousands now. Guys with clipboards, Uncle Sams, serapes and Supp-hose, freaks and vets and, three feet closer to the ground, a kid with a weirdly blank-eyed stare whose fingers are groping in a bowl, slopping small goldfish to the ground. At second glance, it seems he's blind, guided by someone in the crowd. Three nuns, a juggler, and a mime. When Dugan looks back to find the kid, he's vanished as if he'd never been. (Hallucination or fatigue? Perceiving the world in jump-cut mode, like watching a time-lapse hurricane.)

"Hey! Take it easy!"

"Sorry, friend." He's pushing forward towards the front—they've called for priests and rabbis there. "I need to get through," Dugan says.

A family obstructs him, shoving back. The father's sporting a braided beard with fuchsia bows worn Blackbeard-style. A toddler straddling his shoulders smirks and kicks at Dugan with her boot. "There's always one," her mother glares. "What's your hurry?" she says to Dugan.

"I'm late for my dialysis. . . you got a kidney you can spare?" Burrowing past them into a wall of people dressed up like plutocrats. "Excuse me, top priority! Oops, sorry! What? Is this my group? I'm Lepers Anonymous. Thank you, sir. Has anybody found a thumb?" White helmets and a fence ahead.

"No pushing! Hey!"

"I gotta get through."

The bottleneck worsens. One step, two. He must be closer than he'd guessed. Three steps on tiptoe, then a surge in which he's suddenly swept along, the press of bodies holding him up. A murmur followed by a shout, some groans, a laugh, a sweaty stench. "I've lost a contact!" No response.

He sees the front line dead ahead with big celebs like rangy horn-rimmed Doctor Spock. . . and Robert Lowell's quizzical stare, his deckchair angularity in a dapper but rumpled pin-striped suit. . . and what's-his-name, Chicago 7, the lawyer with the famous hair who's standing next to. . . Baba Ram Dass. They're linking arms Red-Rover style with somebody short on Cal Lowell's right. . . it's Norman Mailer, out on parole (for stuffing his wife with Bisquick mix, according to Danny's inside dope) and next to him. . . *Augustus Blunt* (ah, Boris, how it all comes round!) with an unflappable quisling's air.

A bullhorn's beep. They're marching for real past Lafayette's mildly puzzled gaze towards a circle of buses up ahead—a wagon train of rubber and steel like Conestogas in a ring, fencing the White House. Nixon's afraid.

Dugan keeps scanning the crowd for Rose. Blunt looks around, spots Dugan it seems and turns away. The bullhorn's crackle prods the crowd, suddenly restive, like a herd flexing its anonymity. The chant begins from one hoarse throat, "No more. . . no more." Hundreds of voices pick it up. They're out of sync, but it's a roar.

"NO MORE KILLING! NO MORE WAR!

The celebrity vanguard's nearing the troops, mere boys with nervous features set like statues in graveyards in a row with spaces behind them for the press. Dugan has almost reached the front. One step back. They're jostling now. (*At any moment*, Dugan thinks, searching the faces. . . she's not there.) A voice starts up with HO! HO! HO! It doesn't catch on, so someone shouts, "Kent State! Never again!"

"NO MORE KENT STATES!" the bullhorn notes.

"NEVER AGAIN!" the crowd joins in. "KENT. . . STATE! NEVER AGAIN! KENT. . . STATE! NEVER AGAIN! Without a rhyme, it's somewhat flat.

Cameras are bobbing to one side. Headsets, batteries (where'd she be?), guys in jeans with satchels and mikes (look for a mop of glossy black hair!) Word hasn't reached the rear to stop—it's like a glacier grinding on.

"Wherrrre's. . . Dick?" the bullhorn pleads.

"TRIC-KY. . . DICK! WHERE. . . IS. . . DICK?"

There! (*Yes, there!* his brain exults—that stand-up with her back to us. . . her shoulders? hair? He can't quite see. The logo's clear, but. . . *yes, he's sure! He's sure it's Rose!*) He shouts, but his voice is lost in the din. He pushes and elbows, shoulder-blocks, crashing into the celebrity line.

"You little shit!" It's Augie Blunt. Against all odds, he seems to remember.

ONE. . . TWO. . . THREE. . . FOUR!

Now Mailer's glaring at Dugan too from under his fake-palooka lids. TRIC-KY DICK MUST END THE WAR!

"*Bomb!*" gasps Dugan, tugging his waist.

Blunt goes blank but Mailer reacts, shoving so hard that Blunt goes down and Dugan's suddenly in the clear, sprinting towards Rose's camera crew. He shouts again. She doesn't respond, but when he's maybe ten yards away, she turns as if expecting him. He's trying to grasp what's in her eyes when—catching him totally by surprise—the non-existent bomb goes off.

• • •

Silence in a dimly lit room—an office of some kind, it appears. At first he thinks he's there alone, laid out on a hard unyielding couch. . . but not alone, as he quickly discovers. There's a man in a chair at a metal desk, staring into a circle of light like a fisherman on a frozen pond. A young Henry Fonda, Lincolnesque, in rimless specs with a ribbon of beard that's like a strap. Not a doctor, no, but who can he be? He glances at Dugan, looks annoyed, gets up, and quickly leaves the room.

Vague recollections flip through his mid of Lowell, Mailer, Blunt. . . and Rose! He'd seen her, shouted out her name. . . then something must have hit his head. Blacked out, came to—he thinks he did—then what? Not sure. A sedative? That's not protocol—after a bad blow to the head, they're not supposed to let you sleep. He's in some sort of detention now, but where is she? he needs to find out and whether she saw him or not.

He reaches up to touch his head. It's overripe. No more thumping the cantaloupe, he decides. He feels around to see if it's split, nudging it gently back in place. That makes him sleepy, so he sleeps.

He wakes, and this time no one's there. The room is vaguely sinister but clearly not a prison cell. There's the sofa that he's lying on next to a chair that matches the one pulled up to the desk and a photo on the far-side wall of Nixon staring straight ahead with a circular wrinkle nose-to-chin as if he's just doffed an oxygen mask. . . plus, in a corner, spider-legged, a white enameled stool on wheels (hinting at what? he asks himself—that Doctor Mengele will see him soon?) The matchstick blinds have been flipped shut, though he guesses it must be dark by now.

A new guy enters with a nod, moving the chair out from the desk. Bellbottoms with a tapered shirt, monogrammed buckle on his belt— dressed to infiltrate it appears (long hair, moustache, he's got those right. . . except for the buckle, Dugan observes, dead giveaway he's in disguise). Behind Bellbottoms is someone else wearing a shiny cheap blue suit, half sitting, half-leaning on the desk impersonating Warren Oates, last spotted atop a railroad car. He's the one in charge, at least for now.

"Tôn Ny Koung," the Suitman says, reading aloud from some report. Dugan blinks. "You talking to me?"

"Don't screw around, wise guy," he says. Then, ". . . a.k.a Rose Lee," he adds, waiting for Dugan to react and, after it's clear that Dugan won't, "Your slant-eyed snatch, remember her?"

Hardball? Okay. It's what it is. "I know a Rose Lee," Dugan says, trying to sit, then lying back when something seems to rattle loose.

"Who tipped you off?" Suitman inquires as if assured that someone had.

"Nobody. . . or I would have ducked. They must have hit me from behind."

"In Lugton," Suitman growls again.

"In Lugton?" Dugan's throat feels dry.

"That's right, tough guy. You managed to set some sort of trap."

He'd managed? Sure. "You must mean double agent Bob. Bad actor, Bob. I played no part in that at all."

"You didn't?"

"No."

Bellbottoms snorts in disbelief. His voice is low, like Sonny Bono. "Tôn Ny Koung—your friend Rose Lee. . . how'd you know she'd be up here?" Good cop/bad cop's underway.

"I guessed."

"Who told you?"

"Berrigan—we called him Dan. Amazing cat. You got some aspirin I can use?"

Suitman gives a little nod. Bellbottoms frowns and leaves the room, returning with a half-filled mug.

"Two tablets left."

"Gimme," says Suitman, swallowing both.

"Hey!" Dugan objects.

"Can it, hotshot! Whose is this?" Lifting the mug before he drinks and posing the question for his aide.

"I found it in there by the sink."

"It's Hazel's, damn it!" Suitman says. "She's got the goddamned Hong Kong flu!" He rubs his temples. "Well, let's see. . ." he turns to Dugan with a sigh. "Left-wing professor loses job, moves undercover to the sticks, assumes a new identity while copping out on the Reserve, provokes a riot at Fort Bragg, and comes to D.C. yesterday to interfere with an arrest. That accurate?"

"Of course not, no. What am I charged with?"

Suitman smiles. "We'll ask the questions. Yesterday. . ."

"I tried to help a friend of mine."

"Tôn Ny Kuong?"

"I've never heard that name before."

"Your associate. . . one Miss Rose Lee."

"I thought I got to make a call."

"That's in the movies."

"No, it's not."

"Call who?"

"Her mother, Madame Nhu."

Suitman sighs. "Quit fartin' around. In nineteen sixty-eight and nine. . .
"

"What am I charged with?"

"Nothing yet—I told you that. You're making a statement. Sixty-eight and sixty-nine, you frequented a coffee house. . ."

"How 'bout my belt? You want my belt? You worried I'm gonna hang myself?"

"Shut up," Bellbottoms interjects.

". . . called, let's see. . ." Suitman persists.

"Up Yours. That's right—I went there maybe three or four times." Nixon's left eye seems to wink. "I swear that bastard's watching me. You got some hidden cameras here?"

"September, nineteen sixty-nine, in the company of aforesaid Lee, after sabotaging a relay station, you disrupted maneuvers at a military base, Fort Jackson, outside Cumbria, S.C. No charges pressed. Is that correct?"

"Because of General Blatz," he nods. "On orders from Moscow."

Suitman nods. He's not amused. "A few days later. . . get me the files."

"Which ones," asks Bottoms.

"The ones on top of the filing cabinet, the red one. . . and the blue one too." Suit waits for Bottoms to depart. "So why'd you up and quit your job?"

"Medical leave. You need your notes?"

Bottoms comes back with two thick files. Suit leafs through one, then marks his place. "Regular trips to Chantry Mount. You frequented the campus there, meeting with various leftist types, including one. . . Maxine Gewertz."

"Bonnie."

"Right."

"She liked to do it standing up. . . the men's room on the second floor. I tried to tell her it was risky."

317

Suit puts the files down on the desk. "Okay," he says, "let's cut the crap. Rose Lee, okay? She'd managed to give our boys the slip until an informant tipped us off. So I'm going to ask you one more time—how'd you find out about the bust?"

"Well, I dunno. From feeling her up? I gotta go piss. . . is that okay?"

"One joke too many, funny boy."

"I take it back. The Feed & Seed—are they on your list? A regular left-wing listening post. How long you plan on keeping me here?"

What he's just learned is Rose was wrong—it wasn't her guys who'd tracked her down. It was instead, as Ma Beasley said, some agents from the FBI or whoever these jokers represent. But Rose had contacted someone else. . . in a language that In-Ho didn't know. . . her "subscribers" who must have brought her here. They're why he's being questioned now.

Suit and Bottoms leave the room, closing the door and locking it shut. The files on the table are there for him—no oversight, as Dugan knows. The blue one has his name typed out. The red one's labeled "Tôn Ny Koung." He opens it up and sees her face. . . he thinks it's hers, he can't be sure. Younger and starker, not well lit, but something inside him says it's Rose. He pauses briefly on the edge, not looking down, then starts to read.

Tôn Ny Koung
b. 7 May 1934
Kompong Cham, Cambodia

Much older than he'd thought she was, she's listed under various names. Rose Lee is one. A separate entry says Chan Nginn (inside parentheses "Wang Shih"). Her husband? Yes. Two children, it says. "Sudath" is followed by a blank where "Thary" is lightly penciled in. He'd no idea, but that's not it, the missing piece, the revelation left for him. He learns that from a telex sheet: a diplomatic visa—why? Two rows of dots, some sort of code, SUSPECTED AGENT, underlined, and, with an asterisk up top, PRINCE NORODOM SIHANOUK it says.

Aware he's done what they want him to do, Dugan elects to read no more. But then, of course, he's read enough and sits there like a hitching post with Nixon watching him from the wall. At bottom, defiance is what he feels. Even if all that crap is true—husband, children, espionage—if in the end it comes to that, he'll save her again for whomever she loves. It's all the same, he thinks, in the end. Not winning but loving is the game.

• • •

Bellbottoms looks in at half-past three, sticking his head in, pulling it out. The door swings shut without a click. It's left unguarded is Dugan's thought, but they've done it deliberately—don't be fooled. He goes outside and Bottoms is there, deeply immersed in *Business Week*.

"Checkout time?"

"Not yet, dipshit. Still need the head?"

"Tell Warren Oates if he wants to parlay. . ."

"Too late, he's gone. You aim to pee, I'd do it now."

Bottoms obligingly shows the way but isn't around when Dugan's through, leaving the hallway empty and clear. Too easy, though—he's onto that, and, when he finds his own way back, Bottoms is there to usher him in. Another shift's on duty now as Suitman Senior has arrived. . . hulking, with a smallish head, thin hair, big ears, and a feral grin. He looks as if his name is Bud.

"Room service here ain't worth a durn. You smoke?" Bud asks as if they're friends, holding a pack of Pall Malls out and nodding approval when Dugan declines. "Wish I could quit too," he allows, lighting one up and putting the rest inside the jacket of his suit, a baggy wool and nylon mix. His accent's got a menacing edge—southeastern Georgia, Dugan's thinks. Tack on his sly horse-trader's grin, and you'd figure him for aluminum siding.

"You ready to talk?" Bud sucks in deep, exhaling smoke from mouth and nose, seemingly more than he'd breathed in.

Dugan gestures at the files. "Whatever you think you've got on me. . ."

"Nobody's int'rested in you." Bud takes a drag and rubs his chin, his manner coldly genial. "Your smuttiness makes it pretty clear you ain't no Julius Rosenberg. You knew what she was up to, though." He looks around. "No ashtrays? Well. . . I tell you what, just give that trashcan there a shove. Yeah, now you're talkin', lover boy—don't wanna set this place on fire." His message is that he's got all day, a redneck fishing from a bridge. "So let's get started. *Tôn Ny Koung*. . ." He grabs the red file. "Friend uh yours?"

"Your guys fucked up. She's not the same."

Bud wipes some ashes from his tie, a narrow squared-off black knit weave from ten or fifteen years ago. "The same as who?" between two coughs, picking tobacco off his lip. "Your Mata Hari movie star?"

"Well. . ." Dugan pauses. "You tell me. With all your hot Dick Tracy shit, you must've learned her Chinese name—the real one, not the one you said." He hadn't seen it in the file. Bud squints and flicks more ash away, then crushes out his cigarette as Dugan plays his one big trump. "If you don't know—and say you don't—maybe you've made a big mistake."

"Her Chinese name. . ." Bud looks intrigued. "Why don't you tell me, buddy roe?"

"Why should I?"

Bud holds up his palms. "To help her. . . if you think you can. There're some mistakes we still can fix."

"Then you don't know?"

Bud clasps his hands like L.B.J. "The thing you're not quite grasping, Mike—you don't mind if I call you Mike?—is where you are and why you're here. I'm not here to negotiate."

"*Yún Yŭ*," says Dugan. "That's her name."

A silence. Bud unclasps his hands. "What else you learn. . . besides her name?" He nods to Bottoms, who leaves the room.

"She did some acting. Nothing big. I met her on a movie set."

"'The Power Station'—we saw that." He rolls his eyes and cocks his head. "That action scene's a classic, Mike. 'The Army Base' is okay too. The bedroom scene's a little slow—nothin' but audio on our tape—but threat'nin' Agnew was a pisser. . . you think those lines up by yourself?" He coughs and leans back in his chair. "She musta still thought you'd be of use after you pulled things off at the fort, so she wanted something compromisin'. . . but she didn't get much past grunts 'n' groans." He reaches back inside his suit. "My body's cravin' nicotine. Filthy habit. Bother you?"

Ignoring Bud's patter, Dugan broods—on when and if she'd trusted him. Probably never, he reflects. . . except, ironically, at the end. She'd tried to protect him, that was clear—though how can anything be clear with a husband and two of her kids at stake? That scene in his bedroom early on. . . figures, he guesses, in a way. No light to speak of, only sound. But still. Well, hell. "Where is she now?"

"*Yún Yŭ*?" Bud asks. He flicks his zippo—on its side, a globe and an anchor under a bird. . . somehow, it's all about the war, which figures also in a way. "We'll get to that," Bud promises. "But first let's talk about those flicks. You seen 'em?"

"No."

Bud lights and puffs, exhaling smoke. They watch it drift through film-noir streaks that filter past the half-closed blinds. Dawn's early light? Too soon for that.

"And how'd you learn about Fort Bragg?"

"That she'd be there? You serious?"

Bud exhales slowly. "Say that's true. Let's say it's sheer coincidence. You drive there one day on a whim, just lookin' to have a little fun—foment a riot, slam the Man—but, whatta ya know, *Yún Yǔ* shows up! So here's a chance to grab more snatch while baggin' another cameo in one of those flicks you didn't see. . . Say what? Yeah, 'tapes'. . . the latest thing." He rubs his mouth with the palm of his hand, then turns to Dugan with a frown. "That's what you're gonna tell me, right? But sorry, hoss. . . that dog can't hunt, not in the swamp you're wadin' in." He looks at Bottoms, who's just returned. "Playback," he says, and Bottoms leaves.

He smiles at Dugan who smiles back. Smiles fade, and they're still eye to eye. "You knew exactly where she'd be." Bud's head is lowered like a bull's. "You knew what she was up to, too, but didn't care—I'll grant you that. Your mind was listenin' to your dick." He stands and ambles towards the door, filling it like a cork in a bottle while beckoning Bottoms back inside and grabbing a note from Bottom's hand. "*Yún Yǔ*, my ass! Bring that thing in."

A 10-volt, Dugan thinks at first, his childhood nightmare turning real, then sees it's just a TV cart and hears Bud say, "Those goddamn Japs. Our guys invent it, what comes next? We buy our own crap back from them." He gestures. Bottoms plugs it in, hits knobs and buttons and steps back. Skewed images flick across the screen. "Fix this thing, Willis."

"Wallace, sir."

"Just make the fucker work!" Bud barks as Bottoms fumbles with the box. "Annapolis!" he adds with scorn. "Good thing we dropped the A-bum, huh, before they got a look at it?"

The picture stabilizes now. The camera's static, black and white, in softer focus than a film. It's Rose all right, seen upside down, her face a stoical grimace. The guy atop her's leaning back. Not Hector, though it's hard to tell. Some distortion, then a closer shot. She's kneeling, and somebody's hand is holding her by the back of her head. The audio's a gagging sound.

Bud watches it appraisingly. "Must have been for blackmail, huh? Leverage if they think they need it. Or say she's worth a whole lot less, and this was how they let her know it, whatever might keep the prince amused. There're lots of possibilities. That guy Lopez—you know him, right?—he thought she'd got herself knocked up. That something. . . ?"

"No. I wouldn't know."

The onscreen tempo's speeding up as Bottoms helpfully observes, "Cum shot's coming. Check it out."

"You shits!" groans Dugan. "*Cut it off!*"

It stops in freeze-frame, then goes black. Bud looks at him and shakes his head. "I thought Rhodes Scholars used their brains. Somebody says he's Long Dong Wong, you figure that's a put-on, right? A whattaya call it? Sobriquet? So what she told you was '*Yún Yŭ*,' and you, bright guy, you wrote that down because it had to be her name. It's *all* you knew, but you knew that. Know what it means?" He pauses with the note in hand. "I got somebody to check it out. It's Mandarin, not Cantonese, and roundabout in a Chinese way, though they tell me it's something she'd have learned the way you studied Latin or Greek. But I guess, ole hoss, you were outta your league when it came to dealin' with *Yún Yŭ* which basically means "C'mon, l'ess screw" or, even better, just "fuck you!" Maybe you should'a looked it up." Bud gets to his feet and starts for the door, pausing there long enough to add, "Great moniker for a porn star, though. . . sorta like 'Pussy Galore.'"

● ● ●

Reeling, he tries to steady himself, assuming that what they want him to do is panic into betraying her. Attempting to think, he finds he can't— so, dowsing the light, he falls asleep.

At half-past five he lurches awake with sirens loose all over D.C. and thinks of Walt in the hospital wards—kept stocked by what? the insanity factory—so eager to kiss the butchered boys (and "is it all flashes and specks?" he'd asked before he'd seen what the butchers could do). And now the passing stranger's Rose, stamping the duckboards, rubbing her chest ("Ming vase no problem for you, huh?") I am to see to it, he says, that I do not lose you. . . lose you. . . lose you. . .

At six the door clicks open again, and Bottoms, sticking his head back in, supposes Dugan's sleeping still. The door clicks shut, and, drowsing in a waking dream, his mind's at work on what he knows (with acres of rubble after the quake, the light so hazy, so much dust, prodding the laundry with a stick, all that's left of Young Lee's shop and of Lee and his daughter too it seems, but "missing me one place," Walt declaims, peering about the city's ruins, "search another." He waves to Dugan. "Be of good cheer! All goes onward and outward," he drawls. "Everything changes, nothing dies." It does, though, Dugan tries to say. "Nope," Walt signals, chewing his beard while, with a weird seraphic grin, he shuts his eyes and waggles his hips: "How marvelous to see you here!" Dugan ignores his lewd salute, knowing where Walt has cribbed that line. . . but that's okay, wherever it means, so long as she's somehow made it through.) He doesn't think he's sleeping again.

• • •

At six-thirty he's still half-immersed in his dream with coffee in a Styrofoam cup that's slopping onto his shaking hand. Bud enters in time to catch that detail—he's affably dismissive now despite the absurdly early hour.

"Want sugar for that coffee, hoss? . . . Wallace!"

"Sir?"

"Let's get him some sugar."

"Weekend, sir. She's locked it up."

Bud shakes his head and rubs his neck, then sips from a steaming Redskins mug. "This place," he sighs. "You read through those?" He means the files.

"No," Dugan says.

"We might have saved a little time." He bends to pick the red file up, flips through it and puts it down again. "Know how she managed to get to France? The nuns in Phnom Penh had worked things out for her to study in Lyon. She left for Paris in less than a month, met a guy, and shot a few films." He stops to study Dugan's face. "Not what you'd want to show a nun. They do that for a year or so, but then she's suddenly home again and married to a man she'd known—we think she'd known. . . her parents knew. They had their first kid in a year." He stops again. "Come on now, Mike. She talk to you about the kids?"

"No," Dugan says. He feels an odd pain in his back, midway between his shoulder blades, but after a while it eases up.

"No. . . meaning what? You didn't know?"

"Go fuck yourself."

"She talk about Prince Sihanouk?"

"Of course not, no."

"Why would she, huh?" Bud wipes his mouth. "I'll move us right along, okay? Whatta you know about the prince?"

"Nothing."

"Sure. He's on TV—sings rock 'n' roll, remember that? Makes movies too. A movie nut. Directs and stars and, you know what? he used Rose Lee. . . Look out there, Mike! Here, wipe that off! . . . Sihanouk's quite a character. Plays footsie now with Chairman Mao, but, hell, back then, he's ridin' high. You ever heard of Battambang?"

"No," Dugan says.

"It's in the west, a railroad town. Some local farmers staged a coup, the prince's goon squad put 'em down—well, strung 'em up and slit their guts. The only reason I bring this up is Rose Lee's husband comes from there."

"Let's use. . . the other name," he croaks.

"What, Tôn Ny Koung? But that's Khmer. Syun's the one you're looking for, 'Beautiful Jade' in Cantonese. Like being a Jew in Russia, though—when things go bad, you jump the yids. . . You with me, Mike?"

"Go on," he says.

"Things go the way they always go. While this rebellion's on a roll, the farmers think it's pay-back time. They hate the Chinese middlemen—not Sihanouk, who's been misled, at least that's what they'd like to believe. Besides, they think, he's Khmer like them. So, soon as they see they're in control, they hunt down Chinese they can blame. And who do they find? This guy who's there in Battambang to settle some sort of land dispute. . . who's as good as dead unless, somehow, he makes them think he sides with them. Which Wang Shih does. He's in the clear, until the prince's mugs wade in."

"How do I know. . .?"

"Just listen, so maybe you might learn. Sihanouk's thugs are mopping up, hanging the farmers up to dry, when somebody brings up Wang Shih's name. The evidence is he isn't dead—which gets the poor schmuck thrown in jail, along with her, his wife Syun. And here's where Sihanouk comes in. The kids are just collateral to rope her into his big scheme. If she plays ball, the kids survive. . . maybe even the husband too." Bud pauses to let his words sink in. "He'll make Syun a super-spy, a Mata Hari movie queen—'stockpiling targets,' it says here, 'for purposes of strategic disruption.' Yeah, sure, it's lame, what else is new? But then," he picks up Rose's file, "it's not so far-fetched after all, especially if that guy up there," he nods at the photo on the wall, "is more than a little paranoid. 'Stockpiling targets' might be real if backdrops for her hare-brained scenes are places that you'd want blueprints for. For what?" he asks, and Dugan waits, not sure what Bud expects from him or why he's bothered with such a spiel.

"Here's how the game is played, okay? A gangster wants to rob a bank, he gets some pictures in advance. But, say, if what he's after instead is only to make you think he *could* if he's got a mind to blow shit up, so that maybe it's better to deal with him so long as he's acting like a clown. . . *acting*, see? They know he knows they know he knows he's not about to go to war."

Not letting on if that's for real or a parody of Inspector Clouseau, Bud opens the red file up again, running his finger down a page.

"'To designate and reconnoiter for purposes of strategic disruption.'"

He grins and puts the file back down.

"Jargon, right? But that's the catch, that's where this ding-a-ling looks shrewd. He's got his bluffing game down cold. If we squeeze *him*, he'll squeeze us back—he'll escalate the protests here by. . . using what? 'Strategic disruption' of a sort that any dope like you could launch so long as you figure out what to do plus where to go and how to do it. That way he's got a lock on us. . . and who do you think will be his key?"

Dugan's relieved that's all Bud's got. "You know that's utterly absurd."

"And you know that's beside the point."

"She couldn't light a kerosene heater."

"But others could. . . the Weathermen, the S.D.S. Rose Lee produced what they could use."

"And so do the networks' nightly news."

"We're keeping tabs on them as well. Sihanouk's flicks were bush-league crap—which we kept covered pretty good until you screwed things up again. You made us take the Cuban out. . . and that was when she disappeared." He reaches for a cigarette. "But then we found you in the sticks and figured she'd be there as well."

"How?" asks Dugan.

Bud lights up, inhales, puffs smoke out, chuckling softly to himself. "We don't reveal that sorta thing."

Hector, Dugan tells himself, he must have seen me at Fort Bragg—later they went to Gordo too and maybe Dough to piece it together.

"In case you're wond'rin'," Bud resumes, "the coup last month was a surprise. But that's okay we worked things out. Kissinger swears the head guy now—same guy who ran the show before. . ."

"Madam I'm Adam. . . yeah, I know."

Bud looks blank. "Lon Nol, okay? He'll fight the reds, we'll bomb the bush." Bud blows some smoke out through his nose. "You need more coffee?"

"I need sleep."

"But Sihanouk's not a prudent guy. Word's gotten around about his scheme, and people want to see her tapes."

"What for? They're trash."

"Well, you know that and we know that, but how can anyone know for sure unless they see them? Sihanouk hopes his Chinese pals will think he's got good shit to trade."

"But you've got copies."

"Right," Bud nods. "Except. . . for us they're merely bait."

"For her?"

"Her friends. We needed her to flush 'em out."

"Those guys in Lugton. . .?"

". . . did their job. And she reacted pretty quick."

Of course, thinks Dugan, that was it. "She thought her guys had tracked her down, so she called you to cut a deal—and you said if she played along, you'd cover her. You told her Lon Nol had the kids, which may or may not be the truth, but that was what she asked you for. Then she called them, her agents here. . ." He waits for Bud, who takes his time.

"There was nothing left for her to sell." He pauses, and his voice assumes a gelid flatness and contempt. "Don't get self-righteous on me, Mike—not when you're livin' by the sword. Right after the coup, in Kompong Cham, Sihanouk's friends grabbed Lon Nol's brother. . . carved him up and ate his liver with souvenir pieces for the crowd. Lon Nol took umbrage, you might say."

"But not at her."

"No, probably not. But he's eager to meet the prince's friends, and Sihanouk really got around." Bud yanks two photos from the file. "She knew him pretty well it seems." He lays them on the tabletop, three 8x10s in black & white, two of them on a tennis court, one having drinks beside a pool. She's laughing at his moon-faced grin, he's got an arm around her waist, his fingers resting on her hip as if that's where they've been before.

A glance and Dugan shoves them back. "Production stills! They're from a film."

Bud shrugs and gathers them back up. "Well, here's the point about your friend and what she might expect back home, Lon Nol is not a movie buff, and he wants 'em all. . . including her." Bud flashes a sadistic sneer.

Dugan's not sure what happens next. A searing light, a stab of pain, goes flooding upwards through his brain. Maybe he's somehow known from the start she'd turn to look at him too soon, but now that it's happened he's undone in a way that severs his puppet strings. He thinks he hears Bud's voice intone, "I guess that's all we're gonna need."

"*You promised her, you motherfuckers!*" Dugan says or means to say.

"Help this putz up. There, use the stool."

"He looks unconscious," Bottoms says, reaching for the spider-legged stool and holding it steady as Dugan stirs.

"He's comin' around," Bud calmly says, peering back down at Dugan's face. "Look here, dumb ass, before we go, my last name's Boozer. . . *Boozer*, yeah. From Tallapoosa, down your way. My sister Meg's at your old school." (This registers in Dugan's mind—Zhivago's in a frenzy now, attracted by the charnel smell of whatever it is they're working towards.) "Don't s'pose you're one of the sons of bitches who flunked her on her big exam?"

"No," Dugan says.

"I'm glad to hear it. She's had a helluva time down there. When I got her on the phone last night, she was cryin' so hard I couldn't hear. Her weddin' day was yesterday. Pisses me off I had to miss it." He leans his face down eye to eye (his pores are oily, oozing filth). "With your fuckin' march and that guy's wreck, they damn near had to cancel it." He's even closer to Dugan's ear. "Damned kike professor got hisself killed and they went ahead with the funeral plans, not giving a damn how she would feel. They coulda put the schmuck on ice. . . but, no, they buried him right away." Dugan can smell Bud's fetid breath (the old one-two, he thinks too late—no time to duck, it catches him flush). "Meg thinks he had a gentile wife, but that's what yids do nowadays to make you think they're not real Jews. He kept his name, though. . . Rosencrantz or Gildenstern." Bud's money shot is on the way. "Daniel Rosen ring a bell? I guess you must have known him, huh?"

IV

BRAVELY BLOWING KISSES

August 30, 1970

*"He done his damnedest." I think that's
the greatest epitaph a man can have.*

—Harry S Truman

At this point in Caitlin's revery nothing much has changed except for the emphasis of her prayer that's reverted to Danny and altered in tone to something more like a reproachful plea. Though she's still alone in her rumpled bed with the clock still stuck at 5:05, she's brooding on an elusive hope that whatever's existed even once must somehow somewhere always be, if only in the mind of God—to which she trusts she's getting through.

"*De profundis*, Lord, it's me again. . ." which seems a scholastic way to begin, pious but firm in its appeal. "I know You're fully aware of his case—we've discussed it already for nearly four months under the heading of Other Sheep. . . 'not of this fold' is what You said, and maybe You meant—I think You did—possibly even a goat or two who're deeply mired in the trammels of sin—assuming a trammel's some sort of snare and sin goes back to appetite, not love or something resembling love but mindless outright goat-like sex, the bait that lures us to your hook (salvation—right, O Fisher of Souls?) 'Them also must I bring,' You said.

"His sins, Lord? Yes, I'm fully aware—and probably many more than I think. But, still, two things I'd like to ask, just given the couplings You've observed. Are we the creatures You had in mind when bestowing on us such freedom of will? To take, for instance, the issue at hand, did You know how readily we'd succumb to venery when we got a chance, scratching at every sinful itch, indulging it like a credit-card loan with interest compounded minute by minute and hell to pay when the bill falls due? Come on now, Lord, that's usury—and couldn't You guess what the outcomes would be? How many squalid bankrupts there'd be. . . like Danny for one? like Dugan and me?

"And then our brains—designed to keep us untrammeled, I guess—was it actually part of some Catch-22 for hormones to cancel out their use or were we supposed to think in a way inaccessible to the rat or flea? Which is to say, specifically—applied to hard cases like Danny and me, lapsed Catholic wed to wandering Jew—was it chastity that You'd hoped to see?

"Such questions require no answer, Lord, and the wages of sin I understand. But with Danny, who wore his faults on his sleeve, there were virtues I worry You might have missed that made me happy and made us

331

laugh—give him credit for those when You tally the score. And he thought about more than getting his own, he thought a lot about dogs, okay? and students and friends. . . and beetles too. He loved recounting that anecdote when an entomologist tells the world that, no matter how special we think we are, a third of all species are beetles—bugs!—which causes a condescending priest to ask what science has learned from that fact about the Unknowable Mind of God, to which the scientist shrewdly replies that it seems You must have a great fondness for beetles. Worthy of Martin Buber, yes? the sort of thinking You applaud. . . I hope You do, I trust You do. . . and I know You don't negotiate, but I'm asking, Lord, in the name of Saint Roch, to cut my ex a little slack.

"It's been a while since we last talked, but I'm doing my best to know and accept whatever it is You've planned for me and the lessons I've gleaned from all this grief—that nothing can ever stay the same, not for a day, an hour, a minute, that sooner or later bills all fall due and it's folly to hope they're overlooked. . . and maybe—as *amicus curiae*, Lord—if I could add on his behalf that Danny, for all his obvious faults, thought goodness grows out of empathy and not from mere obedience.

"I know such things are for You to decide and I'm less than a beetle in the end, but while we're talking, could I just add that You really did say You'd set us apart, made us accountable for our sins with a chance of reprieve but only for toeing the party line—and there's the rub for creatures like us if we're able to love but encumbered with rules, could soar to the clouds but wallow in stews, make music and war and the Sunday *Times*, feel guilt, desire and endless regret, yearning and groveling in the mud, all of which wouldn't be half so bad if just acting insipid's not the goal or spouting some magical Rippla-Ree. . . but then, what *is*? I'm asking You, Lord, because, though I'm probably way out of line, I loved him more than my own soul, and, forgive me for further presumption here, but it seems your formula's out of whack—too little thought, as Danny would say, and way too much testosterone. . . our fault, I know, but give us a break (though let me observe, as a candid aside, that the estrogen seems to work okay if You could just smooth delivery out—parthenogenesis worked for us once. Maybe it's worth another try).

"Just a lapsed Catholic's random thoughts, trying to fathom the why and what after I've screwed things up again. Help me to find my way, O Lord. Help Danny and Dugan and all of us—including Rose, Lord. . . help her too."

Selah, amen, re-start your engines.

V

LIFELESSNESS IS THE GREAT ENEMY

May – August 1970

Who knows what evil lurks in the hearts of men?

—Lamont Cranston

Two minutes into the Palmetto State, the Pontiac heaves a thunderous belch, shudders along for a few hundred yards, and wheezes to the side of the road at the top of a hill near Pancho's Villa, a sprawling carnival-like motel decked out with faux-bandito themes including a slumbering-Mexican sign whose huge sombrero's brim declares "Mañana's Soon Enough For Me." Big red letters beneath that add:

EL CASA SIESTA
Go-Kart Track
plus
Putt Putt Golf
Gourmet Cuisine
&
Reptile Zoo

There's been a succession of similar signs planted for miles along the road—"La Bomba FIREWORKS Dead Ahead," "MUCHO CATFISH for the kids!" "Last Chance for GAS before Miami (Stock up on Pepto-Bismol NOW!)" with rival billboards interspersed announcing that there'll be "Coming Soon A Jesus-Loves-Me Gospel Resort"—though, judging from the state of those signs, that happy event has been postponed, and, seen in the early-morning light, the Villa itself looks boarded up with the Go-Kart Track in its split-rail corral appearing decidedly moribund.

Dugan himself is dead on his feet as, crossing the highway, he follows a path under a WELCOME AMIGO! sign, hearing a sneeze and a couple of thunks from over by the La Bomba stand. Altering course to peer inside, he encounters a geezer setting up for early-bird pyromaniacs.

"I need a mechanic," Dugan says. "Car broke down just over the road."

"Well, now," the old guy sniffs and nods, gesturing with a sparkler box, "Ronnie Joe Stott, if he wuz hair, could git a dead cat back on his feet. . ."

But Ronnie Joe, as things turn out, "whose wile streak's only been gittin' wuss, went forklift racin' on the track 'n' tore thangs up s' bad he's farred." He's what? "Been farred, done loss his job—so, dead-cat-wise, y're outta luck. . . but take a look at this Gen'l Lee. My bess assortment. Still on sale."

"Maybe a jump start," Dugan says, assessing the odds that he's stumbled across Pa Beasley's long-lost idiot twin—different accent, matching genes.

"Tha'ss a shame," the geezer says. "But hair's the thang, that Stonewall Special's pretty good whether y' got uh car or not."

Dugan looks round for somebody else. He asks, "Where's Pancho?"

"Doin' time."

"Okay, I see the problem here, but maybe you can help me out. I need a ride to Cumbria bad."

"Y' do, huh? Down to Cumbria, eh?" The geezer ponders, chewing his lip, gazing at something far away. "Make me an offer," he suggests.

"You name it."

"Ah." He scans his shelves. "Say, twenty-five even f' Gen'l Lee? An' throw in two Old Glories free."

"Looks like I'm really not getting' through. I got a funeral to attend." He knows it's one he'll hold alone.

"Well, lemme consider," the geezer reflects. His face is like a shriveled fig. "In that case. . . yep, hair's whut I'd do, I'd go with one a-them Fountains o' Doom." He mutters as Dugan walks away, ". . . don' make no noise—jes' sorta fizzles."

Dugan turns round. "How much?" he asks.

The geezer has to stop to think. "Well, now," he perks up, "less see, hair—I reckon I kin let it go. . . f' fourteen-fifty. Second box. . ."

"How much for one?"

"A box?"

"Just one?"

He sucks in hard. "Tha'ss nigh-ny cent. The matchbook hair don' cost a thang—got Pancho's pichure on th' front." As Dugan takes his dollar out, the geezer points up to a shelf. "Y' seen these chicks? They's sump'en else. Hop roun' 'n' lay a little aig."

"Not interested."

"Y' git one free." He drops it in a paper bag, adding a crimson pyramid and pecking out six cents in change. "Shore hope y' fewn'ral goes okay.

Long as y' git y' car cranked up, it's mostly downhill after this." Then, seeing Dugan hesitate, he reaches for a Gen'l Lee.

But Dugan has something else in mind. "What sorta car you driving now?"

"Well, now. . ." His disappointment shows. "I guess. . . my daughter's new Taw-yoda. Sometimes, at lees'." He pauses to suck his teeth again. "She's over to the rayon plant."

"You see that car?"

"That one rite thar?" They study the heap across the road.

"I want you to have it," Dugan says. "Get Ronnie Joe Stott to take a look. There's stuff in the trunk you might can sell. And. . . thanks for the chicken," Dugan adds.

The geezer's gums work up and down. He lets the keys drop in his hand, watching as Dugan strolls away beneath the big sombrero sign. He sees him pass the Pontiac, then stop to wait beside the road. The first car flagged slams on its brakes, a Skylark with a Mo-Town sound.

"Broke down," shouts Dugan. "Need a ride."

"WOO-hoo-oooo!" the music screams. A balding black man cuts the sound. "You headed someplace special, friend?"

"A funeral."

"Amen, ain't we all?" His two front teeth are made of gold. "Don't need no suitcase?"

"Nope."

"Uh-huh. Nekkit we come into this world. Get in, them things don't bother you none." He means the objects piled in back that look like private body parts—plastic nozzles set in disks and ringed with bristly two-inch fuzz. "You lookin' at mah future now!"

"What are they?"

"Washermops, my man! Attach 'em to yo' garden hose an' CLEAN. . . YO'. . . ASS. . . from A-to-Z!"

"Hey!" yells the geezer from his stand.

"Hold on a minute," Dugan says, propping the Skylark's door ajar.

The geezer cranes his neck to the side. "How kin I know this car ain't stole?"

Dugan stalks back to the Pontiac, half-minded to slap it out of gear and let it glide on down the hill. Instead, he finds the title card and props it on the dashboard's rim. The geezer watches with a frown as Dugan pops the trunk lid up and rummages through the stuff he's packed. The Skylark honks and Dugan runs back clutching the Short & Sassy jug and a paper sack half full of clothes.

"So where's yo' funeralizing at?"

He shakes his head. He's not real sure. He knows he's missed the ceremony. "Cumbria ought to fit the bill."

"Uh-huh. I hear you! . . . here we go!"

"WOO-HOO-OOOO!" adds the King of Soul as they're easing back out and picking up speed. Dugan looks round at Pancho's domain and sees, receding on the ridge, a line of blossoming dogwood trees—pink and white and in between, as if, he thinks from far below, the fireworks stand's exploding.

● ● ●

It's gotten close to closing time at Evergreen Eternal Care as Dugan goes shuffling through the gate with the look of a zombie home from work. There's been a changing of the guard—one coming, one going as he arrives. A speed bump slows the day guy down, his Fairlane easing over the hump and down to a saw-horse barrier imposing a left-turn-only rule under the Karnak-like supports that help prop up the Interstate—a speedway over the dead-end spur that Dugan just took to get this far. . . and Danny too, a day ago.

The night guard looks out from his booth and, consulting a clipboard, peers outside—not used to walk-ins it would seem. "You need some help?"

"A friend," croaks Dugan in reply. "Buried here yesterday, I think."

"He got a name?" the guard inquires. His shirt says Clyde across its flap.

"Daniel Rosen," Dugan says.

"Rosen?"

"Yep." He spells it out.

"Don't sound like one of ours," Clyde says.

"Just check, okay?"

"You got a car?"

"It's down the road. I'm here on foot."

"I'll be lockin' up in half an hour. You plannin' to loiter. . ."

"Rosen," Dugan tells him again.

"Well, whatta ya know! He's here all right. Wouldn't-uh thought so." Clyde's perturbed (big mix-up at the Second Coming!) but puts an X down on a map, sketching a route for Dugan to take. "What's in the bag?"

"What bag?"

"Right there."

"Clothes. . . shampoo."

"For what?"

"For what? For algae, Clyde." For scrubbin' that green crud off your graves. "You tellin' me shampoo's contraband?"

"Twenty-six minutes," Clyde declares. "No funny business."

"Funny like what?" Diggin' 'im up 'n' washin' his hair? But Clyde's gone back inside his booth, so Dugan crunches on down the drive, around a circle to the right and, briefly astray, consults the map, pausing beside an obelisk that looks imported from the Nile, then past the Sermon on the Mount and graves of four Confederates with tiny battle flags in the ground. Worried that Clyde has marked it wrong, he veers along the low back slope and there a scalloped awning stands—last hole before the clubhouse turn. The poles are surprisingly cold to the touch, the wired-up flowers without scent. There's a spray with a card from the English Department and a ribbon on which are printed the words

IT CANNOT FAIL THE YOUNG MAN
WHO DIED
AND
WAS BURIED

"Kravitz," thinks Dugan, nodding his head, not bad for a medievalist. He changes his plans for the Fountain of Doom, wedging it at the foot of the mound but lighting the chicken's fuse instead. A shower of sparks shoots out its ass as it hops in a circle and topples over. Two seconds later, he hears a pop. A whitish pellet, two, then three. A tiny sigh. It stops as one more squeezes out.

"Sorry, Dan." He pats the mound. "I shoulda bought the Gen'ral Lee."

• • •

Getting to Caitlin's just before dark, he teeters and sways and rings the bell. It's Millie Doggett who answers the door, recoiling from his haggard look and seemingly more than a little displeased.

"Mike. . . come in. She's resting in back." The room's the same as it's always been except for a pedestal, book, and pen that resemble a Shoney's hostess stand. "You want to sign?"

"What happened?" he asks.

Millie smooths her no-wrinkle skirt. "You know we tried to find you, Mike. Nobody here knew where you were. He wasn't at fault."

"He crashed the Merc?"

"He was driving somebody's else car."

"A g-g-goddamned w-w-white and g-gold Corvette." Caitlin is standing in the hall, looking like Roderick Usher's sister. "Th-They're oh-oh-kay." He doesn't ask who. "D-D-Damned fool was th-thrown out wh-wh-when they wrecked."

"He hit a light pole," Millie says.

In pink pajamas and purple robe, Caitlin's steadied by Millie's arm. "S-S-Sorry, M-Mike." She's shaking her head. "I'm d-d-doped. . . t-to th' gills."

"She's worn out, Mike. She shouldn't be up. You said you'd try to take a nap." This last is said in Caitlin's ear.

"I went to see him," Dugan says.

Caitlin nods and Millie chips in that friends have dropped off lots of food.

"M-M-Millie's in charge. G-G-Get something t-to eat."

"Thanks. That's great. I'll check it out."

A moment of silence while they sit, the women together on the couch and Dugan in Danny's captain's chair. Millie asks him, "Are you. . .?"

"Am I. . .?"

"What?" she says.

"You go ahead," he signals to her.

". . . still camping out in Chantry Mount?"

"I'm nowhere at the moment, Millie."

Like Danny, he thinks. She starts to speak, but Caitlin says, "I'm okay, M-M-Mill. R-Really I am. Y-You g-g-go on home."

Millie pats her. "Are you sure?" When Caitlin nods, she looks around. "Well, let me find my pocketbook. So nice to see you, Mike," she says.

"You too." He stands and follows her out, walking her towards her station wagon.

"School day tomorrow," Millie says. "It's good for her to get back in the swing. But she's really exhausted." Then she adds, "Try to be tactful, won't you, Mike?" She drives off without looking back.

Back in the house, he shuts the door, then stops as if he's lost his way. He's hardly slept for the past three days, and Caitlin's struggling to wake up.

"P-P-Poor, M-Millie. Sh-She's f-found religion."

Discovering that he's really whipped, he sits where the pocketbook had been at the end of the sofa Caitlin's on. She reaches out to pat his hand.

"You l-look t-t-terrible, M-Mike."

"You're one to talk."

A pause, and then it comes to him that none of it's happened after all. It's been a mistake, yet there they sit as if complicit in the charade. Maybe it's true we're flashes and specks, but Danny and Rose? That can't be so. (Rewind the reel and start it over, the movie that changes each time through. Carve something from nothing for their sakes. Sit like a pharaoh, hand on knee, lips compressed like granite slabs into a sneer of cold command.

My name is Mitchell Dugna, pee aitch dee. . .

It's happening. He's almost there. Only his eyes are able to move.) He feels a pain in his diaphragm.

"L-L-Lie down and r-r-rest." She stoops to lift his feet to the sofa.

He'd meant to console but should have known. He's not much good at helping people.

• • •

During the night a blanket appears. He pulls the cover over his head and dreams the thing that lives in the ditch is burrowing all over now, its furrows humped like varicose veins, gorging on people Dugan knows. He watches a tiny rooster run a zigzag path through no-man's land—past fountains of doom with lilies erupting, the tunnel pursuing like a shark.

He wakes up with a plaintive shout, yanking the blanket off his face, and finds it's daylight. By his head, a note's been propped for him to read, but he dawdles until he's pissed away the remnants of his dismal dream

341

(indebted to Goya, he concludes, which being with Caitlin might explain). Finding he's missed his aim at first, he wads some toilet paper up and uses it to wipe the floor. Then he's ready to read the note, which tells him that Caitlin's gone to school—what Millie had meant, they're teaching together. The funeral feast is in the fridge, she'll see him sometime around four.

11:10. He rubs his neck. The watch moves on but not his brain which has a phrase go flapping through like Lickety-Splitters on the lam, words from the poem he'd read to Rose:

I am to wait. . . I am to wait. . .

Undoubtedly, yes, but wait for what? If the answer can't be either of them, not Rose or Danny, what remains? End Times, of course, the body cart (Monday/Thursday pick-up days, remember to leave your stiffs by the curb) or the Peaceable Kingdom Cumbria-style (not that he's certain what that would be—Glubber and Gordo sipping tea while Dexter rolls joints for the students to puff?) His neck again. Waiting can't be the answer, though, since evil is real and loose in the world. What's up, he wonders, with his skin? It's shrunk. Somehow it doesn't fit.

He looks in the mirror over the sink and sees a fugitive from his dream (*Attack of the Mushroom People*—gahhhhh!) His head's a runny swollen lump studded with boils and eyes squeezing shut. He tries to think what he should do. Get something to eat, he tells himself. He finds a baked ham in the fridge (enough like him to be a clone) and picks at a bit—but eating's hard, taking more effort than it's worth. So you're waiting then, the inner voice clucks. He hobbles into the living room and sits in front of the blank TV.

When Caitlin returns at 4:05, the light has grown crepuscular (no jokes this time, he likes the dark) with a sycamore throwing heavy shade along the driveway's side of the house. He hears her in the kitchen next, unpacking some Piggly Wiggly bags along with comfort food from friends and, after a short while, calling his name. So Gregor the Cockroach shuffles in while she's still crouched with her arms in the fridge clearing some space for a carton of milk that nudges a bowl that bumps a jar that causes the three-bean salad to fall, splattering on the vinyl floor. She curses, glancing down and up, sees him, and mutters, "G-G-Good God!"

"What?" he weakly suppurates. She leads him over to the light.

"Ch-Ch-Chicken pox?"

"Had it," he says.

"Sh-Sh-Shingles then." She looks annoyed but, as she speaks, her voice is lost in a grinding roar from a garbage truck that's stopped outside (collecting trash at 4:15?). She tries to shout above the din, but all he hears are question marks. Like where's he staying? Where's his car? What're his plans for teaching again? The truck emits some piercing dings to indicate it's moving on while he, by contrast, merely shrugs. He's got no car, he has no plan. She raises her hands with fingers spread as if to ward off an assault.

"N-N-No way, M-Mike! I c-can't handle that now."

What? he asks with rheumy eyes, knowing she's got an empty back room.

"Y-You kn-kn-know damn well, th-the two of you. . . f-forget it, no!"

"Okay," he nods. "No problem, babe. I'll help clean up, and then I'll go." He reaches towards the shattered bowl, then hesitates. "Like looking in a mirror, huh?" He utters a brief sardonic snort, scraping the beans into a clump and taking two handfuls to the sink, dripping a trail across the floor. "Same problem, you know, that bowl and me. We both got dropped. . . makes a hell of a mess," He smears the trickle with his shoe, observing with another shrug, "*Mais c'est comme ça que le monde se roule*." Then, leering morosely, he's the Heap, displaying the speckled wart-like beans that web the fingers of both hands. "Sorry if that was your supper, babe." She glares at him, then starts to laugh. He gestures weakly, trying to smile. "I'd hug you, but. . ."

"D-D-Don't even consider it!"

"What?"

"M-M-Move!" She grabs a paper-towel roll, then kneels and sits back on her heels, her face contorted by her grief. "G-G-Goddamnit, M-Mike. . ." He knows she's going to relent but thinks it's nothing to do with him. It's all about those fountains of doom past which they try to make their way. "I s-s-screwed up b-bad," she says to him or not to him, then looks away.

"Me too," he says. He's catching on. "I meant t' keep this face in the attic." After a pause he shrugs again. "But considering J. P. Morgan's nose, with looks like these I'll make a mint. Speaking of which, how's my man Dough?"

"Th-That little shit. A sy-sycophant. He. . . n-n-never mind. I m-mean it, Mike. If I l-l-let you stay. . ."

"What?" he says as if Danny was there, drawing these two survivors together.

"N-No d-d-dipsy-doodle."

"I swear it, babe. Just for a while. I'm Fixable."

"L-L-Like hell you are!" She tosses the worst of the mess in the trash, then, wiping the spot and shaking her head, tells him she'll see what nostrums she's got to deal with his loathsome skin disease.

He follows behind her, trailing beans, leaving the door of the fridge ajar.

● ● ●

He knows (O Agnes! O my soul!) how things work out for Copperfield when Dora's gone and, sadder but wiser, the hero screws the girl next door. Zhivago's law should kick in now, but won't because, as he also knows, the principle's electro-magnetic—it works if you live at a headlong pace. . . and he's just moseying at an ooze.

The welcome wagon never arrives to celebrate his moving in. The neighbors dismiss him with a nod, their dogs no longer bother to bark, and, after less than a week has passed, Caitlin's lost interest in his scabs that dry and harden and then flake off. For his part, he's more jaundiced too, noting how heavily she clomps, how studied her stutter sometimes seems (like Brits with lisps, he tells himself), how forbiddingly she keeps to herself—he's merely the lodger, he perceives and, reflexively while she's at school, goes prowling about the empty house feeling self-loathing and remorse like Agee betraying the Gudgers' trust, inspecting her closets, drawers, and shelves—blouses and underwear carefully stacked, stockings stored in clam-like wads—finding it all banal and sad, though never presuming to enter the room she uses as her studio.

For two or three days he watches TV but can't avoid disquieting news. Cambodia's truly falling apart. The NLF and Viet Cong are launching increasingly brazen thrusts. In June, the U.S. troops withdraw to positions inside the Parrot's Beak. The bombing goes on, and Nixon insists the incursion has been a big success.

There's not much else for him to do that wouldn't require more commitment from him than he's ready to give to anything. When he learns his medical leave's expired, he postpones looking for a job, concluding that nothing will matter again unless he deludes himself with lies and finding that lying wears him out. He's got enough cash for a couple of months and, by mooching and scrounging, two or three more. The only fly in his anomie is that Caitlin's recovering day by day while he, in the course of his numb descent, can see that the bottom's still far off. They try to talk but discover they can't, adopting a sort of Trappist regime—wordless and sexless, full of grief, locked in bleak penance for their sins.

He frequents a shopper's matinee at a shopper-less mall on the outskirts of town located between an Oldsmobile lot (owned by a man from the Cotton Boll Ball, the one who'd ventured a dirty shag) and a V.A. facility treating burns for servicemen back from Vietnam. Once or twice he goes on foot, but mostly he gets there on the bus along with maids returning from work plus an affable half-wit in a cap with LOVE stitched rakishly on its bill—the Oldsmobile dealership's name, he learns, musing on what his own might say (SPACE AVAILABLE, he decides). After they've shared the bus for a week, the halfwit waves at him and grins, then dogs his tracks when they get to the mall as if assuming they're a team.

This sometimes thwarts his movie plans—a gibbering seat-mate's hard to take but shaking him off proves harder still. Dugan tries stepping back on a bus or losing his sidekick in the mall while missing the previews and cartoon. No matter, he thinks—it's all the same.

Though Caitlin's V-W is all she drives, he never asks to use the Merc and is not even sure where it's been stowed. But worldliness is not the point. His mindset's like Brad Tittlewhit's as Ahmed the Sufi Movie Buff finds meaning in the humblest things, like smelling exhaust fumes in the street or urinal cakes in pee-stained bowls, evoking a time when things made sense and life was orderly and pure. . . and when was that? (wrong answer to seek—as long as it floats, you cling to it). One day, after faking the half-wit out, he sits through Elvis's *Trouble with Girls* two or three times before he leaves. But most days, when he boards the bus, the driver smirks that his buddy's in back, and Dugan says he should show some respect "for Strontium's illegitimate son." (Who knows? he shrugs, it could be true.)

The movies he takes pretty much as they come until he encounters a Peckinpah film with Mexicans getting shot to rags while some hooky-playing kids down front shout "Groovy!" as the bloodbath grows. It sickens him too much to stay, and after that he doesn't go back.

Needing a new itinerary, he checks the public library out, sitting with fidgety sociopaths looking for pornographic scraps and distracting himself with curious facts picked up at random in the stacks. He learns, for instance, browsing about, that, back in 1924, a Labrador retriever ("Pep") had killed Mrs. Gifford Pinchot's cat. The murder occurred in Harrisburg, and Mrs. Pinchot, the Governor's wife, had the culprit convicted and jailed for life as inmate C2559, "without parole" (and on a leash) until found dead in his prison cell, much grieved for by his fellow cons. He should have become a famous dog.

Then, feeling he might be on a roll, he stumbles across the intriguing fact that, according to Chinese calendars, they're currently in the Year of the Dog. Synchronicity! Jung and Danny would say, though coincidence is Dugan's take. Still, making connections trumps despair in a modestly cabbalistic way.

Enthralled by such arcane success, he spends a couple of feckless days perusing a fifty-year-old edition of something called *The Book of Knowledge*—from "How to Make Splints for Injured Friends" to "Rolling Across the Firth of Forth" and "Things a Boy Can Make And Do" (a table from a cheese box, say) followed by "Chinese Fairy Tales." He puts the heavy volume down and asks a shy librarian—with mailbox torso, stringy hair, and stockings that only a WAC would wear—a question the fairy tales bring to mind. In Chinese, what does *"Yún Yǔ"* mean? Its orthography? He's not quite sure.

"That's quite a challenge," she observes, looking him primly up and down. She'll need a few minutes. While she's gone, he takes a leak, then rolls across the Firth of Forth and studies some things to make and do. She's at her desk when he returns.

"Here's what it looks like in Chinese." She opens a book and points it out:

$$云雨$$

She'd called a Chinese-speaking friend. "The *Yún* means 'clouds.' The *Yǔ* is 'rain.' When added together they make 'a storm.'" She lowers her eyes. "In certain situations, though. . ." A flush is creeping up her neck. ". . . when mountains are also in the mix, it's. . . very erotic."

"Clouds and rain?"

"With mountains especially. Yes," she adds.

"That's very poetic."

She nods at him appraisingly. "It's apparently used in poetry a lot."

Her eyes are steadily on his, but as he leaves he looks around and finds her studying something else. The sound of his shoes is a whispery sluff on the scuffed gray slate of the library floor.

• • •

It drizzles all day on a Monday in June a month after moving to Caitlin's back room. Having prised a kitchen window up and leaning his forehead against the screen, he's watching the runoff from the eaves when Caitlin's V-W comes up the drive, its taillights flaring and going dim. He waits and hears the sound of her heels on brick, linoleum, rug, and floor. Doors open and close, and her voice calls out from her bedroom nearer the front of the house.

"M-M-Mike, you here?"

"Uh-huh," he yells.

In the midst of her usual costume change from teacher to artist in one quick swap, he hears a train five blocks away, and then, in the hall behind him again, her voice approaching the kitchen.

"H-H-How was y-your day?" An open housecoat over her slip, her hairbrush tugging at her hair. He notes her skivvies come from Sears, no lace or fancy scalloped seams.

He offers her a brief report. "I got stuff done. A little research. . . and that window there I got unstuck."

Her brush gets tangled in a knot. She utters a sort of petulant cluck, so matter of fact that it crosses his mind she's using his anomie as a gauge to measure her own recovery by. "There's something I'd like. . ." he starts to say, reverses field and asks instead, "Can I see what you've been working on. . . in there?" he points towards her studio.

"W-Why?" she frowns. She weighs the brush.

"I need a reason?"

She slaps the brush against her palm. Then, turning and leading him down the hall, she opens a door and reaches inside, flipping a light switch, moving a box, motioning him across the tarps past canvas and hardboard stacked ten deep. The odor of turpentine is strong with just a whiff of cantaloupe.

He utters a banality. "You spend a lot of time in here."

She shrugs and lets him look around, not picking out what he should see. He studies two paintings by the door—stripes heavy and dark like power lines writhing across a yellowish sky and knotted like ganglia in the brain or spiders smashed against a wall. A few are fruit bowls, rotting away, but others are force fields teeming with life, intricate whorls like hurricane maps or segments of anatomy—crotches or jungles, who can say?

He looks at her but gets no clue. She's folded her arms sardonically, high haunches propped on golf-club feet (like Popeye's Olive Oil, he thinks, unnerved again by her restraint, unsure if he really knows her at all). He's noticed of late—he can't say why—her ass is not so bony now (the world pads everyone, he thinks, and afterwards many get stouter in some of the padded places). It also sometimes crosses his mind that, in her emphatically Irish way, she's close to looking homely.

"So, t-t-tell me, M-Mike. . . wh-whatta you think?"

"Scary. . . impressive. I don't know. They look abstract, but somehow they're not."

"R-R-Right. Y-You l-l-like abstractions?"

"Is music abstract? It is, and it isn't."

"Uh-huh." She says, dissatisfied. "S-So how about th-this one then?" Plucking one out that faces the wall, she turns it towards him. "W-W-Well?" she says. She waits a beat. "It's Adlai."

"Sure. He's driving a car," he says. "In Danny's hat, I see that now."

"Th-The eyes," she says.

"They look just like him." Not the dog.

"Aw-Awful."

"Yeah."

She lays a finger on her chest.

"I know," he says. He really does.

• • •

On July fifth a Lon Nol court condemns Prince Sihanouk to death, which Dugan discovers the following day while tossing a Coke can into a bin. He's at a bus stop, headed uptown, when, glancing into the pile of trash, he sees a recent *Impeder* on top and, reading a headline, gets the gist.

He gets further informed by the reference librarian who, first, provides the Sunday *Times*, according to which the agile prince has escaped to the arms of Chairman Mao and next, through a bit of field research, reveals that, whatever Dugan might be, he's not so fixable after all.

Things had seemed more promising at eleven when he'd arrived in the reading room. He remembers his sense of mild elation, supposing there'd been a subtle change—not to the winos held transfixed studying Smirnoff ads in *Life* or teenaged boys ogling the models in *Vogue* (seniors out on a study-hall break from Dugan's old high school just next door) or girls with books propped under their boobs like Swedes in March with sun reflectors. Even the overwrought woman scribbling away in Blue Horse notebooks seemed on course for what for her was a typical day. The change was in himself, he thought, and somehow for the better.

By noon the study-hall crowd was gone along with the clutch of restlessly homeless guys who'd move outside when it wasn't too hot. At two the Blue Horse woman left, leaving just him and Edie—short for Edwina he'd deduced from the name on the reference librarian's desk. He was back on his *Book of Knowledge* kick ("Are Stones Alive?" "Why Icebergs Float") when he happened to lift his head and saw that she was closely studying him. Reflexively, he answered her gaze, feeling his libido stir.

She'd looked away, but once aroused, he was conjuring wild scenarios. . . of her cardigan doffed, the brogans gone, her hair unpinned and tumbling down as he came towards her through the rain—through clouds and rain with mountains included—his manhood yearning to be free (Oh, Mike, she'd gasp pedantically, it's truly. . . *brobdingnagian!*)

A half-hour later, the AC fails, and a man comes in to set up fans that rustle *Die Zeitung* on its rack. But heat and humidity thin the crowd that might have gathered that time of day, and, once again, by half-past three, only the two of them are there. . . Dugan and Edie, she in her *Britannica* lair, and he in his *Book of Knowledge* retreat. His trousers are stuck to the backs of his legs. Her glasses have gotten so misted up that it takes both hands to pluck them off, but reaching back to pat her hair, she meets his stare with brazen resolve.

He responds by going to her desk. "I'm trying to find a poem," he says. She rises so they're face to face. "I only remember a couple of words." He leans to write them on her pad, and she leans too—they're leaning together over her pad like intimates in a sauna bath deciphering what he's written down. "Passing stranger. . ." he reads his scrawl (with a twinge of self-loathing for his maneuver, using the poem he'd read to Rose—but there it is, already at work in Edie/Edwina's fertile mind). ". . . you do not know. . ." he quotes the rest. A drop of sweat falls on the pad. "How something or other," he breaks off.

"Right-o," she says. Her cheeks are flushed, the hair in wisps about her ears. "Give me a minute. Let me think. . ." She pats her glasses back in place and hunts through several reference books. No luck so far.

Could it be Whitman? he wonders aloud. He's not sure why but thinks it might.

"We'll try the stacks, then," she replies as if that means the Forest of Arden.

He follows her deep into the gloom.

"Whitmannn. . ." she drawls in a gravelly voice. "Whitman. Whitman. Here, let's see." Cradling a volume with one hand, she flips through its index with the other. Then "Ha!" she cries out huskily, her eyes lit up in triplicate (trifocal allure, he's persuading himself). She points lines out and, as they bend even closer together, their foreheads touch, she leans her shoulder into his, and everything has been agreed. "You do not know. . ." she reads the line,

> . . . how longingly I look upon you

as if he's written it for her. A trickle of sweat runs down his back. The light from overhead is dim. "It's truly beautiful," she declares.

He looks at her as if to say she'd be at least as beautiful too. . . without her specs, her Doctor Scholl's, her sesquipedalian inhibitions—all three of which get quickly chucked when, after an early closing time, she drives them to her hideaway which is strikingly like a Shaker museum except for the houseplants everywhere in pots and boxes, on the sills, trailing from bureaus, tables, and shelves, sprouting and spreading, intermeshed, sending out tendrils under the door. "My babies," Edie lovingly says, stroking a clump of St. John's Wort. He thinks at once of Coach Ray Don and the front porch of his paramour—a vegetative sisterhood.

It's down to business after that. She asks if he'd like something to drink, gesturing vaguely at a shrub. He shakes his head, aware he's in a Circe's den. "This is quite a place you've got," he says. "Yes," she nods complacently, "I like to keep up with my friends."

At first he thinks she means the plants, then notes the copious postcard display she's tacked and taped throughout her pad so that only the pictures can be seen except on the pantry cabinets' doors which, when opened, reveal what the senders had said—like one in Spanish sent by Brad, two from Roberto in Milan, and "*Ciao, chybíš mi!*" from. . . smiley face (people lead unexpected lives).

The bathroom features Xeroxed verse by Roethke, Yeats, and Levertov—all of it carnal, some of it lewd. Franz Marc horses line the hall, a Matisse poster's over the bed, and, though he doesn't see it at first, a large cat's crouching in the ferns like something out of Henri Rousseau.

"What's that?"

"It's Klimt. I love his work."

She evidently means the cat.

"Here, Klimt." He tries to scratch its head while lounging with her on the quilt. But then he sees another cat appearing from underneath the bed.

"Oh, him," she says. "That's Papageno."

"No Klimts except for the cat?" he asks.

"The one on the ceiling," she replies.

"Why, so it is!" When supine, she can study *The Kiss*. "By any chance, you sing to the cat?"

"Why would I?"

Dugan starts to trill, "Pa-pa-pa-pa. . .!"

She utters a noise. He sees she's nude. "Shoo! Get away!" she's chiding Klimt, who dashes at him and disappears.

"You little bastard!"

"What?" she purrs.

"He scratched me! Look!"

"He's envious." She's stretched across the opulent quilt. "He always hates my friends," she yawns, chuckling with myopic lust. Obligingly, he strokes her chest, but finds no handhold, only knobs, looking like bottle caps nailed to a wall. She squirms to redirect his hand. He finds her tongue (it's in his mouth) but finds his mind is wandering. The pain he's been feeling in his back since bouncing the millstone off the bluff has reappeared in his diaphragm, prodding his sternum and fading away, and a memory of Rose returns again as Edie decides to take him in hand—like what? He gropes for similes. A spray attachment for a sink? Or more like licorice in the sun? His own hand's stopped. She does her best to keep him up, tweaking him like a swizzle stick—until, with a contemptuous hiss, she mutters in Latin and turns him loose. "*Inutilis vermis!*" she declares.

"Useless worm," as he recalls, though what she'd meant was *nunc dimittis*. "*Vale*," he grunts by way of reply, wishing that he could share the thought that, anyhow, no matter how horny he might have been, she's too Swarthmoric for him (Danny would have applauded that). It's good-bye to mornings in the stacks, to Books of Knowledge and "Things To Do," but one less thing to worry about as he watches her rise to leave the bed.

In a moment or two she passes back through while slipping a caftan over her head, making it clear their tryst is done—though, even so, he takes his time, still detumescent on his back, hearing her pour herself a drink. When he looks up, it's straight at Klimt who's sizing his wounded rival up. He sees himself through the animal's eyes—less than a postcard-scribbler from Prague, a shagged out sleeping gypsy.

• • •

If Caitlin guesses he's been on the prowl, she's playing it cool or doesn't care. It's time, he knows, for him to leave, but his mind goes blank when he thinks about where. Then, marking time one afternoon, he leafs through stacks of *The Impeder* piled up where Adlai's bowl once stood on the floor of the washer-dryer room.

Old news can't hurt you, he assumes as, browsing through local events and notes, he hits on Billie Swick's feature piece, "War Bride Scores in Beauticians' Olympics." He thinks that must surely have been In-Ho but learns the competitors all were in-state and, furthermore, as a subhead announced, that a "Renaissance Man" was first runner-up." Though a photo left no doubt in the matter, its caption was Billie at her best:

> Balancing brawn with brains and braids, the former Rooster running back and first-round Washington Redskins' pick, J.C. ("Jolie Coiffe") Kingdom.

He remembers his ride, a year ago, in J.C.'s new convertible (a tumbrel cart as things turned out), the sulky glossy-skinned girls in back, his bedlam with Rose just barely begun, and, suddenly, there in the laundry room, it's Danny whose voice he hears again, expounding on his "freedom summer" from back in his halcyon college days—"like Odysseus on a Greyhound bus," his endless trek to a Catskill resort, getting a job, and setting to work only to find a temptress there (What was her name? Now

Dugan goes blank. Clarissa? he fumbles. No, *Clarice*!) "High yallah from Brooklyn," Danny would sigh "like Dorothy Dandridge at nineteen."

She was a salad girl, he was a runner, losing his fool white head on sight and making it plain to everyone there. "One look," he'd groaned as he conjured it up, one meal in the kitchen with the staff, perched on the ladder's lowest rung, mesmerized by her arrogant smirk after she'd leaned across his arm, straightened her back and called him out: "You reachin' beyond yo' means," she said, letting him sniff that heady aroma, matching his accent with her own. After that, he didn't get close. She boogied around with the dishwashing crew who, varied in hue from black to brown and, while sullen or silent with the Man, shot hoops on a backboard by their shack and screwed their way through the waitressing staff ("not all of it smoked," a busboy grinned, the youngest and blackest of the group, known to the older guys as Goat). But Dan was too smitten to stay away.

"Wuss happ'nin', Goat, you seen Clarice?"

Mid-afternoon, their only break. The black guys into some three-on-three when he showed up, the hipster Yid.

"Say what?"

"Clarice?"

"Y'all look out now!" Goat laughed and clapped. "He hopin' to *score*!"

A scuffle ending in a dunk.

"Oh, yeah? With who?" asked the guy with the ball.

"Cla-*rice*!"

"Awright!" A knowing laugh.

"Any you guys know where she went?"

Wiping some sweat off with his arm, one of them looked back with a snort. "Man, you better get in *line*. She been cuttin' the lettuce with Eddie the cook!"—Eddie the Ku Klux breakfast chef, who's supposedly spit in the pancake batter whenever mixed couples came to dine. Danny managed a painful smile. A waiter built like a Watusi prince came over with both hands on the ball. He leaned down close and said with a look that ended up more like a grimace, "You take yo' weenie someplace else."

They assembled a scrum surrounding him, but Danny stubbornly stood his ground. . . and, right on cue, Clarice appeared—her tennis-ball tits strapped high on her chest, her skin like butter melting in syrup.

"Whoa!" said one.

"Hey, girl," hailed another.

Then, like a contestant out to lunch on a re-run of *The Dating Game*, Danny stepped up. "Hi, babe," he drawled with his white Southern twang, "you wanna go look around in town?" He knew, of course, what the answer would be. The brothers, knowing her answer too, waited for her to deliver it.

"For what?" she asked, all innocent.

"For nothing," he shrugged. "For jazzin' around."

"Guess not," she smiled.

"Come on, Clarice!" mocked one of the guys as the Watusi prince started bouncing the ball and straight away the game resumed.

"You sure?" asked Danny.

Of course, he knew she was always sure. But one day when the guys were off, she took him down to where she stayed, just nodded and led him by the belt down past the recreation room. A ping pong game was underway—two white kids tapping back and forth. Petat petok petat petok. . . a dully metronomic sound like something blipped from a machine.

Clarice looked back. She smelled like soap, a lilac scent that was everywhere inside her sparsely furnished room—a chair, a bed, a cheap bureau with doilies and some magazines. . . *Ebony, Jet,* and a *Harper's Bazaar* that must have been left behind in a room. He was wondering where the brothers had gone—when, abruptly, the ping pong noises stopped and she was beneath him on the bed, laid out like half of Africa. The drums were throbbing in his head. Bull elephant in mid-stampede, he plunged ahead through the underbrush, his trumpeting stifling all in his path except his own must-crazed desire.

"White boy. . ." she sniped.

He thundered on. The voice persisted by his ear, as cold as scissors snipping chives.

". . . you fuckin' with yo' brains," she said.

The great trunk drooped. The drums were still.

(Whenever he'd told this in the past, Danny would fold his hands and say, "Make Love Not War, Arbeit Macht Frei. . . the thing about slogans, goyishe one. . . is that they invariably miss the point." He'd wait for Dugan's hand to rise. "A question there?" Yes, Dugan would ask, isn't their point precisely that—that everything's simpler than you'd thought? From Danny there'd come a pitying smile. "The opposite is true, in fact. Nothing is simple," he'd insist. "Not love, not war, not black or white. . . and here's the axiom that you've missed: one of them presupposes the other. Like subject and object, Comrade Mike, like fucker and fuckee, rich and poor. Like man and woman, little brother.")

Sitting in Caitlin's kitchen now, he goes back over what Danny was saying, how difference and danger intermix—and, disturbingly, what he grasps too late is that Danny was right in a crucial respect: what ought to be simple never is if the subject is sex or race or war. What lies at the heart of that anecdote—he now perceives, as he hadn't before—is what he'd merely glimpsed in the ditch, all that he's tried so hard to suppress. . . that, often in ways we can't explain, battle, murder, and sudden death get fused in some inescapable way to sex and race and cruelty. And what if that's unavoidable, locked in the very nature of things? Spotting a hand, a foot, a face, he tiptoes for a closer look. At first just pork chops in a fridge, a jumble of bodies, market-day clothes. . . but then, for an instant, he truly sees and, just for that moment, thinks he knows: that girl again, she's on her back, legs splayed like oars for a single scull (Whoo-ee! Awright! Hey, look out now!) Her head thrown back, she's skimming the ditch, dreamily reaching for the stroke. He tries to shout, but she can't hear—and who will do what we beg to have done, reverse the film, undo the fact? The murderous white boys glare at the throng. Sun glints on their guns as it happens again—at My Lai, Babi Yar, Wounded Knee. Goddammit, thinks Dugan, the time will come, gathering over all our heads and blossoming like the face of God ("on the ultimate beach at the end of the world," he'd said to Rose as they looked at the river, "together we'll watch the sun explode"), settling all our past accounts and filling all the ditches of hell. Gray level waste from here to there. The skeleton of a building's dome. A shadow burned into a bridge.

• • •

When reports of a massacre hit the press, nine out of ten in a St. Louis poll had been certain the story was a lie. When the Army admitted it was true, five soldiers were singled out for blame, prompting some congressmen to declare that the men had been under exceptional stress and not of sound mind on that difficult day. But psychiatrists said that wasn't the case so far as excusing what they'd done, and what most at home were loath to concede began to seem irrefutable—that American troops deployed in the field, out on a routine search-and-destroy, had butchered civilians in cold blood. Men, women, and children had been killed, dozens and possibly hundreds of them.

"Including the babies?" a questioner asked.

"Including the babies," Calley said.

The photographs had clinched the case—so horrifically well that, as Dugan keeps working through the stack of *Times*, *Impeders*, and *Mother Jones* piled up below the Borateem, he finds he's merely skimming accounts while wholly absorbed by what he sees. . . and, bit by bit, they come to life, like peering at a zoetrope, as he studies them obsessively, plumbing the depths of grief and guilt as if to explain what's happened to Rose or, forcing himself to look again, as if he'd been there at the ditch and she that villager, Nguyen Thi Cung, attempting to shield her black-banged child—Sudath or Thary in his mind, whichever of them might be a girl—for that infinite moment at shutter speed as bullets are hovering in mid-air, their flesh not torn, their lives not done. Then Rose becomes the shuddering girl and something short-circuits in his brain as moving by hair-breadths, frame by frame, the bullets continue on their way like the hooves of Muybridge's galloping horse gathered successively out of time. But nothing can call them back again.

Not all that he sees concerns the ditch. Some shots depict the Zippo squad torching a village, hut by hut, or working together to poison a well. One photo shows two shirtless men at ease inside their An Khe bunker with *Playboy* centerfolds on the wall under a tacked-up Stars-'n'-Bars. One of the two is quoted as saying, "We were trying to work with these people, you know. They were basically doing a number on us. You didn't trust them anymore. . . You didn't trust anybody."

That was the case with Company C. They had a duty, which they did—though Mike Wallace had interviewed a vet who was haunted, he said, by what he'd done. "Some days. . . some nights, I just can't sleep. . . They were begging and saying, No, No, No. And mothers were hugging their children" too. But he'd kept firing even though "they was waving their arms and begging."

For many, including that man himself, our soldiers—like the people they killed—were the victims of something out of control. The Tet offensive had been a shock, following which adjustments were made. Company C was redeployed to a dodgier province called Quang Ngai where, on the eve of Task Force Barker, one of their number was shot and killed by an enemy who, as Calley would put it, couldn't be seen or touched or felt. They saw hundreds of villagers during their sweep, though briefings had claimed they wouldn't be there or that, if they were, they'd be VC. "And when you saw children?" the men were asked in a later review of what they'd done. "In the end," said one in Calley's platoon, whoever they might encounter that day "was potentially the enemy." The soldiers were both white and black, and, of those who'd reportedly taken part, some killed, some watched, some walked away. Still others would try to bury reports where nobody else was likely to look—and no one had, until a vet, because incensed, wrote a letter about reports he'd heard to both Congress and the Pentagon. His name was Ronald Ridenhour. He hadn't been present at My Lai 4, he merely repeated what he'd been told, supported by facts he'd managed to learn while still on duty in Vietnam.

Mitigating those facts in some people's eyes were blunders in intelligence, misleading the taskforce launched that day from LZ Dottie towards My Lai, believing that it had been confirmed the string of five hamlets along the coast was the base of the VC 45th. The name itself was in dispute—some called it Song My instead of My Lai. Even before its recent loss, C Company had been under strength and smarting from charges they thought unfair of a lack of initiative in the field. They'd planned to prove themselves that day, and their orders were unambiguous: remove, resolve, eradicate whatever resistance they might meet.

Dugan pauses in his search, steeling himself for what he'll find. March 16th was the crucial day, the year was 1968. By 13:30 that afternoon, the body count had started to rise with 90 VC reportedly killed, two dozen combatants detained, 3 weapons found, one casualty (a PFC whose rifle was jammed had cleared it while aiming at his foot). In later reports the numbers had changed—just 3 or 4 VC said to be killed, none detained, all others described as "collateral damage" for which estimates varied significantly. Combining all units involved that day, CID thought 400 were killed. The Vietnamese said 567, though that included a separate count of 90 civilians slaughtered nearby in a separate but parallel incident.

Irregularities were confirmed: two women were beaten with rifle butts, a girl was forced into sodomy and executed afterwards (a "double veteran" in army slang for killing a woman who'd just been raped). One soldier fired a .45 at an infant found lying on the ground. Heckled about his lousy aim, he'd approached and shot it in the head. In accordance with orders not in dispute, hooches were burned and animals killed and dumped methodically into wells. Having witnessed several similar acts, a combat photographer later said, "I knew it was something that shouldn't be happening, but yet I was part of it. . ." A handful of soldiers opted out, appalled by what was going on. Some took part, they'd later allege, merely to see what it was like. Still others went on a killing spree, unable to stop once they'd begun, ripping up women between their legs and finishing off any wounded who moaned.

Upon learned that such things had occurred, the Secretary of State declared it to be "a shocking, shocking incident" without using the "M" word even once (as was the case with every official discussing it as an "alleged" event), though the general public had been assured that justice would soon be implacably served—a promise preceding a terse report that all charges had been dismissed in the case of Lt. Willingham and officers outranking him. It was Willingham's men who'd carried out the "parallel incident" at Co Luy, but acknowledging that would counter the claim that My Lai was anomalous. So that part of the story was erased.

By mid-July a solution was clear, the My Lai "lone-assassin" conclusion with a message designed to reassure: William L. Calley has shamed us all, get rid of him and the problem's resolved so we can get on with saving the world. "The weed of crime bears bitter fruit" reverberates in Dugan's mind—but just one weed our authorities say. . . one Judas, one Cain, one Typhoid Mary, one SS guard at Buchenwald. What exactly does The Shadow know about what lurks in the hearts of men? Only, it seems, that it's been purged

Dugan's gets this far in his search when he runs across an *Impeder* account—"Local Vet to Testify/A Fracas Under the Microscope"—of a Hollis O. Marlowe PFC, one of the soldiers at My Lai who hadn't fired, who'd walked away, and whose name evokes in Dugan's mind a marginal, obstinate, dangerous guy he hasn't seen since junior high. . . improbable but maybe so as, there in the laundry room's dim recess between the Tide and Borateem, he carves a metaphorical ditch, pours milk and honey, water and wine, and calls the shade of Hollis up.

• • •

In Dugan's mind he'd deemed it Homeric, but only because he'd read the Classic Comic. Though rumored at the time to be as old as twenty, Hollis was probably seventeen, swarthy and hulking like a bear, a "lifer" at Tillman Junior High. He boasted he'd failed a couple of grades plus doing some time in juvenile—though his rival and capo, Jay Dee Sikes, claimed Hollis had just been a ward of the court along with Lester Serio, who spoke some language of his own and tended to slink along the walls in heated discussions with himself. Lester had slunk to a special new school two months into Dugan's seventh-grade year, and, bigger and older than anyone else, Hollis was ceded the elbow room of any large predator on the prowl, trailed by a pasty rat-faced crew kowtowing to him as Number Two in the vaguely menacing riffraff pack the inmates knew as "Jay Dee's Gang"—otherwise labeled mill-kid scuzz headed for First Manassas High *en route* to study time in jail.

For guys just entering puberty, especially from better neighborhoods, Hollis and Jay Dee loomed like trolls under a bridge they all had to cross— and the closest thing to Billy Goat Gruff was a teacher who'd fought in World War II, ex-Sergeant Russell Vigaree, Assistant to the Principal (a fidgety evasive man with nicotine stains on either hand who counted on Vigaree's martial air to help keep order at the school). But Vigaree's POW years had left him with issues of his own, and law-abiders waited in vain for him to butt heads with either troll who, emboldened by Vigaree's restraint, together had cowed the vocational track that centered on Shop class after lunch where Dugan the whiz kid came up lame—a duffer whose tie racks wasted wood. And why was he there in vocational ed? Because his school had phased out art and this was the closest thing they had. The girls took Home Ec, he took Shop and, after Shop, Mechanical Drawing. In a way, this taught him a useful truth, since Hollis, who struggled to print his name, could manage the ripsaw like a pro—as did Jay Dee who, younger and smaller by half a foot, had come from Hollis's part of town, known for its curly-haired sepia whites whose racial pedigrees weren't discussed (not openly. . . though now and then, when backs were turned, the term "brass-ankle" might be heard from those of a suicidal bent). But Hollis and Jay Dee weren't alike. Where Hollis was big, Jay Dee was mean, a fact apparent in his looks—red hair greased back in duck-tail swaths, shirt-collar up (canary or rust), white bucks or blue suede (Elvis style) and pegged pants sporting wide-wale seams, the look of a consummate Fifties hood.

Nobody messed with Jay Dee Sikes. Even the teachers would pull their shots—except for Mister Vigaree (at least in theory, it was said) who'd been on the Death March at Bataan and knew how to kill you with a thumb (just where to put it was much discussed with Danny insisting it went "down low, that soft spot under the diaphragm. . . then twist it around and count to ten, which gives you time to get away before your enemy pukes his guts"). They yelled *banzai!* at the sound of his voice crackling over the intercom, but not when they met him in the hall because they'd heard he was subject to spells in which he was back in the Philippines surrounded by Japs who were middle-school size. That might explain what Vigaree did when a cherry bomb wrecked the third-floor john—a muffled explosion had shaken the school, and seconds later, as if by chance, the long-delayed encounter occurred.

Jay Dee was scurrying down the hall.

"Hold it, big shot!" Vigaree yelled, as if he was back on Corregidor. Jay Dee was wearing a biker's glove and squeezing a tube of rolled-up dimes. "Hold what?" he'd drawled insultingly, ignoring his challenger's half-crazed look.

Vigaree grabbed his tapered shirt and slammed Jay Dee against the wall, lifting him to a tip-toe stance. The two of them froze at point-blank range—Vigaree twitching, Jay Dee calm despite the tight spot he was in. Then Vigaree blinked and let him go while Jay Dee slid around his arm, escaping the fatal flick of a thumb and leering defiantly at the crowd as if he knew that Vigaree's brain was once again in shell-shocked mode. The message was chilling for them all. Jay Dee and Hollis ruled the school.

● ● ●

Dugan gets up and goes to the fridge where Caitlin keeps the Taster's Choice—a dubious quirk, though as a guest he's too discreet to question it. Still, he'd shared the thought just yesterday that, in the natural order of things, toilet paper should spool from the top. . . and Caitlin had not reacted well. "We-We g-g-gotta talk," she'd blurted out, but then, not saying what she meant, she'd left the room and gone to bed. Now here he stands, alone in the house, heating some water on the stove with Hollis and Jay Dee on his mind along with a nagging anxiety that life with Caitlin's getting strained.

Miz Bullard, he thinks—was that her name?—who oversaw post-lunch study hall? She always ducked out to the lounge, leaving Dolores Krebs up front to take down names if anyone talked. For no obvious reason but her name, Dolores was known as "Señorita"—she with the tits so cozily housed in fuzzy pink sweaters with rabbit motifs ("Pat the bunny!" somebody would say, to which Dolores, unperturbed, would answer, "Y'all better hush up now. . . I'll tell Miss Bullard when she gets back.")

But she never reported anyone, so, after she threatened, talk resumed—the boys getting louder minute by minute while most of the girls would giggle and whisper, supposedly working on book reports but posing with sly bust-thrusting yawns as if the guys weren't looking on.

Dugan observed this elaborate game without really grasping how it was played—though during that year, reflexively, he'd started to watch for the fugitive glimpse that sleeveless blouses could provide. He'd grown obsessed with the Reese twin's boobs which, swaddled like mummies in cotton and lace, were flaunted demurely nevertheless, prompting in him a grave concern that the fireworks holstered in his pants might have a self-igniting fuse—mere fantasy until one day, during an afternoon study hall, he heard some thumps from the rear of the room and saw a curious reverie descending over most of the girls, including the Reeses who started to blush when both of them turned towards Hollis's desk and quickly swiveled back again.

The room had gone on red alert, though Hollis himself was undeterred, wearing the tensely focused look of a pinball addict in mid-game. His stooges grinned as if complicit, though Dugan was slow to comprehend on seeing Delores' crimson face, then looking at Hollis, pumping hard, his hands below the lid of his desk as, bucking and slumping, he crowed, "Ah, yessss!" and, like an announcer selling beer, declared with a snort, "It's SCHWEITZERIZED!" (Danny would get it—so would Rose—if Dugan could share the story with them.)

The Reese twins, in their scoop-necked tops, had put their heads down on their desks. To Dugan it seemed almost surreal, like one of those ads for Maidenform ("I dreamed. . . I beat my meat at school!") "Well, Hollis Marlowe!" Dolores huffed, seated behind Miss Bullard's desk, watching him brazenly lurch to his feet and swagger with a disdainful sneer up to the "Use the Trashcan" sign—which Hollis obeyed flamboyantly, tossing some balled-up Blue Horse in. The girls in the class all seemed subdued, like hens with a rooster in the yard.

● ● ●

Dugan's let his coffee get cold. He takes a sip, then puts it down, spilling a little and wiping it up. He's heard the Reese twins live in town. Dolores he's never seen again—she must have married and moved away—

361

though the temptress who's come unbidden to mind is a teenage Delilah named Gail Deloach who, though only a single grade ahead, had a chassis like a Coupe de Ville and reeked of such an acquaintance with sex that even Hollis would look abashed when she alluringly hove into view with socks rolled down and poofed-up hair, smirking at what she'd caused to stir in the britches of any boy who looked as all of them irrepressibly did.

She worked for Mister Vigaree, coming to Shop class every day with notes for "Plessy" Ferguson, the balding excitable middle-aged man in charge of that otherwise all-male preserve. Jay Dee and Hollis were there as well, and both were very tight with Gail ("I'm on the rag," she'd said one day when Hollis proposed a rendezvous, and Dugan, who happened to overhear, was stupefied by what he'd heard. . . he hadn't known girls could talk like that). Then everyone learned about their bet—Jay Dee and Hollis had wagered with Gail she couldn't get Plessy's hammer up (the phrase all three had supposedly used).

Word got around, and, sure enough, when Gail sailed into Shop next day, smacking a wad of Juicy Fruit, she clearly had her game face on— smiling at Plessy, acting coy, brandishing Mister Vigaree's note, then tucking it somewhere out of sight. "You gonna frisk me?" she inquired. He sheepishly told her not to tease, but she'd just perched on a nearby stool, licking her top lip with her tongue while wielding her boobs like an amputee's stumps, the way they'd seen Jane Russell do for her roll in the hay with Billy the Kid.

Plessy had groveled under her spell, ignoring the sniggering from the boys, unable to tear himself away. Gail's undulations were balletic. Dugan still sees her in his mind, stretching the gum into lengthy strands and nibbling it back into her mouth while Hollis and Jay Dee, flanking her, showboated like two Atlanta pimps, applauding her moves and, after a bit, conceding that Gail had won the bet. Nodding at Plessy Ferguson's crotch, she'd popped her gum, slipped off the stool, and, wagging her assets, strolled away.

But what's the connection? Dugan asks, probing for answers in his mind, interrogating his wordless id (nothing but images there, he sees, like silent movies jerking about) and fumbling to translate into words how brutality might relate to sex—from fear and loathing, festering lust, wanting to take and not to share, finding delight in causing pain. . . the opposite of making love? Too pat, he knows, too Augustinian, but there's something there that leads him back to Hollis and Jay Dee's falling out one overcast morning just before school in the churned-up muck of the bicycle sheds.

Jay Dee had reportedly started to brag about a blowjob he'd received—from Gail, he claimed with a wink and a leer, deliberately getting Hollis riled. Hollis had called Jay Dee a liar and told him he'd better shut his trap. Then shoving had started back and forth that quickly attracted a gawking crowd. Things escalated—from open-hand sparring like a game to a sudden sharp rap to Jay Dee's nose that brought forth blood and a shift of intent as, skidding in the puddles and dirt, they circled each other, red in the face, launching some murderous long-range bombs.

When Dugan arrived they were still on their feet—though, as one onlooker gleefully said, Jay Dee "had done been knocked down twict" and his russet pants bore chocolaty smears. Even with rolled-up dimes in his gloves, his buggy-whip arms were flicked aside by Hollis's huge meat-cleaver fists. The crowd was looking on in awe, including a clutch of rat-faced kids who were yelling for Hollis to kill Jay Dee.

Jay Dee was circling in a crouch and brushing a thumb against his nose while Hollis waited for him to charge. A feint, a slip, an off-balance swing and both were flailing away again until, from a punch he never saw coming, Jay Dee went down with Hollis astride whacking his duck-tails side to side. Dugan could hear a sickening sound like pencils snapping one by one. But suddenly, after a curious pause, Hollis's face went very still as if he'd begun receiving a signal transmitted somehow just for him while Jay Dee, concentrating hard with an arm stretched down between their legs, gave a slow deft twist with a black-gloved hand and Hollis pitched forward, open-jawed, silently writhing in the mud.

Nobody tried to stop Jay Dee. He reeled in through the safety doors before the morning bell had rung and reappeared beside his lathe to shave away at a four-by-four. Hollis showed up and did the same, albeit with a gingerly gait, as if it was just a typical day. But nothing would be the same again.

At first there were rumors of revenge, how Hollis was gonna get his own. He didn't, though, and Gail dropped out (ran off with a guy who hustled pool according to rumors unverified) while Hollis and Jay Dee faded away, just got obscure (like Cherokee Bill and Quick Draw Fred when law and order came to Dodge) leaving nothing of note behind except, in "Plessy" Ferguson's class, some lamp stands lined up on a shelf looking like cypresses in a swamp, the works of some fabled Og and Magog.

And now, if *The Impeder*'s right, Hollis, like Dugan, has reappeared—
a teenaged thug who all that time was slouching his way towards My Lai
4.

• • •

He's finished straightening the laundry room up but lingers a moment
nonetheless, knowing there's one more bout to review—from a time
before an aptitude test he'd take for a scholarship competition ("Which
leisure activity would you choose: Polishing Metal/Arranging Flowers?"
and "Answer this question true or false: I think someone is following me")
would reveal a decidedly martial bent which, though on the surface wholly
absurd, seemed, given the history of his clan, almost plausible in a way
since the Dugan who "ain't goan study war" has Great Progenitors who
did—like an Irish adventurer on a roll two-hundred-fifty years ago
marauding with Tuscarora Jack, or a great-grandfather, C.S.A., who'd left
his illusions with his arm in a trench beside the surgical tent on Morris
Island during The Whaw (after a slaughter grisly enough to make My Lai
look almost quaint). But the Dugans have fought enough, he thinks,
musing on his unbroken descent from reckless, obstreperous, violent men,
surviving in pieces to fight again for duty, pride, or getting the girl but
never for mere obedience. . . which is why that aptitude test was wrong
and why he'd turned the scholarship down for a place less geared towards
moneyed success. The Dugans, whatever their uniforms, had always been
unorthodox—good fighters/poor soldiers was the rap, and he reckons that
he's their perfected type—a thought that leads him unfailingly back to a
sorry-ass scrap when he and Danny had duked it out behind the bike shed
after school, same site as the battling titans' clash, for reasons he never
could recall.

Whatever the cause, it wasn't Gail and had nothing to do with ruling
the school—testosterone works in different ways. They'd both been kept
in past the bell, so the yard was deserted when they emerged. Both were
in shirtsleeves, Dugan recalls, though Danny's thick sweater, Kelly green,
was worn like an apron in reverse, and he carried atop a load of books his
giant-pencil pencil box—a foot-long yellow-green plastic tube, pointed at
one end like a stake.

Something had happened (Yeah? You too! You think I care? Well, screw you too!) They'd started to push, he faked a punch, then stiff-armed Danny with his palm, and Danny decided to close his fist and swing as if he meant to kill. Dugan had ducked and swung in return—a clean, crisp shot that prompted a grunt as Danny decided to grapple instead. They'd toppled together into the mud. Dugan was quicker, wriggling free, but Danny was stronger than Dugan had thought, taking a hit to get in close, wrestling until they fell again. The scissors were Dugan's best hope on the ground, but Danny kept slowly breaking his hold and, bigger than Dugan, pinning him down. Eventually, Dugan understood, despite superior swagger and speed, it wasn't a battle he would win—though he was the athlete, Danny was not, so honor of some sort was at stake.

"My nose! Leggo!" He'd dabbed with his hand. "You broke it, you turkey. You'll pay for this!"

"Who started it?"

"You cheater!"

"What?"

"You cheated."

"How?" Danny, bewildered, breathing hard, was tapping his fist against his leg.

"By whacking me with that pencil box!"

They looked at the remnants of the box. During the struggle, once or twice, they'd rolled atop it, breaking its point and emptying most of its contents out. As green as his sweater used to be, it lay on the ground with Danny's books.

"I didn't," said Danny, picking it up, examining one of the broken parts.

"You dirty fighter!" Dugan yelled. He tried to wipe the blood from his nose, smearing some snot across his hand.

"Liar!" said Danny, looking enraged.

"Who's gonna believe you, dirty Jew?"

"You want some more then, dumbass Mick?"

"Fuckin' Jew."

"You got your ass kicked fair and square."

Dugan had gathered his own stuff up and dumped it in his handlebar basket. He waited until he neared the gate. "Next time I'll bring a baseball bat!" Somehow that didn't seem enough. "Jewboy!" he'd added one more time, aware that he'd worsened his defeat—and now another voice intrudes on his séance in Caitlin's laundry room: "Those dirty rotten Jews from New York. . . they're who's behind it," Nixon had said when told of the fallout from My Lai.

Peace with honor means many things.

● ● ●

He hunts through the phonebook looking for Hollis, but none of the first names start with an H, so Dugan heads off to the records office—a cluttered under-lit operation in the basement of a municipal building. It's divided by a countertop with swinging half-doors at either end, and, despite its noisy AC unit, the premises are uncomfortably warm, explaining a large electric fan that oscillates slowly on a stand. *Black Orpheus*, Dugan tells himself while noting the old-style window frames and rows of ceiling-high makeshift shelves crammed with cardboard document boxes and bundles of papers that feebly flap in periodic gusts from the fan. There's a typist at one of a half-dozen desks, absorbed in blowing on her nails, while a clerk sits perched on a Bob Cratchit stool unwrapping a new Life Savers pack and looking annoyed when Dugan says he's trying to find an acquaintance from school.

"Are you a relative, sir?" he asks as if he's not inclined to help.

Proud man's contumely, Dugan thinks. "A lawyer," he barks in a confident voice. "Just checking a will."

"Name?" asks the clerk officiously, examining something on his desk.

"My name or. . .?"

"Yours. And the name of your firm."

"Dugan."

"Dugan and. . ."

"Dugan."

"Nothing else?" He raises his eyebrows. "Just a sec." He gets to his feet and leaves the room. In a couple of minutes he returns. "Richard Dugan?"

"Michael. Look, it's Hollis Marlowe, early thirties. I'm only asking for his address."

"Certainly, Mister. . . Dugan," he says. He leaves again. After another ten minutes or so, he's back with a coffee cup in his hand. He takes a sip and puts it down. "Was that Ollie or Wallace you wanted, sir?"

"Hollis," says Dugan. "Starts with an aitch. Aitch as in hemorrhoids."

366

"Okay. . . sir." His tie has a rooster on one leg extending the other to brandish a spur. "Please take a seat."

The secretary looks at him. He smiles, but she quickly looks away. He notes the countertop's many scars. A seedy office, lousy work. He watches the woman type a form with pauses between the keys as she taps. She hesitates and looks provoked, as if the letter she's looking for has taken a sudden keyboard break. The clerk meanwhile has vanished again. Another ten minutes and Dugan inquires, "Where is he?"

"Sir?"

"What's taking so long?"

She looks at the form she's working on.

"The guy who left. Where is he?" he asks.

She looks surprised. "Who. . . Mister Floyd?"

"The guy I talked to."

"Mister Floyd. He had to run an errand, sir."

"For me. I know. But he hasn't come back."

"No, sir," she frowns. "He won't be back until after lunch. And Mister Grimball's out today."

He cranes his neck in an effort to see what's going on behind the shelves. "It's just a quarter of twelve," he says. The secretary's face is blank. "Maybe there's someone else. . ." He stops. "Excuse me, Miss?" She looks back up. "Can somebody else. . ."

"Sir, Mister Floyd has gone to lunch. I've told you that."

"How long is that?"

"How should I know?"

"How long is *your* lunch, then?" he inquires.

"None of your beeswax," she replies (a couple of months, if she eats like she types). She shakes a bottle of white-out up. When she raises her eyes, her expression's changed. . . so much he thinks she's feeling contrite.

"Hi, Barb!" he hears from near the door as a *Town & Country* type appears bedecked in a monogrammed button-down with a tie in a woven red-and-green plaid. "Is Lester here?"

"I'll check," she beams.

"Thanks, Barb," the monogrammed man replies while turning towards Dugan with a nod. "Sorry to interrupt your chat," he says. He smiles at the typist. Dugan shrugs. Barb pushes a button on her phone.

"It's Doctor Dough."

"And Doctor Dugan," Dugan adds, raising his voice so Lester can hear.

Barb covers the mouthpiece with her hand. "Was that Rutledge or Ratliff, Doctor Dough?"

"HOLLIS MARLOWE!" Dugan persists.

"Ratliff, Barb."

"He'll send it right out."

She smiles and turns to her unfinished form. Dough utters a whinny, turning his head. "Well, well," he smirks, "I do declare! The infamous Dugan back in town? Somebody thought they'd spotted you."

"Dough the Usurper, I presume? How's life at the Dibbledome these days?" He notes the outfit, hair, cologne. "Treatin' you like a prince, I see. Nice tie," he adds.

"It's Dunkie's plaid."

And Robert the Bruce's, but that's okay. "How's Dinkie?"

"Who?"

"The imbecile dog."

"In therapy but doing better. The vet says he was just allergic."

"To what?" he asks, implying *me*?

"To getting dropkicked, I suppose." Dough peers at Dugan along his nose. "You know you're quite a legend here." He whinnies again and throws back his head. "'The Scholar Gypsy,' Doggett says."

"Doggett should know."

"He had us in stitches the other night recounting some of your escapades. We'll be starting back up in a week or so." Barb reappears with an armload of files as Dough continues while looking at her. "Your Joycean hoax I can well believe—at least, as far as Gordo goes. He's a sucker for anything over his head. Even," he chortles, "Timrod and Simms! Oh, here they are," he says to Barb, who jots a series of numbers down. "The run-in with Blunt. . . can you manage that, Barb?" She's clamped the files beneath her chin, her new nails under the bottom tier until she lays her burden down. "I'd call that ill-advised," he grins. "But some of your other shenanigans like dogging it with that Asian whore. . ." He titters and rocks back on his heels.

"Initial here." Barb shows him where, sliding the top file from the stack and squaring the rest up with her arms. She glances at Dugan curiously.

"How's Dunkie?" asks Dugan.

"My wife," says Dough as he takes out his pen, an elegant and expensive one, "is doing just fine."

"Glad to hear it." Dugan leans in as if to watch him sign his name, then reaches out to nudge Dough's arm. "Look out there! Now you've messed it up. Those Montblancs take a steady touch." Ignoring a fixed malevolent stare, he puts his face up close to Dough's. "Same way with Dunkie. What you should know. . ." His voice is even and sincere. "Now that you're dogging her all the time. . . a little foreplay's all she needs."

He winks at the typist who looks away.

• • •

Telling himself the timing is all, he asks point blank to use the Merc, and Caitlin, looking mildly pissed, declares it isn't hers to lend. When Danny died, she'd given it back. . . to his grandfather, Mister Kappelman. It's Kappelman Dugan ought to ask—at ninety-two, he doesn't drive much ("Let's hope not anyhow," Dugan shrugs), though he'd parked the Merc where he thought it was safe and left a set of keys with her "in case of an emergency." He'd forgotten where he left it, though.

"Really?"

No, it's what he'd said. She's sure he'd tell her if she asked. "He's th-th-that acute. He kn-knew how I'd hated s-s-seeing it there, p-parked in his driveway. . . D-D-Danny's ghost."

After a while she'd learned where it was, in a parking garage on Blanding Street. "Is th-th-this r-really an emergency?"

"Well. . ." he says.

He sees her thinking. "Y-You n-n-need," she nods, "to be on your own."

Then she goes to fetch her V-W keys, and, on their way to get him the Merc, she says at a stoplight, "L-L-Listen, M-Mike, y-you understand. . . I n-need m-m-more space. R-Really, it's time."

"Whattaya mean?" He knows, of course. There's no point now in dragging it out. "I'll be gone as soon as this errand's done."

"K-K-Keep the car, ok-k-kay?"

"Okay."

She drops him off at the parking garage, noting she's got some errands too—meaning good luck, *à bientôt*. He finds the Merc and drives it back, packing things up in ten minutes or so. . . two armloads and a cardboard box, including a pile of Danny's stuff that Caitlin's said she'd be throwing out. He leaves it all on the backseat, then pauses to use her telephone, checking the Marlowes one by one. You never know, he might get lucky.

"Is Hollis there?"

Silence. A click.

"I'm looking for Hollis. . ."

"Yuh keep on lookin', yuh sonnovabitch! 'N stay away from mah wife, y' hear?"

"I'm. . ."

Blam! and then a dial tone.

"Hello?" He hears a little old lady.

"I'm looking for Hollis Marlowe, ma'am."

"Hollis?" A pause. "That Big or Little?"

"Uh. . . either one."

A rustling noise. He overhears, "He says which one don't matter none." More rustling, then the old lady says, "Big Hollis is dead."

"I'm sorry to hear it. Is Little. . .?"

A pause. "He's out to Lake Murray."

"S'cuse me, ma'am. Could you say where?"

"Bait shop," she tells him.

"And where is that?"

"Out to Ballentine. . . out that way. Hook Line 'n' Sink."

"S'cuse me, Ma'am?"

"Hook Line 'n' Sinkler's what it said 'fore Buddy's first partner come up broke. An' then the eyes storm took the 'ler' which left it 'sink'—Hook Line 'n' Sink—which Sissie said was too misleadin'. . . though, really, as long as it ain't the boat, that's what you're lookin' for, you know, watching that bobber disappear. A-coarse, nobody's askin' me 'n' Sinkler don't git t' vote no more. . ."

"Excuse me. Where?"

"Right under th' sign that's over th' door, which is off to th' side of th' eyes machine."

"Yes, ma'am," he says. "To Ballentine?"

"Last time I looked that's whare it was."

She cackles, Dugan chiming in.

"I 'preciate that."

"There's a sign that just says 'worms' thare too. Painted it cattywompers, though, 'cause Sissie said she thinks it's cute—a back'ards are. What Bubba said. . ." She starts to cough. ". . . was worms can't read a sign nohow." She gives a dry and raspy laugh, like chinaberries on a shed.

"Yes ma'am."

"You fixin' to go up thare, tell Buddy he better not fergit."

"Tell who?"

She pauses. "Buddy, a-course! Who else you think you gonna see? Lur'lene can't git no help with th' kids."

"Uh-huh," he says. "That's Hollis' wife?"

"If I'm his momma, reckon so. You tell him, now."

"Yes, ma'am, I will."

"Red Man. He promised he wudn't fergit."

"Red Man. Okay. So Buddy is Hollis?"

She makes a noise that sounds like assent. "Them worms can't read nohow," she rasps.

• • •

Two antique pumps and twin screen doors, with racks of novelty cards on display—dwarf Johnny Rebs with fishing poles saluting the unfurled Stars-'n'-Bars ("I Ain't Forgot, Just Goin' Fishin'!") and worms atop the words "BITE ME!" Next to the unlocked soft-drink box are stacks of crates for Nehi, Nu-Grape, and Royal Crown under an ad on a broken clock assuring all thirsty passers-by "We Have Atlantic Ale & Beer."

"Hey, how you doing?" Dugan says, glimpsing a figure in the gloom.

"Don' even ask," a woman replies.

Adjusting into fisherman's mode, Dugan adopts a laid-back stance, lifting the lid of the soft-drink box as if he knows what it contains. It's filled with dirt-stained paper cups. "These worms in here are gettin' sluggish."

"That's sausage, hon. Don' fish with that or you might catch what you can't hannel." She eases out into the aisle and leans against the tackle case in halter-top and toreadors.

"So what you recommend?" he asks, taking it slow like Johnny Cash and catching the breeze from a rotating fan that makes some bright blue streamers wave.

"Depends on whut you're after, don' it?"

Still looking to imitate Johnny Cash, he glimpses a hulk that blocks the light, clicking and slapping as it moves, emerging from some inner room.

"Git back to the kids now, Luraleen."

Shrugging resentfully, she retreats. The man flaps towards him, boots unclasped—aflutter like a fish's fins—and rubber treads squeaking on the floor. He stops to put some spinnerbaits out, half hidden by the metal fan that rattles as it swivels away, tossing the streamers back and forth. "Stripers been hittin' by the dam. . . that where you headed?" he inquires. Rounding the corner, reaching down, he tugs two beers up from the box. Mabel Black Label. "Who's buyin'?" he asks.

"Me. . . if mine's Atlantic Ale."

"Long gone," he grunts while closing the lid, exposing a tattoo on his arm: HELL SUCKS, it says, and, under that, a dagger and heart above a scroll that Dugan's unable to make out—"1/20" it says and then a dash with something or other after that. It's Hollis, all right, it's got to be, though not as brawny as he'd once seemed. He pops both caps and hands one over, lifting his own with the slightest of nods—forefinger hooked about its neck, then tilting it back to take a swig. Dugan does likewise, wiping his mouth as Hollis leans towards him with a squint. "Got all the tackle you think you need?"

"Not goin' fishin'," Dugan says. "Maybe a little huntin', though."

"This time a-year?" He turns to get a better look, contorting sideways like a hen and as he twists revealing why—one eye's like Cream of Celery soup. "Huntin' for what?" he scornfully asks.

"A guy. . . a colleague, you might say—John Duff or Doe. I heard he fished up here sometimes."

"He got a boat?"

"I doubt it."

"Oh, yeah? Well, shit! Lotta John Doe's at that motel—El Matador—just past the dam. Lotta Jane Doe's an' lotta bull." He puts his empty in a bin. "Two Black Labels, sixty cents. . . forget the tax. I get you sump'en else?" he scowls, watching a pick-up truck turn in, then flapping out through the swinging doors with Dugan lagging two steps behind, still waiting for change from his dollar bill. Hollis is slapping the roof of the truck. "So how things goin' there, T.R.?"

"Bitin' real good now down to the hole." A youngish guy in a baseball cap yanks a couple of five-gallon cans from his truck. "Thought you'd play hooky a day like this."

Hollis pumps gas into the cans. "Weather report said look for rain."

"An' Jesus is comin' any day. . . tomorrow maybe," T.R. says, waiting for Hollis to screw the lids and haul the cans back up to his bed. "Always bitin' afore it rains."

"Two-ninety," says Hollis, reading the pump. "Hang on I get you back your dime."

"Gotta go," T.R. nods his head. "Buy Luraleen some roses from me."

"Yeah." Hollis watches T.R. drive off. "Roses, my ass!" he says and spits, turning to flap back towards the store.

"Don't take this wrong, but. . ." Dugan says, detaining him when he's halfway there.

"You got a problem?" Hollis growls, unblinking with his milky eye as, squaring off, he stops and waits. "Donatin' your change for roses too?"

"That tattoo come from Vietnam?"

Cocking his good eye towards the store, Hollis forces some impulse down. "This tattoo here?"

"Right," Dugan nods.

"What if it did? You been to Nam?"

"Nah. Graduate school."

"Uh-huh, I guessed. You been phonin' around. I had you pegged for a 2-S twerp. You from some anti-war magazine?"

He shakes his head. "I'm only asking for myself." He waits a beat. "Just wondering how rough it was. I had a friend. . ."

"Bullshit. You know. . ." He looks to where the highway curves, watching a flatbed rattle by. "It wudn't so bad," he finally says. He starts inside, then stops again. "Think you're the first guy come by here with chickenshit guilt for stayin' home while I was gettin' my balls shot off. . . for which they stuck my ass in jail—or tried to, goddamn bleedin' hearts? Or TV fuzznuts pokin' around wantin' to ask about My Lai. You wamme to tell you what it was like? Go look, asshole. Go see for yourself, and don't come pissin' 'roun' my door. You seen that crap?"

"What crap?" asks Dugan after a pause, sensing a shift in Hollis's tone.

"'bout Calley."

"No."

"It ain't worth talkin' about," he says, his good eye watching Dugan's face. "What they put on a wall outside Cholon—wrote KILL A GOOK FOR CALLEY, see? The guys who're there, who oughta know, and what they know that you ain't heard is Calley wudn't the traitor there. In the middle of all that My Lai shit, a fuckin' bubble touches down. We thought they're comin' down to help. Know what those sons o' bitches did?"

"No," Dugan says, as Hollis sways, his arms like hams hung up to cure.

"Pointed their friggin' M-60 at us. At *us!*" he pauses for effect, shaking his head. "Was like some lame Jane Fonda shit. A bubble, an OH-23. . . a

373

pissant three-man whirlybird." Dugan nods. "Some fucker named Thompson's all I know. 'Cept for him. . ." He scratches his jaw. "Gave him a furlough's what I hear, an' hauled our asses to th' can."

"What happened to you?"

"Fuck!" Hollis shrugs. "I caught a splinter from a mine. Dumb jackass Calley climbed a hill 'n' took me with him. See this here?" He points to his eye. "Know what my disability's worth? A hundred-thirty-six a month—just got reduced since I can work. From 'a grateful country'? Eat my dick!"

They hear a whizzing noise go by as a man on a 10-speed—beanie and shorts, hands in fingerless biker's gloves—appears like a migratory bird and, bent in a picturesque racer's crouch, pumps at a steady rpm, a focused and fit suburban dork pedaling towards the Tour de France. They watch him vanish around the curve.

"Got what you come for?" Hollis asks.

His question takes Dugan by surprise. "Just sorta curious," Dugan says.

Hollis squints up at the cloud-filled sky like he's tired of hooking the same dumb fish. "Some things. . . there's nothin' you can do. Just try to forget it," he says with a shrug. "All but the nookie, know what I mean?"

"Not really," says Dugan. "I don't know much. Which way's the dam?"

"Down towards th' water," Hollis nods, pointing the way the cyclist went as Dugan is getting in the Merc, all his possessions on the seat. "You on vacation?" Hollis asks.

"Homeless."

"Shit! What's your excuse?"

"Dumb luck," says Dugan, turning the key. The Merc coughs twice. He keeps it in neutral, feeding it gas.

"Hey!" Hollis adds before Dugan leaves, his hand on the door as if holding him back. "Remember that hunkie, Gail Deloach?" Blindsided, Dugan attempts to frown as if he hasn't understood, but Hollis appears to know he has, cocking his good eye with a grin as if they're back in Miss Bullard's class. "She was a piece uh work," he says.

● ● ●

Out of the blue on the outskirts of town while listening to "Like a Rolling Stone," he feels a steady insistent pain erupt between his shoulder blades. He's felt some twinges there before, but now it's urgent like a cramp. His first response is to shift in his seat, thinking he'll squirm and stretch it out, but it relocates inside his chest, centering on his diaphragm and spreading outwards, growing worse until it starts to cross his mind that he might be having a heart attack. Too young, he thinks, but all the stress. . . He slows up, panting, then he stops, hurting too much to look for help—though, as he's pulling off the road, he sees a boy who waves his hand and races towards him with a sign. Alarmed by occurrences in his gut, Dugan weakly semaphores back and turns a knob to cut Dylan off.

"CAR WASH!" the boy yells threateningly. In yellow and black, he looks like a bee. Dugan attempts to tell him no, but up ahead there're a dozen more with buckets and hoses, pointing him out and moving excitedly towards his car.

"WASH FOR THE BEARCATS, SIR?" one says.

Dugan weakly shakes his head, but his writhing appears to spur them on. The pain evinced by his grimace is irrelevant to the bee-like girls who're starting to clamber over his hood, chanting some sort of bearcat song. Whatever the hell a bearcat is, they look like bees—a frenzied, aggressive swarm of bees. Somebody's yelling directions out. His car is shaking.

"ROLL IT UP, SIR!" a girl calls out, approaching the tiny gap he'd left to get a little ventilation.

He doesn't ask why. The cramp's become a punji stake, though the shaking appears to help a bit as cheerleaders mount his trunk and roof. That's good, he thinks, half doubled up—just letting the Magic Fingers work. Nobody my age has heart attacks, except my dad (there's that, of course, but he had other problems too, like demon rum and a dogmatic faith). He sees a yellow-pantied rump spread out across his windshield-view and then its owner smiling down through sheets of suds and Washermops. He shuts his eyes to surf the pain.

After a while the shaking stops. Surprisingly, his chest feels better. Almost at once a tapping starts. It's on the roof beside his head. "JUST PULL ON DOWN—WE'LL RINSE HER OFF."

At first he thinks they mean the girl who's wriggled her way atop the car, but it's nautical usage they have in mind. He watches the cheerleader slide to her feet, and, starting the engine up again, eases the Merc back onto the road. The kids are gesturing straight ahead where a gantlet of bees with hoses looms.

What happens occurs without a decision, as if the Merc has a will of its own. One minute he sees them nodding and smiling, the next they're howling and shaking their fists, shrinking into his rear-view mirror as, not quite sure if it's happened or not, Dugan sedately drives away. Ribbons of suds obstruct his view, but it seems two cars are chasing him. Accelerate, the Merc decides. Taking a corner on half his wheels, he sees a guy with a sample case who's jumping back onto the curb. "What's the fucking big rush?" the guy yells out. Killer bees! he wants to reply, gauging a stoplight up ahead. Yellow, then red. He shoots on through as, on his left, a cop on a Harley hog rolls up—leading a funeral, it appears. Traffic stops and Dugan escapes, steering a labyrinthine course as rain begins to spatter down, washing all evidence from his car.

● ● ●

Still free and alive, but what comes next? Evicted, impaled, pursued by bees, he's itinerant in a Twilight Zone. Uppermost is a place to stay, then think about what's wrong in his chest (Vigaree's thumb comes first to mind—how long before he coughs up blood?) He drives around for half an hour before deciding on a room for the night at the Heart of Cumbria Motel, just up the street from the Cock-o-Dome.

"Employer's Name?" the manager asks, squinting officiously at the form.

"What for? It's just a room I want." What is it with dipshits in this town?

"In case of damage. You'd be surprised—I've had guests take the shower knobs." His thinning hair's been deftly combed like the warp on a double-harness loom. "Damn hippie deadbeats, all the same. I'd rather rent rooms to jiggaboos."

"I've got a trust fund," Dugan says.

"I'll need a deposit," Warphead nods, looking past Dugan at the wall. One of his eyes seems to wander a bit, but the other one's like a power drill.

"Just kiddin'. I'm with *The Tarheel Planter*. My company car." He gestures outside, then notes the Merc is weirdly streaked. "Been out in the fields," he adds with a shrug. "Researchin' the kudzu down this way. From Africa, did you know that? Jiggaboos planted it for revenge."

"Thirty-five down, plus eighty a week, plus extra for any out-of-town calls. Maid service free three times a week unless you vomit on the rug. No charge for vomiting on the tile so long as you clean it up yourself. No kids, no pets, no overnight guests."

"Sounds perfect." A week will suit him better.

"And you pay in cash."

"Krugerrands okay too, I guess?"

Warphead's expression doesn't change. "Kudzu's from Japan," he snaps.

Dugan's broke after paying him off, leaving him only a dollar or two. He doesn't unload. He needs to rest.

• • •

When he opens his eyes, it's dark outside. His diaphragm's sore and there's a din, a rhythmic quasi-musical screech, apparently from the room next door—"Do You Know the Way to San José?" trilled in a boisterous male falsetto. Undressing, he stumbles to the john, pees, and steps into the shower. No towels, though. He tries the phone and finds it's dead, but Dionne's going strong next door. Okay. He yanks his pants back on and creeps out from his dismal fen. The breezeway's shabbier than he'd thought—a light bulb gone, paint flaking off. He bangs and waits. The singing stops.

"Who iiiisss it?" asks someone inside.

"The guy next door." A narrow crack, through which he glimpses some push-broom hair and a wary and vaguely sardonic eye. It blinks. The door cracks wider still, revealing a tall dark human-giraffe weirdly clad in a red kimono along with a sash plus powder-puff mules—mimosa pink, a hairy ankle protruding from each.

Dugan coughs. "I got no towels," he explains. "My phone's not working."

"So?" says a Greta Garbo voice.

"I'd like to notify the desk."

"What's stopping you, buster?" Greta replies. His goofy moustache is push-broom too, and his menace contains a petulant lilt. His bearing's oddly regal, though—with shoulders low and head held high. He studies

Dugan, then relents. "Oh, come on in. You look too beat to worry about. Phone's by the bed."

"I'll call the desk."

"You're not a convict, are you, hon?" He watches Dugan try to call and, deducing his own line must be dead, bursts out with a huffy diatribe. "Pluperfect shits! This place is just a wretched dump." Three graceful strides and he's into the head, returning with a towel in hand. "Keep it," he says.

"It's wet."

"It's damp. I used it for a turban, see?" He ties it up and takes it down, checks his watch and tucks his chin. "You look like you could use a drink. Or. . ." making a Groucho, "maybe a smoke?" He watches Dugan hesitate.

"I'm straight," says Dugan.

"That a fact? You look a little bent to me." Flopping across the double bed, he gropes between it and the wall. "You never know until you try. Close the door while I rummage around." One of the pink mules hits the floor. "Scared somebody will rape you, hon? Don't flatter yourself. Ah, there it is!" He's holding what he sought aloft. "Elegant shit," he tells his guest. Picking the mule up with his toe, he sings a Kirsten Flagstad note while rolling a reefer and holding it up. "So, okay, sailor, got a name?"

"Dugan."

"Oh, yeah? Well, close the door—I asked you before. I'm Ready Freddie. Hand me those matches over there. . . on top of the dresser. Dugan what? Don't worry, love, my sex drive's currently in remission." He lights the joint and holds it out. "Listen, sweetheart, close the door. You really that scared?"

"I'm wanted, I think."

Freddie nods and takes a drag. "Must be a nice feeling. What'd you do?"

"Stiffed a carwash."

"Desperate, huh? Now, one more time, just closssse the door. . . gonna get busted if we don't." He kicks it with an outstretched foot. Then, bouncing nimbly to his feet, he puts the latch on, turns and mugs. "Some of my very best friends are straight."

"I gotta be going," Dugan says.

"Face it, hon, that carwash didn't do the job—you need some waxin'. Have a toke." He hands it to him and back and forth. "All the same," he says with sigh, "It's *moi* who's gonna have to scoot. . . so Freddie the Gay Samaritan will leave your gangster ass untouched. I've got a reunion to attend." He poses like a talking head. "Born and raised in this redneck burg, though currently from New York City. . . Freddie Ebert, native son, returns for the First Manassas Bash."

"You went to Manassas?"

"Gimme the roach!" Snatching the butt, he flounces out. Something falls, then several clunks, followed by "Damn!" and then a "Shit!" When Freddie comes back, he's clamped the joint in what seems to be an eyelash curler. "Westside Gold! Too good to waste." He takes a hit and passes it over, holding it up like a lorgnette. "*Went* to it? Hon, does a chicken have lips?" He reaches to get the curler back, then squeezes to let the butt drop free. A single wisp of smoke floats up. "You're looking at Fred the Pom-Pom Boy. You want another? Sure, we do." He rolls and lights it, takes a puff and picks a stray flake from his lip. "A little stage fright at the start? Here you go. This one's a bomber."

Dugan is feeling better now—his legs are fuzzy, and they float. Freddie's an amusing guy.

"Oh, Yeah," sighs Freddie with a twitch, "I had the hots for one o' those bearcats."

"They look like bees."

"Trust me, hon. Tight End was what the program said. I said Uh-huh, sounds right to me. Poor baby." Freddie shakes his head. "Bobby Hicks. . . I loved his ass, and we exchanged a couple of looks that meant a lot more than I knew then—but he married a woman from the mill. . . so I took off. I'd danced a little in pageants and stuff, mostly recitals. Tap. . . you know. . ." He hugs himself. "Oh, God, I lied! When I got to the city, busting my hump. . . Don't hog that shit, love, pass it on! *Man of La Mancha*—I did that. Uptown, downtown, on or off. Whatever would pay. I did it all. Conventions, car shows. . . some TV."

"Like what?"

"Remember the Old Gold dancing pack? That wasn't a floozie, that was *me!*" He sticks a foot out. "Fabulous legs! Don't bother to shave 'em anymore but, way back when, I'd go to sleep thinking of all those sweaty hunks getting a hard-on watching me. Whoo!" he shudders. "What a life! Squandered it, though—I slipped a disk, and Freddie's not so ready now. Oh, well. . ." He squints and waves both hands. "That's why I'm here." He takes a seat on the motel chair.

"Now whattaya do?"

"Windows at Bloomingdales. Men's wear too. And listen. . . what's your first name?"

"Mike."

He eyeballs Dugan, takes a drag and lets the smoke out through his nose. "Your wardrobe needs a little work."

"I'm down and out."

"Hon, ain't we all? Gotta keep dancin', though," he shrugs. "Two months ago, I get a call. . . from Estelle Shealy. 'Freddie, hi!'" He talks to his thumb and little finger as if he's holding a phone receiver. "It's our Big Thirteenth, so come on down!' 'What's so damned big?' I ask Estelle, who thinks Sol Hurok's on the phone. 'Well, turning thirty,' Estelle says, 'nobody trusts us anymore. We gotta consult our Broadway star.'" He pauses. "Me!" He makes a doleful sort of bow. "Hair's getting a little thin back here, but I'm counting on Bobby showing up. Who knows?" he says. "Might be alone. Don't take this wrong, but he looked like you. . . a couple of inches taller, I guess. Same hell-for-leather look in his eye."

"I played for Cumbria," Dugan says. He checks his watch, then looks again. Minutes have stretched into an hour. "Trouble with digital time," he adds. "Can't see where it's going or where it's been. Like TV, huh? But no commercials." This is real funny. Dugan laughs.

Freddie's expression doesn't change, though he tugs with a finger under one eye. "A *Reb*?" he asks in a dubious voice.

"And you're a Bearcat!" Dugan nods. "The only team we managed to beat."

"So when'd you play?"

"Huh?"

"Played Manassas?"

"Who told you that?"

"You did, just now."

"When?"

"That's what I'm asking. . . asking you. When did Mike Dugan. . . play Manassas?"

"Oh, fifty-seven or fifty-eight." He muses on that for a moment or two. Intercepted a pass and ran it back in. . . played loose in the flat and picked it off, as if it had all been choreographed.

"Must have been fifty-seven, hon. *Music Man* was fifty-eight."

At the start of the game, he'd picked it off. Nobody had touched him, waltzed right in. First big-time score of that miserable season.

"Weddings, bar mitzvahs, bachelor parties. Even a funeral. . ."

On the First Manassas run-down field. "It was 'Coley whatchamacallit Night.'" Their superstar fullback. . . hurt in a wreck a month before, but all dressed out like nothing was wrong and put in the game for one sad play.

"A funeral, you hear? Top hat and tails, like Fred Astaire. They played a tape, I tapped along, whacking the casket with a cane. 'What if the guy wakes up?' I said."

"Coley Jeffcoat, that's his name!"

"Coley, sure. 'What if the guy wakes up?' I said. 'That's not included. . .'"

"All-Stater into a basket case—he'd been in a crash."

"What?"

"Coley Jeffcoat. . ."

". . . had a wreck."

"That's what I'm saying. Fifty-eight. After he'd had some sort of wreck, you dressed him out for the Cumbria game and called it 'Coley Jeffcoat Night.'"

"Poor Coley. But it was fifty-seven."

"He could hardly walk. They put him in anyhow. . . just one play."

"I heard about it, but I was gone. Charged extra if I raised the dead—can you believe it?" Freddie says.

The field had been muddy when Coley came in—clean jersey and pants, all Rinso white—with Dugan down low in garnet and gold, red-dogging in between the guards, smaller but quicker, pin-balling around and sometimes finding a way straight through, a clean hard shot like the one that came when their quarterback turned to fake a pass and stuffed it into Coley's gut with nobody picking Dugan up and Coley like some guy wearing gloves about to drop a watermelon. No way to miss, a head of steam, and Coley went down with a pitiful uufff, a laundry sack disgorging socks.

"I heard he got hurt."

"Yeah," Dugan says.

They'd stopped the game for half an hour—the mill-kids silent in the stands. An ambulance.

"Listen," blurts Freddie. "You gotta go!"

"Go where?" asks Dugan.

"With me right now. You *gotta* go!"

Dugan peers stupidly though the haze. "I didn't go to Manassas," he says.

"Mocks nicks," pleads Freddie. "Listen to this, I can't show up all by myself! Big Broadway star *without a friend*. . . while they're all schlepping up with their wives—Crystal or Sharon, God knows what? I just can't face it all alone."

"Sure, you can."

"Really I can't." He starts to cry. . . not sobs, but silent trickles of tears that gather as if on a windowpane, running and sprinkling his moustache.

"I've got no clothes. . ."

"There's stuff in your car. I saw it there when I first came in."

"That's not all mine. It belongs to a friend."

"Like fun! What's wrong? You scared to say it?"

"Really," says Dugan earnestly. "I'd like to go. . ."

"But not with a fag!"

"Not fair. Come on, you said it too. Some of my very best friends are queer."

"Name one."

"What for?"

"You're lying. See?"

"You wouldn't know him."

"How would *you* know?" Freddie glares.

"Okay. It's Walt."

"Walt who?"

"Just Walt." There's also Augie Blunt, of course.

"From where? From here?"

"That's not the point."

"Wear something of mine."

"You're way too tall."

Freddie considers. Then he says, "Let's go through what you got in your car."

Unloading the Merc, they lay stuff out and Freddie's buoyancy revives. "Short & Sassy!" he exclaims. "*Lovvve* that bottle!" he whoops and grins, poking it in between his legs and tossing off a bump and grind. "Outrageous! Unnhh! It's really jumbo!" He roots around through Dugan's clothes. "Now, this is JACKIE! Put it on!" It's Danny's Guatemalan shirt. "Boots and blue jeans, add a tie. . . you're a bodyguard for Papa Doc! Dark glasses too? *Voilà*! A prince!"

"Look. . . Freddie. . ."

"You smoked up all my dope!" He spreads his fingers wide apart, making a window-washing move. "You can't back out. I told you why. Besides, we might see Bobby Hicks."

"On two conditions," Dugan says. "We're taking my pumpkin to the ball. And no matter what Julie Andrews says, don't think I'm gonna dance all night."

"You're such a bitch!" Freddie protests, tucking his chin and blowing a kiss. "It's a once in a lifetime thing."

•   •   •

The Bearcat habitat looks bleak as they approach the Manassas gym after squeezing into a teacher's space. There's a smokestack and a water tank belonging to the shut-down mill and just past that an entry gate with a motto that says We're Free to Work—*Sumus Liberum ad Opus*, it reads, undoubtedly true in a "right-to-work" state, though the mill's been closed for a number of years and Latin's no longer taught at the school (so Freddie says with mock regret).

But the party appears well underway. *Your Hit Parade* is its retro motif with a nostalgia wholly remote from the rock-on neo-Woodstock look that Freddie and his companion flaunt. Yellow and black predominate in the numerous WELCOME BEARCATS signs sporting a cartoon weasel's face that's on the floor at center court and hanging on walls throughout the gym.

The turn-out looks impressively large, as if having grown up and gone to school in the literal shadow of a mill, most of the Class of '57 had liked it enough to stay for good (aside from the army and possibly jail) whereas Freddie who'd dreamed an impossible dream is back with a hope of reliving the past while Dugan himself had naively come home with every intention of shaking things up and blown it because he'd hung too loose, supposing he pretty much knew it all. But he's no longer the person he was (he desperately wants to think that's true) and reckons, however folksy the shindig may be, there aren't many lambs in the sprinkling of goats and no outsiders other than him—which makes it essential to play it cool, not challenging what he thinks are the rules: supporting the Bircherites, Jesus too; not gabbing with the women at social events or drinking the punch if you're a male; discussing the weather and manly endeavors featuring whisky or guns or souped-up cars along with violent contact sports, bass fishing boats, and weekend brawls.

Though Freddie's conversant with none of these, his brio alone seems to carry the day. Like Quasimodo, they've made him king, laughing and clapping wherever he goes—flitting from one group to another, gesticulating like Auntie Mame, decked out like Little Richard on tour (Italian loafers, snakeskin pants, a purple velveteen chemise. . . "heliotrope" to chorus-line friends). His pal, the Guatemalan prince, is left at first to fend for himself—still numb from Freddie's Westside Gold but greeting all strangers with a grin as if he were a Bearcat spouse.

"Hey, hey," they nod. Who's he? they ask, his south-of-the-border deadhead look conflicting with their Fifties theme.

"My mystery guest!" is Freddie's reply.

"Well, Freddie Ebert!"

"Freddie, hi!"

"How's chewing on those New York roots?"

"Ta-dahhh!" says Freddie, riding high, ignoring all comments such as that. So what if he's faggoty? He belongs—and that's what matters most to him, next to encountering long-lost Bobby.

Dugan is meanwhile standing around with a group of guys in open-neck shirts who're drinking from plastic Pepsi cups.

"Harley's out back now fixin' us up. . . out'n his van."

"Fixin' up what?"

They laugh like boys with rabbit tobacco. "Show 'im some, Dale."

"Aw, come on, Earl."

"It's Mickey's Big Mouth."

"Yeah, what else?"

Winking at Dugan, they pour him some. "What you think? It ain't that dainty Kool-Aid punch the ladies is drinking, tell you what. Juss try it."

They snicker as Dugan coughs. "I'll mosey on back there," he declares. He doesn't, though. He's still half-sprung, trying to fathom what he hears—facetious talk of little round balls (baseballs, buckshot, testicles, golf) and fury about an elliptical one, specifically word that Coach Ray Don is fighting off charges from up north that he's feeding his players illegal drugs. . . when all he's done, the wronged man swears, is sprinkle some Gro-Bo in their grits.

"What's Gro-Bo?"

"Stuff you put on plants," says Olin, whose nametag's got a couple of eyes drawn comically inside the O and a tongue that's lolling out of it. "But thuh *Charlotte Observer*'s making a fuss."

"Uh loada crock!" a woman huffs, invading the circle of Bearcat men. She nods to Dugan, sizing him up. "Hi," she says, "I'm Olin's wife."

Dugan nods. He's got no tag.

"Well, did he or didn't he spray 'em down. . ." Dale's got a serious look on his face.

". . . and tell 'em all to go sit in th' sun?" a man named Tubby says to Dale.

"It kinda makes sense, though," Earl replies.

"If pigs could fly," spits Olin's wife, determined to flout the gender rules, discomforting her husband's friends in a way they seem accustomed to.

"Hey, now," says Olin. "Speakin' of pigs, I got a friend who's over to Shiloh. . ."

"Olin believes whatever he hears."

"Shut up, please, Iris. A friend uh mine who raises pigs. . ."

"How'd Sharon Dent get into them pants?" Earl's eyes have wandered across the gym.

"She didn't quite," is Tubby's reply.

"Less pop a nickel in that slot!"

"Don't talk like trash," says Olin's wife. "Hip-huggers like that should be illegal."

"Come on, now, Olin, whattaya say?"

"Well, um. . ." says Olin.

"She's just a tramp. You playboys better keep it zipped."

"You tell 'em, Iris!"

Olin coughs while waiting for Iris to walk away. She doesn't though, so he resumes, "I'm sayin' some critters can get too smart."

"Like what? Like pigs?"

"What's wrong with pigs?"

"Like Coach Ray Don."

"Goddammit, Iris! Lemme talk!"

"Too smart for whut?"

"Their own damned britches."

"Not chickens," says Dugan, chipping in as Iris finally takes her leave. They look at him and at each other. "I used to raise 'em," he explains, aware his switchboard's blinking away that pot and alcohol don't mix.

"How 'bout that?" Tubby interjects.

"Or Roosters either," Dugan adds.

They pause a beat, then Olin shrugs. "Anyhow, whut I'm tryin' to say, can't hardly discourage a pig nohow. You get atween a sow 'n' a shoat. . . an', buddy, that sow'll tear you up! But when it comes to serious snow. . ."

"My chickens froze." He's beaming things down from outer space.

". . . smart ain't enough. Remember how. . . whut? two years ago? it drifted up to two foot deep past Turbeville where Coley lives? Twenny-two inches on his farm! Well, at feedin' time, them pigs come out and trot like always towards the trough. The ground's turned white. . . but, what the hey? Then, halfway there, they hit a driff, and them sharp little hooves juss sink right down. Snow packs down hard and they dangle there. Can't go back and can't go on."

"What happened?"

"Well," he licks his lips. "All uh them piggies died right there, hung up where they couldn't trot no more. Next week it melts. . . an' when Coley, who'd had the flu, goes out, he sees them pigs juss standin' there. Like a passel uh stachures on the grass."

"They all was dead?"

"See, when it melts. . ."

"I put my chicks on cookie sheets."

"Who gives a shit?" says one of the boys, baffled by Dugan's non sequiturs, but Olin attempts to help him out.

"To bake 'em?" he asks.

"To thaw 'em out."

"Can't hardly thaw a pig out, though."

They nod together. Very true. They ponder the thought of pigs in a drift, gazing out over the crowded gym. Dugan sees clumps at either end, some couples dancing, and then a head that bounces up and disappears.

"Flamin' Fred!"

"What?" Dugan says. He's truly stoned.

A laugh. The head pops up again. What Olin has spied is the Man of La Mancha launching a string of *double tours*. One of the bearcats shakes his wrist as Freddie whoops and starts to sing.

>. . . come up and call ole Dan!

"Light in his loafers, wouldn't you say?"

"So's Gene Kelly," Dugan nods.

"Gene Kelly's a fruitcake?" Olin snorts. "I knew he'd danced with Mickey Mouse."

"I came with Freddie," Dugan confides.

Olin blinks and edges away.

SIX-ty. . . MI-i-nit MAN!

A woman swirls up in a mid-calf skirt with poodle-pockets on either side—the dog's festooned with curly pink yarn marking their anklets, ruffs, and crowns. Freddie is following close behind.

"How hard did you try, Estelle?" he chides. "He's just divorced, he isn't dead. He might have surprised you. . . just like me!"

"Dwayne said he's in the Philippines. He talked to some woman in Manila."

"The operator?"

"Freddie, look, we tried to get him. You talk to Dwayne."

"Yeah, talk to Dwayne," a tall guy says, grabbing a poodle from behind as Estelle shrieks and starts to laugh.

I rock 'em, roll 'em all night long. . .

Estelle knows she's looking good, spinning to make her skirt flounce out, smiling at Dugan as she turns. Except for the veins, her legs are fine— and Dwayne's so stoked he feels no pain. He grins at Freddie. "What's your gripe? Who came the furthest gettin' here? I reckon ole Harley wins the prize."

"What prize?"

"That bearcat over there," he says.

"The *stuffed* one?"

"Yeah. Look here, Estelle. . ."

Dwayne's pulling her to him. She resists, ducking and squirming from his grip.

"Harley *Driggers*?" Freddie seethes. "Comin' from where?"

"From Cincinnati. Hey now, Estelle, who's gonna win the booby prize?" He demonstrates what's on his mind.

"You hush up, Dwayne! I'm tellin' Earl."

"I flew from La Guardia!" Freddie says.

"Yeah? Cincinnati's twice as far."

Freddie's indignant. "No, it's not."

"You're still a dumbbell, ain't you, Dwayne."

"Shut up, there, Tubby! Look it up—Cincinnati Ohio's twice as far. Get Earl. . . hey, Earl!"

"What's goin' on?"

"We're decidin' the prize for comin' the furthest."

Dugan sees Freddie spot his shirt—and find a solution for his pique. "Well, guess what, boys?" His face lights up. "I'm now announcing my big surprise. Who wins the prize is Bobby Hicks!"

"But Bobby's not. . ."

"Here? That's what you said. But, Estelle, baby, you were *wrong*! Just look over there. Now who is that?" Freddie's pointing in Dugan's direction. "Come all this way from Guatemala! You thought he was in the Philippines."

They stare.

"That guy ain't Bobby Hicks."

"Sorry, Earl, y'all flunked the test. I brought him with me from New York City. . . but look at where he started from! Bobby wins!"

"So where's his wife then?"

"Still in Manila. Just ask Estelle. They got a divorce three months ago."

Estelle falls silent as Tubby asks Earl, "You think that's him? I thought he'd married Eula Banks."

"Where's Eula, then? In the Philippines?"

Earl looks bemused as he studies the case. "Maybe that's Bobby. I don't know. . . whittled 'im down right good, it seems."

But Freddie's got an answer for Earl. "He's been on the skids since that mess in Manila. Haven't you, hon?"

All eyes are on Dugan's half-hearted nod as he approaches their exchange.

"Rehab works wonders," Freddie says.

"Hold on, there," says the guy named Dwayne. "You told us he's been in Guatemala!"

"*After* Manila. . ."

"I'll be damned!" says a red-faced man who's wearing a second tag next to the first (HI, I'M A MAILMAN! reads the first, the second one says DON'T GIMME NO SLEET!) "Now how 'bout that? How's it goin' there, Hicks? You shore get around." He turns and weaves back through the crowd.

"It's goin' okay."

"So how were the skids, then?" Dwayne demands.

"I had some bad luck."

"Did'ya, now? We tried to call ya, didn't we, Earl?"

"Estelle did."

"So whut you been up to in Manila?"

Dugan frowns. "I can't discuss it."

"Probably not," says Dwayne with a sneer. "Not when you're busy dumpin' your wife. Where were you, then? In Subic Bay? I been there too with the Marines."

"Not there," says Dugan quietly.

"Oh, yeah? Like where?"

"Like screw you too! I told you. . ."

"Eee-sy!" Olin cautions Dwayne. "Ole Bobby's been in Special Ops." (Ole Bobby can kill you with a thumb.)

"Okay," blurts Freddie. "Out with his prize!"

"I didn't dump her," Dugan says, his brain now in another place. "And, actually, she wasn't my wife."

Earl sloshes his drink. "What was she then?"

"I wish I knew."

"Ya shittin' us, Bob!" Earl forces a laugh, turning to Iris. "You hear that? Dumped Eula and says she wudn't his wife."

"For who?"

"Won't say. That still ain't clear. I'm guessing some sorta bigamy."

"With who? With Freddie? Freddie's queer. It can't be bigamy if he's queer."

But Dwayne's not having any of that. "You dumped her for some Asian snatch? Whoever she was, let's get this straight—she's from Manila, she's a gook. From Guatemala, she's a spic. From New York City, he's Freddie the Fag. . . and you're some AC-DC freak who's screwin' your way around the world? That's what you're sayin'? You're fulla shit."

"Jesus, Dwayne!" says a guy with a badge that reads I'M KENNY/KISS ME QUICK. "Less keep it clean. It's Bobby Hicks!"

"She was really Cambodian," Dugan says.

"Who? Eula?"

"No, the Asian snatch." It's Earl, who's looking menacing now.

"Cambodian, huh?" He sees Dwayne wink. "Oh, lots o' them turn up in Manila along with whores from Timbuktu! Don't think we're gonna fall for that. I been there too an' what I learned is what every white Christian oughta know. It's one thing gettin' your ass shot off savin' those folks from Viet Cong. . . or gettin' some poontang—s'cuse me, girls. . . havin' a social life on the side. It still don't mean we *marry* gooks. Their sort ain't mastered toilet paper."

"Oh, shut up, Dwayne!" instructs Estelle.

"No problem," Dugan tells the crowd. For the first time in a couple of weeks, he finds he's remembering Rose's face. For a moment he sees her, then she's gone. "She's dead," he adds, then says to them all, "murdered and raped to win the war."

"In that order? I doubt it," somebody says.

"You been there. . . Merle?" He reads his tag.

"My brother's there. You trying to say. . ."

The music blares out louder now, as if to smother their dispute. The same song's playing over and over.

There'll be fifteen minutes a' huggin'. . .

"Shit happens, Merle. You heard of My Lai?"

"You're some kind of friggin' commie, man. You're weird," says Merle, as Dwayne chimes in, "That's bullshit, Hicks!"

"Or whoever you are," somebody repeats. It's Tubby who's been to see Harley again. "You're as fulla it as that fuckin' Jane Fonda!"

"You watch your language!" Estelle says.

"Keep it up, buddy," Dwayne persists, "you'll get that crap knocked outta you."

The music's growing much louder now, and from somewhere halfway down the gym, there's a chorus of Bearcats singing along: ". . . 'n' fifteen minutes a blowin' my top!"

BOP! BOP! BOP!

"Hey! Hey! Pu-leez!" It's Freddie's turn. "I'm sorry I even brought it up. Line up to do the hokie pokie! Let's. . ."

"Candy ass! Both you and Hicks!"

"You guys lay off. If his wife got killed. . ."

"She wudn't his wife."

"And he ain't Hicks!"

"Whose wife?" The mailman reappears with Olin teetering by his side.

"Bob Hicks," says Kenny/Kiss Me Quick. "And Eula's dead."

"What? Eula Hicks? Her momma ain't heard about it yet."

"How would *you* know?" asks Harley Driggers, returning at last from Thunder Road.

"Well, think, asshole—I carry her mail."

"So who's that there?"

The mailman blinks. "She's still in Manila's all I know. . . I delivered a postcard yesterday, an' Eula's momma was glad to get it. Showed uh couple uh coconuts carved like heads—'Goin' *Nuts* in Manila" was on that side, and 'Eula Banks Hicks' was on the other. She never mentioned no divorce."

Dugan can feel it ticking away, its wires and cogwheels intermeshed (Take Two: The Bomb).

"So who's that there?" somebody repeats.

"Ebert's queer-bait," chortles Earl.

"You heard about the choir director?"

"Aw, shut up, Kenny!"

"Went chasin' the choirboy 'round the church 'n' managed to catch him by the organ!"

"I know that guy," says Harley Driggers.

"From where?" asks Dwayne.

"The Cumbria game." He nods his head.

"Caught him *by the organ*, see?"

"Whut Cumbria game?"

"I swore I'd never f'git his face. The cheap-shot fucker. He's the one."

"No, way," says Merle. "Been over twelve years."

"Since nineteen whut?"

"Since fifty-eight. Put Coley in traction for a month. I memorized that bastard's face."

Dugan smiles. He's not sure why.

"Time to skedaddle," Freddie chirps. He's trying to steer them towards the door when Iris lunges in their way.

"Who's driving that '55 Merc outside?" The crowd draws tighter. Iris seethes. "That car run off from the carwash kids! Same license tag. They wrote it down!" She points a finger. "Freddie's friend."

"That sorry-ass pansy!"

"Stiffed the kids and showed up here?"

"Why'd Freddie bring him?"

"Don't matter, Estelle. I been waitin' to see his ass again. . ."

"S'cuse us boys."

"Just hold your horses, twinkle toes!"

"You speaking to me?"

"I'm speakin' to that liar there. You still maintainin' you're Bobby Hicks?"

"Thou sayest."

"Yeah? You son of a bitch. Coley Jeffcoat, know that name? What goes around is on its way."

There's bumping and pushing. Dugan trips and Harley's face is shoved up close. Pot or alarm, he's not sure which, but something sparks a recollection, not knowing if it's true or not. That face, he thinks. "I know you too. . ." he says serenely speaking to Harley. Harley scowls. ". . . the pulling guard. On a fullback trap."

"You're dead meat now, you motherfucker!"

"You missed your block. That's why your friend got hurt so bad."

He never sees it. Like Houdini. He thinks at first he's lost his breath, then notes his lungs aren't working now. He grabs his chest and feels the stake rammed in between his shoulder blades. He hits the floor, unable to breathe, a thawed-out chicken on its side (the image floats up in his mind).

"That one's for Coley!" Dwayne declares.

"Jesus, Dwayne! Looks like he's kilt."

"Less hope so," Harley Driggers grins.

Dugan is gasping on the floor. He dry-heaves and the crowd thins out as Patti Page begins to sing. Two faces. Three. They're leaning down— not friendly, though they look concerned. There's Freddie, pulling on his arm, and Iris tugging at his pants.

"Whattaya doing?"

"Whattaya think?" She takes three bills, then tosses one back. "Bearcat Club. That's what he owes."

"You shits!" screams Freddie.

There's no reply. Outside, they find the Merc is locked. The keys are dangling from the ignition—but Kenny/Kiss Me Quick steps up, inserts a wire, and then steps back.

"Thanks," Freddie says, and Kenny nods as Dugan collapses on the seat. Doors close and Freddie starts the car. "I hope you're satisfied," he fumes. "You've ruined my fucking coming out."

● ● ●

By the time they're back at his motel room, Dugan's locked in a permanent crouch. He curls up groaning on the rug (goddamn! goddamn! shit fuck goddamn!), though Freddie's TLC is brusque—"You sound like Lennie Bruce," he frets.

The stake inhibits repartee, so Dugan resumes his shit-goddamns. He thinks if he could flatten his back, the pain would spread out evenly—then he could smooth its wrinkles out, the places where the worst knots are. With pain, it's all topography, like underwear that bunches up. He'll concentrate (shit fuck goddamn!)

There's a knock and a thump, then a key in the lock. The wall-eyed manager strides in. "I want you fairies outta here!"

"Oh, shut up! Can't you see he's sick?"

"You bet he is. Now get him out."

"He needs a doctor."

"Listen, you queers, I'm callin' the cops."

Dugan makes gurgles in his throat, ending with a piss-shit-fuck.

"For chrissake, look! The guy can't talk."

"Stop takin' the name of the Lord in vain! You got three minutes, understand?"

"Three minutes? Hah! The phones don't work, so how're you planning to reach the cops?"

"Two and a half." He takes a quick look round the room, aiming his good eye like a gun.

"I paid in advance. I want it back. Don't think you're gonna pull that scam."

"Discuss that with the cops, sweetheart. I smell what you been smokin' here."

"You utter prick!"

Shit-gurgle-fuck.

Freddie examines Dugan's face.

"I'm dying."

"See!"

"Okay, that's it! I ain't havin' no queer oh-dees in here."

He leaves, and Freddie starts to pack, dumping their stuff in two big piles. "Fascist bastard! What a twit! He thinks he'll get away with this. Well, guess what, Igor? Think again. Just try and charge at Bloomingdales!"

Shit fuck goddamn and Warphead's back. This time he's got a Louisville Slugger, slapping its fat end in his palm.

"What's that?" asks Freddie.

Warphead glares. "You get your boyfriend outta here."

"Pattern baldness, caused by stress—you're gonna be hairless, thought of that?"

"You're gonna be toothless."

"Oooo! That's mean! Bite him, Toto!" Freddie squeals. Then "Upsy-daisy!" he entreats, maneuvering Dugan towards a chair. "Come on, now, hon, just sit up straight. The quality of mercy's grand, but Freddie's gonna need a truss."

Warphead feels prompted to reply, "You wanna quote scripture? Chew on this! 'Am I my brother's keeper?' Huh? Not if he's a sodomite."

"That suits you, dickhead," Freddie says. "Cain in double-knit. Come on, Mike."

"Just shoot me! Fuck!"

The manager furrows his narrow brow. "Not on these premises, you don't."

He pokes at Dugan with his bat, as Freddie straightens to his full height, staunch as an Old Gold dancing pack. "Get outta my room! I'm packin' our stuff. I was quotin' Shakespeare anyhow."

"You better be gone when I get back." Warphead leaves but leans back in. "Don't think I'm comin' back alone."

"Bring Jerry Falwell. Judas Priest! He'll want to burn this hellhole down."

Freddie is not a meticulous packer. Whatever he finds he throws in the trunk, including a bathmat, towels, and lamp. "Tacky, but, hey, we've earned a memento." The shade won't fit. He yanks it off. "Want anything else? How 'bout a chair?"

"Unnnh."

"You're right." He tosses it back. "Come on. I'll help you to the car." Some neighbors are watching through their blinds. Freddie waves. "It's okay, folks. I'm Public Health. Looks like it's Legionnaire's Disease."

The blinds flip shut as the car's doors close, and, in seconds—or hours—they're under way with Freddie perched testily at the wheel and Dugan beside him *in extremis*, babbling inside his bubble of pain. (Did I tell you I killed somebody I loved?) "Honey, it happens all the time." (I can't recall, though, who it was. . . if this doesn't stop, I'll go out of my mind.) "Well, won't we all?" (Delayed reaction—what a shot, shouldn't have dressed out for the game. . . back here again? Well, I'll be damned!)

They've traveled, he sees, around the board and back to what you might call Go.

● ● ●

EMERGENCY the big sign says, but inside things are still the same— like a Waffle House whose chef just quit, a bus depot without a bus, a 7-Eleven minus the seven. He curls up in a plastic chair but finds his feet don't reach the floor. The pain has eased up just a bit.

"Jason, you git back ova heah!"

Whose voice is that? It's in and out. He journeys on without the Merc, on wheels again—he's not sure how. Blood pressure, blood work, EKG, a sedative for his withering pain which, mixed with pot and alcohol, propels him towards a very weird place, a rock beneath which he can doze until he starts to re-emerge.

"Look lak he wid us."

Yes, but where? His eyelids seem to come unstuck.

"I'll do the diagnosing here."

A curt reply that prompts a grunt from. . . Hattie McDaniel! Dugan's relieved—though he's back where he doesn't want to be, on a hard flat raft in a choppy sea.

"This patient has been in here before."

That voice, he thinks, a shower cap—and there's the dwarf he met last year. . . his E-R Class of '69! Back from Manila? Where's he been?

"Michael something," reads a nurse. Not Hattie, but Rhonda, he would guess. Red hair with freckles looking prim.

"Whud you just say?" Nurse Hattie leans down, hearing a mumble from the slab.

"Nurse Inez, please, I'll do the talking. Does he speak English? Where's he from?"

"According to his driver's license. . ."

"He tryin' to tell you," Hattie says. "Look lak he come here from Brazil."

"Let's get that blood test run again."

"Too-can, he say—some kinda bird."

"Inez, you hear me? That's my job. You let me be the doctor here."

"Dugan," reads the red-haired nurse.

"He lookin' at you."

"I can. . . *see*. . . that," says the dwarf. "You got a death wish, Mister Dukes?"

"Doogan," he whimpers.

"See whud I say? He done been bit. This man in serious trouble now." The dwarf peers blandly into his eyes. "Just run that test. I'll be right back. I've got a dyslexic having twins two gurneys over. Hold the fort!"

He pulls a curtain along its track, pausing to let the redhead leave. Then he goes too—leaving Inez, who grunts and mutters under her breath, "Go'n' be some changes." Dugan nods, making a sympathetic noise (did that doctor really say what he'd heard?) She gazes at him and shakes her head. "Sicka these know-it-all buckra quacks treatin' me like I'se Hattie McDaniel."

"Unnnhuh," he nods (whatever she says—he's up on his board now, hanging ten).

She pats his arm. "But we're gonna manage dis too-can attack. Don't worry none. You ain' goan die."

He shuts his eyes to check his pain and sees the dark swell rolling in, a face like flotsam drifting by. Rippla-rippla-ree! he cries, or tries to cry, but just before he gets to ree, he catches a comber in the puss. Briny and warm, it makes him gag. He wonders if he's going to drown. If not, is he his brother's keeper? Take brotherless Job knee-deep in dung, or Ready Freddie the Sodomite—and, after Job's endured the shit, is it merely about *The Price Is Right* (Hey, come on down! Here's twice the sheep! New camels and goats and wives? Yahoo!) Is he sedated or still just stoned?

He opens his eyes and looks around. Not Hattie, he thinks, but Miz McDaniel (and yet, he reflects, there must be nights when Hollis wakes up to wind and rain, tent heaving like his overworked lungs, railing against his lousy reward? More camels and goats? Will somebody tell whoever's in charge that people aren't just replaceable parts?) Rose! Oh, Rose! The invisible worm! (But doesn't Bob Barker know the price?) A toucan bit his ass, that's all.

Inez is patting his arm again. "You ress a while. I'm keepin' watch."

He wants to tell her what he means, to beg forgiveness for the ditch (so many ditches, everywhere). Listen, he'd say to Nurse Inez, one night on the road from Chantry Mount where he'd gone to get his turntable fixed, he'd hit a dog with a heavy thunk that seemed to shudder from under the hood—he'd never really seen the dog. He'd stopped and gotten out to look and found it pretzeled in the road, dragging its dead end like a sack, gnawing its haunches in a rage. There'd been a light not far away, a house to which he'd gone for help. White ribbon of sand and moon on the fields, his feet on the porch, and then a voice, feeble and frightened, from inside: "What d'you want?" I hit a dog, it's horribly mangled, next to a ditch. "My husband will shoot it later," she says. "Go on, you better get out of here." Afraid of some hippie cutting their throats, strewing their entrails through the house and ACID IS GROOVY on the walls. He'd known the man would never come out but, helpless to help, returned to his car and driven the killer machine away—the dog still maddened like Ugolino, the moonglint off a strip of chrome.

"Dere ain' no true romantic, honey, who ain' been disillusioned yet."

Like Pavlov's dog, he opens his eyes and stares at her plastic ID badge. Her face is heavy and sleep-deprived, the badge has cracks along one edge. It says Inez—but Inez who? (Were you talkin' to me, Inez? he asks, not talking or thinking anymore until a merciful surge sweeps up and he bobs under, hearing her hum the *Missa Solemnis*. . . O Lamb of God, have mercy upon us.)

"Relax," she says as the music plays on.

Okay, he will. (But what was Caitlin doing here? She knows Inez? He's glad she does.) That takest away the sins of the world. . .

• • •

Still on a gurney, he opens his eyes in a compact low-lit sea-green space watched by two figures dressed in scrubs the same color as curtains drawn on slides. The doctor-dwarf seems half-amused.

"We lifted a heavy object, right? Way too heavy. . . and something ripped?"

Dugan nods. "Then I got hit." His pain thinned out, he's floating in a luminous pool and emptied of what's been troubling him.

"Yep," chuckles the dwarf. "That's how it behaves. Comes at you like a tiger shark and sneaks off like a tabby cat. So how's our shoulder?" Doing okay (my uppercut's slow—but so is life, if you know what I mean). "Let's see. Do this." Windmilling his arm. "That's pretty good, considering. But as for this," he taps his chest and cocks his head as if he thinks they're having fun, "I guess we know what's happening here? The diaphragm. . . it's got a hole—you must have torn it, right through here."

It's not his heart, then? No indeed. "Strangulates and goes back down till something drives it up again. Or just a spasm—hurts the same, except we suck on one of these." He holds a vial up, winks, and says, "Sometimes it'll work, sometimes it won't. We're lucky, though. Just slip it underneath the tongue." What is it? "Nitroglycerine." His destiny as a triple Sadge— will he explode? "Not usually. . . though we might dissolve." Laughter. That was just a joke. "Hiatal hernia is the term—we only fix 'em when they're bad. Cut down on lobster, stress, and booze, reduce our appetite for brawls, and study this bit of sage advice." *Your Hernia & You* it says, its cover showing Dick and Jane matured into the Maalox set (Father's been hooked to life-support, and Mother and Spot. . .) "MISTER DUNCAN!" Dugan, he says. "Please let me finish," growls the dwarf, turning, then bending back again, chewing on something, voice down low. "'Don't ever do nothin' like this again. Don't come back up here. . . understand?'" It's Sheriff Bullard to a T. "'I'd like to see this town die peaceful,'" he adds. "How's our poet?" he wants to know.

Then Inez has him under the arm, guiding him towards the double doors. "That shirt's so pretty," she declares. "You buy that in a Cumbria stow, or yo' frenn pick it out fo' you?" There's Freddie, reading *Modern Bride*. "He be okay now," Inez nods, as Freddie looks up worriedly like an actor in a network soap.

"What was it?"

"Hernia," Dugan shares the news as if announcing It's-a-Boy! "Nurse Inez. . . Freddie Ebert," he adds, still in slow motion from his ordeal. "My friend's just visiting from New York." A man of La Mancha, he almost says as Hattie smiles in a sensible way.

"Oh, no! A hernia?" Freddie emotes, shaking his head theatrically. "Our hopes and plans. Our dream he'd someday bomb Hanoi. All over," he says to Nurse Inez. "All gone in an instant. One fell swoop. This boy is definitely 4-F now."

"Uh-huh," she says. "An' if he still livin' on a farm, he haffa take it easy now." Those 4-F Clubs can wear you out.

"Don't bump me, Freddie," Dugan croons. "I'm full of nitro. I could blow."

"Promises, promises. . . Where's a clock?"

It's two a.m. The bill says August 29—his Blue Cross made it by a day, expires tomorrow. Beat the rap! Maybe he's turned a corner here.

"Listen, hon. As fun as this is. . ."

"Where'd Inez go?" He's more alert.

"She has to work, and so do I. My plane's at eight, and I'm feelin' so whipped I'd rather wait there than sit up here."

The airport then? He nods okay.

"Are you in any condition to drive?"

He will be in an hour or two, after some coffee to perk him up. (It seems we hardly knew yuh, Fred, but planes take off and people die impersonating Bobby Hicks.) "Thanks for the glimpse of S&M. I was lookin' for something exciting to do."

"Yeah, well, you come to the City, okay? I'll fix you up at Bloomingdale's. That wardrobe needs some major work."

He drives while Dugan dozes off—down Blossom Street, across the bridge, and past a geodesic dome, its struts devoid of any skin. Then, after another three miles or so, they're approaching a pair of landing strips. The airport's new, a Sternbolt whim (like Piggie Parlor, based on pork— though fashioned out of yellow brick that looks a lot like barbecue sauce whenever it's wet or lit at night with nobody there but cleaning crews. . . which is clearly the case as they drive up). Was I just dreaming? Dugan asks. All of a sudden, he feels great.

"I think I see a guard," says Freddie. "I'm gonna go in if you're okay. Think you can manage the show from here?"

"Top o' the world, Ma!" Dugan replies. "Hot-chamolly! Shoulder your duds!"

They stuff what fits into Freddie's bags, leaving the lamp in the trunk of the Merc. "Just keep it lit till I get back. My eyelash curler! What happened to it?"

"I'll send it on if it turns up."

"Here's my address." He checks his ticket as Dugan gets out. "Change planes in Atlanta. What a drag! Can't get to hell without that stop."

"They're pretty much the same, I hear."

"Too bad you're straight, but gimme a hug! Keep dancin', honey. You made it real."

The guard looks up as Freddie skips in on his way back to Gomorrah.

• • •

Ah, Lazarus, so it's you again? The town's the same, but you seem changed. So, tell us, hoss, what's it all mean? (He's working on it—give him room. . . he's only just been resurrected.) The Merc creeps slowly towards the hub, circling its periphery (he's packing nitro—merciful God!—whatever you do, don't jiggle his pills!) Speaking of which, a rattletrap Ford veers past him in the right-hand lane, a day-glo sticker on its trunk (JESUS IS COMING BE PREPARED), but after it overtakes the Merc, it runs a light and speeds away. Trailing it is a new-model pick-up— its bumper sticker's much the same (I BRAKE FOR HIPPIES - TRY ME & SEE!) The driver looks like Rolly Dehon, but after a block it turns off too, and Dugan's got the road to himself. No more stickers or slogans. Just the Merc.

Also, he thinks, no place to go and no money left for another motel. But Oedipus-like, he'll solve the riddle, tease out the meaning of this town by driving as long as he's got gas (*systematically*, he tells himself, retrace the layout of the grid until he finds whatever it is that lurks within it hidden away, the minotaur at the heart of it all). But the newly built suburbs where he starts are where logic gives way to realtor chic and streets laid out like tic-tac-toe get twisted into curlicues with names like Windsor and Devonshire gilding their tangled courts and lanes. No answers there, so he'll drive on, heading back towards the section he knows, retracing the route of Lafayette who'd cantered triumphantly up the hill to the Governor's mansion perched on top, making the white-haired patriots weep while rose-crowned maidens, damp in the crotch, watched magnums of champagne going flat as the visiting hero leapt from his horse to hug a black man on the curb. . . his groom throughout the fierce campaign, but still a slave when freedom was won for everyone but people like him (people like Hattie, Dugan reflects, cruising down Marion, Pickens, and Green, then on Sumter past an obelisk for an editor who, having exposed a crook, had gotten a bullet in reply). Down past the mill where poor-white kids had frolicked through twelve-hour six-day weeks, the ballpark, and the Rooster Pit, backtracking up Assembly Street until the Capitol's dead ahead.

My city, thinks Dugan to himself, as if he's finally on the verge of comprehending something or other. He'd gotten this far with Whitman too, and Wittgenstein, and Bessie Smith, but coming so close gets no cigar. He passes a parked policeman's car, a beer truck, and a city bus with one lone rider perched inside. . . the red cap on his head says LOVE (the minotaur he'd feared to find, a harmless dimwit headed home).

He dials up his radio, checking out stations left to right, getting some news he doesn't need (tomorrow there'll be a solar eclipse for those who're living in New Guinea) and news for which there's nothing to do (integration of schools proceeding apace). Eventually, the news runs out, succeeded by some R&B and then a Beatles' sardonic tune. "You may be a lover, but. . ." they jeer,

you ain't no dancer. . .

which he's learned.

There's a sliver of toenail in the sky, littered already, strewn with junk—flags and golf balls, who knows what?—though, even from here, he sees the gash dark as a newly-drained rice field's muck, white as the belly of Sharon Tate. The thought appalls, but he drives on, knowing there lurks on this same road, no more than a dozen miles away, a sign with a neon dancing pig ("*Yún Yŭ! Yún Yŭ!*" it shrieks from its pot, and "Helter-skelter!" sing Paul and Charlie).

● ● ●

He drives back over the river at dawn, approaching the mosque-like Cock-o-Dome aglitter now in the morning sun. Though Herman Munster's still at his post, something about his smile has changed. His mug-arm's stuck in a Nazi salute with his weenie clutched limply by his side. X's are whitewashed on the glass while Herman, with a sad grimace, gazes out wistfully over the road at BUY AMERICAN - DOUBLE WIDE, its lot apparently tripled in size with banners and pennants, red-white-&-blue, above a flashing sign on wheels (SHOP NOW - SUPPORT OUR FIGHTING MEN) beyond which rows of mobile homes fan out across an asphalt beach like errant U-boats run ashore as if summoned by Herman's semaphore.

The Merc slows up. He's not sure why, except, as he watches the tinsel blink next to FREEDOM'S AFFORDABLE - EL CAPRI, he summons up his fellow Rhodes' line ("freedom's just another word. . .") written, they say, while pushing a broom around some Nashville studio with no real job, no prize to win, not even self-respect to lose. "I'm with you, pal," he says to Kris, a thought so compelling in his mood that he stops in front of another sign—George Washington beckoning with a smile and CLASSIC MOUNT VERNON DOUBLE WIDE - BUSINESS OFFICE - COME ON

IN. Below it is a cardboard clock with hands that point to 12 and 2. He sits for a moment in his car, but, noting a Cadillac parked out back with its old-glory mud flaps matched up front by *e-pluribus-unum* bumper flags, he feels there's something there for him, and, despite the clock, he leaves the Merc to peer about inside the lot.

A voice behind him startles him. "Up early huntin' for a worm. . . or just hankerin' for a starter home?"

"Well. . ." croaks Dugan, turning around, confronting a short and sixty-ish man who sports a Mickey-Rooney-like air—everything youthful but the eyes, which have a casino dealer's glint.

Tipping his white ten-gallon hat, the dealer adjusts the clock to 6. "I ain't officially on the job. . . but, like my daddy used to say, strike when the iron gets lukewarm, eh? You want a home?"

"I reckon I'm homeless, right enough."

The man in the hat checks out the Merc. "A snail might say you got a home. Course snails ain't lookin' for a worm, so what you seekin' here, my friend? You in some trouble?"

"No. I was. I got a question."

"Fire away. But join me in that Sanz Soo-see—you look like you could use a rest. As a matter of fact, I'd have to say you look like you could use a friend, some cawfee, and a Tylenol. Had a rough night?"

"You wouldn't believe it," Dugan replies, but adds as he follows him up the steps, "I'm not as desperate as I look."

"That's reassuring. Come aboard." He pauses on the metal porch, turning back to proffer his hand. "I'm Dub-yuh 'Double-Your-Bet' Brazell—call me 'Dub.' I like that shirt."

"From Guatemala."

"You don't say? And how 'bout you?"

"From here in Cumbria. Call me Mike." (Or Ishmael, he's tempted to add.)

"Howdy, Mike. So, you out on the streets?"

"Wrinkled but unbowed," he drawls, finding a touch of Danny in Dub with a hint of the Pancho's Villa guy, a sort of innocence under the scam. "They used to call me Iron Mike."

"And now?"

"Just Mike."

"Well, look here, Mike, tell me the truth. How 'bout that Bell Revv over there? The one with the salmon feelagree. El Hacienda Blanca's next, and then the Bell Revv—classic, huh? That Spanish moss helps set the mood."

"I like it fine."

"Sweet little pad if you're playin' the field—a car like that, I reckon you are. Racin' it stock or soupin' it up?"

"Ain't racin' at all." They look at the Merc, appraising it like two guys at a track observing a racehorse out to stud. Dugan leans back against a rail that yields so much he nearly falls. "Can I level with you. . . Dub?" he asks.

"You bet," says Dub. "C'mon inside. You want it black?"

"I'm really not a customer."

"Slow up there, son," Dub says with a frown, propping the door and gesturing in. "Everybody in life's a customer. You might not be a buyer today, but tomorrow. . . well, just imagine this—you've got a credit card in your hand and, getting' a whiff of what you want, before you know it, there you are, camped out in your customized Sanz Soo-see, surrounded by wimmen who throw themselves at ev'ry sick whim that crosses your mind—Hugh Hefner in a double-wide! Don't tell me you can't afford it, Mike. You kin hock y'r soul an' buy the moon!"

"I'd like to know about Frank 'n' Stein. . . your neighbor there across the road."

Dub looks around with a sidelong squint. "What's that to you?"

"Just curious."

A pause, and Dub gestures to him again. "C'mon!" he repeats like it's a command—he's got the coffee pot on inside. When he turns back, his face has changed (it's more like Jimmy Cagney now). "Siddown, siddown. I hear you, bud. You miss those Monsterburgers, huh? That cup there's yours, this mug is mine." It's got a rooster on its side.

"The sign," says Dugan, taking a sip. "I like that Herman Munster sign. When did the place go belly up?"

Dub sighs, and says reflectively, "What's great about this country, Mike. . . give people what they think they want, an' make yourself a crock o' gold. Provide what they ain't ready for—and, sure as shootin', you get squat." He rubs his jaw. "Leonardo da Vinci said that, son—don't ask me where, that's not the point. We had a concept. It was good. What we got wrong was basically this. . . people want weenies and people want beer, they just don't want 'em with Frankenstein. The writin' was up there on the wall when a kid comes in and was startin' to cry. I told 'em to give him a basket of fries. Here kid, shut up. Know what he says? 'I ain't gone eat no monster shit!'" Throughout his spiel, while shuckin' and jivin', Dub's watching to see what Dugan knows. "So anyhow. . ." He rubs his hands. "I'd sold a franchise here and there but bailed out while it still looked good. Some dentists in Tulsa got upset, but dentists in Tulsa. . ." He pauses as he sees Dugan shrug. "I hear yuh, Mike. No foolin' now. I know it's not what brought you here, but let's walk through this Sanz Soo-see. You won't believe its featurettes."

"I hate to waste your time here, Dub."

"Waste my time? Shoot, what you think? This here's a Sunday." Dub gets up, takes two quick steps, and slaps the metal-plated wall. "I'll sell no trailer a'fore its time. But this is workmanship, my friend. What makes America great," he beams. "Take you yourseff. . . a Veet Nam vet? It's just a hunch. You're lookin' sorta. . ."

"What? Beat up?"

". . . evaporated," Dub observes. "C'mon, I'll show you what we got." He beckons Dugan on out the door and leads him to a steel-gray shell built like a surplus LST. "I call this baby China Beach. Come on, go in." The door appears about as thick as a Swanson TV dinner foil.

"I've been teaching," says Dugan.

"Oh, yeah? Where'bouts?"

He nods uphill. "At CSU."

"Shoot!" Dub exclaims and whacks his hat. "See, Mike, look here. In what I do, it's kinda like guessing people's weight. I'm pretty good at it. . . but with you, I mussta missed some signals there. My boy's up there at CSU—name a Lonnie."

"Sure, I know him." Lonnie Brazell, a.k.a. Mick, the merchant prince of hippiedom. "I taught him. Well, I almost did. . . it's complicated. I dropped out."

"So did Lonnie, durn his soul—just took off on this little bike, hit Monterey and struck it rich, sellin' those geodesic domes." He chuckles. "It's genetic, Mike. Clint Eastwood bought one. . . how 'bout that? Got one of my own out towards Bluff Road."

"That's something."

"Yeah. So tell me, Mike, you want a job? That why you're here?"

"Not that I knew. . . but maybe so."

"Well, now, that's different. Come on in."

The door thuds shut as if it's oak.

"How'd you do that?"

"The foot. See here. That's 'sound construction' in the ads." He thumps his boot against the wall. "You see that built-in couch right there? Go on, siddown. . . a single, seamless Nauga, Mike—one bullet, placed where it don't show. I say that and they laugh, okay? It's human nature, what they think is here's a con man we can trust. That comf'table?"

"Well. . ."

"'Course, it ain't. Now, look at this here kitchenette." He tugs another tin-foil door. "What women want is gadgets, Mike, like that thingamajig a'tween our legs. But this here model's made for men. No doodads, just that one neat hole is what's 'most always on our minds. I ask you am I right, or what? Okay, now take a look in there, just down the hall, right over the bed. You see that mirror? No, up there. That's worth five hun'red in this pad. Don't matter to them the john don't flush. Psychology, son. That's what it takes." He shuts the door. They both sit down, facing each other across a room that feels like a tugboat's boiler-room. "This here's a planet on the move. What I told Lonnie, I'll tell you. This here's a planet on the move. We gotta think global. Yessirree." He pauses while his words sink in. "There's dozens of countries over there. Not just one little measly Veet Nam. You get my drift?"

"Well, I'm not sure. . ."

"Come on!" says Dub. His sudden excitement rocks the boat, making its superstructure creak. "With all that bombin', tell me this, how're they gonna start up again? When the commies are gone, how'll they rebuild?" He lowers his voice. His timing's good. "With mo-bile hooches, son, that's how. And somebody's gonna get that worm."

A mosquito has lit on Dugan's arm. He looks it over, giving blood—but what's the point? He squashes it.

"So whattaya think? Get in at the start. . . or wish you had when it's too late?"

Dugan remembers images—the sun across a wooden sill or pissing in the pristine snow. It's all behind him. This is now. If he can't buy, he might as well sell. Dub zeroes in to close the deal.

"We knock 'em down, we build 'em back. It's gonna take off, I tell you what—this here's a rocket ship we're on." Dub lifts his hat, it fills the room. "It's up to you."

"Well, I don't know."

"Weekends can get right hectic here—'cept during these church hours, never then. On other days you just can't tell. I got two salesmen on the lot—both college grads, you'll hit it off. But listen, Mike, before you speak. . . we glitz it up, we shave it close, but we don't cheat 'em, understand? Past certain limits—that's the thing. Horse-tradin', son, is what it is. Little ole ladies ain't in this game, but out-'n'-out crooks get hung to dry. You follow me here?"

"What sorta pay?"

"Two hun'ed a week, from eight to eight with every other Sunday off. Plus two percent at closin' time. That's where it's at, as Newton said. . . Sir Isaac Newton, heard o' him?"

"You think I got whatever it takes?"

"Up to you, Mike, it's up to you. I'd say you got a worn-out look, but it's appealin' in a way. That shirt might be too fancy, though. The common touch is what you need if you wanna become what my pa woulda called a lollapalooza in this job. You know what I'm sayin'? A *big* success! I got that touch, as you can see. . . an' I think you got the makin's too. You talk to Jeff 'n Randy, hear? the other two guys who're working here. They know the ropes, they'll clue you in." Dub's good at playing out his line.

"Well. . ." Dugan leans against the wall, popping it with a pie-plate sound. One of his grad-school friends had opined that, out of their clutch of pee-aitch-dees, Dugan alone, when the Goths held sway, could make a go of it selling shoes—but his friend had been a southerner too and probably knew that what's-his-name, the schmuck in Eudora Welty's tale, was on the lam from Lickety-Split no matter what his suitcase held and squawked when the job required him to crow. . . whereas Dugan, he said with an ironic smile, "he do the police in different voices" (what useless insider pedantry now!) Toss in the Harvard dean's advice when Dugan defected from the Yard that once you're off the escalator, you're off for good, no way back on (he'd managed to take that too in stride, since, watching his fellow contenders climb, all he'd noticed from them on their way up was a terminal fear of heading down). But whatever his wingspan might have been, this eagle's crash-landed, that's for sure. "I need a day to think it over."

"You got it, son. Now lemme hear those brogans ee-gress with the sound of destiny knockin'."

He thumps the wall and shuts the door. Ka-pok! Ka-pow! He's on his way.

• • •

Strung out but nonetheless energized, he moves from one thing to the next as if working through a grocery list. Two doughnuts and a coffee to go, then a trip to the boondocks outside town where he and Rose had jumped the freight, putting some samples in the bag that he'd gotten his sugar and caffeine in.

Afterwards, since the Merc displays a valid parking sticker still, he parks in the empty faculty lot next to CSU's library building—a lavish white marble edifice regarded as Sternbolt's Taj Mahal but paid for by its marginal use as a subterranean government vault for documents labeled "classified" or Xeroxed duplicates of the same, nobody's sure (that's secret too). It's closed till noon, so Dugan decides to sit awhile, thinking about how things will change for him and Hattie and all the rest (and *ought* to too) until they grow old and get replaced by others with new and different ideas which might be better, though maybe not. . . and, after he's mused a bit about that, he takes his cuttings around in back where, kneeling behind a boxwood screen, he plants the kudzu sprig by sprig, fetching it water in his cup, patting the soil and stepping back as if he's set a bomb's slow-fuse (five years should do it, he reflects, and the place will look like Angor Wat—by which time, in his new career, he'll be known as the princely double-wide czar of a Southeast Asian building boom. . . or who knows what?) The world is wide.

He returns to his bench beside the pool to wait for another hour or two, but wakes with a jolt after taking a snooze, hearing a distant clock strike one. The doors are open. He goes in and, noting how nearly empty it is, ducks down the back STAFF-ONLY stairs into the rarely visited stacks devoted to antiquarian fields. With literature on the mezzanine, he's never explored these depths before. Who has? he wonders, fumbling his way past Babylon, Sumer, Uruk, Ur and Paleontology's meager trove until he encounters empty shelves. Another staircase to the left—collections still unclassified, old journals not yet microfilmed, what seem to be mere blocks of wood safeguarding space for things to come—and deeper still (what lies down there? corridors where they pump in air and hang canaries by the vents?) He sees an elevator door. It's locked but, back behind its cage, he finds a flight of metal stairs—his instincts warning him to desist, his purpose impelling him ever on.

Inside the narrow concrete shaft, the boom of his shoes reverberates— but when he stops, the sound persists. He looks down to the flight below and sees a moving heap of books, a grease-stained sleeve, a balding head steadily bobbing up the stairs. Incredibly, he knows that head. He stops and waits until it nears.

"So, how it's going, Krav?" he says (Young Goodman Brown to Goody Cloyse).

Milt Kravitz does a double take. "Rough stuff," he wheezes, breathing hard. "Medieval's moved. Can't make the climb. Might have to switch to Education." Hitching his load, he pats his brow with what resembles an undershirt or part of one. "God-awful, Mike. . . what happened to Danny. . ."

"Yeah, I know."

Krav wipes his neck. "And Dexter's settled out of court. He's moving to The Citadel."

"I'm happy for him."

"Um-hmmm," Krav says. Then, pocketing his handkerchief and squeezing past Dugan on the stairs, he drops a book that Dugan retrieves, placing it back atop the stack. "Gordo and Meg, has anyone told. . .?"

Dugan nods. They have, he's heard. "So what about you, Krav?" he inquires. "You up for tenure?"

Krav looks down. "I got it," he grunts.

"No shit? That's great! You beat the game."

"Yeah, well. . . you know. . ." He straightens his stack. "I'm working on something new," he says. "You know those novels housewives read? Sell by the millions—nothing but fluff, just variations on one plot?"

"Harlequin romances, right?"

Kravitz nods. "Strictly medieval gothic stuff translated to someplace like Des Moines. So I'm planning to boil the formula down and start churning 'em out to make some dough."

"Krav, you surprise me! Good for you."

"I'll need a nom de plume, of course. . . Gertie McDougal, something like that." He chews for a moment on his beard. "You planning on coming back?" he asks.

"I'm changin' careers."

Krav hesitates, then looks around. "You heard about Glover?"

"Kiddie porn? Caught him corrupting minors again?"

"He's the new chairman. Named last week. Department's antsy."

"Yeah. I'll bet."

Each looks away.

"Well," Kravitz shrugs.

"Good seein' ya, Krav."

"I need a Sherpa." Toiling on, he reaches the landing.

Dugan calls, "Hey, Krav, these stairs. . . how much farther down do they actually go?"

"Depends on what you're looking for."

"Gov Documents."

"The Sternbolt stuff? Go down one more and hang a right. Ignore the elevator, though—without a key, you can't get in. On through the stacks, you'll see some pipes, past shelves they've marked for oversized. Turn right again and there's a door."

"It's for the vault?"

"Who knows?" booms Krav, his voice an echo in the well. "'Government Federal National' and 'Sternbolt Authorized' is what it said last time I looked. . . whatever the hell you think that means."

"Abandon hope?"

But Krav is gone, his footsteps like a distant drum while Dugan listens as they recede. After another half-minute or so, he makes his way on down the stairs, turns right, and finds no elevator. He doubles back the other way, locates some pipes and follows them until he runs into a wall, then splits the difference, shuts his eyes, and ends up by a thick steel door. It's got a square of frosted glass to which is taped an index card, or half of one—he spots the other half on a shelf. When pieced together, what they say is

Government   Documents -
Federal   Records Center
National   Archives
Sternbolt   Extension
Authorized   Staff & Faculty Only

The door's unlocked. He steps inside, finding it dim and icy cold, the A-C churning out a breeze that rushes towards the open door through a passageway formed by high-tiered shelves, some holding volumes already bound but most with boxes still unpacked though coded numerically starting with 12 and running in order through 162. He steps into a larger space where sheaves of papers are lying untied, laid out in piles autopsy-style, some spilling their guts onto the floor. Looking at otherwise empty shelves, he sees scissors and glue sticks, felt-tip pens, and two flat eyes behind a stack, watching intently as he nods. "Hi," he says. "You here alone?"

"I'm cataloguing," a woman says, stepping out from behind the shelves. Her accent might be Portuguese.

"Looks like you've got a ways to go." There's no reply. He notes her stern, reproving look, her mousy-voracious stir-nuts air. "I hate to bother you. . ." he adds.

"Yes?" she says suspiciously.

"I'm. . . looking for some documents."

"Access is restricted here. You're faculty?"

"I've been on leave." But he can produce his I.D. card. He does and lets her check it out.

"You're going to need a new one soon. How can I help you?"

"First," he says, "I'd like to borrow some notebook paper."

She blinks. "How much."

"A couple of sheets. Say, three or four."

She opens a notebook. "Three or four. . ."

He likes the unencumbered way her breasts shift as the sheets are torn, that take-it-or-leave-it body-talk of market women at a stall with nothing but spotty old fruit to sell (whose feigned indifference doesn't conceal their desperate hunger for a sale)—he's willing to bet she's from Brazil. "Thanks," he says. He swipes her pen. "What do you think of Glauber Rocha?"

"I beg your pardon?"

"Never mind. You're a graduate student?"

Yes, she nods. "In Library Science." She looks around the morgue-like stacks, hugging herself against the cold.

"Is something wrong?"

"My pen," she says. "I must have dropped it."

"What color is it?"

"Same as yours." They both bend down to study the floor. He notes her scarlet dancing shoes, with laces crisscrossed up the leg, and she, aware of his eyes on her, commences a guileless monologue, speaking as if he'll understand when she says she knows she's absentminded, that's why they've shut her up down here—it's exile really, she confides. "Where'd it go?" She hunts around.

"Use this one."

Thanks. There're plenty more—more pens than people as a rule. She smiles at him but takes the pen. And where's he from? From Cumbria? Ah, she'd thought. . . oh, well. That shirt, she says, it's so like home What,

Guatemala? He's been there, then? Of course—it's very beautiful. Impoverished, though. Not governed well.

"But that will change." He says to her.

"Yes, that. . ." she answers, stopping herself. She doesn't continue right away, and, when she does, it's in a voice that's like a librarian's once again. "You're looking for something?"

Yes, he is. The Peers Inquiry on My Lai. The General's delivered his report, but only a portion has been released. Sternbolt's on the Senate committee. Have those records been deposited here? She says she knows just what he means. Twelve boxes. All are classified—which one would he be looking for? He takes a shot—the first, he says. A summary narrative is his thought. She twists a finger in her hair, looks down the hallway, sucks on the pen he's handed her—her own, of course, he's given it back. No notes, she cautions. He agrees and says he'll study it right here, in one of the carrels of this room.

"The paper," she shrugs. He hands it back, saying of course he understands. She smiles apologetically. "We don't get many visitors." She goes into an inner vault, returning with a four-wheeled cart on which she's placed a heavy box. A buzz erupts. The telephone. "They're always checking up," she says.

He opens the box and starts to read, aware at once of what he's found, amazed by all that's been suppressed as he skims what the general's group had learned, details he knows are underpinned with things he's never heard before—like the skin flick watched by Calley's men before the next day's horror show; the survivor who, when shown photographs, had picked his butchered daughter out; the woman whose wailing throughout the night had rattled them so, post-massacre, that they'd fired grenades and M-16s, though nothing could shut her keening up. He confirms that, simultaneously, there'd been another "incident," by Bravo Company at Co Luy—another Calley, like the first (the one that Willingham had led). More rapes and murders. More deceit, prompting another cover-up.

But then he spots the name he wants, the curious, half-formed wisp of hope in the back of his mind since talking to Hollis—Thompson, Hugh C. (WO1), reconnaissance pilot, air support, flying an OH-23, backed by two UH-1Bs, from Company B, Aviation Battalion 123, known as the "War Birds". . . the same guy Hollis must have meant. Stone Mountain, Georgia, 25, married, 2 sons. The background info here is sparse, but Dugan's able to piece together a shadowy sort of storyline.

A college drop-out from Troy State, Thompson had served in the Navy Reserve, done active duty for three years, and mustered out—ironically, in retrospect, to operate a funeral home where maybe he'd learned respect for the dead, or disdain for bungling amateurs, or compassion for those who're still alive. . . because afterwards, when he'd re-enlisted, he wanted precision in his job, no wishful-thinking body counts or fragging ascribed to friendly fire or collateral damage written off as business-as-usual in a war. Back as an officer, lightly armed and more or less constantly in harm's way, his rep was as an "exceptional" pilot—competent, brave, and by-the-book—flying his tiny three-man craft into the teeth of enemy fire, supported by Hueys overhead but skimming at times so close to the ground that, firing his twin M-60 guns, he saw the faces of those they shot.

The other two members of his crew were Lawrence Colburn (SP4), a gunner, 18, on his first tour, and Glenn Andreotta (SP4), crew chief, his age not listed here. Then Dugan discovers what he wants—on 16 March 1968, as close support for Task Force Barker, they'd flown their bubble to My Lai.

Pausing, he squirms about in his chair. The air in the archive tastes exhumed, the carrel he's in feels coffin-like (like the Plexiglas cockpit Thompson flew except, of course. . . except. . . he thinks). Hunching his shoulders, stretching his back, he tests the soreness in his chest. At her desk a couple of feet away, the cataloger's ball-point pen is tapping an ominous tic-tac-tic as if some timer's running down (the seventh seal about to be broken, the silo doors sliding open again. . . though, if they're unleashing Armageddon, it occurs to him that, down in this bunker, the two of them might both be safe, surviving to found a better race of super-librarians for the world, a thought that's not so reassuring). He clears his mind and then resumes.

Thompson's bubble set out that day by skirting the village of My Lai 4. He didn't encounter enemy fire but saw several fighting-age males below and followed them as they ran away, hovering above them and making them wait for back-up choppers to carry them off for questioning back at the landing zone. No more possible combatants after that, but wounded villagers in a field that he marked with smoke flares dropped from above, signaling an urgent need for help.

After refueling, he returned to find the injured now were dead with additional corpses scattered about enveloped in drifting clouds of smoke. In a rice field south of My Lai 4, they spotted a woman by a dike, apparently wounded but still alive. From just a few feet off the ground,

Colburn could see her moving her hand, and Thompson called for medical aid. The only contact he could make was with one of the Hueys overhead which, specifically noting Thompson's report of "a wounded civilian under that bubble," relayed it to an officer close by in an adjacent field with ground troops under his command. The officer, wearing captain's bars, walked over to where the woman lay, prodded her roughly with his boot, stepped back and finished her off.

Thompson had seen enough of the war to know what risks might be at stake with friendlies who're friends until they shoot, but what he'd just witnessed was murder. Certain of that, he soared back up, spotting no hostiles anywhere. It was 0900 by his log when, continuing eastward, he looked down on a sizable irrigation ditch piled high with a jumble of bodies while, only a few feet away, a group of soldiers took a break, lounging around with their helmets off, apparently laughing as they smoked.

Unable to fathom what he saw but noting some movement in the ditch, Thompson had landed, clambered out, and, over the chopper rotors' roar, had a shouted exchange with a sergeant there, asking him in a furious voice "if he couldn't do something to help" those in the ditch who were possibly still alive. He was answered with a curt reply that "the only way to help them out is to put them out of their misery." A lieutenant walked over to make it clear that he commanded his platoon and that Thompson had no business there. That officer was William L. Calley.

There's background on him in the file as well, and Calley, like Thompson, had come from the South. A tone-deaf former short-order cook who'd never gotten a traffic ticket, he looked, as one observer said, like a kid from *The Saturday Evening Post*, a Norman Rockwell sort of guy with a touch of Charles Manson in his soul. "Butt the hell out" is how he'd replied in answer to Thompson's urgent request for help for the wounded in the ditch.

Angrily, Thompson had lifted off and circled the area once or twice. Then Andreotta, looking back, reported the sergeant had opened fire, spraying the villagers huddled there. Enraged but powerless, hugging the ground, Thompson had choppered north northeast, locating another large group in flight, women and children rushing to hide in a tunnel or bunker not far off, pursued by men of the 2nd Platoon returning, as later reports would confirm, from a previous rampage at Binh Tay.

It was then that Thomson decided to do what some in the Pentagon tried to suppress as, stung by futility at the ditch, he'd landed like a dragonfly between the villagers and the troops, unfastened his seat belt, stepped to the ground, and, instructing his crew to give him cover, moved grimly towards the advancing platoon—alone, unarmed, proceeding on foot. "Cover you how?" his gunner had asked, and Thompson had given him this reply, "If they start firing, fire on them." Colburn had swiveled his gun around.

In confronting the leader of the platoon—his name in the file is Stephen Brooks— Thompson described what he'd seen from the air. The villagers scrambling underground were clearly civilians he declared. A number were children, some were old. He wanted to get them out of the bunker. Brooks told him that he'd accomplish that with a couple of well-placed hand grenades, then testily tried to brush him aside. But Thompson had shouted for Brooks to wait. He'd get them out himself, he said. . .

A phone rings. There's some murmuring, and Dugan cautiously looks around as silence again pervades the room. Sensing there's something buried here that glitters already through a chink, he knows he's got to dig in a hurry to find the secret hidden there without overlooking it in his haste. He locks in on what happened next as, lifting the tunnel's entrance away, Thompson had coaxed the villagers up while Colburn's M-60 held at bay the men of Brooks' 2nd Platoon who must have assumed it was just a delay before they were once again in charge.

But Thompson had used his radio to call the covering Hueys down to ferry imperiled villagers out. At first the Hueys had temporized, but, describing the stand-off underway, Thompson had made it crystal clear that, if the civilians came under fire, he'd have to defend them using his guns against our own undisciplined troops. The Hueys then did what Thompson had asked, transporting the villagers out of harm's way.

The end of a section, pages of notes, corroboration of various sorts. . . then Dugan picks up with the bubble again, which needed refueling as before—though, on their way to LZ Dottie, they'd made another pass at the ditch. No troops were visible from the air, but bodies were clearly strewn about and jumbled together in a heap. Were some still living? What if they were? Thompson wanted to land, he said. His men agreed and, once on the ground, while Thompson covered both of his crew and Colburn cradled an M-16, Andreotta went down into the ditch.

A short steep slope, some five feet deep. A hundred bodies, blood and filth. Already flies had found the spot. The stench was nauseous. Wading in, waist-deep in hell, Glenn Andreotta couldn't believe he'd found what they were looking for—a child of maybe three or four, covered in blood, but still alive. He saw its eyes move. Nothing else. Then, groping beneath a woman's corpse that lay across it like a shield, he touched its leg and found it was warm. He thought the child was watching him, though as he probed it made no sound. Carefully, he tugged it free, moving entangled limbs aside, and turned to Colburn, lifting it. . .

Dugan stops to take a breath.

. . . lifting it by the back of its shirt and passing it into Colburn's hands, who tucking it in against his side, helped Andreotta scramble up. Together, they checked the child for wounds—a boy, they saw, who was older than they'd thought at first and looked unscathed except for shock. Bundled in Andreotta's lap, the boy was flown to Quang Ngai City. Nobody spoke— though during the trip, as Colburn looked at Thompson's face, he saw that he was quietly crying.

Not far from where the bubble touched down was an ARVN hospital, staffed by Catholic doctors and nuns. A nurse came out. They left the silent child with her, refueled at a nearby strip, and made their way to LZ Dottie where Thompson, tearing his helmet off, rigid with anger and despair, reported a massacre at My Lai 4. Dugan's about to turn the page when a note at the bottom catches his eye. In battle, 8 April 68, Glenn Andreotta had been killed. His wounds had been. . .

"Excuse me, sir!" He turns around. The cataloger looks severe but softens on seeing Dugan's eyes. "I should have explained the rules more clearly. I thought you were current faculty here."

"Is there a problem?"

"Yes, there is. I'll have to ask for that file back." She seems embarrassed as she adds, "This whole collection is restricted."

Through a gap in the boxes, in the hall, he glimpses someone looking on, a face reflected multiple times by glass partitions on the shelves. Dugan shrugs, recalling the lines, *Yea, slimy things did crawl with legs/Upon the slimy sea.* "Has there been a complaint?"

"I'm sorry, sir. . . you've got to leave."

"No problem. . . here." He closes the box, as clenching his fist and holding it up, "*Como en Vietnam,*" he adds.

With glue on her fingers, she clenches her fist. "*Pasará. Hasta luego,*" she says.

"*Hasta luego,*" Dugan replies.

He waves to Glubber in the hall, who tucks his head in like a toad. It's easy to grasp what's happened here, how his nemesis spitefully intervened in a scholar-squirrel's natural habitat—the bottommost vault for stashing

415

his hoard, his nuts and commas and carrion—it all makes sense, he should have known. . . though whether Glubber had followed him down or been informed he'd invaded these depths (maybe by Kravitz, who can say?) is totally irrelevant—as are Calley and Glubber and all their ilk. For, against all odds and despite such shits, he feels such a weird exuberance at having found goodness even in hell that he almost blesses them unawares. . . not their deeds, their reptilian souls.

• • •

It's late in the day but not too late to visit someone he needs to see, though in actual fact they've never met. Max Kappelman's in his 90's now and lives with his wife and Danny's aunt in what had been open countryside when he'd bought the land a half-century back, before its entrance gate was flanked by a garishly tricked out Magik Mart and an Uncle Sam's Factory Outlet Store. But still, with its long dirt-road approach, the property seems a world apart, a Chagall-like old-world hideaway erected on acres of long-leaf pine with stands of hardwoods mingled in.

When he'd bought it during the Twenties boom, his building skills were much in demand for cornices, pediments, bas-reliefs sculpted from stone or cast in cement in ways nobody could duplicate, both durable and delicate with methods brought over from Germany and models transported in his head. A local architect paid his way to help him adorn skyscrapers downtown, the tallest of which was ten stories high. When hard times came, the architect went, and Kappelman switched to things smaller in scale—lawn jockeys holding out hitching rings, banisters, benches, garden urns ("Look at 'em," Danny used to say, "nothing but pink eye spreads that quick!") followed in time, as fashions changed, by cherubs, St. Francis, and nipple-less nudes. Undaunted, Kappelman carried on ("Rabbi Ben Ezra," Danny would shrug, for whom the best was yet to be).

Trees and undergrowth bracket the drive down to another metal gate where there's a sign to HONK YOUR HORN. He honks, and almost instantly a frenzied wolf-like dog appears, hurling itself against the gate. A woman in boots comes up the drive, picking a switch and scolding the dog, gesturing with perfunctory threats. She waves and nods in Dugan's direction as if she's recognized the Merc. Leaning out, he gives his name, at which she smiles and nods again.

"I know, I know," she says in reply. In kerchief and skirt, with rolled-up sleeves, she has a vaguely shtetl-like air.

"I'm here to see. . ."

"Fritz!" she answers, turning her head.

"No. . . Mister Kappleman," he insists, quite certain that Danny had called him Max.

"Go back to the house!" she tells the dog, which he deduces must be Fritz.

The dog complies as she opens the gate and slams it shut once Dugan's through, wagging her switch to guide the way. He rumbles along at her leisurely pace, peering past branches to his right at what resembles a mock Versailles—terraces, stairs, and balustrades cascading down to hedge-rimmed pools, a sort of Watts Towers in cement.

"Come! Come!" she beckons.

He obeys, the Merc's tires sluffing on pine straw and sand until he glimpses among the trees, surrounded by grass and azalea beds, a gingerbread cottage built on a rise. She's gesturing now for him to stop.

"Go down to the workshop," she suggests as if she were addressing Fritz.

Not knowing where the workshop is, he looks around, but, dropping his keys as he's leaving the car and bending over to pick them up, he sees Fritz creeping, ears laid back, as if ready to launch a sneak attack. Fritz freezes when Dugan points him out to the woman who's moved on towards the house.

"Inside!" she hisses from the stoop, scraping her boots and waving the switch.

Fritz bolts past Dugan towards the door, which closes after the dog's inside along with the woman who's tossed her switch into a blooming azalea bed. Still trying to guess where the workshop is, he makes out a gable through the pines and then a footpath down the slope meandering towards a warehouse-like shed so cluttered that, when he peers inside, the far wall can't be seen at all. Over his head, the pine trees creak. He smells their resin-oozing bark.

"Mister Kappelman?" he quietly calls, entering through an open door and proceeding past columns and cement sacks, troughs and ladders, and, farther along, statues with arms and hands so big they lie detached along the floor (*The Scarlet Empress!* Dugan thinks, half-expecting Sam Jaffe to appear, giggling and bug-eyed, bobbing his head). He comes to an empty space in back with a sliding side door and long work bench with tools like chessmen set in place, chisels and sticks with bits of wire, hammers and brushes in a row—an exemplary sight for the order-impaired if merely the tidiness of the old (his grandfather's tackle box comes to mind, but with a more convoluted scheme, smacking, he thinks, of the cabbala, the antithesis of his Lugton hut). He studies the bench as if he's stoned, his brain revved up from sheer fatigue, noticing papers stacked to one side, old sketchpads, and a wallet-sized daybook sitting on top with words and numbers in dark blunt type—"**1918**" first and, under that, in a larger and bolder gothic font,

Soldaten Tagebuch

When he opens its cover, he sees a face that's half familiar in a way—with baleful eyes and a watchful expression, a man in his thirties, wry, bemused. . . the Kaiser's soldier, Dugan discovers: **KAPPELMAN, Maximilian Hans**.

Surreal that it's sitting there ready to hand amid the effigies cast in cement including a bas-relief next to the bench that's wrapped in heavy plastic sheets through which a satyr's gazing out. Its mouth is open and there's a beard, but he notes the resemblance anyhow—the man in the daybook looks the same—a perception that's seemingly crossed the mind of a naked Diana who's turning away with displeasure or fright across the way, hemmed in as she is by other huge works that remind him of Danny's droll account of how *der alte*, at eighty-nine, had one day caused a column to fall, pinning him to the floor for hours before his cries for help were heard—following which, according to Danny, they thought he'd lost a step or two. But in less than a week, there Kappelman was, mixing cement and casting molds as if too busy for trifling concerns like badly wrenched backs and fractured bones.

Dugan looks up and down the shed. Then, trusting that Fritz is still indoors, he follows some flagstones over a bridge to find a Disneyish stone tableau laid out beside a goldfish pool. . . Snow White, six dwarfs, a pair of feet. He counts once more and gets to six when, dead ahead, with a shovel in hand, he sees the last dwarf nod and wink.

"You know vhut I'm doink?"

Dugan's surprised. Expecting Rodin, he's encountered Tom Thumb— wizened, twinkly, and really small (but then, he reflects tangentially as the last two days start taking their toll, Rodin himself was merely wide—broad shouldered, like a pulling guard—though what's this weird recurrence mean of gnomes and midgets at every turn? Is it possibly just a long-term trend, like child-sized armor in museums? How big was Beowulf after all? Or Grendel's mother—Oona's size? We shrink, of course, as we grow older, or maybe our egos need less space—smaller but wiser, happy thought. So, if Kappelman's Admiral Nelson's size, and Dugan and Calley are average height for doughboys off to fight the Huns, why not General Mite with a Gatling gun?) Kappelman's waiting for his reply, but Dugan's too lost in thought for that.

Raising his eyebrows after a pause, Kappelman says with a puckish smile, "I'm puttink life back into zuh erss."

"Uh-huh," says Dugan stupidly. He's been doing a bit of that himself if giving the gift of kudzu counts. Smiling, he bows and nods in turn as Kappelman cocks his head to add as if they're sharing a family joke, "All you need iss a shuffle, see vhut I mean?"

Dugan grins, not speaking the thought that's in his mind—that, in the places he's coming from, what makes a shovel so much in demand is all the horseshit ready at hand. Not here, of course, in this fairy-tale world. . . though Kappelman's confidential air suggests that the Guatemalan shirt combined with the eyesight of old age might have made him appear to be Danny instead. "Excuse me, Mister Kappelman. . ."

"Yes?"

"You know. . ."

"I know, I know." He stops with the shovel poised in mid-air. "You're Danny's friend. He said you'd come."

"He did?"

"Of course." Jabbing the spade into the ground, he shrugs and starts back towards the house.

"I thought I should tell you about the Merc. I've been driving the Mercury. Caitlin said. . ."

"I know. But look, see here," he points. The trunkless feet of the missing dwarf. "If zey ask, I gif zem. Instead zey schteel. I don't know vhy zey chooss to schteel." Shaking his head, he sighs and smiles. "You know?"

"No, sir." Thieves swiping a footless cement dwarf? Maybe it's Fritz.

"Oh, shoor, you do!" He walks with springy light-limbed strides. "You chooss, I chooss. It makes us chooss." Dugan is silent. "Life," Kappelman adds, "it makes us chooss, and vee choos poorly many times. But zat's okay," he says with a shrug, looking back where the dwarf had stood. "It's only meanness zat's truly wrong. And pleasure in meanness." He walks on. "My grandson. . . he vass never mean."

But careless, Dugan ruefully thinks. Where does such carelessness come in? For choosing impulsively, what's the price?

"Listen," says Kappelman, turning around as if he's reading Dugan's mind. "It's luff, you see? Zuh rest doesn't matter." He shakes his head. "Too simple for you? For Danny too." He goes on talking as he turns so that Dugan's unsure what Kappelman says, catching only a sing-song phrase: ". . . *Liebe hab ich nie erfleht.*" Heine and Schumann Dugan thinks, but maybe Schubert or no one at all, just mutterings out of the old man's past.

They reach the house and scrape their feet, smudging the mat with rich black dirt. Inside, as soon as his eyes adjust, he sees the dog and the woman in boots now pushing a wheelchair through the gloom, wheeling in Norman Bates's mother.

"Mootah," says Kappelman, "look whoos here. It's Danny's friend."

He hesitates. "How do you do?"

The mummy glares. An awkward pause. "Mootah doesn't talk today. She underschtands, zough," Kappelman says.

"Mootah wanders," the woman explains. Dugan can picture Mootah and Fritz nabbing dwarf-snatchers late at night. "I'm Danny's aunt," the woman adds.

"I'm. . ."

"Yes. You said."

"Come. Danny hass told me you should see. Venn I vass young as you and Danny, I vass a schtudent. Here, you see?" The dining room wall is ringed with shelves, on which—and on the sideboard too—arranged like tools on the workshop's bench, are silver boxes, plates and bowls, heavily worked and ornamented. "Bevore zuh vaw. . ." He picks up one of the largest bowls. He rubs its rim. It seems to glow. "Ziss vun first prize. You see zuh vay it's hammered here?"

"Wonderful," he hears Danny say.

"*Nymphen,*" Kappelman shrugs and sighs. "You know ziss verd?"

"Nymphs?" he says.

"Yah, nymphs. Ah, but. . . you see—just here? Zey run avay." He turns the bowl. "All-vays. . ." he shrugs, "zey run avay." He puts it back. The room is dark, its panels hued like bourbon casks. Fritz glowers next to Mootah's side as Kappelman takes Dugan's arm, steering him past the shining bowls. "You know vhut I haff to tell you," he says. "Luff. . . okay, you know all zat. But, you see, vhutever hass once been all-vays iss. Each life iss zoh miraculous, and you, me, Mootah, Danny, Fritz. . . vee're just a little part, you see? Zuh whole. . . well, look!" He takes the bowl back down again, tipping it so the inside shows, suffused with a strange reflected light. "It's not illushion. It's okay. You muss luff it, zoh." He squints at Dugan merrily. "I'm zo glad you could come," he nods. "You'll tell her, yes? Vhut I haff said?"

"Who?"

Kappelman smiles. "You know," he says.

● ● ●

When he enters the kitchen, burglar-like, ostensibly he's returning the keys. She's by the sink but dressed for bed, wearing a cotton-print granny gown, her hair pinned back, her narrow bare feet. . . like what? he thinks— gefilte fish was Danny's take. All that's beside the point, of course, because she's made her indifference clear. As a matter of fact, what's she to him—a high-hipped bird that stalks about too unadorned to flutter or preen? as angular as Virginia Woolf, as homely and as hard to read? who drives him crazy, always has, with her enigmatic wait-and-see, her stutter opposed to his wild rush? He can't help feeling a stirring within—and manners require some affable chat. But he's come with a message to deliver.

She's listening to the radio. Her back is turned as he pauses and knocks, amused by his own insulting conceits—a wading bird? Virginia Woolf? a barefoot harridan in a snit?—coincidence kicks back in again as Dylan announces right on cue,

And in comes Romeo. . .

He laughs and ". . . he's moaning," he sings along, watching her cut the radio off and swivel her head in his direction.

"C-C-Christsake!" she yaps, confirming his prophecy of a snit.

"You want a lamp?" He holds it up. "Sorry about the shade," he adds, setting it on the cutting board.

"It's st-st-stolen?" she asks.

"A present from a friend of mine. You got a bulb? This one is broken."
Her gown is blue with parsley and carrots intertwined, harboring rabbits
here and there. "Rabbits?" he asks and gets a shrug. "You want me to, I'll
plug it in."

"G-G-Go away." Her voice is flat.

Clearly, he thinks, she's not amused.

"Rabbits are good, though. Beatrix Potter. . ."

She picks a plate up, hesitates as if considering what to do, then turns
to rinse it in the sink.

"You're weakening, babe." He starts to laugh but coughs and chokes
before he stops.

"Y-Y-You on a b-binge?"

"You might say that." He clears his throat. "I visited Kappelman."

"S-So?" she says, still turned away.

"So. . . I don't know. He catechized me. . . about the earth, the meaning
of life. I had a chance to schmooze with Fritz. And Mootah too. It was
quite a trip."

She bends to open the dishwasher door, reaching inside to move some
bowls. He watches her rearrange the rack, pour Calgonite in, and close the
door, nudging a hip against the knob. He hears a gurgle and a click. A
whoosh of water.

"W-W-Well?" she says, not looking back.

"He's pretty amazing. . ." As Danny had said.

The water slows to a trickle and hiss, then clicks again. The counter
throbs, beginning to churn. She seems to rumba, keeping time, until she
leans her hip away.

"I found a job." He doesn't know why he's telling her this, except he's
sure it's no dead end. Wherever it leads, he'll be okay, something he didn't
know before. "I might even try to write," he says, telling her what he's just
found out about what happened at My Lai. He chokes up when he reaches
the end. "Anyhow, I've got a job. . . though Herman Munster hasn't," he
adds.

She's facing the window, gazing out at lavender clouds between the
roofs. They're covered by layers of purple and pink, dark at the bottom,
mixed with blue and shading again to brighter pink with specks of
incandescent white. The sycamore's turned a stage-lit red.

"Oh, y-yeah?" she finally answers him, turning as if to study his face.
"Y-You came by here to t-t-tell me that? Or w-was it the l-l-lamp?"

He holds the keys up. Neither speaks until she says a second time, "S-So. . ." leaning against the Kenmore again and putting her rabbits in a panic. "Wh-What else d-did he t-t-tell you?"

"Kappelman?"

She straightens her back and the rabbits are still. To him that's regrettable in a way—not thinking about it but vaguely aware he'd liked the way her body moved, like a stutter translated lower down. Surprised by what that triggered in him, he recovers enough to say with a shrug while putting the keys on the countertop, "You make mistakes, you go on trying." He sees her face now in the pane. "He told me I was coming here. I didn't know that. . . but he was right."

She looks as if she listening. . . to what he means, not what he says. They wait together and something melts amid the Kenmore's gurgling sounds, something they've both been waiting for—though neither is sure just what that is. Outside, it's darker in the yard and everywhere there seem to be sparks, like stirring the embers of a fire. "L-L-Lightning bugs," he thinks he hears, though maybe she murmurs meaningless words, slowly easing her hips again against the now frenetic machine.

Whatever she might have meant before, he understands what she's saying now as the rumba resumes, though in reverse, her face half-turned as if to watch the last pale patch of evening sky across which, zipping the sunset up, a jet has dug its luminous furrow. He has a conviction he's always had but never acknowledged. Now he knows. . . it *is* O Agnes O my soul! He stumbles against her, holding her, vibrating in unison hip to hip. Then, reaching out like Farmer McGregor, he ups the ante rabbit by rabbit. Her cheeks are cold, but—stunningly—there're curves he didn't know were there.

He feels her shudder and he responds with what he'd vowed he'd never do, facing the window and, when she turns, fox-trotting across the vinyl floor. The lamp's knocked over. So are they, but, mouth to mouth, the dance goes on.

He hears a furious scrubbing sound, a three-beat rhythm he's heard before. . . but where? He knows. It's in his mind—the Gloria from the *Missa Solemnis*. A spinning and sucking. One cycle. Two. A ratcheting, a convulsive heave. . . and water comes flooding through the seams, drenching her nightgown, dowsing him, and flooding a cardboard Roach Motel just as their own dams burst asunder.

"O Christ! O Christ!"

It dwindles again. A mechanical cluck and then a wheeze. Warm puddles and a whinnying sigh.

Her arms relax. She opens her eyes. "D-D-Don't y-you *ever*. . . !" she gasps aloud, "d-d-do that again!" She reaches behind her with her fist, socking the mute dishwasher door. "G-G-God-d-damned S-S-Sears Roebuck!" she says in despair. He looks around. The lamp, he sees, won't be much good. "Th-that f-fucking shirt!" She winnows the suds. He understands. "He th-th-thought. . ." She pauses.

"What?" he says, aware of the places they'll have to go.

". . . th-that sh-she was u-u-using you all along."

"Oh, I don't know." He contemplates her loose-limbed frame. Not really his type, but there's her mind—he's always loved that steep terrain. "Have you ever heard what Carlyle said to. . ."

"W-Who?" she asks, and they're off again.

He jerks his head. "That appliance of yours is starting to smoke."

"Y-Yours too," she nods. She widens her eyes and he peers in, feeling the same old vertigo. "It's s-s-switching to Dry. . . hot air, okay? But y-you were s-saying. . .?"

"Just more hot air." He lets it go (he'd loved her, though, he tells himself).

He starts to push himself away. She pulls him back and turns her face to let him see her eyes again, then pauses to listen to something else that he hasn't yet begun to detect. . . a whisper from the Kenmore's depths. He hears it too belatedly, a harbinger of wind and rain, before it sputters and falls still. Neither can see the light come on. CYCLE OVER, it says.

VI

THE TRUE MEANING OF A PEAR

August 30, 1970

Had I but time... O, I could tell you.

—Hamlet

They talked for a while to lay some ghosts—he told her a lot she hadn't known, and then, when things had calmed down again, they decided to have another go. . . which is how they'd ended up in her bed where, whatever her present *post facto* qualms, she knows she's somewhat more than complicit. There's not much point in denying that, which makes her further rethink her prayer.

"Forgive me, Lord," she thinks she'll say, "my problem here is not just lust, it has to do with common sense—which isn't to say it's not about sin, though sinners make saints is what I hear, assuming they get things under control. . . and maybe I'm turning a corner here in a way I admit I never saw coming. But You know, Lord, even better than I, that gluttony is my secret sin as I think I've made evident in my work—for which I plead guilty to culpable waste in watching those edibles putrefy and even to wrath if I get to the kitchen and find when I do that the last of the bagels is gone. So let me admit, of the options at hand, I'd make a truly lousy nun.

"I know, I know! a *reductio ad absurdum*, right? But it's not exactly backsliding, Lord, as I'm rolling into the dent he's made and catching the residue of a dream that lingers behind him in my bed—one not about me, and that's okay because I know now where he's been, revisiting bodies in a ditch, a place he's been to more than once except this time there're three men there who've never been in that dream before. . . one of them with a heavy gun that he's got cradled on his arm while another's put down his M-16 to lean with both his hands outstretched to take a child held by the third, who's waist-deep in among the dead as if—and this is in the dream—he's one of them now or soon will be (I hear the dream narrator's voice, a woman I've never heard before: 'He doesn't know he's going to die, or guess dat, in dis moment of grace, all his sins have been forgiven'), a pause before she speaks again ('Cattolick propaganda, huh?')—the dreamer's weeping, so am I.

"End of the movie. . . following which he left for the john, sniffing his fingers and bumping the wall. 'Varsol? Jesus Aitch!' he said, hearing a whining in his ear that interrupts his echoing dream ('Hey, pal, get real, you're screwing my wife!') 'I know that, Dan, shut up, okay?' while sauntering through the semi-dark hall, thumping his chest to summon a burp, a reflex he could identify as a sort of hiatal aftershock, though something was stuck he couldn't get clear. 'You got a suggestion?' ('Sure, I do, squeal lak a pig, c'mon now, boy. . . and gimme my shirt back!') 'Listen, Dan, we've got a situation here. . .' ('A predicament, pal, that's worse than you think. . . as the Adlai Lama wants you to know.') 'The who?" He's belched successfully. ('You oughta know the schtick by now: devout dyslexic searching for Dog. . . it's dharma, right? The Adlai Lama was tellin' me how we got that Famous Dogs baby wrong, but not exactly the way you thought—it's not just countin' 'em up, you see? Count everything else, but *learn* from them, the ones we consider our four-footed friends—they're further evolved, and what are we? a little higher than microbes, Duke, disappointingly lower than the dog. . . they're stalwart, noble, faithful, fun—never malicious, petty, or mean unless we've somehow made them so—no guile or bigotry in them. . . and the message for you here, Brother Mike: be more like them, you copy that?') 'Well, sure, but Caitlin. . .' (After a pause: 'Screw Caitlin!') 'That your final word?' ('And go do that schtick the way we said and nab yourself tenure on the way.') 'Can't do,' he demurred. 'That fishing is tragic—I gotta go sell a double-wide.'"

The voices go silent in her head. "I think that's it, Lord," she'll conclude. "not exactly a prayer, I realize, but maybe—for the moment, at least—something in lieu of a confession."

There was silence in heaven for half a second before she could hear a toilet flush and time resumed with the noise of him in the kitchen next (up to what? she was asking myself—maybe he'd find more clippings to read, how Sternbolt had hauled Hugh Thompson up for questioning by his Senate committee, treating his story with contempt), and maybe he'd guessed what Thompson knew, that, more than a massacre—which it was, though the Pentagon still avoided that term, preferring "alleged atrocity"—such actions as his would be expunged for as long as they could pull it off. Then they'd give him a medal, as they did, along with some not-so-subtle hints that he could have been charged with mutiny, their way of saying, "You sit on this and keep it mum—fragging is one thing, this is worse, forgetting which side you're killing for. . . and don't sound off on Nuremberg, those guys were wackos, not like us." But Thompson's a quarter Cherokee and knows how medals and treaties go.

So back, just briefly, to where we were—with all in the balance, as it were—rising from bed to head for the kitchen, thinking it might have crossed Dugan's mind that the swimmingly gallant thing to do was make us some coffee, check the fridge, and toast that bagel for. . . who'd she be? Still Cinderella sweeping up? "Whatever," she sighed. She'd thought it through as best she could, and, though sex alone can't conquer all, love can, love will. . . she was sure of that—everything else declines and dies. Was that what Kappelman told him too, or was it just the opposite? Hard to say. "It's what *you* said, Lord, that's for sure." And there it was, her prayer's amen.

The clock had jumped to 5:06—she was ready for her close-up now, which meant deciding what to wear. . . the aphrodisiac rabbit gown or hard-luck Guatemalan shirt (unbuttoned, with panties but no bra). The shirt? Okay, she'd go with that, then mosey in and strike a pose. What was he wearing? Couldn't be much—she saw his skivvies on the floor, so no shorts, no shirt, no socks or shoes. . . just trousers (she could handle that), like Battling Butler feigning surprise, wondering if she'd overheard his dickering with you-know-who (the figment that was haunting them both).

Once more into the breeches, then. . . she'd let her outfit take effect and then she'd say her little piece: "yes because I never did a thing at all like that before the chain of guilt is endless you know from Danny to me to you to Rose and on to half of Southeast Asia though sooner or later we'll have to see it's not a splinter festering it's shrapnel lodged so deep inside it's part of us it's who we are no second-guessing no regrets. . ."

She'd get that far, he'd stare at her with an Irish commotion on his face and maybe the new thought in his head that "Holy be-jeesus, she's Irish too!" which he'd never considered, think of that! And how could the two of them bring it off, so much alike there was hardly an Other? "Well, then," she'd say in a Galway brogue, "ask Jimmy Joyce. Aw, what the heck! I'll have a go at it, sure, an' I will!" though she knew, of course, it would probably mean an unending succession of far-out scenes like lying spread-eagled in the sack, declaiming as he came striding in, 'Y-Y-Yes, I w-w-will, Y-Y-Y-YESSSSS!' She was up for that, she thought she was.

So she entered the kitchen and there he stood, eating the last of the bagels.

AUTHOR'S NOTE

The original draft of *Famous Dogs* was begun in late 1989 when I was living with my wife and two of our three children in a small rice-farming village in Northern Thailand. Although much of the story is drawn from personal experience, most of the primary characters are composites and many more are entirely fictitious. All historical information concerning the war in Vietnam, including remarks ascribed to various public figures, is totally factual, but, because memory was at first my only available resource, the sequencing of a few events is slightly inaccurate.

For example, although the details of the My Lai massacre are exact, it was only in November 1969 that reports of that "incident" became known by the general public, and the role played by Hugh C. Thompson and his crew wasn't officially recognized by the U.S. Army until 1998, some 30 years after the massacre and 5 years after I was able to meet both him and Lawrence Colburn. Other slightly inaccurate dates involve the releases of several films (*Deliverance*, *Jaws* and *Little Big Man*) as well as the occasion on which Alan Shepard hit golf balls on the moon (February 6, 1971). Although Bruce Lee had earlier appeared in a number of television productions, his first leading role in a U.S. film was in 1971. Regarding a reference to Augustus Blunt's "Cousin Tony," Anthony Blunt confessed in 1964 to having spied for the Soviet Union, but that wasn't known publicly until 1979; Kris Kristofferson and Rita Coolidge didn't meet until November 1970; and Legionnaires' Disease was not identified as such until 1976. I should also point out that the character of Senator Sternbolt is completely imaginary as are the towns of Cumbria, Lugton, and Chantry Mount along with their universities and inhabitants. However, John Dough's hut actually existed as described, and it was still intact nearly two decades later. James Dickey and I were longtime friends and colleagues, and, although the scene in which he appears unnamed is fictitious, his watches, hat, and dialogue are authentic—as is a passing allusion to the Sunset Lodge, a bordello outside the coastal city of

Georgetown, which until it was closed in 1969 was said to have hosted state legislators for "special sessions" every spring.

Readers who're charitably inclined may agree with the narrator of this work, the former Caitlin Rosen (Mrs. Michael B. Dugan), who attributed such minor mistakes as those I've indicated to what she calls "the inevitable fallibility of memory," citing the work of experimental psychologist F.C. Bartlett whose conclusions on this matter have been confirmed by many subsequent researchers in the field. Regarding the frequency of coincidental encounters throughout the story, repeated references to "Zhivago's law" allude to the manner in which the characters in Pasternak's novel repeatedly cross paths as if their lives were taking place on parallel tracks—a phenomenon which, in my own experience seems to happen for reasons that have to do with quantum physics. . . which is to say I don't know why, but it does.

As for the more problematic depiction of how people saw, heard, and interacted with each other in 1969, much that's considered unacceptable now in matters of language, gender, race, or physical characteristics—an accent, a stutter, one's size or appearance—was simply regarded as how things were regardless of who was offended. As a columnist wrote in this morning's *New York Times* on a day now set aside to honor Dr. King, "We're so fixated on what is wrong today that we forget how much was far more wrong 50 years ago," the consequences of which persist though often less overtly than before. That has led in turn to a general condemnation of devices such as stereotypes and dialect which have long been staples of comedy and satire. On the other hand, I'm inclined to agree that, as a real-life model for Caitlin once observed, their use is "fair enough so long as they're also applied to those accustomed to doing the laughing." Even more to the point, given the parallels between then and now, she also pointed out that "distorting how we view the past risks limiting the future." Many will disagree I know, but insofar as Caitlin herself might be permitted a further opinion, I think she'd want to add that, though our sins may be expiated, they can never be undone because they are, in effect, part of a permanent record. Or, as Ovid is quoted as saying, "everything changes, nothing dies. . ." except Kenmore dishwashing machines.

Ben Dunlap
January18, 2021

Ben Dunlap, 2007

Ben Dunlap is a former Rhodes Scholar who has lived and worked in various parts of the world including Southeast Asia, though most of his life has been spent in the two Carolinas to which he keeps returning.

He has been a prize-winning writer-producer for dozens of programs and series broadcast by PBS, and his 2007 TED Talk, for which he was billed as a "master storyteller," can be viewed on the internet. He has taught a variety of subjects over the years including literature, film, and Asian studies at institutions ranging from Harvard to Wofford College, where he also served as its president for 13 years. For three decades he has served as a senior moderator at the Aspen Institute for which he has helped design and conduct a number of programs and seminars around the world, and for five years he performed as a soloist with a regional ballet company.

At the time his author photograph was taken, he was the player-coach for an unofficial sepak takraw collegiate team which had just completed a tour of Indonesia. He's holding the ball, which had rarely been seen before in places where they competed back home in South Carolina, which partly accounts for his expression.

THE DIVERS COLLECTION

Number 1
Hôtel des Étrangers, poems by **Joachim Sartorius**
translated from German to English by **Scott J. Thompson**

Number 2
Making Art, a memoir by **Mary Julia Klimenko**

Number 3
XISLE, a novel by **Tamsin Spencer Smith**

Number 4
Famous Dogs of the Civil War, a novel by **Ben Dunlap**

Made in the USA
Middletown, DE
06 July 2021